SPACE SPIDERS
ON PROM DAY

Raves for

SPACE SPIDERS ON PROM DAY

"EXTREMELY CLEVER AND BEGGING TO BE a kick-ass, laugh-a-minute, sci-fi romp of **A FEATURE FILM."**
~John Huckert, screenwriter, *DinoCroc* & *The Passing*

"WHAT A BLAST! Mr. Hruby breaks through typical literary barriers to deliver an engaging, exciting, unexpected **PAGE-TURNER** through the territory of teenagers, spiders, prom and **MOST IMPORTANTLY LOVE."**
~Eliza Swords, YouTube Channel - *Best Day Ever With Barry and Eliza*

"STORYTELLING AT ITS BEST - CLEVER, EXCITING AND HILARIOUS with a knack for keeping you reading well past bedtime. With vivid and memorable characters you root for every step of the way, *Space Spiders on Prom Day* is an adventure that's well worth the read."
~Paul Regnier, author, *Space Drifters* series

"GREAT GUILTY PLEASURE! This is both touching and hilarious . . . JD Salinger meets Dave Barry . . . this is the kind of entertainment books were meant to deliver all along . . . give us more Mr. Hruby!!!"
~Steve Chandler, author, *Crazy Good, Death Wish, Fearless*

"John Hruby is **MASTERFUL IN THE ART OF LANGUAGE,** opening a visceral pathway through the power of his storytelling. It is beautifully written infused with a layer of humor and uncanny wit. It **TOUCHES THE SOUL,** opening us to wisdom of our hearts. If you wish to gift yourself with an extraordinary experience, read *Space Spiders on Prom Day*."
~Jody Vehr, author, *Just Hit Send: A Journey to Freedom*

SPACE SPIDERS ON PROM DAY

A CHEVY & SWEETIE ADVENTURE

JOHN J. HRUBY

Let's Do This, LLC

Los Angeles ▪ Oz ▪ Tatooine ▪ Mines of Moria
Restaurant at the End of the Universe ▪ Arrakis ▪ Narnia
Diagon Alley ▪ The Capital ▪ Moonbase Alpha

For Amy, Connor, and Cayden,
thank you for the fun and adventures

Space Spiders on Prom Day
Complete Epic Novel: Includes Book One & Book Two
A Chevy & Sweetie Adventure

Cover design by Ellen Karpenkova

Cover illustration by Liwilljo

Published in the United States.

ISBN 978-0-9984111-1-8
eISBN 978-0-9984111-0-1

Space Spiders on Prom Day

A CHEVY & SWEETIE ADVENTURE

COMPLETE EPIC NOVEL

Now includes Book One & Book Two

BOOK ONE

PREFACE

THIS IS MY STORY and it's the truth.

My name is Chevy. My real name is Eric. Eric's not bad, but everyone calls me Chevy.

I'm going to tell you the real Space Spiders story. Sure, you can get the "facts" from a lot of different sources, and some of those "facts" are correct, but the people telling you those "facts" weren't on the ground where the blood, gore, and fanging happened. They didn't get webbed. They didn't shoot an M4 machine gun with grenade launcher, and they didn't see their high school friends die.

I'm writing *my* story because my Mom told me that she'd get me two 15-inch American Racing Torq Thrust Rims for the '69 Z/28 Chevy Camaro I'm rebuilding. This is Project Freedom. This is why people call me Chevy.

I love her. I do. But my Mom thinks it will be helpful to have my story written down. That doesn't make sense to me. There has been so much stuff already written about the Space Spiders. Military Generals, Astronomers, Bug Specialists.

My Mom says it's never been told from my point of view. That's true. I refused to talk to *Time* magazine and *Rolling Stone*. I feel like I'd talk to them for six hours, and they'll pick out the four dumb things I said and name the article, "How the High School Hick Boy from the Boonies Helped Smash the Space Spiders." My Mom says if I write my story it might sell to Hollywood. My Dad always said we could create whatever we want. I guess my Mom is a believer now. Whatever. It will be nice to get the set of rims and tires for the Camaro I'm rebuilding. And if the story sells, it would be nice if I get enough to pay back the rental company for the Prom tux the Spacers trashed.

Oh, and for the record, we didn't come up with the nickname "Spacers." Me and my high school friends called them Space Spiders like everyone else. I know, not brilliant. They're 16-foot spiders that came from space. Listen, we're simple folk from the farmland. We grow a lot of the veggies and the bacon you eat. Our high school has a hunting club and a Future Farmers of America club, and it's cool to belong to them. We believe in God, living free, and not being killed by Space Spiders. I know, number two and three are kinda the same – living free and not being killed.

Heads up. I'm not so good at grammar and spelling. I made my Mom promise that she's not going to edit one word of this. I'm not really concerned about spelling errors because I'm using spell check and I'm not color bling. I can see the little red lines that appear under misspelled words, and do something about it. My only concern is if I misspell a word with another *real* word and no red line appears. Mom, if you want me to read, proof, and rewrite this, you'll have to promise to buy me the other two rims and tires for the Camaro Z28.

This is my story. I'm not letting anyone mess with it. No one's going to make it cooler, glorious, or pretty.

CHAPTER 1

PROM DAY

A DARK HIGH SCHOOL hallway. Empty. Quiet. The only lights are the red exit lights. Eerie. Spooky. About every thirty lockers there is a classroom door with a skinny window. These windows make sure students and teachers don't have privacy during the school day. Daylight shines through these windows and stabs into the darkness of the hallway.

We tear around the corner as we run down the dark hall. We move pretty fast for a couple of guys who have been beaten up all day long. You're not allowed to run in school, but I guess when the world is ending and you're the only two humans in the building, you can pretty much do whatever you want.

Everyone is gone. When I say gone, I mean home or evacuated. But many of them are gone, gone. You know what I mean: shed their mortal coil, taking a dirt nap, playing a harp in heaven.

We run through the light streaming into the hall from each classroom door window. We dash through each pool of light, our senses on overdrive. My name is Chevy. I'm the first guy running down the hall. I'm 18, a senior, and this is my school. I'm wearing a black tux with a purple bow tie, which was Sweetie's idea. Right now she's out on the battlefield wearing a purple Prom dress. We match but we're not together right now. We should be. It's Prom Day. Sweetie's the love of my life. I hope I get to see her again. My tux has seen some *action*, not the Prom action that most seniors hope for. There's a rip on my left shoulder and dried stuff splattered here and there. Most of it's *their* goo so that's a good thing.

I run down the hall with a guy I call Not Rambo. We hold handguns, which may or may not be safer than running with scissors. Not Rambo also holds a small grey box. He slams into a water fountain that sticks out between groups of lockers. The hallway is dark. He didn't see it.

"Owww." Not Rambo falls in the darkness. His gun slides down the hall.

I say, "The box. You still got it? Is it OK?"

Not Rambo stands. "Thanks for your concern about *me*." He holds up the grey box. "It's fine. I got it." I pick up his gun and give it to him. He rubs his leg and whimpers. Now you know why he's called Not Rambo. Others might call him Not Duke Nukem. Same thing.

I'll tell you what he is. He's 19 and a Private in the Army Reserve. *This is not who I should be sneaking around with on Prom Day.* If you don't know, private is the lowest rank possible in the Army. A private's main responsibility is to follow orders. Don't get me wrong. I love the military, and ideally they'll help us save the world, but me and this particular private don't get along. Not Rambo wears a green Army Reserve uniform. He's got short hair – think buzz cut.

I peer through a window on a classroom door. The light streaming into the hall hits me in the eyes. Man, that's bright. I wipe the sweat from my forehead with the sleeve of my tux.

Not Rambo says, "They're going to charge you a cleaning fee."

"I'd be happy if they charge me a cleaning fee."

"Why?"

"It would mean I'm alive to pay it."

I push the classroom door open. The lights are off, but the

classroom's bright from the sunlight coming through the large windows from the outside world. The purple vest I wear matches my purple bow tie, but the vest has a camouflage pattern made up of different color purples. You can take the hunter out of the woods, but you can't take the woods out of the hunter.

The classroom is clean and the desks are in perfect rows. It smells like orange blossoms and bleach. I inhale and the inside of my nose burns. The chemicals and the cleaning crew did their job; everything that was once alive in the room is now dead.

Someone has spray-painted something on the outside of the windows just above the hedges. The painted words are backwards, but they're easy to make out.

Not Rambo reads them, "School Suc." He pauses, "It should be illegal to do graffiti if you don't know how to spell."

Past the painted windows and hedges are the sand volleyball courts. There's a big push to get kids more active and in the sun. Something about kids being overweight and needing vitamin D to help the body absorb calcium.

Beyond the volleyball courts are the second practice field and the woods. We're in rural Pennsylvania. We've got plenty of open fields and trees, not like the city.

I look but don't see any. "Come on, we can make it."

A large, hairy, white thing scurries past the window just in front of the hedges. It's the size of a small elephant, but it moves fast. We don't get a good look at it, but we know what it is. It's big and has lots of legs, eight of them.

I stop. Private Not Rambo bumps into me.

"Watch it, I'm carrying the detonator." He catches the small grey box as it falls.

"You ran into me. Be careful."

"I know what I'm doing."

As if any of us know what we're doing. If this doesn't work, I'm not sure if we'll be able to save Prom, or, for that matter, the Earth.

Something moves in the hedges right outside the window. It's round, brown, and hairy. It's a little smaller than a basketball. *What evil thing is this?* Oh, it's the back of a human head. I've seen this kid before.

I think he's a sophomore. He has a pasty white complexion. See, he should be getting more sun.

I'm going to tap on the window and talk to him. I whisper to myself, "Stay calm, stay calm." He doesn't see us in the classroom. He looks at the woods beyond the volleyball courts and stumbles out of the bushes before I can make it to the window.

Not Rambo says, "He's not staying calm."

The kid is on the large size. See, he should also be getting more exercise. He wears a flannel shirt over a blue T-shirt with a lunch box on it. I tap on the window, but it's too late. Lunch Box runs toward the volleyball court, heading for the fields and woods beyond it. That was my plan. But Lunch Box is overweight. He doesn't run well.

I say, "He'll make it."

"You're wrong."

Lunch Box holds a can of black spray paint. He pumps his arms but that doesn't help. This kid is not built for speed. The sand volleyball court slows him down. It's hard to run on sand, and he didn't have much momentum anyway.

A web line shoots in from the left. We can't see where the webbing came from, the Space Spider must be around the side of the building. The webbing hits Lunch Box and sticks to him. Lunch Box trips and falls. Arms and legs flail. Sand flies.

I run to the window and raise my Glock right above the small "u" in Suc. It's hard looking through the graffiti. I lean in, but this doesn't help. I can't see the Space Spider because it's still around the side of the building, but I'm ready. I reach my hand back.

"Give me your gun."

"No."

"Come on."

Not Rambo finally offers his Army issued Beretta M9 sidearm. I grab it.

Outside on the sand court, the webbing drags Lunch Box. The teen struggles out of his flannel shirt. He's free. Nice going kid. Lunch Box gets to his knees and shakes sand out of his hair as his flannel shirt gets pulled under the volleyball net and off the court by the web line. The Space Spider is still behind the corner of the building. Lunch Box stands and looks for something.

"Don't just stand there. Move!"

Lunch Box grabs the can of black spray paint he dropped. I guess it's nice to have something to hold onto. He runs in the opposite direction. Yes! He's going to get around the far corner of the school. His feet step out of the sand and onto the grass. Good. Now he'll get some speed. But before he disappears around the corner of the school he stops. He just stops as if he got hit with a freeze ray.

Not Rambo yells, "Keep moving! Don't stop!"

Lunch Box trembles as two big, white, hairy legs come around the edge of the school building. Space Spiders are about sixteen feet big, just a little larger than a full-sized pickup truck like the Ford F-Series or the Chevrolet Silverado. We don't see the Space Spider, just its two front legs.

I raise both guns, but I don't have a shot. Lunch Box is too close to it, and all I can see are the two front legs coming out from around the building. Not enough to aim at and hit.

The Space Spiders mandibles extend out beyond the corner of the building and touch the teen's thick arms. If you don't know, mandibles are the "little legs" that are near a spider's fangs and mouth. They are used like short arms to grab and hold prey.

I flip the safety off both guns. "Come on, show yourself."

Not Rambo says, "Chevy, even if you get a shot, you can't kill it with two handguns, not at this distance. You're only gonna piss it off and give away our position."

I ignore him.

"You're gonna sacrifice the mission and get everyone killed, including Sweetie."

I hesitate. Not Rambo knows which buttons to push, and I hate him for it.

Right behind the Space Spider's mandibles are its big tusk-like fangs. The tips come around the corner of the building. The fangs open but before they strike, the mandibles poke the teen's belly. Wobble. Wobble. Wobble. Lunch Box trembles. The Space Spider hesitates and the mandibles withdraw. The big legs back away from Lunch Box. It's letting the kid go.

Not Rambo says, "What just happened?"

I lower my guns, "See, the kid's not a threat. They're saving him for later. They only attack when …"

But Lunch Box can't leave it alone. He raises his can of spray paint and yells, "I'm the boss of my body." Lunch Box sprays the Space Spider and shouts, "Wolverines!" Which is weird because at Fairland High, we're the Knights.

Lunch Box takes a step forward. For a moment we can't see him because he's advancing beyond the edge of the building.

The Space Spider screeches. Then we hear Lunch Box scream. It was a short victory. Lunch Box steps back into view. He holds the can of spray paint, but he's not spraying anymore. He looks dazed and confused. He looks down. Blood pours out of a hole in his light blue T-shirt making a big, dark purple circle. He drops his can of spray paint and looks to the other side of his body. His hands touch his sides. Both hands come up red. The fangs got him. He's a goner.

Not Rambo lowers my arms until my guns point at the floor. I let Not Rambo take his sidearm back. There is nothing to do now. The teen falls backwards. A web line shoots out from the corner of the building and hits the teen's feet and legs. The web line pulls Lunch Box behind the building so we can't see him.

Lunchtime.

There is nothing we can do.

Not Rambo pats me on the back, "Well, that's what you get for defacing school property."

Now you know why I don't like him. He's an idiot.

Not Rambo and I leave the classroom and run down the hall looking for another way to get back to…

Wait.

I need to start earlier.

I'm gonna start three days *before* Prom. I'll take you back to the Wednesday before Prom for three reasons:

This is the night SNAFU falls in love.
This is the night Sweetie dumps me.
This is the night the moon cracks.

CHAPTER 2

THREE DAYS EARLIER

IT'S THE WEDNESDAY BEFORE Prom,
And all through the school,
Not a creature is stirring,
We think everything is cool.

Just to be clear, my story doesn't start in the middle of a sunny day. It begins at night when all scary stories are supposed to start.

Picture this. I know you can because you already did.

Same high school and hallway as before, but this time the lights are on. Two guys run down the hall again. I'm one of them, but I'm not running with Not Rambo. This time I'm racing my best friend, SNAFU.

I'm in the lead again (because I'm fast), but I'm not wearing a tux. I'm in traditional green and brown hunting camouflage. SNAFU runs right behind me. He's two inches taller than me with about twenty more pounds of muscle and attitude. He wears a black-and-white camouflage jacket with matching pants. SNAFU is a great guy if he's your friend, but if you cross him, watch out. He'll mess you up.

This time I'm not carrying a Glock; I carry my Benelli Nova, 12-gauge 5-shot pump shotgun.

Actually it's a plastic representation of my shotgun. And, representation is stretching it. I carry a small, fluorescent green plastic rifle. We're not allowed to bring guns or anything that looks like a real firearm to school.

SNAFU holds a bright orange plastic toy crossbow that shoots foam darts. This is supposed to represent his 150-pound draw weight, RC-150 hunting crossbow.

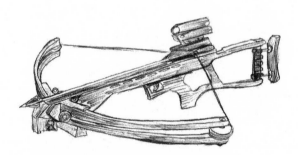

The cool thing is he took the laser sight off his real crossbow and Duct-taped it to the toy crossbow. *Everybody loves his crossbow with laser sight.* We just finished taking our Hunting Club yearbook photos. That's why we're dressed like this.

I am the first one to run past the water fountain and I can tell you it's not easy to run in hunting boots.

"I win."

SNAFU doesn't slow down, he's not a good loser. He comes straight for me, but I've got good timing and I move out of the way. He misses me and slams into the lockers. BAM. He dents one.

SNAFU coughs and spits his gum into his hand. "I almost died." He tosses the wad back into his mouth. "You weren't supposed to move."

"You weren't supposed to try and kill me."

SNAFU rubs his arm. Maybe my Dad is right. I won and I didn't get slammed. My Dad always said you *can* have everything you want in life. Well, maybe this time, but I don't know about getting everything I want *all the time.*

I see a red dot on my crotch. I say, "That's not funny."

"A laser sight on someone's groin is always funny."

Yells and screams come from a nearby classroom. A massacre is in process. I throw open the door and rush in. The classroom is empty and dark. The lights are off and it's getting dark outside. Through the big windows we see the sun set beyond the practice field and distant woods.

The screams come from teens playing volleyball and chasing each other on the sand courts. The coach blows her whistle. "Yearbook picture. Come on, gather up."

Everyone is safe. Everything is fine.

SNAFU touches my shoulder, "You OK?"

I didn't know what I thought was going on, just a bunch of kids having fun. I close the door and we walk down the hall, but a chill runs up my spine.

SNAFU says, "Who's getting their picture taken after the volleyballers?"

"I don't know."

"Yes, you do."

I do know, but I don't like where this is going. I try to change the subject. "I can't believe Benji built a catapult. I can't see how he's ever going to bring down a buck with that thing."

SNAFU turns and walks down a different hallway. "Let's go to the gym." I catch up to him. I have to stop him before we get there.

"That's a bad idea."

SNAFU smirks, "It's my birthday, you have to do whatever I want."

SNAFU is the last guy in our class to turn eighteen. He's the toughest of us all, but he's still the baby of the group. Don't tell him I said that. I suddenly realize why SNAFU wants to go to the gym and it has nothing to do with sneaking into another group's yearbook picture.

"You want to see Darcy."

"Ms. Meyers."

Since when does SNAFU treat teachers with respect? *Oh, man. SNAFU likes Darcy.* Then I realize, of course he does. All the guys *like* Darcy. But it's strange, I never hear SNAFU talk about her. He doesn't have Darcy for a teacher because she teaches the AP classes and SNAFU is not AP. I have an idea on how to stop him. He never remembers my birthday.

"Tell me when my birthday is, and I'll go to the gym with you."

"August 19."

"What? You never get me anything, not even a card."

"That doesn't mean I don't know when your birthday is."

SNAFU's like that. If it's important to him, he'll remember it. Schoolwork is usually not important to him. It's nice he knows my birthday, but it would be nicer if he got me a candy bar or actually said something like, "Happy Birthday" to me. SNAFU is complex. Just for the record, Sweetie's birthday is January 12. I write her a poem on the twelfth day of every month. They're usually short, stupid, and they rhyme, but she likes hearing them, and to be honest, I like writing them. I tell you this now because in a few minutes I'm going to do some stupid stuff, and I want you to know that I'm a well-meaning and a pretty good guy.

We get to the double gym doors. They are closed and the sign says, DO NOT ENTER – PROM COMMITTEE ONLY.

I back away, "Let's go."

SNAFU doesn't follow. He peeks through the windows in the gym doors. The windows are reinforced with metal wires so a basketball won't break them.

I pull on SNAFU's sleeve, "We shouldn't interrupt. Sweetie

will . . ."

SNAFU looks at my hand. I release his camouflaged jacket. Oops. But he puts his arm around me, "Sweetie will be glad to see you. Look, it's an open committee. We go in, get in their yearbook picture, and leave. We won't bother anyone. It will be the perfect birthday gift. It won't cost you any money, which means it won't take anything away from your Chevy fund."

SNAFU is talking about Project Freedom. I haven't told my friends that I call it Project Freedom. They just know I'm rebuilding a Chevy Camaro.

I say, "Tell me what time of the day I was born and I'll . . ."

SNAFU interrupts me, "Chevy, we're seniors. Seize the day. It's like what your Dad says, there's opportunity all around you, all of the time. You've just got to get used to seeing it."

Geez, I guess if someone says something enough times, even SNAFU will get it. I nod thinking he's right. Of course, I forgot what I tell everyone about SNAFU, "Don't *ever* believe a word SNAFU says."

But before SNAFU can open the door, the gym goes dark. The little window in the door shows blackness. I get a bad feeling.

I say, "What happened?"

He shrugs. "I don't know. Someone turned off the lights?"

SNAFU opens the gym door. Thick smoke clings to the floor and rolls out into the hallway over our kicks. I run inside. I'm about to yell for Sweetie, but the gym is more beautiful than ever. The overhead lights are out, but there are hundreds and hundreds of little white lights everywhere.

It takes me a moment, but I can see what the Prom Committee has done. The gym is separated into three sections. There is a big Eiffel Tower of lights in one corner. Obviously not to scale but big enough for a Prom couple to stand next to it. It's amazing. In another corner of the room there is the Hollywood sign made with lights. These lights twinkle. Fantastic. There are even glow-in-the-dark stars on the gym floor creating a mini-Hollywood Walk of Fame.

In another corner of the gym is a gigantic image of a full moon projected on one of the gym walls. It's more than fifteen feet in diameter. The rough cinder block wall makes the moon's surface look rough and rugged.

The far corner of the gym has two magnificent things. One is a river of lights that run through the darkness near the ceiling. Some lights are clustered together and some are spread out. This has to be the Milky Way. I see it every time we have overnight hunting trips. The second awesome thing is fifty or sixty light tubes hang from the ceiling. The lights in these tubes look like they "run" down the tube over and over again. In the darkness, the lights look like falling stars dropping out of the sky. SNAFU and I slowly walk in, partly because it is dark and partly because we are in awe.

SNAFU nudges me, "It's a fog machine. Nothing is burning." He points at the smoke on the floor. I had forgotten about it. I nod. Tiny white lights also shine behind us but I don't turn to look at them.

SNAFU whispers, "Where is everybody?"

Then, as if in answer to his question, a spotlight turns on and falls on Sweetie. She stands on a stage under the Milky Way and the "falling stars." She holds a microphone and looks at the lights. She says, "Beautiful." I look at her and agree.

Fog rolls over the stage, it looks like Sweetie stands on top of a cloud. The hundreds of lights shine in her bright eyes and off her long brown hair. She makes her simple white top and jeans look good. Sweetie's the love of my life, so I'm a little biased.

I smell something. "What is that?"

SNAFU sniffs, "Lavender. Nice." I didn't know SNAFU liked lavender. I thought I knew everything about him. I guess I don't.

Sweetie says, "Welcome to your Reaching New Heights Prom. Your future is as big as your vision!" I step forward as if Sweetie is calling me but I bump into something in the darkness.

Sweetie whispers into the microphone, "This is what your hours and hours of commitment, love, and work created." She talks to the Prom Committee but I can't see them in the dark. I hear clapping from small team from the darkness in front of the stage. I make out four silhouettes sitting in chairs.

One of Sweetie's operating principles is "What you Focus on Expands." She got that from her mother before her mother moved out. I get it now. Sweetie's reason for being Prom Committee Chair was to create an experience that was a *pattern interrupt*. Sweetie says a pattern interrupt is "something different" that changes the thinking of anyone who experiences it.

Let me explain. Many of us seniors at Fairland High never pictured ourselves traveling the world, making it big in Hollywood, or going to the moon. But, if we could get a little help *seeing ourselves* doing these things, by looking at our framed Prom picture over and over again, then maybe this "unthinkable" thought might become a "regular" thought.

And this is how we create our lives, with thoughts. Ten seconds of thinking of something becomes twenty. Twenty seconds becomes twenty minutes. Twenty minutes becomes twenty hours. This "regular" thought then becomes a "possibility." When this happens, we find ourselves taking actions to create the images we hold inside our heads. Every invention starts as a crazy thought that the person just kept thinking. Many success stories started as impossible dreams.

What we focus on expands. Sweetie offers nothing short of an invitation to her classmates to fulfill their heartfelt desires.

Sweetie explains to her committee, "We will wait to do the mirrored ball until the King and Queen are announced." Sweetie looks up at the dark ceiling. "Second spot, please." A smaller spotlight hits a mirrored ball that I didn't even know was there. Little white reflections dance around the gym.

Sweetie moves to one side of the stage. "The King and Queen will come up here, on top of the cloud-stage, and will dance." Sweetie starts to move. Her long brown hair sways. Sensual. She is confident and a little quirky. Sweetie's beauty is more than just her looks. It's her attitude. She genuinely cares *for others*, but she doesn't care what others *think about her*. I want to *beso* with Sweetie more than ever. (Beso is the first Spanish word I learned and the one I use the most. It means *make out*.)

SNAFU whispers, "Where's Ms. Meyers?"

I look at the silhouettes. He's right, none of them look like Darcy.

Sweetie stops moving. "Questions?"

A student raises her hand. Sweetie points to her. "Where is the main photo location?"

Sweetie looks at SNAFU and me. But then I realize she can't be looking at us because we're in the shadows and her spotlight is in her eyes.

"Ms. Meyers, if you will, please move the spotlight to the hot air balloon!" On Sweetie's command the spotlight that was on her, moves off the stage, crawls across the gym floor, and then picks up speed as it zooms through the gym revealing round tables with teal table clothes and white chairs. The spotlight comes straight for SNAFU and me.

SNAFU says, "Smile."

I want to move, but it happens too fast. The spotlight hits us. It's bright. I squint. SNAFU and I stand exactly where each Prom couple will get their picture taken.

Behind us is a big twenty-foot plywood cutout of a hot air balloon. The fake hot air balloon is in the shape of a gigantic heart. It's painted teal to keep with the Prom theme color. "Reaching New Heights" is written across the big heart.

In front of us is a short two-foot high piece of plywood. This is what I bumped into. It's painted so it looks like a big wicker basket. It was short so it wouldn't block the view of the dress and tux of the Prom couple standing behind it.

Sweetie wasn't too crazy about the hot air balloon idea at first. She wanted to have an actual glider inside the gym so Prom couples could sit inside it. You probably know that a glider is a plane without an engine. It gets pulled up into the sky and then rides on air currents. Sweetie said she could borrow one from her soaring association. But with gliders you have to sit one person in front of the other. With a hot air balloon the couple can stand side by side. A symbolic statement that I think is important. She discussed it with the committee. They realized going with the balloon idea would also allow a better view of the tux and dress in the Prom picture. The balloon idea won.

A high-pitched, squeaky voice says, "Sweetie, it looks like Chevy has a new sweetie."

SNAFU and I turn and see the hot air balloon behind us. Yup, the joke is on us. With SNAFU standing next to me, it looks like he's my Prom date.

I wave. It's lame.

16

Sweetie's voice booms over the speakers, "Lights!" The lights do not come on. Sweetie barks, "Rose, put the damn book down and turn on the lights!" The fluorescent gym lights pop on. The little lights still shine but the magic is gone.

Sweetie demands, "What are you doing here?"

It's not the warm welcome I had hoped for. Sweetie jumps off the riser and walks toward the Prom committee's chairs. Four students sit in a circle of seven chairs. Three females and an idiot.

Ladies first.

The Falcon is our only senior to get a varsity letter in three sports. She wears her black and gold varsity jacket everywhere.

She wears it now. The Falcon is one of only a handful of Hispanic students in our school. She is also one of the few students that don't turn pale white during the winter months. I am always a little jealous. The United States may be a melting pot, but not a lot of minorities make it to the southern most border of Pennsylvania. She has long black hair until track season. It's short now. Rumor has it that her dad cries each year when she cuts it. We call her Falcon, but she doesn't look like a bird of prey. She is beautiful and fast. Her other name could have been States because she goes there every year.

The Falcon has a couple of empty chairs on either side of her. Sitting opposite the Falcon is Friendly. Friendly is known for wearing tight clothing. Not something you can put on a college application.

When you walk down the hall and see guys turn their heads, it's often because of Friendly. She gets attention, but I'm not sure it's the attention she REALLY wants.

Friendly stands and points at us. She squeaks, "You guys make a great couple. You'll achieve great success together."

Here's the thing, I don't care how much someone chooses to get physical with others. Pleasure is awesome. God gave us nerve endings; let's use them. But sometimes chicks try to get attention and loving from sexy-time activities. When I was in middle school, my Dad told me, "Son, it's like eating cookies and ice cream, and I mean *only* eating cookies and ice cream for breakfast, lunch, and dinner and hoping to get your daily amount of nutrients. At some point, it will be unsatisfying, you'll hurt yourself, and you'll get sick."

My Dad ended the conversation with, "Don't try to get love, real connection, and self-worth from orifice games. It's not going to happen. If you need help come talk to me or Mom and if you don't want to talk to us, go see a counselor or therapist." My Dad never had a problem asking for help. He said rich and successful people are smart enough to ask for help when they need it. That's part of the reason why they're rich and successful.

On one side of Friendly is Lynn. Lynn is one of the few Asian students in our class. Her long straight hair is dyed teal. Lynn is creative and will probably go into art or advertising. But right now, she isn't happy. She chews on her pen; it's all gnarled on the end. She taps her foot. Yup, she wears her pink ballet shoes. More on these later.

On the other side of Friendly sits the idiot. His name is Roy and he is the only guy on the Prom Committee. He has dark brown hair that is *almost* long enough to touch the collar of his shirt. Never touching, but close to it. He always wears a shirt with a collar, and he's always clean-cut from his head to his dress shoes. Yes, shiny black shoes, which is insane for the amount of dirt and mud around here.

Falcon, Friendly, Lynn, and Roy watch Sweetie as she sits. Sweetie's arm accidentally touches the yellow sleeve of Falcon's varsity jacket. Falcon moves her chair so it won't happen again. Friendly points to SNAFU and me again, "Your boyfriend has a new sweetie."

It is amazing how people who need kindness act in ways where it is really hard to be kind to them.

Roy laughs. See, he's an idiot.

Sweetie says, "I heard you the first time."

Roy stretches his right arm so it wraps around Friendly. She smiles. His fingers wiggle. His hand looks like a spider as it crawls up her arm. Friendly smashes the hand-spider but she scoots closer to Roy. She's not saying "stop," she's just saying "not here."

Sweetie is going to be my ex-girlfriend very soon, but I didn't know that because I'm a guy. Even with how everything was going, I was still thinking we'd be beso-ing in about an hour.

Sweetie pulls her long hair behind her ear and scrunches her eyebrows. I suddenly realize everything is not OK.

I grab SNAFU, "Come on let's go."

But he doesn't look at me, he looks across the gym.

It's Darcy. Holy geez. Private first class Darcy Meyers, in full Army dress. She walks through the sea of teal tables on her way to the Prom Committee. Maybe she's in uniform because all of the teachers were told to "dress in their best" for yearbook pictures. I guess teachers are even told what to do.

Darcy looks good all of the time because she's attractive. And right now, Darcy looks comic book good. Attractive 22-year-old in FULL military uniform ready to make out or kill you at any moment – a young man's strange fantasy. I didn't know she was in the Army Reserve. No one did. How funny is it that we think we know our teachers' lives outside the classroom. The uniform is in direct contrast to how I think of her. In class she talks about going to India and meditating and peace. She just got more interesting.

Darcy looks at SNAFU and me, "No boots allowed in the gym. You get mud on the floor, you clean it up!" That's Ms. Meyers. Direct communication and trying to get us seniors to take responsibility for ourselves.

Darcy is the faculty leader of the Prom Committee. She was placed in our po-dunk town through an organization called *Teaching for the Americas*. They take college kids who didn't prepare for a real job, train them for six months and then drop them in a school somewhere that needs teachers. I'm sure the process is more complicated than that, but you get the idea. I heard the choice is usually inner city or rural. Nobody asked her if she chose our school. The rejection would mess up the fantasy of her being glad to be here.

Darcy walks to the empty chair next to Sweetie. Darcy looks at us. No, she doesn't look at me. She looks at SNAFU. "Gentlemen, join us or leave. It's your move. But don't just stand there. The Universe rewards action."

Roy and Sweetie object, "What?!"

Roy whines, "It's our last meeting. They haven't done anything to contribute."

Sweetie places her hand on Roy's shoulder, "I can't believe I'm saying this but I agree with Roy."

Roy gives me a smug look that's easy to see, even across the gym. Friendly moves closer to Roy, but he turns to Sweetie. She removes her hand from his shoulder. I don't like seeing them agree that I shouldn't be here. I don't like her touching him. Roy has always liked Sweetie. But I can't blame Sweetie for her reaction. She is smart enough to know that SNAFU and I don't think Prom is important, and she knows we might be stupid enough to do something stupid.

I turn toward the door. SNAFU grabs my jacket and stops me from leaving. He doesn't look at me, he stares at Darcy. He pulls me toward the Prom Committee.

This is not going to be pretty.

CHAPTER 3

GODDESS OF DESTRUCTION

SNAFU TOUCHES HIS FOREHEAD as he pushes me toward the Prom Committee. He makes me lead the way so I don't turn and run. Just to be clear, *I don't turn and I don't run.* We zigzag back and forth between the round teal tables. On one switchback, I see SNAFU tap his forehead, right between his eyes. He does it again and again. Is this some sort of OCD I never noticed before?

Then, I think of the first time Darcy and SNAFU met. It was Halloween and Darcy had won the best faculty costume contest. It's not an official contest, it's more of a mental note I make using the talk-o-meter inside my head. The more students I hear comment about a teacher's costume, the higher the score. But this year I saw something I never saw before. With teachers' costumes, it's usually applause or laughter. With Darcy, it was reverence.

She wore a simple and elegant Indian sari. A sari is a garment made of a long piece of cotton or silk fabric wrapped around the body and draped over the shoulder. She also wore a bindi. You know, a red dot.

The red dot, or bindi, was on her forehead between her eyebrows, the same place real Indian women wear them. The sari was a combination of vibrant reds, oranges, and yellows. Dressed like this, she was beautiful and graceful and gracious. I'm pretty sure graceful and gracious are the same thing, but she was so much THAT, I'll use two words to say it.

She bowed slightly to each student as they entered the classroom. Her hands pressed together, palms touching with fingers pointing upwards. She said, "Namasté."

Mouth Wash told me what Namasté means. Mouth Wash is my other good friend. He's kinda the opposite of SNAFU. Mouth Wash is more my size, he's smooth with the ladies, and he always has good smelling breath. I'll tell you more about Mouth Wash later.

Mouth Wash said Namasté means, "The True Self of me acknowledges the True Self of you." I'm not sure what that really means, but I think it's something like, "You're more than a jock, or geek, or wack-head and I'm more than a teacher, or parent, or hot grown-up chick you fantasize about. The True Self that is *you* is actually the same True Self that is *me*. Our True Selves are bigger than our personality, our acne, our grades, our peer group, and our screwed-up parents."

That Halloween, Darcy looked good, but not outrageous, which is unusual because Halloween is often the day good girls get to enjoy and embrace their sexy side. A great holiday for all, really. When you're little, you get a rush by going door-to-door getting candy and unwrapping it. When you get older, you get a rush by seeing how the girl-next-door barely wraps her candy.

But not Darcy. Not at school ever, and, not that day. She was beautiful and covered. She had a box of peel-n-stick bindis for any student who wanted one. They were plastic half jewels: rubies, emeralds, and sapphires. She laughed when the big guys put one on.

Most guys peeled and stuck as a joke, but I noticed a wave of peace wash over most of them when they pressed the bindi in place between their eyebrows. Even our big all-muscle, two-time state wrestler, relaxed when the half-plastic red ruby was pushed into place. I thought he was going to go "Gandhi" on us and give up wrestling right there and then.

SNAFU got in line to enter her classroom even though he wasn't in the class. Darcy gave him a blue sapphire. She bowed and Namastéd him. She then touched the spot on his forehead where he was supposed to place the half jewel. She didn't do that to anyone else. SNAFU didn't say anything. He just turned and walked away. I saw him later. But he didn't have the bindi on. I remember thinking the peace and loving was too much for him. Maybe not.

SNAFU pushes me past the last table toward the Prom Committee. I figure I came this far, I might as well sit down. Falcon puts her hand on the empty chairs and shakes her head no. No one pulls out chairs for us or moves over so we can join them. *Screw them.* We stand outside the circle.

Roy says, "Weapons are not allowed on school property."

Roy is being his jerk self. In grade school he was likely a bully. Now he's just an idiot. Progress I suppose. His family moved here from some big city right before high school. I never cared enough to inquire about his past. But I do give him credit. It's a lot easier to pick up chicks on the Prom Committee than in the hunting club. There is only one female in the hunting club, and she'll karate chop you in your head if you so much as bump into her. Rumor has it Roy has already "dated" one of the Prom Committee girls. A rumor he probably started.

Don't get me wrong; the girls in our school are good shots too. More could join the hunting club. Everyone in our county knows how to shoot, especially all of the first-borns. You can probably guess why. There are a bunch of fathers who wanted a son to hunt with but got a girl first. Sweetie is almost as good a shot as me. Almost. The reason why there are not many girls in the hunting club is because their parents don't want them hanging out with teenage guys in the woods. I don't blame them.

I raise my green plastic shotgun and look at Roy, "You know these are fake. Right?" True, we're not supposed to bring anything to school that looks like a weapon, but these are *not* realistic looking.

I look at Darcy. She still gazes at SNAFU. I say, "We're part of the hunting club. We have permission to carry these tonight. We just took our yearbook picture." I take out a pink permission slip and wave it in the air.

SNAFU doesn't wave nothing. He says, "I know how to handle weapons, even if they don't shoot real ammo. I've been hunting since I was seven." That was true. Here are a couple of other fun facts for you.

There are 900,000 hunters in the state of Pennsylvania. Michigan comes in second with 500,000. In our county, we get three days off from school each year for deer hunting season. Two for bucks and one for does. Hunting and guns are a way of life for us. If the world ends tomorrow, come to the Keystone State and we'll save your ass.

SNAFU looks at Roy, "We know what we're doing." Then SNAFU smiles his creepy smile. SNAFU is telling him to be careful.

Rose, another committee member, walks up to the circle of chairs. She's reading a book as she approaches so she walks slowly. Rose bumps into me with her elbow. Falcon removes her hand from an empty chair.

Sweetie says, "Rose. Sit down."

I pull the empty chair back so Rose can step into the group. I slide the chair forward, under her. Rose sits down without looking up from her book. *A thank you would be nice.* Rose sits between Falcon and Lynn. Rose keeps reading the same book over and over, *The Rose of Camelot.* She found it on Amazon, a five star diamond in a digital haystack. It's about a girl who becomes the first female knight. She reads it on the bus, while she eats lunch, and in class. I think they let her because she's so smart. All A's. I think she's going to be class valedictorian.

Rumor has it that she made her parents move to our district so that she could attend our high school because our mascot is a knight. Rose wears her favorite silver sequined shirt. A little too flashy and dressy in my opinion, she looks like she's going dancing, not calculus. Someone told me she wears tops with sequins because that is the closest thing she can find to chain-link metal armor at the mall. Rose is our mascot for football and basketball games.

This is the only time she pulls back her long brown hair into a single ponytail that comes down to her waist. At games, she waves around a big broad sword and smacks it against her shield. BANG. BANG. BANG. Her ponytail swings around. She looks very *Game of Thrones.* She petitioned the school to let her ride her horse at the games, but it was decided its hooves would mess up the court and football field. I also think nobody wanted to pick up the big horse poop

I watch SNAFU as he turns on his red laser sight. He p͏ͦ ͏ ͏—
little crossbow at the ceiling. The red dot hits the mirrored ball. He moves it around. *What is he doing?* The red dot jumps around on the floor as it reflects off different mirrors. The red dot finally lands right in the middle of Roy's forehead.

Sweetie sees it and laughs. She stops, but it's too late. The committee notices the red dot between Roy's eyes. Even Rose looks up from her book.

Roy says, "What? What?"

Everyone laughs again. Sweetie tries not to smile but fails. I wink at her. She shakes her head and smiles even though she doesn't want to. I think really hard, *everything is going to be alright.* I try to send the thought to her. Her smile gets bigger. She must be picking up my vibe.

Friendly says, "That's not funny." She grabs Roy's head and tries to wipe the dot off his forehead with her thumb. Roy shoos her away.

Darcy says, "Fake weapons on the table."

SNAFU nods, but it's more like a bow. I think he's finally returning the bow Darcy gave him on Halloween. He flips off the scope and sets the crossbow on a round table with a bunch of decoration supplies. This table looks like a Prom workstation with markers, rolls of tape, and other art things. I catch Sweetie's eye. *Time to make everything OK.*

I have to come from a sincere place even if I look like a fool in front of the others. I say, "I'm honored to be here and to see what you've done with the place. It's beautiful. I'm proud to be a Fairland Knight."

Sweetie's shoulders relax. I place my green plastic rifle on the table next to a bunch of glue sticks. I turn back just in time to catch a flying Sweetie. She leaps into my arms. HMMPF. I hold Sweetie. I'm glad she knows when I'm being authentic. She whispers, "Please don't embarrass me."

"I won't." That's a lie. But to my credit, I don't know it yet.

Sweetie smiles and says, "I have good news. We've got teal paint left over. Not a lot, but I think we have enough to paint the tiny bathroom of the apartment we're going to get. Then every time we brush our teeth, we'll think about our Prom together."

I suppose she can do whatever she wants since it's her meeting, but I feel very uncomfortable because everyone is looking at us. I'm also not jazzed about a teal bathroom because I need to tell her that I'm not . . .

I say, "That would be great."

She hears the insincerity in my voice. Sweetie jumps off me and says, "You shouldn't be here." With me, Sweetie has a great bullshit detector, with other people not so much. She walks back to her seat.

Friendly wiggles closer to Roy. It is as if she wants to sit on the same chair together. Falcon stands, pulls a teal tablecloth off a nearby table with a quick pull and walks to Friendly. Friendly moves her chair back. Falcon drops the tablecloth on Friendly's lap.

Falcon says, "Wear a longer skirt and some underwear. Every time you move your legs I see your . . ."

"OK, everyone, let's get back to business," says Sweetie.

Falcon straightens her jacket and sits back down. Our varsity jacket is interesting: black jacket body with a gold collar and two BIG gold sleeves that run from the shoulder all the way to the wrist. It has a matching gold "F" on the front for Fairland High School. There is so much yellow-gold on it that you can almost wear the jacket as a hunting jacket.

Falcon takes her jacket everywhere. Even on summer days. She doesn't wear it when it's hot. She just carries it with her, in case she needs it. I mean, who needs a jacket on a 90-degree summer day with 90 percent humidity? The crazy thing is she'll leave it in your car if you give her a ride. Then she sends a text to everyone asking, "Have you seen my jacket?" I think it's her way of reminding everyone, and herself, that she's someone.

High school is tough. If you don't have a lot of self-esteem you try to get it from others.

"Sweetie," says Roy, "before we get back to business I think you should get ready to look for a new roommate."

Sweetie looks at me.

Roy says, "Unless, your boyfriend is going to do a two-hour commute every day from the city."

No, no, no. Not now.

26

Sweetie's eyebrows scrunch up, she pulls her hair behind her ears, AND she bites her lower lip. Oh, no, the trifecta.

"Chevy?!"

Roy smiles. "Oh, he didn't tell you? Chevy signed up for the summer crew to upgrade the heating and AC for the whole school. Isn't that right, buddy? We had the tour of the basement this morning. Electrical lines, gas lines, and water pipes. It is very exciting. I guess all those tractor repairs paid off. You've got mechanic transferable skills that someone's willing to pay for."

Sweetie says, "But you said we'd get our own place after graduation."

I don't want to have this conversation with an audience. I might as well post our whole damn fight online.

SNAFU pokes me. "Just make sure you don't blow yourself up."

Thanks, friend.

Roy says, "Just make sure you don't blow up the school."

He thinks saying almost the same thing is funny. He laughs. No one else does. Idiot.

"Sweetie," I say, "by the end of summer I'll have enough for my half of the deposit. And, if I don't have to chip in for rent for three extra months, I'll have what I need to complete the Chevy. And, a two-hour commute each way wouldn't give us any time together. We'd be LIVING together but we wouldn't BE with each other. We can leave for the city in September or October or Novem . . ."

"Don't you Sweetie me. I told you I have enough for our deposit. I don't want to wait. I want to take our relationship to the next level. I want to BE with you."

Roy says, "Oh, my God. You guys haven't done it yet."

"Shut up, Roy."

He smiles. "You're moving in with a dame that you haven't even test drove? You must be in luvvvvve."

I move for Roy's throat. Private Darcy springs into some sort of martial arts stance and smacks me in the middle of my chest. All air leaves my lungs. She stops me cold. I drop to my knees. I hear SNAFU sigh. Later I learned that Darcy scored high in demolition and that the Army Reserve had her take a special bomb-diffusing course. I guess

27

she's full of surprises.

Friendly turns and touches Roy's face, "Hey, that's sweet. Don't be mean to them, Honey."

Roy looks at her chest. He says, "Don't ever call me Honey." His hand becomes a spider again and climbs over her shoulder on the way to her . . .

Darcy says, "Hey, hands off. We're on school property."

Roy removes his hand. "Yes, ma'am."

SNAFU smiles another creepy smile at Roy. SNAFU doesn't like him. I'm still trying to breath. I realize how much I enjoy air. Roy keeps his hands to himself and his eyes forward. I am impressed that he listens to Darcy. He doesn't usually respond so quickly to teachers' commands.

I suck in air and slowly stand so Darcy won't hit me again. Sweetie doesn't look at me. I need to play my trump card. I walk toward Sweetie and say, "Sweetie, I love you." I say it like I mean it because I do.

Sweetie tries to stay angry but can't. She says, "I just want to know I'm not wasting my time."

I sometimes forget Sweetie is a Capricorn. She plans everything out. Every little step is important because each step leads to another step that leads to a specific future goal.

I take her hands. They are soft and warm. A wonderful feeling runs up and down my body. I look into her big, beautiful eyes. I focus on how much I love her. I hope she can see the love in my eyes.

"You're not wasting your time. With me you're never wasting time. It's you and me forever."

Sweetie smiles. "I guess I can wait to move in together." She pulls me close, "We'll still have Prom."

I don't say anything. It is a lame response, but it's the best I can do. Sweetie's eyebrows furl again.

"We do have Prom, right?"

This is when I realize I didn't plan this very well. I'm more of a guy that makes things up on the fly. Project Freedom is in direct opposition to Project Prom. I can't do both of them. I only have so much money. My sincere smile becomes a fake, forced smile.

Sweetie steps away from me. "You honestly don't know how important this is to me?" I don't say anything. Then another thought hits her and she says, "You bought the carburetor!"

Her eyes are big and brown. Everything is usually all right when I'm looking into her eyes. I don't want to answer, but I know I have to.

"Sweetie, come on. I can't see spending $400 on one evening. It's a waste of money, especially when we're planning our future."

"That's why you need more time! An old car is more important than spending time together, getting our own place, and BUILDING a life with me!"

"I promise I was only looking, but the guy gave me a killer deal on a Holley 750 double-pumper." As soon as I say it, I realize how stupid I sound. No one else knows or cares that this is one of the best carburetors available for a Z/28.

"Chevy, I'm the Prom Committee Chairperson! I'm nominated for Prom Queen. I'm going to Prom."

Roy stands. "I'll take you to Prom."

Friendly pulls on Roy's arm, "You said you had to work Prom so we can't go as a couple?"

"I say a lot of things," says Roy.

Friendly moves her chair away from Roy. *Good for her. We all have to face reality some time.* Roy doesn't seem to care. He keeps standing ready to take advantage of this opportunity.

I face the love of my life. "Sweetie, ask me to do anything and I'll do it."

"Take me to Prom."

"I can't do that."

"Going to Prom falls into the anything category."

Sweetie walks to Roy, and kisses him on the cheek. "Roy, I'll go to Prom with you."

Roy smiles. "There's an unexpected twist for you."

CHAPTER 4

YOU'VE GOT TO BE KIDDING ME

FRIENDLY STANDS AND PULLS down her miniskirt. Which is wasted effort because it doesn't move much. Falcon covers her eyes. Friendly hands the teal tablecloth to Darcy who tosses it on the table that Falcon took it from. Friendly goes eye to eye with Sweetie even though she talks to Roy. Friendly says, "What about us?"

Roy says, "Do you really think *this* is something long term?" He doesn't wait for a reply, "I can tell you right now my second wife hasn't been born yet."

This confuses Friendly. Falcon explains it to her, "When Roy's 40, he's planning his SECOND marriage will be to a 20 year old."

Friendly gets it. She's been a fool all along. She turns to Roy. "But I got the tattoo." Friendly folds up the bottom of her miniskirt, which is tricky in mixed company. On her thigh is a heart with "Roy" in the middle of it. "And last night, we . . . I let you . . ." A tear runs down Friendly's face. She wipes it away. With her same hand, she pushes Roy out of the way, wiping her precious DNA on his traditional fit twill boat shirt. She stumbles out of the circle of chairs and runs for the gym doors.

I watch her until the metal doors slam behind her. Not a good idea while your angry girlfriend glares at you. I didn't do it on purpose. I am just feeling so uncomfortable that focusing on Friendly's sway gave me a moment of relief from the terrible situation I am in. Nobody says anything. Sweetie sits down in Friendly's seat and moves it closer to Roy. She grabs his arm, wraps it around her, and put his hand on her shoulder.

I say, "What?! Come on, you're going to the Prom with him?"

"And after-party." Roy squeezes her shoulder.

"You know all he wants is . . ."

Sweetie stomps her foot. "That is no longer a concern of yours. Right now, he and I want the same thing, a great Prom experience." She brushes her long brown hair back behind her ear. "Chevy, you've got nothing to contribute here, unless you want to be my date?"

I stare at Roy. He holds my stare. A total idiot but a tough one, I appreciate that. We could be friends if circumstances were different, and if he didn't care about his shoes so much. He doesn't flinch. I don't remember him being so tough when he was a junior. *When did he get so strong?*

SNAFU blows a bubble with the gum he chews. The bubble pops. It's his way of breaking the tension.

Roy smiles. His fingers do little spider-finger pushups on Sweetie's shoulder. He says to SNAFU, "No gum chewing. It's in the school's After School Group and Committee By-Laws."

SNAFU knows that. Every kid knows that. Most faculty don't mind as long as you don't blow bubbles or smack, smack, smack it.

Sweetie sighs. I smile. We know SNAFU and we know what's coming. Roy just told SNAFU he can't do something. Roy put the nail in his own coffin and he doesn't even know it. Sweetie removes Roy's arm from around her. *Smart move, Sweetie.* Time to distance yourself from the idiot.

SNAFU takes the gum out of his mouth. He looks for a place to toss it but doesn't see a trashcan.

He holds the gum. "Sorry, haven't read the by-laws in awhile."

SNAFU grabs two white chairs from the closest table. The group still doesn't open up to us. He sits down on one chair behind the circle. I look at SNAFU. He gazes at Darcy. *That's it?* That's not even a witty comeback let alone a punch in the face. What's happening to the SNAFU?

I say, "Let's go."

SNAFU looks at Darcy. "Not yet." That's all he says. No words of encouragement or comfort. *What was I expecting?* I hear my Dad's voice inside my head, "Don't go to a dry well for water." I realize I'm being as stupid as Friendly going to Roy for loving and comfort. *Time to take care of myself. Forget it, I'm leaving.* I turn and walk.

SNAFU grabs the back of my jacket. My feet move, but I don't. He's strong. He yanks me backwards towards the chairs. I lose my balance and trip over his foot. Why didn't he move it? He tries to catch me, but he loses his balance too. We crash into the circle and slam into Roy. Sweetie scoots her chair out of the way. She isn't going down with Roy.

SNAFU and I knock Roy and his chair over. That's the SNAFU I know and love. Roy stays sprawled on the floor. SNAFU and I stand. I feel better. I return to my chair outside the inner circle. "Excuse me, pardon me." SNAFU stands inside the circle of chairs.

Roy stands, "Did you see that? Throw them out of the committee."

Sweetie says, "They're not even part of the committee."

SNAFU holds his ground. They're close enough to fight. Roy looks away first. He sees SNAFU's gum stuck to the arm of his shirt. Roy says, "Look what he did. This is a brand new traditional fit twill boat shirt."

SNAFU says, "Give me my gum back." He steps toward Roy. Roy moves away, fear in his eyes. *Brilliant.* Roy pulls at the gum, but it's stuck on the shirt.

"You did that on purpose."

SNAFU says, "My Mom used to be a seamstress." SNAFU usually tells a lie before he really messes someone up. And I'm pretty sure this a lie. The only needle his Mom ever used was one that she stuck in her arm.

SNAFU says, "I know all about fabrics, I can get that out."

Roy turns from SNAFU. Roy won't let him touch his shirt or the gum. SNAFU waits. Roy lets his guard down. *Mistake number two.* "First you've got to isolate the gum." SNAFU gently gathers the material around the gum and lifts the gum and material away from Roy's upper arm.

"Be careful!"

SNAFU leans to the table full of decorating supplies and grabs a pair of scissors. With amazing speed, he cut the material and leaves a BIG hole in Roy's expensive new shirt.

"You just cut a hole in my shirt!"

SNAFU says, "Are you always a glass half-empty kinda guy? The gum is no longer attached to your shirt." He holds up the gum with the circle of the shirt attached to it. The hole in Roy's shirt is now a symbol for the hole in Friendly's heart. What goes around comes around. SNAFU returns to his chair outside the circle next to me. SNAFU is the best friend ever.

Darcy waits a moment and then says, "OK, now that that is resolved, let's discuss last-minute updates and address any problems." Darcy gets the Prom meeting back on track.

The fluorescent lights hum overhead. Roy touches his arm through the hole in his shirt. I think about feeding Roy to my older sister's tarantula. I wonder how small would the pieces need to be for Ms. Brazilian to eat him? Or, how large would a spider need to be to crush a human head with its fangs? Little did I know I'd soon get the answer to that pondering.

Sweetie looks at Lynn who twirls the yellow highlights in her black hair. Lynn points her ballet slippers. Oh, ya, I'm suppose to call her Slippers now. Lynn got the nickname Slippers about a month ago when she started ballet classes. That's why I sometimes still call her Lynn. A few kids make it to senior year without a nickname. I'm glad it happened this way for her.

Slippers is the only student with school-colored hair highlights. Go Knights! She uses her ballet slippers to slide Sweetie's notebook across the gym floor to Sweetie. "Thank you." Sweetie opens the notebook. "I have good news." Roy puts a hand on her leg. Sweetie places her hand on top of his. At first it looks like she's just holding his hand, but she grabs his fingers and bends them back. CRACK!

"Aaaaaaugh."

Roy slips out of his chair and onto his knees. *Nice move.* Sweetie releases his hand. Roy climbs into his chair. Sweetie continues, "CelebratingProm.com has received all of the just-in-time measurements that Slippers and I emailed to them. They have confirmed that all dresses and tuxedos will be here tomorrow."

Slippers twirls her yellow hair highlights. She stops chewing on her pen for a moment to smile at Sweetie, and then resumes gnawing.

Sweetie continues, "We got permission to skip second period. We'll lock the gowns and tuxes in the theater department's wardrobe room. Then everyone can pick up his or her formal wear on Saturday morning. We really think having everything brought to us is going to make Prom Day easier and we believe this is reflected in the greatest number of Prom tickets ever being sold. This is going to be the school's highest Prom attendance ever." Sweetie looks at me. It isn't a nice look.

Rose flips a page of her book. Without looking up, she leans over, and taps Slippers on her arm.

Slippers returns to the present. She pulls the pen out of her mouth, "Oh, yes, 92 percent of seniors are attending this year as compared with only 74 percent last year."

Sweetie says, "Farmer Franklin has agreed to lay out the hot air balloon and fill it. He's old and deaf, but he used to assist with balloon flights in New Mexico. He said he wants to be paid with a cashier's check when the balloon is inflated. I'll take care of that."

Darcy nods. "Thank you, Sweetie."

I mumble, "Reaching new heights."

"Yes, Chevy," says Sweetie as she turns toward me. "The Prom theme is a metaphor. Seeing farther, reaching farther, and going farther with the support of our parents, teachers, friends, and *loving partners.*"

I say, "And then going back down, two minutes later." *I shouldn't have said that, but I did.* Two minutes, that's how long each Prom couple will spend up in the air in the hot air balloon.

"I'm all for going down," says Roy.

Sweetie looks at him. Roy flinches. He's afraid she's going to hurt him again. Sweetie leans in and kisses him on the cheek. Just when I think I've got her figured out.

Sweetie says, "I recommend we send Farmer Franklin some cheese and a thank-you note next week. This way, if he's still alive next year, the next Prom committee might have an easier time working with his pompous attitude if they do another hot air balloon."

See, she is always thinking about the future.

"Agreed." Darcy keeps her eyes on SNAFU. I look at him. I won't say he's acting gentlemanly, but he isn't being a jerk. Tamed. That's what he is. *What is going on?*

Rose raises her hand. Sweetie nods at her, but Rose doesn't see the nod because she's reading.

"Rose, you're up."

Rose bookmarks her place. Roy grabs his black and gold Fairland High water bottle. Rose waits until he has a mouthful of water.

Rose says, "We need more *wood* for Prom."

Roy spits out the water. *Brilliant timing.* Rose and Falcon high-five each other.

Rose explains, "We have a bonfire problem. Principal D says we can only get one cord of wood from Mr. Stoltz's lumber yard."

Falcon chimes in, "Something about the fire marshal being an ass."

Roy says, "Are you getting fire wood or cord?"

Roy is a city boy; he's the only one besides Darcy who might not know what a cord of wood is. Rose looks at Roy. "Well, as everyone knows a cord *of wood* is a stack of firewood that is 4 feet by 4 feet by 8 feet." She continues, "One cord is not going to be that big of a bonfire."

Falcon says, "So we're planning to get an additional cord OF WOOD from Jackson farms."

Rose smiles, "That way, we're not getting more than one cord from Stoltz, but we'll also have a bigger bonfire."

They look at Darcy.

"What do you want from me?" says Darcy.

Rose and Falcon say in perfect unison, "Your permission."

"Is what you propose illegal?" says Darcy.

"No, two cords are not illegal. But it's not what we were told to

35

do."

"Check inside," says Darcy. "What answer do you get?"

Rose says, "Huh?" Falcon says, "Como?"

Darcy looks around the circle and connects with each one of us. "Listen, you guys are now grown up. I know the school system pretty much tries to beat independent thinking out of you with the punishment and rewards system, but if you want to be happy and succeed, you've got to learn how to tap into *your* own alignment and then make decisions from there."

"What?"

"If you want to succeed in *your* life then you've got to stop looking for outside approval."

Darcy puts a hand on her chest. It would be nice to be that hand. "Put your hand over your heart and ask your question and then wait for YOUR answer. Not what Principal Domnagel would say. Not what the fire marshal would say. Not what your parents would say."

Rose says, "OK, Ms. Meyers, I'll do that."

Darcy waits.

"I'll do that tonight and get back to you tomorrow."

Darcy says, "Do it now."

"Right now?" asks Rose.

"Yes, this is a teaching moment. Show all of your friends how to do it."

Friends is sometimes a loose word when you're in a high school club. The only club that I've ever been in, where most everyone in the club is a real friend, is the hunting club. Other clubs will have a few friends and a bunch of *acquaintances* with similar interests, or *acquaintances* that want to get to second base with someone else in the club, or *acquaintances* who need to put something on their college application.

Darcy smiles in a way that looks like a creepy SNAFU smile. It's disturbing. "Wait a second. Falcon, you're on the bonfire sub committee with Rose, right?"

Rose lights up. "That's right!"

"I recommend you both do this."

Falcon is not happy. She gives a dirty look to her book-reading friend. Falcon puts her hand over the gold F on her varsity jacket. In Fairland High, we trust.

Darcy says, "OK, take a nice gentle breath in and let it out. Ask your question inside your head and wait for your answer. You may hear it inside yourself or you may just have a knowing."

Everyone else doesn't move or make a sound. We don't want to have to do it too.

Rose puts her hand down, "I got nothing."

I lean over to SNAFU, "That might be the worst affirmation ever."

Darcy looks at me. I shut up. Darcy says, "If you look for nothing and anticipate nothing, you will find nothing."

Darcy smiles at SNAFU. "Ask for the highest good of all concerned. Be open. Then anticipate getting an answer." SNAFU blushes.

Rose and Falcon nod and try it again. This time Rose puts her book down. Slippers gasps and stops twirling her yellow highlight. *Did you see that? Rose put the book down???* Rose and Falcon place their hands over their hearts and close their eyes. Everyone waits.

Rose opens her eyes. "Wow. I saw them."

Falcon laughs, "Oh, my. I heard it."

Darcy nods, "What did you get?"

They answer together, "Get both cords."

Slippers doesn't like it. She puts her ballet foot down, which for dramatic effect doesn't really work because the slipper only makes a muffled sound. "Why is it a good idea to break this . . . this guideline?"

Falcon and Rose say, "I don't know."

Everyone turns to Darcy.

Darcy addresses her cadets. "It's OK if you don't know *why*. Intuition is more powerful than logic and reasoning." That's it. We wait for more of an explanation but more doesn't come.

Sweetie says, "OK, Slippers tell everyone about the plate problem."

Slippers puts down her gnarled pen and points her pink ballet toes. I didn't mention this but Slippers is the oldest girl in the beginners' dance class. Everyone else is 8 or 9. People make fun of her, but I think she's brave. She's following her heart.

She starts to cry, so much for being brave. Everyone's concerned but Slippers is usually emotional so this isn't too unusual.

Sweetie says, "You can do this."

Slippers sniffs up some snot and says, "I can do this."

Darcy looks at me, "A much better affirmation, don't you agree?"

I nod.

"The plates are more of a sea foam green rather than teal," says Slippers.

SNAFU laughs. It isn't because he's mean; it's because he has actually never heard of sea foam green before, and he has no idea how it's different than teal. To him, green is green.

Darcy says, "Gentlemen, you're new to the group, and I'm sure you'd like to contribute to the success of Prom so that your addition to the yearbook photo, which we'll be taking soon, is not just a hollow senior prank. But before you assist us with solving this problem, please introduce yourself for anyone who may not know who you are."

SNAFU nudges me.

"My name is Eric. This is SNAFU." I always give my real name when talking with teachers. Darcy knows me and everyone else knows us. Our class is big but not too big, but I don't think Darcy has officially met SNAFU. If she wants to find out his name, this is one way to do it.

Darcy maintains eye contact with SNAFU. "Eric and Situation Normal, how might you address this problem?"

What a great response. I have known Robert a.k.a. SNAFU for more than twelve years, and I've never heard anyone call him Situation Normal. Most people don't know that SNAFU is military slang for Situation Normal, All *Effed* Up. Robert's old man is ex-Navy Seal Black Ops. He started calling his son SNAFU when he was four. Robert thought SNAFU was a pretty cool nickname until he was in first grade and a sixth grade bully told Robert what it meant. Robert beat up the sixth grader. No one has ever made fun of SNAFU since.

Darcy says, "Well, what would you like to contribute?"

I have nothing. All I know is the astronomy club is taking their yearbook picture after the Prom Committee. The best I can come up with is *let's get out of here and maybe we can sneak into the astronomy club photo.* But SNAFU turns to Slippers and says, "Did you order teal? Or did you order sea foam green by accident?"

Slippers pulls a three-ring binder from under her chair and unclicks the rings. She hands a yellow receipt to SNAFU. "You can see for yourself, I ordered TEAL."

SNAFU looks at the receipt. "Hey, don't get pissy with me. I'm trying to help." He settles himself down and looks at Darcy. "You've got two days before Prom. Call them at 8 a.m. tomorrow morning. That's when they open." SNAFU points to the phone number at the top of the receipt. "They're in the same time zone so you should be fine. Tell them to overnight the TEAL plates and to send a Call Tag and pick up the first order for the mistake they made."

Sweetie looks at me. I'm not sure what either of us expected him to say, but it wasn't something useful. Sweetie's brown eyes sparkle. Her right hand pulls her brown hair behind her ear. She stops. Just last week I was giving her a hard time that she's always playing with her hair. We were in the back seat of the Chevy. It was up on blocks. I love the smell of girls and gasoline.

"Why do you always do that?"

She gave the perfect response. Not that I believe it was true, but it stops me from mentioning it again. She kissed me and said, "I do that whenever I'm thinking about you."

Right then I knew I was going to marry her. That was the moment I decided. I remember thinking, who cares if her father is the Sheriff? With someone that quick and gorgeous, my life will be good.

Sweetie stops touching her hair and looks kinda sad. Maybe she *is* thinking about me. *Maybe.* She moves her chair closer to Roy. *Maybe not.*

SNAFU hands the receipt back to Slippers.

Darcy sits up straight. Her body continues to rock her uniform. She looks at SNAFU. "Mr. AFU, that sounds like valuable advice."

Darcy turns to Slippers. "Slippers, are you willing to make that call tomorrow morning? If you'd like, you can call from my office, and I can support you. This seems like a great opportunity to stand up for yourself." Darcy smiles at SNAFU. Straight teeth and an Army killer. What a great combo. Yup, one weekend a month she runs around in the woods covered in mud with a gun. She's almost as perfect as Sweetie, but in very different ways.

Slippers twirls her yellow-gold lock of hair. She shakes her head yes. Actually, her head shakes yes because her whole body trembles with the thought of standing up for herself. I guess it's time to grow up.

Jeremy, the Bird, walks into the gym with his camera. All the parents think his nickname comes from his photography skills, you know, bird's eye view. But it actually comes from the time Jeremy ratted out SNAFU for cheating on a physics test. Jeremy had just transferred to our school. It wasn't his fault he didn't know SNAFU's reputation. SNAFU made him eat his lunch for three days without using his hands. He had to bend over and peck at his food. And that is why he's called Jeremy, the Bird.

Darcy asks Sweetie, "Is that it?"

"Yes. Nothing else. It's done." Sweetie closes her notebook. I hear the sound of a judge's gavel slam down.

Darcy holds up her hand signaling to the Bird that we need another minute. He nods. Darcy smiles at SNAFU. "Mr. SNAFU, I first thought you and Eric just wanted to get in our yearbook picture. But I see it's a blessing that you're here to assist us with creating a successful Prom."

SNAFU is speechless. I'm pretty sure no one has ever called SNAFU *a* blessing before.

Darcy says, "Well then, I'd say that is perfect timing. I suggest we adjourn. Everyone please walk over to the Eiffel Tower, we'll take our picture there and let the anticipation of a fantastic Prom build."

Everyone claps and stands.

Sweetie steps toward me. "Good bye, Chevy."

She walks to the Eiffel Tower with everyone else. I follow trying to think of something to say. But all I can think of is, *why do we have to take a picture near the Eiffel Tower?* The photographer pushes and pulls bodies into place for the picture.

Roy says, "Sweetie, over here."

I pull on Sweetie's arm. "Come on, Sweetie. It's not goodbye. It's more like, see you later."

She looks at me and I let her go. She doesn't look angry. Anger would have been better than the *nothing* look I get from her. Anger would be something.

Sweetie says, "Right, who am I kidding? It's not goodbye. I'll see you tomorrow, we go to the same school."

That's not what I'm talking about.

Sweetie pats me on the back. *What the hell is that?* She never pats me on the back. I don't even know what that means. She nods and smiles. It isn't a happy or mean smile, it is a thoughtful look, which means something like, life is more complicated than she thought.

"You're right Chevy, I don't need to say goodbye." She looks at the Eiffel Tower, "I could say until we meet again, or how do they say it, *au revoir?*"

Those French words stop my breathing. She walks to Roy. She seems sad, but not the kind of sad, like I'm going to cry sad, but more like bummed-out sad. More like, I see things clearly now, and it's no ones fault but it's just-not-going-to-work-out-between-us sad.

Au revoir. It means see you later or until we meet again, in French. You'd think that might be comforting, *until we meet again*, but you don't know about Frenchie, the foreign exchange student.

Sweetie stands next to Roy. She makes sure she isn't next to me. Everyone is finally positioned. I just want this to be over. The Bird raises his camera but Darcy walks out of the group waving her arms. "No, no, no."

He lowers his camera and sighs as she moves people around. "Your colors would look better over here. Let's balance the picture with you over here. The lights reflect better off your eyebrow ring when you're over here."

And the next thing you know, Sweetie stands between Roy and me, and Darcy has placed herself next to SNAFU.

The Bird gives it another go, "OK, everyone say, 'Reaching New Hei . . .' "

"Hold on," Darcy interrupts. "This has been a very important experience for me. Let's everyone hold hands with the person next to them to symbolize the unity we feel. I'd like to say a prayer."

This is VERY unusual. Now don't get me wrong, we pray all the time here. That isn't the crazy thing she said. I know, I know, in some public schools they don't pray. Heathens. But we do, and no one says anything. We pray before every meal so as to bless our food and

41

neutralize the GMOs and pesticides. We pray before every sports game because we *know* God likes our team better than the other team. JK. Just kidding. And I pray before every hunt because I know animals are spiritual.

I also know us kids pray before every test because we know God knows everything and is therefore the best cheat sheet possible. Sometimes I even pray AFTER a test because I know time is an illusion. I call it retro-pray. So yes, praying is not unusual here but we don't do a lot of handholding. She is asking everyone to hold hands. That's crazy talk.

But no one laughs or mocks Darcy. I used to think it was because she is the teacher or because she is hot, but no one makes fun of her because she's sincere. We know she actually cares about us and she's just being Darcy.

Sweetie and I don't look at each other. We look straight ahead. We don't hold hands. Neither one of us is going to make the first move.

Darcy says, "Come on everyone, take the hand next to yours. We're not taking the picture until we do."

Sweetie's hand bumps into mine, our fingers interlace. My heart skips a beat and I swear I hear her breathing catch. I hope she still loves me. My other hand does "normal" handholding with Falcon. Palm to palm. No interlaced fingers.

I see Private First Class Darcy Meyers take SNAFU's hand. I see a single bead of sweat form on the back of his neck. I never thought Darcy could inflict damage points on SNAFU. Everyone is quiet.

"Dear God, the end of senior year is sometimes exciting and is sometimes hard. No one is going to tell us how to live anymore. No one is going to create our life for us. No one is going to save us. It's time to grow up. Prom is sometimes really glorious and sometimes emotionally difficult. We know even the hard times are useful because when we experience what we don't want, we get a better idea of what we do want. Remind us to focus on what we do want so we move in that direction. We say thank you for all of this, and we ask for your loving and strength to do what we need to do to create a positive, uplifting, and successful Prom Day. And so it is. Amen."

"Amen."

Then two unexpected things happen. Well, one that is pretty normal, except for the circumstance. The other thing has never happened before.

The normal thing happens first. SNAFU lets out one of the loudest farts ever. It must have been some tension fart. It is so loud that I'm concerned that part of his small intestine has actually blown out of his rectum and that he will ask me later to shove it back in. Everyone lets go of the hands they hold except for Darcy; she squeezes SNAFU's hand and laughs.

But it isn't a cruel or mean laugh. It is more like, "Oh, you just got whipped cream on your nose from your hot chocolate" laugh. It isn't even a laugh; it is more like a giggle, like a first-date giggle. Like his butt explosion is one of the cutest and most endearing things ever.

The other thing that happens is Cow Dung runs into the gym yelling, "The moon cracked! The moon cracked! And something is coming out of it!"

CHAPTER 5

THE INCITING INCIDENT

WE RUN OUT OF the gym. I'd like to say the reason I was running was to get away from the god-awful smell that SNAFU blessed us with. But in all seriousness, it was Cow Dung's tone of voice that got me running. Cow Dung is not a member of the Get High at Noon Club, and he isn't known as a practical joker. Unlike most of the other guys, he didn't join the astronomy club to meet girls, stay up late, and beso under the stars. He's president of the astronomy club because he loves all things space. In grade school, all of his science projects had to do with planets and orbits, but it was in ninth grade that he really committed to his soul's purpose.

Cow Dung has brown hair and always wears brown pants, but that's not why we call him Cow Dung. He owns three Galileo T-shirts, and he always wears one of them to school. His mother washes them twice a week for him. In ninth grade, he decided to *only* wear the Galileo shirts. Long story short, his mother said that was ridiculous.

"You've got 30 other perfectly good T-shirts. Pick one."

"No."

Summer came. He turned fifteen. It got hot and humid. He sweated. He kept wearing the same shirts. She didn't wash them. "I only do wash once a week." He sweated more. He smelled bad. He got the name Cow Dung. Finally, his old lady caved and started washing his Galileo shirts during the week. The cool thing is that when kids learn the story behind his nickname, they say it with pride. He got that nickname being true to himself. Deep down, that's what every kid hopes for.

We run out of the gym. It's dark outside. Cow Dung always gets the school to turn off the outside floodlights on astronomy nights. Which, by the way, is also good for "community building" activities a.k.a. beso time. Stars, billions and billions of them. If you ever want to see stars, get out of the city.

The fresh air smells and feels great even though it is more humid than usual because it rained all last week. The ground is still soft. I am glad I have my insulated hunting boots on. I know Roy is going to be cleaning his nice shoes when he gets home tonight. Idiot.

There it is, a big full moon. OK, it's not 100% full, but it's ALMOST a full moon. Trust me, if you're not a star junkie, it looks like a full moon. It takes me a minute, but then I can see it, even without a telescope, a thin, crooked line from the top of the moon to about the center of it. It's weird. I suddenly feel lonely. If you want the actual measurement of the moon crack, just Google it. I think the Russians were the first to get the measurement correct, but who cares?

"Chevy, look at this," Sweetie is about ten feet to my right. She is bent over, looking into the biggest telescope I've ever seen. It is an eight-inch Schmidt-Cassegrain. If we break up, I mean forever, I know I will miss her tight jeans. I love watching her walk down the hall into Spanish. Muy bonita, señorita.

"Chevy, look at the *real* moon."

It's good to hear her say my name. I ask, "How do you use this thing?"

"Stand over here."

I step closer to the telescope as she adjusts it. I see Roy. He stands by a smaller telescope, but he couldn't care less about it. Two cheerleaders hug him as they cry. Some people take change harder than others. He pats their heads pretending he knows how to be compassionate. Jerry, a lanky senior and Roy's best friend runs up to Roy. Jerry wears a black shirt with a skull on it. Jerry tries to pull one of cheerleaders off of Roy. She doesn't want to go with Jerry. Roy tells Jerry to get lost.

"No fair. You have two. I'm a very sensitive guy," shouts Jerry.

Jerry storms away. Roy looks at me and then stares at Sweetie. He's got the same look my hunting buddies have when they spot a rabbit. It's disturbing.

Sweetie says, "Look here."

I look into the telescope as my father's words echo inside my head, *focus on what you want, not on what you don't want.* My Dad is with me. That's good. I am also glad I know how to use the telescope. My cousin has one like this. He uses it to look over the hill at the Hamlin Motel on Route 23. I act like I don't know what I'm doing to see if Sweetie will touch me. She does, very gently on the right elbow. It's nice.

Sweetie brushes the hair away from her face. "Do you see it? The crack runs right through the Sea of Tranquility."

The moon is cool to see through a telescope. Always is. Yes, the crack is disturbing; I'll give you that. The cloud that erupted from the crack has cleared. Cow Dung calls it space dust. No one argues with him. Sweetie touches my forearm. She doesn't need to do that. I smile. *See, I don't need to take her to Prom.*

She says, "Don't think this lets you off the hook. I'm still going to Prom with Roy. The moon cracking is just too big to act stupid about."

Still, with these little touches I know she loves me. I create a desire. *I want Sweetie to be MY girl again even if I don't go to Prom with her.* I hold it for 20 seconds. Now, if all of the manifestation stuff I'm learning is correct, the Universe will present opportunities for me to create my desire.

Someone yells, "Do you see that? That big puff of something?"

It's Cow Dung. He stands at another telescope. His telescope is bigger than the one I am using. I don't know how I missed it. It is BIG. It's a Celestron C11 Aluminum Optical Tube. It looks like a water cannon. Cow Dung is infected with what is called "aperture fever."

Bigger is better with telescopes. Bigger aperture means more light is gathered, which means you can see more. Cow Dung supposedly went out with Rose, and all he talked about was an Orion 50 inch Monster Dobsonian Telescope. There was no second date.

I look into my scope. A puff of smoke shoots out of the moon crack into the air. OK, not air. There is no air in space. It looks like the moon took a big toke and after holding it for ten thousand years, finally exhaled.

Sweetie moves closer to me. "I'm scared." A shiver goes through her body into mine.

"Here," I take off my camouflage jacket and wrap it around her. "You're safe. Now when the aliens come down, they won't be able to see you."

She punches me. "That's not funny."

I suddenly realize how much tension there is. The moon has always been stable. Even when it changes it is a constant you can count on. Not anymore. Everybody is quiet. I hear the crickets. They seem to get louder. I don't think they know or care about the moon cracking. They should be concerned. We all should be. Things are going to get all effed up.

SNAFU puts his arm around Darcy, which I'm pretty sure is illegal. And if it's not, it's certainly frowned upon by the school board. It's a good thing he doesn't care for authority. Darcy removes it. SNAFU puts his arm around her again. She hesitates. I see it. It's only for a split second, but she hesitates and then she removes his arm again and walks away. SNAFU smiles. He felt her hesitation. It's at that moment I realize the world might end. Yeah, the moon cracking is crazy, but SNAFU and Darcy? This could only mean the Earth is about to stand still.

Nobody says anything for about 15 minutes. I notice Roy and the cheerleaders are gone. Good. It's much easier to win when there is no competition. I look around. Damn, there's his black convertible. If he takes Sweetie to Prom, he'll pick her up in that. That car is going to be the death of me. The black convertible is hard to see since it's so dark outside. Roy sits in the back seat with a cheerleader on either side. He turns from one to the other. They don't look scared any more. My first thought is, I hope they're sitting on a sheet of plastic. I'd hate for someone to catch something from that back seat. The second is, good for them. If it's all going to end, that's not such a bad way to go even if they are with Roy. I see Sweetie glance over at him. Good. I'm sure his actions aren't endearing him to her. Or, maybe they are. Maybe she's done with the good boy, even though I haven't been THAT good. Maybe she's looking for a *bad* boy. Geez, life is complex.

Then the phones ring. All of them, except mine. Parents are calling their kids. It is 9:32 p.m. The local and national news interrupt all the radio, television, and Internet news sources.

"I'm OK, Dad."

"I'm OK, Mom."

"I'm OK, Dad."

"I'm OK, Mom."

Times that by about 30.

Then everyone says it again, some three or four times. Jeremy, the Bird, whimpers. Sweetie's Dad puts Sweetie's little sister on the phone. Sweetie walks away from the crowd so she can hear her sister better. Someone taps me on the shoulder. It's Roy.

"So Chevy, no one cares about you?" He sees my phone is silent.

Behind Roy I can see both cheerleaders on their phones with their families. I wonder if they're sharing about their end of the world threesome.

I place my hand on Roy's shoulder. "Looks like she's with me again." SNAFU taught me how to be friendly when I'm actually being threatening. It's a little confusing and always more insulting.

Roy laughs. "All men are hunters. You and your friends go out into the woods and actually hunt. The guys in the city take out hordes of zombies and storm the beaches and castles. I like to hunt attractive girlfriends of other guys." He looks to make sure no one is listening, "You use your big gun, and I'll use mine."

I am about to punch him, but the astronomy faculty teacher walks by discussing gravity and large bodies of mass. He always has two or three nerdy kids with him. He's a good guy and doesn't like seeing kids alone by themselves. He entertains them until they make friends. Then they stop hanging out with him. They don't even say "good-bye." He doesn't seem to mind. I think he understands how it works.

Roy continues, "I don't care if the moon splits in half. I'm taking Sweetie to Prom AND the after-party. I am the better hunter."

SNAFU steps up out of the shadows. *Damn, Roy is a goner.* But SNAFU just stands there. He doesn't do anything. *Damn, Roy isn't a goner.*

SNAFU looks dazed; he's the goner. In the past, SNAFU would have sucker-punched anyone that got in my face. He's gone soft already, probably not literally. I turn. Yup, Darcy's next to him. They don't hold hands or touch, but they are close. Roy takes a step back when he sees SNAFU. I guess Roy hasn't realized that SNAFU is different.

That's when I hear the buzz. People duck, jump in their vehicles, and run back into the gym. Something is in the sky and heads straight for us. The cheerleaders yell, because that's what they do.

"Run, run!"

"They're here!"

"We're being invaded."

SNAFU shields Darcy. Roy hits the ground and covers his own head. It takes me a moment, but I recognize the sound. I laugh. I stand my ground as everyone else freaks out, runs, and hides. It's my Dad's two-seater plane. His crop duster flies over us. He probably thinks it's funny. He must not have heard about the moon cracking.

My Dad loves to fly, but not usually at night. He has always inspired me. When I turned nine, he told me how to succeed in life. We were in the backyard and he was helping me change the oil in our old Ford pickup. I think he knew I was a car guy before I did.

He told me how he always wanted to fly when he was a kid. So he saved up and took flying lessons when he turned 18. He didn't buy a car. He didn't travel. He didn't piss away his money on drugs or alcohol. He taught me saving money was one way to create opportunities and one way to prepare for the future. So he learned how to fly, and was thinking about joining the Air Force because a lot of pilots come out of the armed forces and get commercial airline gigs.

But, as fate would have it, on his nineteenth birthday, he met my Mom at a bookstore. She was in the city to buy a comic book for her younger brother's birthday. See, my Dad would always go to the bookstore and read all of the comics rather than buy them because he was always saving. "If you want to be wealthy," my Dad would always say, "buy assets not liabilities." It took me awhile before I understood what the heck he was talking about. Liabilities cost you money. Assets make you money. But, my Dad wasn't a free loader. He swept, took out the trash, and helped with the early Wednesday morning deliveries at the comic book store.

When he saw my Mom holding Wonder Woman #151, he knew she was his future. She didn't know anything about comics, so he told her more than she ever wanted to know. She left thinking he was a total Comic Con geek. He got her number and called her. That was before texting existed. They became boyfriend-girlfriend. She loved the country and said she would never leave. He said he loved her, but he also loved flying and wasn't going to give up his dream of flying for a living.

He vowed he would have both. He said it was his life, and he wasn't going to sacrifice anything. It took awhile, but he now owns his own plane and is about to buy another one. My Dad got the love of his life, my sister, and me, and he gets to fly every day. He decided what he wanted, and he kept his word to himself.

As the plane roars over our heads, a sign he pulls lights up. He must of flipped a switch. The sign reads, "Chevy heart-symbol Sweetie." The couples sign is his idea to get paid to do some night flying. He's hoping the romantic idea will catch on and high school students will pay for declarations of their love to be pulled through the sky during football games.

Everyone stands. "That's not funny, Chevy."

I say, "That isn't my idea. I didn't ... My Dad didn't mean to scare ..."

SNAFU lets Darcy go. I don't think he wants to, but she is safe now, and it would be awkward if he keeps holding her. Darcy walks away again. SNAFU sees the sign. "Looks like a sign."

Roy accidentally bumps into SNAFU as Roy brushes off his slacks. Sweetie steps between Roy and SNAFU now that Darcy is gone. I'm sure she's trying to stop a fight. She doesn't realize there isn't going to be one. Roy puts his arm around her. "We still going to Prom?"

Sweetie kisses me. *In your face, Roy.* I smile.

Sweetie says, "Good night, Chevy." She turns to Roy, "Saturday, pick me up at six with a white wrist corsage." It's Roy's turn to smile. *Aw, man, not fair.*

She picks up her phone and says, "Ya, everything is fine. Chevy's just being a jerk."

I say, "The plane thing wasn't my idea."

Sweetie continues on the phone, "If you're nice to Dad he'll let you stay up until I come home." She looks at me, "I'm leaving now." That is the worst good-bye ever from someone you love. Sweetie walks away as she talks into her phone. "Everything's going to be OK." I find it interesting how easy it is to lie to someone we love when we don't know if everything is going to be OK.

Everyone leaves. Roy checks in with his two cheerleader prospects. I don't think they leave together. Maybe they will. I don't really care. Everyone gets into their cars and dirt bikes and ride away.

Now my phone rings. Dad wants to know how the sign looks and what do the others think. He has no idea what's going on with the moon. It turns out my Mom doesn't know either. She's streaming some movie, so it doesn't get interrupted with the moon news. I don't want to get into a long conversation so I don't bring it up.

"Dad, everyone got really excited about it."

He's pleased. "See you at home. Don't stay out late."

I look around. It's just me, Cow Dung, and his big telescope. It's silent for a moment and then the ignorant crickets start up again.

"Chevy, would you take a look at this? It's 9:46 p.m. and I'd like you to verify this observation."

I almost laugh, but I don't. Cow Dung is so damn serious. Then I start to freak out. I don't know why, but I do. I walk over to his telescope; it's set up next to his pick-up truck.

"OK," he says, "what you're looking at is the top of the visible moon. You can see the crack, right?"

"Damn, it's even bigger in your telescope."

"Chevy, focus."

"Sorry. Yes. I confirm I can see it clearly." I attempt to be as scientific as I can. There is no more space dust, and the crevice is big and clear.

"OK, now I'm going to move it to the bottom of the fault line, which stops at about the middle of the visible moon tonight."

"Yes. Right in the middle of the Sea of Tranquility." I want to sound smart.

"Not really, but that doesn't matter."

Damn, Sweetie.

"Do you see it? Is it clear?"

He moves the telescope just a fraction and focuses it for me.

"Yes, I see it, and it is very clear."

"Great. Now I'm going to move the telescope up the crack line."

I stop myself from laughing.

He says, "A quarter of an inch is about 10 miles."

I might be making up the inches and miles part. We didn't record this conversation but that's what I remember. I also remember thinking, I'm going to learn something that I would rather not know.

"Eric, do you see the part of the crack that is NOT in focus?" I know this is serious, he uses my real name.

"More moon dust?"

"I don't think so, because if it was more moon dust, it would be shooting in all directions. It would also make a larger section of the fault line blurry. Now keep looking, and I'm going to change the focus of the telescope to 10 miles IN FRONT of the moon."

I keep looking, and what I'm looking at comes into focus. "I can see it." It's really clear now. It looks like a big white crystal. "What is it?"

"Wait, keep looking. Tell me when it goes out of focus again."

He doesn't touch the telescope. He looks at a stopwatch app on his phone. He waits. I look. Nothing changes, the white thing is still in focus. Cow Dung starts counting down, "Three, two, one."

"Now. Now," I say. "It's not in focus any more."

"That's not good."

"Cow Dung, what?!"

"Keep looking!"

I look through the telescope again.

"Eric, this is important. I'm changing the focus to 20 miles in front of the moon. I'm timing this. Tell me when it's IN focus again."

I wait. I stare. "Still out of focus. No, wait … it's in focus."

Cow Dung makes notes in a notebook. If you've seen any of the documentaries, you've seen these notes by now.

"Marvin, what does it mean?" I decide to use his real name.

"Eric, I need you to be detached right now. Can you do that?"

"Shut up. What do you want me to do?"

"I'm changing the focus to 30 miles in front of the moon."

I look again and say, "So you're changing the focus to a space CLOSER to the Earth."

He doesn't say anything.

I say, "It's out of focus. What are you…"

"Shhhhhh. Wait for it." Silence. Crickets. "Now. Is it in focus now?"

A chill runs through my body. I don't say anything.

"Eric, is it in focus?"

"No. No, it's not." *You're wrong. See, we're safe. You're just a stupid high school kid with a big… Wait. Oh, shoot.* "It's in focus. What is it?"

I step away from the telescope. Cow Dung looks at the moon. I finally say, "Dude, what's coming out of the moon?"

"I don't know," says Cow Dung "but it's coming straight toward Earth."

CHAPTER 6

WHAT WOULD YOU DO?

LUCKILY THE GOVERNMENT AND scientists don't tell anyone. Sleep is good. Without sleep, people get crazy fast. Maybe they're giving themselves time to figure out what to do. Maybe they just want to "hold off the weirdness" that's coming. Maybe they're freaking out themselves.

I stay with Cow Dung for about an hour tracking what we think is a slow-moving moon-chip-asteroid. Cow Dung does the math and says it will be getting to Earth about 6 p.m. tomorrow night. He says it's big, but not really big, but it may be big enough to get through the atmosphere before it burns up.

I get home and my Dad is still outside in back with the plane.

"Hey, second-born."

"Hey, Dad."

Since he doesn't say anything, I figure he doesn't know. He must have been jamming to some of his rock oldies.

"Would you help me with this banner?" asks my Dad, "I want to straighten it out."

"Sure."

"Everything OK with you and Sweetie?"

"Yeah, everything's great."

My Dad looks at me. "Listen, son, I love you. I'm OK with you lying to me every once in awhile. That seems to happen between kids and their folks. What I really encourage you to do is stop lying to yourself."

My Dad doesn't know the moon cracked, but he knows Sweetie and I might be breaking up. *How is that possible?*

"Watch your fingers." My Dad presses a button inside the cockpit and the motorized crank attached to the tail of plane pulls in the cord I'm holding. At the end of the cord is a hook that's attached to the banner he's working on. "Tell me when." I keep tension on the cord and banner so the cord's pulled in smoothly. "OK," I say. "I think that's it." The banner is only a couple of feet away from the plane now.

My Dad steps away from the cockpit, and returns to the rear of the plane. He says, "Tell me what you can't have."

"I can't have Sweetie and the car."

"You mean Project Freedom?"

"Yes, Project Freedom." I don't like saying it out loud because it sounds stupid.

My Dad reads my mind. "It only sounds stupid if you think it sounds stupid. Life will be easier if you're not ashamed of what you want or how you're creating your life."

"She doesn't get it."

"Did you tell her about Project Freedom?"

"She knows I'm rebuilding the car."

"That's not what I asked."

"No. I didn't tell her about the plan."

"Listen son, you've got to share your thoughts and plans with the woman you love. Deep decisions create deep intimacy. No wonder she's going to go out with another guy. She thinks you're choosing a car over her."

"How do you know Sweetie's going out with another guy?"

"I wanted to fly and live in a podunk town with your mother. I wanted her, a family, AND to fly every day. A commercial airlines gig was out of the question, I wasn't going to be gone five days a week. I got her, you, your sister, and I'm paid to fly five days a week. I could never have created this if I didn't think it was possible."

"I know the story. You tell it all the time."

"And I'll keep telling it until you get it."

"But isn't there more?"

"Chevy, there is always more. The universe is expanding. Who knows what exciting adventures life will bring. Who knows what crazy situations I will be in and what desires will be born? But for right now, this is my more."

"No offense Dad, but I don't want this."

"Of course not. You want something different. My more is not your more."

"I want my car and my lady."

"I know you do. You can have them both. Go get them."

"How?"

"That is the adventure of being you. But I can tell you something. You will only have them both if you THINK you can have them both."

My Dad flips a switch, and the new banner sign lights up. Roy heart-symbol Sweetie.

I laugh. All the time, I'm holding it and I never looked down. "Roy called you?"

"Right after I passed over the high school. Just to let you know, I charged him double. I'll put half on your desk for Project Freedom."

"Well, that's something."

"Good night, son."

"Good night, Dad."

I hug him. Which wasn't crazy unusual, but there are many times that we say goodnight without hugging. I guess that happens when you get older. Whenever I hug him, I realize I miss him. I'm glad he's still taller than me. I'm taller than my mom now. I got tall sophomore year. It's hard to keep the illusion that someone is responsible for taking care of you when you're taller than them.

"It will be all right," my Dad says, "you're a smart kid."

He has no idea what he's talking about.

56

"Thanks, Dad. Good night."

I don't have the energy to tell him about the moon so I don't. I figure one of us should get some sleep tonight. I walk inside and Mom is just finishing binge watching something. She turns it off. They don't watch the news because if something is "breaking," they get stuck to the TV flipping from one channel to another for hours. I don't say anything because I don't want that type of energy in the house while I try to sleep.

I kiss and hug her. I don't hold on too long, I don't want to let her know something is wrong. I ask her how her day was. She tells me stuff that doesn't matter. She tells me about dropping books off at the library, talking to Aunt Helen, and buying feta cheese for this recipe she's going to try. It's not the information but the act of sharing that builds the relationship, especially with chicks. I am letting her know I love her without saying it. If I were a real writer, I think that would be called subtext.

I also don't bring up the moon stuff because Cow Dung might be wrong. He is a high school senior, and even if he *is* right, there isn't anything we can do about it. She will find out soon enough, probably in the morning, which turns out to be true. I just didn't realize how'd she learn about it.

By early morning the news of something coming to Earth is all over Facebook, the news, and the morning shows. Everyone Tweets and hash-tags. The President says the experts report "the thing" coming from the moon is not too big and that it will burn up when it hits the Earth's atmosphere. In fact, the President says, it will look beautiful. I appreciate the President's efforts to shift the focus from disaster to beauty. However, this is when I start to realize that experts sometimes don't know squat.

My Mom does yoga in the morning on the front porch. She doesn't do social media until she has saluted the sun. This morning, when she looked up to say, "Good morning, Sun," she saw it.

Have you ever heard your Mom scream? It's a horrifying way to wake up. This is what I woke up to:

"Ahhhhhhhhhhhhhhhhhhhh."

I jump out of bed, trip, and run into my bedroom wall. I make it out of my room but I fall down the stairs. I stumble out the front door. I don't find her looking up. She's in a little ball on the porch with her arms over her head, like something is going to drop on her. I look up and see it.

There is a big, crystal-like rock in the sky. It looks like it's gonna drop right on our front porch. I duck and wait to die, but nothing happens. I look again. It's still there. Just hanging in the air. Then I realize it's not a big moon piece crashing to Earth, rather it is the jagged end of what looks like a long Cord in the sky. The one end looks like it is reaching to Earth and is about to slam into our house. The other end goes up into the sky and disappears. The Cord has the diameter of a grain silo. It looks about 19 feet thick (almost 6 meters). It's no small thing.

I look at the Cord and follow it up into the sky, and there, low on the horizon, is the moon. I can't follow the Cord all the way to the moon, but I know that is where it comes from. It has traveled all night. It's 6:12 a.m., and it's about 30 miles from hitting Earth. Sure, Cow Dung is off by about 12 hours, but he's still OK in my book. He made the discovery and the calculations in the field (literally) outside our high school.

I grab my mother. She holds her knees and rocks. She won't let go. For a moment I think I'm going to have to roll her into the house.

"It's OK, you're safe. You're safe." Again it amazes me how easy I say what I do not know for sure.

She stands and I guide her in. I put her on the couch and cover her with a blanket. I wonder how many others are in shock.

It is about 7:20 a.m. when I hear the sonic booms. The jets fly up, down, and around the Cord. That's what they call it. The Long Cord. The Galactic Cord. The Space Cord. One news anchor calls it a Moon String, but that doesn't stick. Whatever it is, it seems to come out of the moon's fault line and drifts or floats through space.

The scientists thought, or perhaps hoped, that it would burn up when it entered the Earth's atmosphere. But no such luck. It moved slow enough that there was no real heat friction, or at least not enough to burn it up. I guess they had been shooting it with missiles all night long. They couldn't break off a piece let alone snap it or stop it. Whatever it is, it's strong.

We watch the morning news and I realize I had heard sonic booms in the middle of the night. At that time, I didn't realize missiles and jets flying faster than the speed of sound were making all that noise. I thought it was a freak thunderstorm. I listened for rain but didn't hear any. I rolled over and went back to sleep. Now don't get me wrong. It took me awhile to go to sleep. I almost texted Sweetie about 100 times the night before. I also opened up my Bible and did a random flip. My eyes zoomed onto Ezekiel 1, part 26. Not part, verse. I may be a heathen, but I know some God stuff.

"Above the dome there was something that looked like a throne made of sapphire, and sitting on the throne was a figure that looked like a man." *What?* I read for a while and then looked up the meaning of the verse. Supposedly it's God telling Ezekiel that God has a mission for him. I took it as a sign. I got down on my knees because that is what you do when a big piece of space shit is about to hit your planet.

"God, this all seems pretty effed up. I don't really mind the world ending. I mean, if it's going to end, it's going to end. But to tell you the truth, I really don't like the idea of Roy making out with Sweetie if the world *doesn't* end. Now here's the thing. I know I have to do what I know is right for both me and her, even if she doesn't know it's the best thing for us. If I go to Prom because of her demands and postpone my future, this is not going to benefit her or me in the long run. She needs me to be a strong man if we're going to have a fighting chance at a good relationship. I've always heard to not pray for an easy life but to be a strong person. I request strength, God. Lots of it. And perhaps a little more smarts too because I may not be seeing this situation as clearly as I could be. Thank you."

I felt tired after that. Not tired defeated but tired relaxed. I mean, what more could I do? I climbed into bed and went to sleep. That was 3 a.m.

My Mom sits and hums on the couch. My Dad isn't much better. He sits and I lose him to the news. They flip from one channel to another. My older sister Seven-Thirty comes down the stairs. She wears a cropped T-shirt, baggy pants, and an army jacket. She was big into hip-hop in high school and kept it up through college. Sometimes she dresses normal, but most of the time she's more colorful.

Seven-Thirty is twenty-two. She graduated from college last year, but she wasn't sure what to do. My father said it didn't really matter what she did, just so long as she did something. Then she just needed to listen to the feedback she received. For example, did she like what she was doing? Was it working out for everyone involved? Did she want to keep doing it? He said if she enjoyed what she was doing and everything was cool, then keep doing it. If not, then be smart enough to do something else. She told my Dad that she wanted to help him with his business. He wasn't expecting that, but embraced the idea. He loved flying and marketing but not the book side.

So my sister moved back home. Seven-Thirty also told Mom that she wanted to learn how to cook. She was done with fast food. She said it didn't make her feel good and didn't help her with her dancer's body. She wanted to eat healthier and learn how to slow cook. So she's bonding with my parents in meaningful ways, which was much better than when she was a teen and they bonded through fighting.

Seven-Thirty is east coast hip-hop slang. I don't know if this is true, but seven-thirty is supposedly the time mental patients get their medication. Seven-Thirty is a colorful way of saying someone is crazy. My sister can definitely be seven-thirty.

My friends, of course, also want to come over and *bond* with my older sister. That's when Seven-Thirty decided to get Ms. Brazilian, which just reinforced the meaning of her name. She had always been fascinated with spiders, and she told me that my friends would keep their distance if there was a tarantula crawling all over her body. I didn't say anything, but I laughed inside. I thought, that's why she might be single; she doesn't know guys very well.

My sister sits on the couch next to my parents. She surfs the web on her phone for additional moon info. She reports interesting stuff that has not been said on the news.

"Even though Americans have planted six flags on the moon, it doesn't mean we own it." Seven-Thirty goes on to say that the astronauts in *six* different Apollo missions planted a flag on the moon each time they went there. To tell you the truth, I didn't know there was more than one lunar landing.

The last thing I hear while I eat my scrambled egg and bacon sandwich is that the first American astronauts left a plaque on the moon. She passes her phone around so we can see it.

I read one of the lines on the plaque a couple of times, "We came in peace for all mankind." I think, *if someONE or someTHING made the Galactic Cord, did it read that plaque? And if it did, is it in agreement with coming in PEACE for all us humans down here?*

Another good question is, do you go to school, or work, or milk the cows on a day like this? It is Thursday, two days before Prom. I am supposed to read my history report about the Panama Canal in class today. It all seems rather unimportant now. Who cares what the Untied States military did to get ownership of that strip of land (Isthmus of Panama) so that international maritime trade (check out my use of big words here) could travel from the Atlantic to the Pacific Ocean under the U.S.A.'s control? Sure, we played pretty dirty to control the Canal, but does that really matter on a day like today?

I realize I'm living history, right now. I think living life is more important than talking about it. Maybe it always is. I think about skipping out of all of the insanity and work on the Chevy. But if today is going to be the last day of my life, I don't want to be alone. I think about hanging out with my family, but Mom and Dad are already fixed in some sort of hypnotic trance in front of the TV. So much so that they don't even notice when Seven-Thirty takes a whole bag of cookies, dumps them into a mixing bowl, pours milk on them, and eats them like cereal. My parents do, however, notice when she throws up in the bathroom thirty minutes later. That's the worst part of eating cleaner, you really feel it if you go back to eating junk food.

I shift from what I *should do* to what I *want to do*. I think of Sweetie, but realize that's probably not an option. Next idea. I would rather be joking around with SNAFU. I text him to see if he's going to school. He writes back, "Headed toward school. Got surprise for Darcy."

He's going to be worthless. He should just leave that alone. He's only going to get his heart broken. I think about texting Sweetie again, but she hasn't texted me. I'm not going to be the first one to send a text on the last day of my life.

I jump onto my dirt bike and head to school.

I get to school at about 9:30 a.m. It's suppose to start at 8:50, but I figure no one is going to be taking attendance, and if they are, screw them. Actually, I don't make it to school. I get stuck in the traffic jam and roadblock *on the way* to school, which is about a quarter mile down the road.

FYI, there is a two-lane road that runs to our high school. It passes the cemetery and the Wellness Medical Center and then goes on for about a quarter mile through some fields before getting to the high school. That's where I stop. That is where traffic stops. Cars are also pulled over on the berm to look at the Galactic Cord just hanging over the high school admin building. I look back over my right shoulder and can just see the Civil War memorial statue in the cemetery. It is a 1/8 reproduction of the one in Washington D.C. It is the Civil War statue of a solider on his horse. Not a lot of people know this but our town saw some action during the Battle of Gettysburg.

OK, the action wasn't a battle; it was more like a small skirmish. And the guys from our little town lost the skirmish, but the point is they fought hard and tried. Trust me, I know this is the point because they tell us this *every year* when we celebrate the fight. Our town can't celebrate a win, but we do celebrate trying.

Oh, and for those of you who don't know, the Battle of Gettysburg was one of the bloodiest battles of the American Civil War that was fought from 1861 to 1865. And, a lot of people died. The Northern States and the Southern States weren't agreeing on a few things, one of them being slavery. The Southern states broke off to form their own country. President Abe Lincoln and the North said, "No." There was a big, horrific war and the United States stayed united.

The monument in the cemetery is a Calvary soldier riding on horseback with his sword drawn. He points his sword as if he's charging. At the moment, the sword kinda looks like it's pointing at the Galactic Cord up in the sky. Again, foreshadowing, but I didn't see it.

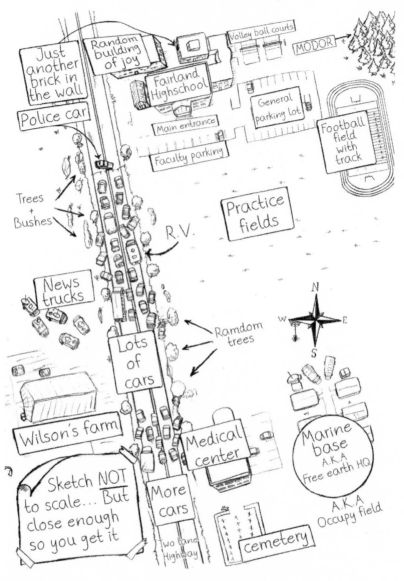

Over my left shoulder, on the other side of the two-lane highway, is Wilson's farm. There are already seven different news trucks set up in the middle of his squash crop. In Pennsylvania we grow veggies that get shipped up and down the coast. His field is going to be ripped up. Later I heard he got paid a pretty good amount before the trucks drove onto his land. I never found out exactly how much, but I do know that he took some of the dough and bought four one-way tickets to Florida. He and his family flew out and watched what happened from a luxury suite in a five-start hotel in Miami not more than 40 feet from the ocean. I mention this here because they might have been the smartest people in town that day.

The Wellness Center used to be named after some major disease but then someone said, "Hey, let's not focus on being out of balance; let's focus on healing and health." So they changed it to the Wellness Center. Smart. I can tell you it feels better driving past the *Wellness Center* everyday. As Sweetie would say, focus on what you want, you will always move in the direction of what you focus on.

It turns out the big Cord from heaven is going to hit Earth next to our high school. I mean, I guess it's got to land somewhere. If it hits farmer Wilson's Barn, or my house, everyone would say, "What are the odds?" It just so happens that *the somewhere* is near our high school.

Someone calls it Luggi. I think it's Cow Dung. Some people get groggy from staying up all night. I guess he gets funny. He has his big telescope set up on the back of his pickup truck. He's mobile. Well, not anymore. His truck, like everyone else's, stands still on the two-lane highway. He has a step stool and helps kids up and down so they can get a good look at it. I guess he has the "teacher" gene.

The two-lane road is not really a two-lane road any more. People drive on the berm on both sides of the road. It is now four cars wide with all of the traffic going one way, toward the high school. Cars and trucks get stuck in the dirt berm. Wheels spin. Mud flies. People yell. You see, it rained a lot last week. The ground is still soft with big puddles. Not ideal conditions for going off road.

All of the news crews make up stuff because they have to keep talking hour after hour. At home, I remember hearing the local station W-PAL repeat its tag line about twenty times in thirty minutes, "W-P-A-L has your back. We are your news pals." And, they kept giving updates like: "Experts still don't know what it is or why it's here."

And then they have important breaking news like: "This just in. The Galactic Cord is NOT 19 feet in diameter; it's 19 feet AND 3 inches in diameter. It is bigger than first calculated. We'll be right back to discuss what these 3 extra inches mean to you, me, and the fate of the world!" Come on, an extra 3 inches might make a difference to my girlfriend, but it isn't going to change how the Galactic Cord is going to effect Earth.

I weave through traffic with my dirt bike.

I could go off road, but as I said the ground is still wet from the rain last week, and I don't want to spray mud up onto the back of my shirt. I also don't want to shower it on everyone I pass. Racking up bad karma is not a good way to start the end of the world.

I head toward a huge RV that is near the front of the blockade. It has a canopy on top. *That's the way to watch the Apocalypse.* There is a young man in a suit and tie on the roof of RV under the canopy with a megaphone. I can't hear what he's saying, but he's the most interesting thing going on so I head there. To tell you the truth, I keep looking for Sweetie's car, but so far I don't see it.

CHAPTER 7

FRONT ROW SEATS FOR THE APOCALYPSE

AS I GET CLOSER, I realize the preacher kid on top of the RV looks like SNAFU. *That's funny.* The kid picks up the megaphone again.

"God spits on our school."

It *is* SNAFU. He wears a white shirt, navy blue jacket, and tie! He even combed his hair. SNAFU doesn't look like SNAFU. The way he looks is actually *more shocking* to me than the 19 ft. 3 inch Galactic Cord that is about to plop down near our school. I'm so glad to see him. I don't think I could have gotten through the day if it was going to be all-serious doom and gloom.

"Chevy, get up here!"

I park my dirt bike and climb the outside ladder on the back of the RV. The car next to me honks, and I almost fall off the ladder and crack my head.

The guy in the car yells at SNAFU, "God does not spit on our school. That is not funny."

God spitting on our school is funny. Me almost dying isn't funny.

I've got to be more careful on this strange day.

Bible Thumper honks his horn again. He shouts, "Non-believer, put down the megaphone." Bible Thumper looks funny when he's upset. His face contorts, twitches, and turns bright red. He gets out of his car and slams the door. The funny thing is Bible Thumper is dressed just like SNAFU. White shirt, navy suit jacket, and tie. The tie is not exactly the same, but it's close.

SNAFU sees Bible Thumper and notices they're dressed the same. He yells into the megaphone, "It is my brother from another mother. He has returned home. Father, kill the fatted calf."

I smile and step away from the edge of the RV roof even though there is a small railing all the way around it. No reason to tempt fate. The roof of the RV is beautiful. It has a bright blue canopy over the top with built-in couches along the sides. The roof can easily host a 20-person party. SNAFU's father comes up through a hole in the roof. He wears his Navy Seal uniform and carries a pitcher of pink liquid with ice. SNAFU's father is ex-Black Ops. SNAFU says his father existed outside military protocol, engaging in off-the-books operations, and bending or breaking international laws. If that's true, then I understand why SNAFU is the way he is. Maybe it's genetic.

SNAFU's father shakes my hand. "Chevy, I'm glad you got the text.

Excuse me while I prepare. There is always so much to do on a day like today." He places the pitcher on a small table.

"Is that pink lemonade?"

"Yes, would you like some?"

I do but I don't answer. The contrast between Navy Seal and pink lemonade is too great for me to grok. SNAFU's father pours me a glass. "I'm glad you found us, son. It's a beauty, eh?"

Did he just call me son? I look at the RV. "Yes, sir, she's a beauty."

I remember some of our past conversations. SNAFU's father talked about buying a "fifth wheel" so that when he retired he could tour the country. Fifth wheel is slang for RV. I don't know why. I check my phone and see the text from SNAFU. *On RV at front.* I don't hear text dings when I'm on my bike.

SNAFU's Dad sweeps his hand. I realize he's giving me a tour. "Rooftop deck is accessed from an internal stairway." Yup, that's the hole he stepped out of. "With the sky deck you literally double your social space and you also get a 360-degree view of your vacation." Not vacation. We aren't really on vacation. But we do have a 360-degree view.

I see a cop car about six cars in front of us with orange cones and barricade things. An officer stands next to his car. He stops traffic from getting any closer to our high school. The first car at the barricade is Slippers' yellow Volkswagen bug. I can read her bumper sticker, "Dance And Know God." I guess she's ready to stand up for herself and make that call about the sea foam plates. *Good for her. I guess it's time to grow up.*

The high school is further down the road past Slippers' yellow car and police roadblock. The Galactic Cord hangs in the air over the field with the sand volleyball courts.

To my left, I take another look at the news vans in farmer Wilson's fields. To my right are woods and open fields. Behind us, to our right is the Wellness Center, and a little farther back is the town's cemetery with the Calvary man ready to charge. I think it's a little strange to put a medical center next to a cemetery. Sure, it's convenient for those who don't make it, but is a tombstone an image you want to see when you're driving to see the doctor?

I turn around. Directly behind us, the road is jammed with cars. Students get out and climb on their vehicles so they can see better, others visit each other. Some hug, some cry, some drink. Students standing in the back of a pickup truck point to the row of trees and bushes that line the two-lane highway. No, they point at something on the other side of the trees.

Oh, I see it now.

They point at a makeshift Marine base that has been setup on the fields on the other side of the medical center and cemetery. I count 15 camouflaged canopies and tents. This must be where they are coordinating the air assault. I'm assuming the Marine base was dropped in during the middle of the night. It's nice to see they can move fast if they need too. When I was on my dirt bike, I couldn't see the camouflaged tents, due to the row of trees along the road. (And, because the tents are camouflaged.) But up here, with my 360-degree sky roof view, I can see it all. SNAFU's father is right. I'm sold. Let's buy one.

Just then a navy blue pickup truck zooms along the berm. It spins out in the mud, but keeps going. I see a single shotgun in the gun rack against the back cab window. What is the driver going to do? Shoot at the Cord? The truck drives on the muddy berm. The officer yells at the driver as the truck passes the barricade and cop car. The truck swerves back onto the road and heads straight for the school. Mud from the back tires of the pickup rains down on the police officer. He calls it in on his walkie, but remains at his post. The pickup races to the high school.

The pickup screeches to a stop in the parking lot about twenty feet from the school. All eyes are on it. People climb on top of their cars to see what's happening. A guy wearing a red flannel shirt gets out and walks toward the school. He looks up at the Galactic Cord. I think he graduated last year.

He gives the Galactic Cord the finger. The crowd cheers. And I don't mean polite applause, but I mean yelling, howling, and whistling. With my 360-degree view, I see hundreds of people expressing their enthusiasm and fighting spirit. Wow, people have lots of feelings about this. I see something move on top of the Wellness Center. Yes, there are people up on the roof of the medical building cheering. One guy with dark hair and a beard, in a pale blue hospital gown, raises a crutch and shakes it at the Galactic Cord. I can't hear him, but he's saying angry words.

The police officer realizes no help is coming and he has to handle this himself. He jumps into his squad car, flips on his lights, and races toward the school. The flannel ex-Knight lowers his finger. He reaches into his navy pickup truck and gets a can of something. He drinks the rest of it. He takes a few steps toward the school and throws the empty can at the Cord. I don't know if you have ever tried this, but it's really hard to throw an empty aluminum can. It doesn't weigh anything. It goes about three feet and falls to Earth. The can doesn't even get close to the Galactic Cord. It's disappointing, after all of the hooping and hollering.

The cop car squawks its sirens. The kid realizes the law is coming for him. He jumps into his pickup, slams on the gas, and crashes into the only light pole in the parking lot. The cop car boxes the truck in. The officer pulls the kid out, handcuffs him, tosses him into the backseat, and drives off. See, don't drink and drive even if it's the last day of the world.

Everyone climbs off of their cars; they think the show is over. Little do we know it hasn't started yet.

Bible Thumper's girlfriend, Nancy Potter, comes running up to him. He hugs her, but she can't hug him back. She carries a big book and lighter fluid. I can see the library sticker on the spine of the *Goblet of Fire*. Did she break into the library this morning? Or has she been saving this copy for a special occasion? They run off to the side of the road to burn the book, like sacrificing popular teen fiction is going to appease the gods and stop the end of the world. Their attempt to fix things this way seems like a throwback to the stone ages.

Note: don't make fun of Nancy's name and don't ask her if she has a brother named Harry. Nancy Potter is 100% Muggle. She and Bible Thumper are an item. They purchased three Harry Potter books last year and burned them because they said the books encouraged kids to do witchcraft. Yeah, and *Iron Man* encourages kids to make exoskeleton body armor and fight crime. Buying books and burning them sure showed the publisher and the author. Nancy and Bible Thumper gave them more money for doing something they don't like. Brilliant.

SNAFU's father pours more pink lemonade.

"Thanks, Dad." I never heard SNAFU call him Dad before. Life is changing really fast. I hope I can keep up. "Life is short, maybe shorter than we know," SNAFU continues, "We may soon be covered with some sort of moon phlegm. And when I say we, I mean Earth. It could be starting right here."

I say, "What could be starting right here?"

"The end times."

You'd think this wouldn't shock me because I've been joking about the apocalypse all morning, but when someone says it in a calm mater-of-fact way, it's very disturbing.

SNAFU's Dad pours himself a glass of the pink stuff and says, "Which is somewhat fitting."

Fitting that THE END starts here?

He smiles. *Good, he's joking.* I smile too. He raises his glass; we toast. *Wow, happy and witty too.* Is it the sky roof? Is it the pink lemonade? Is it the fact that this could be the last day of our lives and we're all realizing what's important?

The pink lemonade is cold, sugary, and sour. My mouth puckers.

SNAFU looks at the Cord. "Who knows how much of this stuff is inside the moon and is going to grace our fair planet." I never considered that. *What if it keeps pouring out like an endless lava flow like in MineCraft?*

A voice in the wilderness yells, "SNAFU, repent now. The time is near."

We walk to the edge of the RV and look down on the peasants below. Bible Thumper and Potter are back. Behind them, I see black smoke as the book burns on the side of the road. I look up. Nope, the Cord is still there. I guess the sacrifice didn't work.

SNAFU raises his megaphone, "Do you really want to die angry?" Bible Thumper and Potter look at each other.

SNAFU says, "Take the wood nymph and have your way, young Knights!" SNAFU points to the trees behind them that run along the highway. There are just enough trees and brush to get lost in.

"We are saving ourselves!"

For what? But I don't say it out loud.

SNAFU says, "You don't have to go *all the way.*" He pauses and then adds, "Is it better to *make out* or *be hostile?*"

Bible Thumper takes his girlfriend's hand, they run, and disappear into the foliage.

SNAFU yells into the megaphone, "Another couple saved." Applause erupts from the small crowd that has worked its way up to the front of the barricade. Even without the officer and cop car, the line holds. Most people are smart.

I smile. "It's the old SNAFU and at the same time, the new and improved SNAFU."

He slaps me on my back. "It's all about the loving."

Ow, that smack hurts. I can't tell if he's serious or joking. SNAFU's father raises his glass. "To loving." We toast. We drink. His father wipes something from his eye. Is that a tear? A tear of joy? This is weird.

Just then something comes up from the hole in the roof of the RV. I jump but it's only Darcy. Darcy??? How long has she been in the RV? She comes up the same stairs that SNAFU's father used. She looks like an angel as she floats up onto the roof. No army uniform. Not today. She wears a white summer dress. She looks softer today. She kisses SNAFU. Not a gross, get-a-room kiss but a nice kiss, as if they have been dating for a while.

SNAFU turns to me, "I'd like you to be my best man."

"Best man for what?"

He laughs as if I don't know what he's talking about. I don't.

"My Dad went online this morning and got ordained in the Church of the Whippoorwill. He's now a nondenominational, interfaith minister." I nod as if I understand what he's saying. SNAFU takes Darcy's hand and continues, "We stayed up all night talking. Just talking. We talked about everything. It was like we have known each other forever but haven't seen each other for a long time."

I look at them holding hands in front of the retired killing machine turned minister. I realize what's going on. *Holy. Holy. Holy.*

Darcy yells, "Sweetie!"

Darcy runs to the back of the RV. Sweetie climbs up the outside ladder. The wind tosses Sweetie's hair. *How can I miss her so much in just one day?* Darcy gives Sweetie a big hug.

Sweetie says, "You can borrow this." Sweetie hands Darcy a small, old cheerleader trophy.

Darcy looks at the trophy. "I use to be a cheerleader."

Sweetie smiles. Sweetie touches her jeans pockets but they're empty. "Sorry, but I can't find the blue pen I had." Sweetie looks down off the RV as if she's looking for the pen on the road below. "Why do you need these?"

Darcy looks down over the side of the RV too. Darcy looks sad.

SNAFU opens his wallet, "It's OK. It's OK. I came prepared."

I think, *don't pull out a condom. This is not the right time or place for a condom.* SNAFU pulls out a scrape of notebook paper. He unfolds it to reveal a blue, plastic jewel. It is the sapphire bindi that Darcy gave to him on Halloween. He has carried it with him ever since.

SNAFU hands Darcy the blue dot.

Darcy says, "You didn't tell me that you kept this."

"I didn't think about mentioning it because I now have you."

"Yes, you do."

Gag me with a fork.

Darcy smiles and they both turn toward SNAFU's father who stands facing them. Sweetie walks over and joins us. I realize we are in place. I stand next to SNAFU and Sweetie's next to Darcy.

Sweetie says, "You're not even going to say hi to me?"

All I can get out is, "Do you realize what's happening?"

"Yeah, the world is ending and you're being a jerk."

"No, I mean right here. Do you know what's happening right here?" I look at the Lieutenant, SNAFU, and Darcy. I touch the sleeve of Darcy's WHITE dress. Sweetie looks at everyone. Darcy picks up a small bouquet of flowers. SNAFU's father reviews a handful of index cards.

Sweetie gets it. "Oh, my God." Sweetie turns to Darcy, "You're committing a felony. You're not allowed to be involved with a student."

Darcy smiles. "I resigned this morning at 7 a.m."

SNAFU says, "You gave up your career for me?"

"This was just my first year of teaching and I can always ..." But then Darcy realizes SNAFU means it as a sign of her love for him. "Yes, yes I am giving up my past to create something new with you. I'm not going to do what I should any more. I'm going to honor all parts of me."

SNAFU's father says, "Dearly beloved, we are gathered here ..."

BOOM. BOOM. BOOM.

Huge explosions rock the Space Cord. Jets zoom in. People take cover. Some duck into their cars, some duck behind them, and some duck under them. SNAFU grabs Darcy. I hold Sweetie.

BOOM. BOOM. BOOM.

We sit on the semi-weatherproof, semi-comfortable couches on the RV roof. We hold still until we realize we aren't going to die. I continue to hold Sweetie, her body against mine. I smell her hair. Coconut and Sweetie, fantastic. I feel her forehead against my cheek. My hand on her back, holds her to me. If I'm going to die, I want to go out like this.

The Galactic Cord doesn't break. Each missile that hits it sends a shock wave through it. The Cord snaps violently in the sky with each blast. The pilots focus their barrage at the same place on the Cord, a point about a half-mile up. I believe they're seeing if they can break it. It isn't breaking but it's sure flailing around, slicing through puffy white clouds like Indiana Jones' whip.

BOOM. BOOM. BOOM.

Then the explosions stop. It's quiet.

Darcy turns to Sweetie. "When SNAFU told me that Chevy was going to be his best man, I knew I wanted you here. I don't have a lot of young friends since I'm new here."

"And, you were our teacher."

"But now that you're graduating and I'm marrying Chevy's best friend, I'm hoping we can become besties."

Sweetie hesitates and thinks. She means what she says so sometimes she takes some time to respond. Sweetie finally smiles and nods.

"Sure."

Darcy gives her hug, relieved. Sweetie hugs her back. I think Sweetie would say more because she thinks Darcy is cool, but her brain has probably locked up like mine. This is a lot to process.

And then, we hear singing. "And the rocket's red glare, the bombs bursting in air..." The crowd surrounding the RV belts out *The Star Spangled Banner*—which seems strange and appropriate at the same time.

An army helicopter flies up to the RV. A voice barks from the copter's speaker system, "Private First Class Darcy Meyers, what are you doing? Your reserve unit has been called in. Your country needs you."

Sweetie says, "How did they know you're here?"

SNAFU's father says, "Cell phone. If the batteries aren't out they can track it."

Darcy hands her bouquet to SNAFU. He accepts the fact that his woman is needed to play a bigger part in whatever is unfolding. His personal wishes and desires are going to have to wait. Darcy picks up SNAFU's megaphone and replies, "Yes, sir."

A rope ladder drops out of the helicopter. SNAFU and Darcy kiss. SNAFU says, "I'll wait for you."

SNAFU's father grabs the rope ladder. Darcy steps on the ladder and says, "I'll be back." She climbs the ladder as SNAFU's father holds it steady. He turns to SNAFU, "Son, the time for waiting is over. No one creates a life they love by waiting."

SNAFU looks up at Darcy, he looks under her dress. I don't think he intended to do that, but he smiles. SNAFU hugs his Dad, "Thanks, Dad. Thanks for everything. I know it hasn't been easy..."

SNAFU's Dad hugs him back. "Son, life isn't supposed to be easy. If it was we'd never get strong. You're a good kid. I love you."

"I love you too." SNAFU tosses the bouquet over his shoulder and Sweetie catches it. He climbs up the ladder after Darcy. SNAFU's Dad lets go of the ladder and salutes. The helicopter flies away with SNAFU still climbing up.

"I thought it would take him longer to leave the nest." SNAFU's Dad turns to Sweetie and me. "You know, Eric, I still have a marriage ceremony in me."

Sweetie turns to me. I take her hand. "I do love you."

More jets zoom overhead. BOOM. BOOM. BOOM. They try again to break the Cord.

I don't know what I was thinking. You know how it is when you go to a wedding and all of a sudden you get caught up in weddingness? You look around the room thinking, *who can I marry?* I mean, two days earlier you're thinking relationships suck and you're thinking of becoming a monk, but you get close to a wedding and you want to do it. Plus today, add the fact that the world is ending, and I'm not thinking straight.

Sweetie says, "You won't go to Prom with me, but you'll marry me?"

Ash floats down, the sky roof stops it from falling on us. The ash is like confetti. It makes me want to get married more. The crowd cheers. Everyone thinks the missiles are damaging the Moon Thread, but little do we know that the ash is actually little bits of missile raining down on us. The Galactic Cord holds strong.

I look at Sweetie and nod. *Yes, I don't want to go to Prom, but I do want to marry you. Is that a crime?* Sweetie shakes her head and puts down the bouquet.

The Hocker Cord from Heaven hits the school. It comes down hard as if God has snapped it himself (or herself depending on how you ponder God). The shock wave from the last three missiles snaps the Cord something fierce. Not snaps off, like the military is trying to do, but snaps like the end of a wet, twisted towel in the boys' locker room after gym class. SNAP. CRASH. BOOM.

The Earth shakes.

The Galactic Cord SMACKS down on top of the main school building and the front parking lot. And it sticks. It smacks hard and it latches on. Another set of jets swoop in and blasts the Cord. The missiles explode and send vibrations through the Cord but it stays stuck, no more flailing around.

The RV shakes, and Sweetie goes over the edge, head first. I reach for her and grab her arm. Right before I fly off the roof I reach for the railing with my other hand, but I miss. I go over the edge with her. But then someone grabs the waist of my jeans. It's the Lt. Minister. He's got me and I've got Sweetie. But the ex-Navy Seal does more then hold the waist of my jeans, he's also got my underwear. He saves my life but not my ass. It's a terrific wedgie.

He pulls us up. We thank him even though my voice is now higher than Sweetie's. SNAFU's father apologizes, "The rails are not safety rated for end-of-the-world weddings."

We look at the large Cord from space attached to the school.

Sweetie says, "Thank God, the Prom is in the gymnasium."

You're still planning to go to Prom? But I say isn't any better, "That thing just hit Earth and is stuck to our school, and you're still thinking about if the sea foam green plates are going to be shipped overnight so the colors don't clash?"

"Teal. The plates we want shipped overnight are the teal ones. Your ability to pay attention to what is important to me is outstanding."

"We're talking about plates."

"No we're not. Chevy, a relationship, a MARRIAGE is caring about another person. Sometimes that means caring about what the other person cares about."

"I am not spending $600 on one night out."

"Now it's $600? Whatever. Get your carburetor."

"It's already bought, rebuilt, and installed." *I didn't need to say that.*

"Marry your freaking Chevy, Chevy."

She walks down the steps in the middle of the roof into the darkness of the RV. The Lt. Minister hugs me and holds me. It's awkward. He won't let go.

"Just let it out. It's OK to let it out. You have to get the DIS-ease out of the body so you don't get a *disease.*"

I hate it when the world ends. People act weird.

I look past the Lt. Minister at the Solid String of Goo and I realize something I never considered. No wonder they blast it with everything they have. Well, almost everything. *Everything* is on its way. The Galactic Cord is not taut; there is slack in the line. Actually, a lot of slack. It came from the moon, drifted over and stuck. But as I look at it, the Space Cord is getting more and more straight. It's as if the moon is reeling in the Earth, or perhaps it's the other way around.

As we all know, the moon is stationary or at least in a stationary orbit around the Earth. However, the Earth turns. Something like 1,000 miles per hour. We don't notice it because we're on it, and everything is moving together so there's nothing whizzing by us letting us know how fast we're moving. But now the moon is attached to the Earth. The

Earth still rotates even though the Cord is connected to it. I watch the Phlegm String tighten. In just a few minutes, the Cord goes from looking like a sagging clothesline to a taunt line at a 45-degree angle from our school to the moon. The Lt. Minister lets me go, but now I want him to hold me. *Oh, Holy Man of God with the many medals denoting bravery, keep me safe.*

I say, "SNAFU's Dad." I don't know his first name. "Look, the Earth still rotates but the moon does not."

"Actually Chevy, the moon does rotate, but it's tidally locked with one side always facing the Earth."

"Okay, you're right, but that's not what I'm talking about. What I'm saying is there's going to be a tug of war between the Earth turning one way and the moon being *tidally locked* and going the other way."

The Lt. Minister gets it. "We better hold on to something."

He sits down and grabs a furniture leg that is bolted to the top of the RV. I join him.

I yell, "Sweetie hold onto something!"

There is no answer from inside the RV. I look at the Cord. It gets tauter and tauter as it stretches. It looks more and more like a zip line to the moon. The crowd starts screaming. Others figure it out too. I keep waiting for the jolt when the rotation of the planet fights against the moon, but the jolt doesn't come. The Cord gets straighter and straighter as the Earth rotates. Everyone knows the Cord is lightweight and strong, but no one knows how flexible and stretchy it is.

Then I feel it. It isn't a jolt. It's a tug. I guess the Earth is towing the moon. Towing is not really the right word. They're pulling each other. Then I think, if the Earth stops rotating, will gravity stop and we'll float away?

CHAPTER 8

SO FREAKING CLOSE

I GRAB HOLD OF the RV a little tighter. I realize this isn't going to matter because the RV will float away too. But I don't float. Nothing floats. It turns out the rotation of the Earth on its axis is not what causes gravity. Believe it or not, no one really knows what causes gravity. Some say it's the relationship of objects that are near each other in space, as well as, movement and time.

You can skip this paragraph if you want to. I would if I were you. I will now explain MY understanding of Minkowski's theory of gravity, called General Relativity. It will probably make no sense to you. I'm guessing this because it makes no sense to me. *When an object has mass and it travels through space, it also travels through time and thus gravity is created.* This supposedly explains gravity as a space-time distortion rather than a force. See, now you understand as much about gravity as I do. Crystal clear, eh?

So anyway, my point is gravity keeps doing its thing. As the bumper sticker says, "Gravity Sucks." No one floats away. Everyone waits for something to happen but nothing does.

Let's review. Moon connected to the Cord. Cord connected to the Earth. Earth stops turning or really slows down.

The jets fly away. They didn't accomplish what they set out to do. The Cord hit the Earth and now it's attached to our high school. The good news is the world hasn't ended. *Sweetie, I need to find Sweetie.*

I look down into the RV. "Sweetie, you OK?"

"There." SNAFU's Dad points to the parking lot behind the RV. I look and see her making her way through the cars. No, our relationship can't end this way. Not on a day like today. *If I hurry...* she starts to run. She runs right into Roy's arms. They hug. *Really?* Roy gives me the finger. If love makes the world go round, it certainly isn't the love that Sweetie has for me. Oh ya, I forgot, the world isn't going round.

Roy guides her to his convertible. *No!* But his love machine is stuck in traffic just like everyone else. *Good.* He leans into the car, starts the ignition and presses a button. The roof starts to rise. *What?* He's creating privacy. *Oh, no, not the back seat, not now.* I hurry to the ladder. Sweetie must have said something or he saw me coming. The roof stops and lowers back down. By the time I get to the ground, I see Roy handing some kid a whole lot of green from his wallet. Roy and Sweetie jump on the kid's dirt bike and ride off. *I can still catch them.* I go for my dirt bike but it isn't there. I watch some chick ride off on it.

"Ahhhhhhh, come on."

I watch Roy ride off with my lady.

"Ahhhhhhh, come on."

It's lunchtime. The world didn't end and everyone gets hungry. People leave. Most walk because the highway is jammed with cars. It's a two-lane highway, but when they stopped traffic, a bunch of idiots decided, *hey, let's drive up on the OTHER lane so we can see what's going on.* It's a two-lane road with cars on both sides facing the same direction. Idiots. There is no space to back up and turn around and the idiots up front left with their keys. Some 4x4s drive on the berm or right through the fields. Cars and even a few trucks get stuck in the muddy berms and gullies. It's a mess. So a lot of people just walk away.

I'm too tired to walk. I go down into the RV and make a tuna fish sandwich with mayo and pickles. I think I'm eating the reception food.

I can tell you it's one of the best sandwiches I have ever eaten. I'm hungry. I hear Sweetie's voice inside my head, *No tuna for youna.* I laugh. I miss her. I text SNAFU but get no reply. He must be busy doing something stupid. Or, perhaps the satellite is out of range now that the Earth isn't turning so good, or maybe the cell phone towers are all jammed up with activity.

The Lt. Minister also makes a sandwich. "I'm going to see if I can help." He leaves while taking a big bite. I look around. Cord is still attached. No other people around. No jets fly in the sky. The Marines and Air Force must be figuring out what to do next.

I fall asleep in the driver's seat of the RV because my sleep the night before was lousy. When I wake, it's spooky quiet. I turn on the radio. I hear news reports about the Earth not spinning and more military being called out. I open the door of the RV and there is no movement outside. I sit back down in the driver's seat and look at the taut cord out the front window. I feel alone. I get goose bumps. I wish I had everyone from my Z.A.S.T. here. You know, a Zombie Apocalypse Survival Team. Right now, my Z.A.S.T. only has two members: SNAFU and Sweetie. SNAFU is the muscle and Sweetie knows how to fly a glider. My worst-case scenario is Sweetie would fly me out of danger while SNAFU provides ground cover. Gliders only have two seats so SNAFU would help us get to the air field and then he would sacrifice himself to give us time to fly away from the evil horde. We, in exchange, would promise to name our first son after him. We would then fly to some paradise island and start repopulating the Earth. These thoughts always move me. But right now they just make me feel alone. The RV creaks. *I'm sure it's nothing.* I decide to lock the door. I get up and walk to the door. I reach for the handle. The door flies open. I scream. It's Sweetie.

"Good to see you being brave. You're not answering your phone."

I stand in the doorway, not letting her in. "I don't think it's working."

"I didn't know where to go," says Sweetie. "My family has been praying for the last six hours. It was nice at first, but I can't keep praying. And I have no desire to beso with Roy for another hour."

"ANOTHER hour?"

Sweetie smiles. "Can I come in?"

I think about saying no. I have no idea if she is serious or not and beso is *our* word. I don't like it. I open the door for her. "Get in here." It's good to see her but I make a mental note: *open enrollment for new members in my Z.A.S.T.*

She hands me her phone and I call my Dad. "No Dad, it's me. I'm using Sweetie's phone. Mine isn't working. Tell Mom I'm fine. Yes, we'll stick together." Sweetie rolls her eyes. I pretend not to notice.

I lean out and look at the cars. No movement, I feel the quiet. My Dad tells me everything is going to be OK. I tell him, "Of course it is. See you soon." I shut the RV door and lock it. Sweetie sits at the little booth-like table in the RV. I slide her phone to her. "Thanks. My family's stuck on the couch. If the world is going to end, I'm not going out watching TV."

"You could be working on your Chevy."

"You could be with Roy."

"No, he got a call and had to go."

"Where would he have to go on a day like today?"

"I don't know, but he started throwing up."

"There's a keeper for you."

She gets up and goes to the fridge. "Well, at least he doesn't scream when I open a door." She brings back two beers and puts them on the table and says, "You still want to get married?"

I could hear the hum of the refrigerator. The two brown beer bottles stand tall on the table, identical really. They're so close that they almost touch, but they don't. Condensation, like sweat, gathers on the bottles, and I watch a drop of water run down the side of the bottle closest to me.

I decide to be honest. Then I decide to lie. Then I decide to be honest. I say, "The moment has passed."

Sweetie smiles. I open both beers and slide one to her. We each take a sip. She shivers and pushes the beer away. "I hope I like the taste of it by the time I'm legal."

I put my hand on the table. She takes it and says, "Maybe we should have sex, you know, in case we're going to die."

I push my beer away. I think sex is a good idea. Death or no death.

"I agree."

"I thought you would."

I stand. I raise her hand to my lips and kiss it. Her skin is so wonderful. I figure I will be a gentleman until it's time not to be. Her hand is warm and soft, so much nicer than a crescent wrench or lug nut. I walk to the back of the RV. *Look for the room with the bed. It can't be hard to find.* Yup, here it is. Sorta looks like a hobbit's room.

"You know," she says. "I love you and I hate you."

"Let's focus on the love part."

We beso. Good, I got past "another comment" pre-sex banter. Any comment could easily derail sex. SNAFU says the key to having sex is not to start an argument when you're undressing.

She stops kissing me. "Why do you hate Prom so much?"

My hands stop undressing her. Do you see how if I answer this question that the only thing that will happen is *us not happening*? If I say, "I don't hate Prom." Then she replies, "Yes, you do." Then if I say, "You're right, I hate Prom." She says, "I can't believe I ever loved you. The one thing, blah, blah, blah…"

It doesn't matter how I answer this question, our underwear's not coming off. But I'm not one that gives up on my dreams. So I reply with an unrelated comment.

"I'm so glad I'm not alone."

"So it doesn't matter that you're with me? You're just glad you're not alone?"

Oh, she wants an argument. Time to go on the offensive. Perhaps I can throw her off track.

I push her away from me. "You don't want to have sex with me."

"I do. I do," she says. "My body wants you so much. I'm so ready, if you know what I mean, but I want my heart to be involved too. The love I HAD for you is not enough. I need to love you NOW."

She looks out the window. The musty smell of the RV lingers in the air. Hot air and new carpet smell. Some one should have opened up a window.

"Sweetie … "

"And, I don't. Right now, I don't love you like I did."

All right, do or die time. I move toward her. The sunlight cuts through

84

the room from the blinds making horizontal strips across my chest, like I'm in prison. The room is hot. I see the sweat on her forehead and neck. I want to taste it. I decide it's DO time; forget about dying, even though I realize that may be coming soon.

"Sweetie, I want to tell you something."

BOOM. BOOM. BOOM.

Really loud explosions shake the RV. The windows on the right side of the RV shatter. Sweetie and I are thrown across the room. I grab her and turn so my body hits the wall first. See, chivalry isn't dead. Her elbow hits me in the gut. We crumble to the floor.

BOOM. BOOM. BOOM.

The RV shakes again but we're OK. We pull ourselves up and peek out the window. If you ever get a chance to see a tank roll over an empty news truck, do it. Treads crush metal. Tires pop. It's very cool. While the blast sounds like it is just outside the RV, it isn't. The tank is about 20 yards away shooting at the Goo Line. We cover our ears. BOOM. BOOM. BOOM. The shells hit the Cord, but it doesn't look like its affecting it. The tank advances up and over another news truck. But then I realize if they think the news trucks are empty, they probably think the cars and RVs are empty too.

"Everyone's been evacuated. No one knows we're here. Come on."

I stand and extend my hand to Sweetie as she completes buttoning her shirt. She tries to stand, but when she puts her weight on her right leg, she falls.

"Go without me."

"I'll be right back."

I grab two dishtowels and run up the stairs to the top of the RV. The sunlight and fresh air feels great. I look around; good, there are no tanks about to crush us. I wave the dishtowels, but the tank we saw through the window turns its turret away from the Cord and heads back. It moves fast. It's disturbing to see a big tank run away. I realize, if a tank hightails away from something, you can bet it's a good idea that you should also get out of there.

I run down the stairs. Sweetie leans against the refrigerator, favoring her hurt leg.

I say, "We got to go. We're the last two here. The tank thing didn't work. I think they're going to try something bigger."

Sweetie hobbles to the door.

I say, "How is it?"

"Not bad."

I throw open the RV door. "Where's the dirt bike you guys bought?" I can't get myself to say Roy's name.

"It ran out of gas by the creek. I walked the last quarter mile."

She can't hobble that far. "Let's go to the roof and see if we can flag them down. If they see us, they'll come and get us." I help her up the stairs. It takes forever. I'm glad we didn't try to run for it. I could have carried her, but it would have been a slow go and I can't carry her forever.

Sweetie says, "Thanks. I've twisted it like this before. I just need to rub it and get a good night's rest."

Exactly, that's what we all need. A rub and a good nights sleep.

By the time we get to the roof, the tank is gone. The 360-degree view is great. But right now all we see is a whole lot of stillness. I grab the tablecloth, but the Sky Roof hinders me from waving it. Sweetie sits down and props her leg up. She turns on the radio.

Experts thought the Cord would not attach to the Earth, but it did. Experts thought the spinning of the Earth would snap the Cord, it didn't. Experts thought everything was going to be OK, but it isn't. I see the pattern. The experts aren't experts. I hope they aren't getting paid.

I step up on the short safety railing. I hold onto the Sky Roof with one hand and lean out. I wave the tablecloth. I can see the Marine Base through the trees. I don't see any movement over there. That's not good. Marines always leave last.

A scientist comes on the radio and tells everyone that the Earth isn't moving much. Half the Earth is going to experience daylight for weeks. The other half night for weeks.

I look at the trees; they look the same to me. The science expert says if the Cord holds, it will take about four days of "no nights" before leaves wither and fall off. Africa is getting screwed with constant night. Plenty of farmers, animals, and people are going to freak out. Maybe plants freak out too, I don't know. Plants are going to die either way – too much sun or no sun. Being raised here in the farmland of America, I'm very aware that the plant kingdom is the base of the food pyramid for all living things on Earth.

A jet soars overhead speeding AWAY from the Galactic Cord. I stop waving. We didn't hear it approach because it's going faster than the speed of sound. Then the sonic boom rocks us. BOOM. The guy on the radio is interrupted by a more serious guy. I miss SNAFU; he would make fun of them. Serious guy says, "The president has talked with the governor. The governor has given the OK to use a nuclear weapon."

Sweetie and I look at each other. We then look at the jet as it starts to make a wide U-turn in the sky. It's coming back around.

Sweetie says, "How big is a nuclear blast?"

The radio guy seems to answer our concern. He says it will be a *small* nuclear bomb. Sweetie and I look at the Cord that is attached to our high school about a quarter-mile away.

She says, "I don't think we will survive a small nuclear blast. I mean, how small is a small nuclear blast?"

I turn off the radio and take Sweetie's hand. She lets me pull her to me. She leans into me for support making sure not to put any weight on her ankle.

"Do you know why I'm rebuilding the Chevy?"

"What?"

"Do you know why I'm rebuilding the Chevy Camaro Z/28?"

"I don't want to fight right now."

The jet is half way through its big U turn in the sky. We can't hear it. We listen to the silence. I run my fingers through her hair, "Do you know why I'm rebuilding it?"

She wipes a tear from her eye. "Because you love it more than me."

I smile. I can't believe how lousy of a boyfriend I've been.

"No, I'm rebuilding it BECAUSE I love you. No one is going to hire me to work on tractors in the city. We both know that. So I did some research. I can get a job as a mechanic. I had a couple of interviews set up in the city. But then I found this classic car place. The pay is almost three times the hourly rate of a regular garage and I get to learn what I want to learn. But they only want mechanics with three years of experience and I don't want to wait that long. I had to get that carburetor. I need to finish the Chevy so I can drive it into that shop. That Chevy is going to be my resume."

I take a deep breath and continue, "I need that job so I can take care of you. I want to buy you a house. I want to buy you a real diamond ring and not some little chip that looks like it came out of a cereal box. I want to buy us two tickets to Florida so we can go to spring break. I want to honeymoon with you in Vegas. I'm rebuilding the Chevy because I want to buy you the good things in life."

She kisses me. I kiss her back. I have her heart again. And, boy oh boy, I want the rest of her body. *Too bad we're going to die.*

The jet is almost overhead.

She punches my shoulder. "Why didn't you tell me your plan?"

"I didn't know if it would work and I wanted to surprise you."

"Your timing sucks."

We watch the jet fire its missile at the Cord. We watch the missile head straight for the Cord. It seems like it's in slow motion. Even though the radio is off, I imagine the announcer guy saying, "Target has been acquired. Payload away. The world waits."

I say, "I'm sorry."

"Don't be. It was a pretty good run."

The payload is going to hit the Cord about two miles up. This is where the experts say a lot of stress is focused on the Cord as it holds the Earth and keeps it from turning. They declare this the weak point, the sweet spot, the Achilles tendon.

We kiss one more time. It's a nice tender kiss.

"See you later."

"You bet."

CHAPTER 9

BOOM

THE SOUND OF THE jet breaking the sound barrier shakes us. The jet turns in the sky and gets the hell out of the way of the blast. The missile hits the Cord. Time stands still.

BOOM.

The shock wave hits us. Part of the Sky Roof rips off. The blast picks us up and throws us through the air. We fly over parked cars; my hand is torn from hers. There's so much light and sound. We land in the berm, you know, the dirt strip that runs along the side of the road. A few tall trees stand about ten feet farther back from the road. Good thing we didn't hit them. I'll be honest. I don't remember the landing part. I black out as I fly through the air.

But I do remember thinking, *it's nice we're in love again before we die.*

CHAPTER 10

LOOKING GOOD IS IMPORTANT

I NEVER THOUGHT DEATH would hurt so much.

My mouth is parched and I am actually stuck in the Earth. I didn't realize it, but it's a blessing it rained last week. The dirt is soft. It broke my fall. The blast knocked me at least ... no, wait, it knocked *US*.

I whisper, "Sweetie. Sweetie."

I attempt to yell, but can't. I pull my arm out of the dirt. It isn't mud anymore. It dried. *How long have I been stuck here?* The sun is still up. It seems like only minutes have passed.

"Sweetie."

I get on my knees. Nothing is broken, but everything is sore. I feel like I just wrestled SNAFU. I see Sweetie. She's about ten feet away from me. Thank God, she hit the mud too. I gently shake her. She moans. I pull her arms and legs out of the Earth. She yells when I touch her left arm. The underside of her arm is red. We landed in the shade of the tall trees but Sweetie's left arm wasn't so lucky. It's in the sun, and it's burnt.

How long were we out?

She mouths, "Hey," but looks past me.

I squint and look up. *Yup, there it is.* The Cord still streams down from the moon and is attached to our school. I pull out my phone. It is 4 a.m. *What?* And, it's Saturday. *Saturday?* We were unconscious for all of Friday. Geez, bright sunlight at 4 a.m. in the morning. That's right, the Earth is not spinning so good. I look at my phone. Thirty-seven texts and six messages, I'm Mr. Popular.

Sweetie pulls on my arm and whispers, "Water."

I look for the RV. I don't see it at first; it's on its side. Some other cars have also flipped over. I run to one of the cars that's upright. OK, *my run* is more of a hobble. I find a bottle of water and bring it back to her.

We drink. She brushes crusty dirt off one of her legs. She rotates her foot in small circles. Sweetie coughs and then laughs.

"Hey, my ankle feels good. The rest of my body feels terrible. But my ankle feels good."

"You were right." I say, "It just needed some rest."

"What do you mean?"

"It's Saturday."

She looks concerned and says, "It's Prom Day."

This is not her vision of what Prom Day should look like. I stand and offer my hand. "Well, at least we're alive."

She takes my hand, and I help her up.

"You know," Sweetie says, "Even though we're talking, we're still dead." I have to think about that for a moment.

I nod. "We were pretty close to that blast."

"How long does it take before you die of radiation?"

"I don't know. I think it has to do with how much radiation you're exposed to."

We hold hands and look into each other's eyes. We are dirty and beat up. We look and feel terrible, but it doesn't matter. We have each other.

"Chevy?"

"Yes, darling."

"Can we find someplace more comfortable to die?"

"Sure, that's a good idea."

We find some more water in another car and a protein bar. We split it, it tastes great. *Our last meal?* We turn toward the RV. I'm still starving. I touch Sweetie's burnt arm.

"Ow. Radiation burn."

"I don't think so. The rest of our bodies are fine. I think your arm was in the sun. We've been out a while."

I guess they don't make nukes like they use to. I pull a backpack out of a car. I rifle through it. Just school books. I realize how *not* useful they are. I spot a first aid kit under the drivers seat. I open it.

"Look what I've got."

I hold up a tin of *Mama's Magic Skin Salve*. It's good stuff. I use to forget to put sunscreen on the back of my neck. Talk about a red neck. My mom found *Mama's Magic* online. Her skin salve is all-natural with *organic remedies to sooth and heal* sunburns. *Mama's Magic* also makes really great organic body oils for massages. Sweetie and I like the lavender essential massage oil, but this isn't really the time or place to get into specifics about that.

Sweetie pulls her phone out of her pocket, it's crushed.

"Better your phone than you."

Sweetie turns her arm over. Yikes, the underside of her arm is burnt pretty bad. I smooth the salve on her arm. Her whole body relaxes.

"That feels good. Thank you."

She gives me a kiss. *Thank you, Mama.* We walk toward the RV.

Sweetie says, "Let's die in better clothes. I'd rather we look good when they find our bodies."

To be honest, not really important to me, but I'm not going to start an argument. I say, "I'm starving. I'd rather die with a full stomach. There may be more food left in the RV."

Sweetie walks to a black and gold van. It's the CelebratingProm.com van. She smiles one of her best smiles ever. I think it's a terrible idea, but how can I say no?

She dresses first. It takes forever. I chalk it up to her being blasted 40 feet through the air, and the fact that she is about to die at any moment. I climb into a nearby Honda Civic. The keys are gone. I hot-wire it. Being a mechanic has its perks and I can pretty much drive almost anything. I blast the AC. I roll down the passenger window and yell, "The AC is on and it feels great!" This might get her to move faster. I don't want to die waiting for my girlfriend to change.

I turn on the radio. They talk about how the attempts to burn the Cord didn't work. I look up and notice a thirty-foot section of the Cord is black. I guess they were busy while we were out. I would have liked to see it on fire. The commentator says, "Well, the Blockbuster bomb didn't work and they couldn't burn it. I guess we've got to bring out the big guns." *What?* It turns out the Governor GAVE the approval to use a nuke IF the Blockbuster bomb didn't work. Then they tried the fire thing because no one really wants to set off a nuke on American soil. But now that both of these didn't work, the nuke recommendation is being revisited.

We survived a blockbuster bomb, not a nuke. *We're not dying!*

I jump out of the car and run to the van. Again, not really a run, more like a shuffle. I'm just about to yell to Sweetie when I see her teal bra hanging on the open van door. I stop. I forget all about the bomb news. I peek around the open back door. She looks good in her teal thong. She steps into her dress. That's Sweetie; Prom colors all the way. She zips up the back of the dress. *I wish we weren't going to die.* Then I remember, the bomb wasn't a nuke. *We're not going to die!*

I yell, "We're going to live!"

I surprise her and she jumps. Her hair flips from one side to the other and that's when I see the tattoo on her shoulder, a heart tattoo with Roy written inside the heart.

"Chevy, give me some privacy!"

I look at her tat, turn, and leave. I stop at the car I hot wired. I'm not sure what to do. I find out that I'm going to live and then Sweetie kills me.

She comes out from behind the van. I'm so angry until I see her. She looks great. She wears a strapless high-low Prom dress. If you're a guy and don't know what that means it means the dress part in back is longer, full length to the floor. The front part of her dress is shorter like a party dress so I can see more of her legs.

I didn't want to say it but I couldn't stop myself. "You're beautiful."

She smiles.

Then I remember the tat. "But why did you..."

"I didn't get a tattoo!"

"But I saw it!"

"PEN! PEN! PEN! I drew it on after the committee meeting. I was so angry. That's what you get for spying on me." Sweetie crunches her eyebrows. A gentle wind blows her Prom dress. She looks great.

I say, "Why did you draw a fake tattoo?"

"I wanted to get you mad. I needed to know you still love me."

"Well ... it didn't work. I'm not jealous and I don't love you."

Sweetie laughs. "Yeah."

What's really great is she's not wearing high-heel shoes. She's wearing her sneakers, her high-top ones that lace all of the way up the front, almost to her knees. They look cool with the dress. Sweetie walks to the van, and then comes back with a wardrobe bag. She hands it to me. I keep my hands in my pockets. I'm still angry. She waits until I finally take the bag. She doesn't let go. She leans in and waits. I can't resist. I kiss her awesome lips.

She says, "I love you."

"Yeah."

She laughs and lets go of the wardrobe bag from CelebratingProm.com.

I say, "Is this Roooooooyyyyyyyyysssssss tuxedo?"

"No stupid, it's yours."

"But I didn't get measured."

"Yes you did."

"No I didn't."

She pretends to pull an imaginary tape measure across my chest. She bats her eyes and says, "Eric, you're so big and strong."

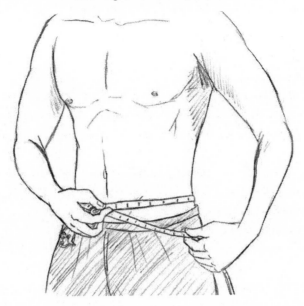

I flashback to the night we were fooling around with a tape measure. We measured *everything*. We had fun. We said we wanted to make sure things would fit.

Ever since then whenever I see a tape measure I get excited and feel vibrations in my first chakra, if you know what I mean. So, that's the night she got my tux measurements. She's smart, sexy, and sneaky. Just how I like my women.

I go to the van to change. Not easy but I do it. This is my first time with a tux. I look in the side view mirror. I feel like I have super powers. I usually don't like tight fitting clothes, but I look good. I hear music.

Sweetie blasts music out of the Civic. The doors are open and she dances next to it. She keeps dancing until she sees me. She says, "Damn, I knew you'd look good all cleaned up."

We dance. I take her hand and pull her close. We kiss. I say, "I find it interesting that the moment your girlfriend gets all dressed up, the first thing you want to do is take off her clothes."

"You *always* want to take my off my clothes."

"Well, I want to take them off faster now." I pull her toward the RV. "Come on, let's get something to eat."

"You want food? Right now?"

"I do want food but I was thinking we could do something else first. I was just trying not to be rude."

"That's what I thought. Wait a second." She turns to the Civic.

"What are you doing?"

"I can't leave it running with the AC on."

I look at the destruction surrounding us. *Really? You're concerned about our carbon footprint right now?*

Something happens up in the sky. There is no sound, just color. Silent fireworks by the Cord. They aren't the exploding fireworks like you see on Fourth of July, or the Queen's Birthday, or the Chinese New Year, but more like glowing lights with an assortment of fluorescent colors.

The first Space Pebbles are hitting the atmosphere and are burning upon entry. I know I haven't mentioned the Space Pebbles yet, but this is how we experienced it. We didn't know what was happening.

What now?

Sweetie leans into the driver's side of the car, but instead of turning the car off, she tries another station.

"Sweetie, what're you doing?"

"I'm finding out what's going on up there."

"We probably know more than they do. We're a lot closer to the ..."

"Shhhhhhhh."

Sweetie sits in the drivers seat as she flips around looking for a station with talking. She looks up through the windshield at the show. I open the passenger door and get in.

She looks at me. "Barry?"

What? But then I get what she's doing. I smile and play along, "Yes, Eliza."

We mimic our favorite YouTube Channel – *Best Day Ever with Barry and Eliza.*

She exclaims, "You're looking good today!"

And I mirror her enthusiasm, "You're looking good today!"

"You know who else is looking good today?" says Sweetie.

We both look an invisible dashboard camera – pretending to be Barry and Eliza – and we say, "YOU'RE looking good today!"

We continue to talk to the invisible camera. I say, "Yeah and you know what else? You're amazing!"

Sweetie leans toward the dash and asks, "Hey, are you getting ready for Prom too?"

And that brings us back to reality, not even Best Day Ever with B & E can get us out of the doo-doo we're in today.

Sweetie returns to searching the radio for someone knowledgeable, maybe an expert. The quiet fireworks in the sky are not important to me. I want to make my own noisy fireworks. But Sweetie continues to search. I look up and see three balls of light burning as they come down the Cord. Space Pebbles, that's what they are first called. And they come down the Cord in groups of four. The fourth one is on the other side of the Cord so we can't see it. As far as I know, there are only 3 coming down.

I say, "Maybe parts of the moon are coming down the Cord and we're seeing them burn up when they hit our atmosphere."

Sweetie finds a station with talking. "Experts confirm that they are Space Pebbles, which are also being called moon chips. They're coming down the Cord and are burning up when they hit our atmosphere."

I feel very pleased with myself.

"You're an expert now."

"I am NOT an expert," I say. "Those guys don't know anything. Come on. I saw a pair of hunting binoculars in the RV. Let's get a better look."

"You just want to get me back to the RV."

I smile.

"How big do you think they are?"

The guy on the radio answers her, "They're each the size of a fully loaded SUV or mini-van. For those of you not into cars, they're about the size of a small elephant."

Sweetie looks at them. "They're beautiful."

I take her hand and pull her close. I move in for a kiss. She closes her eyes and leans toward me. I stop. I don't kiss her.

She opens her eyes. "What?"

"I'm serious," I say. "I saw binoculars in the RV. Let's go."

I need her to want me. Sweetie looks at my lips. "Yeah, that's a good idea," she says. She turns off the car and we run to the RV. We're feeling good now.

The RV is on its side and what's left of the blue Sky Roof canopy looks like a big shield. However, there are rips in the fabric. We step through a large rip and find ourselves looking at the couches and tables that are still bolted to the roof. Sweetie points to the hole in the roof that has the staircase leading into the RV. Now that the RV is on its side, it's hard to climb in, but we do it.

One of the sides of the RV is now the floor, the other side is now the ceiling. The good news is the big side window has shattered and acts like a sunroof. Light streams into the RV. At first our eyes focus on things we expect to see such as books, papers and pots and pans. It's true what they say, your *outside* world is a reflection of your *inside* world. Yes, it's a mess in here too.

But then our eyes recognize shapes we don't expect to see.

"Are those guns?"

Machine guns, rifles, and handguns are everywhere. There are also boxes of ammo. We can't believe what we're seeing. It's like an NRA Christmas dream. I see some small pineapples. *Come on, you've got to be kidding me, grenades?* I pick up a grenade and then carefully put it back down. *Grenades are not toys.* I place it next to a missile launcher. *A missile launcher? Really?*

Then I shift gears. *Cool!* I suddenly have the desire to blast something. I feel better about all the chaos around me. God bless the Tier-One Counter Terrorism Teams.

Sweetie says, "What's with all the hardware?"

"Ex-Black Ops. You've got to love their obsession with weapons and their paranoia of an upcoming apocalypse."

"I don't think you can use the word *paranoia* any more."

Sweetie makes her way to the front of the RV and turns on the radio. *No. No. No. The bedroom is the other way.* She says, "Battery works. That's good. The fridge should still be cold."

Curses, the moment is lost. A serious woman on the radio says, "It has been confirmed, the Space Pebbles are each about the size of a Jeep Grand Cherokee or a big pickup truck."

Sweetie picks up a handgun and checks it. "Not loaded. Good. He's gun crazy, but not stupid." She puts the handgun down. She climbs over a few things on her way to the fridge. See how important comfortable shoes are to being a successful woman? Prom Dress and sneakers. She's my 21st Century Princess.

Serious Woman says the experts are amazed that the four Space Pebbles are coming to Earth at the same time, one on each side of the Galactic Cord. Sweetie lifts the fridge door. The light comes on. She grabs two individually wrapped sandwiches and tosses one to me.

I say, "Do you want a grenade?"

She's already eating. "Tat's the hest Prom Day esent ever."

I put down my sandwich, which is a mistake. Z.A.S.T. training 101: if the world is ending and you have a chance to eat, eat. You don't know when you're going to get another chance at food. But I am already captured by the thought of protecting ourselves. For some reason it seems like a really good idea to be armed. I locate some ammo and am playing the matching game with the firearms.

"Is a grenade a better present than a corsage?"

Sweetie wipes the mustard from the corner of her mouth. "No. Don't ever mess with the corsage."

I pick up two grenades. I toss one to Sweetie. She catches it.

"Easy with the grenades, Romeo."

Serious Woman on the radio clarifies, "The Space Pebbles are spherical in shape. They're round with an estimated diameter of 16 feet."

I pick up a triangle-folded American flag that's sitting on a pile of weapons and respectfully place it on a seat cushion. I gently slide a M16 machine gun out of the mess of weapons. "Wait a second! If they're moon fragments, how in the world are they ALL the same size AND round? That doesn't make any sense."

Serious Guy replies, "The Space Pebbles seem to be using the Galactic Cord as a guide. The Experts, of course, say that's ridiculous. It's just random that they're traveling next to the Cord. If you want to see them, look now. Everyone agrees that they'll never make it to Earth because they're small and they will burn up in our atmosphere. Enjoy the show while it lasts."

Small? A 16-foot pickup truck is not that small. I look around and grab a bent 30-round magazine. M16's originally used a 20-round straight magazine. I'm glad I got the new and improved magazine, the 10 extra rounds might make a difference. I click the magazine in. I feel better. I find a smaller mag, and slide it into my little friend, Glock. I check the safety and slide the handgun into the waist of my pants. Gangsta style.

Sweetie watches me as she shoves the last bit of her sandwich into her mouth. She nods as she moves aside some place mats and picks up a Choroszmanów submachine gun. It's a Polish gun created by a guy with the same last name. The gun was used by Polish freedom fighters during the German occupation of Poland during World War II. It's a beautiful gun with a polished, wooden stock. Leave it to Sweetie to find a beautiful but deadly weapon. She pulls the magazine out of the submachine gun. Yup, the weapon is fully loaded and ready to go. She shakes her head. It's not smart to store loaded weapons.

She picks up her grenade and walks to the front of the RV. "Let's go take a look."

I'm armed now so I say, "Sure."

Sweetie climbs out of the RV through the missing front windshield. She crushes broken glass as she walks. See, sensible shoes are important. Don't get me wrong, high heels are great, but now is not the time nor place for them. The right place is, of course, the bedroom. Which sadly, is in the opposite direction.

I see the hunting binoculars next to a skillet. *I knew I saw binoculars.* I grab them. We stand outside the RV. The radio is on, but not loud enough for us to hear it. Sweetie looks beautiful. The Space Pebbles continue to make pretty colors in the sky. Reds, blues, greens, yellows.

I can't keep my mouth shut. I try to be funny. "I ordered the fireworks in celebration of Prom Day."

"Even though you weren't planning to take me to Prom, you ordered fireworks?"

"I know how important Prom is to you." *I cringe as soon as I say it.*

"You know how important Prom is to me but you won't ... shut up." *Boy, I just killed the mood. Stupid.*

She says, "I wonder what Roy's doing? I hope he's OK."

Really? You've got to mention Roy? Relationships suck.

I raise the binoculars. I see three Space Pebbles burning up as they enter our atmosphere. The fourth one is hidden from me because it's behind the Cord. Up close, the colors look like they're on fire. Quite spectacular.

I hand the nocs to Sweetie. She places her submachine gun and grenade on top of a red four-door Ford. The grenade rolls off the roof. Sweetie catches it before it hits the ground. She's fast. She hands the grenade to me. Prom dresses don't have pockets. I decide to put her grenade in my pocket, then I'll have two bulges in my pants because I already put my grenade in my other pocket. But a fighter zooms over us. The sonic boom is loud. BOOM. The noise surprises me, and I drop her grenade before I can secure it. It rolls under Lynn's ... I mean Slippers' yellow car. No time to get it. I hope she has insurance. I yell, "Grenade." We both take cover. We wait. It doesn't explode. I guess the pin didn't come out. I walk to get the grenade but Sweetie grabs my arm.

"Don't. Leave it."

One arm wraps around me. She doesn't want to be left alone. We share a weird moment: it's nice. She takes another look at the Space Pebbles burning in the sky with the nocs. I can't make myself leave her.

I look at the fighter jet race away from the Cord and us. Then I watch it make a wide left turn.

Oh man. The nuke bomb being flown in. It's on that jet. It's here already.

"We've got to get out of here." Even as I say it, I know we can't make the distance we need.

She holds my arm. "It doesn't really matter, right? I mean we're dead already from the radiation of the nuke." She sighs, "I really wanted to go to Prom."

"No no, that bomb wasn't a nuke."

"We're going to live? I can go to Prom?"

"No, I don't think so."

"Chevy, you're not making sense."

"That bomb, the first one." I look up at the jet in the sky. "It wasn't the nuke."

"Why didn't you tell me?"

"I was going to but I saw you dressing, and I forgot."

"That's so romantic."

She kisses me. I don't kiss back. I should have, but I was feeling like an idiot for not getting us out of there faster.

She says, "Everything's going to be OK, right?"

The Excited Guy says, "I interrupt this newscast with the Governor live from the secret government base in the Ohio Appalachian Mountains."

Sweetie says, "What's the Governor doing in a secret mountain base so far away?"

The Governor says, "I love this state, the farmland, and the people who live and work here. And I love this country. Fifteen hours ago, the Blockbuster bomb did not work..." He gets emotional and has to drink some water.

The Governor swallows. "It was at that time that I told the president that if that Blockbuster did not work, I would agree with the Pentagon's recommendation to use a small nuclear explosive device."

I look up. The jet makes a wide turn in the sky,

Sweetie watches it. "*That* jet has the nuke on it."

I nod.

Sweetie buries her face into my tux. "I'm not going to Prom."

CHAPTER 11

TIME TO MAKE SOME NOISE

"PLEASE KNOW THAT I'VE been assured this is a small device," says the Governor.

Small device? It's a bomb, say bomb.

"It's not like the big devices that were exploded at the end of the second World War." The Governor blows his nose. Is he crying? He continues, "I have also been assured that everyone in the small radius of this focused device has been evacuated. My one condition for agreement was that no Americans would be killed in this blast. This is a time for action but not a time for panic."

I sling my machine gun over my shoulder and duck into the RV. I come back out with the American flag. "We're not dead yet. If they see us, they won't drop the nuke. The whole world has to be watching. You're not allowed to blow up high school seniors on Prom Day. It would be really bad press." I look around. The tallest thing I can see is a flipped over car on top of Cow Dung's pickup.

"Come on."

I parkour up the pickup truck and jump off of the bumper of a Ford truck. I land on top of the flipped over car. I shake out the American flag and wave it.

The jet continues its wide turn in the sky.

Sweetie yells, "Wait! What's that?"

I look at the Galactic Cord running through the sky. I see the black section and the pretty Space Pebbles burning up. I don't see what she's talking about, the Cord looks the same as before. But she's not talking about the Cord. She points. Then I see it. On the ground, about a hundred yards from the high school and where the Cord is attached to it, in the middle of the football field, is a big red dome rising. It takes me a moment, but I realize what it is.

"It's the hot air balloon." I feel better. Life is never as bad as you think it is when you're looking at a hot air balloon.

She shouts, "Help me up."

I grab her hand and pull her up onto the flipped over car on top of the truck. I'm shocked to hear me say, "Everything is going to be OK." I guess that just comes out when you're dealing with loved ones and imminent doom.

I wave the flag, but the jet keeps flying. It comes out of its wide turn and is ready to make its final approach. It isn't going to be OK. I lower the flag. They don't see us. It's too late. Sweetie sees me lower the flag. She raises the nocs. She looks at the burning rocks fall to Earth. I fold up the flag.

"They're so beautiful. Chevy, you've got to see these colors. If we're going to go, it's not such a bad way to go."

I set the flag down in the pickup truck. I can't disagree with her more. This is a sucky, dumbass, stupid way to go. She hands me the binoculars, but I only want to kiss her again. I think that's a better way to go, but she wants me to take another look. I'm about to raise the nocs when the President of the United States comes on the radio. "I'd like to thank the Governor for agreeing to make the tough decision. But just to clarify, the United States military will not be detonating a nuclear device."

Sweetie and I hug. "We're going to live."

It turns out if you detonate a nuclear bomb in the atmosphere it is

BAD. Supposedly far worse than blowing one up on land. The President doesn't explain. However, the President does say, "After much discussion it has been agreed that a pre-nuclear device will be used to break the Galactic Cord."

So they're going to use something a little less strong. Something they call a pre-nuke. Great.

I say, "Cool. We survived the last one. We'll be OK."

See, I did it again. I said, we'll be OK. *What the hell am I basing that on?*

Sweetie looks at me as if I'm a complete idiot. The announcer agrees with her. "The pre-nuke will be about 10 times stronger than the blockbuster. Everything within five miles will be wiped out unless it's in some sort of safety bunker or container."

OK, so we're not going to be OK.

Sweetie hugs me. I guess this is as close as we get to a Prom slow dance. It's a little tricky to sway on top of an upside-down car with machine guns slung over our shoulders, but we wrap our arms around each other and manage. I still hold the binoculars.

I raise the nocs to take one more look. The fluorescent colors are beautiful. Reds, yellows, greens, and blues. I focus on one Space Pebble. All of a sudden, the colors stop. The Space Pebble is still there, but it's white now. It looks like a big white snowball or, rather, a big white boulder.

I knew something was going to hit Earth. Experts are idiots. A white, round boulder is going to hit Earth. Then something really disturbing happens. The boulder blinks. Two big, red albino eyes look right at me, with six smaller eyes opening up under the big ones. *What the...?*

"The colors stopped," says Sweetie. "What's going on?"

I can't answer. The big, white boulder wiggles. Then it unfurls. Big long, hairy white legs unfold.

"Look, it's opening like a flower," says Sweetie.

I guess she can't see it so well without the binoculars. It isn't pretty and it isn't a flower. The legs extend. It looks like it's using its legs to catch the air just like skydivers do with their arms and legs. This thing uses its legs to balance and slow its descent. Then it rotates, and I can see its eight red eyes again. And then I notice the scariness under its eyes, two twitching fangs, the size of elephant tusks.

"Chevy, what's happening?"

I think of my grandmother, *God bless her.* She always said, "If you don't have anything nice to say, then don't say anything." I realize I might not be talking for a while.

The fighter jet with the pre-nuke sees the hot air balloon and the old guy filling it. The pilot calls it in. The military ignores the intel. Half the world is burning up and half the world is wilting. They were told the area has been evacuated and they were given the OK. The pilot is given the green light to proceed with the pre-nuke. The time for patience is over. Farmer Franklin is going to be collateral damage.

What we don't know is that W-PAL, the local television station, is broadcasting footage of farmer Franklin filling up the balloon. Even though the local news crews have been evacuated, W-PAL is buying satellite feeds and is running them through its sister station in Ohio. Farmer Franklin and the balloon are being watched around the world. For the first time in my life, W-PAL is really "my Pal" and really "has my back."

This might not have been enough to stop a military operation in which the world is at stake, but W-PAL did something the military could not ignore. In addition to getting footage of old man Franklin and his 1920s (literally) pickup truck, they also got video of his cute pet goat. Yes, his cute little goat is now as famous as Santa Claus. People on the other side of the planet who can't even speak English have already fallen in love with the little black and white goat, which, by the grace of God, gets nicknamed "Hope."

It isn't right to blow up Hope with a pre-nuclear bomb when what the world needs most is Hope.

The pilot doesn't see the goat. But the military general, General Kensington, is at the secret base in the mountains with the Governor. Some of the local law enforcement that helped set up operations in the field next to the high school are also at the secret base. The General has monitors showing local and national new stations. The General doesn't like PR, but he's smart enough to know it matters. One tweet can ruin his whole career or at least make his life hell and ruin his retirement book deal; that is, if we all survive this.

The General can't believe he's watching an old man fill up a hot air balloon. *WTF?* But what makes him laugh, on the inside, is that it seems like a baby goat is now the poster child of this operation. Just to be clear, the General never laughs on the outside while in uniform.

Here's the fun part.

Included in the law enforcement at General Kensington's side is the sheriff of our county. Sheriff, you-better-not-be-touching-my-daughter-or-I'll-shoot-you Sheriff. That isn't his real name, but that's how I know him. The sheriff is Sweetie's Dad. He stands next to the General, who is, get this, standing next to SNAFU and Private First Class Darcy.

Yes, SNAFU and Darcy. They watch Hope, the goat, on 9 of the 20 monitors. With each moment, Hope pops up onto another monitor. News channels realize the cute farm animal is the big story right now.

Let me tell you why SNAFU is eating pretzels with the General.

The Sheriff, a.k.a. Sweetie's Dad, saw SNAFU trying to sneak into the Marine compound on the practice fields behind the medical center. Darcy's helicopter had landed next to the Marine compound. This was before the command center was evacuated. SNAFU had jumped off the ladder before the helicopter landed because he figured they wouldn't be too excited about a high school senior hitching a ride into a secure military situation.

SNAFU was looking for Darcy when the Sheriff saw him. That's not completely accurate. SNAFU was being dragged away by two MP's (military police) when the Sheriff saw him. SNAFU didn't make for good, stealthy ninja because of his large size and because he's wearing a suit. The Sheriff asked for SNAFU to be brought to the operations center. The Sheriff did this because every guy, including the adults in our town, has hunted with SNAFU at least once. SNAFU is the only guy who has a crossbow with a red laser sight, and he always lets others try it. Everybody loves the crossbow. It's very medieval.

SNAFU, of course, befriends the General by telling him some great hunting stories. SNAFU also tells the General about Private First Class Darcy. The General, not being averse to being in the company of a beautiful woman, and wanting to show off his clout to his new buddy, calls for PFC Darcy to join them. Darcy joins them and then everyone evacuates to higher ground. The General relocates the party to the secret mountain base via a souped-up Tony Hawk helicopter. This time, they let SNAFU ride inside the helicopter.

Now, everyone watches the farmer, the balloon, and the goat. The General thinks his whole career is going to be screwed by a goat. They watch the goat eat some grass. They watch the goat walk to Farmer Franklin's truck. They watch the goat pee on the front right tire. Brilliant. Let's HOPE the critics don't refer back to that image when they review the General's military memoir.

Somebody says something about *Hope springs eternal* and somebody thinks of Sweetie and me. I don't think it's the General because he doesn't know we exist. You see, Sweetie's Dad doesn't bring up his missing daughter because the Governor had already been escorted out of the war room for blubbering. The Sheriff is waiting for the right moment to ask about *her*. Notice I didn't say *we*. SNAFU studies the other monitors. He finds one that is a satellite camera feed that shows the flipped over vehicles on the road. Everyone likes a good car wreck. The camera passes right over Sweetie and me, but we are too small to be noticed.

Sweetie and I slow dance and kiss. She stops. "I have a feeling someone is watching us."

Sweetie sticks her hand into my pocket, *yes, this is the way to go!* Who would have guessed she's into voyeurism? Or is that exhibitionism? But she doesn't grab me, she pulls out my grenade. She says, "I need an open window!"

I point to vice principal Crawford's sporty BMW. "There."

Sweetie pulls the pin and tosses the grenade. Nice arc. Good throw, but it's going to fall short. Sweetie's got great aim and is strong but doesn't have a lot of upper body strength. The grenade hits the roof of a Corolla. Fail. But it bounces right into the BMW's open window. Epic.

"Nice."

"Thanks."

Then we realize what's about to happen. We jump and take cover. The BMW explodes into a big ball of flames.

I hug Sweetie. "You're really good with making things explode."

The sky-high camera comes back to the burning BMW. We jump up and down and it finds us. We are more exciting to watch then a peeing goat. We flick onto one monitor after another.

SNAFU points at monitor six. "There. There." The General looks.

SNAFU says, "You've got to save my best friend."

The Sheriff says, "You've got to save my daughter."

Darcy says, "You've got to save Hope."

The General had already thrown the Governor out of the room for getting too sentimental. Everyone holds their breath and waits. The General curses. He asks the fighter pilot if he has enough fuel for a fly by, a pass around the Cord, to inspect and confirm the location of the "sweet spot." The General is asking if the pilot has enough fuel to postpone his bombing run for about ten minutes.

The pilot confirms he has enough fuel for a fly by. I think it's pretty amazing my life is being saved by a full tank of gas. The General orders Darcy and SNAFU to get a helicopter and pick up Sweetie and me. He sends another helicopter to pick up Hope and the damn fool farmer.

Sweetie and I don't know any of this is happening. We think we have failed and we're going to die.

We watch the jet fighter approach the Cord. I don't have time to tell her about the Space Spiders, and at that moment, I figure the pre-nuke is going to take them out anyway. She snuggles into me. No more kissing, even though, to be honest, I wouldn't have been opposed to it. We turn toward the Cord; we're going to face *this* explosion.

"Chevy."

"Yes."

"You're a big dork."

I smile and pull her closer. "It takes one to know one."

"I love you."

"I love you, too."

We time it pretty good. We get the witty line out and we tell each other, "I love you." Then we hold in the silence. But the jet just flies right past the Cord. I don't want to say I'm disappointed, because I am happy to be alive, but it's really weird to be given another chance.

Sweetie says, "Did it miss?"

"I don't think so. Maybe they saw us after seeing your explosion."

"I hope the vice principal didn't see me blow up her car."

The fighter jet makes a big wide turn. Then I remember the Space Spiders. "This is not good."

"What?" she says.

"You're not going to believe this." But before I give her the nocs, I realize if one Space Pebble is one Space Spider than the other ones are probably... I look. Yup, more hairy legs flail about. No, not flailing, very much in control. I swear the moment I look at the next Space Spider it turns and looks right at me. All eight red eyes glare at me. Its fangs do a little fang dance. I hear a singsong inside my head, "I want to eat a human. I like human meat. I want you."

The scary, hungry, angry-looking bug shoots a web. And I know spiders aren't bugs. So don't send me an email telling me that.

"Chevy, what are you looking at?"

"I don't know. Hold on."

I look at another Space Spider. Yes, it shoots a web and connects to the next Space Spider in the group. You can see great footage of this in the "Space Spiders: The Moon Is an Egg Sack" documentary. I wasn't sure what was happening, but I took a guess. Each Space Spider shoots a web to its buddy. Webbing now links one Space Spider to the next around the Space Cord. All four Space Spiders are connected. Six of the Space Spider's legs extend out, causing wind friction. The front two legs of each Space Spider pulls on the web line that connects it to the one in front of it. They form a ring around the diameter of the Galactic Cord. They pull themselves closer to the Cord. The connecting webbing RUBS against the Space Cord. They use the friction to slow themselves down. The experts are wrong. The Spacers are going to land in one piece.

That is when I see the beautiful colors again.

The radio guy jumps back on again, "Hey, more Space Pebbles. Aren't they beautiful?" I'm not really listening, but he babbles on about how the rocks didn't burn up upon entering the atmosphere. Duh. He says they seem to have movement now, that the atmosphere must have burned off parts of the Space Pebbles and now the aerodynamics of their windfall is making the rocks shift around. Stupid.

I'm not sure if I'm the first person to see them. There has to be a bunch of scientists and military people watching. I do believe we're all thinking the same thing, *what the...*

The radio guy keeps talking. "So many of us got caught up in Operation Save Hope that we didn't see this next set of Space Pebbles coming down the line. They seem to be the same size again, each one sixteen feet round. Good news, I've just been informed that there are a whole bunch of these groups coming down from the moon. In fact, I've been told it looks like an endless supply of them. Which, of course, the experts say is impossible, but overall it's going to be beautiful skies for a while. Isn't this our lucky day?"

It takes me a moment, but then I realized that today, all 40-plus hours of it, is turning out to be the best and worst day of my life.

Best day ever: I finally share Project Freedom with Sweetie and she doesn't make fun of me. In fact, she knows that I love her more than ever.

Worst day ever: Earth is being invaded by Space Spiders, and I'm wearing a tux.

For some reason this makes me laugh. Not a big guffaw, just a chuckle. Sweetie looks at me as if I'm Seven-Thirty. "What?" I kiss her. It's always beso time. I look back up at the falling Space Spiders.

This is my school. This is my planet. And this is my girlfriend's Prom Day.

I flip the safety off of my machine gun. *Bring it.*

"The jet is coming back around," says the happy announcer. "It's going to pass close to the Galactic Cord and visually inspect the target sight. Good news everybody! The pilot's going to swing wide to give the military time to rescue Goat Hope and evacuate some civilians before the pre-nuke is used."

The radio guy keeps talking and I get concerned. He says, "The pilot better watch out for those Space Pebbles. They're only going to be about a quarter mile above him by the time he swoops back around the Cord." The announcer must have thought of his international audience listening via the Internet. He adds, "A quarter mile is just a little more than 400 meters."

That seems pretty close to me. I remember the hungry look in the Space Spider eyes. The pilot is meat, and pretty soon he's going to be the closest human meat to them.

Sweetie touches my shoulder. I jump, "What!" I don't like people sneaking up on me, which she didn't.

"Freak. Let me see."

I hand her the binoculars. "Look at the Space Pebbles. They're not rocks."

"What do you mean?"

I don't answer. I decide to let her make her own discovery. A picture is worth a thousand words, and, to be honest, I don't have a thousand words in me right now. And if I start explaining, she will think I'm an expert. Then she will pelt me with a thousand more questions, questions I don't have answers to. Then she will get angry. That's what people do to people who act like experts who don't have answers.

The jet is far away and starts to turn before it comes back toward the Cord. The jet is going to pass really close to the Cord on its "inspection run." I look further up the Cord. I see the four white, ninja Space Spiders unfold. They're out and they're falling fast, even though they are still high up. My fears ease a bit. I don't know the mathematics, but it looks like the jet should pass well under them with no problem. I relax.

Sweetie keeps looking through the binoculars; her hand touches my shoulder, "Holy ... " She doesn't say anything else. Sometimes Sweetie isn't good with words either.

The jet gets closer to the Galactic Cord. One of the Space Spiders drops out of formation around the Cord. The other three wave their arms. Perhaps they're saying, "Good bye, good luck." I don't know.

I take the binoculars from Sweetie, she doesn't object. Shock will do that to you. The free-falling Space Spider becomes a hairy, white, red-eyed cannonball. It tucks its legs in and wraps its legs around itself. It shoots down like a bullet. I look at the jet coming around the Cord under the Space Spider. *Oh, man, if it doesn't pick up speed that Space Spider is going to hit it from above.*

The speeding Space Spider rockets down with its head and fangs first. It looks like a big ugly dog sticking its head out of the passenger window - the hair on its face is pushed back and its red eyes bulge out.

The jet pilot shouts, "There's something on my radar and it's coming in fast. It's on a collision course."

The General yells, "Get out of there!"

The pilot hits his booster rockets. The extra power shoots the jet forward. The jet looks like it will scoot past the Cord just before the kamikaze arachnid will hit it.

The plummeting Space Spider stretches its legs out. It sorta becomes a Space Spider glider—you know, a plane without an engine. The legs on the sides are wings; the ones in back, the tail fin. The Space Spider zooms away from the Cord toward the jet. It uses its legs to change its trajectory. It still falls, but now it's flying. The Space Spider is going after the jet.

The pilot screams, "It's coming after me!" On the black box recording, you can hear the pilot smack the jet with his fist as if to make sure it's working correctly. "I repeat, whatever that thing is, it's locked on and coming in fast!"

Sweetie grabs my arm. "It's going to take out the jet."

She's right, it's going to crash right through the jet.

The General orders the pilot to remain calm. "Get a hold of yourself and fly that bird, solider. That's an order." It works. The pilot replies, "Yes, sir. Evasive maneuvers, sir."

The Space Spider pulls its legs in and drops hard and fast. The jet is right under it. Then, as if in slow motion, the jet rolls—one wing points to the ground, the other points to the sky—and the white ball of death drops past it. I can see with the binoculars the Space Spider's face is only a foot away from the glass of the cockpit dome. The pilot looks at

113

the eight red eyes just outside the cockpit. I can imagine the red eyes reflecting on the pilot's mirrored face mask. The Space Spider's pointy tusk-like fangs shoot out and grab the cockpit, but it can't hold on. I know this isn't possible, but as the Space Spider falls past the jet, I hear the fangs scratch the cockpit glass. It sounds like fingernails on a chalkboard. The Space Spider continues to fall to Earth, and the jet continues its roll.

Damn that was close. Sweetie and I jump up and down as if we just won the Homecoming game. I point at the falling Space Spider and yell, "Gravity is going to squish you like a bug."

The pilot shouts, "I'm clear! I'm going to get some distance. Please get the friggin' goat out of there, and I'll turn this thing around and deliver the payload."

I don't hear what the pilot says, but I see two army helicopters in the sky. They are big. One is going to pick up Goat Hope and his Farmer. The other heads toward Sweetie and me. We don't know that SNAFU and his PFC Bride are in the copter coming for us.

Sweetie yells, "Aaaaaaaaaaghhhhhhhh!"

She points at the Do or Die Space Spider who just missed the jet. This white cannonball of death flips over. It's upside down as it falls. Web shoots out of its silk-maker. The web line shoots up at the jet and hits the underside of the jet's wing and sticks. Sweetie lets out another squeak, or it could be me.

The pilot yells, "I've been hit."

The Space Spider balls up again. I expect the wing to rip off, but it doesn't. The web stretches, and since the Space Spider doesn't hold on to anything, the jet pulls it through the air. Since the web is attached to the right wing, the jet starts to make a huge arcing turn in the sky.

As the jet turns, the Space Spider continues to fall. It pulls on the right wing. The jet makes a huge turn in the sky and heads toward the medical building. The pilot fights to keep the jet above the Wellness Center. All is not well.

No one is left on the roof of the medical building. Everyone has been evacuated. But if they were up there, the guy with the beard in the hospital gown could have reached up and touched the jet with his crutch. That's how low the jet is. The Space Spider and webbing turns the jet and continues to bring it down.

The Space Spider lets out more slack and drops onto the field in front of the school's main parking lot. It hits hard and dirt flies up. It faces the school, the web line still comes out of its back end and it's still attached to the jet. *The webbing holds.* Maybe it's true what they say, a spider's webbing is the toughest thing around.

When the Space Spider hits the field, all eight legs dig into the earth. This turns the jet even harder and faster. The jet pulls back and drags the Space Spider backwards through the field. Grass and dirt fly into the air. The Space Spider looks like one of those barefoot water skiers. Strips of sod are thrown into the air on either side as the jet drags it backwards. I'll bet a farmer somewhere is thinking, I wonder if we can get them Space Spiders to plow my fields next year.

Then the Spacer digs in, and the back two legs pull in the webbing. The jet turns even harder. The jet crashes through the thin tree line that borders the two lane road we're on. The jet stays in the air and zooms over our heads. It's loud. It's a good thing the RV is down on its side; otherwise, the wing of the jet would have ripped off its Sky Roof. The Space Spider pulls hard and the jet turns back toward the high school and crashes through the trees outlining the road again.

This time it's too much for the jet. The wing rips off. The jet flips over, it's going to crash in our practice field. For a moment it looks like it's going to slam into the Space Spider that brought it down. That would be poetic justice. But the Space Spider scurries out of the way. No poetry and no justice.

The jet crashes. Sweetie and I duck. Not that ducking will protect you from a pre-nuclear bomb a hundred yards away, but fear sometimes trumps logic. We wait for an explosion, any explosion, but it doesn't happen. The jet just smashes into the ground.

I look at the Space Spider on the ground about a hundred yards away from us. It looks at me. My left arm pulls Sweetie behind me. Instinct. In all reality, her being a few more inches away isn't going to make a difference, but it makes me feel more masculine and that feels good. My right hand holds my machine gun. Sweetie steps out from behind me. She keeps a watch on the Space Spider as she walks over to the red car where she left her World War II submachine gun. She picks it up and turns off the safety. She walks backwards to me, never turning her back on the thing. She stops at my side.

The Space Spider gnashes its fangs and looks up. We look up. The next set of Space Pebbles unfurl into four white Space Spiders.

I turn and see the sky dotted with over thirty troop helicopters. They're too far away to hear, but they're big enough to see. The troop copters are behind the ones that are coming to get Hope, Farmer Franklin, Sweetie and me.

The General is sending in troops. I smile and nod at Sweetie. I'm glad she's so beautiful and strong. I say, "I guess we're going to have a ground war."

CHAPTER 12

FREQUENT FLYER FRIENDS

THE ACCOMPLISHED SPACE SPIDER moves a leg around in the dirt. I think it's testing the soil. It's the first time its kind is on our planet. That's one small step for a Space Spider, one giant leap for Space Spider-ness. It looks at us. *I took down a jet and I just hatched. All you did on your first day of your life was piss and spit all over yourself.* The Space Spider winks – a big red eyewink – which I believe is impossible because spiders don't have eyelids. My body tenses, I hold my machine gun down low like a GTA hoodlum. I hear SNAFU's whisper of long ago, "Don't tense up, take a gentle breath in and out. And when you pull the trigger, do it nice and slow."

We were both 10 when he first said that to me. SNAFU started hunting when he was 7. But this was my first time out. My dad was more of a fisherman than a hunter. I remember raising the 22 rifle and shooting at a wild turkey. I missed.

I realize today is not a day for missing.

Sweetie's hair and Prom dress moves with the gentle breeze. Her eyes remain locked onto the Spacer Spider. She's got great focus.

The helicopter coming for us is still a ways off. The Space Spider shakes the dirt off its legs. It twitches its fangs. It runs back to the school. I let out a breath. I didn't know I was holding it. *Breathe, Chevy. You've got to remember to keep breathing.*

Sweetie watches it run. "See, it's afraid of us."

I'm going to let her believe that, but I think she's wrong. I think it just has other priorities. I imagine when you invade another planet you've got a whole list of things to do. But I don't have the energy to argue; I think I'm in shock. She probably is too, perhaps the whole world is.

The daredevil Space Spider stops scurrying. It stands in the parking lot of our high school and looks up. At first I think it's looking at the big school logo of a knight on horseback on the front of the building. The logo is black and yellow like our varsity jackets. The knight's lance extends out in front of it. I say "it" when referring to the knight because all of the guys think it's a guy and Rose thinks it's a girl.

You might remember Rose; she's our class valedictorian who always reads the book *Rose of Camelot* that is about the first female knight. She'll argue all day that it's a young woman up there on our logo. *"See, her chest plate comes forward more than if she was a guy."*

Guys will sometimes stand in the parking lot and argue with her. It's not that most of us are male chauvinists. It's more that we're in awe of the female body and usually don't get to talk about it with anyone but our guy friends. And if she gets really upset she'll throw out her chest and yell, "See. See." And, we're allowed to look rather than just trying to steal a glance while walking down the hall. In this world of contrast you can't have UP without DOWN just as you can't have YIN (feminine) without YANG (masculine). I believe when a guy appreciates the feminine it heightens his experience of being masculine.

The horse in the logo is up on its back two legs, ready to crush something. Maybe it's coming down on a big spider. Maybe.

The Space Spider raises its front legs like the horse with the knight on it. The Space Spider isn't looking at the logo; it's looking up at the Galactic Cord. The other three Space Spiders still fall from outer space. I assume the moon is considered "outer space." I wonder what Cow

Dung would say about that?

They fall with their legs out wide trying to catch as much air as possible. They are left with only this option because they don't have their fourth buddy to hold webbing and rub it against the Cord to slow down their descent. The fourth guy is, of course, the cannonball Space Spider who left his post to take out the jet. Now it's on the ground looking up.

The three come down faster than they had planned. The Space Spider on the ground steps, steps, steps, steps, steps, steps, steps, steps back. It actually only takes one-step but it's got eight legs. It's trying to gauge something. Then it scurries off of the parking lot and back onto the practice field. It waits for its three frequent-flyer friends. It opens its "arms" wide. Oh, it isn't waiting for its buddies, it's getting ready to catch them.

But even I can see this isn't a good idea and I'm NOT a physics guy. The other three Space Spiders are coming in too fast.

Sweetie says, "They're coming in too fast. They don't have a jet to slow them down."

Like three fury meteorites, they crash in the field just in front of the main parking lot. One of them nails the Space Spider with open arms, I mean legs. I think of Friendly. See, about every thirty seconds guys supposedly think of *beso-ing*. Note: I haven't tracked this to confirm or deny this claim, but as far as I know, we don't do it on purpose. It's just a guy chemistry thing. But, that doesn't mean we don't enjoy it. And, to be honest, sometimes the thoughts are annoying because they just pop up and distract me from what I'm doing.

The Space Spider survived the crashing jet but does not survive trying to catch its hairy pals. Fail. *See you don't always get what you want.*

We feel the impact from where we stand. The three Spacers hit about 100 feet from the navy blue pickup truck that was left in the parking lot. But even at that distance, the pickup truck bounces 20 feet into the air and flips over. It lands on its side. We hear metal crush as the side mirror snaps off and glass shatters all over the asphalt.

But what's really gross is a fountain of Space Spider guts flies straight up into the air about 50 feet. I almost spew chunks. The sound of the SPLAT is OK, but when the goo rains down, that's when the

119

acid crawls up the inside of my throat. The slapping sound of wet guts falling all over the *Reserved for Faculty* parking spots is horrible.

Then I see the colors again. Sweetie points at them way up in the sky. She doesn't say anything, just points. This is not the next set of Space Spiders. The next set has already burned off their pretty colors and are unfurling as they fall. I guess we missed the pretty colors while we watched the goo smack down. The pretty colors we see are the THIRD set coming down. The blues and greens are beautiful; I'll give you that. I appreciate how nature can mess with you. Just like a fish that is really pretty, and then it stings you and you die in ten seconds. I guess alien nature can be tricky just like Earth nature.

I haven't told anyone this, but it's true so I'm going to tell you. I promised myself I would tell the whole story, or nothing at all. The first Space Spider that landed – you know the one that ripped the wing off the jet – raised its right mandible which is one of its short leg-like arms. The mandibles are near a spider's mouth and fangs. The mandibles grab and hold food (or humans, I'm guessing) when the spider eats. Well, I saw the Space Spider touch its mandible to its forehead. It saluted. I'm serious about this. I don't know, maybe it was saluting its three comrades that were still falling. I believe the Space Spider was proud of itself. I know, call me crazy, but I saw it salute before it was crushed by it's three comrades.

Note: the YouTube video showing the Space Spider pulling down the jet has 983 million views as I write this.

Nobody thinks the Space Spiders are telepathic. Idiots still argue about it. But I was on the ground that day fighting them. They seem to have some sort of spider sense that can tell them if something is attempting to do them harm. I swear to this. And they will go after any threat without the thought of dying themselves. They are all about group survival.

A different radio guy comes on and tells us what we know. "The jet carrying Little Bob is down." That is what they nicked named the pre-nuclear weapon. He continues, "The bomb did NOT explode." *Yeah, no duh.* Then there is radio silence. I assume some body is telling him something HE doesn't know, perhaps: Space Spiders are coming to Earth. Experts are a bunch of eff-ing idiots. I think they're having a hard time dealing with reality. I know I am.

Sweetie and I watch the sky as the second set shoots webs between themselves around the Galactic Cord. They use their legs and webbing to slow their descent. They pull the webbing and it rubs against the Cord creating friction, decreasing their speed. They know what to do. But they're still moving pretty fast. Are they going to smush or land? We both know that whatever happens in the next minute is going to determine how difficult our lives are gonna be. And it just might determine if Sweetie goes to Prom.

Sweetie touches my hand. I shift and hold my machine gun with one hand so I can hold her hand. She squeezes. "They're coming down too fast. They're going to crash on impact like the other three."

I think she's wrong. These guys are slowing themselves down pretty good. But I don't blame her for saying it; positive thinking can be powerful and often influences our behavior so that we actually create what we desire. But, in this case, all the nice thoughts, affirming words, or ideal-scene-mind-mapping-picture-collages in the world aren't going to stop these guys. I don't plan on disagreeing but it just comes out.

"I don't think these guys are going to splatter. The other three didn't make it because one of them broke off to take down the jet. That's why they're coming down in fours. So they can work together to land safely."

To be honest, I hadn't really thought it out but once I started talking, the words just came out. We watch the descending Space Spiders. I wonder if this was how Little Miss Muffet felt when she sat on her tuffet eating her curds and whey. My stomach tightens just like it did the Tuesday of finals week sophomore year. I found out the History final was on Tuesday and not Thursday. I hadn't studied yet. Oops. I wasn't ready that day and I don't feel ready now. Good thing Sweetie is here. Together we can do any …

Sweetie lets go of my hand, turns on me.

"Wait a second, you're telling me that the first one sacrificed itself? That it wanted to take down the jet because it KNEW it was carrying Little Bob?"

"I don't think it knew the name of the bomb. But I don't think it was an accident."

"So it took out the jet on purpose?!"

"Come on, we all know spiders have a spidey sense." I see all of the Spiderman movies.

"You got a C in biology and now you're telling me that you *know* the Space Spiders read the pilot's mind?"

The wind gently blows her hair and Prom dress. Her eyebrows crunch up. I can still smell wet flesh, which I assume is the alien mess in the parking lot. I remember thinking, *I'm glad we're down wind, that may assist us if we need to battle this out.* Then I smile, *good, the shock must be wearing off, I'm starting to think like a hunter again.*

Sweetie pulls a rebel strand of hair away from her face. I can tell she's afraid that I'm right because she attacks me personally. I never told her how I got a C on that biology final. I had cheated off of SNAFU that day. I know, that's crazy, but he digs animals and Earth science so he actually does all the reading. That's how I got the C. In all reality, I didn't even get a C because I cheated. But bringing that up now would not help my argument. So I go with …

"I don't know if the Space Spider could read *EVERYTHING* in the pilot's mind. Like what different things he was hoping to try with his wife next Saturday night but I do believe …"

"What? Did you just bring up sexy-time activities?"

"You're talking about reading minds and I …"

"Space Spiders are landing on Prom Day and you're still thinking of…"

News flash, I'm always thinking of … I don't have time for this. *We* don't have time for this. I'm not sure exactly what we're suppose to be doing but somehow I know arguing is not it. I stop her rant. Sometimes chicks need us to reel them in and save them from themselves.

I say, "I'm just mentioning something specific as an example so … "

"So why is the pilot not happy with the stuff he's doing with his wife?"

"I'm not saying he's not happy. I'm just saying he might be more adventurous than she is and he … "

Sweetie steps toward me. "Did he tell her?"

"What?"

"Did he tell her that he wants to try something new? Does he have the courage to say what he wants or is he being passive aggressive?

"I don't know what that means."

"It means someone who waits for an alien invasion to mention the fact that they're not happy with what they're *doing* with the person *they love* because they're too afraid to come out and say it *in the moment*."

I yell back, "All I'm saying is Space Spiders knew the pilot wanted to kill them and they acted to take out the threat! Don't make this about us!"

"Too late, you already did!"

I glance up. The second set of Space Spiders continue to work together with webbing and friction as they descend. We both take a big, deep breath. We realize we're being crazy.

Sweetie whispers, "I'm sorry I yelled. I don't want to yell. My parents yelled."

"It's OK," I say. "You're right. I hadn't thought about it before, but I was aggressive and passive."

"Passive aggressive."

"Do you really have to correct me? I mean, right now?"

"Sorry."

"I mean, I'm trying to apologize and connect with you and you…"

"I said I'm sorry. Don't push it."

She's right. I let it go. I take Sweetie's hand. I want to connect *here and now* because I don't know how much longer we may be *here,* or how much *now* we may have left. "It's my intention to be more courageous in the moment and ask for what I want."

"Good. I believe we'll BOTH benefit from it." She kisses me and says, "I'm open to adventures." *Yes, she is. She's great.*

She straightens my bow tie. Super. You know a chick likes you if she fixes your clothing. I brush the hair out of her face. Our timing does suck, but we smile. *Man, relationships are harder than they look.* We almost kiss again, but touchdown is imminent. I wait for the post-argument agreement.

Sweetie says, "They're falling a lot slower than the first group."

I reply, "Yup."

After an argument, one of us always says some neutral statement that the other person can agree to. If we're driving it might be, "The sun is sure hot today," or "That cow is really big." If the other person agrees out loud, "Yes, it is," then we both know the argument is over and we're alright. Sometimes our relationship is even better after a confrontation. I think it's important to say what you really think and feel in a relationship even if it's sometimes with a loud voice.

Sweetie lays her submachine gun on the road and tightens the laces of her sneakers. She knows it's important to have the best support possible for her feet. She's very intuitive.

I realize that I don't hear the helicopters. I look and see the one going toward the hot air balloon. *Lucky old farmer coot.* Remember, at this time I don't know about Hope yet. I didn't know the standing order was, "Save that damn Goat." But the helicopter that's coming for us doesn't look any closer. In fact, it looks like it's getting smaller. *Is it flying away from us?* That isn't good, not with four Space Spiders about to land in the practice field.

Sweetie stands with her machine gun ready. I decide not to mention that our limo isn't coming to pick us up. Panic and dread does not assist with creative thinking. I look at the four newbies coming down the pipeline. *Well, what's it going to be: land or splatter?*

The Galactic Cord is attached to the main school building, but before they smack into the main building they break formation and pull away from the Cord. They drop straight down onto the school's practice field *in front* of the front parking lot. And, to tell you the truth, it isn't even a drop. It's sorta a glide and swoop move. I don't like to admit it but it looks cool.

The four Space Spiders hit hard and a big dirt cloud rises from their impact that blocks us from seeing them. For a moment we think they smushed, or at least we "goated" so. OK, I apologize; I will NOT use the word *goat* for the word *hope* for the rest of the story. For example, Sweetie *goats* to go to Prom. I'm sure it would be really annoying. (I'll just secretly substitute the word inside my head, but I will not type it so you won't be bothered by my musings.)

The dust cloud is big and I see no movement. Maybe they are dead. Then movement. *Damn.* A large, dirty white, hairy leg steps out of the haze. One can always *hope* … I hate being right sometimes.

124

Everyone calls this second set of Space Spiders the scouts. I think it is stupid that they're called *the scouts*. They aren't. The first four were the scouts. They ended up dead. These guys are called scouts just because they're the first ones to land and live. *Whatever.* I'll call them scouts because everyone else does, but that still doesn't make them scouts.

The four Space Spider scouts shake the dirt off and inspect each other, yup, all eight legs OK. The dirt cloud settles and we see their eight angry eyes, two big red ones with six smaller ones underneath them. Below the eyes their big tusk-like fangs twitch. Maybe they're signaling each other; maybe they're just making sure they work. All four scouts turn and look at us. We're still pretty far away, but a chill runs through me as we stand in the bright, hot sun. I grab Sweetie's arm and pull her close.

"Ow, be careful. That's my burnt arm."

"Sorry."

We raise our guns. All four Space Spiders gnash their fangs at us. Even at a distance, they look scary. I think they're assessing us. Are we a threat? I remember thinking, *go ahead and underestimate us, we'll see how far that gets you.*

They turn toward the school and look at the Space Cord. One of them touches the edge of the parking lot and then touches the edge of the field. Then it touches the parking lot again. All four of them step toward the school. Their butts face us. They stop and their back ends jerk back and forth, *are they twerking? Perhaps some sort of happy planet landing dance?* Then webbing sprays out. They direct the webbing along the edge of the parking lot and the practice field. They work together and spray the webbing into a mound, which grows into a Wall. Two feet high, then four feet, then six. They spray fast. Pretty soon we can't see them. One peeks over the top of the Wall and looks at us. Eight eyes glare, fangs twitch.

Sweetie says, "Don't worry, the chopper is coming to get us."

I don't say anything. I read this book by Steve Chandler. He's a smart guy that helps people get out of their own way. He says don't ever correct someone you love. I thought that was really, really stupid at first. I mean, *what about saying what is true?* But the more I practice it, I find it's a good relationship builder. When people figure out they're wrong *on their own* they are less likely to be argumentative and you don't need to "prove" their inaccuracy. Proving your girlfriend is wrong never builds a relationship. So I don't reply.

We look at the helicopters. The one coming for the mammal called Hope gets closer to the hot air balloon. The one coming for the mammals called Chevy and Sweetie turns around and goes back to base.

"Chevy, where's it going?"

"I don't know."

Sweetie raises her hand and shields the sun from her eyes. She looks at the bigger troop copters. "Well, at least the big ones are still coming." But they aren't. The troop copters are just hovering. They're still up there, which is good, but they aren't getting bigger. They aren't moving toward us. They aren't coming to fight. They aren't coming to save us.

Darcy and SNAFU's helicopter was called back. The helicopter was too expensive a piece of equipment for the Army to lose for two teen civilians that didn't matter. I added that last part, "that didn't matter." But that's the truth. As of right now, the Goat is getting more press then we are. The whole world is focused on Hope and needs Hope, so Hope has to live. I think the General could see the front cover of his memoir and he saw himself holding that damn Goat (or one that looks a lot like it).

To be fair, the Space Spiders on the ground aren't that close to the Goat and the Farmer right now. The Space Spiders are closer to us as they build their Wall. The pilot probably let the General know, "I can get the Goat (and Farmer) with no problem because there aren't any hostiles nearby."

I also think the General left us on our own because he didn't like the idea of landing a bird so close to the front line with only a minimal crew on board. He didn't send a full extraction team in our helicopter because he wasn't expecting any action. For goodness sake, he had let SNAFU go and he's a freaking civilian. The General isn't going to lose the first engagement with the Space Spiders. That wouldn't be good for morale. He knows the whole world is watching, and he has no Intel on

126

these guys yet. So he called back our copter.

But I can't figure out why the big troop transport copters aren't landing. Then I realize that Sweetie and I are the lab rats. We are the ones that are going to gather the intel the General needs before he makes his next move. He wants to see. Perhaps even *needs to see* what these Space Spiders can do before he makes a decision on how to respond. *It's up to us.* Not only do we need to engage the enemy on our own, but if we're going to survive, we're gonna have to save ourselves.

Time to grow up fast.

Here's what happened when Darcy and SNAFU's helicopter was ordered to return. Darcy and SNAFU thought about making the pilot pick us up. In fact, Darcy held her 9 mm, semiautomatic Beretta sidearm to the back of the pilot's head. Luckily the ride was loud and bumpy and the pilot never knew a gun was pressed to the back of his helmet. SNAFU gently pushed her gun down.

"Don't."

"What?"

"Don't!"

"What?!?!"

Darcy couldn't hear him because it was so loud in the copter. SNAFU decided if she couldn't hear him the pilot couldn't either. He picked up one of her ear muffs and yelled directly into her ear. "CHEVY IS WOODS SMART AND SWEETIE'S A GOOD SHOT TOO. LET'S NOT DO SOMETHING STUPID AND JEOPARDIZE RESCUING THEM LATER."

To tell you the truth, I'd have thought SNAFU would have been the one to pull his piece out, but he wasn't. Falling in love can do strange things to a fella. He got calmer. I was also surprised SNAFU used the word "jeopardize." That's a pretty big word for SNAFU. Perhaps love also increases your vocabulary.

The Space Spiders on the ground, work side ways on the Wall. I'm guessing there are two on each side. I'm guessing because we can't see them, and the Wall continues to get wider and wider. We had just learned about the Berlin Wall coming down in history class. Well, the Great Wall of Stick is going up.

Sweetie asks, "What're they doing?"

"They're building a base." I'm glad they're busy. It gives me a moment to think. *OK, the General needs more intel before he comes to get our asses.* I hear my dad's voice inside my head. "Son, whenever you need information, don't say, I don't know what to do. That's a terrible affirmation and will never lead to an answer that will help you. Instead say, I wonder? I wonder invites inspiration."

I can tell you I've tried this and it works, or at least it works for studying. Recently I was getting ready for finals and I said, "I *wonder* how I can cram for this final so I can remember all this stupid crap? I said it about 50 times and then I got a crazy wonderful idea. I took all the stuff I needed to know and made a song. I sang it till I remembered it. I got a B+. *But will "I wonder" work in a life-and-death situation?* I look up at the next bunch of Space Spiders coming down. I realize singing to them isn't a good idea. I say to myself …

I wonder how I can stop these guys?

I wonder how I can give the General what he needs?

I wonder how I can keep Sweetie and myself alive until he unleashes the Marines?

Sweetie and I watch the next four Space Spiders free fall. They web each other and use friction to slow their descent.

Sweetie says, "The good news is the Wall helps block the smell from the three that went splat."

That's it. *Four come down now. Three went splat. Four came down with a swoop and glide, but three came down with a smack and splatter. Three! That's what we need. Three not four.*

I grab Sweetie's face and kiss her on the lips. Mmmmm, peppermint.

I grab her hand, "Come on, I have an idea."

"Not now, Chevy."

"No, not *that idea.*"

She screams, "Aaahhh!"

I look. She points at a Space Spider as it comes over the Wall toward us.

"Hurry."

The Space Spider climbs over the Wall and scurries toward us. We're about a quarter of a mile away. Speedy, my track friend, can run the 440 in 51.3 seconds. He went to states last year and got the silver. He's got two legs. This thing has eight legs. I figure 51 divided by 4 is about 12-point-something seconds.

I look at the RV. We aren't going to get there in 12 seconds. So many weapons, so little time. I look at the Space Spider scurrying toward us, *That Space Spider just read my mind. It knew when I was thinking of killing it.* This confirms my hypothesis. *Space Spiders know when something is meaning to do them harm.*

We turn and face the Space Spider. Sweetie pulls the magazine out of her Choroszmanów and slams it back in. I check my M16. *OK, my idea would have to wait.* I guess it's time to make a stand right here, right now, and give the General some down-and-dirty intel that he's waiting for.

CHAPTER 13

NO LONGER VIRGINS

I SAY, "PRIVATE LAB RAT reporting for duty!"

"What?"

I don't answer Sweetie. We don't have time for a conversation. I lean up against a hot truck. Temperature hot, not style. It's an old beat-up pickup that has actually done some work in its day. It's hot because its been sitting in the sun for days, literally. It burns my arm. "Owwww." I raise my M16. She pulls part of her Prom dress from behind her and placed it on the hot metal, she rests her arm on it and raises her submachine gun.

"Short controlled bursts." That's what they say in the movies.

Thirty feet. The Space Spider gets closer.

"Hold." *I wish I would have shot off a few practice rounds.*

Twenty feet. "Hold." *I don't even know if these guns work.*

Ten feet. *Oh no, what if these are collector pieces and the firing pins have been removed?*

Sweetie yells, "Now!" BAM. BAM. BAM. BAM. BAM. BAM.

Bullets fly. They work!

The Space Spider stops less than ten feet in front of us. It looks at its right legs and then its left legs. It's fine. It isn't hurt. Not because it's impervious to metal bullets. No. It's fine because we missed it.

You see it takes a lot of force to shoot a round out of a gun. This force pushes the gun back and up. This is called the "kick" of a gun. And the more fire power (the bigger the caliber of the gun) the more kick there is. The machine guns have a bigger kick then rifles and shotguns. We shot right over the Space Spider. I'm glad I found the bent magazine with 10 extra rounds. I guess those WERE my practice rounds.

I say, "Aim lower."

The Space Spider walks toward us. It doesn't seem worried, and I don't blame it. We just made a lot of noise, and we didn't even touch it. So far its intel on "land humans" is *noisy, but not dangerous.*

Bad choice on its part.

It gives us the time we need. We slam the butts of our machine guns into our shoulders. BAM. BAM. BAM. BAM. BAM. BAM. BAM. BAM. We rip it up pretty good. Metal slugs dig into it. Legs, head, and body. Little pieces of Space Spider fly up and away as the rounds welcome it to Earth.

Sweetie yells, "If it goos, we can kill it."

Then click, click, click. It's about 6 feet (only 2 meters) from us and we're out. Not out of danger. Out of bullets. Stuff oozes out of the Space Spider. It doesn't look good, but it still stands. It takes a half-step toward us. We back up and bump into a flipped-over car. *Smart Chevy, not enough ammo and no escape route.* But I'm not too hard on myself. I have never hunted "big game" before. I mean, I never shot at anything that can take me out if I don't kill it. No need to call myself names, it's just "a learning." I hear my Dad's voice, "Go easy on yourself when you're learning new things. You can't know what you don't know."

However, this looks like a costly life lesson. It approaches and we try to get out of there. I go left and Sweetie goes right. We try to slide between the cars we're stuck between. But the Space Spider is one step ahead of us. Two big hairy legs reach out. One blocks Sweetie and the other blocks me from escaping "out the sides." It stretches its mandibles for us. It's fangs twitch. I guess it's going to do a taste test. *Just gathering human intel, nothing personal.*

Sweetie presses hard into me. At least I'm going out feeling her body. *There's a better feeling thought for you.* Its mandible thumps me right on my tuxedo vest and pushes me against the car behind us. It drips lots of Space Spider goo. Some of the goo bounces off the old truck and splatters on my vest. The Space Spider smiles. OK, maybe it doesn't smile, but all eight red eyes sparkle.

I wipe the goo off my vest and feel something in the waist of my pants. Yes! I am brilliant. I grab the Glock and blast the Space Spider. BAM. BAM. BAM. It screeches a terrible Space Spider screech. BAM. BAM. BAM. I shoot until it's empty.

A big glob of Space Spider brain slips out of its head. SPLAT on the road. *I think I'm going to puke.* It wobbles. Then it drops. It's dead. We are no longer Space Spider virgins. I kiss Sweetie on her cheek.

I say, "Thanks for knowing how to shoot."

"You too."

I raise my hand into the air and give the General a "thumbs up." Inside my head I can hear everyone in the command center cheer. I remember what my Dad told me, "Remember, when you're doing something new, the first time is always the hardest. The next time is easier." I'm not so sure the next time will be easier but I'm glad *there will be a next time.* I vow to be better prepared.

I pull the fake purple handkerchief out of my tux pocket and brush the goo off of my vest. I guess it isn't so fake, it works. The goo is sticky.

Sweetie says, "Hey, it looks like you just … "

"Not now, honey."

I know the General has "eyes" on us. I don't want Sweetie to say anything *like that* out loud if he also has "ears" on us. I toss the gooey hanky aside. Long white Space Spider hairs fall to the ground.

"Damn thing shed on me."

"They look just like your little … "

"Not now, honey."

Sweetie points at the rising Wall. Three Space Spiders peer over the top. They don't look angry; I mean, not more angry than they normally look. It seems they're studying us. Taking in what just happened, thinking, calculating. They return to building the Wall.

I look up. The next set of incomers stop making pretty colors. More are coming.

Sweetie says, "They don't know we're out." She means ammo. "Let's get back to the RV and load up."

We run for the RV.

Back in "video land," everyone in the local and national TV stations cheer. They cheer for us and for themselves. They're glad the Space Spiders didn't rip us apart because that means they can show the footage of us taking out the first one. Ratings, baby. The stations didn't show our encounter "live" because they didn't want to show a Space Spider ripping apart two teens. The real good news is they recorded it. Everyone "rewinds" digital footage. Producers argue who is going to narrate it. The sports guy in a play-by-play way, the lead anchorman in his this-is-tragic way, or the hot weather girl in her sultry put-on-your-raincoat-it's-going-to-get-wet-tomorrow way. They also have to decide when they're going to cut back to the damn Goat being rescued. At the moment, a solider carries Hope to the copter. and it seems to have gotten even cuter.

Can life get any more absurd?

But then something unexpected happens. The old Farmer grabs the soldier's arm and says, "When am I getting paid? Agreement is C.O.D. You know, cash-on-delivery."

The solider loses its grip on the Goat. The solider loses Hope. The Goat jumps and runs toward the Wall. Little Hope runs fast. There is no way that the solider can catch it on foot. The General yells, "Don't come back without that Goat or there will be no hope for you." The General doesn't say, "… there will be no HOPE for you." I just like the play on words.

The Solider grabs the old Farmer and pulls him to the copter. The old guy pulls back. The Solider releases him and says, "Your check is in the copter." The Farmer lets the Solider help him onto the helicopter. Smart solider.

Hope continues to run toward the Web Wall. Some viewers around the world start to call the goat stupid. Others call it baaaaaaaa-d goat.

By the time the copter gets in the air, Stupid Hope is almost to the Wall. A Space Spider comes out from behind it. Little, helpless Hope stops. The Space Spider towers over the bad goat. They look at each other. People around the world hold their breath. The Space Spider extends a front leg and pushes the little goat. It falls down. Everyone calls the Space Spider baaaaaa-d. The Space Spider turns and walks back to the Web Wall. The Space Spider decides the goat is not a threat and it has more important things to do. The General and the world breath a sigh of relief.

But Hope is stupid. The little goat FOLLOWS the Space Spider back to the growing Web Wall. The goat bleats. The Space Spider faces it. The cute goat bleats again and again. The Space Spider picks up the goat with its mandibles, turns the goat around, and gives the goat a little push. *Go away.* Hope stumbles forward but turns back toward the Space Spider and bleats again.

Everyone around the world yells, "Shut up. You're pissing it off."

The Space Spider screeches, but the little goat holds its ground and bleats again. Some of the darker, meaner people of the world shout, "Eat the damn thing." The helicopter approaches. The Space Spider crouches down and watches it. Hope, empowered by the arriving copter, bleats again.

The Space Spider has had enough. Big hairy legs grab the little goat.

Citizens of the world yell, "Nooooooooooooooooo." The General slams his fist down. But it's too late, the Space Spider passes the little goat to its back legs and flips the noisy little mammal over and over as the Space Spider webs it into a cocoon.

The General orders, "Take that bug out."

The pilot fires two Tomahawk cruise missiles. The Space Spider drops the cocoon and jumps to the side. The missiles just miss the Space Spider. The explosions are huge. The cocoon rockets into the sky.

Sweetie and I crush glass on our way into the RV when we hear the explosions. We turn and see the fireball reach into the sky. We see something fly through the air toward us.

Sweetie says, "What's that?"

It looks like a small equipment bag filled with a couple of soccer balls. I run to catch it.

Sweetie yells, "What are you doing?" She glances at me, the RV, and then the Wall to make sure more Spacers are not coming for us. They're not.

I have to catch it. I don't know why, but I have to catch it. I remember Darcy saying intuition trumps logic. She's not the first to say that, but she said it so clearly. I promised myself then that I would listen to that little voice whenever I heard it, and right now it says, "Catch it."

I run off the road toward the tree line, but the flying thing is not going to make it over the trees. The "white laundry-sized bag" crashes through branches, which slows it down. I lay down my M16, dive and catch the "bag." Umph. I hit the ground hard, but I save it, whatever it is. I am pretty proud of myself until the cocoon thing moves. I freak out and push it off of me.

Sweetie catches up to me. She carries a M16. She must have ducked into the RV and grabbed one for herself. Sweetie also leans my M16 against a tree. *Thanks for picking it up for me.* The white laundry-sized bag moves. Sweetie points her M16 at it. Sweetie glances at the Web Wall to make sure we aren't being followed. "We should get back to where the trees are thicker. They provide more cover." My momentum had carried me and the surprise package into the open. The cocoon moves and we hear a muffled bleat.

Sweetie says, "Is that a goat?"

It bleats again. I rip open the webbing. Goat Hope's cute face blinks at us. I rip off more webbing. The baby goat stands, shakes, and jumps out. People around the world cheer.

The news anchor on W-PAL wipes a tear from her eye. "They saved the goat." The producer yells something into her ear bud. The news anchor says, "They saved Hope." Which is better, but not good enough. The producer yells again into her ear bud. This time it's so loud the news anchor pulls her bud out and tosses it on the desk. Even the camera crew can hear the producer cursing through it. The news anchor regains her composure. She leans toward the camera in her best girl-next-door voice and says, "Because of those brave teens, Hope

Lives!"

My parents still sit on the couch watching the news. My Dad slaps his knee, "Chevy saved a goat."

Seven-Thirty, my older sister sits on the love seat next to them. She lets her pet tarantula climb over her. She wants to make sure it knows that humans don't hate all spiders, just the ones from Space. My Mom asks, "Why can Chevy rip the webbing when the jets can't blow up the Galactic Cord?"

Seven-Thirty says, "Earth spiders have different types of webbing. Webbing for framing is the strongest. Webbing for prey is the weakest. Webbing for prey doesn't need to be really strong especially if the spider bites the prey, because the prey is paralyzed."

"The Space Spider didn't bite the goat, did it?"

"No, it didn't."

"Why?"

"I don't know. Maybe it's saving its venom for humans."

That's a nice thought isn't it?

The little goat bleats at me. I try to think, but I can't think with all the bleating. I finally yell at the goat. "Get out of here." I need quiet to think. The goat bleats again and again. Sweetie shoots a few rounds into the air, Hope runs away.

Then I remember what I was thinking, *Three not four.* "Come on." We run back to the downed RV. *Three not four. Three not four.* We enter the RV and I lean my M16 against the ceiling. Remember, the RV is on its side. *Weapons, weapons everywhere but not a missile to launch.* There's the launcher; I grab it. *OK, that's part one.*

Missiles, come out, come out, wherever you are.

Sweetie rummages around in the mess looking for more M16 magazines. It isn't easy. I continue my search for a missile. There, next to the fallen vacuum cleaner, there's a missile. *Come on, if you buy one, wouldn't you get a second one? Maybe at half price? Maybe to keep the first one company?* I say, "I'm not leaving without two." I've never shot a missile before. I need a mulligan.

Sweetie sees what I'm searching for. I see a cabinet lying on the floor. *A missile might be stored in there.* Sweetie sees the cabinet too. She pulls up the tall doors. Nope. Brooms and mops. Her hand goes in and it comes out with another missile. *God, I love her.*

She hands the missile to me and goes back to looking for more ammo. "Why would you need 50,000 different types of guns?" says Sweetie.

There aren't 50,000 guns and magazines on the floor. She is frustrated and exaggerates. The matching game gets old pretty quick. But I answer, "Because there are 50,000 Space Spiders coming to Earth right now."

I carefully make my way to the door. You don't want to run through weapons when you're carrying missiles. Sweetie kneels down and pushes aside pots, pans, and oven mitts. She scoops up magazines and drops them into a brightly colored, reusable grocery bag. The bag has vegetable characters on it. Written above a smiling tomato is, "Do Your Part to Save the Earth."

Sweetie picks up a cute little handgun. She put it down and picks up a bigger Russian handgun. I hold the launcher and two missiles in a way I think is safe but feels awkward. I notice a laminated tag attached to the launcher. *Who knew they came with instructions?*

I say, "Let's go."

She loads a few more magazines into the bag, "OK." She grabs our M16s and the Veggie ammo bag. She leans out of the RV. "All clear." Sweetie leads the way. I keep reading as I exit the RV into the bright light of Prom Day.

"Look the instructions are in both English and … " *Stop, don't say it out loud.*

"What?"

"Nothing."

"You were going to say French."

Damn it. I say, "The sun feels good." I look up. Four more burn off pretty colors. "We should get ready." I try to change the subject.

"That makes sense," says Sweetie. "French is an international language."

I don't say anything. *Come on Sweetie, let it go.*

She smiles at me. I smile back, OK that was awkward, but it's over. Let's get back to what we …

She says, "It's funny that the weapons directions are in French.

French is usually considered the language of *love* not destruction."

She walks away from me. She leans my M16 against a teal car. *What are the odds?* She sets the bag of assorted magazines on the road. *Damn it. This is really not a good time for this. It was just one night. Sorta. And it's over now. You were with the group that drove her to Cleveland to catch her flight back to France.*

Focus. I look at the Wall. Two of them, sixteen eyes stare at us.

"Hit the one on the left," she says. "It's sticking out more."

"No."

"What do you mean no? What are you going to do?"

"Something else."

"What?"

"I can either do it or talk about it." That was aggressive-and-passive. *But hey, Honey, let's not bring up the past when we're fighting for our lives.*

She says, "You need to learn how to multitask."

Sweetie takes a magazine out of the plastic grocery bag, tests it in her M16. It doesn't fit. She tosses the mag as hard as she can and yells, "Aarrrrgh."

She picks up the next mag and tries it. I go back to reading the instructions. She tosses it and yells. She tests another one. Each one with a yell. It's hard to concentrate with your girlfriend throwing BULLETS. But I don't say anything. I look up at the helicopters hovering oh-so-far away. I give the General the finger. *We might as well fight the whole goddamn war by ourselves.*

She says, "Chevy, take your time. We have all day. And I mean ALL DAY, I don't think night's coming."

"Look, if what I'm doing works … it could be a way to save Earth … and you can go to Prom." I should have left it there but I don't. I add, "With Roy, if he can clean the vomit off his black, shiny, rental shoes."

Sweetie throws another ill-fitting magazine in the direction of the growing Web Wall. I review the missile launcher cheat sheet.

"Do you even know how to use that?"

She wants a fight, but I'm not going to give her one. *I'll save my fight for the Space Spiders.*

I say, "The best way to learn is by doing."

Sweetie laughs. She laughs because that's what I said when we first beso'ed. We didn't know Spanish then. She was concerned she didn't know how to kiss. She wouldn't get close to me. We were both each other's firsts; neither of us knew what we were doing. Her laugh makes me smile.

She says, "Ah, the Zen of killing Space Spiders."

I wait for her to smile but she doesn't. That's OK; I'll take the laugh with a witty comment. She tosses another mag aside. No yell. Good, she's just tossing now, not hurling and screaming. Progress.

I say, "I love you."

"Yeah, yeah, yeah."

I get down on one knee.

She says, "What are you doing? Not here, not now."

I point the missile launcher at the school, at the Latch Sight. I don't know what she's talking about. Then I realize I'm down on one knee.

She says, "Oh, I thought you were … " She hurls another magazine that doesn't fit. The sun glistens off the shattered glass that covers the surrounding cars. It's bright and hard to see. The mag bounces off the hood of a silver pickup. I duck but nothing happens.

"Sweetie, I want to. I do. But now isn't the time and … "

"Shut up, Chevy."

Another Space Spider peeks over the Great Wall of Web. I follow the Cord up to the pretty colors coming down. A few more sets of Space Spiders have swoosh-landed behind the Wall. I don't know how many but its time to put a stop to it. They seem to be coming down faster now.

The peeking Space Spider comes out to introduce itself. It must have "heard me" thinking about killing its siblings. It moves slower than the first one we shot. I guess it heard the other one screech before we killed it. *Be careful, Fangee, there's more where that came from.*

Sweetie yells, "Yes!" She finds another M16 mag. She slams it into my M16. I gave her a thumbs-up. She nods. *I think we like each other again.*

Sweetie looks at the Wall, a second Space Spider slips out through a Wall flap. You can probably picture it. It's a camouflaged, hinged door at the base of the Wall. Now that's sneaky. The Wall is twenty to thirty feet high now and continues to be extended out on both sides. They build fast.

She swings her hair out of her face. "Did you see that?"

I nod.

"I think you should do whatever you're thinking of doing." She tries more mags, but faster.

The first over-the-top Space Spider scurries from the open field to the line of trees along Route 43. Route 43 is the two-lane road that runs past the high school. Route 43 is the road that we, the RV, and other cars are on. Smart. It's running along the tree line. Some cover is better then no cover. Helicopters keep watching from a distance. The Space Spider continues to move toward us. It ducks and weaves between the trees and bushes along the side of the road.

The second Space Spider, a.k.a. Happy Fang Face, also runs to the tree line. It's about 20 or 30 feet behind the first one. I point the launcher at the next group falling down the Cord. I can still see pretty colors burning off. They're still too high.

"Chevy! I've got an idea. You take the first one when it clears the trees, and I'll take the second one."

"No. You're doing great. You take them both."

"What??"

"I have an idea."

"I do too," she says. "My idea is that we keep living."

"You're smart, you'll figure something out."

"Chevy, I appreciate your confidence in me. It's one of the things I love about you, but right now it's irritating." She straightens her Prom dress, "If you have a plan, share it with me."

That's what my Dad said about Project Freedom. I have to let her in. *How can I get her support if I don't share?*

I turn to her. "You're right. I don't need to be so secretive especially with stuff that includes you. Sometimes I think I may not be able to pull something off, so it's better if I don't tell anyone, so if I fail no one will know."

The first Space Spider leaves the tree line, gets up on the road, and comes straight for us. Ballsy. Sweetie raises her M16 and aims. BAM.

BAM. BAM. One big red eye pops. The Space Spider screeches and ducks. It hides behind a car that has flipped over.

Sweetie says, "We don't have time for this."

The Space Spider hurries from the flipped-over car to a little Smart car. The Space Spider tries to hide, but its legs stick out on all sides. It's funny in a horrifying way. Sweetie fires a couple of rounds at the Space Spider breaking windows of the Smart car. The car alarm goes off. The Space Spider attacks it. Good, that will keep it busy. The Space Spider webs the little car.

Sweetie says, "You don't need to do everything yourself. Some people will make fun of you when you try to do something grand, but *I never will*. And if you fail at what you're doing *right now*, you won't be able to hide it. So just tell me. You need to realize that a woman hates feeling alone when she's IN a relationship. That's worse then being alone alone."

I feel terrible. I make her feel alone.

The second Space Spider joins the first one and they both web the Smart car. The alarm gets muffled. If the Spacers can work together, so can we. I say, "I only need to hit one. All four are needed to land safely."

She gets it. "Yes, if you blow up one. The other three will fall like rocks."

"Exactly."

"Thanks for letting me in."

God, I love her so much. I hope we don't die today.

The two Space Spiders pick up the Smart car and drop it. Gravity brings it down hard. The muffled alarm wheezes out.

Sweetie rests her M16 on the hood of the car in front of her. She winks at the Space Spider who edges closer. They are both about six or seven cars ahead of us. Sweetie tilts her head to the right, her neck cracks. She says, "Who's ready for a slow dance?"

CHAPTER 14

25% IS 100%

THE SPACE SPIDERS SPLIT up. Space Spider 1 darts behind a 4x4 truck. Space Spider 2, Happy Fang Face, scurries behind the downed RV. Damn sky roof provides cover for it. Sweetie lets a few shots fly. She wants them to know their mission isn't going to be easy.

The instructions are clear enough. There are four switches on the missile launcher. I realize it has to be simple. The last thing you want to do is give a soldier a complex thing to do when she's under fire. I look at the next group of four "space pebbles" coming down. They stop making pretty colors. *Good, I need one to be out of its shell before I blast it.* The last thing I want to do is hit one and help it crack its way to freedom.

Sweetie looks around. Her frown turns upside down when she sees a big black pickup nearby. She gently puts the bag of magazines into the back of the F-150 truck. She places both M16s into the bed of the truck and she climbs up into the bed of the truck. She now has the high ground on the intergalactic arachnids. With all things being equal,

142

and they aren't in this scenario, the side with the high ground in a battle usually wins.

Space Spider 1 scampers from behind the 4x4 to a RAV 4, which is two flipped-over-cars closer to Sweetie. It screeches at her.

Sweetie says, "Oh, that makes me so afraid."

"Remember," I yell, "short controlled bursts."

"Hey, don't tell me how to kill *my* Space Spiders and I won't tell you how to kill *your* Space Spiders."

Why is this thing not locking on? I look through the viewer at one of the falling Space Spiders. I read the instructions again. Press and hold. Keep it on the target. Move with the object ...

Space Spider #1 scurries and leaps at her. Sweetie shoots short, controlled blasts. *See, I know what I'm talking about.* The blasts spin the Space Spider in the air and two legs fly off. Nice shooting. The Space Spider crashes into a car. Sweetie looks for Happy Fang Face, but she can't find it.

"I lost the second one."

"Don't worry, you'll find it." I finally get confirmation. "I'm locked on."

"Good. Shoot the damn thing already."

I fire. The missile shoots out of the launcher tube but it doesn't leave with a lot of oomph. I'm concerned. The missile only flies about ten feet up into the air propelled by a weak-ass rocket. *Damn, the missiles are old and worthless.* Then a second rocket kicks in and the missile streams up into the air. *Ahhhh, that's how they get rid of the "kick back."* Smart. *The powerful rocket kicks in AFTER it leaves the launcher.* That way the person shooting the rocket isn't thrown backwards. We humans can be really creative when it comes to killing each other.

If this was a 3D movie: The missile would "hang" in the air right in front of everyone – in the theater – for a few seconds, and then the second missile blast would shoot red, fiery flames – right into the faces of the audience – with a ROAR. Everyone in the audience would jerk backwards as they try to get out of the way of the blast.

Space Spider 1 stands with six legs. It limps-scurries toward Sweetie. She stands tall holding both M16s, one in each arm. "Say hello to my little friends." She blasts. BAM. BAM. BAM. She rips up the

Space Spider. It dives behind a Mustang that is on its side. Sweetie sends a few bullets into the car's roof to let the Spacer Spider knows she's got plenty of ammo, even though she doesn't.

I pick up the second missile. Time to hang out with my lady. There is an upside-down car that looks like a ramp. I run up it and leap. I fly through the air and land in the bed of the truck next to Sweetie.

"Hey."

"Hey."

Sweetie hands me my M16. "I kept it warm for you."

"Thanks."

Space Spider 1 peeks out from behind the Mustang. Sweetie shoots a few rounds. I turn and watch our backs. I see Happy Fang Face. "I found the second one."

"Thanks, I knew I left it here somewhere."

Smart, it circled around us. It charges from behind. Which, of course, is by invitation only. I fire my M16. BANG. BANG. BANG. I keep shooting. I don't kill it, but it doesn't like metal slugs hitting it in the face. Happy Fang Face ain't so Happy now. A couple of eyes pop, it rethinks its rear attack plan and ducks behind some vehicles. I track it. When it's far enough away, I look up. BOOM. I see the missile I shot hit one of the descending space invaders. Payload delivered.

Sweetie hears the explosion and takes a quick look. "You hit something." *I wish she didn't sound so surprised.* The other three fall away from the Cord and plummet to Earth. Sweetie says, "Hey, 25 percent. That's better than your Statistics midterms."

That's not true. I'm not super smart, but I don't flunk stuff.

Fang Face pushes a white Ford Focus at us. The Space Spider uses the car as a shield and a battering ram. Creative. I blast my M16. BAM. BAM. BAM. Click. Click. Click. "I need a little help."

Sweetie slides the bag of ammo over with her foot. She's a giver. My hand dives into the veggie bag of wonder as I search for another magazine. Fang Face pushes the white Ford into an upside-down car. The upside-down car slams into us. We almost fall out of the truck. The Space Spider crawls over the Ford Focus. *Focus, baby, focus.* Sweetie blasts the Space Spider as it crawls up and over the cars at us. The force of the rounds make it pause.

I grab a pistol out of the grocery bag. Yes! It is the Makarov Russian semi-automatic pistol that Sweetie packed for our day trip. *I can't wait to see what special treats she'll bring when we actually vacation together.* I join in the blasting. It's nice when you can do things with the one you love.

I have heard love is NOT about two people looking *at each other.* Rather love is when two people stand side-by-side looking (and moving) in the same direction. When MY soul's purpose matches YOUR heart's desire, then a grand love journey is possible. Sweetie and I are united in such a way: Save Prom!

We hit it pretty good. Red, angry eyes pop like firecrackers on the Fourth of July. Let freedom ring. Fang Face drops. It can take no more.

Space Spider 1 decides to take advantage of this distraction. It charges the front of our pickup. We turn but it's already in the air, leaping toward us. Maybe it got a bad push off, or perhaps it's the flurry of metal slugs we pellet it with, but the Space Spider isn't going to reach us. It crashes headfirst through the windshield of the truck we stand in. The impact knocks Sweetie and I backwards; we slide toward the tailgate. She hits it first and the tailgate pops open. Now that the gate is down, I slide right off the back of the truck. I fall and hit the road hard. Sweetie looks down at me.

"You OK?"

I moan, "I'm fine," even though I'm not. I lay on my back. *Oh, what a pretty blue sky.* I want to stand but I can't. I wiggle my fingers. I'm glad I can do that.

Sweetie walks to the cab of the truck. The head of the Space Spider crashed through the front windshield and is still stuck inside it. The Spacer makes all kinds of screechy, gnarly sounds. It settles down as Sweetie approaches it. Its face presses against the shotgun in the window rack, its one good eye looks through the little back window. It uses its legs to push against the front of the truck. It tries to pull its head out. But it's not easy. As it pulls, the broken glass of the windshield cuts into the Space Spider's neck—even though spiders don't really have necks—but you know what I mean. It's stuck.

In one last-ditch effort, its fangs rip up the back seat and pull the shotgun off its rack as it tries to get Sweetie on the other side of the glass. Sweetie steps closer to the window. Fangs reach for her, scratching and cracking the back window of the pickup. Sweetie slides the little window open with the muzzle of her M16. One mandible reaches out for Sweetie. She puts the muzzle through the window, right on top of its one good eye. The mandible pushes against the machine gun but Sweetie steps on the mandible with her foot.

Sweetie says, "Reaching new heights."

BAM. BAM. BAM. The Space Spider's head explodes inside the cab.

You'd think that the General would have been watching us since we were the guinea pigs on the ground. But I guess a General has many responsibilities during a space invasion. One of his assistants had to tell him to look before the missile I shot hit the Space Spider. He saw it happen in real time. SNAFU and Darcy had returned to the command center just in time to witness the explosion on a couple of the screens.

The General said, "What the hell was that?"

SNAFU said, "That's my friend, Chevy, on the ground."

A Sergeant sneered, "Good for him, he got one."

"No, sir," SNAFU says. "He got all four."

When the missile hit the Space Spider and it went BOOM, goo and fur splattered onto the Galactic Cord. The explosion pushed the other three Space Spiders away from the Cord. They were still attached to each other with webbing, but without the Cord to rub against the three of them fell and gained speed.

Fun fact: Gravity accelerates objects toward the center of the Earth at 32.2 ft. per-second-per-second, which can also be written as 32 ft. per second squared. In other words, an object's velocity will increase by 32.2 ft./s (or 9.8 m/s) for each second the object falls until it reaches its terminal velocity, which you can think of as a kind of speed limit.

Important: Terminal velocity is reached when air friction of a falling object equally opposes the force of gravity. Do you know what is the terminal velocity of three Space Spiders falling? It's our school's parking lot. They ain't going any faster once they hit asphalt. SPLAT! SPLAT! SPLAT!

The three of them hit and they hit hard. Sweetie and I hug. Darcy and SNAFU hug. Everyone at the army base cheers. They want to hug, but the military is still working on expressing emotions in the work place.

SNAFU says the General and Sweetie said the same thing at the same time but there's no way to prove it. Supposedly the General and Sweetie said: "Nobody stops Prom." For the record, I don't believe the General said that.

The three Space Spiders hit the asphalt really, really hard. They SMACK DOWN next to the abandoned pickup truck in the parking lot. This is the blue truck that was left by the guy who threw the empty aluminum can at the Cord.

Well, when the three Space Spiders hit the parking lot, it's like an explosion. Chunks of asphalt, as well as the blue truck flies into the air. The truck flips end over end. It would have been cool except that the debris rockets in our direction. As I climb into the bed of the 5150 truck, I look up and see chunks of asphalt and the blue pickup truck flying through the air right at us.

Sweetie yells, "Get down!"

I just got up. I don't have the energy to jump out of the truck. I'm still moving slow. Sweetie pushes me over the side and then jumps behind me. The flying truck flips in the air and crashes above us. It bridges the 5150 truck we jumped from and the car next to it. Glass rains down on us as we duck for cover. What we don't see, because we are too busy confirming we're still alive, is two more Space Spiders slip through the hole in the Wall.

SNAFU sees the two scurry to the tree line and continue toward us. He points at the monitor and yells, "Get someone in there!"

The General looks at a clean-cut guy with glasses dressed in business casual attire. I think he's some sort of analyst or strategy guy. The Guy nods and says, "It's fine." He lets the General know that they have the intel they need from Sweetie and me. It's now OK to save us (or let us die).

The General orders, "Sting Ray One do you see the two approaching LR 1 and 2 on the ground?" Again, never confirmed, but LR has to stand for Lab Rats.

"Yes, General."

"Do not interfere. Four more are burning off colors. You are the closest asset to the Cord. Take out one of the Creepy Crawlers with a missile or your big guns. But *only* one. Save your ammo. Do *not* get too close. Do you copy?"

"Yes, sir."

The Strategy Guy steps forward and whispers in the General's ear.

The General says, "Remember 25% is 100%."

SNAFU yells, "Do not interfere? My friend just showed you how to stop them before they hit the ground."

"Yes, he did," says the General, "And, I'll make sure he's remembered."

SNAFU approaches the General. Soldiers step closer to intercept.

The General says, "Do you think he'd rather have me save him and his pop tart or do you think your friend would rather have me save the world?"

Darcy puts her hand on SNAFU's shoulder. "How about both?" Everyone looks at Darcy. "It will be really great press if they survive," says Darcy. "Give me a bird with a team. Let me bring them in."

SNAFU shakes off his wife's hand, "That will take too long." Soldiers step closer to the General. They are ready to stop SNAFU and protect the General.

"Stand down, son."

Darcy whispers to SNAFU, "Chevy is woods smart and Sweetie's a good shot too. Let's not do something stupid and jeopardize rescuing them when we can."

SNAFU laughs. *His words.* She uses the same words he said to her on the helicopter. *How can he argue with himself?* His wife is smart and beautiful. SNAFU steps back, "You're right, sir. Chevy would put the world before his own needs."

The General nods and his soldiers stand down. The General looks at the monitors. Some screens show the two Spacers sneaking toward us, other monitors show Sweetie and me climbing out from under the truck brushing off broken glass. The General says, "What are they wearing?"

Darcy replies, "It's Prom Day, sir."

I have no idea if that made any difference, but he says, "Take the copter with the 44 mm gun and a full extraction team. You're a private.

You follow orders."

Darcy salutes. "Yes, sir."

The General says, "Let's see if we can get them cleaned up before the dance." He looks at SNAFU, "Your passion isn't going to get in the way of you shooting straight, is it son?"

"No, sir."

"Then get out there and help your friends."

The two Space Spiders scurry down the road toward us. We could have seen them, but we aren't looking. They pause behind some flipped over vehicles. The rest of the world sees them on their TVs, laptops, and smart phones. People jump up and down in their homes, apartments, and shanties. Some are in daylight, while others watch from the other side of the planet in the dark of night. But the one thing they have in common is they all scream.

"Behind you! Watch out!"

"Two more! Turn around!"

"Deux plus! Tourne-toi! "

"二つの毛深いものはあなたのために来て"

"Detrás de ti! Ten cuidado!"

"बाहर देखो, नुकीले आप के लिए आ रहे हैं!"

Spás Spider teacht! Ahhhhhhh!

Spójrz wygląd wygląd!

La Douleur est mieux que la mort!

Aragog riddikulus!

Es lebe Prom!

Sweetie and I pull glass out of each other's hair like monkeys picking bugs on a Sunday afternoon at the zoo. Picking stuff out of someone's hair is a surprisingly intimate and sexy thing to do. Maybe that's why there are so many little monkeys running around in the jungle.

"Don't move," I say.

Sweetie freezes. I pick a small piece of glass from the front of her dress. My finger brushes her skin.

"You put that piece there on purpose."

"You know me too well."

She shakes glass from her dress and spins in a circle. Beautiful. She says, "They say to allow 90 minutes for Prom prep. I guess I should have factored in another 10 minutes for glass removal."

I almost kiss her, but the helicopter in the sky fires its big guns at the next four Space Spiders coming down the Cord. It's loud. She turns to see. Her beautiful lips no longer near mine. The big guns blast a Spacer, but I curse the pilot. *Nice timing, idiot.*

"Three not four," says Sweetie. She turns toward me, "Nice shot."

"Thanks. And you did a great job holding them off."

The two Space Spiders sneak closer, but we still don't see them. We look at each other. The adrenaline of the fight heats us up.

Sweetie says, "Flattery will get you everywhere."

That's exactly where I want to go. *Everywhere.* We kiss.

My mom and dad yell, "Turn around! Turn around!" My sister screams, "You can kiss her later! They're right behind you!"

Sweetie's Dad paces in the command center a few feet from the General and his advisors. The Sherif pulls the Mary medal from under his white undershirt and kisses it.

The two Space Spiders get closer. We are a threat to their landing operation and we're scheduled to be terminated. They ignored us before because we were just a one-on-one danger and we weren't attacking them. That's smart. *The Art of War* says, "Don't fight a battle you can't win." But with our missile launch, we forced their leg.

"I love you," says Sweetie.

I see something move behind her. It's got eight eyes. We duck under the truck bridge. Kneeling on glass sucks. She grabs her M16. I pick up my Russian hand job.

"How many?" she asks.

"I only saw one."

We check our magazines. "One," I say. "I've got one round left."

"I've got two."

I look for more Spacers. "Oh, by the way, I love you too."

Sweetie smiles.

I see the launcher and the second missile on the ground not to far from us. I hand Sweetie my Markarov. *Markarov ... Polo.* I grab the launcher and load the second missile. The pickup truck starts to rock and sway. Sweetie leans out with her M16 and goes face-to-face with the Space Spider. BANG. BANG. She's a good shot. The Space Spider backs up. It doesn't know the M16 is out of ammo. The truck stops rocking. The Space Spiders are being more cautious. With reinforcements being compromised, they aren't willing to sacrifice any more members of "Team Arachnid" that are already on the ground.

"Two," I say. "I think there are two out there."

"You said one before."

"I changed my mind."

"You've got one missile," she holds up the Russian semi-automatic pistol, "and I've got one round left."

"Perfect."

"This is not the time for optimism."

"It's always the time for optimism," I say. "We have what we need. This is great."

She shakes her head and turns in the cramped space. Her right knee just misses my special parts. "If there weren't two Space Spiders trying to kill us, I'd kick you in the balls."

"Thank God for the Space Spiders."

I wonder how this is going to work? I look up. The pickup is still above us. I see the sound system in the cab. Maybe I could throw a CD at it. *I wonder* how we can survive this? Opportunities are everywhere. All I've got to do is look and I'll find … a shotgun. Yes, in the cab of the truck above us is a shotgun. I reach up into the cab and wrestle the shotgun free from its rack. I hand it to Sweetie.

"You've got to be kidding me."

I reach back into the cab but can't get to the glove box. *Awww come on.* The rocking of the truck starts again, the glove box opens. Maps and a box of shells fall out. I catch the box of shells and hand them to Sweetie.

"See, God wants us to win."

She loads the shotgun. "I think I should get to use the missile launcher?"

"But I've got experience."

"One. You shot one missile, Chevy."

"And I hit what I was aiming at." Which isn't exactly true. I aimed for the one on the left, and I got the one on the right. *No need to bring that up right now.* "Sweetie, you're good with a shotgun, think of it as a really big buck."

"A really big buck that wants to eat us."

Sweetie checks the gun's sight. The truck stops moving. Stillness. The Space Spiders are planning something. I look at the pickup that covers us. "They're going to pick it up."

"How do you know that?"

"Crayfish. When we hunted them in the stream when we were little, what did we do when they hid under a rock?"

"Picked up the rock," she says.

"Where did we hold the cup to catch them when they ran?"

"On the side."

"One of them is going to lift the truck. The other is going to be waiting for us to make a dash."

We ready the best we can under the truck. I brush aside some glass for her and she kneels with one knee on the road.

Sweetie says, "I'll take the one with the truck."

"I'll take the one on the side."

We wait. She looks good kneeling in her Prom dress. I say, "We are never given more than we can do."

Sweetie says, "That's stupid. What about the people who do something and end up dying like the jet pilot? Everything sure turned out all right for him. He wasn't given more than he could handle." Besides being good looking and smart, she doesn't like bullshit.

She says, "Where do I aim?"

"The heart."

"Where's a Space Spider's heart?"

I don't know. "Forget that, aim for the head. The eyes."

"Which ones?"

"The big ones."

She says, "I have a different idea."

Suddenly, the pickup truck isn't above us. A Space Spider lifts it over its head.

"Don't stand, it will drop it on us."

Sweetie blasts the shotgun. The blast rips off the right leg which holds up the truck. Without that leg, the truck falls on the Space Spider.

I look to my right, nothing. I look to my left, past Sweetie. There's the second one. It's not charging, but its butt points toward us. Its web-shooting hole opens and closes. Gross, I really don't need to see that.

I yell, "Duck!"

I shoot the missile over her head. The missile hangs in the air above Sweetie as she reloads the shotgun. *The missile is too close.* I push her to the ground and covered her with my body as the second rocket kicks in. I feel the heat from the second booster rocket on my back. The missile zooms right into the Space Spider's web dispenser, yikes. The missile pushes it about 15 feet back before the Space Spider blows up. BOOM!

The pickup truck rises into the air, on the back of the first Space Spider, as it stands. Goo drips out of the holes the bullets made in its body. The Space Spider shudders, I guess a pickup truck is heavy. The truck rolls off of the Space Spider. Sweetie stands and pulls the trigger. BAM BAM. Both barrels hit it. Chunks of Space Spider hair and flesh fly away. But she had to fire before she could get a solid stance. The kick from the 12-gauge knocks her backwards. I catch her.

"Thanks."

"Anytime."

She reloads. I wave the Russian pistol and shoot its last round. The Space Spider ducks behind a car. It screeches. I know I'm out, but it doesn't know that. It picks up a smaller car, a red Volkswagen Beetle. I make a fist and turn to Sweetie. She says, "Don't you dare." I lower my fist, but she can't stop me from thinking it, *punch buggie no punch backs.*

The Space Spider throws the Volkswagen Bug at us. I roll out of the way. I see weapons on the ground outside the RV. I might be able to help if I can ...

Sweetie yells, "Go already!" as she runs behind the tossed punch buggie. I run for the RV. I hear Sweetie yell at the Space Spider, "Come on! You scared of a girl in a Prom dress?" She blasts it two more times in the head. It staggers. Goo leaks out.

I scramble into the RV. I grab another machine gun, but it's stuck under the stove. *Damn.* I look around. There's a magazine with bullets inside a white coffee mug. The mug has a picture of a solider with a machine gun on it, the words on the mug reads, "We Make House

Calls." I recognize the slender magazine in the mug. I pull my empty Glock from my waistband. The magazine is a high capacity mag that holds 30 rounds. A standard mag only holds 15 rounds. *Yes!*

I slam it into my Glock and run out of the RV.

The Space Spider stands in front of the blue pickup truck. Sweetie reloads again. Purple venom drips from its fangs. It sniffs for her. The grossness of its face causes me to hesitate, but I point the handgun at it. BAM. BAM. BAM. BAM. BAM. BAM. BAM. BAM. I'm probably not going to kill it from this distance, but I just want to hit it to give Sweetie more time to reload.

The Space Spider doesn't like bullets. It looks at me, even though it doesn't have eyes any more.

She yells, "Hey." The Space Spider turns toward her. Sweetie raises her shotgun, "I don't care how many legs you've got, you're not gonna stop Prom!"

The Space Spider rears up on its back legs, it's going to crush her. BOOM. BOOM. She hits it with both barrels. The Space Spider stops in mid-air and then falls forwards. Sweetie steps backwards. It drops in front of her. For a moment, one hairy, white leg moves. Then it stops. It's dead. She found its heart. That makes sense. She found mine too.

I say, "You just brought down a 500-point Buck."

"At least."

CHAPTER 15

TAKE BACK THE (PROM) DAY

SWEETIE STEPS CLOSER, BUT not too close, to the dead Space Spider. We look around to make sure nothing else sneaks up on us. I see a missile shoot from the helicopter. It takes out another incoming Space Spider. Three more drop to Earth. This is gonna work.

Sweetie fixes her hair and rests the shotgun on her shoulder, "Take a picture, social media me."

"I don't have my ... I'll be right back."

I jump into the RV and come back out with the Lieutenant Minister's camera.

"Say Spacer." She smiles. I take the best pre-Prom photo ever.

I put the camera back in the RV. *I hope the camera's still here when this is over. I hope WE'RE still here when this is over.* I kick the stove about six times. It finally moves. I grab the machine gun that was stuck under it. I grab more random magazines. Sweetie meets me at the RV. She puts down the shotgun and picks up one of the machine guns. I hand her a couple of mags. I'm getting better at the matching game.

155

Give your girlfriend a fish, feed her for a day. Prove to her that she's great with a machine gun, and give her a lifetime of killing Space Spiders.

Chicks dig guns once they know how to use them. Granted, guns can be frightening at first. They hold a lot of power. I believe they can act as an extension of the small amount of testosterone that women have. Most women cannot lift or punch as hard as men can (of equal size and weight). I said most. Please don't send me a million emails telling me that you know a woman that can kick my ass. It's nothing personal; guys just normally have more testosterone than most women. Guns equal all that out real fast, and then some.

Another Space Spider peeks over the top of the Wall. It ducks back down. A moment later the flap at the bottom of the Wall opens and it comes halfway out and waves.

Sweetie points. "What's it doing?"

I look at the Space Spider. It isn't coming for us, but I'm sure I see it smile. The problem is the smile makes its fangs more prominent. "It's inviting us in." Then I remember something I read a long time ago. "Step into my parlor, said the spider to the fly."

Sweetie yells, "No thank you!"

As Sweetie politely turns down the Space Spider's invitation to death, the military PR team tells the General that people all over the world LOVE seeing Sweetie kill a Space Spider with a shotgun. The world wants to know this young woman's name.

The General doesn't know our names. He didn't asked SNAFU or Darcy, because he didn't and still doesn't care. Perhaps I could be a little more generous. Perhaps he knew it didn't matter to the mission what our names were so he never asked. Or perhaps he had read that people who do animal testing don't name the animals because they don't want to get attached to them before they're sacrificed. That's what we were to him, lab rats that he's ready to sacrifice.

The General turns to Sweetie's dad, the Sheriff. The Sheriff doesn't say anything. He knows how to follow the line of command. He waits to be called upon before talking. He waits for the General to ask him what his daughter's name is. To the General's credit, he doesn't ask the Sheriff. I guess the General knows how to take advantage of a PR opportunity. The General says, "We call her Prom Queen with a

Shotgun."

The Sheriff smiles. He knows Sweetie will like that.

You should have seen Sweetie's face when she heard that the press and social media picked up the General's nickname for her. She was so happy. In less than ten minutes, people from Albania to Zimbabwe knew her as Prom Queen with a Shotgun.

Nobody knew her real name, yet folks all over America clapped, cheered, and high-fived each other as their daughters begged to go to the gun range for shooting practice. There was even a low budget comic book that was started in a garage in New Jersey called "Prom Queen with a Shotgun and Tuxedo Glockenstein."

Without us knowing, Darcy and SNAFU head toward us for the second time. Another four incoming space invaders stop making pretty colors. The Black Hawk copter doesn't shoot, it flies away. *What? Don't leave now when it's working.* A missile zooms in and explodes one of the hairy beasts. A fighter jet soars overhead. *Cool, jets are getting in on the action.* We see a line of jets in the sky. It's nice when we can all play together and take turns. We look for more sneaking Space Spiders. We don't see any.

"I don't think we're a high priority any more."

"I think you're right. I'm sure the Space Spiders are more concerned about the Black Hawks and fighters." Three more go SPLAT. We go back to the RV for shade and something to drink. I stay outside and keep an eye on the Wall. Sweetie lifts the fridge door again.

"You want another beer?"

"No. I want to think straight if I need to. Water would be great."

I see the next four Space Spiders burn off their colors and unfurl. I look for another jet, but a Black Hawk copter blasts away. The Space Spiders seem to be coming down faster now. After the explosion, the other three Spacers fall fast and hard. I look at the Cord. I can only see so far up, but they keep coming. *Is it possible there could be an endless supply?* That's crazy.

Three helicopters fly over us and stop a hundred feet or so from the Great Wall of Web. I expect them to open fire, but they just sit there. I suppose they are tasked with keeping an eye on the Spacers that are already on the ground. I'm not sure how many are left on the ground since the "25% is 100%" campaign began. There can't be too many left, because we took out a few ourselves. I'm thinking some genius is trying to figure out how to capture the remaining ones so they can be tortured, I mean tested on, in some secret military base. I can hear them thinking, *Oh the secrets we could learn.*

What takes her so long in the RV? I get scared. Something rumbles around inside the RV. "Sweetie?"

I look in at the same time she looks out.

"Ahhhhhh."

She hands me a bottle of water. "Freak."

She went to the bathroom. Her hair is combed and make-up

reapplied. I'm so glad I'm not a girl. I drink half a bottle and pour the rest of it over my head. I run my fingers through my hair, combing it out. Water drips down my face.

Sweetie says, "I'm so glad I'm not a guy."

We hear a chopper slow down. It lands not too far from us. Darcy and an army guy that looks like SNAFU jumps out.

"That guy looks like SNAFU," says Sweetie.

"That *is* SNAFU."

"Where did he get the fatigues?"

"Where did he get the suit this morning?"

Sweetie laughs. "How many wardrobe changes do you think he's going to do today?"

The pilot remains in the chopper. Three more Army guys jump out. They look either eager or scared. Perhaps both. They're on high alert. One Army guy stays with the chopper. The other two make their way toward us. They signal Darcy and SNAFU to follow. We jog toward them.

The Army Guys stop about halfway to us and let Darcy and SNAFU come the rest of the way. SNAFU says, "Nice shot, dude." We run and hug them. I keep holding SNAFU. It gets awkward, but he hugs me again. He whispers, "It's OK. It's going to be alright now." I am far more emotional than I'm comfortable with. I am so glad to see him that my bullshit detector doesn't go off. *How in the world can he know if we're going to be alright?*

Darcy and Sweetie hug. "Nice shooting." Sweetie wipes her eyes. Darcy holds her and places a hand on the back of Sweetie's head. "You did good. Real good." Sweetie sniffles, it's been a big morning.

Sweetie says, "And I just redid my makeup."

Darcy looks at her. "You look good."

"No I don't."

That's enough tenderness for SNAFU. He pats me on the back and stops the hug. "Hell of a way to end the year."

I touch his uniform, "What's this?"

"Darcy deputized me."

"She can do that?"

"On a day like today, you can do anything you want."

SNAFU, Darcy, Sweetie and I watch another Space Spider peek over the Wall. One of the helicopters above the Wall blasts it. The Space Spider drops back down. Yup, those copters are there for containment.

Darcy says, "Did you see the way that thing looked at us?"

SNAFU says, "They look a lot scarier when you're on the ground."

"You should see how scary they are when they're trying to kill you."

"Let's get out of here," says Sweetie.

That's when we hear the gunfire. The two soldiers that are halfway to the helicopter stand on a car that's stuck in the mud. They yell at us.

"Come on! Move it!"

We see five Space Spiders approach our getaway copter. The solider near the helicopter shoots at them. They must have escaped from behind the Wall before the Black Hawks arrived. There are five Space Spiders circling the lone soldier and the copter. The pilot can read the writing on the Wall (of Web). Or, perhaps, the pilot could read the writing on the coffin (his coffin). Both work here. The helicopter rises into the air. *Oh well, there goes our ride.* The Space Spiders focus on the commando left on the ground. He hurts the Spacers with rounds from his M4, the new and improved version of the M16 that's a little more compact. However, one guy can't take out five Space Spiders.

A Space Spider charges him. The decorated solider BLASTS. Alien flesh flies. Another Space Spider charges from behind. The commando spins. His courage and aim are great, but a Spacer grabs and fangs him right through the helmet. The soldier's muscles must have locked-up because his gun keeps shooting. Before he dies, his machine gun rises right under the Space Spider's head and continues to blast. A fountain springs from the top of the Spacer's head. The Spacer and the solider drop. See, karma. Do unto others as you would have them do unto you. You reap what you sow. You have to eat the lunch you packed.

The two other soldiers return to the chopper to take on the remaining four Space Spiders. I appreciate their enthusiasm, but I don't see the need to rush.

Darcy yells, "Come on!"

We run. By chance or agreement, the two commandos shoot at the same Space Spider. Flesh flies and goo pours.

The helicopter gets about twenty feet in the air when a Space Spider turns, raises its butt, and shoots a web. The web line hits the front windshield. The helicopter attempts to lift and run, but it isn't going anywhere. Tug of war time. The Space Spider pulls one way, the helicopter the other.

One solider waves to the pilot to come back down. If you can't fly away you might as well land before you crash. Two Space Spiders charge the soldiers who blast their hairy leader. That's when Sweetie, Darcy, SNAFU and I get in range. We aren't as close as the two Army guys on the ground but we're close enough to make a difference. We get into position and wait for the front Space Spider to drop so we can blast the two Spacers behind it. But that doesn't happen. The two Spacers behind Mr. Wobble Legs hold it up. They push the dead Space Spider forward, using it as a shield.

The helicopter, still in a tug of war, comes down to land. One of the soldiers jumps in. The helicopter doesn't land; it goes back up. The solider gets behind the 44 mm gun. *Ah, I see what he's doing. Why use a small gun when you can use a big one?*

The pilot wants to shoot a missile at the tug-of-war Spacer but the chopper is too close to the ground. It might miss at this range and the explosion would damage the chopper.

The big guns BLAST and rip up the Space Spider that's being used as a shield. Legs fly off. The big rounds make the carcass jump and leak. The dead Space Spider is no longer an effective shield. The two

Space Spiders hiding behind it toss their dead comrade at one of the soldiers on the ground. It crushes the solider. That's a yucky way to go.

The big gun from the helicopter rips up the two Space Spiders that no longer have their dead buddy to hide behind. The four of us also shoot at these two Spacers. They stop advancing. We push them back. Yes! The pilot gets an idea. It is a bad idea, but kudos to him for thinking. He tilts the helicopter forward.

Sweetie says, "He's going to try and cut the webbing with the chopper blades."

I yell, "No, it's too strong!"

This seems to happen in slow motion. The first blade hits the web line. SNAP! The blade cracks. The blade flies. The blade zooms at us. I mean, right at us.

We jump out of the way. It sticks in the ground between SNAFU and me. Second blade hits the webbing. CRACK! This blade flies into one of the other Space Spiders, right through the body and pins it to the ground. The scale isn't exactly right but it looks like a bug pinned to a board at a museum. The Space Spider tries to push itself away from the blade. The blade slices the Space Spider in half. Both sides fall as it splits itself open. Gross.

The helicopter comes crashing down. The Space Spider who pulls the webbing is too close. Too bad, so sad. The helicopter bursts into flames and so does the eight-legged winner of the tug of war. Winner takes nothing. All of the other members of the extraction team are gone. The last Space Spider turns toward us. It has been hit by the big gun and is a little shaky but it screeches at us. The hairs on the back of my neck stand.

SNAFU looks at us and then at the Space Spider. "Four on one. Doesn't seem fair."

A car alarm goes off behind us. A Space Spider fangs the hood of the two-seater hybrid until the alarm stops. The Spacer is pissed that the little car gave away its position.

Sweetie steps up on the front bumper of a Honda Civic, "They're sneaking up on us." She steps up on its hood, then roof. "One, two, three, four ... five."

Odds are now four to six. *This sucks.* Either a whole bunch of them snuck out before the three containment helicopters arrived or they have dug an escape tunnel. I don't like being out in the open and far away from the RV, our weapons stash. I look up; no more helicopters are landing for us. I say, "Come on, back to the road."

We run back up onto the road and between the cars. We are still a ways off from the RV.

SNAFU says, "Who wants to play Hide and Screech?" SNAFU and Darcy shoot at the Spacers. Sweetie joins them. She calls to me. "Come on, Chevy, it's fun."

SNAFU says, "Come on, Chevy, everybody's doing it."

Peer pressure in high school can be brutal. "No," I say. "I've got to do what's right for me." That's the proper way to respond to peer pressure. You must hold to your own convictions. "Cover me."

I run to the RV. I make a lot of noise rummaging through stuff and probably almost blow myself up, but I get what I want: another M16, a few matching mags, and more grenades. I see something scurry outside the RV. I peer through the tattered holes in the Sky Roof, and I see a Space Spider. It runs and hides. It waits for me. I decide to hunt the hunter. I go back to the ammo stash. *I wonder what would be useful right now?* I smile as I pick up a new toy. The Space Spider sticks its head into the broken front windshield. I surprise it with a stream of fire to its head. It scurries backwards. I shoot the flamethrower again. A long stream of fire shoots out of the RV windshield and ignites the Space Spider. This is great. But, I also get a little fire inside the RV. OK, not a little bit, a lot. Oops. Learning curve. Flames jump everywhere. Fire dances around the rest of the ammo and weapons. Not good.

I head for the Sky Roof exit. The RV is still on its side so the stairs are crazy difficult to climb through. The fire burns all around me. I feel the heat and cough on black smoke. I can't maneuver with the flamethrower on my back. Rounds explode. I slip out of the flamethrower and drop it harder than I want to. I wait for it to explode, but it doesn't. I grab my M16 and other supplies and run.

The RV explodes behind me. BA - BOOOOOOOOOM.

The blast picks me up and throws me toward Sweetie, SNAFU, and Darcy. They shoot at Space Spiders hiding behind cars. I crash-land and tumble to Sweetie. She stops me with her foot. I lay on the ground as she taps out some flames with one of her sneakers.

"You alright?"

"Yah, I'm fine," I say. "I wanted to do that. How many you got out there?"

Sweetie looks at the decimated RV. She shakes her head but decides to let it go. "Six."

"Six are better than seven."

Sweetie laughs. "That is not much of a better-feeling thought. I'd like something with a little more oomph to it."

I stand and hand her another mag. "How about, you're beautiful, and I'm so glad to have such good friends in my life with so many high powered semi-automatic weapons."

Sweetie locks and loads her M16. "That's a better better-feeling thought."

One of the Space Spiders breaks off from the pack and joins the wobbly Spacer that attacked the helicopter. They circle around behind us.

Darcy barks out orders, "SNAFU, don't let Charlotte and her friend crawl up our ass." Darcy points to Sweetie, "Pretty girl, you got the other perimeter." She turns to me, "You and me got the center."

I say, "Hey Buddy, I know why you love her so much."

SNAFU grins. "That's my wife!"

Sweetie and I respond, "Wife?"

Darcy holds up her left hand. We see the grenade she holds. She turns her hand. We see SNAFU's high school ring.

"Your high school ring? Nice."

Darcy beams, "The chaplain married us while we were waiting for the pre-nuke to drop."

Sweetie says, "Hey, that's when Chevy and I fell back in love."

I check my mag and switch off my safety, "Who says we should end nuclear proliferation and the arms race?"

Darcy says, "I'm going to invite everyone in the military industrial complex to our reception."

SNAFU shoots a few rounds. His blasts are warning shots. Or ... he could have been aiming at the Space Spiders and he's just experiencing the learning curve. He might still be getting the hang of his M4.

Sweetie sends a few rounds at the Space Spiders on the other side. They peek over a mini-van. She hits one. They duck back down. She looks at Darcy, "Give me a moment and I'll give you another hug."

Darcy smiles, "Thanks for accepting me into your group." She tosses the grenade. A Space Spider sticks his head out. BOOM. Almost got him.

I respond only half jokingly, "Hey, I can finally move to the city with Sweetie. I needed to find someone to take care of SNAFU before I left."

Sweetie chimes in, "We're not losing an insane friend, we're gaining a tough, smart, and powerful new friend." Darcy beams.

The first two Space Spiders approach Darcy and me with caution. Maybe it's the smell of their dead brothers and sisters that give them pause. Maybe it's the fact that they don't feel any fear from us. I often wonder what they would have done if we would have started doing the Chicken Dance, Macarena, or Cupid Shuffle. But not right now, the dancing will have to wait for the reception.

I take two grenades and pull the pins. I wink at Darcy, "I got you a wedding present." I throw them really high into the air. The two Space Spiders in front of us look up. "Sitting ducks."

She and I let go with a burst of M4 machine gun fire. We rip up the two hairy Space Spiders. By the time the grenades come down, they look like soggy fur balls my 12 year-old cat, Grouchy, coughs up.

Then...BOOM. BOOM.

The grenades finish them off. Grenades are cool. I turn to check on Sweetie. Darcy turns to her husband. *Her husband?! SNAFU is married!* That's nuttier than us fighting Space Spiders on Prom day.

The two Space Spiders try to outflank Sweetie. They move pretty fast. She blasts and shoots out car windows as they make their way around her. They duck and jive. She hits them. It looks like she has them pinned down behind a truck. They peek. She shoots. They hide. I realize they might be buying time.

"Watch out, you're going to run out of ammo."

Sweetie looks at me, "Then come over here and help."

I run to Sweetie. Darcy joins SNAFU. I hear BAM BAM BAM.

"You're sexy."

Sweetie says to me, "Get ready, they're going to jump."

"How do you know?"

"Because we're going to light them on fire."

Sweetie looks at the truck's gas tank. We blast together because that's what you do when you're in love. We tear up that truck real good and then BOOM! Metal, glass, flames and two big hairy Space Spiders fly out of the explosion.

I yell, "Pull!"

Sweetie takes the one on the left. I take the one on the right. RAT-A-TAT-TAT. Itsy bitsy spider ... parts. Nobody's going back up the waterspout.

Sweetie and I turn toward the newlyweds. I remember hoping that their honeymoon hadn't started yet. I don't want to see SNAFU naked. Darcy and SNAFU blast a big pile of webbed up cars. *What? When did that happen?*

Charlotte and her friend webbed together three cars and a pickup truck. I can also see the front end of a PT Cruiser sticking out. The last two Space Spiders have made a little bunker for themselves and they're hiding behind it.

CHAPTER 16

WEB MOUNDS

BY THE TIME SWEETIE and I get over to SNAFU and Darcy, the
two Space Spiders are completely hidden behind the Web Mound of
cars. It's a standstill. Everything is quiet. SNAFU and Darcy crouch
down between a pickup truck and a black convertible. They're about
twenty feet from the Web Mound.

SNAFU and Darcy hold hands. *Really?* I join the two lovebirds in
their metal bunker. Sweetie climbs onto the roof of a blue Hyundai
Accent. A little compact car that I'm sure gets good gas mileage. She
looks around for more Hairy Party Crashers.

I call out, "Darcy, you've got a radio, right?"

"Yeah."

"I don't think the Black Hawk copters should be that close to the
wall."

Darcy looks at the copters patrolling the Wall. A flap opens in the
front of the Wall. A Space Spider tries to sneak out. The copter on the
end drifts over and blasts the flap. The Space Spider goes back in.

168

Darcy says, "At least they're stopping the leak."

I look up at the Galactic Cord. Four more Space Spider rock pods hit the atmosphere and burst into beautiful colors. The process of birthing Hairy Babies of Joy is breathtaking. So is fighting them. *Is it every 20 seconds now? It seems faster.* Helicopters and jets take turns. Very organized. It's nice when war can be civilized. They still blast one of each four-pack; sometimes with a big gun, sometimes with a missile. One Spacer pops and the other three drop.

I follow three as they fall. They wave their arms trying to stop gravity. Good luck with that. SPLAT! SPLAT! SPLAT!

There are two or three inches of Space Spider goo around the school now. That's going to be one heck of a mess to clean up. My female classmates better have some tall CFMPs to keep their dresses goo free when they enter the gym tonight.

Whenever a fighter jet approaches the Cord, the helicopters get out of the way so the jet can blast a Space Spider. The jet then makes a WIDE turn around the Cord. Everyone keeps their distance. It gives me a good feeling. *The bipeds might come out on top.* I see huge transports in the sky, tanks and 100s of Marines parachuting down. Marines are sexy.

This is going to be easier than I thought.

Let's do the math. They came down for about four minutes before the jets lined up. Four Space Spiders every thirty seconds equals eight per minute. Eight Spacers times four minutes is thirty-two Spacers. We and the helicopter Marines killed about ten. About 22 intergalactic arachnids are left including the two on the other side of the Web Mound. I guess most of them are guarding their base and are theoretically contained. I look back at the three copters hovering near the Wall of Web. They still look too close to me.

SNAFU salutes the tanks and Marines who parachute down, "The Great Wall of Web is going to fall."

It's nice to have more Freedom Fighters on the field. It's nice the Space Spiders have others to be concerned about. And it's nice how good Sweetie looks in her Prom dress.

"Darcy," I urge, "I think the Black Hawks are too close to the Wall."

"The General's not going to like hearing suggestions from a high school senior."

"I don't really care what he likes or doesn't like. I just want the humans to win. The Spacers are planning something."

SNAFU says, "Yeah, how they're going to die." SNAFU raises his fist, but I don't bump it. "Man, a Space Spider invasion happens and you go all serious on me."

Darcy turns to SNAFU, "You got these guys while I call in?"

SNAFU says, "I'll cover you."

"In what?" She bats her eyes.

SNAFU blushes.

Sweetie says, "Gross."

Darcy and SNAFU kiss. He stays focused on the car-web-mound with the Spacers behind it. Darcy calls on her walkie, "This is Private First Class Meyers. I have information that the General may be interested in." She slides her way out from between the cars. She steps away so she can hear.

I have never seen SNAFU blush. Today is a strange day.

The two Space Spiders peek from behind the Web Mound. SNAFU blasts. They duck back down. Sweetie joins us between the pickup truck and the black Mustang convertible. Oh, man it's *Roy's* convertible. I hit the side view mirror with the butt of my M16.

Sweetie yells, "Hey, hey!"

But it's too late. I hit the mirror again. SNAP! The side mirror dangles.

"Was that necessary?"

"What? It was sticking out. I didn't want anyone to bump into it and hurt themselves." *Screw Roy, he's an idiot.*

We listen, but we don't hear anything from the other side of the Web Mound. SNAFU watches Darcy, but talks to us, "What do we do now?"

It's funny that we are the Space Spider experts now. SNAFU's gun glistens in the sunlight. A few jets have formed a line, they pick off one out of every four. Black Hawks provide back up. Marines advance on the ground. I smell gasoline, which is better than Spacer guts. The ground troops get the OK and a group of soldiers fire a really cool

170

rocket launcher. Different model than the one I shot. A rocket streams up to their hairy targets. BOOM. It explodes and the other three drop like rocks. I'm about to answer SNAFU's question when I remember how the other experts are always wrong.

"Well, I'm no expert so I'm not going to guess what they're planning."

Sweetie adds, "But they're dangerous."

"I don't think it would be wise to go in and attack them," I say, "just like it's not wise to go after a grizzly."

SNAFU says, "Which we've never hunted."

"No, we haven't. But remember the wolf that got trapped in Mr. Steven's barn?"

"We didn't go in."

"No we didn't. We got it to come out."

Darcy jumps back into the car bunker with us. "The General says the Marines should be here soon. He says to hold tight; the Marines will take them from behind."

Sweetie snickers.

"Waiting is not a good idea," I say. "They seem to be able to adapt."

Three more Space Spiders SMACK down into the parking lot of death.

Sweetie looks for options. "The best defense is a good offense."

SNAFU puts his arm around Darcy and pulls her close, but he agrees with us. "Waiting sucks."

I say, "What do you think Private First Class Meyers?"

"Waiting gives them all the power," says Darcy. "It's not the General's life on the line out here." She picks up her walkie, "I'm sorry sir, I didn't read. Would you confirm, should we wait for the Marines?" Darcy turns off the walkie, "I never received confirming orders."

I like her more and more. Darcy takes the last two grenades off her belt. She gives one to me. SNAFU takes his last two grenades and gives one to Sweetie. *Our last four grenades, they need to count.*

Darcy says, "I guess we're on our own."

"It's been that kind of day," I say.

SNAFU smiles. "OK then, we flush them out."

Darcy leads. "I'm going to count to three. Pull the pin on two, toss them on three."

Sweetie practices her throw. She pulls her arm back, she's planning to throw it like a football. Darcy says, "No. Underhand. So it goes high and drops on the other side of the mound."

"That makes sense."

Darcy counts, "One, two," we pull our pins …

Sweetie yells. Aaaaaahhhhhhh! It isn't a war cry; it's more like a rattlesnake bit her. She points in the direction of the school. We fumble. I drop my grenade before I can put the pin in. We've got ten seconds before it explodes.

SNAFU yells, "Fire in the hole!"

The grenade rolls past Sweetie and bumps into SNAFU's boot. Seven seconds. He reaches for it, but he kicks it under Roy's black convertible. Darcy reaches under the car and comes out with the grenade. Four seconds.

She yells, "Pin!"

Sweetie yells, "Just throw it!"

"No. These are our last four grenades. Pin!" Darcy needs to put the pin back into the grenade so it doesn't explode.

"I don't have it. I dropped it," I say.

Darcy pulls the pin out of her grenade and sticks it in my mine, buying us time. "Find it! We don't have grenades to waste."

I get down on my hands and knees. *I'm finding it. I'm finding it. I'm finding it.*

"I got it!"

I toss my pin to her so she can put it in her grenade. I throw it too hard. Her hand whips up and grabs it. She slides it into her grenade. We wait. No boom. That was close. I realize she and SNAFU might go the distance. She's got nerves of steel.

I turn to Sweetie, "You OK? Why'd you yell?"

She points to three Space Spiders as they fall. I didn't see if a jet, copter, or land missile took out their buddy but it doesn't really matter. They are on their way to their Death-by-Gravity sentence.

"What?" I ask her.

"I don't know."

"What do you mean, you don't know?"

"I know what I saw, but I don't know WHAT I saw. Just watch. I'll keep an eye on the two behind the mound."

So SNAFU, Darcy, and I watch as the three fall and hit the ground behind the Wall. Wait, no splat. No goo flying up. No death behind the Wall. Then we see what freaked out Sweetie. The three Space Spiders spring back up.

"What?"

Previously, the three falling Space Spiders hit so hard that goo shot up into the air, but not anymore. The Spacers bounce up. I'll say it again, "What?" We watch them flip once over-easy and then land behind the Web Wall. We don't see them land because the Web Wall is too high, but there is no splat.

SNAFU uses the binoculars, "I can't see past the Wall."

Darcy says, "A web trampoline. The survivors built a web trampoline."

We can't see it, but it is the only logical conclusion. The three helicopters along the Wall move forward.

I say, "No, too close. Back up!"

They get closer to the Wall so they can take out the trampo-web and the Space Spiders who made it. Three Space Spider butts appear on the Wall.

Sweetie whispers, "They're too close."

Webs shoot out of the Space Spiders on the Wall. Each hits a helicopter. The Space Spider on the right scurries to its left. The one on the left, scurries to its right. They each pull their helicopter towards the one in the middle. Both copters fire. A missile flies out and hits the Wall just missing the Space Spiders that drags it to the center.

The Black Hawk in the center climbs into the sky. It pulls the middle Spacer to the top of the Wall, but the Spacer holds onto the Wall. The web line stretches.

Sweetie shouts, "Blast it, now!"

The helicopter in the middle starts to unloaded its payload; one, two, three missiles zoom out while 44 mm rounds pound into the Wall. Two missiles shoot over the Wall; one hits the Wall. Big explosions, but minor damage. Big rounds rip up the middle Space Spider and it disconnects from the web line pulling on the middle copter.

We cheer.

Then we stop. The copter on the right swings in fast and so does the copter on the left. They are going to SMACK the middle one. But the middle copter flies up just in time. The middle copter looks like a balloon that someone let go; it goes up while the web line string waves in the air. It's free.

We cheer again. Then we stop. The right copter CRASHES into the left one underneath the middle one.

The middle pilot radios, "I'm free. I'm going to take out the trampo-web."

But he isn't fast enough or high enough. The crash of the two copters under the middle copter explodes into a massive fireball. Unused missiles and rounds explode. The detonation extends in all directions. Left, right, down, and UP engulfing the free Black Hawk copter.

The pilot radios, "Cancel that. Not free. Going to die."

The third copter EXPLODES. Two more Space Spiders bounce safely to the ground behind the Wall. We look up. Another set of four burn off colors and unfurl as they zoom toward Earth.

SNAFU says, "They're coming in faster now."

I say, "No, not faster now. They were waiting for this. They sped up a awhile ago."

Darcy says, "What do you mean?"

I said, "It takes time to travel from the moon to the Earth. The 30 and 20 second intervals must have been the first wave."

Darcy adds, "They needed time to learn, adapt, and secure a base."

"If the first wave was to secure a base," asks SNAFU, "what's the next wave for?"

"Invasion."

SNAFU turns to the Wall. "When?"

"I don't know. I'm not an expert," I say. "They're probably going to build up a swarm first. They know we're fighters and we're dangerous. Only by sheer numbers can they overrun our military."

The trampoline of webbing is still safe behind the Wall. Holy Geez, the Wall is about thirty or forty feet high now. I wonder how much webbing they carry in their butts.

The trampo-web is in front of the school (and ten yards behind the Wall). This is where gravity pulls the Space Spiders to their death in the "Three not Four Campaign" (also known as the 25% is 100% Campaign). The trampo-web is made on four short mounds made of broken asphalt and webbing. Two mounds are slightly higher then the other two making a 40-degree angle so that the Spacers that hit the trampo-web and bounce up are directed OFF the trampo-web. This way, the Space Spiders using the trampo-web do NOT bounce straight up and hit the next set of Spacers coming down. Smart.

The General orders the troops to take out ALL of the falling Space Spiders now that they're doing gymnastics. Jets, helicopters, and land troops shoot missiles and rounds. Other fighters receive orders to take out the trampo-web. The first missiles hit the trampo-web. Yes! But they bounce off it. Luckily the missiles fly over the school and blow up in the woods.

Sweetie says, "That was close."

Fighters are ordered to blast the ground next to the trampo-web to dislodge the support mounds. Smart. But more Space Spiders land before the fighters arrive.

Knocking all four Space Spiders out of the sky isn't as easy as it sounds. The jets, Black Hawk copters, and ground troops aren't ready for the new arachnid aerobatics. Some Space Spiders pull in their legs and fall fast. Then they pop open like some horrible, deadly flower, which slows their descent drastically. Missiles and rounds fly under and over their bodies, just missing them. Missiles blast into cornfields miles away. Some missiles create fires, which creates popcorn. Some Space Spiders stick out a leg, this ROTATES the four Space Spiders around the Galactic Cord as they fall. Missiles are locked on, but they JUST miss them and hit the Cord. The Space Spiders even learn how to time it right. They tuck in their legs and drop fast to avoid a missile when they see one coming. Adaptive hairy freaks.

Don't get me wrong; Space Spiders still get hit, one, two, and sometimes even three in a group, but now that they are coming down faster and doing maneuvers, many get through. There are also other problems. Now that ammo is being blasted at a frenzied rate, jets and helicopters leave more often to reload. And with more birds in the air, fuel is being used at a faster rate.

Two jets zoom over the Wall and blast the ground around the trampo-web. Three Space Spiders fall and SMUSH. Once again we see the fountain of goo. We cheer. The troops cheer. The folks watching cheer. The General smiles. But the ground Spacers are fast. They create new mounds and reattach the trampo-web before the next two come down. They bounce to safety.

I realize the easy part is over.

Four more burn off colors and open up. A jet takes out the first one. A helicopter shoots two missiles and blasts the second. The helicopter flies away to reload. Two fall to safety. But wait, a tank rolls through the practice field and fires. A third Space Spider blows up. Nice. *That's what we need, a tank. Forget the limo. Tanks rule.* Space Spiders fall, disappear behind the Wall and bounce up. They tuck their legs and flip over a few times like high divers going for the gold.

I say, "We've got to stop them from coming down the Cord."

SNAFU says, "How do we do that boss?"

But before we can discuss, Sweetie blasts the car mound with her M16. "They keep peeking. I think they're up to something."

I'm glad she's watching them. I forgot they were there. Sweetie is right. We're in trouble. We gave them WAY too much time to think. And, the Marines that were promised must have been called off to take out more of the incoming Spacers. I get it, I do, but thanks again for nothing, General.

Suddenly, a web line shoots over the bunker, over our heads, and hits a Mazda that is parked on the other side of Roy's black convertible. The web pulls the Mazda up and over our heads. I never thought a car that weighed about 2,860 pounds could go from standing still to "zooming" over our heads so quickly. It flies over our heads and crashes into the Web Mound. Windows shattered and glass shoots in all directions. A few pieces bounce back at us. Then the Mazda is pulled up and over the top of the Web Mound. One of the Space Spiders looks to see if it worked.

Sweetie says, "They wanted to pull that car into us."

SNAFU says, "Technically, a Mazda 5 is not a car. It's considered to be a family wagon." I think that too, but I'm smart enough to not say it out loud. Sweetie looks at him. *Really?* SNAFU isn't being a jerk, he just likes cars as much as I do. *No need to correct the car ignorance of the people you love at a time like this.*

Darcy returns fire. The Eight Legged Freak ducks back down.

Darcy says, "Pull the pin on two and toss on three." We get ready. She counts, "One, two," pins out, "three!" All four of us under-hand the grenades up into the air. They come down on the other side of the mound.

CHAPTER 17

HONEY & SWEETIE

WE WAIT FOR THE booms. Darcy says, "Honey and Sweetie, you get the right side when they run out. Chevy, you and me, the left side."

Note: This is the first time I've ever heard someone call SNAFU honey.

I think it's smart that we don't always work with our significant others. Space Spiders are a lot of stress. Add relationship expectations and Prom on top of that, and that might prove to be too much for a bunch of high school seniors on the battlefield. The grenades explode. BOOM. BOOM. BOOM. BOOM.

We flip the safeties off and raise our M4s and M16s. SNAFU and Sweetie face the right side of the mound. Darcy and I cover the left. But no Space Spiders run out. Well, if they aren't dead, they're deaf.

One leg flops out on the right side. SNAFU and Sweetie shoot it until they realize there isn't a Spacer attached to it.

SNAFU yells, "We killed a leg."

We wait. Nothing happens. Suddenly, another web line comes

shooting over the mound. This time it's a little lower. It flies right at our heads. It's going to hit me in the face. *Good shot from the blind.* I duck behind the pickup. I feel a rush of air as it zooms over me. The web line hits Roy's car behind us, but we're safe behind the pickup.

Note: In North America, a pickup truck is often simply referred to as a pickup or truck. It is a light motor vehicle with an open-top, rear cargo area that is also called a "bed." Other countries have their own terms for a pickup, such as "utility" or ute in Australia and New Zealand, or bakkie in South Africa. In Europe, light lorries are commonly used for similar roles.

Look at that, another educational moment.

If you're a kid reading this and your mom or dad tells you to stop and do your homework tell them you're learning something. Parents will almost always let you continue doing something if:

One: You're not bothering them,

Two: You're able to convince them it's educational.

Three: You're willing to connect with them about whatever you're doing.

Parents love the idea of "learning" because learning means you're preparing "for the future." And, if you're doing that then they feel like good parents. Remember, your parents love you. Share some of the story with them. That's what "connect" with them means. Just be smart, if they don't like the gross stuff, don't freak them out. Be nice to them.

The web line hits Roy's mustang behind us. It sticks to the passenger side door. SNAFU is on one side of the web line; I'm on the other side. I look at the web line that separates us and attaches to Roy's nice, shiny convertible.

I say, "That sucks for Roy."

Sweetie looks at the web line. "One's still alive."

Then another web line shoots over the top of the mound. This time it hits and sticks to the back end of Roy's car near the rear bumper. This web line is on the other side of me.

I laugh. "Missed again, sucker."

Darcy says, "Number two's alive."

I try to focus, but I have an incredible urge to limbo. I should have but I talk instead. "Maybe they're trying to hit us."

SNAFU reaches over the web line that separates us and hits me. "You think?"

The Space Spiders pull on the web lines and Roy's car slams into us, pushing us into the pickup in front of us. We're being crushed. Nice move. I didn't see that coming. I correct myself, "Maybe they're trying to do what they just did." I should save my breath, because once I exhale, I have a hard time inhaling.

Roy's convertible doesn't crush Sweetie and Darcy. Sweetie slipped down and hit the ground when Roy's car was pulled into us and Darcy jumped up. Darcy now stands in the back of Roy's convertible. SNAFU and I weren't so quick; we are left between the two vehicles. We're like Han and Chewie in the trash compactor. We push with all our might with no result. I'm, of course, Han Solo.

I think about telling Darcy to watch out for STDs in the back of Roy's car, but she has boots on so I figure she's OK. With our backs against Roy's mustang, SNAFU and I attempt to keep it from completely smashing us into the pickup truck. Thank God for forearms and rib cages. SNAFU howls like a wookie, "Arrrrruggghhhhh." I think that's his last breath. I can't ask him, though, because I'm lacking the ability to breathe.

Even in the midst of all this, I don't lose sight of the fact that Roy's car is crushing me to death. Poetic, ironic and/or twisted. If I were a writer, I would know which one.

Sweetie rolls out from under the pickup. She moves toward us with worry on her face. I hate it when chicks look at you that way. As if you can't handle the mess you're in and you might die. I shake my head no and then look at the Web Mound with the two Spacers behind it. *If she's going to help us, it has to be by taking out the enemies behind the bunker.* Darcy leaps from the back of the convertible to the bed of the pickup. She runs her fingers through SNAFU's hair as she jumps over us. I think SNAFU would have smiled if oxygen was getting to his brain. Darcy and Sweetie know what to do, they run to the side of the car-web-mound.

They jump behind the mound. The two Space Spiders have their butts in the air. I know, I've been calling them butts for a while. The scientific name is abdomens. This is the big bulbous part that is the web-making factory. But abdomen is three syllables and takes longer to say (and write) and who doesn't like the word butt? So their butts are up and a web line extends out of each one at about a 45-degree angle. The web line goes over the web bunker and attaches and pulls Roy's car into SNAFU and me.

The Space Spiders are not in good shape. That's why SNAFU and I are still alive.

SNAFU and I would have died right away if the grenades had not been so successful. Sure, they didn't kill the two Space Spiders, but when Darcy and Sweetie pop around the edge of the mound, they see eleven legs flip-flopping on the ground. One Space Spider has only three legs to stand on, the other has two. It's pretty gnarly looking. Spacer fluid oozes out of joints everywhere. The one with two legs wobble. This is why, when they pull the webbing, they aren't crushing us. They are weak because they're hurting so bad and they can't get much traction or leverage.

A leg that lays on the ground, twitches and flips in the air at Sweetie. She ducks just in time as it flies over her head, droplets of goo spraying her. Darcy blasts the tripod Space Spider. Sweetie kneels down with her elbow on her raised knee—classic hunter position plus a Prom dress—and blasts the wobbly one.

They screech and bare their fangs. I'm talking about Darcy and Sweetie, not the Space Spiders. The girls show no mercy. Bullets fly. Bullets hit. Bullets rip up alien flesh.

Darcy yells, "Nobody crushes my husband but me!"

Darcy shoots the spinneret off of her Space Spider. You know, the back part of the butt where the web comes out. Webbing blobs out. Gross. The Space Spider looks at her, then its legs buckle and it falls down dead.

Sweetie blasts the other one. Her rounds hit the Space Spider between the head and the abdomen. And, just to be clear, a spider doesn't really have a head. It's got two big bulbous parts. The front part is called the Cephalothorax. How might you remember that for a test? Ce-phal-o-thorax. Much easier when you break it into parts. (See, *this is* educational.) The fangs, eyes, and all eight legs of a spider connect to this front part. The back part, as I said, is the abdomen. I did a report in seventh grade about spiders, I know stuff.

Sweetie blasts until she unloads her weapon, so much for short controlled bursts. She's out of ammo. The Space Spider looks at her. Sweetie ejects the magazine and slams in another one. She blasts again. The cephalothorax separates from the abdomen. The abdomen (or butt) falls with a thud. Again, gross. The front part with the legs wobbles and falls over. The fangs twitch, and then they don't.

SNAFU and I push. Without the Space Spiders pulling on the web lines, Roy's car moves a fraction of an inch, which is just enough for us to inhale and climb out. Air is good. We cough. I'm concerned I might hack up a piece of lung.

A tank shoots at our school.

Sweetie yells, "Hey, that's our school!" *Is she still holding onto the dream of Prom?*

But the blast doesn't hit our school. It curves down and blows up the trampo-web. *How is that possible?* One of the Black Hawks has a laser sight on the trampo-web. A tank fires a missile over the Wall of Web and then the missile "zeroes in" on the laser and comes down fast. BAM. It blows a hole in the ground and busts up all four trampo-web supports. Cheers. But two Space Spiders jump up, spin a web and attach it over the hole. They move fast. They get out of the way before the next two fall and bounce to safety.

I stop coughing. I look at Roy's dangling side view mirror. "Stupid car." Then, in the mirror, I see something horrifying. Something hits a jet and the jet explodes. *What is that?* I turn. Everyone looks at the explosion in the sky.

Then we see a jet break out of formation. It flies all Willy Wonka. A Space Spider stands ON TOP OF the jet. The jet rolls, but the Space Spider holds on. The Space Spider bites down into the cockpit. Fangs bust right through the glass and into the pilot's chest. Blood sprays up and covers the inside of the fighter's cockpit. The jet nosedives. The Space Spider jumps off before it crashes. It scurries away as the jet explodes.

Sweetie says, "What the ... ?" *How are the Spacers getting airborne?*

A fighter zooms toward the next group of Spacers coming down the Cord. Another Space Spider shoots up into the air. It's beautiful in a Cirque du Soleil kind of way. The Space Spider is balled up with fangs leading the way. The fighter rolls to miss the flying Space Spider. The Space Spider misses, but the jet never gets off a shot off at the other Spacers coming down. A land missile zooms up at the flying Space Spider cannonball, but just misses it. The Space Spider lands on the ground.

Sweetie says, "It missed." But the land missile wasn't aimed at the circus Space Spider. The missile continues upward and hits one of the four coming down the Cord.

SNAFU says, "It hit!"

As usual, the other three pick up speed, disappear behind the Wall of Web and bounce to safety. *How are they getting such height and accuracy? How are they attacking jets?*

There it is. *Damn, they're smart.* The Spacers have turned one of the football goal posts it into a giant slingshot. A Space Spider climbs up the goal post and onto the web between the two posts. The Space Spider shoots a web line down to three Spacers that are on the ground behind the goal post. The three on the ground, grab the web line and pull the shooter back so hard that the goal posts bend backwards. Then they wait. The Space Spider in the slingshot-goal post searches the sky with all eight eyes. A jet approaches. It shifts its weight and cuts the web line with some unknown alien-butt-muscle.

ZOOM!

The furry cannibal shoots into the air. It pulls its legs in and rockets toward the jet. This one hits the jet wing and takes it off. The jet explodes. Well, at least it's a one for one trade. But no, the Space Spider flies out of the fiery ball of death. It's on fire when it lands, but it drops and rolls and extinguishes the fire. The Space Spider is blackened and its fur smolders, but it's OK. However, it has landed in the middle of the battlefield. Fifteen Marines open up with machine guns. The smoky Space Spider screeches and dies.

I take a moment to steal a glance at the Latch Site, you know, our high school where the G-Cord is attached. I to try and calculate some rough numbers. It isn't looking so good for the humans anymore. More keep coming down and the Wall of Web gets bigger and bigger.

Sweetie says, "What are they doing back there?"

I say, "I think they're waiting. I think it's a numbers game. They need to have more before they come out. Otherwise, they'll lose." I think about how quickly the fifteen Marines took out one Space Spider.

SNAFU says, "That gives us time."

Darcy says, "Time for what?"

"Whatever Chevy comes up with."

They turn to me.

I say, "I see three objectives. Take out the goal post … "

Just then two jets zoom overhead. A Space Spider flies out of the goalpost at them. The first jet opens up with its guns and rips the flying Space Spider in half. Tough and sweet. The second jet fires two missiles at the goalpost as another Spacer climbs up it. The ground crew pulls it back. The Spacer zooms right into one of the incoming missiles. BOOM! The Space Spider blows up. The second missile hits the goal post. BOOM. The goal post explodes and the ground crew scatters.

A Black Hawk copter blasts the other goalpost and end zone as a preventive measure. Another copter joins the first one and they whoop-whoop-whoop overhead as they fly to the Web Wall.

I say, "The second objective is to take out the trampo-web."

The helicopters open up with all kinds of craziness. The Black Hawks rain down madness onto the other side of the Wall. The trampo-web blows up. It's replaced with a lot of negative space. In other words, a really BIG hole. The copters blast any Spacers that come near it.

SNAFU says, "The third objective is for the four of us to be picked up by a fully loaded and manned copter and taken to safety." We wait. Nothing happens.

Sweetie says, "Chevy, you say it. Go ahead and say it, and we'll see if it happens." I look at her, *really?* I'm about to continue, but Darcy and SNAFU nod their heads in agreement. *Well the first two objectives occurred right after I said them.*

"The third objective is that a fully loaded and manned Black Hawk copter lands and picks us up and flies us out of here." Everyone looks around. We see copters, but they don't fly toward us.

SNAFU punches and dents Roy's convertible. "It was worth a shot.

What were you going to say?"

"OK, the third objective may seem a little more challenging than the first two."

Sweetie scrunches her eyebrows. "Just say it."

"We need to disconnect the Cord from Earth and get it out of here."

They all look at me. SNAFU says, "When you say WE need to do this, are you talking about the human race or do you mean WE, as in the four of us?"

"I mean we, the four of us." I'm surprised at the conviction in my voice, but I'm a on a roll so I follow it up with, "We need to disconnect the Cord from Earth and get the Earth end out of here."

All three laugh. *See, that's why I'm so secretive about my plans. You share what's important to you and people will mock you.*

They notice I'm upset. They stop laughing. I flash back to my Dad handing me a gasket. We are in the barn. He's helping me put in the new four-barrel carburetor. He says, "When people react to you it has very little to do with *you*. The key is to NOT take it personally. If you can do that, then you can understand that their reaction actually means something about *them*."

I remember standing in the barn thinking, *what?* I ask, "Why did you just say that?

"Just planting a seed. You'll get it one day." Then he gets back to the conversation we were having. "You're right. This thing will be fast."

For some reason, on the battlefield that day, I get what he meant. *I decide* if their laughter means anything about my me or my idea. I decide not to take their laughter personally. As soon as I do this, I realize their laughter just shows me that they haven't caught the vision yet of what I know is possible.

Sweetie says, "You're serious?"

"I try not to be, but right now, I am."

I'm not angry any more. I wish they could see the possibility I'm creating, but I'm not angry they don't. They see my calm. I realize I can love them now because I'm not feeling hurt. They feel my unconditional positive regard and they relax—that is, as much as they can in the middle of a battlefield. Note: It's very quiet except for the war raging around us.

"The Universe never gives us an idea without providing us with the means to achieve it."

SNAFU can see the seriousness in my eyes. He says, "OK. It's a crazy enough day. How are we going to do it?"

"I don't know."

"But you just said the Universe won't leave us hanging."

"It won't. I just don't know how to do it *yet*."

That's all I have. I mean, I know we *can* do it, I just don't know *how* yet. They want to know what they should do. They want to know what the next action step is, but I'm not aware of that yet. Everyone waits for me to say more, myself included. Darcy takes SNAFU's hand. I realize I have to start talking.

"Listen," I say, "This could go on for a long time. We don't know how many ... " I pause. *What is a group of spiders called? A herd? A pod? A gaggle?* I continue, "We don't know how many Space Spiders there are over there." I point to the Wall. "Right now, we might not be losing, but we sure aren't winning. I mean we have plenty of troops and ammo. I don't know what the latest numbers are but between 2001 and 2011, our base defense budget soared from $200 billion to over $500 billion. A lack of weapons is not the problem." *See, learning facts can make your arguments stronger.* "And I'm sure the Untied Nations is already talking about offering troops." *Which is true.* "But the question is how fast can more troops and ammo get here? The other concern is, when are the Spacers going to make their move? Right now they are kinda contained behind the Wall. We need to cut off their supply before they scurry and spread out across North America."

We wait for more, but that's it. Sweetie says, "We're with you, but what are we going to DO?"

Darcy says, "What's the next step? Even something small?" It seems Darcy and Sweetie think alike. They will be good friends, if everybody lives.

SNAFU says, "Give him some space to think." He turns to me. "Think faster."

I say, "Let's imagine us celebrating."

All three say, "What?!"

SNAFU turns to Sweetie and Darcy. "Jinx, you owe me a beer."

Darcy lets go of SNAFU's hand, "Really? Right now?"

Sweetie pats Darcy on the back. "Get used to it, sister."

A jet blasts another falling Space Spider. The "One is Four" campaign is back, now that the trampo-web is gone. But the Space Spiders don't fall the same way. They try something different. This time, the three falling Space Spiders PUSH OFF of the Galactic Cord. They fall to Earth in front of the Wall of Web.

Four ground Space Spiders scurry over the Wall. They climb on top of each other. Now there are two stacks of two. The bottom two Spacers face each other. Fangs move as if to communicate via some sort of fang sign language. The top two face the other way—butts over the heads of the Spacers on the bottom.

Because the next set of Space Spiders push off of the Galactic Cord they're going to drop and smush IN FRONT OF the Web Wall. This is where the two double-stacks of Space Spiders prepare themselves.

The top Space Spiders shoot webbing at each other. The webbing forms a stretcher. The bottom Space Spiders walk backwards, away from each other. The web lines get taut. The three falling Space Spiders do different things. One tucks in its legs and falls fast; the other two throw out their arms and slow their descent. At the last second, the cannon ball Space Spider opens its legs and hits the stretcher. The webbing bends down and HITS the Earth. They catch the falling Spacer, but it isn't enough. The Space Spider doesn't splatter, but by the time the webbing springs up, the Space Spider is dead. It flops to the ground with a thud.

A sigh of relief passes through the military community.

But two more Space Spiders scurry over the wall and crawl under the bottom two Space Spiders. There are now two stacks of THREE Space Spiders. The next Space Spider falls into the web hammock. This time it stretches down and doesn't hit the ground. This 16-foot Space Spider springs up and lands gracefully. The stacks of Space Spiders move and catch the next one too. Good for them, not for us.

They don't rebuild the trampo-web, but they don't need to. They create a bunch of web hammocks and then scurry about catching their falling friends. Sure jets, helicopters, and tanks blast some of these circus freaks, but they move fast and aren't easy to hit. A lot more get to Earth. Some run back behind the Wall--they must be planning something. Others join the fight.

Then they turn the tables on us humans. The goal posts may be down, but the idea is still alive. Instead of bouncing out of the hammock after being caught, some Space Spiders stay in them as two hairy friends pull the hammock back and let it go. Yup, they create portable slingshots. Space Spiders catch their falling comrades and then shoot them up into the air.

Helicopters fly low and take out hammock towers (that's what the military called them). But the Space Spiders return fire and by sending their friends into the low-flying choppers. It becomes more and more of a ground war with groups of five or ten Space Spiders leaving the Wall and attacking the ground troops. One tank or one helicopter provides cover for each unit of Marines and Army soldiers with missile launchers. Space Spiders attack. Sometimes a tank blasts them or a helicopter shoots them. The U.S. Armed Forces are doing a great job, but we can't keep doing this forever. More Space Pebbles kept coming. Space Pebbles. *Somebody should kick the experts in their space pebbles.*

Five Spacers attack a "missile launch site." They move like white, fury ninjas. A tank takes out one beast. A helicopter takes out two more. The Marines on the ground take out a Creepy Crawler with a missile that screams maybe only eight feet off the ground till it explodes goo all over the place. But the fifth Spacer engages the three Marines. One soldier gets a hairy foot through his chest. Another gets fanged in the back and goes stiff like a board, the venom paralyzing him. The last solider gets hit so hard by the Space Spider's abdomen that the soldier's skeleton flies out of the solider's skin. The soldier's body stands there for a moment and then, because it has no support, just crumples into a bag of flesh.

Sweetie says it first, "You want us to celebrate? Now?"

"Yes," I say. "Let's celebrate."

It takes everyone a moment to come back to what we are talking about. We got lost in the horror. I say, "Whenever you're starting a project, it's always good to start with the end in mind."

Darcy says, "*They* can't even break the Cord, and you want *us* to remove it from Earth?"

SNAFU says, "Now you get to meet the real Chevy."

Darcy shakes her head. "Is he crazy?"

"No, just optimistic. Right now, he probably sees the planet as half-saved."

CHAPTER 18

START WITH THE END

SWEETIE COMES TO MY defense, "He does have the uncanny ability to create what he would like to create." She hesitates, "It would have been nice if he would have realized how important Prom is to me."

I step toward her, "Sweetie … "

SNAFU gets between us and says, "Don't. We need both of you. The planet needs both of you. I love you, but this is bigger than the two of you."

He's right. I can try to fix our relationship when this is over, if it's ever over.

I say, "This is going to sound simple but we don't have time for complex. We need to see the end result we'd like to create and believe it's possible and ideally that it has *already* been accomplished." Sweetie played this game with me when she wanted to be the Prom Committee Chair Person. I decide not to bring up that example.

I continue, "So let's picture success."

A jet crashes near us. We duck. Metal flies over our heads. The Earth shakes and dirt rains down on us. A Space Spider screeches and two Marines fire M4 machine guns while another Marine gets ripped in half.

As we watch, Sweetie says, "That doesn't help."

She's right. No one wants to say it, but it doesn't look good for us. The battle has turned. I know it's only a matter of time before the General decides to do something that can't be undone. We are officially losing, and the U.S. military doesn't like to lose.

I say, "The key is to see the future we'd like to experience. See us living it. Feel the feelings." I realize how stupid this sounds right now but this is Creating 101, which is, start with the end in mind.

I get nothing back from them. They look tired. SNAFU says, "What do you mean ... exactly?"

I decide to go for it. I raise my hand as if to "high-five" SNAFU. He doesn't raise his arm. I pick up his arm with my other hand. I "high-five" his hand with mine, "Yeah, we did it! They're dead! They're gone!" I let his arm drop.

I go to Sweetie. I give her a big hug. I say, "We did it! We saved the planet!" She doesn't hug back, I don't let go.

Come on Sweetie, I know it's a stretch, but if ever you believed in me, do it now. Sweetie takes a deep breath and hugs me back, "Yeah." She doesn't say it with much enthusiasm, but then she looks me in the eye and kicks it up a notch. "We did it. We won!" I'm about to say I'm sorry, but Sweetie turns to Darcy and says, "You're the best girlfriend ever. Damn, you were great out there. Let's start planning your reception!"

Darcy hesitates, but *reception* gets her. When she hears reception she smiles. The smile energizes her. "Yes, that would be great. I'm glad we ... played our part. I'm honored to call you my friends. I'm thinking a big sit-down dinner with a DJ and dancing!" Darcy hugs Sweetie.

I turn to SNAFU, "Big energy, bring us home."

SNAFU yells, "Humans are awesome! We're awesome! We kicked their hairy asses!" He jumps up and down like a madman. He runs to Darcy, "Let's go honeymoon!" He kisses her big, right on the mouth. His tongue brushes her teeth.

Darcy pushes him off her, but laughs.

Suddenly something blocks the sun. It's a Space Spider, and it's going to crush me. I think it was shot hammock-slingshot-style but it doesn't really matter. Fangs come down for me. I guess I'm going to die.

BOOM.

Something really BIG behind us shoots something really BIG. The Space Spider freezes in midair, as if time stops. It takes only a second, but the tank shell reverses the momentum of the Space Spider. No, that's not correct. The Space Spider doesn't fly backwards, just the middle of the Space Spider where the tank shell hit – flies backwards. A perfectly round piece flies away from us, into the air, and into about a zillion pieces.

The shell leaves a hole in the middle of the Space Spider. I see the blue sky through the hole. I can't die. We just 'won' in our 'celebration game.' My brain does not accept dying because that will not assist us with achieving the vision we just created. I see the opportunity that's present. There's always at least one.

I drop my M16, pull in my arms and tuck my chin. I go pencil thin. The Space Spider lands on top of me. I stand in the hole with a front row, panoramic, 360-degree view of Space Spider guts. Not as glorious as the Sky-Roof view. The Spacer's heart beats right in front of me. Then it stops and the organs start to ooze toward me. I climb up and out of the Space Spider, because I don't want to swim in alien innards. It's true, *knowing what you don't want* helps you to *know what you do want*. I pull myself up on top of the Spacer.

There it is, a M1 Abrams tank. It rolls toward us. Nice shot, Tank Boy. Sweetie spits and tries to get something out of her mouth. I jump down from the Space Spider. SNAFU checks all of my limbs and says, "Beginner's luck."

I say, "We're way past the beginning." I point to Sweetie. "She alright?"

"She screamed when the Spacer was about to crush you. Goo guts got in her mouth." Gross. Disgusting. I make a mental note: keep mouth shut when in close battle with Space Spiders.

The tank is loud. It stops next to the Web Mound where Sweetie and Darcy killed the legless Space Spiders. SNAFU climbs on top of the dead Spacer and takes the lookout. "All clear."

Darcy and I walk toward the tank. As ranking officer she's going to interface with the tank commander. I, being the saved civilian, am ready to give the tank commander a big kiss. Sweetie spits out goo. She yells, "Does anyone have gum?"

Darcy tosses her a water bottle. Sweetie rinses her mouth.

On the side of the tank is the Army Reserve logo. It's a picture of a 1800's guy in a colonel hat with gold leaves. I guess the Army Reserve was started in pioneer times. I'm glad they have machine guns and tanks now instead of muskets and horses. Humans have gotten really good at killing people. I wonder how I'd look in an Army Reserve sweatshirt.

The tank latch opens and Tank Boy sticks his head out of the hatch. It's a young soldier who wears a helmet. He looks familiar. *No, is that?* It is. It's Roy with a helmet.

Roy shouts, "Hey Chevy, you got a bug problem you can't handle?" He turns to Sweetie, "Don't worry Sweetie, I'll get you to Prom on time."

What? It can't be! Roy is my hero?!

I ask, "Roy knows how to drive a tank?"

"Hey Chevy. Fix any tractors lately?"

I turn to Darcy. "What the hell is he doing in the Reserve?"

Darcy looks at Roy. It's a look that's an order. Roy obeys, "I joined the high school senior Army Reserve test program. I've been earning credits toward college all year long." *Damn, Roy plans ahead like Sweetie.* He jumps out of the tank and walks to Sweetie. She gargles with the last bit of water from the bottle and spits it out.

Roy gives Sweetie a hankie. *Who carries a handkerchief nowadays?* She wipes her tongue. Roy continues, "I didn't want anyone to know until I moved up in rank."

"Thanks," says Sweetie.

I think about punching him. It's amazing how fast I go from gratitude to smack-itude.

Roy continues, "Because we all know chicks like to give it up to officers."

Sweetie punches him in the gut. He doubles over. I sigh with relief.

I realize I don't need to keep Roy away from Sweetie. *Roy* will keep Roy away from Sweetie. Sweetie drops Roy's handkerchief. She walks away from him. Roy picks it up and licks it. Gross. I wish Sweetie had seen that.

I say, "I'm glad that whole Prom thing is over."

Sweetie looks at me, "You don't get it."

"What?" Then I quickly add, "I love you," just to be safe.

"I love you too but it's not enough."

"Love's not enough?"

"No Chevy, it's not. Not if we're going to create a life together."

"Come on, the world is blowing up and all you care about is going to Prom?"

"Wait a second," says Sweetie, "with all *this* going on, *you* think I still care about going to Prom?"

This seems like a trick question to me so I say, "A little?"

Sweetie shakes her head. She's more disappointed with me than angry. I try to defend myself. "But you just said ..."

Sweetie looks at Darcy and says, "Do you think I care about going to Prom right now?"

"No."

I am so confused. I know it's not a good affirmation to assist with gaining clarity, but I'm so confused. I plead, "Then what is it?"

"I can't tell you," says Sweetie. "You need to know otherwise what I thought we had we never did."

"Sweetie, you know that I love you."

"No Chevy, you may *think* you love me but you can't love someone you don't know and respect."

I turn to Darcy and mouth the words, 'help me,.' Darcy turns away from me and faces the battlefield. I know this is not hers to fix, but I'm desperate. I don't know ... I haven't figured it out yet.

Roy says, "Well, I know what I've got," he turns toward Sweetie, "A Prom date. Pick you up tonight after we exterminate these bastards?"

"Sure Roy, we'll go party and have some fun when all of this is over."

"Yes, that's what I'm talking about." He's such an idiot.

Darcy turns from the big, bad, *impersonal* war raging around us and faces the big, bad, *personal* war raging between Sweetie and me. Darcy asks Roy, "What happened to Sergeant Hamling, your tank master?"

"He went home."

"He went home?"

"Yeah, it turns out he's afraid of spiders."

SNAFU finds a piece of gum. He tosses it to Sweetie. "Gum."

Roy steps back, "Hey, be careful with that. I don't want a hole in my uniform."

I smile remembering what SNAFU did to Roy's shirt. My smile gets bigger. *Yes, I get it.* I get the answer I've been looking for. Not the 'What is going on with Sweetie?' answer, that one's still coming to me, but the answer to all of our problems. *Thank you, Universe.* I still want to kill the messenger, but I decide to take the road less traveled, because I hear it makes all the difference. I move toward Roy. He steps back. I extend my hand.

"You may be a total scumbag, but you're a great shot with the tank."

Roy shakes my hand. "I beg to differ on the first part but agree whole-heartedly with the second part."

I whisper to him, "You touch Sweetie and I'll kill you." I pat him on the back and say, "Everybody, come here. Roy just told us how to disconnect the Galactic Cord."

"What?"

I lead everyone to the other side of the Web Mound of cars. I walk past the Space Spider whose butt exploded. *Nice shooting, Darcy.* I think of SNAFU when he farted in the gym. I subconsciously take a deep inhale. *Why do we breath deeply when we smell other people's farts? That has always disturbed me.* But I inhale any way, because I have to know. Yup, I'm right. The Space Spider's butt doesn't smell as bad as SNAFU's.

I look at the Space Spider that Sweetie shot. *Perfect, the abdomen is still in one piece. This might work.* I climb on top of the dead Space Spider's abdomen. A jet screams overhead and I duck. I tap my foot on top of the Space Spider.

Roy says, "What are you doing?"

SNAFU shushes him.

I look at the Web Wall that shields the front of the school. It guards something. I think I know what it's guarding. The battle rages on. We are not the focus of the Spacers. *Good, that might give us the time we need to attack.*

SNAFU puts his hand on Darcy's waist and pulls her close. "Hi wife."

"Hey husband."

Darcy kisses him. SNAFU laughs. "I can't believe I'm saying this but we should pay attention to Chevy. I've seen that look in his eyes. He's thinking and … "

But Darcy kisses SNAFU again and he doesn't stop her. It's a slow passionate kiss that makes your body ache for more.

SNAFU says, "We starting the honeymoon early? I'll show you what I can do with a slipknot."

Darcy smiles, "Fifty Shades of SNAFU?"

Roy says, "Aw, come on, it's bad enough the world is ending but do we need to listen to … "

Darcy says, "At ease, Private."

Roy shuts it. I like Darcy more and more. I stomp my foot on the back of the dead Spacer's butt. It sounds like a courtroom judge slamming down her gavel. "OK, everybody, why did the Space Spiders build a thirty-foot wall around the school?"

Roy whines, "To get to the other side."

"Come on, there are no stupid answers, just stupid people."

Roy wipes Space Spider goo from his boots, old habits diehard.

I say it again. "Why does anyone build a wall?"

Sweetie blows a bubble, it pops. "The Space Spiders are protecting something?" I look at Sweetie and smile. She doesn't smile back. At least she's talking to me.

"Right," I say. "What?"

Roy wipes his boots on the dead Spacer. "The vending machines in the cafeteria."

"Close. They don't want us to get to the school, but why?"

I walk on the big bulbous back of the dead Space Spider. Every now and then I stomp. I finally hear a hollow thud.

SNAFU yells, "I can't see the school, the Wall is too high"

Sweetie watches more Space Spiders travel down the Cord. She steps to her left and the next breeze brings her to me. Instead of the smell of death, alien guts, and gunpowder, the breeze graces me with the smell of Sweetie. It's beautiful, empowered, and sensuous. I now call the fragrance Dangerous Princess. *My Dangerous Princess.* I inhale. What a great break from the war.

She points at the next four Spacers coming down the Cord. A jet blasts one. The other three push off and fall fast. Hammock towers catch them and two Spacers bounce to safety and run away. A Black Hawk copter comes in low. One Space Spider doesn't pop out of its hammock. Two Spacers pull the hammock backwards as the Black Hawk gets closer. *Oh, no.* The two Space Spiders let go of the hammock-slingshot. The Spacer shoots out toward the Black Hawk. The helicopter pulls up. The Space Spider gnashes its fangs but misses the copter and starts to fall. The pilot gives the Spacer a hand gesture. The Spacer drops headfirst. Sucker! A web line shoots up out of the falling Spacer and hits the underside of the Black Hawk copter. The pilot struggles but keeps the bird in the air. The Space Spider crawls backwards up the web line. Inside my head, I yell to the Black Hawk pilot, *get out of there!* The other Marines inside the copter lean out and shoot the Spacer climbing up the waterspout. The jarheads blast the piñata to see if they can break it open.

The copter rises. Another Space Spider jumps and grabs onto the Spacer climbing up the web line. The weight is too much for the copter. The Marines continue to hang over the side and shoot. The second Space Spider climbs over its buddy. Bullets don't stop it. The Space Spider pulls itself into the copter, it crawls over the soldiers and knocks one out. The Black Hawk starts to spin. The hanging Space Spider detaches and scurries away.

The Spacer inside the helicopter attacks everything and destroys the copter from the inside out. Missiles and rounds shoot in every direction. A jeep full of soldiers explode. Marines on the ground are shot up. Holes are made in the practice field and dirt rains down on us. The Space Spider rips out the pilot's seat with the pilot still in it. The copter falls out of the sky. It crashes. BOOM. Black Hawk down.

I shudder. And, to make things worse, Sweetie steps out of the gentle breeze. I get a nose full of horror again.

"The Cord comes down," says Sweetie, bringing us back to the Roy-inspired plan to disconnect the Cord from the Earth. She adds, "and the Cord disappears behind the Wall."

Darcy says, "We can't SEE where the Cord attaches to the school."

They're getting it. Sweetie brings it home, "The Galactic Cord is too strong to break or blow up. The Space Spiders don't need to protect the Cord. But they do need to protect the Main School building. They're protecting the Latch Site."

Darcy says, "That's the weak point and they know it."

"Yes," I say. "If we blow up the school, then the Cord is no longer attached to the Earth."

They look at me. *Blow up the school?* Sweetie turns away. She may not care about going to Prom right now, but if we blow up the school, all of their hard work goes up in smoke. Darcy thinks it's a good idea. She picks up her walkie-talkie. "Get me the General. We have an idea." She walks away from us while she waits for the General. SNAFU watches over her.

I jump up and down on the butt of the dead Space Spider. They think I'm excited, but I have another idea. I keep jumping. Roy steps closer, "OK, Chevy, we get it. It's a good idea. A little extreme, but it makes sense. You can settle down now."

Finally, I hit the spot I'm looking for and webbing shoots out of its butt at Roy's face. He screams, "Aaaaaaa." He ducks but he isn't fast enough. The webbing hits his helmet and sticks to it. "Aaaaaaa, it's still alive." Roy throws off his helmet. The helmet doesn't go far because it's stuck to the web line. More webbing comes out and coils up on top of his helmet. Roy looks different; he has a crew cut. Goodbye collar-length hair.

Roy draws his pistol. He shoots the dead Spacer almost hitting my feet. BAM. BAM. BAM. I jump out of the way. SNAFU lands next to Roy and punches him. Roy goes down hard. SNAFU climbs back up and resumes his watch over Darcy. *For a big guy, he moves pretty fast.*

"Give me that," Sweetie picks up Roy's pistol. Roy reaches for his gun, but she doesn't give it to him.

Roy looks at me. "What are you doing?"

"Hold on. That's not it. That stuff is too sticky."

I stomp again on the Spacer butt. *This sounds like a good place.* I jump up and down. More webbing comes out of its spinneret and coils on the ground next to Roy's helmet. Roy stands clear as he rubs his jaw. *This has to be the right stuff.*

I say, "Sweetie touch that webbing with your M16. It won't be sticky."

Sweetie hesitates, but she knows this is bigger than just us. She touches her M16 to the new webbing. Her M16 sticks to it. She gives me a hostile look. She tries to shake the webbing off but no luck.

"Good idea, Chevy."

I apologize. "OK, that wasn't a good idea. My bad."

Sweetie ejects the magazine out of her M16 and lays the M16 on the ground. *She'll get another one.* There are plenty of men and women all over the place who are not using their weapons any more.

I jump off of the Space Spiders abdomen and punch its big bulbous butt. "Damn it, damn it, damn it."

Webbing comes out again. It's not as thick as the first or second thread. Sweetie reaches into a car and pulls out a baseball bat. She touches the end of the new webbing with the bat. The bat doesn't stick to it. She slides it into the pile of the webbing and moves it around. She pulls the bat out clean. No fuss. No muss.

SNAFU says, "Chevy, what the hell are you doing?"

"Third time's a charm," I say. "That's framing web. It's the strongest webbing and it's not sticky. Earth spiders can make six different ... "

"Eight," Roy interrupts. "Earth spiders can make eight different types of webbing."

"Whatever. Six, eight, does it really matter?" *Seventh grade was a while ago.* I look at Darcy. She's still on her walkie.

"I'll tell you what I'm thinking as soon as your wife returns. It's important she's on board." I grab the webbing now that I know it isn't sticky. I hold it, it's pretty light. "We're going need more of this. Would you help?"

SNAFU punches the abdomen. Webbing shoots out of the spinneret. I punch. You punch. He, she, it punches. We punch. Sweetie and Roy – they punch. Conjugating verbs is fun.

I throw one end of the webbing to SNAFU and he pulls on it. It stretches and it's strong. We get into a tug-of-war. Darcy returns and we settle down. I start the biggest sell job of my life. "OK, here's the plan. Tank Boy and I go to the school. We're going to the basement with as much explosives as we can carry, open up all the gas lines, and blow the school."

Sweetie bites her lip and smooths out her Prom dress.

Darcy says, "You can't do that. The General said your idea was a good idea BEFORE they started coming down, but now it sucks."

We look at her.

"OK, he didn't say suck, but you know what I mean. If the Cord gets disconnected the Earth will turn. That's good for the plants and animals. However, the Galactic Cord will be dragged across the Earth as it rotates. The Space Spiders will be dropped across the United States and then the ocean, which might be good if the freaks can't swim. But, if they keep coming down the Cord will be dragged across Europe and the Spacers will cover the Earth. The U.S. Generals and the Untied Nations want to keep them in one place. He said to hold tight, it will all be over soon."

That's not comforting. We know what that means. A real nuke.

Darcy puts her hand on Sweetie's shoulder.

Sweetie says, "That's OK. Chevy's plan was going to do the same thing as the General's but on a smaller scale."

I say, "Darcy, I hear you, and I hear what you're saying, but this," I hold up the coil of webbing, "changes everything."

"What changes everything?"

I wave the coil of webbing around, "This."

"I see the webbing you're waving around. I don't know what it means."

"This can let us blow up the school and get rid of them," I say. I hand the webbing to SNAFU. He takes it but looks at Darcy. He says, "Buddy, don't make me pick sides."

"There are only two sides here," I say, "Space Spiders and humans. Hear me out and then everyone can decide what we do." I smile at SNAFU, "Trust me, I don't want to cross the Mrs. either."

Darcy doesn't smile.

I continue, "Blowing up the school and detaching the Cord is just part one." *When forming an argument always agree with the opposition. This will let the people you're arguing with know that you've heard them.* "The General is right, part one without part two would be a disaster. Space Spiders dropping all across the United States and then the entire planet is a terrible idea."

Sweetie says, "So what's part two?"

"You're part two. All three of you, if everyone agrees." *When attempting to change people's minds remember to ask for their agreement rather than telling them what to do.* "You, Darcy, and SNAFU will make your way to the hot air balloon."

"The hot air balloon?"

I look at SNAFU. "You're going to fill that thing up and get it in the air." I don't look at Sweetie when I say we need to separate. This is a shitty boyfriend *or ex-boyfriend* thing to do on the day of Armageddon.

I continue, "You then attach one end of this framing web to the Galactic Cord. Don't be a hero and mess around with the incoming Space Spiders coming down the Cord. Let the military handle them. Your mission is the Cord only. After you attach one end to the Cord, attach the OTHER end of this thin webbing to the basket of the hot air balloon. When the school blows up, you jerry rig the balloon so it goes up all by itself."

SNAFU nods. "I can't believe I'm saying this, but I get it. The school blows up and disconnects the Cord from Earth. The basket then goes up, pulling the Earth-end of the Cord up and away."

"Right. Once the basket lifts this end of the Galactic Cord up, the Space Eggs won't hit the atmosphere and they won't burn off. Instead the eggs will just shoot out into space."

Sweetie says, "And float forever more." She looks up at the Sun. "Or maybe into a fiery death."

Great, Sweetie's on board. But in this case 25% is not 100%.

Roy says, "Wait, is that even possible?"

SNAFU says, "Chevy doesn't deal with what's *possible*. He doesn't even embrace what's *probable*."

I say, "Hot air balloons can go as high as 65,000 feet."

Roy says, "Is that outer space? Does anybody know?" No one

answers him. Roy looks at me, "Chevy, you're out of your mind."

"Yes, I am. I am *out of my mind*. Do you know *where* I'm at?"

Roy says, "You're right here. Is that a trick question?"

Sweetie interrupts, "That was a rhetorical question."

I repeat, "I am *out of my mind*. I'm not listening to my limited thinking. I've tuned to my gut. I'm connected to my intuition. I'm listening to my heart. The mind is useful but it's limited to only what it knows."

Darcy remains silent. It's not a "yes," but it's also not a "no." *That's something.*

SNAFU says, "Yeah, sure. And maybe I could also make everyone a pizza and we could have a picnic? Are you crazy?"

"Wait a second," I say. "You just sounded like you were on board with the plan."

SNAFU hesitates and then says, "The farmer guy is the only one who knows how to fill the balloon."

"Chevy and I watched a bunch of YouTube videos with hot air balloons," says Sweetie. "I think we can fill it."

"You think?"

Darcy says, "It's a balloon and there's hot air. We'll figure it out."

SNAFU raises his hands, he surrenders. "Great, got that handled. How do I attach the webbing to the Cord?"

"I don't know," I say. "I trust you'll figure it out."

"I'm not good at thinking of things and creating what I want."

"That's the old SNAFU. The one that wasn't married to one of the most amazing women around."

SNAFU thinks. Maybe his life is changing. He says, "I need some sort of plan. Can't you come up with something? You're the one that belongs to the Optimist Club."

"I don't have anything for you right now. But I'm focusing on the fact that you're a smart and creative guy."

"What?!"

"You got me through the Biology Final."

SNAFU shakes his head, "No, no this is not the same thing. I don't agree to this. This is a stupid plan."

Remember this. This is important. When someone says, "no" to what you propose, always ask WHY before you argue. Sometimes their objections are something you haven't thought of.

"Tell me, what's the problem with my plan?"

"Only about 100 things. But if we fail, my wife ends up in the brig for 30 years for disobeying a direct order."

See, I would have never seen that objection, but now that I'm aware of it, I can address it. If I hadn't asked that question I would have been arguing stuff that didn't mater to SNAFU, and I would have lost his support.

I say, "If the Spacers keep coming down, nukes will be used. You know that's what the General is talking about. If that happens we'll be in a big pile of ash and radiation. You won't be spending the next day with Darcy let alone the next 30 years with her. But let's not think about us. Where is that cloud of fallout going to go? It's going to cross the United States. When Japan had that nuclear power plant meltdown after that tsunami in 2013, radiation floated across the ocean and was picked up in California and Washington. Radiation knows no boundaries."

"But let's talk best-case scenario. They drop one bomb and kill all of the ones on the ground. Fantastic. Sometimes there are sacrifices in war. If that's the end of it, I'd be OK with going out that way. But what about the ones that keep coming down? Do they drop another nuke? How many? And maybe the Space Spiders land in the radiation and die. Maybe they mutate. Maybe they don't mind radiation. Maybe they *like* radiation. Do you know how much radiation there is in space?"

"And here's another thing," I pause for dramatic effect.

"Do you really think the school is going to remain attached to the Earth if they drop a nuke? The Cord is going to be ripped up. Sure, maybe half the Cord is destroyed IF a nuclear bomb is stronger than the Cord. MAYBE. But let's go best-case scenario again. Let's say the lower part of the Cord is destroyed. Now the Spacers have to drop to Earth without a Cord. Maybe they will all smush and die. We've seen that happen. But we've also seen their persistence. We've seen how they adapt. If they keep coming maybe they'll learn how to create web parachutes or gliders or something."

I pause because this is the first time I think of web parachutes and gliders. I wonder if they can do that. But the time for thinking is over. It's time to convince everyone that it's time for action.

"We've got to detach the Cord and we need to get the Earth end of the Cord out of here. If we don't, we not only lose Prom but we will also lose the planet."

CHAPTER 19

TAKING ACTION

"WE DON'T KNOW HOW to do this," says SNAFU. "We're not ready." I smack him on the back. "That's OK, buddy. Sometimes you've got to take action before you're ready."

"That's stupid."

"No it's not," I say. "If people wait until they're 100 percent ready, they'd never do anything. All you need to be is about 70 or 80 percent ready before you start something. The rest you figure out as you go."

"You're just making that up."

"No, Chevy's right," agrees Darcy. "If people wait until they're ready they would never get anything done, because they'd never start anything. I wasn't 100% ready for true love."

SNAFU blushes. Roy gags. *Good, Darcy's in.*

SNAFU looks at me. "I hate talking with you. You always win."

Great, that's Sweetie, Darcy, and SNAFU.

I turn to Roy. He says, "What do I have to do?"

"Drive the tank, blow up the school, and stay alive."

"I was planning on doing two of those things anyway, I'm in."

Darcy says, "OK, we don't tell the General what we're doing, otherwise he'll order me to stop you. I'll let the General know what our plan is AFTER the balloon is up. I'll ask him for air support to blast off as much school as possible from the Earth-end of the Cord after we disconnect it."

Roy rubs the peach fuzz on the top of his head. "Wait a second. You're serious? We're going to blow up the school?"

Everyone ignores him.

Sweetie says, "Why? Why do the jets need to blast off the school parts stuck to the Cord?"

I could see her imagining the gym with all those little lights attached to the end of the Cord. And then jets and tanks blast those lights into tiny pieces. I walk to Sweetie and she lets me take her hand. "We've got to get the Cord as light as possible if the hot air balloon is going to lift it up and out of here." I don't say it, but I think it. *We're gonna have to blow up Prom.*

Sweetie releases my hand and takes the mag out of her machine gun, inspects it, blows on it like you do with an old Atari cartridge and slams it back in. A strand of hair blows gently across her forehead. The light shimmers off her Prom dress. She's *not* going to Prom.

"Whatever."

Darcy puts a hand on her shoulder. "Hey, I never attended my Prom. I turned out all right."

"You just married SNAFU, a high school senior with no plans for the future, your marriage is questionable at best." Sweetie turns to SNAFU, "No offense SNAFU. I love you, but you're not the easiest guy to be in relationship with."

SNAFU nods, "I'd be the first to agree with you about that." But he looks hurt. Sweetie lets out a sigh. "I'm sorry. You're a good guy and *nobody* knows anything about the future." She turns to me, "I certainly don't. You know what the worse part is?"

I'm thinking the worse part is four more Hairy Friends coming to Earth every twenty seconds. I also think the worse part is somewhere they're loading a nuke onto a bomber, and I'm wasting time being touchy-feely. *Chicks and their emotions. We've got to get this space show on the road.* But I don't say any of that. Instead I hold both of her hands and say, "What? What's the worse part, honey?"

"Now, I'm overdressed."

I kiss her gently, "You look great."

"No I don't. I look foolish."

"I'll take you out dancing later."

"It won't be the same."

"You're right, it won't be the same. It will be better. I promise."

I smile inside. It's a done deal. Sweetie is *not* going to Prom with Roy and he's *not* going to be slow dancing and climbing all over her. I win. Then I see Sweetie's face and I see her disappointment. She *really* wanted to go. A pain shoots through me, it isn't physical, it's in my heart. This was really important to her and I'm happy she can't do something that is really important to her? *What does that say about me?*

Sweetie pats me on the back, "Have fun with my date." She runs her fingers through Roy's short black hair, "See you later, fuzzy."

What? Really? She's still not letting me off the hook? It's not even *possible* for me to take her to Prom when the school blows. I should tell her that I've changed. I should yell it out loud to her, I WANT TO TAKE YOU TO PROM NOW!. But I don't. The compassion I was feeling is replaced with anger. I'm pissed she's still talking about Roy. Sweetie turns away from me. *Nobody turns away from me.* I turn away from her and climb on top of Roy's M1 Abrams tank.

Roy says, "Careful with the hardware."

"It's a tank," I say. "I'm not going to break it."

A Humvee pulls up about twenty feet behind us. We watch six Marines pile out of it and set up a mobile missile base. I don't think much of it, but it's problematic. *Why?* Because once they start blasting Space Spiders the Spacers will get angry and they'll need to go *through us* to get to the Marines.

Enough talk, we need to get out of here. *I need to get out of here.* I yell to SNAFU, "The hot air balloon is on the side of the school and is not in the main path of war! I don't think there will be a lot of Space Spiders around it!"

"You don't *think*?!"

"One more thing, I believe they're telepathic. They can sense when someone is planning to do them harm. So when you're climbing into the hot air balloon make a clear mental thought that you are NOT planning on hurting them, you're just using the balloon to escape. Perhaps you could even send them positive thoughts. I think that will buy you the time you need to get it up and away."

"Can you give me anything more concrete to use then nice thoughts?"

I point to the coil of webbing he holds, "You got that."

"I get this," he holds up the webbing, "And you get a tank."

I yell, "Love and appreciation. If you can radiate that, I'm pretty sure you'll be safe."

"I'm not even going to respond to that." He kicks some rocks. "Any idea on how I'm going to attach the balloon basket to the Cord?"

"You're good with knots," I say. "You'll figure it out. You're a smart guy."

"You know, just because you keep saying something doesn't make it so."

"Some people would argue that."

I realize I'd like to hug SNAFU, but I'm already on the tank. I should want to hug Sweetie, but I don't. SNAFU says, "Hug me later, after we kill all the mother ... " BOOM. A jet explodes over our heads. We duck.

I turn to Darcy, "You fill the balloon, attach the webbing, and get the balloon about six feet in the air. When I see the balloon up and ready, we'll blow the school. I figure we can both be ready in about an hour."

I think someone is going to question that time frame. We are planning to do insane things in the middle of a hostile alien invasion. How the hell do I know if it'll take an hour for us to do what we're going to do?

But nobody says nothing.

SNAFU and Darcy look across the battlefield in the direction of the balloon. It's a lot of rough terrain to cover. They hold hands. She says, "Piece of cake." He says, "Well, if I'm suppose to focus on love and appreciation, I can keep looking at you." Darcy kisses him.

Not the SNAFU I know, but great, SNAFU's in.

I say, "It's simple really. The school goes up. The balloon goes up. The Cord goes up. And then the Space Spiders go up, up, and away."

Sweetie looks at me. "Reaching new heights." For a moment I almost feel compassion toward her, but I hold onto my anger.

Roy walks to Sweetie. She holds her machine gun in front of her preventing him from hugging or kissing her. Is she still rooting for us? But why does she say she'll go to Prom with Roy even though that's impossible? I just want to blow something up. I yell, "Roy, get in the tank!"

Roy shakes his head at Sweetie, "Battle is messing you up. You must have STDs."

Sweetie laughs. "Roy, that would be PTSD. Post Traumatic Stress Disorder."

Roy climbs onto the tank. "No, I mean STDs." *See I'm right. Let Roy talk, his mouth is a Sweetie repellent.* I should say something to her. But the war interrupts me. Three missiles blast over our heads toward the Space Spiders. The Marines get ready to shoot more.

Sweetie yells, "I'll see you later!" I look at her, but she's looking at Roy. Sweetie blows Roy a kiss, *right in front of me.* "Be safe." He catches the kiss and rubs it all over his body. He slips into the tank smiling at me.

I can't believe I wanted to take her to Prom. I climb into the tank. I try to stay angry, but I can't. I'm in a TANK. I am living every guy's "other" fantasy. I'm in a real TANK with real ammo. *I hope we get to blast something.* The tank is bigger than I thought. *What's that smell? Locker room?* Yes, I smell body odor. I try not to think that I am breathing Roy's sweat. Roy pushes and flips a lot of cool buttons and switches. He says, "Keep your hands to yourself."

Well, I guess that's fair. I don't want him touching my girlfriend, and he doesn't want me touching his tank. I look out the little window. Roy jolts the tank forward. WACK. My body smacks into a wall of instruments.

Roy says, "Don't touch the controls."

I rub my arm and shoulder. "Don't drive like an idiot."

"Get use to it."

It's a bumpy ride. Roy is a terrible driver. I watch SNAFU, Darcy, and Sweetie as we roll away. *Come on, Sweetie. Turn around and look. Fight for our relationship.* She doesn't turn. The tank bumps. I bang my head. Ow. I look back at her. She turns and looks at the tank. She looks at me. Yes, she's still fighting for us! Then I get it. *I'm the problem.* I'm not fighting for us. I mean, I am, but not the way that *she* wants me to. I never apologized to her. She doesn't want me to take her to Prom, it's not possible now. And she doesn't want me to save the world, OK, she wouldn't mind that. But what she wants me to save is *our world, our relationship.*

She wants me to say I'm sorry. Not for the Space Spiders or for blowing up Prom but for not realizing what's really important to her. She wants me to apologize for not treating what matters to her as important. That's what she's projecting into the future. She can't be with a guy that doesn't realize what's important to her. And I saw it on her face, I felt it in my heart, *and I didn't say anything.* She's afraid I am going to be like her father. No, she's not afraid I'll be like him, I'm *already* acting like her father! I'm telling her what should be important to her. I'm telling her what should not be important to her. She had to live with that growing up. She isn't going to choose to live with that for the rest of her life.

"Roy, stop. Turn this thing around."

"There is no going back, solider."

"Roy, shut up. I've got to talk to Sweetie."

"We've got a mission, son. You got to know when to hold them and know when to fold them. There will be time enough for dames when the dealing's done."

What?! He's morphed into a strange combination of General Patton and the Gambler. I try to grab the controls from him. He touches his sidearm, "Do you know what happens if a gun is shot inside a tank? The bullet just ricochets around until it pierces everything inside."

I settle down. He keeps driving. Idiot.

I beat myself up. Sweetie needs me to apologize for not honoring what is important to her. She was the Prom Chair Person for goodness sake and was nominated for Prom Queen. She lived in that gym getting it ready. She wants me to say, "I'm sorry for not knowing how important Prom is to you." And she wants me to mean it.

This is going to be a long and terrible ride.

As the tank pulls away, SNAFU says to Darcy and Sweetie, "Well, at least Chevy can't come up with any more brilliant ideas for us to do."

Darcy looks at the Marines and their Humvee. "Let's see if we can get some more ammo."

The Marine Unit fires more missiles and knocks down Space Spiders as they zip-line to Earth. LEADER Marine has a chiseled jaw, piercing eyes, and a the word *Repent* tattooed on his neck written in cursive. He turns his piercing blue eyes toward Darcy, SNAFU, and Sweetie. "What are you kids doing here? Don't you know school was cancelled today?"

"Really?" says Sweetie, "Did he just say that? Does that qualify as battlefield wit?"

"I'm right here," says Leader. "I heard you."

Darcy says, "We're on a special mission. We'd like to borrow a few mags of ammo and whatever grenades you can spare."

BIG Marine comes out from behind the Humvee. Big Marine is XXL and he's all muscle. He looks at Darcy and says, "Damn, she's good looking." SNAFU steps forward, ready to fight. Big Marine says, "And she's got a pet Hobbit." Compared to Big Marine, SNAFU looks small. SNAFU doesn't start a fight. *Is he growing up?* Perhaps. Strange things happen on a battlefield. He may be putting the mission ahead of his pride. And, he must know fighting a Marine isn't going to help them achieve their goal. However, he does give the Big guy a creepy smile.

STOCKY Marine runs up. He's a thick human being. He looks like a section of a Redwood tree with short legs. He taps Leader Marine on the shoulder. Stocky whispers. Leader curses, "Gosh darn it, friggin gumballs!" These aren't the real words he uses. He continues in more appropriate language, "We don't have time for this!"

Leader yells an order to the last Marine of their unit. "Calhoun, escort the purple princess back to Free Earth HQ." That's the name of the military base set up on the practice field. Leader looks at Sweetie. "You'll be safe there."

Calhoun loads another missile before she looks up and says, "Sir, with all due respect, I'm probably the least maternal here and I ranked second in the land-missile competition. I'm more valuable on the field, sir." Leader shakes his head. He knows she's right, but what is he suppose to do? Calhoun preps the rocket. She turns her body so Sweetie can see what Calhoun's doing. She calls out, "Prepping Rocket." Calhoun waves her in closer so Sweetie can see better. Calhoun whispers, "Remember slow is smooth. Smooth is fast."

Sweetie nods.

Leader knows Calhoun's right, the female Marine IS more valuable on the battlefield, but she's the newest to the unit and no Marine ever chooses to leave a fight. Leader is about to say something but Calhoun yells, "Rocket ready."

Calhoun looks behind her. She says to Sweetie. "Don't stand behind me." Sweetie moves. Calhoun shouts, "Back blast area secure." Calhoun shows Sweetie how to look through the launcher sight. She taps the trigger with her finger. Sweetie nods. Calhoun aims the launcher at the Spacers coming down the Cord and yells, "Rocket!"

Calhoun fires the missile. A huge blast shoots out of the back of the rocket. Sweetie takes another step away from launcher. Calhoun laughs. The missile winds its way up into the sky and connects with a Spacer. It explodes. Goo and a burnt leg falls.

Sweetie walks up to Leader Marine. She says, "Why do I need to go?"

"Because you're not military," says Leader as he gives Stocky a long cold stare, "and I'm reminded that we MUST escort all civilians to safety."

Sweetie points at SNAFU, "He's a civilian too." SNAFU gives her a what-the-hell-are-you-doing look.

Leader looks at SNAFU. "Hey baggy uniform, what's your story?"

"I'm not a civilian. I was sworn in today."

Leader laughs, "Like a deputy? What do you think this is, the Wild West? I know the Army Reserve is not the Marines, but you can't just be sworn in and fight."

"Why not? I know how to shoot. What am I suppose to do? Sit and do nothing?"

Leader can't argue with that. In fact, he agrees with SNAFU. Leader didn't sign up to follow stupid rules and politics. Leader signed up to kick ass. "Rocket," yells Big Marine and another missile streams skyward.

Stocky barks, "You can't just be sworn in because this is the United States military! We've got rules! I'd tell you to take off that uniform, but we don't want to see you naked!"

SNAFU nods, "You're a smart, *little* man." *So much for growing up.* "Besides, I only strip for my wife." He looks at Darcy.

Leader addresses Darcy. "You're married to him? Can this day get any weirder?" Leader addresses Stocky. "Calhoun's right, she outshoots all of us. I need you to escort these two civilians off the battlefield."

"Rocket," yells Calhoun as she blasts another rocket. She smiles. Sweetie gives her the thumbs up.

Stocky says, "Wait, I remember something." Stocky runs back to the Humvee.

Leader says, "Hey, take your time!" *What kind of freaking war is this?*

Darcy says, "I'll watch our back."

"If you think it's necessary."

"Trust me, it is." Darcy takes up position behind the unit.

Stocky returns with papers. Stocky whispers something to Leader and hands him the papers. Leader laughs, shakes his head, and hands the papers to Sweetie and SNAFU, "Sign these, and then you can get yourself killed."

A missile that Big fired misses and explodes against the Cord. The four Spacers push off the Cord, trusting someone will catch them.

Stocky explains what the papers are, "These are battle waivers. We need you to sign them. They say we offered you an escort off of the battlefield to safety but you're choosing to stay. If you're killed or maimed neither you nor your family will have the right to sue the Marines or the United States government."

Sweetie asks, "Do you have a pen?"

Stocky's face lights up. "You're Prom Queen with a Shotgun."

"What?" *This is the first time Sweetie is hearing her new nickname.*

"The whole world saw you take out that Spacer with a shotgun. You're famous."

Sweetie beams with pride.

Stocky gives Sweetie a pen. But, before they can sign, Stocky says,

"Can I get a picture with you?" Stocky doesn't wait for her reply, he stands next to her and pulls out his phone. She bends down for the selfie so Stocky won't look so short. Sweetie's like that. Considerate. I'm not. I'm a freaking idiot. Stocky puts his arm around her. *Click.* "Thanks." He returns to the Humvee with a smile.

Calhoun loads another missile into her launcher as six Space Spiders scurry over the wall. They form two stacks of three and shoot webs between them. The create another hammock tower.

Big Marine yells, "Two side orders of short stacks. Who's hungry?"

Leader says, "Calhoun, you eat breakfast this morning?"

She yells back, "Sir, I don't even know what time of the day it is." The other Marines laughs.

Leader yells, "Calhoun, that's not my question."

"Yes, sir! I'm hungry!"

She blasts the missile. It whistles away and hits the middle Space Spider of the first triple stack. The middle one BLOWS UP. The one on top is ripped into pieces. The bottom Spacer is blown into the ground, smashed to death, under the force of the explosion. The web hammock drops just in time to NOT catch a falling Space Spider. It hits the ground hard and splatters. A goo fountain shoots thirty feet into the air and rains down. BIG CHEERS. Guts cover the other Space Spider hammock tower. These three Spacers turn toward the Marines and screech.

Leader yells, "I love my Momma's pancakes in the morning."

SNAFU and Sweetie sign the forms and give them to Stocky. He checks them and says, "Come here." Stocky leads SNAFU and Sweetie to the back of the Humvee. Stocky grabs something from the Humvee. It looks like a black dumbbell. He says, "Give me your M4." Sweetie gives her machine gun to him. Stocky ejects the thirty-round box magazine and gives it to Sweetie. "That is now your backup." Stocky attaches the black dumbbell thing onto Sweetie's M4 where the magazine use to be. He says, "This is a 100-round double-drum magazine."

Sweetie says, "Thank you," and kisses him on the check.

Stocky blushes. He grabs a backpack and says, "Let me pack a gift bag for you," jokes Stocky, "everyone who attends the war today gets a little something-something." He puts grenades, water bottles, and protein bars into the backpack. He adds two more drum magazines. He looks at SNAFU, "One for you and one for the little lady. Good luck and God bless."

"Thank you," says Sweetie. " You, too." SNAFU shakes his hand.

Darcy watches a missile zoom toward the next four pack of descending Spacers. This Marine Unit is good at blasting them. That is good AND bad news. Darcy knows it's just a matter of time before a hairy arachnid unit will come over the Wall to say, "Stop that." The real bad news is they're going to say, "Stop that," with their fangs.

Darcy yells to SNAFU and Sweetie, "We've got to go."

Sweetie nods. *Yes, it's dangerous to stay here.* She says, "They've been hitting a lot of them."

A Space Spider explodes in the sky as Calhoun's rocket hits another one of them. And then IT happens, Space Spiders come over the Wall. Darcy yells, "You got incoming! On the ground!"

Leader yells, "Land troops!" He turns to Darcy, Sweetie, and SNAFU "Try to kill something before you die. That way the ammo we gave you won't be wasted."

SNAFU slaps his 100-round double drum magazine into his M4. It looks like there are two little loaves of burnt bread on either side of his gun. He's ready.

Sweetie asks Darcy, "Do we help these guys out?"

"No. They're going to provide us cover. Our mission is more important."

SNAFU yells to Big Marine, "K-MAG YO-YO."

Big Marine laughs and yells, "Get out of here, Marines don't babysit!"

Leader sees the concern on Sweetie's face. He says, "Don't you worry that pretty little head of yours. I eat spiders for lunch." He winks at her.

Darcy, SNAFU, and Sweetie run. They hear the Marines shout and blast.

"We've got a whole bunch coming in fast!"

"Good, I hate this one-at-a-time crap!"

Darcy, Sweetie, and SNAFU don't look back. They don't want to turn to salt. They run from the gunfire and grenade blasts. Finally the three drop of exhaustion. They hide behind a webbed-up tank. They sneak a peek at the Marines and the carnage. Stocky shoots the 44-caliber rifle that is mounted on top of the Humvee. Others blast and throw grenades. The Space Spiders explode. Alien flesh and limbs blow back towards the Wall.

Sweetie catches her breath. "What is K-MAG YO-YO?"

"Kiss My Ass Guys, You're On Your Own."

Sweetie almost laughs, but it isn't funny right now. SNAFU always says he never learned anything from his old man. I guess he's wrong. SNAFU attaches the big drum magazine to Darcy's M4. She nods and puts the box magazine into one of her uniforms pockets.

They watch as Leader, Calhoun, Big, and Stocky blast lots of Spacers, but there are just too many of them attacking. The Space Spiders close the gap.

Darcy says, "Thanks, guys. Let's go."

The three friends don't watch to see what happens. They jog in the direction of the hot air balloon hoping it's still in one piece.

CHAPTER 20

2,000 FEET PER SECOND

IT'S A BUMPY RIDE in the tank. I hit my head again. Roy sucks as a driver. I watch him while I think of Sweetie. I compliment him, "You really know how to cruise a tank." I almost throw up from the ride and my bullshit comment. But it works, he tells me more about the switches and buttons. I need to learn how to drive the tank just in case I've got to do it myself. Right now I need Roy and I don't like that. It feels icky. I look out the window and see a Space Spider walking next to us.

"Roy, nine o'clock, we got company."

Roy turns the tank turret but the Space Spider moves out of the way. It sidesteps just out of our range. It smiles. It's teasing the tank.

"I can't turn fast enough."

"I can."

I grab my M4 and pop the top. The Space Spider looks surprised to see me. I remember thinking, *What, were you born yesterday?* Then I realize it was actually born today.

"Happy Birthday!"

217

I shoot. Tiny metal presents travel at speeds topping 2,000 feet per second. This is the best surprise party ever. The Spacer stands its ground, perhaps out of shock or perhaps because of pride. Whatever the reason, it's a mistake. The metal slugs take their toll and the tank turret catches up to it.

Roy shoots. BOOM. The tank shudders.

The Space Spider explodes.

I go deaf.

CHAPTER 21

WORSE THAN WE THOUGHT

DARCY, SNAFU, AND SWEETIE continue across the battlefield. It isn't a pretty nature walk. They pass lifeless soldiers, exploded Space Spiders, and smoking jet parts. Sweetie stops when she sees a young, dead Marine. She removes the standard issue eyeglasses from his face. She wipes Space Spider goo off of his dark rimmed glasses.

"He's our age," she says.

"Well, at least he died trying to make a difference," says SNAFU.

Sweetie doesn't know what do with his glasses. They're clean now, but he doesn't need them. Should she put them back on his face? Should she drop them in the dirt? But if she does that, they'll get dirty and she just cleaned them.

SNAFU says, "Give me the BCDs."

"What?"

"His glasses, give them to me."

She hands them to SNAFU.

The military standard issued glasses are nicknamed BCD, which is slang for Birth Control Device. They are *not* stylish. SNAFU decides this is not the time to tell Sweetie this. It would make it look like he's trying to be funny at a time that isn't funny. *Wow, he's being appropriate.* Maybe he is growing up.

SNAFU folds the BCDs and slides them into the Marine's shirt pocket. SNAFU takes the magazines, grenades, and a knife that the Marine won't be using.

They pause for a moment of silence.

CHAPTER 22

THIS SPACE INTENTIONALLY LEFT BLANK

… FOR A MOMENT OF silence.

CHAPTER 23

AFTER THE SILENCE

THEY CONTINUE TOWARD THE other side of the school and the hot air balloon. A jet zooms overhead filling them with hope and energy.

"Yeah, go get them!"

Three web lines shoot up into the air. One web line hits the fighter and pulls the jet into a nosedive. It crashes with great violence. Metal explodes. Flames jump up. Black smoke pours out.

Sweetie can't see anything beyond the burning wreckage and dark smoke. "I think the explosion got them."

The wind blows and scatters the black smoke. They get to see the big hole in the ground that the jet made. *Yup, no more Space Spiders.* Black smoke from the wreckage fills the area again. Darcy, Sweetie, and SNAFU continue walking when a brown Space Spider wobbles out of the smoke, the three warriors hide behind wreckage, the Spacer hasn't noticed them. The Spacer shakes itself like a wet dog after a bath. Dirt flies off its body. The dirty-white Spacer picks through the wreckage.

Darcy points to a tank, not too far away. She whispers, "Let's go." They quietly walk away. SNAFU whispers, "At least the jet got two of them." Another Space Spider walks out of the smoke. This one is pristine white, as if it was just laundered. Sweetie whispers, "One is better than none."

They're almost hidden behind the busted up tank when the third Spacer walks out of the smoke. SNAFU and Sweetie shake their heads and sigh. The jet didn't get any of the Spacers. In unison the three Space Spiders turn and twitch their fangs at them. Darcy gives SNAFU and Sweetie a stern look, but says, ""Alright, if they've got a death wish, we'll grant it."

No more sneaking around. Darcy faces the Spacers. She's in the middle, SNAFU's to her right, Sweetie's to her left. They raise their M4 machine guns. Darcy says, "Wait till I give the order."

The burning jet snaps, crackles and pops. The three Space Spiders are easy targets with the black smoke behind them. "Wait." Four more clean, white Space Spiders step through the smoke.

Darcy says, "Good, a party." She taps her 100 drum magazine. Another breeze clears the black smoke. Fifteen more Space Spiders approach from behind the first group.

Sweetie says, "Maybe they have something better to do." All twenty-two Space Spiders screech at her. She says, "Chevy's an ass. Positive self-talk does not work."

SNAFU says, "It's a good thing that SAT study course you took prepared you for your future."

Darcy orders, "Grenades first." But SNAFU and Sweetie seem frozen.

"NOW!"

SNAFU and Sweetie move. They put down their M4s. They each have a few grenades. This is good.

Darcy says, "On my orders." She whispers, "Mama gonna knock you out."

More Space Spiders step through the black smoke. The gaggle of Space Spiders stop. They don't advance. Perhaps they're being cautious or perhaps they're scared. Or, perhaps they *do have* something better to do.

Darcy says, "Hold." Nobody does anything. "I'm OK with a truce. Prepare to back up, nice and slow. No running."

The black smoke from the jet gets less and less as the fuel burns out. When it clears, they see more Space Spiders. Thirty. No, more like another forty coming up behind the first group of twenty.

Sweetie says, "That's a lot."

Darcy doesn't know if they can't take sixty of them. Maybe thirty or forty, but not sixty.

Sweetie turns to SNAFU. "Thanks for making life interesting."

"No talk like that," orders Darcy. "We've got a mission." It's a nice try, but optimism is dead. Since Darcy isn't embracing reality, SNAFU hands his grenades to Sweetie. He says, "Here, cover me."

"What are you doing?"

"There's only thing we've got left to do," says SNAFU. He drops to his knees and bows his head. Sweetie gets ready to throw.

"Wait," says Darcy, "they're not close enough for your girl throws."

"Don't direct your anger at me. I'm not the bad guy." But Darcy wasn't trying to be mean, she just didn't want to waste any grenades. The Space Spiders move closer but they don't like SNAFU kneeling. They haven't seen this before and if he's doing it now, under these circumstances, it must be BIG magic.

SNAFU says, "God, I know it's been awhile; and I'm a failure. But Darcy and Sweetie are good people. So if you could ... "

Darcy yells, "Stop that!" She bumps SNAFU with her knee and almost knocks him over. She says, "You're going to live! If you die, I'll kill you! We're married now. If you're in pain, then I help you. That's our agreement. You're not a failure. All things heal with love."

Sweetie shouts, "Hey guys, I think they're in range of my *girl arm*."

SNAFU starts again, "God, an angel just spoke to me." Darcy smiles, but responds to Sweetie, "I didn't mean anything by that, I just want ..."

"Forget it," says Sweetie.

SNAFU continues, "God, I'd like to say if you help us that I'll be a better person, but there's probably not a lot of truth in that. But, maybe, just maybe, I'll be able to use Darcy's love for me to heal some of my old stuff so I won't be such a bastard."

Darcy gets a tear in her eye. The Space Spiders edge closer.

SNAFU continues, "I also know we've only been married for a day and I'm no expert about the possibilities of a long-term relationship. But I'm willing to give it a shot. But God, to do that we're going to need some time. Which means we're going to need a little help right now. Amen." SNAFU stands. "Is that better?"

Darcy wipes tears from her face. "That's perfect."

"Thank you for your love and support."

"That's what wives are for."

SNAFU smiles. "They're also for *other* things." He smacks her ass.

"Oh, yes they are!" SNAFU and Darcy kiss. The Space Spiders pause and look at each other. *What strange voodoo do you do?*

Sweetie says, "Hey, let's focus." Sweetie hands SNAFU's grenades back to him. "Thanks." Sweetie softens and says, "That's one of the nicest things I've ever heard a married couple say to each other. You sounded like Chevy's parents." She raises her grenade. "But I think we should throw these now."

Darcy says, "Pull and throw."

One, two, three grenades. Nice throws. They land right in front of the confused Space Spiders.

Darcy says, "Everything you've got."

They don't wait for the first three to explode. The fourth, fifth and sixth grenades go flying. The Space Spiders snap out of it. They've seen grenades, they know what's coming. All that kneeling, praying, and kissing must have been a trick. Just a tactic to get them bunched up. The Space Spiders charge.

They throw the rest of their grenades. The first ones explode. BAM. BAM. BAM. Parts of Space Spiders fly. Some assembly required. BAM. BAM. BAM. More go down. BAM. BAM. BAM. Space Spiders rip apart. Some blowback, some blow sideways, some blow up.

SNAFU, Darcy, and Sweetie drop to one knee, and raise their M4s with the 100 round magazines. Darcy orders, "Clean, short bursts. Save your ammo for the ones in back. They all want to die."

The last grenades go off. BAM. BAM. BAM. Burnt fur and alien flesh. Funny how a really terrible smell can put a smile on your face. Morale is high. This is possible. Optimism is resurrected.

The Space Spiders come at them fast, but they blast faster. The M4 shoots between 700 rounds per minute. They practice control so they can increase their accuracy, but they still empty their 100 round magazines in less than thirty seconds. The barrage of rounds rip into the Space Spiders heads and bodies. Brass shells fly from their guns faster then they can see them. Space Spiders pile up on the battlefield. It's awesome.

The grenades mess up a bunch of them, but they keep coming. Darcy, Sweetie, and SNAFU discard the empty drum magazines and slam in their *back-up* mags and blast some more.

Note: most GIs only load 28 rounds in their box magazines because 30 rounds puts too much pressure on the magazine spring and if its not used within a period of time dust, dirt, and moisture causes the spring to fail, jamming the machine gun. But in a firefight, ammo is freely expended, and 30 rounds is charged into the magazine because the gun is going to be emptied/fired within seconds anyway.

Darcy, SNAFU, and Sweetie don't know if their box magazines holds 28 or 30 rounds. *Who's got time to count?* They just pop out their *back-up* mags and slap in last magazines. They use ammo fast. They don't have enough.

Some lucky shots must have hit tiny Space Spider brains or ripped through their hearts because a handful of Spacers just drop. But the majority of them take the hits and keep coming. Sure, legs fly off here and there, but Space Spiders can move pretty good with only five or six legs.

Three Space Spiders break away from the pack and come rushing in. Overachievers suck. Darcy and SNAFU stand. BAM. BAM. BAM. Three legs of the front Space Spider drop. It falls and rolls. The other two climb over the first one and scurry even faster toward them.

Click. Click. Sweetie yells, "I'm out!"

The two front Space Spiders leap into the air. They're on their way to crush her. This is it. Time to die. It's amazing how quickly things can go from hopeful to hopeless. Even if these two Space Spiders don't land on them, the next thirty plus Spacers will overrun them.

And then everything happens in slow motion.

Darcy smiles at SNAFU. "I love you."

"I love you more."

"I wish we would have consummated our marriage," says Darcy.

Sweetie has a vision of SNAFU and Darcy doing it. It doesn't seem safe. He's big. He might crush her. But then Sweetie remembers it's all right because Darcy does Pilates. Sweetie flashes back to the tantric sex book she and Slippers found in her mom's nightstand. Ah, to be flexible and strong. So much life yet to explore. She thinks of Chevy. I love you. Maybe in the next lifetime we'll get to ...

Then she has a weird thought.

If Space Spiders overrun the world and they're the only thing left on the planet, will she and Chevy be reincarnated as Space Spiders? And if so, how do Space Spiders have sex? She knows black widow spiders kill the male spider after they mate. Sweetie vows not to kill Chevy if they come back as Space Spiders and they do it.

CHAPTER 24

TAKE A TANK TO SCHOOL DAY

THE TANK RIDE CONTINUES to throw me around inside. The good news is the silence has been replaced with ringing. I can't hear anything else. I feel like barfing. The only blessing is when Roy talks, I can't hear him. I watch him drive. I think I know how to do it now. I look out the little window. I see three Space Spiders in the distance.

"Roy, we've got three more! Go to your right!"

"You don't need to yell."

"What?!"

"You don't need to yell!"

I can't hear a thing he says, but I get it. "Go to your right!" I still yell, but I think it's not as loud.

"Why?"

"Just do it!"

"Everybody likes to give orders!"

Roy rolls the tank to the right. By turning he puts a downed Black Hawk copter between the Space Spider patrol and us. The Space

Spiders keep coming. I guess they aren't afraid of tanks or crashed copters anymore.

I yell, "Can you hit that?"

"The busted up Black Hawk?"

"Yes."

Roy looks at me as if I'm crazy. "Of course, I can. I'm sexy and I know it."

He stops the tank. He gets the Black Hawk copter in sight. "Chevy take a look, the targeting system is cool. It looks like a video game."

I look in the viewer. The crosshairs are right on the crashed Black Hawk. I can see unexploded missiles. I figure it also has lots of rounds just waiting to go boom. I wish he'd let me shoot the big gun. He pushes me out of the way.

"Wait till they're next to it," I say.

"I know."

Roy puts on sound-canceling earmuffs. I tap him. He hands me a pair to use. Thank goodness, the ringing is just starting to go away. They scurry next to the copter. One of them climbs over it.

"Shoot before they move."

"I know. Shut up."

Roy fires. BLAMO!

The Space Spiders jump, but it's just a little jump; they're familiar with tank blasts and don't seem concerned. What they aren't expecting is the BLAST from all the ammo still left on the Black Hawk. The impact of the giant explosion hits the closest Space Spider, and rips it apart. The second Space Spider flies twenty feet into a Ford pickup. Ram tough, not Space Spider tough. Its head is pushed into its body, fangs puncture vital organs. It drops. The third Space Spider is engulfed in a ball of flames and catches fire. It put its right foot in, it put its right foot out, it put its right foot in and shakes it all about. It does the hokey pokey and ... burns itself to the ground ... and that's what it's all about.

Wow, we made it this far, we might be able to pull this off.

Roy says, "Au revoir!"

Au revoir. That's what Sweetie said to me in the gym when she said she was going to Prom with Roy. Now that I have a few moments, I think about Frenchie.

Frenchie, was a junior foreign exchange student. Sweetie was assigned to be Frenchie's buddy. Sweetie was supposed to show her around America or at least as much as she could while living in our small town. But Sweetie was busy that semester. She was too busy for me let alone having time to babysit a foreign exchange student. Sweetie was on the volleyball team and she was also taking a SAT study course. I told her to tell Madame Smith that she needed to assign Frenchie to another student, but Sweetie wanted Foreign Exchange Escort on her resume, so she asked me to cover for her. Sweetie handed Frenchie off to me every day after school with direct orders to keep her a vegetarian. What that meant was, keep all Yankee Doodle boys away from her.

Ah, what we fear we create.

Frenchie was a normal teenage girl, with normal hormones and an abnormally high appetite for adventure. That makes sense, she was willing to go to a foreign country where she didn't know anyone and she only a teen. But let's be clear, Frenchie didn't wanted to sleep with everyone, but she was also not opposed to it, she just wanted to live life and have fun. Ah, the French zest for life.

This isn't really the time or place for any details, but Frenchie and I hung out. She went hunting with the club. She was a terrible shot but enjoyed pulling the trigger. Her laughter chased animals away, but most of the guys didn't seem to care. Not to make excuses but I was lonely, she was available, and Sweetie wasn't. At first we just talked a lot. Then we fell in love. Well, love might be an overstatement, but we were young. We liked and cared about each other. It was more than physical. OK, that's enough explaining, you either think I'm a dog or you don't.

One night, Sweetie comes over expressing great joy about her pre-SAT test scores. She finds Frenchie and me alone in the dark. Sweetie tells us all about it as she walks around my family's living room turning on the lights. She never saw us groping, but it couldn't have been more obvious. We congratulate Sweetie on her score. She doesn't congratulate us on ours. Sweetie took French home. It turns out Sweetie can honestly put on her resume, Foreign Exchange Escort.

Frenchie left three days later.

We never talked about it, but when senior year started we both chose to take Spanish to fulfill our second year of foreign language requirements. Everyone kept saying, you took one year of French, you might as well take the second year. My parents never questioned me. I never told them what happened, but they're not stupid. Taking Spanish was our way of telling each other it was over, and we still liked each other.

I guess we decided to not make a big deal out of it. We were teenagers; life is like that some times. We never talked about it or alluded to it. The closest we came to it was when we went out the night after Frenchie flew home. We got burgers. Sweetie asked me, "Do you want some French Fries?"

I looked her in the eye and said, "No." She nodded and got me some anyway. She knew we were talking about a lot more than deep-fried potatoes.

When Sweetie said "Au revoir," to me in the gym, it was the first time we said words in French since the incident. And, when Sweetie said she was still going to Prom with Roy when I climbed up on the tank, it was Sweetie's way of saying, *I get it. I understand now. You weren't really an ass for hanging out with Frenchie. We wanted different things, and I was not there for you. Now, we want different things again. I want to go to Prom and you don't. This time you're NOT going to be there for me. But going to Prom is important to me. And it's important to me that you know what's important to me. This is a deal breaker.*

I realize life isn't finding someone you can *look at*. Rather it's about finding someone *that looks and is going* in the same direction as you. That way you can do things together and create a life together. Or something like that. I wish I had my Dad, SNAFU, or Mouth Wash to talk to. There is no way I'm discussing this with Roy.

I wonder how Sweetie, SNAFU, and Darcy are doing. I sent my girl, my best friend, and his killer wife to the enemy camp armed only with machine guns, a few grenades, and a coil of unsticky webbing. *I'm such an ass.*

CHAPTER 25

YOLO

SWEETIE STARES AT THE two Space Spiders as they fly through the air … they're going to crush her. She looks at all those legs and tires to figure out how they might "fit together." Strange that this is her last thought. No, she has one more. *I can't die. Chevy, owes me a dance.*

Something black flies over her head. Tires. Three large truck tires. Perhaps spare tires from a Dodge or Ford. She can't read the brand or model number, but they're big and fly over SNAFU, Darcy, and herself. It's all slow mo now. The tires head toward the incoming Space Spiders. SNAFU and Darcy kiss. *That's nice.* The three big tires float, but they aren't floating; they're zooming with a purpose. Back to real time speed. Two of the tires hit the first air borne Space Spider and flips it head over spinneret. The third tire smacks the second Space Spider and knocks it back.

OK, that buys us another 15 seconds of life. Just enough time to get a good look at the horde of Space Spiders charging toward us. Then Sweetie thinks, "Where did those tires come from?" She turns and sees

232

one of the most beautiful sights ever. Five teens dressed in camouflage run toward her. Three teens kneel and shoot missiles right at them. I mean, right at them.

Sweetie yells, "Get down!"

Darcy, SNAFU, and Sweetie duck. The missiles zoom over their heads just missing them. The missiles hit the two tire-smacked Spacers and one of their eager friends. The missiles push them back and then BOOM! BOOM! BOOM! Explosions rip them apart and blow back other rushing Spacers.

The five teens are guys from the High School Hunting Club. Two big football guys run to Darcy's side. They carry something heavy. *Oh, yes, a really big weapon.* The gun looks like one of the guns that Han Solo and Luke used on the Millennium Falcon to shoot down Tie Fighters. A weapon like that deserves a nickname. Something like "Take Back The Prom Day," or "Last Dance."

The other three teens run to Sweetie's side. The first two, the Chip Brothers, drop next to Sweetie letting their stubby gun with a metal box crash to the ground. The Chip Brothers are identical twins with red curly hair, nice smiles, and cute dimples. They are both a little shorter than SNAFU, but they're muscular, thick, and strong.

The Chip brothers position the medium-sized, metal box and point its stubby gun toward the rushing pod of Spacers. Sweetie always liked the Chip Brothers. Now she loves them. Both brothers are wrestlers and the rumor has it they sometimes pretend to be the other brother during meets. Their opponents expect the moves one brother is known for, but by the time their opponent figures out he's wrestling the *other* brother it's too late and he's pinned.

The tripod for their weapon is short so that it's close to the ground. One of the red heads sits behind it and shoots. It looks like it's shooting cupcakes. The weapon is a MK 19 Grenade Launcher, an American made 40 mm belt-fed automatic grenade launcher with an effective range of 1,500 yards. The Space Spiders are closer then that. That means the grenades hit the Space Spiders HARD. Grenades take off legs with the shear velocity they're traveling at. Some hit the front line and cause them to pause. *Good, we could use another second to get ourselves together.* Some grenades embed themselves. Others, if they don't hit anything hard, make their way right through the first Space Spiders and land in front of the next ones. The internal damage forces Space Spiders to crumble or bump into their neighbors.

The MK 19 grenade launcher operates on a blowback principle, which uses the chamber pressure from each fired grenade to load and re-cock the weapon. I don't understand that, but it sounds cool.

They shoot forty grenades per minute. Fantastic any day of the week. Really fantastic on Prom Day.

But even with all this, the front line of Spacers are going to be here in less than ten seconds. That means the first ones are going to get to Sweetie before the grenades explode. You see, it takes longer to write this than for the action to actually happen. They need something to take out the frontrunners NOW before the grenades go BOOM. A precision machine gun starts ripping up the Spacers.

Who's the short guy in the hood next to the Chip Brothers with the firepower?

The hood kicks back. Hey, that's not a guy; it's Crystal, the only chick in the Hunting Club. Sweetie makes a mental note: *don't tell Crystal I thought she was a guy, she wouldn't respond well to that.* Actually, she's beautiful when she smiles. The problem is she never smiles. And she always wears big, oversized clothes so it's hard to see any curves. Right now she wears a long sleeved camouflaged shirt that is probably her Dad's shirt. It looks like it's two sizes too big for her.

Damn, Crystal with a gun. That never seemed like a good idea, but today it's brilliant. Crystal lies prone, her M249 light machine gun is up on its folding bipod that's attached at the front of the gun. The M249 provides infantry squads with the heavy volume of fire of a machine gun combined with the accuracy and portability approaching that of a rifle. In other words, she's blasting off parts of the closest Space Spiders with great accuracy. Chunks of head and brain fly through the air with the greatest of ease. Spacers crumble. She makes every round count.

Crystal's M249 light machine gun is gas operated and air-cooled. Space Spiders go down with their heads ending up in a mess of goo. Crystal helps buy Darcy and the teens the time they need before the Chip Brothers' grenades go off.

Other Space Spiders sense it's "do or die" time. YOLO. *You Only*

Land Once. They made it onto the planet; now it's time to conquer it. Another ten or so kick in the speed from the next line back. The Spacers are going to out run the grenade explosions. Crystal can't stop them all. Then, the big noise next to Darcy starts. Sweetie looks past Darcy and SNAFU and sees what all the commotion is.

The weapon making all the noise is a M2 Browning heavy machine gun. The big guy working it is Daisy. Daisy is six feet two and weighs 252 lbs. Sweetie knows that because Daisy is the biggest guy at school, and he plays on the defensive line for our football team. She doesn't remember the name of the position but on every play Daisy tries to break the offensive line and sack the other teams quarterback. He averages 10 sacks per game.

The M2 Browning weighs 88 pounds. That's a lot of weight to run with. Only a big guy can do that. Next to Daisy is Michelle. She's just a little smaller than Daisy, which means she's a big girl. She's Daisy's girlfriend so you don't want to be caught saying that out loud. Michelle had carried the Browning's tripod, which is no small feat in itself. It weighs 44 pounds. It's a good thing she's big and strong.

Daisy sits behind the M2 Browning, grabs the squeeze-triggers (which are mounted to the handgrips) and blasts. Damn, the Browning is loud. This could be the difference that makes the difference. Michelle swings her M4 into position and joins in the fun. The M4 machine gun is very useful in *close quarters combat*.

Close Quarters Combat (CQC), is a physical confrontation between two or more combatants usually at very short range. In the typical CQC scenario, the attackers try a very fast, violent takeover of a vehicle or structure controlled by the defenders who usually have no easy way to withdraw. The M4 is perfect for today.

This is the 21st Century Breakfast Club. Attitude with firepower.

Darcy hands Sweetie two more 30 round magazines for her M4. They are brand new except for the human blood and dried alien goo on them. Sweetie doesn't know who gave them to Darcy, but it doesn't really matter. Probably Michelle. She's always nice to Sweetie. Sweetie slams one in and starts shooting. It feels good to be back in the game.

Spacers keep coming. *Come on, when are the grenades going to go off?* One of the Space Spiders crumble and slides toward Sweetie. She raises her foot and stops it from knocking her over. She lowers her M4 ready to blast it, but it's already dead. *Good, that would have been messy.*

One of the Chip Brothers gives her a thumbs-up. She smiles and has an ah-ha moment. One of the best ways to get through high school is with friends. It's the feeling alone part that really sucks. But even with all this firepower and love, she isn't sure if they're going to survive this hairy herd. There might be too many of them.

CHAPTER 26

ALMOST

ROY HAS HIS HEAD sticking out of the top hatch. He wants a better look at the Black Hawk and Space Spiders he blasted. *He always has time to admire his own work.*

"Come on, we've got to keep moving." I think about trying to drive on my own.

Roy closes the hatch and drives. I look out the little window at one of the smoldering Space Spiders. It adds a nice touch to the overall battlefield scene.

Roy says, "You know what?"

"What Roy?"

"If the Space Spiders take over we'll probably be OK."

"What are you talking about?"

"The Human Farms."

I don't want to ask but I can't stop myself. "The Human Farms?"

"Yeah, Human Farms. It's where the Space Spiders corral all the humans together with web fences. They feed us, let us breed, and then

237

eat us when we grow. Sorta like what we do with cattle, pigs, and ostriches. I figure I'll be alright because they'll make me have sex twice a day with all types of hot looking women. I'll be the number one male breeder."

"Everyone would call you The Big Dick."

"You know it! Or, Emperor of All Surviving Humans. And Chevy, I know you don't know what the heck you're doing, but I could teach you. I could be your Obi Wan."

"You're not going to teach me anything!"

"Alright. I'll bang all the chicks myself."

"Shut up, Roy."

Roy opens an Army protein bar. I can smell the chocolate. I realize I'm starving. I wish I hadn't told him to shut up. "Do you have another one of those?"

"Now you want to be my friend?"

But he must have seen my sad face. "All right, I'll give you one, but I think I would make a great Emperor of All Surviving Humans." He searches his bag as he eats another bite. He pulls out a water bottle, "Orry, tat's pfht lass bar."

He spits chocolate crumbs as he speaks. One lands on my tux. I realize I am going to eat it. I'm so hungry that I'm going to eat Roy's crumbs and I'm excited about it. *Not a proud moment for me.* I grab it and toss it in my mouth.

"Dude, you just ate food that fell out of my mouth. Here."

Roy hands me the rest of his Army Protein Bar. I guess he's not such an idiot after all. I rub off a few crumbs—but not many—from the end that he chomped on. My pride is gone, but for some reason I'm suddenly concerned about Roy germs. I pop the rest of the bar into my mouth. It's the worst-tasting dehydrated-cardboard thing I ever ate. It tastes great! Roy slaps me on the back and I spit it out. Just like that it's gone. It sails through the air and skids across the dirty tank floor. I would brush it off but the bar slides behind a control panel lost forever.

Roy says, "Sorry. But I figured it out. You could be my cock assistant. You could be in charge of my calendar and the woman's schedules. You would bring the women to me when they're ovulating.

You'd be good at that. It would be like that summer job you and SNAFU had when you artificially inseminated dairy cows."

I don't even look at him.

"Hey," Roy says, "the Spacers seem to burn pretty good. What if we light the school on fire?"

"The Cord won't burn. We've got to cut off the Cord's attachment to the school and the Earth like SNAFU did with the gum and your shirt." I bring that up hoping to piss him off and shut him up.

"I wasn't thinking about burning the Cord. I know they tried that. I'm not stupid. I'm talking about creating a fire for them to deal with. Maybe the Prom bonfire will cause them some grief. Let's light it up and keep them on the defensive. If they're on the defensive maybe they'll be less on the offensive for Sweetie and the rest of the military."

That's the closet I ever got to wanting to hug Roy. "Roy, that's a great idea."

"Don't act so surprised."

Roy may not be an epic fail after all. I decide to compliment him, "No wonder women find you so irresistible."

"That's right, Chevy. Now you're getting to see some of the Magic of Roy."

What an ass. I say something nice and then he says something really stupid. Roy punches some calculations into his computer. He looks through the view finder. "The cords of wood. How close do you think they are to the school?"

"It's between the school and the football field. About 200 ft. from the school?"

"Good enough for government work. One incendiary coming up."

I grab my noise canceling headphones and press them against my ears. Roy shoots. BLAMO. The tank shutters. The shot goes high and then comes down. It hits close enough to the wood. Fire explode all over. The bonfire ignites. Space Spiders run and burn. They flip over. You know, stop, drop, and roll. They must have had fire drills on the moon.

I don't think about it, but the more we cause them trouble, the more we become a target. But I don't have time for troubling thoughts, I'm happy. I'm in a tank shooting things. And, we're getting close to the school. I can see around the end of the Web Wall. I can see the school. I can see the side entrance. *We going to make it.* I want to hug Roy, but then I realize I have *no desire* to hug Roy.

"Chevy, can I ask you a question?"

You just did. But I don't say that out loud. I don't want to start a fight inside a tank. It would be too loud and too many things can explode.

"Roy, in a situation like this, whatever you want."

"Do you hate me?"

"Hate is a strong word."

"Do you like me?"

"No. No, I don't like you."

"That's OK. I like myself enough for the both of us."

"Cool."

The tank comes around the end of the Wall of Web and treads up to the side of the school. We're about 30 feet (roughly 10 meters) from it. There isn't much Space Spider action or fighting going on this side of the Wall.

"Coast is clear. Keep going."

The side entrance door of the school gets closer. If we can get inside and get past the Chem lab, Faculty offices, and down the stairs, we can be in the basement in about ten minutes. We can do this. We'll be in gas pipe heaven. They run back and forth to every part of the building. Thank God for cold winters.

The tank stops moving. No, that's not accurate. The treads keep moving but the tank stops going forward. *Damn, we are only 10 feet away.* I look out the back window. A Space Spider has webbed up the rear of the tank and pulls us backwards. We get farther and farther away from the school.

"Turn the turret around, we've got a bogey at 6 p.m."

Roy corrects me, "Six o'clock."

Damn, I knew that. I just said it wrong. The turret turns and then it stops.

"What happened?" I ask.

"The turret. It's stuck," says Roy. "It's not moving."

"That's the definition of stuck: not moving."

"Actually, Chevy, the definition of stuck is to push a sharp or pointed object into or through something: for example, I stuck my thumb into your girlfriend's..."

"OK, OK, you're better at words than me."

The tank jerks. I look out the side window. I see three of them. My guess is that they've webbed up the turret and treads. Nothing moves. They learn fast. The tank continues to be dragged away from the school. This is not good.

Roy says, "Well, we're safe as long as we stay in the tank."

The tank starts to rock.

"You're an idiot."

The tank goes up on its side. Roy slams into me. His elbow hits me in the gut. It could be worse. Then the tank flips over. My head smacks a hard piece of metal. Roy's foot kicks me in the balls. It is worse. But even though the tank is flipped over, we aren't completely upside down. The ground must be uneven. We hit something, and we're at an angle.

"Roy. Your foot."

"Chevy, the Space Spiders made me kick you in the balls."

"I know Roy. Move your foot."

"I can't."

He's upside down and jammed into the side of the tank. *I don't want to die with Roy stepping on my groin.* I wish Sweetie was pressed against me. Oh, Sweetie! I should have made Roy turn around.

The Spacers rock the tank. I slide further down. My head hits the top hatch. My hands grab the wheel. I push with all my might to try to get myself up right but instead I turn the wheel and the top hatch opens. But the hatch only opens part way because the tank leans against something. My head slips out and hits the dirt underneath us. The Spacers kept rocking the tank. My neck feels like it's going to snap. I bang on the hatch but it won't open enough to let me crawl out. We're in an impossible situation, but I've never let impossible stop me. As my Dad says, "The willingness to do gives the ability to do."

Roy says, "We're all going to die." Remember, when you go on a creative adventure it's much easier if you surround yourself with people that are positive. Roy is not demonstrating that trait.

I figure Sweetie, SNAFU, and Darcy are about half way to the hot air balloon. *I'm sure they're just fine.* Any other thought would kill me.

"Roy, move your foot. Carefully."

The tank shakes again and Roy elbows me in the head. "Sorry."

"No time for apologizes!" I yell. *Except for mine to Sweetie.* "Pull yourself together, Private, and move your foot! We've got a school to blow up. We're not dying on Prom Day!" *I promised my lady a dance.*

CHAPTER 27

THE GOOD, THE BAD, AND THE SEXY

GOOD: SWEETIE AND THE others are alive.

Bad: Grenades from the grenade launcher need more time before they explode. Sweetie, SNAFU, Darcy and the rest of the teens don't have more time. They need to stop the first wave of Space Spiders now.

Good: They only need a few more seconds.

Bad: If they wait a few more seconds, the first group of Spacers will be on top of them when the grenades INSIDE the Spacers explode. This will be bad, very bad because the Spacers will be so close to the teens that the teens will be pierced by grenade shrapnel.

Good: Daisy fires the Browning M2, heavy machine gun. The Browning M2 can take out lightly armored vehicles and low-flying aircraft.

Very Good: Space Spiders are a lot closer in makeup to Jell-O then lightly armored vehicles or a low flying aircraft. Daisy's M2 rips up the Spacers something fierce.

Very Very Good: The M2 heavy machine gun shoots fifty caliber rounds. That is a BIG ass round. And, if you don't know guns or hunting, a "round" is the technical term for bullet. Sorta like glute is the technical term for ass. You could say, "That is one big glute round," but no one would ever say that.

Here's the sexy part. The M2 fires up to 800 rounds per minute, which is more than 12 rounds per second. That's insane. The teens only need a few more seconds before boom time. Daisy, the big man with the big gun, buys them the time they need.

BAM. BAM. BAM. BAM.

Daisy pumps five rounds into a Space Spider and then moves to the next one. It takes less than two seconds to "go down the line" of the first wave and BLAST all nine of the scurrying Space Spiders. Less than a third of a second per Spacer. Rounds rip right through them. They stop, drop, and goo themselves, sometimes in that order.

The M2 offers long range, accuracy and immense stopping power. STOPPING POWER is the ability of a weapon to cause a penetrating ballistic injury to incapacitate the target where it stands.

A man-stopper is any combination of firearm and ammunition that can reliably incapacitate, or "stop," a human target immediately. For example, the .357 Magnum revolver has a firm reputation as a "man-stopper."

The M2 heavy machine gun now has a reputation as a "Space Spider-stopper." The eight-legged, hairy Jell-O shots with fangs look like mechanical toys that someone switches off. Gravity sucks them to the ground. The last two of the front-runners smack, collide, and tumble. More Spacers rush up from behind the ones that fall, but that's OK, the grenades start to explode.

BOOM. BOOM. BOOM. BOOM. BOOM.

Darcy orders, "Take cover!"

The explosions are big, loud, and dangerous. The grenades in the first bunch of dead Space Spiders explode as the next bunch of Spacers scurry over their fallen comrades. BOOM. BOOM. BOOM. Some of the second wave slip and slide into each other. Legs tangle. More grenades explode. BOOM. BOOM. BOOM. Space Spider parts and goo rain down. Sweetie closes her mouth. BOOM. BOOM. BOOM. Times ten. The blast range of the grenades is fantastic. Then silence. Darcy and the teens stand. There are about twenty to thirty yards of Space Spider casualties. The teens rub their ears and take a deep breath. Daisy smiles his biggest smile ever. Michelle high-fives him. A moment of calm then forty more Space Spiders charge at them.

Darcy yells, "One more wave. We can do this."

Sweetie turns to the Chip Brothers. The brother who is the grenade loader looks around and grabs another box of grenades. He sees Sweetie and yells to her, "Coco Bean." He doesn't like being called his brother's name.

Sweetie yells over the noise, "Coco Bean, I knew it was you!" She didn't, she actually thought he was Bender, his brother. Oh no, she told a lie. She gets nervous and blurts out, "Coco Bean, I apologize, I thought you were your brother." You see, Sweetie picked up one of my books the last time she was at my house. We don't have magazines in the bathroom. She flipped to a random page and read that when you're dishonest you forfeit Spiritual Assistance. This is no time to be lying. Sweetie realizes she and her friends could use all the help they could get right now, seen and unseen.

"That's OK Sweetie, no big deal," says Coco Bean. "I thought you were Chevy." Coco Bean is a funny guy.

Sweetie knows better than to read books lying around my house. The first time she read something at my house, she read about this Tibetan monk that was being tortured in some prison. To avoid death and to continue to be useful, his soul "walked into" the body of a Seattle, Washington man as this guy committed suicide. The monk then lived out his life as this American guy who wrote a bunch of Tibetan Monk books. It was at that point that she realized she only knew a very small fraction of what's possible in life. She also decided some of the books in my house are too deep of a read when you're just trying to take a dump.

Michelle shouts to Daisy, "That's the last belt of rounds." Daisy slows down to 60 rounds per minute so he can save his ammo. He's also more accurate at a slower speed and this helps since the next group of Spacers are farther away. It turns out the M2 is able to drop them at a distance. Forty charging Space Spiders soon become twenty maimed and limping Space Spiders.

Bender keeps shooting the grenade launcher. The grenades take out Space Spiders at thirty yards. This is fun now. Bender smiles and chips fall out of his mouth. Good God, even in the middle of the battle to save Prom, they eat chips.

Coco Bean is a good-looking guy. His brother is, too, since they're identical. They're the only two students in our class who have red hair. Sometimes they have different haircuts so you can tell them apart, but most of the time they don't so they can mess with teachers, their parents, and girls.

Coco puts another handful of chips into his brother's mouth so Bender doesn't have to stop firing. It's obvious why they're called the Chip Brothers, but if girls ask, "Why are you called the Chip Brothers?" They always respond with a smile and say, "Because you can't have just one."

The brothers work well together even though they don't lead identical lives. Bender does yoga. He tells everyone, "Stress is the root of all diseases." He says stretching and yoga release stress, which then allows the body's natural healing abilities to kick in. I can hear him inside my head now, "Deep breathing calms the body and assists with releasing toxins, which also promotes healing." He taught us how to stretch before going hunting so our muscles don't cramp. I taught Sweetie Downward Dog. Yoga is hot. He also taught me breathing exercises so I could calm myself before tests. It's much easier to think and do well when I'm breathing deep.

Coco Bean looks for the next box of grenades, but there isn't one. I guess that's what sucks about heavy artillery. It's heavy and hard to carry extra ammo into battle. Coco Bean yells, "Slow it down. This is our last box of Girl Scout cookies."

Sweetie doesn't have a good feeling about that.

It's bright and shiny in the "noonday" sun. The glare off of their shiny red hair makes Sweetie squint and turn from the Chip Brothers. They must use good shampoo and conditioner. Sweetie wonders, "Might their hair attract the Space Spiders or scare them away?" I'm sure you've heard about snakes that bother blue lizards because SOME blue lizards are poisonous. It turns out the snakes can't tell which ones are deadly and which ones aren't, so they don't eat anything blue.

Maybe there is something deadly on the Space Spider's home world with red fur on the top of their head. One can hope.

SNAFU looks up and down the line. Of course Hunting Club members are here, where else would they be? He looks at Daisy and the Chip Brothers. See prayer works. You get on your knees and a bunch of teens with weapons appear. God works in mysterious ways.

But who's that little guy on the end? *That's not a guy.* SNAFU realizes that's Crystal with the nifty machine gun. Then SNAFU realizes that she isn't a GIRL. She's a young woman. In fact, it's been a long time since she's been a *little girl*. Crystal is angry, which is nothing new, but instead of directing her rage at guys, she snarls at the Spacers as she sends rounds of metal death into their alien flesh. She has valid reasons for her hostility toward men, but this is a better use of her angst. She looks at SNAFU; she can tell he's looking at her. Her green eyes sparkle and, for a moment, there is a hint of beauty in the midst of her rage. SNAFU smiles. She doesn't. He knows he should have answered her texts. She turns back to the advancing Space Spiders and shoots them in the face. A small quartz crystal on a gold chain swings from her neck. SNAFU slams another magazine into his machine gun and blasts the incoming Spacers. He remembers the first time he saw that necklace.

It was freshman year, first week of Algebra. SNAFU sits next to Crystal. They haven't talked yet, not really.

"Hi."

"Hi."

One day SNAFU drops his pencil and she picks it up for him.

"Thanks."

"Sure."

But lack of conversation doesn't stop SNAFU from wanting to kiss her. He has already wrestled with her about 250 times inside his head. Crystal doesn't have her nickname yet. In fact, SNAFU doesn't even know her real name because she never raises her hand in class. She's just another teenager trying to make it through the gloriously awesome first semester of high school.

One day, there is a BIG test and SNAFU can't get the cheat sheet out of his underwear. *Why in the world did he put it there?* Oh, yeah, he figured a teacher would never want to get into his pants. He's wrong, of course. He thinks of Darcy even though she isn't a teacher any more. SNAFU comes back to the present and turns to Darcy. Darcy sees his smile, "Twenty left! What are you smiling about?"

"If I had a cheat sheet in my pants, you'd go after it."

Darcy shakes her head. "Shut up and shoot."

SNAFU blasts as he flashes back to that Algebra class. He remembers jamming his hand in his underwear to find the cheat sheet. Crystal sees him with his hand in his jeans. It looks like SNAFU is having "a party with himself." Mrs. Havendash sees him. "Mr. SNAFU, get your hand out of your pants."

Kids laugh. Somebody in the back howls, "SNAFUUUUUUUU."

Mrs. Havendash responds, "Shhhhhhhhhh!"

Crystal gives SNAFU a smile. Such beauty. He forgets about the test and just watches her. How her hair falls next to her face. How her quartz necklace hangs and almost touches her paper. How she takes off her necklace ... *hmmm. Why is she doing that?*

Crystal holds the gold chain. The quartz crystal is about an inch above her test. It swings back and forth. She marks her paper. Then she closes her eyes and the crystal swings again, but this time, side to side. *What?* Is that possible? Is her necklace helping her take the test? She pencils in another oval. When she gets done, she slides her paper to the end of the desk so SNAFU can see it. She keeps an eye on Havendash while SNAFU copies. After the tests are collected, SNAFU says, "Thanks, Crystal." And the name sticks.

SNAFU got a B+ in that class. The highest grade in any math class he ever took. His Dad drank a beer with him when he came home with his midterm grades. They toasted to SNAFU's brilliance, a beautiful, disturbing, and hollow moment.

More grenades explode. Back to the present. The BOOMS take out the Space Spider frontrunners. Then it gets quiet. The grenades stop exploding and Daisy fires the last round from his M2 Browning. Crystal shoots two more rounds and then goes clickety, click, click. Only five or six Spacers limp toward the would-be teen saviors. The war rages on around them, but it seems like white background noise now.

SNAFU can't tell exactly how many Space Spiders are left. They form a tight "ball" with the intention of protecting the ones inside. The Space Spider at the front of the little group sacrifices itself. It leaks, dies, and falls. The Space Spiders reorganize themselves.

Darcy yells, "Inventory."

Michelle holds up her M4, "Half a mag."

SNAFU searches his pockets, and surprises himself. He pulls out a grenade, "One Grenade."

Michelle says, "Be careful with SNAFU. He doesn't know about the firepower in his own pants." Darcy doesn't laugh. She turns to the other teens. Sweetie shakes her head, no ammo left. Crystal pulls out two handguns from her waist. "Glocks." Her baggy shirt covers more than her femininity. Bender turns over an empty bag of chips. Crumbs pour down. "We're out."

Darcy is out too. She unsheathes her seven-inch ASEK Survival Knife. The Air Crew Survival Egress is a knife that entered into service with the U.S. Army in 2003. It has a 7-inch carbon-steel blade with a serrated edge on the spine. The generous crosspiece means the hand won't slip forward when the knife is used as a weapon.

The pack of wounded Space Spiders is not in a hurry to get to the teens. However, they do advance with resolve. One Spacer drags a couple of legs that don't work, but didn't get blasted off.

Jets zoom overhead. Sweetie hears explosions, gunfire, and even shouts. A strand of hair falls in front of her face. She feels alone in a crowd and it sucks. It's like being in High School before you make friends. Being alone in a crowd feels like the world is ending. Funny, *her* world is ending. Perhaps *the* world is ending. I guess high school does prepare you for real life. Same feelings. She looks around for someone to help, but the Marines, Army, and Air Force are busy. She looks at the Spacers slowly advancing. These are theirs to handle.

Sweetie turns to Darcy. "Isn't this when the cavalry is suppose to show up?"

Darcy says, "The Spacers ate the horses this morning."

"That's not funny."

That might have been funny if our high school had an equestrian team or if Sweetie didn't love horses so much. But not today. Sorry, no funny points for you, Mrs. SNAFU.

SNAFU looks at the others and says, "I think they were the cavalry. We're all alone now."

Sweetie looks at their friends and realizes something different, "No, we're not alone. We have each other."

And that is the real truth. It's what let Sweetie survive High School in relatively good spirits. It's what is going to help her survive the Space Spiders. Friends. Thank God for friends. Things are *never* that bad when you have friends. She looks at the small but fierce group of Space Spiders. She looks at her friends with almost no weapons. OK, things *are* that bad.

Chevy, where are you?

BOOK TWO

And now, the exciting conclusion.

CHAPTER 28

FOLLOW THE IDIOT

THE SPACE SPIDERS ROCK the tank. I feel like the cheap no-name brand candy that is stuffed inside a piñata. At any moment we're gonna break open, spill all over the ground, and be considered worthless. We're upside down in the tank now. Roy pulls his handgun.

I yell, "What are you going to do with that?"

"I don't know!"

"Put it away!"

The bullets will ricochet until we're both dead. *He's the one that told me that.* You see, guys who play too many hours of first-person shooter games sometimes forget they have to solve *some* problems without a gun.

I don't like being upside down. It's not natural. My entire body weight comes down on my head as it hits the hatch. As I wiggle around trying to right myself. I accidentally open the hatch and my face finds dirt. I have an idea. I open and close the hatch smacking it into a car part that lays on the ground. I finally get the hatch open far enough for

255

us to crawl out.

"Roy, you got smoke?"

"Smoking isn't good for you and a lot of people say vaping might not be good for you either."

"The tank. Does the tank have smoke bombs?"

"Yeah, We've got smoke."

"Good. I need a smoke screen all around us. Can you do that?"

"Lots of smoke coming up."

Roy hands me a gas mask. It looks like a cooler, hipper version of the old World War II spooky gas masks. Roy hits some buttons and we wait. I pull myself up and look out a window. It looks like we're inside a white cloud. I let myself slide back down. My foot hits Roy in the groin and I step on his nuts. *Oops.*

"You did that on purpose."

I didn't. Not consciously, but we supposedly act from our subconscious about 85% of the time. So … I probably did do it on purpose. I just didn't know it.

I slam the hatch open a few more times and I pull myself out. I crawl away from the tank. Good thing I'm slender. Damn, I've been hanging around Sweetie too much. Guys don't say slender. Guys say thin or skinny. I whisper, "Roy, can you grab the explosives and use them to blow the tank?"

"You want me to blow Sweetie?"

White smoke swirls around us. We look like freaks in the gas masks. I'm not sure if I heard him correctly. "What?!"

"Oh, you didn't know that's what I call my tank," says Roy. "That way every time I climb in I say, Sweetie I'm coming inside you." He holds up a big package of C4 in front of his groin. "My package is explosive!"

No wonder Roy has so many friends.

I say, "Not too big. I don't want you to kill us with tank shrapnel." *Idiot.*

Roy rips off a chuck of the C4 and shoves the rest of it into a camouflaged backpack. He attaches a detonator to the smaller piece and smushes the C4 into the tank controls. He releases more smoke. The Space Spiders shake the tank again. Roy gets tossed around and the tank almost crushes me. The cloud gets bigger and he gets stuck as he tries to slide out of the tank hatch. "Chevy, a little help." I pull him out and we crawl. We could be crawling right toward the Space Spiders because we can't see anything, but we have to get away from the tank. I bump into something. It's metal and not hairy, *thank goodness*. The breeze blows. We look back and we see the smoke move. We watch the three Spacers turn the tank right-side up.

Roy points and laughs. The Spacers turn and look at us. *Nice work, Roy*. But the tank explodes. The tank is like a really BIG grenade. Tank shrapnel shreds the three Space Spiders. The smoke wafts around us and then clears. In front of us, another Space Spider scurries and attacks a downed jet. We freeze and it doesn't see or hear us. The Space Spider fangs a webbed-up jet. *What?* But it's not biting the jet. As the Spacer moves over the fighter, the webbing disappears off of it.

I pull Roy behind some debris. "What's it doing?"

"It's eating the webbing."

"Really?"

"Spiders can't make an infinite amount of webbing," says Roy, "they can only make so much. Then they eat what they made so they can reuse it."

"Are you making that up?"

"No Chevy, I'm not *making that up*. I did a report in 8th grade about spiders." I guess Roy's 8th grade report was more in depth then my 7th grade report.

We're quiet as the Space Spider eats the rest of the webbing and hurries off into battle. After it's gone, we look around. When we were in the tank, we got pulled back to just beyond the Web Wall. We're about thirty yards from the school building. I guess we didn't get pulled back too far. Luckily there aren't any Space Spiders extending the Wall on this side. This side of the school hasn't seen a lot of action. We peek around the Wall of Web. Coast is clear. We move toward the school with the Wall behind us. Then we hear what sounds like a stamped of cattle.

"Oh, no."

Fifty or sixty Space Spiders charge. We step back until we're up against the great Wall of Web. They stop between the school and us.

257

They just stop and wait. We realize they don't see us. *How?* I notice they don't look at us, they're looking in the direction of the Cord and the front of the school. *Are they guarding it? Are they waiting for further orders?* We were so close to getting into the school and now this area looks like it's the next staging area for the Spacers.

I whisper, "There's no way we're going to get past them. How many do you think there are?"

Roy doesn't answer. I turn around and Roy's gone. *Did he get eaten?* That would be terrible, he's got the C4.

"Psst."

I look up. Roy climbs the Web Wall. I want to yell at him, but I know yelling will draw attention. I climb up after him. He lays on top of the Wall studying the herd of Spacers and the school just beyond them. More and more Space Spiders join the gathering. All of them waiting.

"What are you doing?"

Roy says, "I count over 100 of them and they keep coming."

I repeat myself, "What are you doing?"

He smiles, "Well, we're not going to get past them, but how about OVER them?"

"What?"

Roy stands on the Wall. *Get down.* But the Spacers look zoned-out. *Are they at attention?* They don't look at us and I don't think they care. They're waiting for something. A red-eyed, fanged, battalion is forming right in front of us. They stand in staggered rows evenly spaced from each other. It's impressive. I stand next to Roy. I guess we're not a threat. The closest ones stand only two or three feet from the Wall.

Roy says, "Their fangs face down. They can't bite us if we're on top of them."

"They're not statues," I say. "They can move."

Roy tightens his backpack straps and jumps. He lands on a Space Spider's back. Actually, he lands on its abdomen, the big round part, and bounces up. He runs and jumps to the next abdomen. He bounces and leaps to the next one, each time getting closer to the school. Their abdomens are bouncy. The Space Spiders don't attack Roy. Perhaps this is so new, random, and non-threatening that their reactions are minimal. Perhaps orders are orders and they're not suppose to move.

This is crazy. But then I notice the Spacers that Roy bounces on don't look back at me, they turn and look at Roy as he continues jump-running toward the school. And, they don't seem upset. I don't think they have any intel on this type of activity and it doesn't look like Roy's antics cause them any pain. The Space Spiders seem focused and on-purpose. They aren't going to let this little fly-of-a-human distract them. *This might work.*

I jump off the Wall and land on top of a Space Spider. All Spiders can't turn their heads. They're not like humans or owls. Their necks are more like those of body builders, solid and fused. To turn, they need to turn their whole body. I wait too long to jump. The one I'm standing on starts to turn. Roy yells, "Chevy!" *Hey, cut me some slack, it's the first time I'm jumping on a giant 16-foot spider.* The Space Spider next to mine picks up its head and looks at me. Its fangs twitch.

Roy yells, "Come on, Chevy. It's fun."

Roy jumps up and down on a Spacer's abdomen like a trampoline. He's getting some height. I run and jump off the back of the next Space Spider. The abdomens are springy. I jump to the next one. Oh my gosh, it's like being in a kid's bouncy house. I haven't been in a bouncy house in years. I bounce to the next one. This time I get more air.

"Woooooooo." Bounce. Spring. Land. Bounce. "Woooooooo." *I'm flying!*

Roy yells, "Where are you going?!"

I land on another abdomen and bounce up high. I pick up my head and look. I'm bouncing in the wrong direction. Roy and the school are behind me. Roy may not have a good moral compass, but he knows where the school is. I'm heading toward the front of the school. I turn and so does the Space Spider I stand on. It seems like the grace period is over. Eyes and fangs pop up everywhere.

Roy shouts, "Next level."

I guess that was the training round. Run, jump, and bounce. *Abdomens. It's important to land on abdomens, they give the bounce.* I land on the next abdomen and then bounce to the next one. I know what I'm doing now. I bounce and leap from one to another without running or taking any steps. *Excellent.* But then I land too close to a head. I step on it, right between its big red eyes, and jump. Mandibles reach for me. Fangs slice the air.

I keep bouncing. More fangs reach for me and almost grab my leg. Only twenty more Spacers to go before I get to the side door. They start to move like a herd. *This is different.* The Spacer I'm heading for gnashes its fangs at me. Now that they're moving it's a little trickier. *Next level.*

Timing is important. I don't want to fall between the Spacers. That would not end well. Jump and run. Sometimes in mid flight, I shift my weight and land on a different Spacer than the one I was going for. It's hard, but still fun.

I look up. *Where's Roy?* He lands next to me. I lose my balance and fall off of the Space Spider. He grabs my arm and pulls me back. "Saved your life."

Idiot. Roy drops to his knees and runs his fingers through the hairy back of the Space Spider. "Chevy, look at this." One of the Spacer's right legs starts to do that "kick move" that dogs do when you scratch their "magic spot."

"What are you doing?"

"I dropped my keys on one of these guys," says Roy. "Without them, we're not getting in."

"You know, it's a $1,500 fine for losing a master key. They'll have to rekey the whole building."

Roy looks at me. *Yeah, that was stupid.* We're on top of a Space Spider moving away from the school we're planning to BLOW UP in the middle of a war that may decide if humanity goes bye-bye. Nobody is going to fine anyone for losing a master key.

"Forget it," I say. "I've got my keys. We're going to have to pick up the pace if we're going to make it to the side door."

Roy stands and balances on the moving Spacer. He smiles, "I think this is as close to surfing as we're going to get in Pennsylvania." We're getting farther and farther away from the side door as the battalion of Spacers march toward the front of the building. A web line shoots at Roy. I pull him down. It just misses him.

"Saved *your* life."

Roy shouts, "Next level!"

I look at the side door and say, "First one there wins." I leap before he can answer. We run, jump, and duck our way there. Webs shoot from the left and right. Their aim gets better. Sometimes we have to jump over web blasts.

We get closer to the side door as we get to the end of the battalion. Only a few more to bounce over. Roy jumps ahead of me. *No, I want the high score or he's going to be impossible to work with.* I turn on the speed. I bounce down hard on a Spacer. It makes an umph sound, *sorry.* I spring up and pass Roy in the air. Laters, Baby. I come down hard on the last Space Spider. My downward force pushes the Spacer to the ground, but my bounce is going to be big. I'm gonna win, but I realize my speed is going to carry me into the school building. Not good. I brace for impact. SMACK. I just miss the light fixture, but the brick is hard. Winning isn't suppose to hurt so much. I crumble down the wall. Roy lands on the ground behind me.

"You won. Nice bounce at the end."

I mumble, "Thanks."

The last Space Spider I bounced on slowly stands behind us. My "super" bounce must have winded it. The rest of the Space Spider battalion has moved to the front of the school. This Spacer is on its own and is no longer part of the "group-think-mob-mentality." It seems to have regained its free will. The right side of its head is covered in black, including its right fang. It looks like it got burnt in battle.

Roy says, "I will call this one Scar Face."

Scar Face twitches its fangs at us. Carbon flakes off its body.

Roy says, "Hey, I think we toasted this guy with our fire rocket."

Great Roy. Let's make it personal. We slowly walk up the 12 stairs to the side door, but it's locked. Scar Face scurries after us. Roy pulls his M4 off his back and blasts Scare Face as he yells, "Keys, keys, keys." I'm already pulling out my teddy bear key ring that Sweetie gave me.

"Ahhhhhh, that's cute."

Roy shoots the charging Scar Face. Burnt flesh puffs up into black smoke.

"Nice shot ... "

"Get the door open!" BAM. BAM. BAM.

I open the door. Scar Face jumps at us. I grab Roy and pull him in. The door shuts. Scar Face slams against the door. There's a tiny window in the door. It has thin lines of metal running through the glass. Even with the reinforcement, the glass cracks and a few pieces shatter. Roy gives Scar Face the finger. It screeches at us and scurries away. We back away from the door.

CHAPTER 29

PARTY SNACKS

SWEETIE, DARCY, SNAFU AND the rest of the teens face the last group of wounded Space Spiders. The Spacers shuffle closer. There are only five or six of them and they're limping and goo-ing, but the teens don't have many bullets left. Darcy steps forward and raises her knife. She says, "Everyone with ammo, wait until they're close. Every round HAS to count."

Adrenaline spikes. The ones with the empty weapons raise them like baseball bats. They take fighting stances. Sweetie hears something attacking from behind.

"They're sneaking up our rear." *That's not right.*

Darcy and her Knights turn, ready to fight with what they've got left. But it's not fangs at their backsides, it's a catapult. It's Benji's catapult. This is how the flying tires got launched. This is how spare tires knocked down Spacers that were going to crush Sweetie. She thinks, *that seems like that happened a week ago.*

Benji and B+ pull the catapult through the battlefield and it isn't easy. Sweetie swoons when she sees B+. All the girls do. More about these guys in a moment, but first something about their "weapon of not-mass destruction." The catapult is the size of about four shopping carts, and it looks like something from Trojan horse times. It's Frankensteined together with scrap lumber from Old Man Gotham's barn. Later, Sweetie would find the plank with a heart carved on it with two names: Eric + Theresa. That was before Sweetie and I got our school nicknames.

We were in first grade when we held hands. In second grade we went on "dates," which meant we shared crackers on the playground during recess. Then we broke up for awhile. Nothing dramatic. Just me hanging out with "the gross boys" and Sweetie hanging out with "cootie girls." In eighth grade we kissed behind Old Man Gotham's barn, and I carved our names into it. In tenth grade we did other things. It's interesting how I somehow became *less gross* and she no longer *had cooties*. I guess that happens when you grow up.

Sweetie flashed back to me carving our names into the barn. We had just got done licking the juice off our fingers. Strawberries taste best when they are wild, fresh, and free. I said, "You're sweet, sweeter than strawberries." That became Sweetie. Only a few nicknames start before high school.

The catapult looks like it doesn't work, but I guess it does.

Benji yells, "How we doing team?"

Benji is cute, fun, and friendly. He has short, curly hair. If he had a tail, it would be wagging most of the time. There are old movies with a cute, little dog named Benji. I think that's where it comes from. Not the greatest nickname, but he could have gotten one far worse. Sweetie takes a moment to look at B+. Even with "bombs bursting in air," she can't help herself. He's so good looking, underwear model good-looking. B+ cranks the catapult; his muscles ripple under his tight camouflage T-shirt. Sexy. And, what a great glute. One more turn and the catapult's big arm comes down and locks into place. The girls call him B+ because he has everything they want except for the desire to climb all over them. Benji and B+ are boyfriends. They have been since sophomore year.

Sweetie yells back, "We got a six-pack of leaky cans. What are you bringing to the party?"

B+ loads two tires without rims into the big, net-scoop of the catapult. Benji wedges a can of gas into each empty tire. He jams a rag into each gas can and flicks a lighter, but no flame appears.

Benji shouts, "Jalapeño Poppers. Be careful, they're hot." He tries the lighter again. But still no flame, only clicks. B+ holds up two grenades, "What about these?" Benji kisses B+, "How'd I get so lucky?"

"We're the only two gay guys born in the middle of nowhere."

Benji laughs. "You're such a sweet talker. Pull the pins, we're already fashionably late."

B+ pulls the pins and shoves the grenades into the spare tires with the gas cans. Benji pulls a short piece of lumber which is the release pin on the catapult. SPRONG! The big arm springs up and hits a massive eight-by-eight cross bar of wood. The arm and net stop, but the spare tires, gas cans, and grenades fly.

Two fire bombs away! Two Jalapeño Poppers! Two tickets to the next life!

They fly over the teens and head for the tight group of Space Spiders. The hairy freaks look up. The one leaking the most goo collapses, succumbing to a mixture of despair, dread, and internal damage. The other five Spacers watch the tires fly over their heads. I mean, way over their heads, about 20 feet over their heads. The tires keep going. They land about 30 feet behind the Space Spiders. Then, to add insult to injury, the tires roll AWAY from the Spacers. They finally explode. BOOM. BOOM.

Flames shoot up. Nice explosions, but they're so far away that the Space Spiders don't even have to duck. They're safe. The Space Spiders snicker at the error in calculation. They bob up and down and twitch their fangs.

"What are they doing?"

"I think they're dancing."

The Spacers stand taller, all of them except for the one with the dangling legs. The teens look at Benji.

"It's a catapult," says Benji. "How accurate do you think it's gonna be?"

The five Space Spiders form a single-file conga line and approach the teens. The Spacers have learned a frontal assault, even with really big numbers, is not a guaranteed win. The *Art of War* says, don't ever fight a battle you know you can't win. The Space Spiders realize they need to try something different.

SNAFU raises his last grenade. Crystal thinks he's waving at her. She softens and waves back. Then, she realizes he isn't waving to her. *Damn, I hate that when that happens.*

Darcy grabs SNAFU's arm. She says, "Wait." He waits. He doesn't like it, but he waits.

Crystal touches her necklace and moves closer to Sweetie. "Hey Sweetie."

"Hey Crystal."

Crystal whispers to Sweetie, "What's up with Ms. Meyers?"

Darcy still holds SNAFU's arm. She's been holding it for a while and SNAFU seems OK with it. Sweetie realizes this is not the time or place for explanations. "I'll tell you in a moment." Sweetie shouts to Darcy, "What are they doing?"

"They're adapting. The first one is acting like a shield with the intention of protecting the others." Darcy turns to SNAFU, "Can you throw the grenade so it lands on top of the second or third Space Spider?"

"Of course. For you, the world." Darcy smiles and lets go of his arm. Crystal rolls her eyes.

Darcy yells, "OK everyone, get ready to pick up the scraps."

Michelle kneels on bended knee and raises her M4 machine gun. Crystal points both Glocks. SNAFU pulls the pin and tosses the grenade. It's a nice toss. It's going to land on top of the second Space Spider or right between the second and third one. That's pretty good aim for only one day of grenade throwing.

One of the Spacers in back turns, puts his butt in the air, and shoots a web. The webbing shoots up and hits the grenade. The webbing wraps around the grenade and it drops, like a rock, right in front of the first Space Spider. It's slightly bigger than an American football. Or, if you know rugby, it's the size of a rugby ball, which in Australia is called a "footy." They hear the sound of a muffled explosion. Something like Zmmmft. The grenade explodes inside the webbing, not even the first Space Spider gets blasted.

This is a big win for the Spacers. They wave their legs in celebration. The one with the flappy legs accidentally shakes them off. Oops. The Spacers raise their heads (and fangs) and march toward the camouflaged teens.

Darcy yells, "Now."

Michelle and Crystal open up on the first one. The Spacer takes the rounds with great pride and screeching. It doesn't look good for the Knights of Fairland High. They only have enough ammo to eliminate two or three of the five Space Spiders. The last two will engage them in hand-to-fang combat. Even Darcy realizes her big knife is not going to be enough to win the day.

Crystal's Glocks blast. Sweetie attaches the bayonet to her machine gun. She thinks back to the Civil War reenactments her town does every year to commemorate the brave soldiers that fought against overwhelming odds. Who would have ever thought she'd be attaching a bayonet in real life? She didn't even know they still used bayonets. War sucks.

Sweetie doesn't hear the four-wheeled, white ATV drive up behind her. It's Mouth Wash. He's dressed different than everyone else because he's different from everyone else. Sure, he wears white, gray, and black camouflage pants, which is not too different, but he wears a white T-shirt. It's a T-shirt he got from the school bookstore. It has a capital F on the front of it for Fairland High. The top of the F runs across his strong and well-defined pecks. The bottom of the F clings to his washboard abs. He wears tight T-shirts. *I wonder why.* Sweetie doesn't see it until later, but he has written the word "it" with a black permanent marker at the bottom of his shirt. *Get it?* "F it."

Mouth Wash gets off the four-wheeled ATV and raises a Shoulder-launched Multipurpose Assault Weapon (SMAW). It's a missile launcher, but it's a little lighter and sleeker than the one I used from the RV to bring down that first Spacer. Which makes sense because even though Mouth Wash is my friend, he always tries to one-up me when it comes to Sweetie. Sweetie looks at Mouth Wash with the SMAW rocket launcher and thinks of the plastic army guys her cousins used to play with. In her mind, she can see the little green guy on bended knee with the bazooka on his shoulder.

Mouth Wash wedges himself between Sweetie and Bender. Bender shakes his head and moves. Mouth Wash always worms his way next to Sweetie. Most everyone agrees Mouth Wash is good looking and has a great smile. *Whatever.* There is Space Spider goo on his right knee and splattered across the F on his shirt. Good for him.

Sweetie puts out her hand. Mouth Wash reaches into his pocket and hands her a mag for her M4. She's glad she doesn't have to use the bayonet. She didn't like the idea of getting that close to a Spacer. Sweetie isn't surprised that he has a fully loaded magazine for her. Mouth Wash is psychic and Sweetie knows it. He would have gotten a different nickname when he was a freshman, but nobody suspected it at the time. He was either not psychic yet or he kept his abilities hidden when he transferred in. That is, by the way, the meaning of esoteric: hidden. Hidden knowledge. I'm thinking esoteric might have been his school name if we had known of his abilities. Esoteric is not bad, but four syllables is kinda long for a nickname. It probably would have been shortened to Eso or Eric, which would have been weird because his school nickname would have been my real name.

Mouth Wash and I often hunt together. The main purpose of our expeditions is to talk mystical and spiritual stuff. We hunt by ourselves because these conversations usually freak-out or bore others. You know what they say, likes attract.

Sweetie loads the mag and blasts her M4. This is the straw that breaks the Space Spiders back. The one in front goes down.

Michelle shouts, "Now serving number two."

Mouth Wash flips switches and prepares to shoot the launcher. He asks, "How's it going?"

"Super," says Sweetie. "Ninety-six down with four to go. How about you?"

"Minty fresh."

Mouth Wash always says that because it's true. His breath is always minty fresh. Sweetie sits behind him in Home Room because of alphabetical seating. Whenever Sweetie needs a pen, he hands it to her BEFORE she asks. He also whispers funny stuff about Mr. Lancaster.

Sweetie leans forward to hear him. She enjoys catching a whiff of his winter-mint musings.

Sweetie watches Mouth Wash kneel with the SMAW bazooka on his shoulder. She says, "You're just in time."

"I heard you asking for help."

What he means by that is that he can hear *her* inside *his* head. Nobody knows if he can really hear people inside his head or if he just has really good timing. Perhaps they're the same thing. But if you remember, Sweetie did ask Darcy, "When's the cavalry arriving?" Perhaps Sweetie was calling Mouth Wash and she didn't even know it. I don't like thinking that they're that connected, but I'm glad he showed up.

She points to the rocket launcher. "How did you get one of those?"

"My good looks." He winks. "Step back."

She knows the drill. Sweetie moves to the side. Mouth Wash is just about to fire when Darcy says, "Stop." It's an order. He stops.

"We got them all lined up," says Darcy. "Wait until we drop another one, and then your rocket can take out the rest. We've got enough ammo to take down the front man."

Everybody nods and blasts. The first Spacer takes the hits. It looks drunk and wobbles side to side. It goo's all over the place because that's what Spacers do when they battle the Knights of Fairland High. But it doesn't drop. *Why?* The second Space Spider holds up the first Spacer. Amazing. The front man allows itself to be used as a shield for its buddies. You've got to respect that. It keeps taking more and more rounds. Michelle shoots out her magazine. Crystal's Glocks stop. The Spacer line moves closer. It's about 20 feet away.

Darcy puts her hand on Mouth Wash's shoulder. "Hold."

Sweetie thinks, you can do this Mouth Wash.

He replies out loud, "Piece of cake."

Imagine a colander, you know a large bowl that's usually made of white plastic or metal with little holes that's used to drain pasta? Now imagine a hairy colander but instead of it holding pasta—it holds Space Spider guts—and instead of draining water it's drains Space Spider goo from all of its holes. That's what marches towards these guys. Crystal slams two more slender magazines into her Glocks, but Darcy holds up a hand. "Save your ammo."

Crystal says, "Don't tell me what to do." But she doesn't shoot.

The Spacer stands for one more moment and then it drops. Actually *drops* is not the right word. The Space Spider behind it can't hold up the leaky Spacer any more because it just falls apart. Crystal lowers her Glocks.

Michelle yells, "Now serving number three!"

The next Spacer shakes off the rest of its friend, goo flies in all directions. An effective way to clean up, but rude. It screeches and charges.

Darcy taps Mouth Wash and says, "Now!"

Mouth Wash fires. The missile comes out with amazing force. An equal blast comes out the back. Firing a SMAW rocket is not the same as shooting the other rocket launchers where the missile "sits in the air" and then blasts off. The SMAW missile flies with GREAT speed. It hits the charging Space Spider with such force that it enters its head and pushes right through its body without exploding. The missile hits the next Spacer and pushes it and the ones behind it backwards about fifteen feet. The rocket explodes. BOOM. The explosion engulfs and rips apart the last two Space Spiders. Flames explode in all directions including forward. The flames shoot right through the rocket-hole in the first Space Spider making it look like a fire-breathing Space Spider. Darcy and the teens duck. The flames shoot toward them and over their heads. The flames roast the inside of the Space Spider. It crumbles into a pile of burnt alien flesh. The smell is wonderfully awful.

That is the last of this Space Spider group. They did it. Daisy, Michelle, the Chip Brothers, B+, Benji, Mouth Wash and Crystal cheer. They helped saved Darcy, Sweetie, and SNAFU.

SNAFU hugs Daisy and then Michelle. The Chip Brothers open their arms to Darcy. She hesitates, but hugs them to their great satisfaction. Bender hollers with excitement. Sweetie hugs Mouth Wash a little bit longer then all of her other hugs. SNAFU notices.

Crystal hugs B+ and Benji. B+ swings her around, muscles rippling, wind blowing back his hair. Very model like. B+ and Benji are Crystal's only guy friends. Probably because there's never sexual tension between them.

Mouth Wash looks at Sweetie's Prom dress. "What's a nice girl like you doing in a place like this?"

Everyone gathers to listen. Sweetie explains, "We were on a mission to save Prom, but that doesn't seem possible now. It seems like we're going to have to settle for saving the world. We need to get to the hot air balloon."

Bender says, "That's near the Latch Site."

"We know," says Sweetie.

Benji says, "There will be a lot more Spacers over there."

"We know," says Darcy.

Michelle says, "That seems dangerous and kinda stupid."

"We know," says SNAFU.

Mouth Wash takes Sweetie's hand, "Why don't we come with you. We'll pick up more weapons on the way." Sweetie wipes tears of joy from her eyes and hugs Mouth Wash. "That's one of the nicest things anyone has ever said to me."

Bender rolls his eyes, "He volunteers *all of us* and *he* gets another hug."

Daisy says, "That's Mouth Wash for you."

B+ pulls something off of the catapult and hands it to SNAFU. It's his crossbow and arrows. B+ says, "I thought you might need this. Thanks for letting me borrow it. I got a six-pound trout by the old cabin." B+ pauses, "That kinda seems trivial now."

SNAFU looks at his crossbow, it doesn't compare with his M4. He's ready to put the crossbow down, but then SNAFU looks at the fishing arrows. SNAFU looks at the hole at the end of one of his arrows. This is where the heavy-duty fishing line gets tied to arrow so the fish can be pulled up after it's shot. He gets an idea. *This could be the opportunity Chevy was talking about.* SNAFU picks up the thin coil of webbing that he had put on the ground. He tries it. Yes, the webbing is thin enough to fit through the hole at the end of the arrow. SNAFU smiles. See, I was right, an opportunity presented itself and SNAFU's smart enough to recognize it. *Prom day is magical!*

SNAFU hugs B+ and says, "Thank you. You know, if I was gay, I'd steal you away from Benji."

"I don't think so." B+ walks away from SNAFU.

Mouth Wash looks around. "Where's Chevy?" *Nice of him to stop hugging Sweetie and notice I'm not there.*

"He's on his way to school to blow it up with Roy," says Sweetie.

Mouth Wash nods. "But of course. Where else would he be?"

When I heard how the Hunting Club showed up at just the right time, I thought of a poem Brother Clark recited at the Bright Light Retreat a couple years back. The poem is by St. Teresa of Avila. The retreat for high school students is interesting. A lot of teens beso during quiet time. Who says organized religion can't be fun?

First, I'll tell you the St. Teresa poem. Then I'll tell you my Space Spider version. And, if you want to substitute Buddha, Sakthi, Krishna, Mohammad, Mother Goddess, or Obi-wan into the poem, that's fine with me. I'm pretty sure they're all representatives or agents of the All.

Christ has no body now but yours,
No hands on earth but yours,
No feet on earth but yours,
Yours are the eyes with which he looks Compassion on the world,
Yours are the feet with which he walks to do good,
Yours are the hands with which he blesses all the world.

Here's my Spacer version.

Jesus has no machine gun but yours to cut down Space Spiders,
No grenade launcher but yours,
No M2 Browning but yours,
Yours are the weapons with which to blast the Spacers,
Yours are the Friends to cover your glutes,
Yours are the Courage and Strength to save Prom.

I'm sure Saint Teresa wouldn't mind my version. Saints forgive stuff. That's what they do.

CHAPTER 30

THE HITS JUST KEEP ON COMING

CRYSTAL STANDS ON TOP of a downed jet keeping an eye out for more Space Spiders. She's smart and a loner. Maybe she's being both right now. The other teens break into groups of two to collect weapons and ammo from the fallen. Not pleasant, but necessary. Darcy and SNAFU work together. SNAFU keeps a lookout while Darcy frees an M4 from a solider who's not going to be using it. Sweetie watches for Spacers while Mouth Wash finds more grenades. He gives a couple to Sweetie. Sharing is caring. B+ and Benji work together. B+ looks like he's in a men's cologne ad. Daisy and Michelle, the big couple, turn over a jeep to gather supplies. Bender and Coco Bean, the red-headed twins, move dead Spacer legs off a solider to get more ammo. They get into a fight with the Spacer legs and beat each other with them. These brothers have a hard time being serious even for a war.

It's great that everyone stays to fight. But who's going to miss an opportunity like this? There are only two possible outcomes. Either the world will not be saved and everyone dies or a straggly band of teenage freedom fighters save the world. Then, future high schools (without Galactic Cords attached to them) will be named after these heroes. All the guys realize there will be a line of grateful, young women (or men) wanting to *wrestle* with them to show their gratitude. There may be something different that motivates Sweetie, Darcy, Crystal, and Michelle. I'm not sure, I don't know females that well.

Mouth Wash stands too close to Sweetie. He likes her. A lot of guys do. I realized a long time ago that it isn't up to me to stop Sweetie from going out with Mouth Wash or other guys. No, that isn't my responsibility. My job is to stop Sweetie from *wanting* to go out with other guys. My job is to be the best guy and boyfriend I can be. I only really crossed the line that one time and now I'm screwing it up with the whole "Prom isn't important" fiasco.

Four Marines arrive in a High Mobility Multipurpose Wheeled Vehicle also known as a Humvee. This is a four-wheel drive military vehicle that is like a jeep on steroids. The Humvee has proven itself by negotiating treacherous desert sand and rocky terrain with ease. The Humvee proves itself now by ripping up our practice field with its big ass tires.

The Humvee stops. The driver and a few other Marines jump out with weapons drawn. "Clear." "Clear." "Clear." Sergeant Killer opens the front passenger door and gets out. He's handsome and strong. He looks the teens over. His gaze stops on Crystal who's still perched on top of the downed jet. Sergeant Killer smiles and waits for the leader of these misfits to step forward. Darcy approaches.

"Sergeant."

"Private." He doesn't say it with any disdain.

Darcy doesn't go into specifics about the mission and blowing up the school. Sergeant Killer isn't a man of words, few Sergeants are. He just wants to help win the war, especially if it involves killing Spacers. Darcy's smart enough to get that. All she says is, "We need your help. We're on a mission to stop them from coming to Earth. It's going to be dangerous."

He nods. "We're in." He's happy to have something specific to do.

Crystal jumps down from the jet and lands in front of him. Sergeant Killer says, "You can't come. You're too young." Crystal stands her ground. "I'm eighteen." He looks her up and down. "Are you sure?"

"Yes, sir."

"OK then, you're with me."

Crystal smiles and says, "Ooh Rah." She likes the bad boys.

Sergeant Killer turns to Darcy, "Which way?"

Darcy points in the direction of the football field and the balloon.

Sergeant Killer nods. He says, "How much fuel we've got left?"

One of the Marines says, "We're way past empty, sir. Probably driving on fumes."

Killer says, "We'll walk. Our big gun is out of ammo anyway. Distribute whatever we've got with our new friends." The Marines pass out weapons and supplies. Coco Bean puts on a helmet to cover his red hair. It might be a good idea to not be so noticeable.

The new unit walks toward the hot air balloon. Sergeant Killer leads because that's what Marines do. SNAFU holds Darcy back.

"I really should be up front with the Sergeant."

SNAFU whispers, "No, I don't get a good feeling about this. It's not about who's first. It's about getting there and completing the mission. Let the professionals run block."

She stops. "*I am* a professional."

"Yes, you are. Don't get defensive."

Darcy says, "What does run block mean?"

Michelle steps up. "Run block is a football term. It means a player who blocks and shoves members of the opposing team *out of the way* so the running back, the guy carrying the ball, can score."

SNAFU says, "We're going for the touch down."

"OK," says Darcy, "I'll let them *run block*."

Daisy, the big football player says, "Well, in that case, get out of the way. More big people moving up front." Michelle hits him in the arm, "Speak for yourself." Daisy blows Michelle an air kiss. Michelle ducks it and teases, "You missed." Michelle runs to the front. He chases after her.

Bender runs his hand through his red hair as he passes Darcy and SNAFU. He's going to the front too. Bender says, "The important thing is that you *score*." SNAFU isn't sure if Bender is joking around or if he's saying the mission *must succeed*.

Darcy says, "We'll score."

Coco Bean smirks as he jogs behind his red-haired brother. Coco Bean secures his helmet and is about to say something but Darcy says, "Keep moving."

"Yes, ma'am."

B+ points to one of the younger Marines who is really cute. Benji nods and says, "We're going up front to keep an eye on Crystal." Benji and B+ also catch up to the Marines.

Darcy, SNAFU, Sweetie, and Mouth Wash are now the last four in the squad as they march to the balloon. Darcy waits until B+ and Benji are out of earshot. She asks, "What's Crystal's problem? I don't have her in any of my classes. Why is she upset with me?"

"I don't know," says SNAFU. "Where do you want to honeymoon?" SNAFU is dumb, but he's not stupid. He mentions their honeymoon to change the subject.

Darcy says, "What about Turkey?"

"What about Florida?"

"You've got to be more exotic than that."

"I can be exotic."

"I bet you can."

Kiss. Kiss. Slap someone's butt. Growl. Snicker. Laugh.

Mouth Wash gags, "OK, OK. That's enough."

He stops and grabs Sweetie's wrist so she stops walking. SNAFU and Darcy continue without them. Mouth Wash is *not* going to listen to *that* all of the way to the balloon. He waits until a gap forms between the newlyweds and him and Sweetie, then he starts walking again. Sweetie wipes tears.

He says, "Are you hurt?"

"What if Chevy's dead?"

"Then you and I get to have angry sex."

"Mouth Wash, I'm serious."

"Me too."

This time Sweetie stops, but Mouth Wash pulls her along. "There's a difference between a gap and being left behind."

"Stop it. You're one of Chevy's best friends."

"And that is why I'd be there to support you."

"What!? With angry sex? You and me?"

SNAFU and Darcy turn. Sweetie and Mouth Wash smile and wave.

Mouth Wash says, "Sounds kinda good, doesn't it?"

"No, it doesn't."

"Just a little?" Mouth Wash flashes his pearly whites. Sweetie tries to stop herself but she smiles.

Mouth Wash says, "Listen, if Chevy dies, or is dead already, you'll be depressed. Then, we'll have angry sex to help move you out of your depression."

"I thought anger is worse than depression."

"It's not. When someone is depressed they just stay in bed or sit on the couch. Depression is often the result of unresolved sadness and a person may focus anger *inward*. *I'm stupid. I'm dumb. I'm a loser.* People sometimes get scared when someone moves from depression to anger because with anger their hostility is directed *outward*. When depressed people move into anger they often become loud and scary. Most people don't realize anger may be a great next step out of depression. But we wouldn't stop with angry sex."

"No, of course not. Then what? Go to an amusement park to grieve?"

"No. The amusement park is later. We'd then have Blame Sex."

"More sex."

277

"Yes.

Sweetie scrunches her eyebrows. She doesn't want to ask but does, "What is Blame Sex?"

"It's where we move out of anger by blaming others. We'd have really great sex and then blame Chevy for dying, blame the Space Spiders, and probably at the very end, blame God."

"What kind of sex would we have after that?"

"Now you're getting the hang of it. Disappointment Sex. I mean, the sex wouldn't be disappointing." Mouth Wash smiles.

"No, of course not, not if it's me and you."

Mouth Wash nods. "Then we'd have Pessimist Sex."

"Pessimism with an orgasm?"

"It's really the best pessimism there is."

Sweetie laughs, but then twirls her hair. "Something like, life sucks, it's never going to get better, I'll never be happy again, touch me here, that feels good, faster, harder, yes, yes, yes!"

SNAFU turns again, but this time Sweetie and Mouth Wash don't see his glare.

Mouth Wash claps. "Exactly."

"What kind of sex is after that?"

"Boredom Sex."

"But just to be clear we're not bored with *the* sex. We're just bored and then have sex."

"Right," says Mouth Wash.

"Sex with *me* will never be boring," says Sweetie.

"Never thought it would be. Then, we continue having sex and we realize, 'life's not so bad. Things happen to everyone. We're still alive and we actually have pretty good lives."

"Sounds like we'd be having Contentment Sex?"

"Yes," declares Mouth Wash. "And once we turn this corner we're not too far from Hopeful Sex and then Positive Expectation Sex."

"We start feeling better about life and anticipate more and more fun and good things. We realize Chevy loves us wherever he's at and would want us to be happy."

"Right."

"Would we then stop having sex?"

"No. Not by a long shot."

Sweetie nods. "I probably could have figured that out by myself."

"Then we have Joy and Gratitude Sex."

They duck behind a broken down jeep because everyone else takes cover. Mouth Wash reaches into the jeep and pulls out a couple of magazines for their M4 machine guns. Sweetie smiles, she feels better, partly because of the conversation and partly because she has more ammo. Mouth Wash finds a bottle of water, opens it and offers it to Sweetie. She drinks and hands it back to him. He drinks the rest. He drops the bottle. This is not the time to recycle. Save the Earth, yes. Recycle, no.

Five more Space Spiders run past them. Sergeant Killer stays down. He signals to everyone to hold. Darcy signals back when it's all clear. No reason to fight if they don't have to. The mission comes first. Everyone stands and continues.

Mouth Wash says, "And then we'd have Empowered and Absolute Freedom Sex."

"Really?" says Sweetie, "you'd do that for me?"

"Of course, what are friends for?" Mouth Wash smiles. "Then we continue our relationship or we don't. But because we feel great and have recaptured our *own alignment with who-we-really-are*, we'd be in a position to design the rest of our lives from a place of wholeness and adventure."

Sweetie says, "Some how I feel like you're being a good friend AND a little self-serving and manipulative."

"I do what I can." Mouth Wash sticks out his hand.

"You want to shake on it?" says Sweetie.

"Hold my hand."

"What?"

"Friends can't hold hands?" asks Mouth Wash.

"No. No they can't," says Sweetie. "Not if they're in America and in a relationship with someone else. Especially if the other person is the opposite sex and has talked about having sex for the last 10 minutes."

"Friends, even in the United States, can *now* hold hands. It's the 21st Century. The rules are changing."

Sweetie doesn't buy it. Mouth Wash keeps his hand out. He says, "Listen. Why would two friends, who love each other," he touches his heart, "Real love, not possessive, grabby, I-need-you-to-be-whole love, stop themselves from holding hands when they're walking through the final verses of Revelations?"

Sweetie smiles, "But possessive, grabby love is sometimes just around the corner when two friends," she makes air-quotes in the air, "hold hands especially if they're in the middle of the End of Times."

Mouth Wash laughs, "Point well made, Ms. Steel, but it's the Age of Aquarius. Don't act out of Fear. Shit happens when we act out of fear. Check inside. We need to act out of Loving. Is this OK to do right now?"

Sweetie smiles, "I would like to hold your hand but ... "

"No buts."

Sweetie takes his hand and they walk. Awkward silence. Then she says, "This is weird."

"Only if you think it is." They take a couple of more steps. "It takes time to get used to it."

"You've done this before?" asks Sweetie.

"No."

"Then how do you know it takes time to get used to?"

"I'm making this stuff up as I go."

SNAFU and Darcy look back. SNAFU's ready to charge Mouth Wash and punch him in the face, but Darcy grabs SNAFU's arm.

"Not our business," says Darcy. "They're adults."

"Barely legal," says SNAFU. He gives Mouth Wash a dirty look.

Sweetie straightens her Prom dress, She says, "This is making SNAFU angry."

"That's OK."

"Really?"

"Hell no. He scares the jeepers out of me." Mouth Wash squeezes her hand. "But how does *this* make you feel?""

"Good. Great."

"Do you want to stop because of what others think?"

Sweetie says, "No, that's surviving. I don't want to survive any more. I want to live."

"Then screw them and their ignorance. Oh, and by the way, Chevy's alive."

Sweetie hugs Mouth Wash. After the hug, she doesn't hold his hand.

"Thank you," says Sweetie. "I know you don't usually use your powers to tell people stuff."

"I do on dates. It usually gets me some action."

"How is he? Is he OK?"

Mouth Wash inhales, tries to "feel" the answer. His smile goes away. "He's hurt."

"Wounded? How bad? Is he going to make it?"

"No, not hurt-wounded. More like hurt-irritated."

Sweetie laughs, "Well, of course he is, he's with Roy. Thank you."

"Sure, that's what Soul Friends are for."

Everything gets quiet. It seems like someone hits the pause button on the battle. A shiver goes through Sweetie's body. She says, "Mouth Wash, say something. Tell me a story."

Mouth Wash shakes his head, "Sorry Sweetie, the time for talking is over."

CHAPTER 31

SAY SOMETHING, YOU FOOL

MOUTH WASH ISN'T TALKING and Sweetie doesn't like it. Nothing ever happens when Mouth Wash talks. Nothing important. He has perfect timing. Let me explain. If a teacher leaves the classroom and Mouth Wash tells a joke, the teacher *always* enters after Mouth Wash finishes. I mean immediately after the punchline. Every time. And then everyone else in class has to hold in the laughter or the teacher busts them for "acting out." The teacher never enters when he's in the middle of the joke or even a second too early. Never. Sweetie unconsciously knew everything was going to be OK as long as Mouth Wash kept talking. That is why she was so comfortable having a conversation as they walked through the Valley of Death.

The "next thing" always happens *after* Mouth Wash stops. He isn't talking any more and that means "bad things" are now possible. Mouth Wash and Sweetie catch up to Darcy and SNAFU. The Marines and the rest of the Hunting Club are about 30 feet ahead of them.

SNAFU stares at Mouth Wash. "If you kiss her, I'll punch you in the head."

"And the ignorant shall cling to the past and complain that things are getting worse. And in their focusing on what they do NOT want, they shall create more of it." It isn't a quote from the Good Book but the way he says it makes it sound biblical.

SNAFU swings at Mouth Wash. Mouth Wash ducks. He doesn't have to be psychic to see that coming. Darcy steps between them, "This is not the time to fight each other."

The Marines, Crystal and the rest of the Hunting Club stand still. Darcy doesn't know why they stopped but she isn't going to yell to them. Then Sweetie sees it and breathes a sign of relief. It lies on the ground about 60 feet beyond Sergeant Killer. It's the red, orange, and yellow striped hot air balloon laying on the football field. It's a little crumpled, but it looks like it's laid out in an organized way. The basket sits upright.

Sweetie points, "There it is." *Good, something to look at. Something to distract the boys' so they don't focus on each other.*

SNAFU says, "I'm glad it's so bright and colorful — maybe the Space Spiders won't see it when it goes up."

Darcy laughs. Laughter on the battlefield is weird but good. Darcy laughs again and then snorts. A funny sound from an attractive young woman. It's also a little too much because what SNAFU said isn't THAT funny.

They see what she's looking at. It's Daisy, the big football player. Daisy is doing his 250+ pound, I-just-sacked-the-quarterback dance. He's happy they're so close to the balloon. Daisy's a big guy who dances with amazing fluidity. His outrageous moves leave the viewer inspired. When he does his dance during a football game, the crowd stands in the bleachers and dances with him. It's fun to see.

Nobody gave Daisy a nickname freshman year. Daisy got his name during the last football game of the regular season.

At the time, Daisy was just called 43. "Hey 43, looking good." He was called 43 because that's his jersey number. Not creative but safe. Nobody wanted to call him a name he didn't like. Nobody wanted to get their face broken. It was the fourth quarter of the game and Daisy hadn't sacked the quarterback yet, which is very unusual. The Center was a really big senior who had already signed a college deal with Ohio State University. Go Buckeyes! O-H. I-O. The Offensive Line was strong and kept Number 43 away from his quarterback.

There were only two minutes left in the game. We were up by one point. But, the other team, the Vikings, was on our 30-yard line and it was first down. Here's what that means if you don't know American football. The other team, the Vikings, the bad guys if you will, had a short distance to score a touchdown, which is six points (maybe seven if the kicker gets it through the uprights). If they score this touchdown, they will win the game, and this will end the hopes of *our* team winning a really big trophy, lots of bragging rights, and probably a bunch of chicks wanting to beso them.

The Vikings' coach calls a time out. Our team also huddles. Daisy is at the back since he has been neutralized the whole game. Neutralized in sports means ineffective as opposed to neutralized in war which means dead. Nobody thought Daisy was going to be the savior of this mess. Daisy slipped out of the huddle and walked over to the cheerleaders. It was Once-Over-Easy's Birthday and someone bought her flowers. Her name actually comes from her ability to flip on the field, not in bed. She has never had a boyfriend. Rumor is she's either focused on grades or she flips for her cheer mates, if you know what I mean.

Daisy grabs a bright yellow daisy from Once-Over-Easy's bouquet. The whistle blows. The time out is over. He breaks off the stem and hides the flower in his big hand. He returns to the line of scrimmage. Everyone lines up. He takes the Gerber daisy and puts it on his uniform. The Center with the promising college career looks at him and laughs. The offensive line sees the flower and laughs. The ball is snapped. Daisy plows the Center over because he's off balance. Daisy breaks through the line and hits the quarterback. The ball pops out and is recovered by Sticky, one of our rushers. Sticky runs down the field and scores a touchdown. Our team wins the game. Celebration and heavy petting ensue.

The story spreads fast. By the time our team gets to the locker room, our coach walks up to 43, shakes his hand, and says, "Nice play, Daisy."

Michelle dances with Daisy. She knows the Daisy Touchdown Grove by heart. She was on the football team freshman year. That is how she met Daisy. You see, when Michelle was born, her parents named her Michael, which made sense at the time because Michelle was born with a penis. Her parents were doing the best they could at the time. She certainly looked like a boy. It wasn't until much later that Michelle decided it was too painful to try to live like a guy even though she had a guy's body.

SNAFU and Sweetie also dance. Darcy hasn't learned the Touchdown Grove yet, but she dances. Mouth Wash rarely goes to football games. He says it doesn't make sense that people run into each other as hard as they can over and over again. The human body isn't made to handle that type of punishment. However, he has seen the Daisy Touchdown Grove at pep rallies and he does enjoy watching the cheerleader's version which is a little bit nasty. But Mouth Wash doesn't dance. He never learned The Grove and he's not in the dancing mood right now. Mouth Wash isn't talking. He knows what that means: the *teacher* is returning. Mouth Wash flips off the safety on his M4 machine gun.

There are two groups dancing on the battlefield. The advance squad made up of the Marines with Crystal, Daisy, Michelle, the Chip Brothers, B+, and Benji. The Marines don't know the Touch Down Grove so B+ and Benji teach it to the cute Marine. Crystal and Sergeant Killer are doing their own thing. More like dirty-dancing-twerking. The other two Marines do the Sprinkler and the Robot. The group that is farther back has three dancers: Darcy, SNAFU, and Sweetie. Mouth Wash isn't dancing. He's being a buzz kill. He's not shaking his cutie-booty nor is he thrusting to an imaginary beat. He scans the area. This sobers up Darcy, SNAFU, and Sweetie real quick.

Sweetie wants to hold Mouth Wash's hand again. Not out of friendship but out of fear. But she can't. His knuckles grow white from gripping his M4. Sweetie switches off her safety and breathes deep. There will be enough time for fear later.

The teacher *is coming back.* The coast looks clear even though something's not right. Maybe the teacher is already *in the room.* Sweetie realizes that she'd rather see the enemy. She taps her purse to make sure the extra magazines are still in it. She had to toss her foundation and blush to make room for the ammo. *Next war, bring a bigger purse.*

That's when Sergeant Killer steps on the Space-Spider-land-mind. In his defense, it's hard to see and no one was looking for it. No one was looking down. It was just a little mound, a little bump, a little speed hump with "white grass" on top. Who doesn't enjoy a little hump now and then? Not this one.

When he steps on it a Space Spider rises straight up underneath him. Dirt rains down. Sergeant Killer falls off the Spacer. Eight red eyes stare down on him. Sergeant Killer rolls and raises his machine gun, but the Space Spider grabs the Sergeant's leg with its fangs. He screams. The Space Sider flips the Sergeant like a pancake. It's not a gentle once-over-easy flip, it's a SMACK. Sergeant Killer is going to be served up bloody with a side order of crushed. Another flip and the sergeant's leg rips off. But he doesn't suffer because he's already dead. Sometimes you've got to be grateful for the little things.

Four more Space Spiders pop up from the ground. It's a trap! There are only five of them, but they have the element of surprise. The Spacers literally knock the teens and the Marines over as they rise from the dirt. One Spacer fangs Bender and rips him apart. So much for Yoga helping you live a long life. The humans can't act fast enough. Another Spacer sits on Benji and smushes him. Perhaps brutal payback

for all the Earth spiders that humans have stepped on over the years. B
+, with tears running down his face, blasts the Spacer that crushed
Benji. A Space Spider approaches from behind and hits B+ with one
of its long front legs. B+ flies, hits the ground and never gets up. He'll
probably still make a good coffin model. The other Marines shoot, but
they're too close to their targets. The Spacers attack.

SNAFU watches as a mound of dirt rises under Crystal. She drops
to her knees on the Spacers back. She's good on her knees. The Spacer
shakes. Dirt flies off, but Crystal holds tight. Her left hand grabs onto
the short and curlies, her right hand waves in the air. She looks like
she's in an alien rodeo.

There are six Space Spiders. Michelle pulls a grenade but before she
can throw it a Space Spider blasts Coco Bean with webbing, which
pushes him into Michelle. They get stuck together with the grenade in
the middle.

Coco yells, "Throw the grenade!"

"I can't."

"This is a shitty way to die."

Michelle looks for Daisy and finds him. He blasts his M4 in slow
motion. She smiles. Daisy sees her smile and smiles back until he
realizes it's not good. BOOM. Michelle and Coco Bean explode. The
webbing holds everything together except the human parts. That stuff
scatters.

Darcy, SNAFU, Sweetie and Mouth Wash watch in shock. The
Spacers are too close and too fast. Darcy says, "Hold. Our mission is
more important." Sweetie, SNAFU, and Mouth Wash are torn. Are they
just going to watch? Sweetie whispers, "No," but she holds her ground.

Crystal rides the Spacer. It can't throw her; when Crystal decides to
hold onto something, she usually does. SNAFU runs to her.

Darcy orders, "Stop!"

SNAFU doesn't stop. Darcy says, "They're dead! We've got a bigger
mission!" He keeps running. Sweetie and Mouth Wash look at Darcy.

"Damn it," says Darcy, "he's got the webbing and the crossbow."
SNAFU also has her heart. Darcy runs after him. Sweetie and Mouth
Wash follow.

Cute Marine opens up with his M4. A Space Spider bites off his head from behind. Not so cute anymore. His M4 keeps blasting. The Space Spider grabs the headless body and turns it so the M4 blasts the last two Marines, Robot and Sprinkler. The Space Spider tosses Cute-Headless-Marionette aside. Everyone in the advance unit is dead except for Crystal. It was a quick and painful ambush.

Only one Space Spider lays crumpled on the ground. The Marines had got it before they were taken out.

SNAFU runs to save Crystal. She holds on tight. Her free hand pulls out her nine-inch hunting knife and jams it into the side of the Space Spider's head. She turns the knife. Her Space Spider walks sideways bumping into the other Spacers, as if it's drunk. One Spacer tries to fang her. Crystal realizes if her ride drops, she will be easy-pickings for the other five hairy bastards. Crystal changes tactics. She doesn't want to bring her Spacer down. She stabs and cuts the back of its head.

You know when I say everyone in the first group is dead except for Crystal? Well, that isn't true. Daisy only pretended to be dead. He looks like a big speed bump on the ground. A Space Spider has to slow down when it steps over him on its way to the one-woman-alien-bronco-show. Now that everyone else is neutralized (see, sounds better than saying they're DEAD especially when you're talking about friends), the Space Spiders turn to Crystal and her Spacer ride.

The five Spacers realize SNAFU and the others are coming to save her. That's what the Space Spiders want. The Spacers stop trying to fang Crystal. They want their attackers to rush in. The Spacers realize the other humans aren't using grenades because of the one riding bare back.

Darcy orders, "Stop! They want us up close! Open fire!"

They are only 10 feet away. This time SNAFU listens. They all do. SNAFU drops his crossbow and the coil of webbing as he and Mouth Wash drop to one knee and blast. Darcy and Sweetie stand and blast, but they're too close. *Emotion on the battlefield will get you killed.*

Daisy, the big football guy, decides this is a good time to rejoin the fight. He was just playing dead. He rolls over and empties his magazine into the underside of the nearest Spacer. It collapses and dies. Daisy shoots a grenade from his M4's grenade launcher at another Spacer. At such close range, it enters the body of the Spacer with great force. Thumpft! It lodges itself next to Spacer's alien liver. Unfortunately for Daisy, it takes ten seconds for a grenade to go BOOM. Ten seconds is a long time when you're fighting a Space Spider. It's about seven seconds too long. It takes one second for the Space Spider to turn. It takes another second for it to charge. Daisy blasts the charging Spacer but one gun isn't enough. Fortunately, Darcy and Sweetie join him and blast the rushing Spacer. The Spacer goos, leaks, and screeches. It dies but its momentum carries the hairy invader toward them. It collapses on Daisy's legs. Daisy tries to push it off but can't.

"Grenade!" yells Daisy

"Where?"

Daisy points at the dead Spacer on top of him, "Next to its liver!" How Daisy knows that is anybody's guess. He's pre-med and loves science so maybe that has something to do with it. Darcy punches her hand into the dead Spacer that lays on top of Daisy. She fishes around and pulls her arm out. Her arm's gooey. The grenade is in her hand. She tosses it at the next closest Spacer. Darcy and Sweetie dive over the dead Spacer lying on top of Daisy just in time. BOOM. The grenade explodes in front of the other Spacer. No more fangs. No more head.

Three Space Spiders left. This includes Crystal's beast of burden. Crystal's ride turns so the other two can fang her. She's not going to last much longer. SNAFU can't shoot because he might hit her. Then SNAFU has an idea. Taking out the legs won't kill the attackers, but it may make the other Spacers shorter so they can't fang Crystal. He opens up. BAM. BAM. BAM. BAM. SNAFU cuts off four legs of an attacker as Mouth Wash rushes up.

SNAFU yells, "Come on, everybody's doing it." See, peer pressure can be used for good.

Mouth Wash blasts off the other four legs. Stubby drops to the ground. It's still alive but can't move well. SNAFU high-fives Mouth Wash. *Friends who blast together stay together*. Then SNAFU remembers that he doesn't like Mouth Wash.

One *standing* Space Spider left. It turns toward Sweetie and Darcy. They blast it.

Crystal cuts another whole in the back of the head of herSpider

289

ride. Goo splutters up. Her Spacer drops to the ground. It's dead. The last Space Spider turns from Sweetie and Darcy because they're too much trouble. The Spacer approaches Crystal now that she's easy-pickings. Crystal jams her hand into the back of the head of her Spacer and grabs its brain and spinal cord. Crystal pulls and her Spacer stands. This surprises the attacking Space Spider. Crystal yanks the cord again and her Spacer turns and hits the other Space Spider, knocking it over.

Crystal sticks her other hand into the back of her Spacer's head and pulls. Her Spacer's fangs open and close. Crystal shouts, "Look, I found the fang controls!"

Sweetie and Darcy's weapons go empty. Click. Click. Click.

Crystal tries to "drive" her Spacer forward to intercept the Space Spider going for her friends, but Crystal's Spacer walks backwards. "No, no. Forward not backward." Crystal looks at Sweetie and mouths, "Sorry."

Sweetie says, "Darcy, hoist me up."

"What?"

Sweetie laces her fingers together to show what she means. She wants Darcy to create a platform for one of Sweetie's feet so Darcy can toss Sweetie into the air. "Throw me in the air. Then you get that." Sweetie glances at the M4 with a grenade launcher on the other side of the last Spacer. Sweetie runs at Darcy. Darcy puts her hands together and bends. Sweetie puts her foot into Darcy's hands and Darcy tosses Sweetie. Sweetie goes high. It looks like she's in slow motion. Both arms and legs stretch as she reenacts her signature "starburst" cheerleader move. The Space Spider looks at Sweetie. *That's the plan.* Darcy rolls and grabs the M4. The Space Spider realizes it's been duped. It turns toward Darcy, but she's ready. RAT-A-TAT clickety-click-click. It's out of ammo. *Aw, come on.*

SNAFU and Mouth Wash pull their triggers but nothing happens. They're out too. SNAFU realizes he's going to watch his wife and friends die. The Space Spider lunges at Darcy. At the last second, Crystal's Spacer grabs the attacking Space Spider with its fangs.

Crystal pulls back on the fang-controls and her Spacer drags the attacking Space Spider backwards. It screeches and falls to its knees (if spiders had knees). Crystal's Spacer rips a hole into the other Space

Spider. Guts pour out and it dies.

Crystal walks her Spacer over to SNAFU and shows off. Her Spacer does some fancy footwork. SNAFU says, "It's a hybrid, part Spacer part human."

Crystal says, "It's more fuel efficient."

Crystal pulls something and her Spacer screeches. She does it again. "Look, I found the horn." She does it again, but the screech peters out. "I think I broke it."

Her Spacer crumbles to the ground, just like most of the guys who allow Crystal on top of them. Her Spacer gives one last shudder as Crystal rolls off and jumps up. She was a cheerleader in 7th and 8th grade. That's when she and Sweetie became friends. But Stubby, the Spacer that got its legs shot off, stretches out a nub and hits Crystal's foot. She trips and falls. She scrambles to get away.

Darcy grabs an M4, steps on top of Stubby, and blasts it in the head. BAM. BAM. BAM. Now, all of the surprise Spacers are dead.

Mouth Wash offers Crystal a hand up. She refuses. She stands on her own. I've never seen her accept help. Darcy and Crystal look at each other but neither of them say thanks.

SNAFU helps Daisy out from under the dead Space Spider. Daisy can't stand by himself; his right leg turns to the side. His football career might be over.

Sweetie pulls Crystal's knife out of the dead Space Spider's head. She gives it back to Crystal.

"Thanks."

"Nice ride."

Crystal looks at SNAFU. They hold each other's gaze for what seems to be a hundred years.

Darcy says, "I don't like it."

Crystal says, "Get use to it." Crystal thinks Darcy doesn't like SNAFU, her husband, still having feelings for Crystal. Crystal is telling Darcy, *SNAFU still loves me.*

Darcy turns to Crystal. "Relax. You two can have your *moment.* Don't be so immature."

Damn. Nobody calls Crystal immature. Crystal steps forward. Darcy doesn't back down.

Mouth Wash tries to diffuse the situation. He looks at the bodies of his friends, "I know what you mean. I don't like it either."

Darcy adjusts her bra strap. "No, that's not what I mean either." Darcy walks away from Crystal, which is more insulting then going head-to-head with her. Darcy pokes one of the dead Space Spiders with the muzzle of her gun. "They keep getting smarter and sneakier."

They hear something move. Everyone tenses and readies their weapons. Then, they hear coughing. B+ slowly stands. He isn't dead. He was just knocked out. Good-looking guys get all the breaks.

Then they hear, "Over here."

"There's a voice coming from under this one." Darcy and the teens pull on a Spacer. Benji crawls out. His right arm is at a crazy angle. Gross.

B+ says, "You lucky dog."

Benji says, "Shut up."

Darcy looks at Daisy and Benji. "These guys need medical attention." Everyone knows what that means. Somebody has to take them. Somebody isn't going to the balloon. Somebody isn't going to finish the mission.

B+ says, "I'll take them back. My head is ringing so loud I can't even think." It makes sense. He's the only guy that is big enough besides SNAFU that can support Daisy.

Darcy checks her magazine, slams it back in. She hands the weapon to Benji. He holds it in his good hand. Daisy leans against B+. B+ grabs Daisy's arm and wraps it around himself. B+ asks Daisy, "You good?"

"Yay, fantastic thanks." Daisy isn't used to leaning on others. He looks for Michelle. B+ says, "I'm sorry."

Mouth Wash puts a fresh mag into his M4 and gives it to B+. B+ says, "See you later." B+, Daisy, and Benji hobble away.

Mouth Wash looks at the other bodies. "What do we do about them?"

"We honor our friends by saving the planet." Darcy doesn't mention Prom. *Let's hope they didn't die trying to save Prom.*

Sweetie says, "Come on, we've got a balloon to blow up." Time to grieve later. Darcy leads. Sweetie looks at Mouth Wash and then looks at Crystal. Mouth Wash gets what Sweetie wants him to do. He'll hang back with Crystal. It's a good idea to put some distance between Crystal and Darcy.

Sweetie and SNAFU catch up to Darcy. They walk in silence. They're almost to the football parking lot and field. It looks like the hot air balloon is laying between the 20 and 30 yard lines.

Mouth Wash hangs back with Crystal. She says, "I don't need a babysitter." He doesn't say anything. He just smiles and nods. They walk in silence.

Crystal says, "You're looking at her."

"What?"

"You're looking at her Private First Class ass."

Mouth Wash wasn't, but he looks now. To be honest, he was probably looking at Sweetie.

Mouth Wash touches Crystal's arm, which is a definite no-no. She grabs his wrist and twists. Her right leg extends behind his and she pushes him. He falls backwards, tripping over her leg. He hits the ground hard. He forgot she knows karate. An overreaction on her part, for sure, but that's what Crystal does. Overreacts. She stops. She didn't mean to hurt him, but she doesn't apologize. *Nobody touches me.*

Mouth Wash doesn't let Crystal see him smile. *This is what he wants.* No, not to be on the ground hurting, this wasn't part of his plan, but the others keep walking and that's what he wants. He wants more space between Darcy and Crystal. It's time to settle things down, not throw gasoline on the fire.

Mouth Wash and Crystal have always been *friendly* toward each other. Not *friends* but *friendly*. He never makes cracks about her. There's no reason to hit a person when they're down. One time when they were on an overnight hunting trip, she climbed into his sleeping bag. Mouth Wash always thought it was just a mistake. Crystal was the only female to go camping with the Hunting Club. Nobody messed with her until SNAFU did.

Mouth Wash slowly gets up and brushes himself off before they start walking. "Yes, I've looked," says Mouth Wash. "It's a whole lot better then looking at all of the death and destruction around us."

"Guys are all the same."

"Yes, in that way we are. We like to look at females. It triggers something inside of us. It feels good."

"You disgust me."

"Answer me this." Crystal looks at him. He continues, "As we've been traipsing through this wasteland have you *glanced* at SNAFU?"

Crystal doesn't say anything. He grins a little, just a tiny bit. Not enough to be insulting. Just enough to say, "Come on, we're not that different." It also helps that his eyes sparkle. Not with meanness, but with fun.

He says, "Come on. Tell the truth."

She finally gives in.

"Maybe once." Her voice smiles but not her face.

"Just because a guy likes to make out doesn't make him a bad guy. There are a lot of good guys who like to wrestle."

"And, you're one of the GOOD guys."

"Of course."

She can't stop herself from smiling. Sweetie hurries back to them. She whispers, "Guys, come on. Hump time."

Mouth Wash and Crystal snicker. Sweetie looks at them, *what? Are you in fifth grade?* But Sweetie says, "Another Space Spider land mine. Pull yourself together."

Sweetie, Mouth Wash, and Crystal silently catch up to Darcy and SNAFU. Mouth Wash can't see it. He takes a step forward.

Darcy raises a fist in the air. Mouth Wash stops. SNAFU smiles. He knows what that hand signal means. Thank God for the movies.

Sweetie glances at the hot air balloon. She can see the deflated red, orange, and yellow balloon stretched out on the football field. *Is it still in one piece? Will it be able to fly?*

Crystal says, "I see it."

Mouth Wash looks left and right. There are no cars in the student parking lot, just webbed up tanks, turned over army trucks, and dead Space Spiders and soldiers. Mouth Wash asks, "They're under the parking lot?" Crystal grabs his head and turns it. The mound is about 12 feet in front of them *in the dirt* in front of the parking lot. Mouth Wash nods and takes a step back.

It's a little mound of dirt, easy to miss if you weren't looking for it.

White hair pushes up from the ground like short, albino grass.

Crystal says, "Do you see any others?"

Darcy raises her fist again, *stop, no talking*. Crystal rolls her eyes. Darcy motions everyone to step back behind a flipped over Jeep.

When they're in the safety of the Jeep, Darcy answers her. "We scanned the area. There is only one of them." SNAFU nods in agreement. Crystal thinks, *they make a right jolly team.* She doesn't know why she's thinking with an English accent. Their safeties are off. They're ready. They wait. Nothing happens.

Darcy says, "Ideas?"

Sweetie raises a grenade. Darcy nods. Sweetie pulls the pin. "One, two, three … " She lobs the grenade underhand. It lands in front of the Space Spider mound and rolls right up on top of it and stops. Nice. Sweetie's an expert at Corn Hole. You know, that yard game where you toss and slide beanbags into a hole in small wooden ramps. The white-haired volcano mound erupts into a Space Spider. The grenade remains perched on its back. It looks right and left for its prey. Then, it spots the teens behind the upside down Jeep.

Sweetie stands and makes the peace sign, "Peace."

The Space Spider hesitates. BOOM. All of its innards blow straight down to the ground. The Space Spider looks underneath itself at its own guts. Then it makes a sound, something like, "Huggggghh?"

Sweetie leans over to Mouth Wash, "I should have said *pieces.*" Mouth Wash gets it. Witty. For some reason Crystal doesn't like Sweetie joking around with Mouth Wash. Crystal realizes she's jealous. She likes the feeling and doesn't like it at the same time.

The legs of the Space Spider buckle. Its body drops and it meets back up with its guts, but it's not the same. Everyone is on high alert for another jack-in-the-box Space Spider. Silence. Nothing else happens.

Darcy says, "Alright, let's get that balloon up."

The jeep they're hiding behind shakes.

Darcy turns to SNAFU, "Stop that."

"I'm not doing it."

Crystal looks under the jeep and watches as a Space Spider lifts it. "Spacer!"

Crystal rolls away from the jeep. The jeep slides off its back and pins Darcy, SNAFU, Sweetie, and Mouth Wash to the ground before they can scramble. They aren't going anywhere. SNAFU hits his head which knocks him out. Dirt rains down on them as the Space Spider stands in all its glory. The Space Spider looks at the four friends trapped by the Jeep. Mouth Wash's leg sticks out. The Space Spider walks toward his leg.

Sweetie yells, "Pull your leg in!"

"I can't. I can't move it."

The Space Spider gets closer. It's fangs do a happy fang dance.

Crystal calls, "Hey, big guy, over here."

The Spacer looks at her. She sits on a tank about ten feet away. The tanks tracks are all webbed up, it's not going anywhere. The top hatch is open behind her. Both of her hands are behind her back. She holds a grenade, which no one can see.

"They're trapped," says Crystal as she bats her eyes. "They're not going anywhere. Don't you want desert before you have lunch? It's me you want to feast on." Darcy rolls her eyes.

The Space Spider walks toward Crystal. She pulls the pin from the grenade behind her back. She drops the grenade into the open hatch behind her. The Spacer charges her. She scrambles over the hatch and jumps off the back of the tank.

The Space Spider scurries over the tank after her. The grenade explodes. The blast shoots straight up out of the hatch. The blast catches the left side of the Spacer taking off four legs as well as a chunk of its abdomen. The Spacer slides off of the tank and plops next to Crystal. She put a machine gun to its head.

"I wish I had my chemistry goggles."

She closes her eyes. Sweetie closes her mouth.

Click. *Really? Out of ammo?*

Sweetie yells, "Run, Crystal run!"

Crystal doesn't need to run, it only has four legs, but Crystal does need to move. The Space Spider drags itself toward Crystal. Don't get me wrong; the Spacer is going to die soon. The question is, is it going to die before or after it kills Crystal?

Crystal steps back and smirks, "I will call you 50 Percent." She taunts the Spacer as it pulls itself toward her. "Look a discount sale. Space Spiders half off." 50 Percent lunges for her and grabs Crystal's boot with its mandibles. She under estimated it. Fangs ready to … Crystal's other boot stomps on the Spacer's face. Crystal falls and scrambles away. 50 Percent continues to drag itself with its four good legs toward Crystal. It leaves a trail of goo behind it. Crystal spots another machine gun near the tank. Because 50 Percent only has legs on one side, it starts to turn itself around. Stupid Spacer. Crystal grabs the machine gun and stands in front of the tank. 50 Percent is now completely turned around and *faces away* from her. "You're facing the wrong way." Crystal hesitates. She doesn't want to shoot it in its back.

That's a mistake. Even though part of the abdomen is gone, 50 Percent shoots webbing. The blast of sticky stuff hits her and plasters her against the tank. The machine gun sticks to her oversized camouflage shirt. Crystal can't move herself or the machine gun. The weapon is stuck to her chest and she's webbed to the tank. *It wasn't facing the wrong way, it turned around on purpose.* 50 Percent turns back around with its four good legs and drags itself toward Crystal.

Darcy, Sweetie, and Mouth Wash try to push the Jeep off them, but they can't get the leverage they need. Darcy claws for her M16, but it's out of reach. Sweetie grabs her gun, but the tank blocks her shot of 50 Percent.

The Space Spider screeches a victory cry that's almost a laugh. Crystal pulls on the gun but it's stuck to her. And, she can't get away because she's stuck to the tank. 50 Percent gets closer.

Crystal says, "Hey, I saw your four legs back there. You might want to use some of your sticky-tack to put them back on. You know, before the flies start eating them. You eat Space Flies all day long and now Earth flies are eating you. You know what that's called? Karma. You sow what you reap."

I have no idea if there are Space Flies, but I wouldn't have said anything if I was there. When Crystal starts getting crazy, you just shut up and hope her rage doesn't come your way.

50 Percent looks back at its four legs on the ground. One twitches. Flies buzz around the gooey parts. The Space Spider screeches again.

Crystal struggles with the oversized camouflage shirt. She pulls both her arms into the shirt. The arms and sleeves of the shirt are still webbed to the machine gun, which sticks to the tank. She tries to push the gun free but the webbing is too strong. She can't get the gun to point at 50 Percent.

50 Percent raises the stub of its front leg. Goo drips onto her shirt, machine gun, and webbing.

Darcy shivers from the sight. Disgusting. She pushes on the Jeep again.

Both of Crystal's arms are still inside her shirt. She wiggles around and then her arms shoot back out the sleeves of the big shirt. This time each hand holds a Glock. She can't straighten her arms but she turns her wrists. Both handguns point at 50 Percent.

"Stupid Space Spider."

BAM. BAM. BAM.

Rounds rip apart 50 Percent.

BAM. BAM. BAM.

Chunks of exoskeleton fly away revealing Spacer brain.

BAM. BAM. BAM.

Chunks of brain explode leaving an empty space.

BAM. BAM. BAM.

The wounded Spacer drops. Crystal pulls both arms in toward her body again. She bends her legs and wiggles down and out of the large shirt. The oversized camouflage shirt and machine gun remain webbed to the tank. Crystal wears a camouflage tank top, which shows her strong muscular body. #motivation

Something moves behind her. Crystal raises her Glocks and turns with lightening speed. Both guns are now just inches away from Darcy's face. Adrenalin pumps through Crystal's body.

"Whoa whoa whoa," says Mouth Wash. "She's a mammal."

Crystal doesn't lower her handguns, "You were going to leave us. You said we were all dead."

Damn, Crystal has good hearing. Darcy doesn't flinch. Mouth Wash slowly lowers Crystal's arms till the guns point at the ground. Mouth Wash says, "Nice guns."

SNAFU rubs his head as he joins everyone. He looks at Crystal's tank top as he says, "What I miss?"

Crystal looks at Darcy, but motions to SNAFU, "What's going on between you too?"

SNAFU doesn't say anything. Darcy says, "I'm SNAFU's wife."

Crystal laughs. "Right, and I am Sweetie's lesbian lover."

Crystal turns to Sweetie. Sweetie nods yes. Then Sweetie clarifies, "I mean, yes, they're married, not yes we're same sex partners. But you know that already."

"Since when?" demands Crystal.

"This morning," says Darcy.

"Nice day for a wedding, partly cloudy with a chance of arachnid," says Crystal. "A day you'll always remember. Something borrowed, something blue. Like, I blew its brains out of its head."

Crystal walks over and kicks 50 Percent. It's better than kicking SNAFU. Nobody stops her. She kicks the dead Spacer again. Goo spurts out. It's best to let her burn herself out. Crystal holsters one of her Glocks in the front of her jeans. She grabs Darcy's hand and turns it over revealing SNAFU's High School ring on her wedding finger.

"I bought you that ring," says Crystal.

"Only half," he says.

Darcy and Crystal look at him.

"OK, two thirds," says SNAFU.

Darcy says, "You didn't tell me that."

SNAFU doesn't reply. *Anything you say can and will be used against you in a court of love.* Darcy takes the class ring off and hands it to SNAFU. She walks away.

Crystal turns to SNAFU, "You've got big freaking fingers. How'd you ever make that ring fit her tiny, pretty hand?" Darcy stops walking and turns.

Sweetie touches Darcy's shoulder, "Come on. Chevy and Roy are getting ready to blow the school. We've got to get that balloon up."

Darcy turns to Crystal, "We wrapped band aids around the ring so the opening would be more my size." Darcy says, "Why do you care so much?"

Crystal says, "Let's make this official. Hi Ms. Meyers. I'm Crystal, SNAFU's girlfriend."

"Girlfriend?" Darcy looks at SNAFU. He doesn't say anything.

Crystal continues, "Well, I guess I'm actually his ex."

Darcy asks, "Since when?"

"This morning. I suppose we officially broke up when you two got married."

Darcy looks at SNAFU again. This time she waits for an explanation.

SNAFU says, "We had been growing apart for a while."

Darcy shakes her head and walks away.

Crystal still has a Glock out. She waves it around. SNAFU's eyes dart between the gun, her shirt, and her eyes. Sadly, she always catches him looking at her shirt. He says, "I was going to text you, but the whole Galactic Cord thing happened. I didn't want to make your morning any more difficult."

"What? You afraid us breaking up would be too much for me? That I'd end my life because you're leaving me? Don't flatter yourself."

Crystal holsters her second Glock. SNAFU relaxes. He never thought she'd end it all if he broke up with her. He was just afraid to tell her. Crystal waits for him to say something but he doesn't.

Sweetie puts her arm around Crystal, "Come on Lover, let's walk it off." Crystal lets Sweetie guide her away from SNAFU.

Mouth Wash walks to SNAFU. "You've had a full day."

SNAFU smiles, "That went better than I hoped. Nobody is dead or bleeding."

"And when you say 'nobody' you really mean *you're* not dead or bleeding."

SNAFU slaps Mouth Wash on the back. "Yes, that's exactly what I mean."

CHAPTER 32

POWER UP

ROY AND I ARE inside our school. I've never been so happy to be *inside* our school. I lean against the door we just slammed shut. It's quiet. The outside war is muffled. The lockers on both sides of the hall stand at attention, awaiting orders from high school students that will never return. BAM. Scar Face slams itself against the door propelling me onto the floor. It screeches at us through the door and then leaves. I attempt to stand, but a pain stabs me in my belly. I fall back down.

"What? You drunk?"

"Aaaaaaawwww. My stomach."

Roy kneels next to me. "Are you hit? Did you get fanged? Next time, when you jump, you've got to pick your feet up higher."

Don't tell me how to jump Spacers. But I'm in so much pain I can't talk. "Aaaawwww." He rolls me over and moves my hands off my stomach.

"Chevy, I don't see any blood." A loud rumbling noise comes from my gut. He says, "Is that you?"

"I think I'm hungry."

"What?" Roy stands. "Get up!"

"It's been two days since I ate."

"You are such a wuss."

I slowly stand and take a step, but I double over again.

Roy walks to a row of lockers. He raises the butt of his gun and smacks a combination lock. He hits it again and again. The lock jumps off and shoots down the hall. He goes through the locker tossing out books and a Knights sweatshirt.

"What are you doing?"

Roy smacks open another locker. He rummages around and pulls out a small apple and tosses it to me. I've never seen one so small. I don't complain. I eat it.

"Protein. I need real food."

Roy smacks another locker, this time showing mastery. One hit and the lock sails off in the direction of *my head*. I duck. Roy pulls out books, folders, and a flute case. They fall to the floor. He's having fun now. He finds a brown paper bag.

"Winner winner chicken dinner." He pulls out a sandwich. "Looks like turkey."

He tosses the sandwich to me. I pull it out of the baggie. *Yes.* I take three large bites. Then I smell it. Awwwwww. I spit it out, but it is too late. I throw up. Barffffffffffffff. It isn't that big of a deal. The only thing that comes up is three bites of sandwich covered in tiny apple chunks.

Roy says, "I guess you've got to refrigerate something like that."

I just lost all my energy points. Roy smacks another locker. "OK, looking for chilled protein. The end of the world is always a good time to start getting picky. Perhaps something gluten free?"

The locker door swings open. He unzips a red backpack and pulls out a sandwich. He sniffs it, "Peanut butter and jelly. These don't need ice." He tosses it to me.

I sniff it.

"Almond butter."

"What, you don't like tree nuts? Shut up and eat it." I eat.

Roy throws me two more things. "Applesauce cup and a bag of trail mix."

I don't ask for a spoon. But I hesitate. Applesauce is what just came up. I read the expiration date.

"Chevy, eat it!"

I pour the applesauce into my mouth. I throw in a handful of trail mix. I chew.

"Come on," says Roy.

I don't get up. It takes a few minutes for the food to hit my stomach, blood stream, and brain.

"Chevy, come on."

I feel better. I start thinking again. It's true. Glucose assists thinking especially during stressful times. I see the stairs at the end of the hallway. *That's right.* Down the hall, down the stairs ... we're close.

I stand. Yes, full energy level. I'm ready. I pick up the red backpack Roy tossed on the floor. I put the bag of trail mix in it. I'm not leaving the food behind. I put the backpack on. "We'll take the stairs at the end of the hall. Let's go."

"Been waiting for you, Princess."

Sweetie! I finally get a moment to think about something besides surviving. Maslow is right. When you're on the bottom of the pyramid, you've got to take care of the basics first. I have to believe she's OK. I have to think everyone is OK. Any other thought will just suck the energy right out of me.

Roy and I walk down the hall. I feel much better. It's nice that the majority of my barf didn't land on me. We turn a corner. The hall is clean. The custodians must have spiffed up the place the night the moon cracked. I guess nobody told them it isn't important to scrape gum off the floor when the world is ending. I look around. *This is the last time I will walk down these halls.* The school is going to blow up or I'm going to die trying. Or, perhaps both.

We walk past the Chem Lab. A desk falls over inside the classroom. Roy and I freeze. He flips off his safety.

"You open the door and I'll blast."

"Roy, what if it's a freshmen that got locked in somehow."

"If it's human, I say we don't kill it."

"Good idea, Roy."

I didn't know about the Space Spider ambush so I didn't think this was a trap. Unlike Space Spiders, humans can only telepathically communicate one-to-one. You know, like when your friend texts you right when you think of them. But if a Spacer experiences something, it seems like their whole race "learns" it immediately. But things are changing for us humans. The 20th Century gave us social media which allows us to "group communicate" almost instantly. Our grandparents had to "group communicate" through newspapers and TV and the flow of information was only one way. Perhaps the 21st Century will give us the time to develop our abilities to "group learn," and experience "direct knowing" —you know, the ability to just KNOW something *without* the need of learning it. Maybe these will be the benefits of us being Indigo and Crystal children—or whatever they're calling us nowadays. That'll be cool.

We hear another noise in the Chem Lab as something moves around. I try the classroom door. It's unlocked. I open it. A glass jar hits the inside of the door pushing it closed. CRASH! The container was filled with water. I know because the liquid seeps under the door and into the hallway. Roy taps his boot in the growing puddle.

"Chevy, this doesn't smell like water."

Then another glass SMASHES on the inside of the door and flames flare up inside the room. Flames also shoot out under the door into the hall. The liquid is not water, it's highly flammable something. The flames in the hall surround Roy.

I yell, "Get out of the liquid."

"I'm trying to, but I'm on fire!"

I grab the fire extinguisher off the wall. Roy stomps and splatters flames onto nearby lockers. Flames jump.

"Stop that!"

"I'm on fire!"

His pants are on fire. *He's packing heat.* I blast his legs and boots with foam. I lather up the floor, the lockers, and everything around the door putting out the flames.

"Damn it. Look at my boots."

"Give it a rest about your footwear."

Roy checks his camouflaged backpack with the C4. It's OK. Then we hear a kid scream from inside the Chem Lab. "Don't leave me. I don't want to burn to death."

Roy says, "He's the one that threw the fire bomb."

"Tell him, not me."

Roy yells at the door. "You're the one who threw the fire bomb!"

"Help me! Help me!"

I say, "Just because he's stupid doesn't mean he should die."

"Are you sure?"

Am I sure it's important to save *this one particular* moron? I don't know about that. But what I'm thinking is he's human and right now we may be heading for extinction so it might be wise to save everyone we can.

I look at Roy until he reluctantly sighs. "OK, we'll save him," says Roy, "but next time someone does something really dumb we let them die."

I step back and Roy kicks in the door. We feel a blast of heat. Flames everywhere.

I yell, "We're human. We're human." I don't know how stupid, scared, or dangerous this kid is. When all three of these are combined in one person, it's sometimes hard to make good things happen.

A tall kid cowers at the far end of the room against the classroom windows. He wears big safety goggles and a breathing mask. Flames jump around him.

Roy steps back from the heat. "There's no way one extinguisher is going to put that out."

He's right. There's too much fire. I can't see the tall kid's face. The goggles and mask covers his eyes, nose, and mouth. He holds two large glass beakers filled with water, one in each hand. That isn't enough to put out the fire either.

I yell, "I'm going to make you a foam path. It's the best I can do. As soon I do, put DOWN the beakers, and come out. DON'T run; it'll be slippery."

I spray a path from the burning doorway toward him. I spray until I run out of foam. I back up but Beaker Kid runs straight for me before I'm out of the way. I told him NOT to run. And, he doesn't put down the beakers. I told him to PUT DOWN the beakers. *Idiot. I'm not signing his yearbook.* I try to get out of his way. I almost fall. The foam's slippery.

Roy tries to see around me. "What's happening?"

I yell, "Get out of the way!"

But it's too late. Beaker Kid hits the foam path and slides towards Roy and me. That's when I realize the liter-sized beakers he holds aren't water; they're another batch of Insta-Flame. If the liquid in those beakers mix, we'll be "neutralized" by a big ball of fire. I swear, if people just listened to me, life would be a lot easier.

We try to get out of the way, but we slip and slide. Roy elbows me in the jaw. My fist hits him in the stomach. The Tall Kid moves toward us, arms swinging with the beakers of liquid death. One beaker aims for Roy's crotch, the other for mine. All those good people dying out there, and I end up trying to save this loser.

Beaker Kid wears a shirt and tie. *That's no kid, it's Mr. Damerstain.* I should have figured. Damerstain. A Damn Shame of a teacher. A STAIN on humanity. Mr. Damerstain is the Chemistry Teacher that gave me a D+ in my Junior English Lit class last year. He was filling in for Hoops the regular English teacher who was stupid enough to get himself hurt playing basketball with the varsity team. Old people need to learn their limits. The D+ that Damn Shame gave me cost me two months of allowance. Money I would have put toward my car a.k.a. "Project Freedom." What a jerk. I told Damerstain that if I get a D that I'd lose my allowance. He could have given me a C-, but instead he gave me a D+.

Idiot.

I told him I CAN'T get a D and he gives me a D+. *Hello, a D+ is still a D.* Mr. Per-i-o-DIC Table. He told me that I didn't ask for a C- that all I said was that I didn't want a D. He said, "I'm teaching you a valuable lesson. It's really important to be clear and ask for what you want in life."

What an ass.

He yells, "Get out of the way."

"Turn! Turn sideways!" I yell. He turns so the beakers move just in time. I stick out my arms. I need to slow him down. Maybe he won't end up Catching Us On Fire. I don't think we'd look as good in flames as Katniss.

Roy manages to get OUT of the way by grabbing my shoulder and pushing me toward the teacher. *Thanks, Roy. I owe you one.* Damerstain SLAMS into me. I crash into the lockers. The beakers don't spill or break. *That's good.* Damn Shame stands as I crumble to the floor. I can't breath, but we're alive.

Roy says, "Are you OK, Mr. Damerstain?"

Damn Shame gives the beakers to Roy. Roy holds them far apart. Damn Shame pulls off his goggles and face mask.

"I'm OK." He wipes the foam off the rest of his face. "Roy, isn't it? So good to see you. Thanks for saving my life."

What an idiot. He looks at me. "Who are you?"

Nice. He screws me over with the grade, I save his life, he credits Roy, and he doesn't even know who I am. I step out of the foam as I try to breath. I want to say something, but I think of Mouth Wash, *the time for talking is over.* Something REALLY big crashes through the Chem Lab classroom window. Shattered glass and chunks of wall explode, throwing bricks out of the classroom door into the hall. We duck. Through the open door we see a Space Spider in the still burning classroom. Oh, geez. The Spacer stands amidst the flames and sees us through the burning doorway.

I have a feeling that's exactly what hell looks like. An evil, angry Space Spider surrounded by fire. Then I realize this isn't just *any Spacer*. Half of its face is burnt and blackened. Scar Face has tracked us down. Oh, man. This is the same Space Spider that chased us into the school building. It doesn't want to kill us on principle. It's personal.

Scar Face picks up its front leg and points at the burning ceiling.

Roy says, "What's on the ceiling?"

"It's not pointing; it's flipping us off. It's giving us the leg."

All we have left are our handguns. We don't have the firepower to fight. Scar Face smiles. Fangs twitch. Damn Shame freaks out and shouts, "They're everywhere. They've surrounded the school. Don't worry kids, I'll protect you."

What?!

Damn Shame takes the two beakers from Roy. I look down the hall; I can see the stairs leading to the basement.

"Come on, run. We need to get down the stairs." No one moves. I add, "Now!"

I'm asking for what I want and I'm being clear. Dame Shame doesn't move toward the stairs. *Idiot. I can't believe I helped saved the one freak that can screw all of this up.*

I touch his arm and speak slowly, "Put down the beakers and run to the stairs with us."

He doesn't move. He's not taking orders from me. He turns to Roy, "Do you have a plan?"

Roy gives him the most confident, "Yes, sir," that I have ever witnessed. Maybe it's the uniform, but Damn Shame relaxes, his eyes tear up with joy and confidence. Then Roy says, "We're going to the basement to blow up the school."

Damn Shame starts to shake so badly the beakers knock together. I reach for them but he yells, "Get your hands off my boomy chemicals." I make a mental note. When you're with a guy who's really scared, don't tell him you're going to blow up the building he's hiding in.

Scar Face webs out the fire that surrounds the door. Mr. Damerstain freezes. Sometimes it's not a good idea to confront your fears. Scar Face is the size of a small elephant.

Roy says, "Don't worry, it can't get through the door."

As soon as Roy says it, I know it's getting through the door. The reason Roy is always wrong is he thinks he's an expert. I pull Damerstain toward the stairs but he won't budge. He watches in horror as the Space Spider lowers itself onto the foam runway and slides itself toward the door. It scoops up foam and rubs the foam on itself.

"It's trying to make itself fireproof," says Roy.

"No. It's making itself slippery."

Two front legs reach through the door. Dame Shame whimpers but the Spacer isn't trying to grab us, not yet. Scar Face grabs the doorway and pokes its head through.

I say, "Come on. Let's go." But we don't move.

Two more legs come through the door. Scar Face wiggles, four powerful legs pull its body through the door but its abdomen catches. It's too big. Maybe Roy's right, even all foamed up, it's still too big and can't get through. *Yes, it's stuck!* Damn Shame smiles. Roy slaps the teacher on the back. Foam shoots off of Damn Shame and hits me in the face. Then, as if to prove Roy is an idiot, Scar Face wiggles again and pulls itself through the door. A big "round peg," with force and foam CAN fit through a small "square hole." My dad's right. When someone wants something and is willing to do the work, they can usually accomplish it.

Now we move. We run toward the stairs.

The wet-dog of a Space Spider crawls into the hallway and shakes the foam off. We get to the stairs and look back to see if we can make it down the stairs before we die. But Scar Face and Damn Shame are not with us. I assumed he was right behind us. It's not rocket science. Big, hairy alien wants to eat you, you run. But it's only Roy and me at the top of the stairs. Scar Face and Damn Shame are still in the hall by the classroom. Damn Shame holds out his arms. The beakers are between him and the burnt Spacer. Damn Shame backs away until he hits the lockers. He looks down, avoiding eye contact with the Spacer's eight eyes.

"Shoo shoo shoo."

Roy says, "Is he trying to shoo it away?"

I look at the pack that Roy carries. I look at the stairs. We're pretty close to accomplishing our mission. Maybe we should leave him.

Roy misinterprets my glances, "I can't use the C4. Scar Face is too close to Mr. Damerstain and if those liquids mix ... "

I yell, "Damerstain, come on! Keep the chemicals between you and the Space Spider and keep thinking fire. They can read minds. You can make it to the stairs."

Roy says, "They can read minds?"

"I'm pretty sure they can."

"What if they can't?"

"Then Damerstain dies."

"Chevy, that's not very nice."

"Do you think his odds are better standing there hoping it will go away?"

Roy yells, "Mr. Damerstain, do what Chevy tells you to do!"

Damerstain says, "I can't make it."

My dad always says *our word is law* in *our universe*. If *you say* you can't do something, you can't. If *you say* you can do something, you can.

I yell, "If you think you can't make it, you can't."

"I'm going to die!"

Scar Face grabs and punctures Damerstain's head with its fangs. *Yup, he was right.* I'm glad I'm at the end of the hall so I can't see the yuk. He was a waste of a human, but that's still a hard way to go. I realize why my Dad would "bite my head off" whenever I'd say I can't do something. My old man was just trying to help me. Just trying to save my life.

Damerstain's body doesn't fall. It's too soon for rigor mortis, he must be leaning against the lockers. And he must have been so scared that his body locked up even though his head is no longer useful. Scar Face looks at us. I glance down the stairs. They're wide. Twenty kids can go up and down at the same time. There's more than enough room for a Space Spider to scurry down and fang us from behind. We have three flights to descend. Space Spiders can move pretty fast. I don't think we can beat it to the basement and survive.

Roy says, "Come on, let's make a break for it."

"No. It's waiting for us to make the first move. We've got three flights of stairs. We're not going to beat it."

"What do we do?"

"We wait."

"Wait for what?"

"An idea."

"How long is that going to take?"

"I don't know."

"Chevy, that's not comforting."

"Roy, do you believe this is possible?"

"What? Making it down the stairs alive?"

"No. I'm talking about winning. Do you think beating the Space Spiders is possible?"

"Yes, I do. This is our planet. They don't belong here."

"Good. If we think we can do this, then we'll see the opportunity that will present itself."

"How long will that take?"

"You already asked that."

"Oh."

I see the beakers in Damerstain's hands. In slow motion, his arms begin to drop. They're going to hit the floor and mix. Scar Face will go up in flames. Yes, the old fart is going to save our lives. *Thank you, Mr. Damerstain. You may be a terrible human being, but you're an awesome chemist.*

Roy moves toward the stairs.

"Don't. We need to keep Scar Face next to Damn Shame."

The Space Spider looks at me and then at Damerstain. It looks at the beakers.

I say, "Stop thinking."

"What?"

"Oh, did I say that out loud?"

Scar Face turns away from Dame Shame. The ex-teacher's arms lower. *Stupid Spacer, you're going up in flames.* The beakers will drop! But webbing shoots out of the Space Spider's butt. The webbing pins Damerstain against the lockers. Both of his arms lock in position. The beakers are *not* going to fall. Scar Face is safe.

I tell Roy, "Blow it up."

"I can't. I only have one detonator. If we use it here, we can't blow the school."

"That's a damn shame."

"Chevy, was that the idea you were waiting for?"

The Space Spider screeches at us. "No, that isn't the idea I was waiting for." I smile and pull my sidearm, "*This* is the idea I was waiting for."

I raise my Glock and take aim.

Roy says, "You can't kill it with a pistol."

"Yes, I can."

BANG. I miss the Space Spider. I hit Damerstain in the chest. A small red spot shows through his white shirt.

Roy yells, "You shot Damerstain!"

"Shut up, he's dead."

The Space Spider walks toward us.

"Come on Chevy, let's go!"

"No, if we don't run, it won't chase us."

"Chevy, you can't kill it if you can't hit it!"

"Yes, I can."

I shoot again. I hit the beaker in Damerstain's right hand. It shatters. The liquid splashes onto the floor and runs under Scar Face.

"You're going for the beakers."

I shoot again. The other beaker explodes. Dame Shame bursts into flames. The flames run under Scar Face. Flames engulf the Spacer. I love chemistry. It's now my favorite subject. Scar Face screeches and scurries toward us.

"Run!"

We haul down the stairs, two and three steps at a time. We leap down a flight of stairs. We don't look back. In the corner of my eye, I can see a big ball of fire chasing us. Second flight of stairs. I feel intense heat behind me. Red and orange lights dance in the stairwell. I smell burnt hair. Roy and I jump again. We hit and roll onto the next landing. Stairs are hard. One more flight to go. Burning fangs reach for us. We grab the railing and leap over it crashing down onto the last set of stairs. Scar Face scurries behind us. We tumble down the last bunch of stairs. We're in the basement, but we're hurt. We can't stand. Scar Face rounds the last landing and crumbles down the last set of stairs behind us. We manage to roll out of the way as Scar Face crumples into a heap of smoking, charcoaled flesh at the bottom of the stairs. It doesn't move, but we get up.

Suddenly, Scar Face stands and lunges at us. Roy and I fall backwards. Its fangs stop moving and it drops. It's dead.

We catch our breath. "Come on. Let's blow this popsicle stand."

CHAPTER 33

THE FAULT IS IN OUR SPACERS

MOUTH WASH RUNS FAST and in good form. Head straight. Arms pumping. Breathing steady. His eyes focuses on something in the distance. *He looks where he's going, not where he's been.* Mouth Wash is on the track team and has learned how to run. He focuses on an abandoned Channel 5 news van. Mouth Wash is fast so it's no surprise that he gets to the empty news van first. He throws open the back doors and tosses out a few chairs.

"Come on, you can make it!"

He watches them and hopes they'll make it. It will be really lonely if they don't. Two Space Spiders chase Darcy, Sweetie, Crystal, and SNAFU. His friends have a good lead, but the Spacers are gaining on them.

"Damn."

They had to run AWAY from the balloon. Not a smart move, logistically, but sometimes you've got to do what you've got to do. The two Spacers came in fast before they were able to find enough ammo to make a stand. It was run or die. Sweetie spotted the news van. Darcy said run. It's not a tank, but it will have to do. It's funny that they think a tank will keep them safe.

Sweetie and Crystal speed up and pass Darcy. I believe Darcy lets them pass her. Darcy leads even while she's falling behind.

SNAFU catches up to Darcy. They run together. Darcy tosses him a grenade. "Something borrowed."

He catches it and smiles.

Mouth Wash urges Crystal and Sweetie forward, they're almost there.

The two Space Spiders are about 50 yards (about 45 meters) behind Darcy and SNAFU. The humans still have another 45 feet (about 16 meters) before they reach the news van. The Spacers close the gap.

SNAFU pants, "How you doing, honey?"

"Better now that we're talking."

SNAFU nods. Marriage is a long journey. The odds of surviving are small. *It's a good thing I got a warrior to do it with. We might just make it.* Darcy looks over her shoulder.

"Pull your pin, but don't throw it."

Darcy and SNAFU pull their pins.

"Wait for me."

"Always."

Darcy smiles at him and then gets serious. "I'm serious, wait."

SNAFU mutters, "Dear God, this woman's gonna teach me patience."

"What?"

"Nothing." The Spacers get closer.

SNAFU says, "Honey, you still holding your grenade?"

"Not yet."

"Now?"

"Not yet!"

Crystal gets to the van before Sweetie. Mouth Wash is inside waiting for her. He says, "Give me your hand."

Crystal ignores him. She runs to the front of the vehicle. She looks around and grabs an M4 off of the ground and slings it over her shoulder. She steps on one of the front wheels and then pulls herself on top of the van. She lays prone on the roof and starts to shoot at the Spacers catching up to SNAFU and Darcy. Each round hits one of the Spacers in the head.

Sweetie ducks as she jumps into the van next to Mouth Wash. Sweetie doesn't trust her aim enough to shoot past her friends with a gun she only started using *today*. Or was it yesterday? She's good, but that seems too risky.

Sweetie yells, "Come on! You can make it!" *Once a cheerleader, always a cheerleader.*

The first Space Spider gets very close to the married couple. SNAFU says, "How about … "

"Not yet!"

"I love you."

"Not yet!"

"Honey, I think we …

"On my mark, throw it straight up five feet. Wait for it. Mark!" Darcy and SNAFU toss their grenades into the air.

Mouth Wash and Sweetie climb back into the van and raise the M16s they found. They're ready to help as soon as they get a shot.

Darcy and SNAFU still have 20 feet before they get to the news van. The Space Spiders gain on them. The first Spacer lunges for the newlyweds as Darcy's grenade comes down first. BOOM. The grenade explodes next to the Spacer. The explosion doesn't kill it, but one leg flies off and the force of the BOOM knocks it into the second Space Spider. The second Space Spider trips on the first one. SNAFU's grenade lands right behind the second one. BOOM.

Good News: SNAFU's grenade blows off the abdomen of the second Space Spider. It isn't dead but will be soon.

Better News: The force of the second grenade forces the second Spacer into the first one. They are now a tumbling mess of fangs, hairy legs, and goo.

The Not So Good News: The force propels the 1.5 Space Spiders into Darcy and SNAFU. Sweetie watches as her friends get tangled in the rolling ball of aliens.

Sweetie yells, "Crystal, hold on!" The boulder of humans and Spacers is going to CRASH into the van.

Sweetie and Mouth Wash close the back doors just in time. Crystal leaps off the van as the mixed-up ball of Spacers and friends hits the van. It's a HARD hit, the whole van shakes. Sweetie and Mouth Wash throw open the doors and jump out. The ball has broken apart. Darcy, SNAFU, and the Spacers lay dazed on the ground. The question is, blast the Spacers or help your friends? Mouth Wash grabs SNAFU. Sweetie runs to Darcy. The half Space Spider, the one without the abdomen, reaches for Darcy with its fangs. Sweetie grabs a leg from the other Spacer and puts it in front of Darcy. The Space Spider bites its friend. The other one screeches. The half Space Spider releases its comrade and tries to stand. Half-er falls back down. I guess that's what happens when you lose your ass.

Darcy and SNAFU get into the van. Crystal comes around the side and blasts the Space Spiders, causing them to hesitate, but she knows one gun is not going to win against 1.5 Spacers. Not at this range. Crystal jumps into the van. Mouth Wash and Sweetie slam the doors shut. It's pitch black. Everyone hears SNAFU pant. Sweetie finds the light switch. Lights go on and everyone watches SNAFU pant.

Darcy kisses SNAFU. He kisses her back. Crystal clears her throat and spits onto the editing console in the back of the news van. "Funny, with everything that's happened today, that's what I'm going to see in my nightmares."

Mouth Wash shhhs everyone. It's quiet. Suddenly a Space Spider bangs against the van.

Mouth Wash says, "I wish this was a tank. If it was a tank we'd be safe." *Ya.* The Space Spider hits the van and it almost tips over. Crystal flies into Darcy.

Crystal presses against her, "Excuse me."

"Sorry."

Crystal says, "Don't be, it's not your fault."

They aren't talking about bumping into each other. It's nice they're being friendly. SNAFU looks at Crystal pressed up against Darcy. Perhaps they could ALL be real friendly. Perhaps ...

Crystal shakes her head at her ex. Darcy looks at SNAFU, "Don't get any ideas."

Mouth Wash pulls Crystal off of Darcy.

Two fangs pierce the metal roof and purple venom pumps out of the fangs and squirts onto the floor. Everyone stumbles backwards. SNAFU's hand touches the luggi Crystal spit on the edit bay. Gross. He wipes it on his pants.

Crystal grabs one of the fangs and holds tight. Sweetie grabs the other one. Purple venom continues to shoot out. Crystal and Sweetie stick their machine guns to the roof of the van.

Sweetie says, "I always liked you."

"I always thought you were a little too clean, but you're alright."

They pull their triggers. RAT, A TAT TAT. TAT A TAT TAT TAT. Right through the roof of the van. The van stops rocking. The venom slows to a drip, drip, drip and then stops. Sweetie lets go of her fang.

Crystal punches the roof of the van. "Drained you!"

No one moves. No one knows what to say. Darcy turns to Crystal, "You've got anger issues."

Crystal laughs. "Sister, you have no idea."

Darcy says, "You might be surprised."

Crystal and Darcy share a moment. Maybe they aren't so different. Maybe Darcy is just a little bit older and has healed some of her childhood trauma. Maybe instead of an enemy, she could be a sister-guide-mentor. Maybe.

Everything is quiet.

Darcy picks up a pair of dark sunglasses off the floor and holds out her hand. "Sweetie." Sweetie gives Darcy her M16. Darcy nods to Mouth Wash. He opens the van doors. Sunlight streams in. Everyone covers their eyes except Darcy. She raises her M16 and surveys the area. She jumps out of the van. "Secure." SNAFU, Crystal, and Mouth Wash squint and climb out. They look at the dead half-Space Spider.

Sweetie stays in the van. Mouth Wash turns to her, "Come on, they should be in the basement now." Sweetie doesn't jump out. She attempts to smooth her Prom dress, but it's ruffled, ragged, and ripped. It's a mess. *Prom is dead.* She looks at the battlefield. There's nothing but death all around them. She wants to cry, but she isn't going to. Not now.

She glances at a white T-shirt hanging on a hook by the edit bay. She holds it up. There's a picture of a pipe on the front of the shirt with the French words Ceci n'est pas une pipe, under the picture is the translation: *This is not a pipe.* Sweetie puts the shirt back. *I can't do anything French right now.* She looks down and sees something under the console. It's a pink colored gym bag. Sweetie smiles. She says. "Give me a moment." She closes the van doors.

CHAPTER 34

GETTING DOWN IN THE BASEMENT

THE FLUORESCENT LIGHTS GIVE the place an eerie feeling. So many pipes run back and forth across the ceiling. I'm at the top of a ladder. I use an oversized wrench to loosen a big-ass nut. Roy tosses the backpack aside and molds the C4 into a familiar shape.

"Look what we're going to do to the Space Spiders." He moves it up and down.

Really? After what we just went through? But I can't stop myself. "Mine is bigger."

"We'll see what Sweetie has to say about that."

If I kill him now, do you think anyone will find out?

Roy says, "It's nothing personal, Chevy. You're not giving her what she needs." Roy moves back and forth. I push and pull on the wrench as I grit my teeth. *My – rage – must – be – chan – neled – into – the – task – at – hand.*

"I'm going to call mine C4," says Roy, "because it goes off with a BANG!"

With a final burst of energy, the wrench moves. I did it. A few more turns and we'll have all the gas we need to blow this sucker. Now I've got to wait for Roy. He's a lousy partner. Sweetie and I are always one right after the other. "Come on, Roy."

Roy cracks the fuse box lid, but can't get it open.

I say, "Easy, gentle."

"Sometimes you've got to be a little rough to get the job done."

"Yeah, no doubt, but there's a difference between rough and abusive." I wonder if I should have a stop word with Roy.

Roy shoves the C4 into the opening between the fuse box and the wall. "It won't all fit. What do I do with the other half?"

I bet he's never said that before.

Roy says, "I hope we don't get in trouble for blowing up the school."

"We won't if we save the world."

"I'm going to rewire the electrical system so when … "

"Roy, don't do anything fancy just … " A fuse POPS. Roy falls down. *Did he electrocute himself?* He doesn't move.

"Roy, get up. You can die later." Roy rolls over and moans. I can't believe how happy I am. He holds up the other half of the C4. It's flattened. "Oh man, I smushed it." The fuse box sparks and pops again. We duck.

"You're lucky I didn't open up the gas yet."

Another POP, SPARK, and ZAP and the lights go out. We're in total darkness.

"Nice work, idiot."

The emergency lights come on. The red glow is spooky, but it's enough so we can see. This is my red room of pain, but it's not as much fun. Now that we have no electricity, I figure it's safe to let the gas out. I turn the end of the pipe some more and the end falls off. Gas hisses out. I put my face close to a red emergency light and make a crazy, villainous laugh. "Ha ha ha." Then I start to cough and can't stop. *Air, I need air!* I fall off the ladder and roll. I grab the camouflage backpack and press it against my face. I try to use it as a breathing mask to filter out some of the gas.

Roy says, "Stay down. I'll … " Cough, cough, cough. He jams the rest of the C4 around the fuse box and shoves in the remote fuse. He grabs my arm and we stumble out of the basement.

We almost trip over the dead Spacer at the bottom of the stairs. I'm hoping for fresh air, but all I get is the smell of burnt hair and charbroiled alien meat. We climb the stairs. Returning to the main floor is a lot easier then getting down. I almost toss the camouflage backpack, but then I have an idea. I take off the red backpack I'm wearing and transfer the trail mix to the camouflage pack. I eat another handful first. I put the camo pack on. Red is to flashy. And besides 'm a spring not a fall. I jest. I have not idea what my colors are.

I figure we'll take a detour past the teacher's offices and then we'll exit the building the same way we entered. I haven't learned yet that you can't go back. Perhaps that will be something I'll learn at our 20th high school reunion. Of course, the reunion will need to be held offsite because in about 20 minutes there will be no school to return to. And, of course, I'm assuming that we'll stop the Space Spiders, or, I suppose, we could have our reunion at a Space Spider farm with Emperor Roy as our host. Man, that doesn't sound like fun.

We make our way to the side door. I avoid stepping in my apple and turkey barf. The door is all webbed shut. *Thanks, Scar Face.* We can't open it. There is no need for it but we draw our guns. Fear can make you do that.

Roy says, "I don't like sneaking around. I'd prefer a face-to-fang fight."

I look at him, *why are you acting tough?* "Shut up and follow me. I've got an idea on how to get out of here."

We run down a different hallway so we won't have to see and smell the burnt Chemistry teacher. We turn again. The only lights in the hallway are the red exit lights. It's empty and quiet. About every thirty lockers is a classroom door with a skinny window. Daylight shines from these skinny windows and stabs into the darkness of the hallway.

We dash through each pool of light as we run down the hall.

Roy runs into a water fountain that sticks out between lockers. He falls; his gun slides down the hallway. I pick it up and give it to him. Roy is Not Rambo.

I say, "The box. You still got it? Is it OK?"

"Thanks for your concern about ME." Roy holds up the detonator. "It's fine. I got it."

I push a classroom door open. It's bright in the classroom. Someone has spray painted "School Suc" on the window. It's written backwards, but we can read it.

About twenty yards past the painted windows and hedges are the sand volleyball courts. Beyond the volleyball courts are the second practice field and woods. *That's where we're going.*

Something moves in the hedges right outside the window. It's a plump, pale sophomore. The teen looks at the woods beyond the volleyball courts. He wears a flannel shirt over a blue T-shirt with a Lunch Box on it. *But you know that already and you know what's going to happen to this kid.*

I make my way to the window. The teen stumbles out of the bushes and makes a run for the woods. He's a big kid and doesn't run well. Webbing hits Lunch Box and drags him across the sand court. The teen struggles out of his flannel shirt. The flannel shirt gets pulled under the volleyball net and off the court by the web line.

Lunch Box runs in the opposite direction but stops before he gets around the back of the building. A Space Spiders blocks his way. At first, it looks like the Spacer isn't going to eat him because the teen is not a threat. But Lunch Box sprays the Space Spider and yells, "Wolverines!"

The Space Spider screeches and fangs Lunch Box. The kids screams. Lunchtime. There's nothing we can do. We're too far away with too little firepower.

Roy says, "Well, that's what you get for defacing school property." *Idiot.*

Roy and I run down the hall looking for another way out. We look through classroom windows, but Damn Shame is right, the school is surrounded by Space Spiders. We aren't going to be sneaking out a window even if we could. Technically getting out is not the hard. The challenge is not getting ripped apart after we leave the school.

Roy runs into the men's restroom. "I've got to drop the kids off at the pool."

I scan the hall as I wait. It's quiet. Our high school is pretty big and like a big maze. I expect to hear the click and whirl of a creeper. Then I notice the teachers' offices are just down the hall. I get an idea.

Roy comes out of the restroom into an empty hallway. He freaks out and starts screaming, "Chevy! Chevy!" All he gets in return is silence. He yells again, "Chevy!"

I step out of Ms. Meyer's office and he almost shoots me.

"Whoa! It's me!" He settles down and lowers his weapon. I say, "Were you scared and lonely? *Did you miss me?*"

"Shut up," says Roy.

We run down the hall and get to the front doors of the school. We approach the doors quietly. "This is not going to work," says Roy. He's right, there are about 500 Space Spiders outside between the school and the Web Wall. And, more keep coming.

Roy shakes his head, "I'd much rather die having sex."

"Is that an option?"

"OK, what if we don't blow the school and we just wait it out here?"

I unlace my shoes. "What do we wait for? Nuclear bombs? Do you think they have something that will take out them but not us?"

"Maybe the military and Orkin are working on something like that."

"You still think someone is coming to save us?"

Roy kicks his boot against the wall. Burnt Spacer and dried foam flake off.

I take off my second sneaker and kick it to the wall near the first one. "No. We're not little kids any more. Waiting and hiding is not an option, not if we want to get what we want. We're old enough to get involved. We're going to get on the other side of that Wall and when we see the balloon go up we're going to …

"IF it goes up."

"WHEN it goes up. They're working on it right now. Sweetie and SNAFU are very persistent. And WHEN it goes up, we're going to be there to help." *No more whining. No more complaining. No more wishing things were different.* The time for feeling sorry for ourselves is over. We didn't create this situation, but this is what we've got. It's time to take action. More and more action until we create what we want or until we're dead. I don't say all that out loud. All I say is, "Shut up, Roy."

I turn so he won't see what I'm doing. I pretend to be studying the Space Spider situation out front, but I put my hand over my heart. I inhale. I exhale. I try to remember what Darcy said to us in that Prom meeting. I need to hear that *still, small voice* inside me so I know what to do. I should have paid attention. My shoulders relax. It's much easier to be creative when I'm calm. I say to myself, "We're smart kids."

"Don't tell me to shut up."

I smile, but not in a mean way. Of all the things to get upset about, he chooses that. And, I'm pretty sure I've already told him to shut up about 100 times today.

"Wipe that smirk off your face," says Roy. "No one tells me to shut up."

"I apologize. I shouldn't have said that." This is not the time to fight with the guy you're working with. But geez, now he's sensitive. I guess we all have our limits.

Sometimes you have to be humble when you lead. Leaders don't tell people what to do. I mean, they do. But ideally, leaders evoke a desire and commitment from others to follow. You know, follow the leader. Good leaders have a mission and they inspire others to get out of their gaming chairs and take action. It's time to inspire.

"Seriously, Roy. I shouldn't have said that. Look how far we've come. It's pretty amazing."

Roy says, "Shut up."

So much for inspiration. Roy looks out the window at the Space Spiders. "What are we going to do?"

"We're going to blow the school and detach that Galactic Cord from Earth. We're going to help SNAFU take the Cord up so the hairy babies stop coming down to this blue-green jewel of ours."

"How are we going to do that?"

"We're going to be ready for the opportunities that present themselves.

"That means you have no idea how this might work."

"There are always opportunities present."

"What if there are no opportunities?"

"There are ALWAYS opportunities" I say. "We will see them if we expect to see them. We'll know it here," I touch my head "and we'll know it here," I touch my heart.

Roy shakes his head, "I don't think that's going to work for me. I pretty much just take orders from here," he touches his groin. "And, my weenis is saying there's NOT a lot of opportunities out there."

"Did you know your weenis is actually the extra skin on the end of your elbow that allows you to bend your arm?"

"Really? I thought it was just a cute name I came up for my ..."

"I get it. And, we just need one."

Roy says, "Of, course we just need one. Especially, if you got one like mine."

"I'm talking about opportunities not your ... we don't need *a lot* of opportunities. We just need one. They come by all the time. Most people are not looking for them so they don't see them or they're too scared to act."

"I'm not scared."

Bullshit. We're all scared." But I don't say that. Instead I say, "All we need is one chance."

"You're talking about sacrificing ourselves to save everyone."

I didn't mean to bring that up right now, but that's what I'm thinking. But even if *that* type of sacrifice is needed, this isn't the time or place to discuss it. *Stay present, Chevy. Focus on what needs to be done right now.*

"Roy, I need your help. I invite you to be bigger than you think you can be. This is your time. This is our time."

Roy looks at me as if I'm talking Chinese. He says, "Relax Chevy, I'm not going to die. I would disappoint too many women."

I almost laugh. But then I realize he's not joking. I'm glad I didn't laugh. I turn and pretend to cough. *He is a BIG idiot.* He looks out the front doors at the horde of Space Spider troops. He says, "We're going to die a slow and painful death."

"That is NOT a positive focus."

Roy opens the front door and points at the Space Spiders. "How the hell are we going to get past 1,000 Space Spiders?"

"Shut the front door!"

I pull Roy back into the school. The door closes. Luckily the Spacers look toward the battlefield preparing for world domination.

And, there aren't a thousand of them: 500, maybe 600 tops. Roy is scared and exaggerating. Sometimes people need to hear a concrete plan before courage kicks in and and they can buy into doing something stupid. "I have a plan." I'm about to tell him, but he continues to whine.

"How are we going to get to the other side of the Wall without a pair of fangs jamming into our eye sockets and eating our brains?"

"They're Space Spiders, not zombies," *as if one is better than the other.*

I unbutton my shirt and unzip my pants. *I wonder who would win in a fight? Space Spiders or zombies?* Roy looks at the shoes I kicked off and then at me. He realizes I'm undressing.

"Chevy, what the hell are you doing?"

I come back to the present moment. Action, not words. *The time for thinking is over. And the time for talking is over.* I throw my tux shirt at Roy. It hits him and falls to the floor. I'm glad I'm wearing a white, classic, tag-less tank undershirt. The last thing I want bothering me is a tag at the back of my neck in the middle of battle. I say, "I have a theory."

Roy steps away from me. "I am not going to have gay sex with you even if we're about to die."

I take off my pants. I'm glad I'm wearing boxers. It's good to let the boys roam free. "Good," I say. "Because if you were listening, I said I have a THEORY. I didn't say I have a ... " BOOM. A jet soars over the Wall and crashes in front of the school. The main building shakes.

Roy says, "Are those Christmas boxers?"

I look. Yup, little red and green mistletoes with "Kiss Me" written all over. Sweetie got them for me last year.

"Is taking off your clothes one of the opportunities that's going to save the world?"

"It is, if it works. If it doesn't, it's just an embarrassingly bad idea."

"How is stripping going to help?"

"My idea is based on two things. They can read minds. Which I know you don't fully buy, and that Space Spiders are planning to be here for a while."

"At our school?"

"No, I mean Earth."

"How do you know that?"

327

"I don't."

"So your plan is founded on something I don't believe and something else you don't know? Your ability to inspire and evoke courage sucks."

"They're planning on being here for awhile because I don't see them preparing an exit strategy."

"That's stupid. If someone watches me when I go to a party they'd never say, Roy's planning to be here forever because I don't see him looking for the door."

"When you go to a party, do you go around punching everyone?"

"That would be stupid."

"Why?"

"Because I just got to the party and I want to stay …"

"Exactly."

"But the Space Spiders are 'punching everybody.'" He does the invisible quote signs in the air with his fingers. Roy means *ripping off heads and worse.*

"Not everyone." I continue, "They're not going around and killing all of their food on the first day of their pilgrimage. Or, if you want to continue the analogy, on the first day of their party. That would be stupid. I believe they're only killing whatever fights back."

"And they KNOW when somebody is going to fight them?"

"Right. Lunch Box was fine until he fought back." FINE might be a strong word.

"Who is Lunch Box?"

"The kid on the volley ball court."

I take off my socks. Roy paces. He takes the magazine out of his handgun, looks at it and then pops it back in. "I get it. You mean they can read minds like they have a spidey sense?"

"Yes, exactly.

"That makes total sense."

For a moment Roy and I share a moment. *I'd rather not connect with him while I'm in my boxers.* I click my fingers remembering. "Olecranal skin. That's the official name of the extra skin on the end of your elbow. It's called the olecranal skin."

"Who cares?"

I pick up my sneakers and put them on.

Roy says, "If we're almost naked, they won't see us as a threat."

"That's right. Come on and don't take any weapons except the detonator. We can't be seen as hostile."

"What about the goat? They didn't ignore the goat."

What goat? Then I remember unwrapping the little fellow and its awful bleating.

"That goat was very annoying. Don't be annoying."

Roy gives me the finger.

"And, they didn't kill the goat. They just wrapped it up for later."

"That's comforting."

"Come on, they should be filling up the balloon right now."

Roy looks out the front door at the Spacers. "I still don't see how we're going to get past them?"

"With joy," I say, "Now hurry up and get undressed."

"That's what your mother and sister said to me last night."

CHAPTER 35

SEE ME

SNAFU CROUCHES NEXT TO the hot air balloon basket. The basket lies on its side now. The balloon looks like a beached whale with a red head, an orange middle, and a yellow tail. It's rising but not straight up. Sorta like when Sweetie had me read parts of *Fifty Shades of Grey*. SNAFU read the entire Grey trilogy but never told anyone, not even me. I knew he read the books because I saw *Darker*, in his backpack between his world history and geometry books. He also said, "Laters Baby," for about a month instead of his regular, "See you tomorrow, Squirrel."

One day I said, "Laters Baby" to Sweetie.

"Are you reading *Fifty Shades*?"

"What?" I had no idea what she was talking about. Then we read some sections together. That's when I learned women folk could be just as adventurous as us guys.

One day, during art, I decided to bust SNAFU's chops. I held up my drawing and said, "Do you think Christian Grey would hang a picture like this in his place?"

I took him by surprise. He pointed at my drawing and said, "I like your border." You see we made an agreement not to mock each other's work. We agreed to only say what we *liked* about each other's art. That compliment was as close to an insult as I was going to get.

Ten minutes later he said, "Do you think it's possible?"

I know how slow SNAFU's brain works so I figured we were still discussing Christian and Ana. "Well, I've been reading that working women have to be in control a lot more in their life, so sometimes they may want men to be in charge and ..."

"What are you talking about?" he said.

"I thought we were talking about whether it is possible to find a woman who likes blindfolds and handcuffs."

"No, that's not what I'm talking about," said SNAFU. "I find women like that all of the time."

What? Where? I don't share *everything* Sweetie and I do with SNAFU, but I didn't think he was keeping secrets.

"What I'm asking," said SNAFU, "is do you think it's possible for a woman to love a guy so much that she helps him heal? You know, like Ana did with Christian? So that he isn't so *dark* anymore?"

I hadn't really read the books for the plot. I only read some of the special parts. I didn't know there were meaningful character arcs between the freaky couple. But I did say, "I think that's the journey of all human relationships. To love each other so much that the other person changes how they see *themselves,* so they can heal from their past."

I was surprised I said that in the middle of class, but it just came out. I would probably say it a little bit different now, but I didn't have time for a rewrite. Real life doesn't afford that. I thought SNAFU was going to make fun of me, but he didn't. He nodded his head and went back to his drawing. He said, "That's nice. You've got a good brain inside that head, Squirrel."

I laughed. The teacher shhhhh'ed us.

Another burst of flames shoots toward the opening of the balloon filling it. The sound is loud, but can be talked over. SNAFU holds the switch and more flames push hot air into the balloon. The red, orange, and yellow bulge gets bigger. Mouth Wash is on one side of the balloon opening and Crystal is on the other. They pull the ropes, which centers the mouth of the balloon so the flames and heat shoot inside it. They pull hard and remain steady so neither the balloon nor themselves get burned.

It passes the half-full mark. The big red, orange, and yellow-stripped beached whale comes to life. It can't be more exposed and vulnerable.

Crystal looks at Mouth Wash. "This is taking too long."

Mouth Wash takes a quick glance at Crystal's body.

"Did you just look at me?"

"Yes, I did."

SNAFU stops so they can have a conversation. Crystal yells at him, "Keep filling it." SNAFU bursts more flames.

Crystal yells at Mouth Wash. "Get away from me."

Mouth Wash yells. "I'm all of the way over here."

"That's not far enough. You're disgusting."

"No, I'm not. I'm normal. You're the one messed up."

"You did NOT just say that!"

"I'm not going to apologize for being alive. Do you not feel safe near me, or do you not feel safe generally?"

Crystal crosses her arms in an attempt to protect herself.

"I know stuff happened in your past. I know you don't trust men."

"Who told you?"

"No one. But I'm not stupid. My question is, do you feel unsafe with *me* because of *me*, or do you just feel unsafe with *me* because you feel unsafe around *all guys* ... that aren't gay? I'm not gay."

"I know that, stupid."

"I need you to see me for who I am, not who you think I am," says Mouth Wash. "Am I giving off a dangerous vibe?"

"You like me ... and that's dangerous."

"Am I a threat to you?"

She wipes tears from her face. "I don't know."

"What?"

"I don't know!"

Mouth Wash softens, "I'm sorry. It's not my intention to make you feel unsafe, but you're beautiful, both your body and your spirit. I'll try and leave you alone."

She turns so he won't see the tears run down her face. She whispers, "No, don't do that." But he can't hear her over the roar of the flames.

Three Space Spiders amble toward the front red part of the balloon. Darcy and the teens don't see them approach because the balloon is so big. The Space Spiders aren't in a rush. They seem curious. The first Space Spider touches the balloon with it's front leg. It pushes the balloon down. The Space Spider removes its leg and the balloon regains its shape. The Space Spiders laugh. What fun! The second Space Spider does it. More screechy laughter. The third one is just about to jump on the red part of the balloon when it hears.

"Hey!"

The Spacers are caught off guard.

Darcy and Sweetie come around the side of the balloon. Darcy still wears her Private First Class uniform. Sweetie now wears the sports top and yoga pants she found in the pink gym bag.

Darcy waves her gun. "Back up."

The Space Spiders take a couple of steps back. SNAFU stops filling the balloon. Crystal and Mouth Wash hold the ropes that hold the balloon steady, but they glance at their nearby weapons.

Sweetie keeps her eyes on the Spacers and yells, "SNAFU keep filling it." SNAFU flips the switch. Flames roar and hot air shoots into the balloon. Crystal and Mouth Wash shift from holding their ropes with two hands to one hand. They lean and pick up their weapons.

The Space Spiders turn to Sweetie and Darcy. Fangs twitch. No more giggles and laughter. Darcy readies her M4, and readies the grenade launcher, but doesn't raise it. The Spacers are really close to the balloon. She's gotta be careful.

Sweetie turns to Darcy. "I got this." Sweetie walks toward the Spacers. She keeps her weapon pointed down. The Space Spiders look her up and down. She rocks the new outfit. She waves her hand in a "back-up back-up" gesture. The Space Spiders take a step back. Sweetie steps between the balloon and the Spacers. She draws a line in the dirt with her foot. She steps away from the line toward the hot air balloon.

It's right behind her. She points at the line with her M4.

The first balloon-poking Space Spider approaches the line in the dirt. Sweetie takes another small step back from the line and bumps into the balloon. Balloon-Poker crosses the line with its front leg. Sweetie raises her M4. The Space Spider screeches. It doesn't like being threatened.

Darcy yells, "Hey! Back up!"

Darcy raises her M16 just a bit. Balloon-Poker withdraws its leg.

Sweetie says, "Easy Darcy, don't be a threat." Sweetie leans toward the Space Spider. "Hey you, Balloon-Poker, come here."

Darcy says, "Sweetie, what are you doing?"

Sweetie ignores her. She leans toward Balloon-Poker and whispers, "Psst, you, big guy, come here." Sweetie knows all guys like to be called big. The Space Spider looks at its two comrades. *What do I do?* The other two Space Spiders shake their heads. They're clueless. Balloon-Poker moves closer to Sweetie, but makes sure it doesn't cross the line. Sweetie smiles, "Me and my friends. We'll be a tasty treat *after* you conquer this rock. But, if you kill us, we'll be stale and yucky by the time the battle is over. We're not a threat to you right now."

Darcy gently pulls Sweetie back. "Get away from them." Sweetie steps away from the Space Spiders.

The second Space Spider taps Balloon-Poker on the back. Balloon-Poker jumps. It turns and hits the second Space Spider for startling it. The second Space Spider points to the battlefield. Balloon-Poker steals one more glance at Sweetie and then nods in agreement. The Space Spiders run off to join the war.

Darcy pats her M4. "Laters, Baby."

SNAFU blasts more hot air into the balloon. Darcy and Sweetie look at each other and laugh. Then they quickly look around to make sure nothing is sneaking up on them.

Darcy walks to SNAFU. "You OK?"

"I'm fine. Who would have ever thought it takes forever to fill a damn balloon." He pulls hard on the switch. Flames erupt. Hot air blasts into the opening urgently, violently. The balloon shifts and another fold pops out. The bulge gets bigger. SNAFU grabs Darcy. They kiss each other.

Crystal turns, unable to watch.

Mouth Wash says, "Hey, Crystal, remember when one door closes, God opens a Mouth Wash."

"Is that supposed to be funny?"

Darcy says, "That just creepy."

Mouth Wash nods. "Yah, it sounded better inside my head. I tried the heartfelt approach and that didn't work so well so I thought I'd try the humor approach."

Crystal looks at him. "How do you know the heartfelt approach didn't work?"

"Did it?"

"How many approaches do you have?"

"How many is it going to take?"

She smiles. She's beautiful when she smiles. "Do you have a slow approach?"

"My least-liked approach. But for you, I'll give you the special Prom Day Slow-Approach Special."

Crystal smiles. She is beautiful.

Darcy pats SNAFU on the butt and walks over to Sweetie.

Sweetie says, "Chevy's right. They can sense threats. I also think that when one of them learns something they communicate it to everyone else, maybe instantly. They don't just learn from THEIR experience, they learn from ALL of their experiences. That's how the newbies know about us. These guys are fresh out of the egg, but they know that an assault on humans who are ready to fight is not going to be easy especially if we're equally numbered and not afraid."

Darcy adds, "I wish humans were able to do that. Instead we have to take history classes and 'learn' from books, which are written by the winners and the people in control. We learn a tweaked version of what happened. Our thoughts and emotions are manipulated so that our behaviors and actions, or lack of them, are influenced."

Sweetie studies Darcy, "You're a lot darker then I thought."

"Why do you think I went out of my way to seek the Light? You know, nobody from Alabama accidentally ends up in an ashram in India for 6 months."

SNAFU flips the switch and more flames burst. Crystal and Mouth

Wash tug on their ropes. Mouth Wash smiles at her. She blushes. SNAFU sees this. He nods and gives them the thumbs up. Crystal gives SNAFU the finger.

Darcy readies her walkie. "I'll let the General know we're in place and tell him what we're planning to do. I'll request air support to knock off any parts of the school building that remains attached to the end. I think this will give the balloon a better chance of lifting the Cord out of the atmosphere."

Darcy looks at Sweetie. This is it. Darcy is breaking a direct order. She and her team are either going to be heroes or are committing treason. When you're in the armed forces, it's not a small thing to "do what you think is best." Sweetie hugs Darcy. Darcy is grateful for the silent support. Darcy walks away from Sweetie for privacy.

Sweetie takes Crystal's rope to relieve her. Crystal rubs her hands and readies her weapon. She walks around the basket and stands next to Mouth Wash. She doesn't face him. They are back to back. They are close enough to talk but they don't. Small steps. The slow approach. The fighting out on the battlefield continues. Jets zoom overhead. Every 30 seconds four more come down the Galactic Cord.

Crystal doesn't look at Mouth Wash but says, "You think this is going to work?"

"I don't know."

"I thought you could sense things."

They continue to look in opposite directions. They pretend to be keeping a lookout for other Spacers.

"I can," says Mouth Wash. "But when I'm next to someone I'm really attracted to, my desires sometimes screw up my intuition."

"You're cute." Crystal steps backwards so her butt bumps into his. "I like this approach."

"I love this approach," says Mouth Wash. "This is now my most favorite approach ever." Crystal laughs.

Darcy returns. She holds the walkie away from her. Sweetie hears the General scream. Everyone hears the General scream.

"That is a direct order, Private! You and your crew STAND DOWN, right now! Do you understand me?! Is that clear?!"

Darcy motions to SNAFU, to cut the flames, she needs to hear the

General. *Or, is Darcy obeying orders?* Sweetie looks at the balloon. It's almost ready to stand on its own. It just needs a little more help. It could be big and impressive. It could be successful. It could be.

Darcy whispers to Sweetie, "I need you to hold for me."

Sweetie looks at the rope in her hand, "Darce, I am holding."

Darcy smiles. This is the first time Sweetie called her Darce.

The General says, "PRIVATE. Are you there? Do you understand me?"

Darcy lowers the walkie. She lets the General scream. Darcy looks at Sweetie. "What I mean is I need you to hold WITH me. I need you to look at me and remember we're strong. I need you to remember that we're powerful. I need you to remember what we're fighting for. Let me *see you*, the real you. I'm going to use you to help me be strong."

Sweetie nods. "I get it. I can hold for you." Sweetie stands tall and strong. Darcy feels her strength.

Darcy picks up the walkie. "Sir, I mean no disrespect and I know this sounds crazy, but it's my experience that it's usually the younger generation that comes up with the crazy ideas. Sir, don't shut us down. How many nukes do they want to drop?"

She holds the walkie away from her head. The General yells, "Private, when is the last time a General ever explained battle plans to a Private while in the middle of a war? We're going to drop as many as it takes!"

Darcy's eyes remain on Sweetie. "That's my point, Sir. The first one will take out the high school and the latch site. Not to mention a good part of Pennsylvania and West Virginia, killing men, women, children and livestock and making the soil worthless for growing crops."

The General says, "War sucks, Private."

Darcy says, "But that's not the worst part. The Earth will turn and the Cord will be dragged across the United States. The Spacers will keep coming, four of them every 20 or 30 seconds. They will be distributed across the United States, until the Cord gets to the ocean."

"That's the plan. Let them drop in the water."

"What if they can swim?"

"We'll take our chances."

"Are you going to follow them across the country with more

nukes?"

"That hasn't been decided yet. Probably not. It depends if we have the firepower to neutralize them as they land."

"What if there are more then you can handle?"

"We'll do what we need to do."

"Sir, the Earth will start rotating again. The Cord will be dragged to other countries."

"Then the Space Spiders will be their problem."

"Sir, that's short sighted. If they take over South America or Europe they will make their way here. It may take time, but they will.

"We'll take our chances."

"And the Earth will keep turning and if they keep coming down the Cord they will come right back to the United States. What are you going to do, drop nuclear bombs all over the country?"

"We'll take our chances."

"Sir, that's not good enough. You're taking chances with our future. Permission to speak frankly."

"No!"

"Sir, your plan sucks. If the Space Spiders don't kill everyone, humans will. I ask that you listen to the next generation. Don't shut us out. It will be our chance soon. We have ideas and courage. We've got energy and passion. Support us and we'll surprise you."

Darcy and Sweetie listen for the General's reply. There is no reply. Darcy points to Crystal and waves her over. Crystal takes the rope from Sweetie. Sweetie whispers, "Thanks. Keep filling the balloon. We're going to walk over there because Darcy needs to hear the General."

Darcy and Sweetie walk away from the balloon. Crystal gives SNAFU the head nod. SNAFU flips the switch; flames burst again.

Sweetie whispers to Darcy, "What did he say?"

"Nothing. He either hung up or he's thinking."

"You're doing great," says Sweetie. "Give him everything you've got."

"I did."

"No you didn't. Don't hold back. The time for holding back is over. It's way over."

Darcy hands the walkie to Sweetie. "I don't have anything else. It must be your turn." Sweetie doesn't know what to do. She sees the balloon filling and the hopeful looks on her friends' faces.

Darcy points to the button on the walkie that Sweetie needs to press to talk. Sweetie takes the walkie and presses the button, "Excuse me, Sir."

"Who is this?"

"It's Sweetie."

"Who the hell is Sweetie?"

Sweetie almost cries, but she doesn't. She breathes deep. Now, Darcy *holds* for her. Sweetie sees the strength in Darcy's eyes. Sweetie takes another deep breath and stands strong. "Sir, you probably know me as Prom Queen with a Shotgun."

"Well, little lady, what can I do for you? I didn't realize this was a conference call."

"General, just because I'm 17 and won't ... " Sweetie stops herself and decides to approach the General from a different angle. "Sir, I'd like to talk to you, warrior to warrior."

The General laughs. "OK, you've got my attention, Prom Queen with a Shotgun. I guess you've earned that."

Sweetie brushes her hair behind her ear. "Sir, I need you to *see me* for who I am. *We* need you to *see us* for who we are." The General doesn't respond. Sweetie bites her lip and gives it another go. "Sir, no disrespect, but in 20 or 30 years, you and your generation will be dead. However, we will still be here with our kids. To be frank, we're more invested in the long-range outcome of today then you are, and sometimes that can lead to greater inspiration."

"How old did you say you are? I'm older than all of you put together."

"Yes sir," says Sweetie, "it may be argued that we don't have years of experience to fall back on. But that might be a good thing. General, we're too young to know what will and won't work. We're in a better place to try the impossible and succeed."

Sweetie waits. A jet breaks formation out of the sky and dives towards the balloon.

SNAFU says, "It's going to strife the balloon." He thinks, *this balloon couldn't be an easier target.*

Darcy and Sweetie watch the jet approach. They listen to the radio silence. Sweetie holds down the button, "Sir, if you're in the mood to take a chance, take a chance on us."

The General yells, "Cancel that order!"

But it is too late, the jet continues to dive toward the balloon. Everyone ducks and covers their heads. The jet pulls up. The guns never fire. The jet rolls as it zooms overhead and the pilot salutes them. Darcy salutes back. The jet soars away. The force of the jet sends ripples through the rising balloon. Mouth Wash and Crystal hold the ropes to steady it.

The General barks, "Put Meyers on." Sweetie hands the walkie to Darcy. "Alright private, you've got your air support. God bless you, your misfits, and that god-damn balloon of yours."

"Thank you, Sir."

"And Private, would you tell Prom Queen with a Shotgun something for me?"

"Yes, sir." Darcy holds the walkie so Sweetie can hear the General.

"Tell her she reminds me of myself when I was younger minus all that girlie stuff. Tell her that I believe in her."

"Yes, sir!"

CHAPTER 36

45 Degrees is Better Than Nothing

THE RED, ORANGE, AND yellow humpback whale puffs up even more. *It is alive!* The basket tilts up at a 45-degree angle to the ground. It's still a large lump but it's going to stand on its own soon. This is a big win for the ground crew.

SNAFU yells, "Do you see that?"

Crystal gives SNAFU a high five. Then she remembers she's supposed to be angry with him.

The balloon is more than a big, beautiful, speed bump in the middle of a death and destruction highway. It's a bright symbol of possibility in the midst of bleak colors of despair. The hot air balloon is on the twenty-yard line of the football field. They are within scoring range. It has been a long, hard drive to get to here. Sacrifices were made, and team members were lost. But with each blast of fire, the impossible seems more possible.

It also helps that the General believes in them. Or, at least, believes in them enough to give them a chance. A nuke is still being flown in.

Just in case. The General didn't tell them, but Darcy and Sweetie are smart enough to realize this on their own. The General does believes in them, but he also knows they're just a bunch of crazy kids. And, to win a war, you have to have a Plan B because the truth is, every thirty seconds four more 'space pebbles' come down the Cord, burn off pretty colors, and then four more Spacers join the fight. Sure, some get blasted, but some drop safely into web hammocks. It's funny how this, too, has become part of the background "white noise."

SNAFU calls Sweetie over. She takes over blasting hot air. SNAFU turns his attention to his crossbow and the coil of webbing. He laughs. *This is ridiculous.* Mouth Wash and Darcy tie the ropes to keep the balloon anchored. One rope is tied to a crashed jet, the other to a charred Humvee. Crystal forages for more weapons and ammo. SNAFU turns a fishing arrow over and over again in his hand.

Darcy edges closer to him. "Everything alright?"

SNAFU doesn't look up. "Yeah, everything's great."

Darcy knows he's not OK but she gives him some space. She motions to Sweetie. *SNAFU needs help.* SNAFU threads one end of the webbing into the opening in a fishing arrow. He ties the webbing to the arrow with a big knot. It seems secure. He stares at it.

Sweetie watches SNAFU zone out. She calls Mouth Wash over and shows Mouth Wash how to fill the balloon. He flips the switch and flames blast, the balloon gets bigger. Sweetie walks over to SNAFU. SNAFU looks up and sees Mouth Wash filling the balloon. *That makes sense, Mouth Wash is usually full of hot air.* Sweetie pulls SNAFU further away from the balloon so they can talk.

"You alright?"

"I'm fantastic." SNAFU glances back at Mouth Wash. "Listen Sweetie, if we survive, you've got to talk to Chevy. He needs to KNOW that you KNOW that he said 'no to Prom' because he DOES care about you and your future together."

Sweetie touches SNAFU's shoulder. In the midst of everything going on, SNAFU's thinking about his best friend. "SNAFU, you're such a good guy. I know. I get it now. Chevy was thinking more about our future than I was, which is weird. I mean, I still think he was overreacting for thinking going to Prom is going to ruin our future, but

I get his point of view. Relationships are hard."

SNAFU looks at Crystal and then at Darcy. "Yeah, you should try marriage."

"I just wish Chevy wasn't so stubborn."

"You'll be glad he is when he stops the Spacers."

"So you think it's possible?"

"No, but I know Chevy does," says SNAFU.

"Which means *it is* possible." Sweetie smiles.

SNAFU watches four more come down the Cord. Things keep getting worse. A Space Spider scurries to the top of the Web Wall. The Spacer jumps up onto the Galactic Cord. That's something new. The Cord is slowly being pulled down onto the Web Wall as the Earth rotates and reels in the moon. They better disconnect the Earth from the moon soon, if they don't the moon will come crashing down on them. The Spacer scurries up the Cord but stays on the underside of it so it can keep an eye (or all eight eyes) on SNAFU, Sweetie, and the balloon.

Sweetie points at it. "Hey, Neo, we've got a squidy watching us. You better start hustling."

SNAFU says, "I'm not Neo. I'm more like Dozer."

"Dozer dies in *The Matrix*."

"Spoiler alert."

Sweetie touches SNAFU's arm. "It's easy to die for a cause. Get all-fanged up, ripped apart, and put in a web coffin. That's easy. You know what's hard? Living for a cause. Cleaning up the mess we inherit. Cleaning up the mess we make."

SNAFU pretends to agree with her. He raises the crossbow. Sweetie puts a hand on it. With her other hand she points to the Space Spider above them and whistles. Darcy sees the sneaky Spacer climbing up the Cord looking down on them. Darcy nods and says, "I'll watch it."

Sweetie turns to SNAFU. "It's hard to be part of the solution. It's hard to believe in ourselves after we've been called worthless. It's hard to take action after we've been drugged for so long by people who tell us it's for our own good. Losers don't save the world. Losers don't design a future with people who love them. Losers don't have fun and make out with their hot wives."

SNAFU doesn't want to smile but he does.

"That means you either CAN'T have those things or you're going to have to stop calling *yourself* a loser. And, if you stop calling *yourself* a loser then you're NOT one"

"What?"

She touches his big scruffy face. "Do you get that? You decide what you are. Not anyone else. Sure, everyone has their opinion and they WILL share it with you, but none of that matters unless you agree with them."

"Sweetie, it's not that easy."

"SNAFU, don't argue for your limitations. You are not a loser. You have great friends who love you. And you saved Crystal."

"Crystal kinda saved herself."

"If it wasn't for you, we wouldn't of been there to help."

"I couldn't save everyone."

"We're high school seniors in the middle of an alien invasion. Nobody's having a perfect day."

SNAFU looks down at his crossbow.

"Look, you can focus on what you didn't do. You can find evidence to put yourself down. You can make yourself feel like dirt. We can all do that. **What you focus on expands.** I need you to focus on the good you've done. I need you to focus on the possibilities you'd like to create. You're right, Chevy is out there doing what he's doing. And, we know him well enough to know he's almost in position by now. Why? Because he believes it's possible. Even if he's got to do it with a guy that he hates and that wants to bang me into tomorrow. If you don't believe this is possible, then don't go up in the balloon because you won't succeed."

SNAFU holds up a hand. "Sweetie stop. I can't handle all your words. You're talking too much."

Sweetie takes his hand and holds it with both of hers. "Listen, and this is really important. If you were truly a loser, then EVERYONE would agree about your lack of worth. But if you've got just ONE person who believes in you, then YOU have to decide to whom you're going to listen. SNAFU, you've got three people right here who believe in you. Darcy, Crystal, and me. And I can speak for Chevy. He always tells me SNAFU shouldn't be so hard on himself."

Darcy and Crystal walk up behind SNAFU.

SNAFU says, "Darcy and Crystal hate me."

Darcy laughs, "Listen. It would have been nice if you didn't have a girlfriend when we got married but I don't hate you. I love you."

Everyone turns to Crystal. She says. "I hate you, but I pretty much hate everyone so you don't need to take it personally. I'll get over it. Remember, when God closes a door he opens a Mouth Wash."

Sweetie, Darcy, and SNAFU make a gross face. Crystal laughs and walks back to Mouth Wash. He blasts more flames.

Sneaky Spacer continues to walk upside down on the Cord above them. It continues to watch them. Darcy watches it back.

Sweetie says, "You know the saying, it takes one to know one?"

"No."

That doesn't stop Sweetie. "Look at Darcy and Crystal. I'm inspired by their courage. I can see that positive quality in them because I've got that quality in myself. But the opposite is also true. If people can't see the good in THEMSELVES, then they can't see the good in YOU. So, if they don't see how valuable you are, eff-em."

"Or bless them," says Darcy.

"Bless them?"

Darcy nods. "Yes, bless them. You know why? Because if they're in judgment of themselves then they're in a self-created hell. Bless them when they call you names. Bless them as they twitch their fangs. Bless them as they strike with their words, fists, and webbing. Why? Because every time someone calls *you* a name they're letting you know what they think about *themselves*. Bless them because they're in so much pain AND they think others are causing it. Bless them because it's really their own judgments causing their suffering."

SNAFU says, "You really think so?"

Darcy nods.

Sweetie says, "When we were kids, we use to say. I'm rubber you're glue, whatever you say bounces off of me and sticks to you."

SNAFU laughs.

"Exactly," says Darcy. "My favorite was, 'I know you are, but what am I?' We were very wise when we were young." Darcy runs her fingers through SNAFU's hair. He savors her touch. "Honey, you're not a victim, you're a creator. But here's the kicker. As a creator you can create being a victim. It feels terrible, but you can do that. All you have to do is *think you're not good* and *think you're not worthy* and you're a victim. A lot of people do that. I did it for years."

This gets Sweeties and SNAFU's attention. Private First Class Meyers didn't have a first-class life.

Sneaky Space Spider above them jumps. It pulls in its legs and comes down like a cannonball. A Hellfire missile streams through the air and blasts it. It explodes. Everyone dives for cover. Sweetie closes her mouth. The goo rains down on the balloon. An Apache copter flies overhead. Crystal yells, "Thank you!"

Darcy lays her hand on SNAFU's chest. He takes a deep breath. She says, "I need you to focus on your good. Focus on what you love and appreciate. Focus on the people who love you. I need you to know you're good. Maybe not in all of your *behaviors* but in *here*." She looks at her hand over his heart and taps his chest. "You're good. Not for what you say or do but because of your inherent goodness."

SNAFU wipes a tear from his eye. He looks around at all of the destruction. Broken machines. Broken bodies. Broken dreams. "This is how I feel inside."

Darcy says, "I know. I'm sorry."

"It's not your fault."

"I'm sorry not because I'm responsible for how you feel, I'm sorry because I love you and you're in pain."

SNAFU lets Darcy hug him, but he doesn't hug back. She holds him. She keeps holding him. He finally hugs her. She whispers, "A loser can't pull this off but my husband can."

SNAFU nods. "Thanks." He wipes his eyes. Darcy wipes her eyes. Sweetie wipes her eyes. SNAFU and Sweetie hug. It's a hug fest.

Sweetie says, "If you believe Chevy's plan is crazy enough to succeed and, if you believe there's a chance we might be able to do this, then I'll let you climb into one of the biggest, most colorful, and easiest targets that has ever graced a battlefield in the history of Earth."

"Well, since you put it that way, how can I refuse?"

Sweetie looks up at the Cord. "Is it too high up? Can your

crossbow reach it?"

"I think so. The bowcaster has a 40-yard range and the webbing is light enough," says SNAFU. "It's a good thing the Earth is pulling the moon closer to the planet."

"There's something I never thought I'd hear you say."

SNAFU raises his crossbow. The red laser dot lands on the Cord above their heads. He pulls the trigger. The arrow flies, pulling the lightweight webbing. The arrow sticks into the Galactic Cord.

"Nice shot," says Darcy.

The lightweight webbing hangs down in front of SNAFU. He hands the crossbow to Darcy. They kiss. He says, "Thank you." She nods. He pulls on the webbing. It stretches, the arrow doesn't pull out. He jumps and grabs the webbing. It stretches, and he comes back down to Earth. The arrow stays in. He bobs up and down on the lightweight cord.

"What are you doing?" says Sweetie, "you want to rip it out?"

"I'm testing it. It's going to be lifting a lot more than the weight of me."

Crystal walks past them with a handful of weapons and says, "I don't know about that. You're pretty big."

Darcy loads up the basket with a bunch of magazines and a handful of grenades. Crystal meets her at the basket and puts in an M4 with a few more magazines. Mouth Wash stops blasting flames so Crystal and Darcy can talk.

Crystal yells, "Keep filling it. You want to be here all day?!"

Mouth Wash holds down the switch. You don't argue with Crystal. Not when she's like this. *Which is weird, she was fine a moment ago.* The flames roar. It's loud.

Crystal yells at Darcy, "You were going to leave us to die!"

Darcy yells back, "You beat the odds!"

"I always do!"

"Listen, you're not more important than the mission." Darcy points at dead soldiers on the ground. "*They're* not more important than the mission. None of us, *including me*, are more important than the mission. The Spacers had you by surprise. I made the call to sacrifice you. I'm not going to apologize for that. If we would have died saving you, the whole planet might be wiped out by nukes and radiation. Was it worth the risk?"

"Somebody thought it was."

They look at SNAFU. He bobs up and down on the web line, and he's getting some good height now. "Yee-haw." *It's good to see him feeling better, but this is really not the time or place to be acting like this.*

Crystal says, "Look at us, we're fighting over a piñata."

Darcy smiles. "He may be goofy looking, but he's got good stuff inside."

"I know." Then Crystal blushes. "I mean, that's not the 'good stuff inside' that I'm talking about. I mean ..."

"I get what you mean. Stop talking."

But Crystal can't let it go. "I guess that's why we're fighting over him."

Darcy shakes her head. "You know, we're not really fighting for him," she says. "The decision has been made, we're together. We're married."

"I get it. I guess I'm still angry." She looks at Mouth Wash. "I'm pretty sure I don't even want SNAFU now. I want more. My more is not SNAFU. Your more is SNAFU, which is very surprising, but my more is someone else. I've been dumped before, and I hate it, but I've never had a boyfriend *marry* someone else while we were still going out."

"SNAFU's social skills need some work."

"Good luck with that."

"I'm glad you're alive," says Darcy. "Please don't fight me. Fight them. If you do, we might just pull this off."

"I hate it that you're so smart, nice, and beautiful."

Darcy smiles and says, "It takes one to know one."

SNAFU walks his end of the lightweight web line to the balloon basket. The web line stretches; the Galactic Cord doesn't move. He studies the Cord. It's as thick as a grain silo. It has to be about twenty feet in diameter. *Nineteen feet three inches to be exact.* He looks at the faded "day image" of the moon up in the sky. He follows the Cord from the sky, over the Web Wall to the high school. *This is NOT going to work. Wait, what does Chevy say, find a better feeling thought. I'll bet there is a one in a million chance. That's a better feeling thought. And, Chevy is a one in a million type guy. And since likes attract, maybe I'm a one in a million type of guy too.* SNAFU smiles. *God knows how many people have told me I'm a special case.* He laughs as he ties the web line to the basket. He looks inside the basket and sees all the hardware. *I am loved.*

Crystal pulls on her crystal necklace. It catches on another necklace she wears. The pendant is a twisted nail.

Darcy says, "What's that?"

Crystal hesitates, but decides to show Darcy. Darcy touches the 3-inch bent and looped nail and feels the braided leather "chain."

"That's nice," says Darcy.

"SNAFU gave it to me."

Darcy let's it go.

"Listen," says Crystal, "you seem like a good person. SNAFU gives one of these to all the girls he … *dates*."

"He didn't give one to me."

"You've just started *dating*."

"Actually we've never *dated*." Darcy thinks, *is her husband going to treat her like all of his ex's?*

"Whenever he gives one of these," says Crystal, "he always says, I've never given one of these to anyone before."

"He doesn't lie to me," says Darcy.

Crystal ignores her, *everyone* knows SNAFU lies to *everyone*. Crystal continues, "And, he also always says, I made it myself. But my dad says it's impossible for a high school kid to bend a nail it's just … "

"We have a different type of relationship!"

"OK," says Crystal. *You can't blame a girl for trying.* Crystal was just trying to save Darcy some heart ache. Crystal slides the quartz and nail pendants under her shirt. She walks away from Darcy.

About 30-feet away, Sweetie approaches SNAFU at the basket as he inspects one of the M4's. He wipes some goo off it and checks the magazine. Sweetie says, "I miss Chevy."

SNAFU's glad she mentions me. He doesn't want to think about himself any more. Sweetie hands SNAFU a grenade. "Happy late birthday. I'm sorry I missed your day."

"Don't worry about it. You were busy with Prom, the moon cracking, and the end of the world."

"Mouth Wash is just a friend," says Sweetie. SNAFU looks at her. She adds, "A good-looking, flirty friend, but I'm with Chevy. Besides he wants Crystal."

"I don't think it's mutual."

"Look."

Mouth Wash flips the switch and flames shoot into the balloon. Crystal provides cover, her back toward Mouth Wash. They're not being romantic. They don't even look at each other.

"They're just standing there," says SNAFU.

"When's the last time Crystal stood next to a guy who isn't gay?"

SNAFU thinks. "Wow. She really does like him."

Sweetie looks happy for them. SNAFU gets it. Sweetie's heart doesn't belong to Mouth Wash. Then Sweetie looks sad.

SNAFU hugs Sweetie, "I miss Chevy too, but he's OK."

"You think so?" asks Sweetie.

"Yeah, he's stubborn and he loves you."

"But he won't take me to Prom."

"I didn't say he's smart."

She defends me. "Chevy's smart."

"I know he is," says SNAFU. "Just not all the time."

Let's review. The moon is attached to the Earth by the Galactic Cord. The moon hasn't completely stopped the Earth from spinning. I know, some people say the moon stopped the Earth. It didn't. The Earth is too big. The moon just slowed it down, but the Earth still rotates and actually pulls the moon. Sorta like reeling it in. But, please note, this is happening really, really slowly. Because the Earth is pulling in the moon, the Cord is no longer going straight from the school to the moon. The Cord lays across the front parking lot of the school all of the way to the Wall of Web and, in fact, crushes the top of the Web Wall. From there, the Cord goes up into the sky toward the moon. The good news is as the Earth pulls on the moon, the Galactic Cord gets closer to the hot air balloon. This will decrease the distance between the balloon basket and the Cord, making it easier for the whole "Lift the Cord Out of Here" mission. It's nice to catch a break like this.

Crystal marches up to SNAFU and Sweetie. Crystal pulls Mouth Wash with her. *Who's filling the balloon?* Sweetie see Darcy blast more hot air into the balloon. Sweetie mouths a question to Darcy, *What's going on?*

Darcy mouths back, *Closure.* Sweetie's suddenly scared for SNAFU.

Mouth Wash says, "Hey Sweetie, SNAFU."

Crystal says, "Don't be nice to him." Crystal punches SNAFU in the arm. "Owwww." SNAFU grabs his arm and steps behind Sweetie. Crystal can hit hard.

Crystal yells, "Don't you ever break up with me again." She kisses Mouth Wash and yells again, "What do you say to that?"

Sweetie doesn't like being used as a shield but she understands. SNAFU wants to be safe and he's not going to fight Crystal. SNAFU says, "I can't break up with you again because we're not going out any more. I'm married."

Crystal gets really angry, "I know what I'm saying doesn't make sense, but so help me you'd better agree with me."

Sweetie elbows SNAFU. He says, "I promise to never break up with you again."

Crystal pushes Sweetie out of the way and grabs SNAFU. He freezes; his worst fear is happening. Crystal hugs him. She keeps hugging him. SNAFU pats her back. But she doesn't let him go. SNAFU finally hugs her.

Crystal whispers, "I'll miss you."

SNAFU says, "I'll miss you too."

Crystal lets him go. "Good-bye." Mouth Wash takes Crystal's hand. This time Mouth Wash leads Crystal away.

SNAFU walks over to Darcy. She asks, "Everything OK?"

"Yeah, I'm not allowed to break up with her again."

Darcy nods.

Four more SUV sized "rocks" zoom along the Cord overhead. The four burn with pretty colors and then open up into Space Spiders. One gets blasted. The other three continue down the Cord, past the arrow that SNAFU shot into the Cord. Without their fourth buddy, they fall away from the Cord and drop to the Earth. One smushes and the other two land in web hammocks. One scurries over the Wall. *What are they doing back there?* The other Space Spider hurries into battle. Take the battle to the enemy and they won't have time to attack your arachnid troops back at the base.

Come on, Chevy. They're growing in number and we're running out of time.

CHAPTER 37

1,000+ Not 500+

I NEVER THOUGHT I'D be taking the battle to the enemy in my underwear. Roy unzips his pants and says, "Do you want me to dance while I undress?"

Idiot. I turn to give him privacy. I look outside at the horde of Space Spiders at the front of the school. *This is going to be fun.*

Roy says, "You can turn around."

He's wearing a white muscle undershirt, camouflage briefs, and white socks. *Camouflage briefs*, this dude's all in. Roy pulls off his socks.

"You can leave your socks on."

"You took your socks off."

"But I got sneakers. You've got boots and ... "

"Don't tell me what clothes I can wear." He jumps on one foot as he puts a boot back on. He loses his balance and falls. I snort. It's childish, but I'm glad he fell.

"I'm OK," says Roy. "But Seven-Thirty usually helps me to undress so I ..."

"Stop talking about my sister."

Roy smirks. He sits on the tile and laces his boots. He picks up his socks and stands. He folds one. *What? OCD? Folding dirty socks when facing death?* He turns around so I can't see what he's doing. He adjusts his briefs. The camouflage material hugs his butt. *I did NOT sign up for this.* I wait but he doesn't turn around. *What's he doing with his socks?* Then I get it.

"Did you just stick your socks in your underwear?"

Roy turns. It looks like he has a tennis ball in his groin. I laugh. "Dude, you've got to fix that."

"If we get on the world news, I'm going to have chicks texting me in all different languages."

"Yah. They're going to be asking you if you have a tumor on your dick."

Roy doesn't like being laughed at. "OK," I say, "it's not a bad idea, but you've got to shape it a bit so it doesn't look like one of your balls is about to explode." He turns for privacy. He pulls out one sock and tosses it. He folds and molds the other one. He turns.

"Better?"

"I'd rather not comment on your misinformation campaign but yes, better."

Roy picks up his handgun.

"Put it down," I say.

"No."

"Is that really going to help against a thousand Space Spiders?" I overestimate to prove my point. Roy looks out the window at the Spacers. He puts down his Berretta. I slap his shoulder and he winces. I pick up the camouflage backpack and put it on. "We need to act as non-threatening as possible. I recommend happy thoughts."

Roy looks at me as if I'm the idiot. He picks up the detonator.

"Do you want to put that in my pack?"

"No," Roy says, "I'll carry it."

The front doors of the school bust wide open. Roy and I march arm-in-arm and sing as loudly as we can, "Itsy bitsy spider went up the water spout, down came the rain and ... "

We march straight toward the 500+ Space Spiders and the Web

Wall. The Spacers turn and bare their fangs at us. Spooky. Chilling. We hesitate. Our voices crack, but we keep singing and marching. The Space Spiders look at each other, as if someone should know what to do, but they don't. This is unusual. The Spacers go back to what they're doing.

One Space Spider comes within 10 feet of us as it walks across the front parking lot. We slow down so we don't bump into it. I could reach out with my hand and touch it. Roy does.

"Roy!"

"What?"

We let the Space Spider pass us. It doesn't give us a second glance.

Roy looks around. "Do you see any cameras?"

"No. I don't," but I want to keep Roy upbeat so I say, "But that doesn't mean they're not focused on us right now." Roy straightens. Chin up. Chest out. Operation propaganda big-boy ready to go viral.

"I wish I would have put both socks in."

"No, bad idea. All the petit girls with small vaginas would be scared to contact you."

"You're right. Good thinking."

Idiot.

Roy tosses back his hair, which is too short to be tossed back since he got the military buzz cut this morning. Or perhaps that was yesterday morning. I don't know, it's been sunny for a while. We continue to march, so far so good. Roy raises his hand with the detonator, "I hope all these guys are here when we blow the school. It will be nice to take out a bunch of them."

A Space Spider charges at us. It "heard" Roy's threat. We have nothing to defend ourselves with. Roy's sock isn't going to help us here. I grab Roy's arm and say, "Don't run. Think happy."

The Space Spider screeches to a halt. Literally, it screeches as it slides to a stop right in front of us. Its strong legs dig into the parking lot. Chips of asphalt fly up. The hairs on its body continue forward because of its momentum. It's so close to us that the hairs on its face almost touch Roy. Its eyes and fangs are inches from him. I see Roy's scared face in the reflection of each of the Space Spider's eight red eyes. I feel goose bumps on Roy's arm. I want to let go, but I figure this is the time he most needs to know he isn't alone.

I whisper, "Happy thoughts. Mountain streams. Birds flying."

The Space Spider's mandibles touch Roy's face as if the Spacer is a blind person "seeing" Roy for the first time. The Space Spider looks down at his trembling hand with the detonator.

I whisper, "Happy thoughts. Puppies. Chocolate ice cream." Then I remember I'm talking to Roy. "Making out with cheerleaders in the back seat of your Love Machine."

Roy's eyes glaze over. Fangs twitch, but Roy is now in the Roy-Boy-Toy zone. He says, "Sexy," to the Space Spider. It doesn't understand. The Spacer looks at me for clarification.

"Yes, it's true. He's a real ladies man."

The Space Spider lets go of Roy's face. The Spacer studies us for a moment. We are not a threat. It walks away.

I let go of Roy's arm. I point to the hole in the Wall, "To the hole."

"A fine mantra indeed. Let's go."

Roy locks his arm around mine. We skip like Dorothy and the Tin Man. I am, of course, the Tin Man. We sing, "A hundred bottles of beer on the wall, a hundred bottles of beer … "

If we are streaming live, foreign babes are NOT looking at us with any sort of desire.

The happy-go-lucky underwear-skipping-friends get closer to the Wall. I believe that's how we are going to be described in the General's autobiography that someone else will write. "Friends" might be a strong word. I don't think Roy and I are friends, but I don't think we're enemies any more.

Roy and I get closer to the Wall. Space Spiders run back and forth through the hole in the Wall. Sometimes a Spacer runs out into battle, sometimes a charred one scurries back in. It's good to see the battle is still happening. Before they run out they always stop and look for incoming traffic. They're smart.

I think it's *simple* now. (Thoughts get a little skewed when you find yourself out in public wearing only underwear.) I think, *all* we have to do is get to the other side of the Web Wall, wave to SNAFU, who will be in the balloon, wait for his wave so we know the basket is attached to the Cord, and then blow the school. *No big deal. That's not so hard.*

Easy peasy. We get closer to the hole in the Web Wall that the Spacers use to rush into battle. There's something inside it.

I drop Roy's arm and slow down to a walk. "What's blocking the hole?"

"Nothing," says Roy. "Just keep picturing success. Your actions and behaviors will follow whatever picture you hold in your mind."

It disturbs me that Roy is coaching me about intention and visualization. It's good to focus on what you want, but sometimes you've got to deal with *what is*. Something *is* blocking the passage. Oh. It's a BIG Space Spider. I knew Roy was wrong.

Roy adjusts his sock. "It's guarding the exit."

"No, It's facing the other way."

"OK, then it's *blocking* the exit and guarding the entrance. Does it really matter?"

He's right, either way, we're not getting past Guard Space Spider. We approach slowly. Guarder doesn't turn around. Guarder moves the camouflage flap and peeks out. We get a glimpse of the battle beyond the Wall. Maybe Guarder is assessing how it's going. Maybe it's planning something. Maybe it's learning our strengths and weaknesses and communicating them to the others. We move closer.

"Chevy, get it to move."

"How? Should I push it out of the way? Wait, I got an idea, why don't you just smack it with your giant … "

"You said you could talk to them."

"I never said I could TALK to them."

Roy sits down on a Humvee tire that has somehow managed to get on this side of the Wall. "Fine, we'll just sit this part of the battle out and fail."

I hate him. I take back the possible friend comment. We are mortal enemies. I walk up to Guarder. "Excuse me." It doesn't turn around. "Excuse me." It doesn't even know I'm there.

I move closer and tap one of its hairy legs. I step back. Nothing. I tap it again and jump back. Nothing. No movement at all. Maybe Guarder is dead. Maybe it got wounded, ran back to base and died in the hole. No, that's stupid I saw it move the camouflage flap. Or maybe Guarder didn't move the flap. Maybe a gust of battlefield-wind moved the flap. I grab a handful of white hair on back of its leg and pull hard. RIP! Before I can step back Guarder spins, grabs my head with its mandibles, and screeches. Fangs ready to eat my face. The hair on my head blows back as if I'm in a wind tunnel. Hot sewer breath with a hint of peppermint blasts me. I clench my fists. I feel its coarse hair between my fingers.

Guarder releases my face. It looks me up and down assessing my threat level. Then it looks at Roy.

Roy steps away from me. "I'm not with him."

Guarder looks at me again, but then does a double take of Roy. Guarder stares at the bulge in his underwear. Guarder shakes and makes little chirping sounds. It looks at Roy's crotch again, the chirping sounds get louder.

"It's laughing at your C4."

Roy puts a hand over his unit. "Shut up." Guarder laughs so hard it falls on its back. All eight legs hold its belly. Roy walks toward it. "It's not that funny."

Guarder laughs so hard webbing shoots out of its spinneret. I smack Roy on the back. "It laughed so hard it webbed itself."

Guarder stops and jumps upright. It looks past Roy and me at the Space Spiders that gather between the school and the Web Wall. The 500 plus Space Spiders turn toward us at the same time, as if they're back-up dancers in some Taylor Swift video. They look right at us. No, they're looking through us. Spooky. The 500 plus Spacers charge.

"Here they come," I yell. "Get out of the way!"

We turn to see how we can get past Guarder, but the big Spacer has already moved. The hole is empty. Smart Spacer. We run through the Web Wall. The pounding of the 40,000 plus hairy legs behind us shakes the ground and echoes inside the Wall. It's deafening. We push the camouflage flap out of the way and run to the other side. I see the Galactic Cord pressing down on the top of the Web Wall. I wonder how much longer we have before the moon is close enough to be sucked into Earth's gravitational field.

On the other side of the Cord, I see the hot air balloon. Damn, it isn't up yet. I see the Knight Squad on the ground. I count. One, two, three, four, five. Five? Is that Darcy and SNAFU or two other soldiers?

I can't make out their faces. I don't see Sweetie's Prom dress. Did Sweetie not make it? Suddenly, I'm not able to move.

Roy is smarter than me. He doesn't stop to look. He pushes me out of the way as the Space Spiders come pouring out of the Wall. I almost stumble into a crater made by a big bomb or perhaps a helicopter that crashed with a lot of unused ammo.

Roy saves my life by grabbing my backpack and pulling me behind a webbed up tank. We stay close to the tank. We're right on the edge of the crater. I almost slip and tumble down into it. Space Spiders jump over the tank, over us, and land in the crater. They scurry out. Others run around the tank and crater. Pretty soon, they only run around us. The first ones must have told their buddies to watch out for the big hole on the other side of the tank. I sneak a peek around the tank. I watch Space Spiders stream through the hole in the Wall and scramble over it. They keep coming. Hundreds of them. The invasion is now.

I realize Roy's right. There are a 1,000 plus Spacers. A lot more than I thought.

"Damn," says Roy. "I was hoping we'd get some of them when we blew the school."

I look at the balloon hoping to see Sweetie walk out from behind something. It's hard to see the football field because of the bleachers. I think I see Darcy.

"Should I blow the school?"

"No. The balloon's not up yet." I hesitate. "Roy, I don't see a Prom dress."

"Maybe Sweetie changed. It can't be easy fighting in formal wear."

That's it. Sweetie must have changed. I want to kiss Roy. But I'm not going to do it. We could be streaming right now. I don't want some yahoo editing the video showing our kiss then cutting to Roy's "surprise" package. I don't need that kind of press.

"It looks there are two other females besides Darcy. The taller one could be Sweetie." Yes, that looks like her tight …

"Chevy, the Space Spiders are going over the Wall in ALL directions."

I get what Roy's saying. A lot of Space Spiders scurry for the football field and the balloon. They're going to get there before it can get off the ground.

Roy says, "How much more time do they need?"

"I don't know. But whatever they need, they don't have."

"Why are they invading now?"

"I don't know!" I say. "How would I know?!"

We're getting hostile with each other because there isn't anything we can do. I realize the invasion isn't Roy's fault. I add, "They must have realized they could only win with sheer numbers."

A jet with a Space Spider on it nose dives for us. We don't have time to run. We jump into the crater in front of us and duck. The jet hits the tank we were hiding behind. BOOM. Dirt fills the air and covers us.

CHAPTER 38

RUNNING ON EMPTY

I HOLD MY BREATH as we get buried alive. I can "see" the balloon almost standing in my mind's eye. We're so close. I remember telling Sweetie *touch it, it grows*. Not really applicable with a hot air balloon. But memories are triggered when they're triggered. I start wiggling.

Darcy sees the gaggle of Space Spiders come over the Wall. "Now would be a very good time for this to happen!"

Mouth Wash yells, "I'm working on it!"

"They don't need to fang us, they're going to trample us to death."

"The balloon," yells SNAFU, "is not launching before they get here."

Darcy takes command, "Sweetie and Crystal, to the front. SNAFU and Mouth Wash you get this thing up."

Sweetie, Crystal, and Darcy run to the front of the balloon. Girl Power! The Space Spiders climb over the Web Wall. It's an all-out attack. They're going to secure the battlefield by force. Jets zoom in with bombs and firepower. It seems like the military is ready.

Darcy locks and loads. "We shoot only the ones coming directly at the balloon. Let them run by us on our left and right. We only need to kill a few and they will transmit that info to everyone else. We ARE protecting the balloon. We are NOT stopping all of them."

Space Spiders scurry over the football box office and the short wall around the football field. They run straight for the balloon. Facing one Space Spider is scary. Facing hundreds charging right at you is horrifying.

"Hit them early," orders Darcy. "I want a mound of Spacers that the others will go around." When the Space Spiders enter the end zone, the three young women unload their fury. The Space Spiders make it to the five-yard line and the grenades explode. They start to pile up. Space Spiders scurry left and right of the female warriors and run past the balloon on both sides.

Darcy yells, "Stay focused. Blast only the ones coming right at us. Let the others go around."

The pile gets bigger. The rushing Space Spiders take the path of least resistance. The Space Spiders part like the Red Sea around the young women and the balloon. Hundreds pass on both sides.

Darcy, Sweetie, and Crystal cheer. SNAFU and Mouth Wash also cheer.

But what they don't see are the Space Spiders as they trample and fang ground troops, break through the military lines, or overrun the makeshift military bases and push into nearby townships. There is not a lot of cheering going on.

Sweetie yells, "It's working." She doesn't realize that the Spacers that ran by them are invading America. She's just talking about keeping the balloon in one piece.

SNAFU runs to the three amigas. "If the balloon gets crushed, I've got nothing to go up in. Mouth Wash can fill it on his own."

Darcy looks back at Mouth Wash. He salutes her. Darcy smiles, but not for long. The Space Spiders do what spiders do. They climb. They climb right over the mound of dead Spacers on the 10-yard line.

Darcy, Sweetie, Crystal, and SNAFU blast. Darcy yells, "I'm out." Sweetie's M4 also goes silent.

SNAFU and Crystal blast, but their weapons also run out. Sweetie and Darcy hold hands and stand tall. The Spacers will have to go through them to get to the balloon. SNAFU takes Darcy's other hand. Crystal stands alone. SNAFU extends his other hand to her. She takes it. The time for being petty is over.

Red rover, red rover let spidey come over.

I'm covered in dirt. It's really hard to move when you're buried alive. It's quiet, dark, and cool. For a moment, I think about staying. I'm out of the hot sun. It's quiet and nothing is trying to kill me. Then I realize I want to breath. My lungs burn as my arms push the dirt. My hands claw for the sky. *Dear God, let this be the way up.* My head pushes through the dirt and I breathe. I see Roy's foot sticking through the dirt. It disappears as he wiggles down. He's going the wrong way. Typical Roy. I work my way to where his foot disappeared. I reach into the dirt, grab his leg and pull. He fights me, but I manage to pull him out of the dirt. He coughs.

"What are you trying to do?!"

"Save your life!" *Idiot.* I hear buzzing. I think it's in my head.

"Do you hear that?" asks Roy.

I guess it's not in my head. I try climbing up the side of the crater, but I slide down on the loose dirt. Spacers run along the edge of the crater. They stare down at me. I realize I'm OK where I'm at. The only bad thing about being in the crater is that I can't see the football field. We're too low, but I can see the top of the balloon now. Yes, it's almost straight up.

The buzzing gets louder. I look for jets even though it doesn't sound like jets. I don't see anything in the sky. But then I do. A swarm of black dots zoom toward the balloon. My guess is 20 or 30 of them.

Roy says, "Crows?"

"If those are crows, they're really big crows and they're moving fast."

I take another look at the balloon. It should be ready to go up soon.

"Get ready with the detonator."

"I don't have the detonator."

I yell at Roy. "What did you do with it."

"I don't know! I got blown up! I lost it!"

I turn around and show him the backpack that is still on my back. He should have let me carry it.

"Shut up."

We look at the place where I pulled Roy out. We dig.

The Goddess of Destruction and her Knights are going to be trampled by Space Spiders. The balloon and Mouth Wash will also be crushed. One of the commanders says to the General, "Oh well, the kids gave it their best shot." The General doesn't respond. The Sheriff doesn't want to watch the death of his little girl, but he can't look away.

Darcy hears the buzzing and smiles. "Drones."

Sweetie says, "Thank God for Homeland Security."

Predator drones use to have a snowmobile-type motor that ran off regular gasoline. They are probably different now but that's the buzzing we hear. They're coming in at more than 200 miles per hour (313 km/ h). Drones normally fly at 20,000 feet. At that height, the TOI's (Targets of Interest) on the ground can't see or hear the drones because the drones are so high they're virtually invisible. However, when drones are closer to the ground, they can send better images back to the command center. And, to be honest, I think the General and his cohorts want to get a good look at the Spacers.

Nobody knows how many drones are flying in. That's probably not true. Let me be more accurate. Somebody knows, but the people who know aren't saying. The estimates range between ten and a hundred. Every time the Pentagon mentions the drones, they give a different number or they say, "We have a committee looking into it." Anyone with any type of brain realizes they just want to confuse people long enough so they stop asking. It's a lot easier to focus on the latest Hollywood sex scandal than the drone count that keeps changing or is going to be confirmed tomorrow, tomorrow, tomorrow. Confusing people is a strange way to manipulate them to talk about something else, but it works.

This chapter has a few pictures. A picture is worth a thousand words and I'm at the end of the book, and I don't have many words left in me. So I'll give you pictures. If you don't like pictures in a book, then don't look at them. If there are five pictures in this chapter then that equals a 5,000-word chapter. Wow.

I can identify Reaper, Avenger, Sentinel, and Sky Warrior drones. God knows if there were other ones ripping up the Space Spiders. I'm in my underwear and busy so I may not have all the info. I emailed the Pentagon and other branches of the military with a list of questions. Surprise surprise, they told me they had a committee looking into it and they would get back to me tomorrow. Tomorrow. Tomorrow.

What we don't see are the Global Hawks (pictured above). These are about the size of a regular fighter jet, but they don't carry any ammo. Their job is to be way up in the sky to provide military field commanders with high-resolution, near real-time imagery of what's happening on the ground.

Global Hawk drones: 48 feet (14.5 meters) long with a wingspan of 130 ft.

Here is what the General and the other commanders see via the drones: Six Space Spiders scurry over the mound and charge at Darcy and the teen line.

The Predator drones send two little "love gifts" called Hellfire missiles.

They probably could have gotten away with sending just one, but things are happening fast, and it's important that none of the Spacers

get to the balloon. Hellfire missiles are the primary 100-pound class air-to-ground precision missile for the armed forces of the Untied States. The missiles hit the big mound of dead Space Spiders in front of the balloon. The six Space Spiders scurrying over the top blow up.

The blast knocks Darcy, Sweetie, and the rest of the gang down. Sweetie, Crystal, and Darcy roll and jump up. Cheerleading skills last a lifetime.

"Ready?! OK!"

It takes SNAFU longer to get up. The blast hits the balloon and sends ripples through it. Mouth Wash grabs the ropes and holds it in place.

One hairy Space Spider leg lands on the 18-yard line. Not enough for a first down. Push 'em back, push 'em back. Harder. Harder.

The Predator, Reaper, Avenger and other drones circle above the balloon. Some witnesses say they set up a figure eight in the sky. That sounds too complicated to me, but I'm no military expert. Drones need to keep moving or they'll fall out of the sky.

Here's a fun fact, Predator drones only weigh as much as a pickup truck, which is about 2,000 pounds. This means they can stay in the air for a long time. The sensor operator controls the video camera, the infrared camera (used at night), the SAR (Synthetic aperture-radar) and the laser. The SAR emits successive pulses of radio waves to "illuminate" the target scene. The echo of each pulse is received and recorded to create an image of what's happening. The Operator points the laser at the target on the ground. They use the word TARGET so the pilots and sensor operators don't focus on the fact they're blowing up men, women, and children. The military doesn't usually try to blow up women and children, but it happens. Anything that blows up when a target is ENGAGED - that isn't supposed to be blown up - is called Collateral Damage. As you might have guessed, the military doesn't keep track of Collateral Damage. Nobody really wants to hear about homes being destroyed and innocent people dying. Information like this doesn't make war fun.

When Sweetie and I get ENGAGED, I hope we don't obliterate or destroy each other.

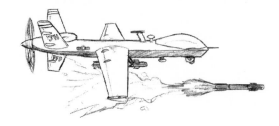

The General sees the images of Darcy, Sweetie, and the others being blown back by the Hellfire explosions. The Predator drones start using Griffin bombs. A Griffin is a lightweight, precision-guided bomb and is laser guided just like Hellfire bombs. The difference is that the Griffin is only a 13-pound warhead, which reduces collateral damage. This is important because right now, if Darcy, Sweetie, SNAFU, and Crystal blow up, they would be collateral damage.

The explosions stop the Space Spiders from trampling Private First Class Darcy Meyers and her teen unit. The smaller Griffin explosions also allow Darcy and the teens to remain on their feet.

Some drones release Viper Strike GPS-aided laser-guided glide bombs. The GPS assists with making the bombs precise, which is important when you're attempting to blow something up. I can imagine a Viper Strike GPS computer voice saying, "Make a right turn in 500 feet." The glide bomb then turns a little to the right. The voice says, "Your destination is on your right." And then, "You have arrived." BOOM!

The drones increase the distance between the balloon and the Space Spiders. Bodies of dead Spacers outline the balloon. The glide bombs also make big holes in the ground filled with goo, guts, and assorted smoldering Space Spider parts. I imagine it must seem like some kind of crazy video game bonus round. The operators sit in their comfy chairs with their controllers blasting away as they protect the balloon and the unit on the ground. The more Space Spiders that rush in, the faster the operators must blast.

Darcy looks at the balloon; it's almost up. "SNAFU, get back to the balloon. Tell Mouth Wash to stop putzing around." SNAFU leaves. Darcy turns to her girlfriends. "Sweetie, Crystal, secure more weapons."

Darcy points to an Avenger drone flying overhead and yells, "Cover us."

It's hard to find more ammo with explosions raining down dirt and goo. The General orders the drones to stop pressing forward and to fall back to the balloon. They need to keep a perimeter, but they don't need to spread themselves too thin. Someone else will need to take care of the other Spacers running around the balloon and invading America.

Drones only carry so much ammo. Some of the Predators have already unloaded their Hellfire Missiles. They;re now just "eyes" for the General. The Reaper drones carry four Hellfire missiles, two Paveway laser-guided bombs, or two Joint Direct Attack Munitions (JDAMS). Some of the drones carry SDBs (Small Diameter Bombs). The good news here is that a drone can carry a pack of four SDBs in place of a single 2,000 pound bomb. Please note, small has nothing to do with its size. The SDBs are almost 6 feet long (which is about as tall as I am). Small also doesn't have anything to do with price: about $250,000 each.

Perhaps you were lucky enough to have seen the unedited footage of when the drones first approached the balloon. The video footage got leaked for about 12 hours before the military took it down. I would have made a copy of the video, but I didn't realize it was leaked and that it was going to disappear.

I've nicknamed the pilots and sensor operators the Digital Drone Boys and Girls of Prom Day. Many of them control their drones from New Mexico and Wisconsin. Some sit in single-team trailers, but many of them sit in groups so a single commanding officer can watch over them. The Digital Drone Boys and Girls are clean-cut and wear military uniforms. They're in there twenties and thirties.

I emailed the Pentagon many times to get more info about the Digital Drone Boys and Girls. I received one reply, "Because offensive uses of the Predator, Reaper, Avenger, etc. are classified, U.S. military officials report an appreciation for the intelligence and reconnaissance-gathering abilities of UAVs (Unmanned Aerial Vehicles) but declines to publicly discuss their offensive use." I'm sure someone will get back to me tomorrow. Tomorrow. Tomorrow.

Here's what I remember from the video I saw of these gaming Warriors. The Digital Drone Boys and Girls sit in front of monitors with controllers with joysticks. They sit in front of a lot of monitors. The monitors are black at first.

Thank God they all grew up playing those first-person shooter games. See, it's true, what you focus on expands. All those hours logged stealing cars, assassinating foes, and blasting zombies helped create the reality they experienced on Prom Day. Shooting real live things.

As the drones enter Pennsylvania airspace, the Commanding Sergeant in the New Mexico Command Drone Rooms shouts, "You are hovering above and in front of the balloon! You are protecting the balloon and the unit on the ground! Operation *Reaching New Heights* is on! You WILL let the Space Spiders go around the balloon! You will stay focused and pick off only the ones threatening the balloon! You will remember what your mission is! Your mission, and I repeat, your mission is to protect that balloon and the Team on the ground!"

"Yes, sir!"

Someone yells, "Sir, we'll have eyes on the ground in two minutes."

"We've got some young kids on the field," the Commanding Sergeant continues. "They think they know how to save the world. Can they do it? I don't know. Saving the world is a pretty big task for a bunch of hoodlums. But I can tell you, the General believes in them. And this means I believe in them. And if I believe in them, then that means YOU believe in them."

The Sergeant pauses for dramatic affect.

"We are going to give them the support they need. We are going to give them the opportunity they need. We are going to give them the resources they need. They've got a hair-brained scheme that involves a hot air balloon in the middle of the goddamn apocalypse! But if there is one thing I've learned in life, it is at times like these – when everything looks like caca – that genius comes forward to save our butts. And, let's be clear, this is one of those times."

"Sir, we're within range."

The black monitors flick on. All of the monitors show the same approaching footage from the first drone. You can see the balloon almost standing. If you look closely, you can see Mouth Wash by the basket.

The monitors show hundreds of Space Spiders charging the balloon. They can see the mound of dead Space Spiders that have piled up in front of the balloon. They can also see Darcy and the others in front of the balloon blasting the rushing Spacers.

The Sergeant says, "Steady everyone. Remember, today we are not just drone pilots. Today we are hope providers. Today we are *Reaching New Heights.*"

The Digital Drone Boys and Girls grab their controllers and joysticks.

"Sir, switching to individual UAV views."

The monitors in front of each pilot switches from the group view from the first Black Hawk drone to the point of view of each individual drone. Some of the monitors show Darcy, Sweetie, SNAFU, and Crystal holding hands."

One pilot whispers, "Are they holding hands?"

Another pilot whispers back, "I guess it's time for us to be heroes."

"Sir, ending auto flight in three, two, one."

The six Space Spiders run up and over the mound. The Spacers don't realize they're about to die. The Sergeant says, "Happy Hunting."

BOOM. BOOM.

The Digital Drone Boys and Girls do it. They save the balloon and the unit on the ground. They give hope. They *Reach New Heights.*

SNAFU runs to Mouth Wash, "What happened?" The blast from the Hellfire missiles had kicked the balloon's ass and it had lost some hot air. Mouth Wash is not happy.

"What do you mean, what happened?" says Mouth Wash. "We're in the middle of a freaking war!"

Others get frustrated too. The Space Spider situation isn't being seen as just an American problem. The Chinese and Russians have readied nuclear missiles. They aren't happy that we, the Americans, haven't "isolated the problem" yet. And, Free Trade or no Free Trade, Canada and Mexico don't want us exporting Space Spiders. The Chinese and Russians realize if the Spacers keep coming it's only a matter of time before they spread across the North and Sound American continents. Which, by the way, the Chinese can live with, but they figure America has to be considering using nukes on their own soil and the Chinese and Russians don't like that idea. They figure the Cord will be dragged across the globe as the Earth starts turning. China and Russia don't want the Spacers dropped all over Europe and Asia. The Untied States goes to DEFCON 4. The Chinese and Russians also don't like the fact that the Earth is stretching the Cord and reeling in the moon. Their scientists say the moon hasn't left its orbit yet, but they're concerned it will. Better to cut the Cord now before the moon gets sucked into our gravitational field. Our president responds with, "If you launch nukes, then we'll retaliate. Stand down. We've got our best and brightest working on this situation."

That's funny. SNAFU and I are part of the president's "best and brightest."

Darcy, Sweetie, and Crystal scatter within the "safety zone" of the drones to find more weapons. The stampeding Space Spiders are not that far away. Sometimes 20 feet, sometimes less. Most of the time if a Spacer drifts too close, it explodes. Thank you, drone pilots.

Sweetie sees an M4 with a grenade launcher in the arms of a fallen solider. He's a little too close to the invisible border of rushing Space Spiders, but the time for thinking is over. The strap of the M4 wraps around the fallen private's arm. Sweetie rolls the soldier over so she can get the gun. But it's not a guy. The soldiers a she, just a few years older than Sweetie. Sweetie hesitates.

A Space Spider breaks from the herd and charges her. Sweetie pulls on the weapon, but it won't come free. Sweetie drops on the ground in front of the solider. She points the M4 at the incoming Space Spider. She fires. BAM, BAM, BAM. She hits the Space Spider. Sweetie launches the last two grenades. PFOMPT. PFOMPT. They hit the Space Spider where the rounds broke its flesh. The grenades enter the Space Spider. But it's too close; it's going to get Sweetie before the grenades explode.

Sweetie grabs the dead soldier and rolls pulling the dead body on top of her. Space Spider fangs sink into the dead solider. Once, twice, three times. The Space Spider tosses the dead body aside. Sweetie lays exposed, but she's still got the M4. She blasts the Spacer in the face, forcing it back. But it's too close. The grenades are going to blow and take her out too.

A 66-foot black winged angel, a.k.a. a Predator drone, that is out of Hellfire missiles, swoops down and SMACKS into the 16-foot Space Spider. The drone knocks the attacking Space Spider backwards into the torrent of rushing Spacers. The drone flies up as the Spacer goes BOOM BOOM. The grenades explode making a messy hole in the stream of Spacers racing by. The hole quickly fills in with more Spacers. Sweetie blows a kiss to the drone that has returned to the sky.

Inside the Drone control center, a monitor shows a close-up of Sweetie blowing a kiss. The operator is Mackenzie, a female solider. The operator next to her looks over and sees Sweetie blowing the kiss. He says, "Ooooh, Mackenzie has a girlfriend."

On Mackenzie's monitor: Sweetie takes unused magazines from the dead soldier. Mackenzie says, "Prom Queen loves me."

Sweetie runs back to the balloon. Darcy and Crystal are at the basket with Mouth Wash. Darcy sets a loaded M16 on the ground next to Mouth Wash who continues to re-fill the balloon.

The big wave of Spacers is over. More keep coming down the Cord and a few scurry by now and then, but the Christmas rush is over. Darcy and the teens look around. *Where's SNAFU?*

Darcy looks at the balloon. Mouth Wash says, "I'm on it." The others scan the horizon for SNAFU.

SNAFU hears the muffled BOOM BOOM of the grenades that Sweetie pumped into the Spacer that Mackenzie's Predator crashed into. He has no idea what happened because he's on the other side of the balloon. SNAFU walks with a machete. Yes, an actual machete. It's amazing what you can find on the battlefield. SNAFU walks around three dead Spacers. He sees the web hammock they were carrying. The hammock looks like it's all in one piece. He shakes his head, "Damn, Chevy's right, you look for an opportunity and you'll find one."

SNAFU hears something unusual for a battlefield. *Is that spoken word poetry in a foreign language?* The sound comes from the other side of a webbed up tank. SNAFU checks the sky. The safety zone of the drones has pushed beyond the tank. He glances back at the balloon. It's not up yet. *Is someone hurt and delusional?* Whatever it is, he's got time to investigate. SNAFU makes his way around the tank. He steps over a dead Marine. The Grunt's head is webbed up. Tough. But the solider has a brand new M4. SNAFU picks it up. He searches, but there are no clips of ammo to grab. SNAFU hears the foreign-language-song better now. SNAFU peeks further around the tank.

Something surprises SNAFU. He swings the machete before he realizes Tall Marine is human. Tall Marine ducks the machete. It hits the tank. CLANK. Tall Marine grabs SNAFU's arm and punches him in the gut. The machete and SNAFU fall to the ground. Tall Marine presses a finger to his lips, "Shhhhhhh." SNAFU isn't going to talk or get up. He just wants to breath. Tall Marine points to another Marine who stands about 10-feet away.

Praying Marine continues to chant in Arabic. He bows with his hands to the knees, and then stands. He gets down on the ground and places his forehead to the earth in front of him.

SNAFU slowly stands.

Tall Marine whispers, "Give him a moment. He's in the middle of Fajr Salat."

SNAFU nods and whispers, "Sorry. Didn't mean to interrupt morning prayers." SNAFU looks right and then left and says, "Northeast seems about right. How'd he know which way to face?"

"He's got an app."

Praying Marine sits and then returns his head down to the ground. He stands and repeats the cycle.

SNAFU gets nervous. *This is taking too long.* "Is this really a good time to ..."

"Shhhhhhhh." Tall Marine translates the chanting for SNAFU, "Allah, I ask You for the best the day has to offer, VICTORY, support, light, blessings and guidance; and ... I don't remember the rest."

SNAFU continues, "...and I seek refuge in You, Lord, from the evil in it, and the evil to come."

Tall Marine turns to SNAFU. "Are you Muslim?"

"No, my father had Islamic friends. One of their daughters was my babysitter. She was cool. Used to give me two scoops of mint chocolate chip when my Dad said I could only have one." SNAFU scans the area for Spacers. "Do you guys take turns covering each other during prays?"

Tall Marine laughs. "I'm not Muslim, I'm Baptist."

Praying Marine pauses in a kneeling position, and then continues.

SNAFU whispers, "I know Prophet Muhammad's companion, the guy that is said to have a photographic memory, what's his name?"

Tall Marine whispers, "Abu Hurairah."

"Yeah, him. I've heard he said prayers are more important than Calvary, but I'm not sure if the literal translation is useful right now."

"Prayer gives us the opportunity to connect with that which is greater than ourselves."

"Yeah, but ... "

"When we take action from *that place of connection*," continues Tall Marine, "we operate in sync with the Power and Majesty of God. If we take action from a place of Lack – unhappiness, despair, unworthiness, then death will follow."

A wounded Space Spider peeks over a nearby Humvee. SNAFU and Tall Marine ready their weapons. Praying Marine sees the Spacer too. He stops his prayer, grabs his M4, and stands.

SNAFU says, "If prayer is so important shouldn't you finish?"

Praying Marine smiles, "There is the letter of the Law and the Spirit of the Law."

"And you've got the Spirit?"

"We will see by our results," says Praying Marine. He joins SNAFU and Tall Marine. They stand side by side waiting for the Spacer to come out and play. Praying Marine justifies stopping his prayer and says, "The Qur'an teaches that necessity makes the forbidden permissible."

SNAFU says, "I like practicality in a religion."

The Space Spiders ducks behind the Humvee. It's more disturbing not to see it. Tall Marine says, "God grant me the serenity to accept the things I cannot change ... "

The Spacer scurries over the Humvee at them. SNAFU and the Marines blast. All three shout over the gunfire, "... THE COURAGE TO CHANGE THE THINGS I CAN ... "

RAT a TAT TAT.

" ... AND THE WISDOM TO KNOW THE DIFFERENCE!"

RAT a TAT TAT.

All three shooters step back as they blast the advancing Spacer. The Marines empty their weapons and reload. SNAFU wants to reload, but he doesn't have another mag. The Spacer reaches for them with its mandibles and fangs. SNAFU blocks with his M4. The Spacer grabs the M4 and tosses it aside. SNAFU picks up the machete. He swings and cuts off the end of one of its front legs. The Spacer screeches. The Marines keep shooting.

RAT a TAT TAT.

The Spacer leaks and drops. It's dead. SNAFU turns to Praying Marine, "That is the St. Francis prayer. He isn't Muslim."

Praying Marine says, "Actually, that is the Serenity Prayer, it was written by an American theologian named Reinhold Niebuhr. St. Francis wrote, "Lord, make me an instrument of your peace … "

"Which is not applicable today," says Tall Marine as he inserts another magazine and keeps the look out.

"Yeah," says SNAFU, "but how do *you* know that?"

Praying Marine looks at Tall Marine and slaps him on the back. "We teach each other stuff. It's fun to learn about other religions."

Mouth Wash keeps his hand on the switch. Flames and hot air bellow up. The balloon is close to standing again. Sweetie walks away from the balloon.

"No," Darcy orders. "We don't know which way he went. We're not splitting up. He'll be back. When the balloon is ready, the SNAFU will appear."

It's got to be hard being concerned for your spouse in the middle of a war.

The good news is that the wave of Space Spiders is over. The war is back to *normal*, except there are fewer humans on the battlefield now.

Spacers scurry by, sometimes one at a time, sometimes in small groups. The drones blast a few, but the Space Spiders are kinda free to move around now.

Then it happens. The balloon stands! It's ready to go.

The Digital Drone Boys and Girls cheer. People around the world cheer. The General cheers. But not out loud. The General cheers on the inside. Rumor has it he almost smiled once in 1967. Sweetie's dad cheers. The Sheriff turns to the Private next to him, "That's my baby girl."

"Which one?"

"Prom Queen with a Shotgun."

"She's hot."

The Sheriff glares at him. The Private stands at attention with eyes forward and says, "She's hot, Sir."

SNAFU glances back at the webbed-up tank and sees the balloon standing behind it. Yes! Even though only the Knights and the General know the plan, everyone all over the planet realize the balloon is important because of the effort to protect it.

Praying Marine talks into his walkie. "Copy that. Over." He says to Tall Marine, "Come on, we're being called back. They've scattered everywhere."

The Marines look at SNAFU. "You coming with us?"

"No. I've got a thing I've got to do."

SNAFU comes around the webbed up tank. He smiles at Darcy, Sweetie, Crystal, and Mouth Wash. Darcy has her fists on her hips. *Where the hell have you been?*

Sweetie yells, "Get in the damn balloon already!"

SNAFU runs and jumps into the basket. Well, that's not true, but that's how I heard it. SNAFU tried to leap into the basket. I've seen unreleased footage that shows SNAFU falling into the basket. SNAFU is kinda big, so this makes more sense.

Darcy hugs and kisses him after he stands in the basket. "You OK?"

SNAFU nods. "Of course I am, Sugar Pie."

"Sugar Pie?"

SNAFU looks at the thin webbing tied to the basket. *Thank the*

Lord, it's still there. His eyes follow it up into the sky to the crossbow arrow stuck in the Cord. Good. Darcy and SNAFU look at each other. Their smiles fade away. It's time to do this. Darcy steps away from the basket. Crystal and Mouth Wash untie the ropes securing the balloon.

"Wait!" says SNAFU. Crystal and Mouth Wash grab the ropes stopping the balloon from rising.

SNAFU points to the web hammock. "Get that hammock and stretch it between that tank and the busted Humvee. I'll jump into it when I get this thing going."

Darcy nods. SNAFU smiles and blasts flames into the balloon. Crystal and Mouth Wash release the ropes. SNAFU and the balloon rise. Darcy and Sweetie work on the web hammock.

Crystal shouts, "Remember, you signed the battle field waver. Don't do anything crazy up there."

SNAFU slips on a grenade. "Thanks for the reminder, I'll play it safe." He kicks the grenade out of the way. SNAFU cuts off sandbag weights with his knife. They drop. He pulls the lever. Flames roar. The balloon lifts faster.

SNAFU tugs on the thin webbing as the balloon rises. The thin webbing stretches. Since the Cord is still attached to the school, the balloon can only pull and lift the Cord so high.

SNAFU looks at the Web Wall and the school just beyond it. "Come on Chevy, be alive. Blow the damn school."

CHAPTER 39

LOVE IS A BATTLEFIELD

THE BALLOON GOES UP, but we don't see it. We're having too much fun playing in the dirt, digging for the detonator. "I got it." I pull out a small piece of fighter jet.

"That's not the detonator."

"I know!" I toss it away.

Roy points over my shoulder. "It's up! It's going up!"

I see the balloon rise. Someone stocky is in the basket. It's SNAFU. Good job, team. They did it. He blasts more flames and waves. I wave back, but he doesn't see me. He waves toward the Wall. He's giving us the signal, but he doesn't know where we are. Space Spiders are positioned on top of the Wall. There's one about every twenty yards. They don't move. They stand very still, just watching. It's spooky.

I continue throwing dirt. Roy jams both his arms into the Earth and pulls out the detonator. "I got it. I got it."

"Nice work. Do it."

Roy brushes off the detonator. "Do you think we're far enough away from the school?"

"We'll find out soon enough."

Roy flips the cover and pushes the button on the detonator. Nothing happens.

"Roy, you suck."

Then … KA-BOOM. The whole school blows. I mean the entire building. The force of the explosion throws some of the watching Space Spiders off of the Web Wall into the air. A few Spacers burst into flames. Screeches fill the air. I don't know why but one section of the Wall explodes. Maybe pockets of gas had gathered in the basement under it.

Roy and I cover our heads. Dirt rains down on us. I yell, "I take it back! Roy, you're a superstar!"

The force of the explosion shakes the battlefield. Darcy and Sweetie steady themselves as they stretch and secure the web hammock. Mouth Wash bumps into Crystal. They fall down and lands on top of her. It sounds like the planet is exploding, but Mouth Wash and Crystal are lost in their own world.

He says, "Hi."

Crystal is about to tell him to get off, but she smiles. "You smell good."

"Minty Fresh."

They both smile.

"Now you can get off me," says Crystal.

"Are you sure?"

It could have gone really wrong, but it doesn't. Crystal laughs.

"Think of this as exposure treatment," says Mouth Wash.

"I've had guys on top of me before."

"Yeah, but only guys that were emotionally unavailable so you were always safe from being hurt. I mean REALLY hurt. We've connected more today then you and SNAFU probably did over the last six months. I'm here and I like you."

"I know," says Crystal. "I can feel you on my hip."

Crystal sees something in the sky above Mouth Wash. She yells, "Move!" The balloon falls out of the sky. But Crystal is more concerned about the Spacer plummeting down towards Mouth Wash and her.

Here's what happened.

When the school exploded, one of the Space Spiders on the Web Wall got blasted off the Wall and flew into the balloon. Luckily, it wasn't one of the Spacers that had burst into flames. And luckily, the flying Spacer didn't hit the balloon fangs first. But that's where the good luck ran out. I saw the Space Spider fly into the middle section - orange stripe - of the balloon. I thought the Spacer might bounce off the balloon, but it didn't. It went right in. The balloon tilted to the side as it swallowed up the Spacer. It took a moment, but the balloon started to fall. SNAFU panicked and pointed his gun at the balloon. He had a hard time *accepting the things he could not change* but he had *the wisdom to know the difference.* He realized shooting the balloon was not a good idea. He dropped his gun and blasted more flames. SNAFU found the *courage to try to change the things he could.*

The balloon puffed out as it fell.

The balloon *spit* the Spacer out as if it realized it ate something that didn't taste good. The Spacer's lifeless body rolled out without a fight. The blast from the school must have killed it. But the dead carcass was still deadly. It came straight down and it was going to crush Mouth Wash and Crystal.

Crystal yells at Mouth Wash again, "Move!"

Two things happen at almost the same time. The Spacer drops and the basket and balloon come down about twenty feet away from Crystal and Mouth Wash.

The basket hits the ground before the dead Space Spider hits the young couple. SNAFU grabs the sides of the basket and braces for impact. BAM! The basket hits the ground hard. SNAFU and Darcy are on eye level again. They look at each other. The momentum of the drop pulls the balloon down around SNAFU. First the yellow stripe, than the orange, than the red. No, wait, the red top of the balloon doesn't make it all of the way to the ground. It stops. Everyone holds their breath.

The red top lifts, then the orange section rises, and then the yellow. The balloon lifts and reveals SNAFU still standing in the basket with a big silly grin. He gives Darcy a "thumbs up."

Darcy yells, "Yah!"

SNAFU blasts more flames. The basket rises again. Yes.

That's when the shock waves start. It turns out the molten metal in the Earth's core keeps churning even when the Cord "stopped" the Earth from rotating. Now that the Earth is no longer attached to the Cord, shock waves ripple through the Earth as the molten metal twirls and whirls, getting the rest of the planet to come along for the ride.

As this all happens, Mouth Wash grabs Crystal, and rolls them out of the way of the falling Space Spider. The dead Spacer falls, but it doesn't go SPLAT. Right before it hits the ground, it flips over. The Spacer isn't dead. The blast only knocked it out. It lands right where the couple had shared a moment. Even though the Spacer lands on its legs, its momentum brings it down fast, and its body SMACKS into the ground. It takes a moment before it stands. It screeches a wheezy out-of-breath screech.

SNAFU sees the Space Spider and thinks about shooting it from the basket. Darcy shakes her head no. He decides to focuses on the balloon. He blasts more hot air. The basket goes up, stretching the webbing that will lift the Cord.

The wheezing Space Spider twitches its fangs at Darcy and Sweetie. Another molten core shockwave ripples through the Earth, sending Darcy and Sweetie into the web hammock. The Space Spider almost falls over too. The outer crust does its best to catch up to the speed of the inner core.

The Space Spider steps toward Crystal and Mouth Wash, but the Spacer walks sideways. Crystal and Mouth Wash raise their weapons, but the tremor knocks them over.

Crystal stumbles into Mouth Wash. "Is the explosion causing

earthquakes?"

They catch each other and fall down. This time she's on top of him. Mouth Wash smiles. "I don't think so. I think the Earth is starting to rotate again."

Shockwaves register all over the Earth. Short old buildings crumble. Tall modern buildings sway. The good news is the Earth is not going from 0 to 1,000 miles per hour quickly. That's right, the Earth normally spins at 1,000 miles per hour. We just don't notice it because we're all moving at the same speed. Some scientists estimate that the Earth would have to stand still for 10,000 years before our molten core would stop churning. There's a piece of info you'll never use.

The shock waves aren't big, but they keep coming. The teens decide to stay down. The Space Spider doesn't look concerned; its cellular memory is probably kicking in. I'm sure this type of thing has happened before to other Spacers as they planet jumped through space.

Sweetie sees Crystal lying on top of Mouth Wash. *Really?* Accidentally knocked on top of each other again?

Crystal says, "We should stop meeting like this."

Mouth Wash moves a piece of hair away from her face so he can see her better. "I was just thinking the opposite."

The Space Spider gets its sea legs and approaches.

Crystal rolls off Mouth Wash. Both teens blast the Spacer while remaining on the ground. The Space Spider has lost its surprise attack. It moves toward them, but its close proximity is now an advantage for the Knights of Fairland High. They shoot, and even though their M4s move back and forth with the shockwaves, the majority of their rounds hit the advancing Spacer. Darcy and Sweetie blast too. They're off to the side and are on bended knee for better control. Four guns are too much for the weakened Spacer. It leaps at Mouth Wash and Crystal, but the shock waves and the rounds knock it over. This time it doesn't get up. Mouth Wash and Crystal continue blasting. They yell together as they finish blasting at the same time. Very satisfying.

Roy and I climb up the crater. We're almost to the top when a shock wave hits and knocks us back down. The crater is steep and the dirt is loose.

Roy stands and brushes himself off. He looks at his underwear. "Oh man, I can't be running around with dirty underwear." He gets ready to run up the side again.

"Wait."

He waits. Nothing happens. Roy looks at me. *You're stupid.* He runs up the side of the crater. The next shock wave hits and knocks him down again. He tumbles. *Idiot.* I smile. It's the little things in life that make it so enjoyable.

SNAFU pulls the lever and the flames blast. The balloon rises. The balloon pulls the webbing. The webbing stretches as it pulls on the Galactic Cord. The far end of the Cord still stretches out toward the school and has a lot of school attached to the end of it. The lightweight webbing pulls on the Cord, but it's slow going. The end of the Cord is too heavy for the balloon to lift it.

Sweetie looks for Roy and me. She scans the busted-up Wall, the new holes in the battlefield, and the school building debris. "That was a big explosion."

"I'm sure they got far enough away before they blew the school," says Darcy.

"I don't see them."

"Maybe they're hiding."

"Yeah, Darcy," says Sweetie, "They're hiding in the middle of a battlefield of a million Space Spiders. Where?!"

"I'm sure they're OK."

"You're sure? What did they do? How did they survive? Oh, I know. Maybe they sang songs and skipped their way through the Spacers." *I call that intuition by sarcasm.* The next shock wave interrupts Sweetie, which is good, because no one else is stupid enough to do that. The shock wave is less dramatic and everyone gets the hang of riding them out.

Darcy uses the shock wave to step closer to Sweetie. "You know why I'm sure? Because Chevy is smart and Roy is lucky. That boy has the most dumb luck of anyone I know." Darcy puts a hand on Sweetie's shoulder, "I can't do this without you. I need you stay positive and focused. This isn't over yet."

Sweetie nods.

The Earth continues to get back up to speed. Mouth Wash stands and offers Crystal a hand; she hesitates, but takes it. He pulls her up.

"Thanks."

"Anytime."

Mouth Wash looks for ammo. Sweetie runs to Crystal, "You let him help you up."

You'd think Crystal might grunt or push Sweetie away, but she doesn't. Crystal blushes, another first on Prom Day. *Ah, love. It makes the world go round, again.*

Sweetie ejects a magazine from an weapon she finds and confirms it still has some rounds in it. She steps next to Mouth Wash and punches him. "Nice head's up, Romeo. What happened to your timing?" He smiles but doesn't answer.

Darcy checks the web hammock and makes sure it's secure. She looks up and sees the bottom of SNAFU's basket. Good. Close enough.

The balloon slowly lifts. As it does, the lightweight coil pulls and drags the Cord over what's left of the Web Wall. There's still a lot of debris on the end of the Cord and it catches on tanks and other wreckage slowing down the process. It's going to be awhile before the end of the Cord leaves planet Earth.

Crystal says, "Let's hope the balloon can lift it up and out of here."

"It will," says Mouth Wash.

"Are you saying that because you know it or because you hope it?"

"I'm not sure. I'm standing too close to you. You're jamming my radar."

Crystal blushes again.

Sweetie touches Darcy's arm. "When do you think he's going to jump?"

"As soon as he can get it on autopilot."

Private First Class Meyers commands, "Take cover. There are some flipped-over tanks on the other side of the football field, near the end zone. It will be a good place to hole up while we wait for SNAFU to bail."

Mouth Wash says, "You mean that one?"

There's an upright tank that's all webbed up just a few yards away. A dead solider is halfway out of the hatch.

Darcy says, "No. There's two tanks over there."

Darcy points to a Boeing CH-47 Chinook troop transport helicopter. It's a twin-engine, tandem rotor heavy-lift helicopter. The CH-47 is among the heaviest lifting Western helicopters. But right now, it's crashed at the 50-yard line, in the middle of the football field. The backend of the Chinook stands 40 feet in the air. Most of the back rotor blades are busted; only one of the blades is 30 feet long. Darcy continues, "The tanks are on the other side of that troop carrier. We'll see them once we get around it."

As they hustle past the downed troop transport. Crystal says, "I wonder how they got that thing down?" One of the drones covers them from above.

They slow their pace whenever they need to ride out a little shock wave. It's like riding the subway or a bus without holding onto the handrails. Even Mouth Wash and Crystal remain vertical. Sweetie considers it a miracle.

Two Space Spiders scurry out of the transport carrier as they pass it. The drone fires a Griffin missile and explodes both Spacers. The blast throws Darcy, Sweetie, Mouth Wash and Crystal. Mouth Wash and Crystal end up entwined with each other again. Sweetie shakes her head. It figures. But the fact is, it's not safe to be out in the open.

The drone is out of missiles. All four of them wave to the drone as it flies away. It seems all of the other drones have already left. The balloon is up and the Spacers are invading America. The teens are now on their own because the drones are out of ammo or are needed elsewhere. Darcy and crew make it past the troop carrier. Crystal provides cover as Darcy, Sweetie, and Mouth Wash climb between the two tanks and set up fort.

Sweetie says, "We can't see the web hammock we set up for SNAFU. The transport blocks our view."

Darcy says, "I know, but it's the best we can do. We'll keep an eye on the balloon. We'll see him jump. We can't remain out in the open."

"Yeah, there are too many of them roaming about," says Mouth Wash. "Anyone out in the open is dead for sure."

Darcy and Crystal glare at Mouth Wash. *What?* He sees how devastated Sweetie is by his stupid comment. *Oops.* Mouth Wash adds, "Except for Chevy and Roy. We know they're amazing. I'm sure they're OK." Crystal hits Mouth Wash. *Shut up.*

Sweetie scans the battlefield for the boys.

So far so good.
1. Balloon up.
2. Cord attached to the balloon basket.
3. School blown.
4. Cord slowly being lifted.
5. Earth rotating again.

As SNAFU slowly lifts the Cord, the end of the Cord drags across the ground. The next step is to make the Cord lighter so the balloon can lift it out of here.

Jets scream overhead. Tomahawk missiles hit the end of the Galactic Cord and blast off chunks of school. The air-to-surface missiles make the Cord lighter, and the balloon rises faster. It's working! The end of the Cord drags up and over the Wall as the balloon lifts.

Drones and Apache helicopters get in on the game. They blast off more school parts from the end of the Cord. Debris flies in every direction. Sweetie sees something shinny flying through the air. It reflects the sun. It's bright. The round object hits the ground and shatters. It's the cracked and busted mirrored dance ball from the gym.

Sweetie whispers, "Good-bye Prom."

CHAPTER 40

BETWEEN A TANK AND A HARD PLACE

ROY AND I CONTINUE to travel light, in our underwear, without weapons. The walk to where the balloon launched is uneventful. Random Spacers run by us every now and then. They hesitate to glance at Roy's bonus package.

He yells, "Keep moving! Shows over!"

"Yeah," I say, "there's nothing to look at."

After awhile, Roy looks at my backpack. "You got anything in there we can use?"

"Some leftover trail mix."

"Anything else?"

"No."

"Good thing you keep carrying it."

While setting up fort, Crystal realizes the second tank isn't a tank. She yells, "This one is an upside down Humvee." You can't tell it's a Humvee from far away because it's covered in webbing. Crystal and Mouth Wash look for supplies. Darcy and Sweetie keep the lookout.

Now that the "school anchor" has been blasted off the end of the Cord, the balloon rises a little faster, dragging the end of the Cord through the battlefield as the balloon lifts. They can't see SNAFU. They only see the bottom of the basket and the balloon above it.

Crystal reaches into the upside-down Humvee and pulls out water bottles. Each person gets two. Everyone drinks. Mouth Wash chugs the first one and starts on the second one.

"Go easy," says Darcy. Mouth Wash nods, but he keeps drinking.

Darcy shakes her head and then smiles. Sweetie asks, "Why are you smiling?"

Darcy points at the hot air balloon lifting the Cord. "It's working."

Darcy laughs. Sweetie laughs. Crystal and Mouth Wash think they're crazy, but they start laughing too. It's working! #Crazysuccess

I watch the hot air balloon slowly climb its way toward heaven. The basket rises and pulls on the lightweight webbing that stretches and pulls the Galactic Cord. The Cord continues to drag on the ground.

They blasted the end pretty good so it looks like it has tentacles.

A few pieces of brick and mortar still cling to the end of the Cord. I guess they couldn't blast off everything.

Up, up, and away in my beautiful ... SNAFU. He tries to rig it so the lever stays on, so the balloon can go up by itself. He smiles; *if we got this far we can probably go all the way.* He thinks of Darcy. That's a better feeling thought.

Then, SNAFU's heart skips a beat. It actually skips four beats, one for each of the four Spacers coming down the Cord. SNAFU looks down. The web hammock is under him but it's getting smaller and he's drifting to the right. He has time to jump and land in it but he better jump soon. The lightweight webbing stretches as it continues to pull the Cord up. The Cord is under the basket as the next four Space Spiders come down it. The Space Spiders look up at SNAFU and the balloon as they zoom down the Cord toward Earth. SNAFU grabs a gun as they pass under the balloon.

An Apache helicopter hovers near the Cord and releases two Stinger missiles. All four Spacers drop. They zoom-glide down to the planet, but the missiles have locked on. When the Spacers land, two blow up. The blasts shake SNAFU and the balloon. The pilot looks at

SNAFU to make sure he's OK. SNAFU gives him the thumbs-up.

The surviving two Space Spiders look up and study SNAFU, the basket, and the balloon. Maybe they're sending new intel back to the others coming down the line. Maybe the next Spacers will be better prepared to deal with this new "balloon" complication to their plans of world domination. One Spacer jumps on the webbed-up tank with the solider hanging out of the hatch. This tank is almost directly under the balloon. The Space Spider eats the webbing, cleaning it off and then the two Spacers run off into battle.

Here's what happens next. The Earth rotates and the moon pulls the Cord toward it. At the same time, the balloon rises, which pulls the Cord in the other direction. This means the Cord starts to be on the same level as the basket and SNAFU. SNAFU may not get physics, but he's not stupid. As the balloon rises, the Space Pebbles coming down the Cord are NOT going to pass under him; they're going to come straight at him and his basket.

I'm not that good with physics either, but I can see it too. The Spacers are NOT going to drop off the Cord. They're going to come down and SLAM right into SNAFU and the basket.

"We've got to help SNAFU."

"What?!" says Roy. "Are you crazy? We're in our underwear."

The balloon lifts higher. The end of the Cord finally lifts up off of the ground. It's only a couple of feet above the Earth, but the entire Cord is in the air. *The time for talking is over.* I run for the end of the Cord.

Roy yells, "What are you doing?!"

The end of the Cord continues to lift. It's now a few feet off of the ground. I jump and grab hold of cement bricks attached to the end. I pull myself up and hold on as the Cord rises.

"Chevy, jump down from there!"

I climb up the dangling part of the Cord. I'm going to get into the basket with SNAFU and help him fight off the incoming Spacers.

Roy yells, "You don't have any weapons with you? What are you going to do, spit and curse at them?"

I continue climbing, but there are only a few more chucks of cement to use as hand and foot holds. I try to pull myself up the

Galactic Cord, but it's too smooth to climb.

"Chevy, you've got nothing to fight with."

I can't climb higher, I've got no weapons, and I'm in my boxers. I look down. I'm about 20 feet in the air. That's a big distance to drop. I see the web hammock tied between two busted-up pieces of military gear. *Who did that?* I realize that doesn't matter. *I can make it!* I jump and hit the web hammock. I bounce off of it and hit the ground. I tumble into a downed fighter jet.

I watch the Cord lift higher. That didn't work.

The crashed jet I'm next to has missiles that aren't launched. *I wonder how can I use these to help SNAFU?* Next to the jet is a Marine sprawled on the ground with an M4 next to him. A Space Spider runs by us. It doesn't pay me any attention. It's on a mission and I'm not a threat. Roy waits for the Spacer to pass and then runs up to me. He eyes another machine gun not to far from him.

I say, "Forget the M4. Think happy thoughts."

Roy looks around. "It's gone," he says. He's right, the Spacer has moved on and there are no Space Spiders nearby. He steps closer to the machine gun. "Coast is clear. I can get it."

"Roy, don't do it. They're everywhere. Think happy thoughts."

Roy stops. *Thank God, he's finally listening to me.* It's important to NOT be a threat until we figure out what we're going to do. Then I see Roy eyeing the tank a few yards away. It's upright with only remnants of webbing on it. A dead solider hangs halfway out of the hatch.

Roy claps his hands. "That's our ride back."

"A tank won't protect us. We were in a tank. Remember, it didn't end well."

"It's better than nothing."

"No. It's death."

Roy whistles as if he doesn't have a care in the world. He saunters toward the tank.

"Roy. Don't!"

Roy looks around. Still no Spacers. Roy runs for the tank.

"Damn it."

A Space Spider scurries through some smoking wreckage not so far away. *Where was it a moment ago?* It sees Roy climbing onto the M1

Abrams tank. The Spacer scurries toward Roy with twitching fangs. Roy has a good lead; he's going to make it. Roy climbs onto the tank and pulls on the dead solider, but the body's stuck in the hatch. The Space Spider is almost to the tank. Roy can't pull the body out. Roy's *not* going to make it.

I grab the M4 from the dead Marine on the ground and blast the Spacer as it leaps for Roy. The Space Spider flinches and Roy slides down the other side of tank just in time. The Spacer's fangs pierce into the dead solider hanging out of the hatch. The Space Spider yanks the body out of the hatch. *Thank you, Alien Freak, for clearing the way for Roy.* I empty my mag into its butt. I eject the mag and slam in another. It's fun to shoot a big gun in your underwear. The Space Spider turns on me. Roy climbs onto the tank. I see another Spacer heading toward me. I can blast one by myself, but not two. Not in boxers.

If Roy is going to save my 100% organic-cotton-covered ass, he doesn't have time to climb into the tank. Instead Roy gets behind the 0.50 inch caliber machine gun mounted on the top of the tank a.k.a. the commander's station. He fires the big gun. The rounds shred the Spacer closest to me. Goo and guts explode. The second Spacer jumps between the tank and me. Smart. Roy can't shoot at it. If he misses the Spacer he'll hit me.

Roy yells, "Get out from behind it!"

I slide over the downed jet next to me and duck. Roy blasts the Spacer. A few rounds hit the fighter jet I'm hiding behind. I stay low. Roy's big gun gets the Spacer before it can fang me. The Space Spider splits in half, the left side falls one way, the right side the other. Vital stuff glops out.

Roy shouts, "Chevy, you OK?"

I look at the unused missiles on the crashed jet. At $1.6 million apiece it's kinda a waste to just let the missiles lay there collecting dust. I look up. The balloon has drifted a bit, it's almost over our heads.

"Chevy, you OK?"

SNAFU looks out of the basket and stares at the Galactic Cord. He's pretty much eye-to-eye with it. The Cord looks like a long web runway that will deliver Spacers right to his front door. *Come on, SNAFU, tie that thing off and get out of there.*

"Chevy!"

I stand up and finally say, "Roy, I'm fine."

He's relieved I'm alive and pissed it took so long for me to answer. "You're a … " BOOM. A jet crashes not too far away.

"What?" I ask.

"Shut up."

I look at the web hammock below the balloon, that's brilliant. He must of done that. I've been telling him for years that he's a smart guy. I'm glad he saw the opportunity available, because it saved my life. I look up. I don't see SNAFU climbing out of the basket. I hear the flames blast. The balloon continues to rise and drift. He better jump soon if he plans on hitting the hammock. *What's he waiting for?* I watch four more Spacers burn off colors. I get it. He's not planning on jumping. If he bails the balloon will be defenseless. He's going to try and protect the balloon as it lifts the Cord out of the atmosphere. He's going to ride this thing out.

Roy sticks his head out of the tank hatch. "Chevy, come on. Get in the tank."

"SNAFU's not gonna jump."

Roy ignores me. "Chevy, we should be safe. Right? We're driving AWAY from the Space Spider's hive. We won't be seen as a threat."

"Bees have hives. Spiders have … "

"Whatever. Shut up. Come on. Sweetie's waiting for you."

Roy may be stupid, but he's not dumb. He knows how to get me to move.

"No. I've got to help SNAFU protect the balloon or this whole thing will be an epic fail."

I raise my M4. Maybe I can shoot the newbies coming down the Cord. But I don't have a scope and the Cord is too high. I could empty a whole magazine and only hit the Spacers once before they get to SNAFU. That isn't going to be the difference that makes a difference.

Roy watches me as I point my M4 at the sky. "You can't shoot Spacers coming down the Cord. You might hit SNAFU or the balloon."

I'm not that bad of an aim. I laugh.

"What are you laughing about?"

"SNAFU's going to save the world."

Roy doesn't think it's funny, but then he laughs. "Yeah, that's nuts."

Back at the tank and Humvee fort: Darcy and Sweetie whisper to themselves as Crystal leans into Mouth Wash. She says, "You hunt small game. Rabbits. Isn't that right."

"Yes," he says as he edges closer to her, "I like small, *cute things*. You seem to go after *big* game."

"I bring them down."

Sweetie snickers, but looks away when Mouth Wash glances at her. It's hard to have privacy in this cramped space.

Mouth Wash says, "Going for the big insensitive beasts. How's that working for you?"

Darcy says, "What did you say?"

Oh, yeah. Mouth Wash can't insult SNAFU, because he's Darcy's husband now. Mouth Wash looks at her. *You're not supposed to be listening.* Darcy glares back at Mouth Wash. *Don't say anything mean about my love.*

Sweetie puts a hand on Darcy's shoulder, "He's right, SNAFU wasn't so caring or sensitive until he met you."

Darcy keeps her focus on Mouth Wash, but talks to Sweetie, "You take that side, I'll take this side." Darcy says, "We'll take the first lookout."

Darcy peeks over the Humvee. Sweetie gives Mouth Wash her raised eyebrow look: *Don't piss off Darcy.*

They don't have much space or privacy so Mouth Wash whispers to Crystal, "You go out with the big, mean lugs because you think guys only want ONE thing." Crystal moves closer to him to hear. That's good. Her hand accidentally touches his. She pulls it back, but the touch clears his brain. What was he saying?

Crystal smiles and helps him. "I go out with jerks because I think all guys are jerks."

"Right. Thank you. You think all guys are that way so you FIND the guys that ARE that way. Don't you see, it's a self-fulfilling prophecy. Then you blame ALL men, but it's not ALL men, it's just ALL the guys you hook up with."

Crystal thinks about it for a moment. "Which way is this?"

"What?"

"Is this your psychological bullshit approach?"

"What?"

"This approach of wooing me sucks. You were doing really well before, but blaming me or trying to get me to blame myself is a terrible way to *get with me*."

"Oh."

A group of Space Spiders hustles in front of the makeshift fortress. Crystal raises her weapon and takes aim. Darcy places a hand on Crystal's M4. "Save your ammo. When SNAFU hits that web hammock, we'll jump out and give him cover. We're going to need everything we've got."

Crystal nods. The Space Spiders scatter. Crystal turns to Mouth Wash. He mopes. She softens. Crystal touches his hand and whispers in his ear. "Your fun, carefree approach is much more affective." Mouth Wash smiles, but before he can say anything, Crystal goes on the offensive. She pokes him in the chest. "Why are you so confident?"

"Ahh … I've learned the best way to get what I want is to ask for it."

"Do you always get what you want?"

He isn't sure how to answer. He might end up sounding like a dog. She smiles. She's playing with him. He returns the smile and decides to go on the offensive. He presses her against the Humvee. "Usually."

"Do you think you're going to get what you want from me?"

Mouth Wash clarifies. "With you."

"What?"

"I don't want anything FROM you. I want to live WITH you."

"You want to LIVE with me?" asks Crystal.

"No, not like MOVE in with you and your parents. I don't think they'd approve."

Crystal laughs.

"What I mean is that I want to experience life WITH you. I don't want anything FROM you. I see it as co-creating and living life WITH each other." Mouth Wash moves away from her and starts pacing in the small gap between the war vehicles. He seems excited.

Crystal says, "You're good with words."

"I'm good with many things," Mouth Wash winks at her and dances and wiggles.

"What are you doing?"

"I need to pee."

Crystal covers her face with her hands.

Sweetie turns. "Really?"

Mouth Wash jumps around. The three women watch him. Sweetie thinks, *he must have it bad, his timing is way off.* He grabs his own crotch.

"OK, OK," says Darcy, "Climb back over, I'll cover you."

"No," says Crystal. "I'll cover him. He's my boyfriend."

Mouth Wash stops dancing. He moves toward Crystal for a kiss, but he can't stop himself from wiggling again.

"I'm not going to kiss you now! You can't even stand still." Crystal pushes him. "Go already before I change my mind."

Mouth Wash grabs his M4 and climbs over the tank.

CHAPTER 41

GIRLS JUST WANNA HAVE GUNS

I LOOK AROUND FOR the girls, but all I see is the destruction of the battle. I focus on the Chinook transport copter again. Roy says, "They've got to be close. I'm sure they're watching SNAFU and the balloon right now." *That makes sense.* Roy's comment breaks me out of my stare. Darcy wouldn't leave SNAFU and I'm sure Sweetie and Darcy wouldn't leave the fight. They're too strong for that. But I also know Sweetie *is* strong enough to leave me.

"Tell me which way to go," says Roy "and I'll start the tank up."

"We're not moving until we know where they are. We could drive in the opposite direction and get farther away from them."

I look at the big helicopter troop transport again in the middle of the football field. Maybe they're in there. Then I realize, there might be extra weapons in that big Chinook. A Space Spider runs out of the crashed transport. I decide that's not the opportunity I'm looking for. But I glance at it again. It's strange; I have a feeling about that transport. I could swear that's where they're holding up.

The next four Space Pebbles zoom down the Cord. They're going to land in SNAFU's lap.

SNAFU watches the Pebbles coming at him. The colors are beautiful, but this doesn't shift his mood. He can only see three coming down the Cord. He hopes the Spacer on the underside of the Cord will drop to Earth if he's able to blow up the other three. He can't see the one on the bottom of the Cord so best not to think about it.

Help me to accept the things I cannot change,
the courage to change the things I can,
and the wisdom to know the difference.

SNAFU checks his M4 with the grenade launcher. Good it has grenades. This might be the best wedding present ever. He could kiss Darcy. He'd like to kiss her. The Space Pebbles burn off their pretty colors and reveal snow white, 16-foot fury, angry, fluffy boulders of alien joy. Birth is such a wonderful experience. The Space Spiders unfurl and shoot webs to each other as they race toward SNAFU and the basket. They pull on the webbing, creating friction on the Galactic Cord. Sometimes they pull hard, sometimes they let go to vary their speed of descent. They have learned from their predecessors. All eight eyes are not focused on each other. More than a few look at SNAFU and the balloon. The Cord isn't attached to the planet anymore. Something has threatened the stability of the Cord and the Spacers are zooming toward it.

SNAFU fires one, two, three grenades. He doesn't want to waste ammo, but if one of the Spacers gets to him and the balloon, then it's game over. And, as we all know, it sucks to die with unused firepower. It's happened while playing video games. It's not going to happen in real life. One grenade flies past the Space Spiders, but two hit the Spacer on top of the Cord. BOOM. BOOM. The top Spacer explodes, as does half of the Spacer on the right side. The chain between the four Spacers is broken. The other two and a half Spacers fall to Earth.

The two healthy Space Spiders land just fine on the ground. The half Spacer doesn't fair so well. SPLAT! I duck to avoid being hit with splattering goo. The two Spacers look at the tank and me. Roy stands tall behind the 50-caliber gun, but he doesn't engage them. They run off.

Roy yells, "That's right! Run home to mommy!"

Mouth Wash stands with his back to the tank and Humvee hideout. He wiggles until he gets his zipper down. He pees on a burned-up Jeep. Now that Mouth Wash is out of the tank and Humvee fort, he can see past the death and destruction carnage of the troop transport helicopter that blocks the view of Roy and me from the others. But Mouth Wash doesn't look in that direction. If he did, he'd see Roy in his underwear on top of the tank.

Just moments ago: The two and half Space Spiders fall to Earth. The half Spacer goes SPLAT.

Darcy yells to Mouth Wash, "What's happening over there?"

Mouth Wash hates it when people talk to him when he's trying to pee. By the time he looks in our direction, Roy is inside the tank and I've stepped behind it. Mouth Wash only sees the tank.

Mouth Wash yells, "The same thing is happening. Two more just landed."

Crystal yells, "Are you still peeing?"

"Every time something explodes or someone talks to me, I stop. It takes time to relax and get things flowing again."

Crystal yells, "We don't need details just hurry!"

"Stop talking to me!"

A Space Spider comes out of nowhere and charges at Mouth Wash. He stops peeing again and screams, "Ahhhhh." Darcy and Sweetie raise their weapons and slide next to Crystal. Darcy says, "It's too close to him." Crystal yells to Mouth Wash, "Move to the left!"

Mouth Wash glances at his M4 that leans against the burnt Jeep.

Sweetie yells, "Don't go for your weapon! Don't move! Don't be a threat!"

"That's easy for you to say!" he yells.

Crystal glares at Sweetie.

"I know Crystal, doing nothing sucks, but he can't be seen as a threat. The Spacer is too close to him."

The Spacer gnashes its fangs at Mouth Wash. Mouth Wash raises his hands. His pants fall down revealing his boxer brief underwear – a boxer and brief hybrid that does well in revealing the shape of his butt. The Space Spider looks Mouth Wash up and down and rushes off. Mouth Wash turns and yells to Crystal, "See, if I act really casual, they don't see me as a threat!"

"Pull up your pants and get back here!"

But before Mouth Wash can pull up his pants, he sees Roy climb back onto the top of the tank. Mouth Wash yells, "Roy, I see Roy! He's standing on a tank in his underwear." Mouth Wash winces and shivers. "It looks like something is wrong with his … thing."

I don't see Mouth Wash peeing, which is fine with me. I look up instead worried about my best friend. I can't see SNAFU. I only see the bottom of the basket. I hear the flames roar into the balloon. SNAFU's not looking over the side of the basket. He's not planning to jump.

"He's going to ride that thing all the way up," I say.

"Chevy, come on let's go. We can't help him from down here."

"We're not going anywhere until we know where to go."

I watch the balloon rise. *There's got to be some way I can help him.* The next set burns off their shells with spectacular colors. I don't know how much ammo SNAFU has up there. A missile streams out of the basket and hits the Space Spider that is on top of the Cord. The explosion is big. The range of the blast extends out and burns the two Spacers on the sides of the Cord. The burnt Space Spiders crumble into ashes. The two side Spacers and the one under the Cord, all fall to Earth. All three hit with a thump. They look at us and hobble away.

"Chevy, he's doing just fine without us."

SNAFU can't have an unlimited amount of ammo. The balloon *is* going up but it's not *racing* skyward. This is taking too long.

Bits and pieces continue to shake loose from the end of the Cord. Bricks fall and dirt rains down on us. Something black and gold drops from the end of the Galactic Cord. It floats for a second and then falls. It's a varsity jacket.

"Come on Chevy, let's go."

SNAFU crouches down in the basket. It swings side to side like a pendulum from the blast from the missile he shot. The Spacers were pretty close when they exploded. SNAFU holds on until the basket settles. He looks around. No more missiles. He tosses the launcher over the side. He does a quick inventory. Two more M4's, grenades that roll around, *yeah, that's safe*, and three more magazines.

"Chevy, he's fine. He's got a rocket launcher."

Something falls out of the sky and CRASHES on the jet wing next to me. I jump. It's the rocket launcher. "He doesn't have any more rockets."

"We can't help him from down here," says Roy.

"If SNAFU goes down, the Spacers take over. If the hot air balloon stays in the air, then you and I are heroes and you'll get laid by everyone. You can even fuck guys, if you want to."

"Chevy, I'm pretty sure that's the most insensitive and politically incorrect thing you've ever said, and that certainly doesn't motivate me, but I get what you mean."

See, I knew if I used Roy-speak, he'd get it. I wasn't sure how we could help SNAFU. *Come on, think.* An opportunity is right here. There is always one available. *Come on, let me see it.*

Roy climbs into the tank. "Let's go. We can't help him from down here."

"Stop saying that! Wait. Say that again."

"Let's go."

"No, the other part."

"We can't help him from down here?"

Roy's right. We can't help him from *down here.* "Roy, you're brilliant." I look at the dead pilot strapped into the downed jet next to me. "Bring the tank over here."

I look at the balloon. I think it's still close enough. I pick up the varsity jacket that fell out of the sky. Roy looks at me, the tank isn't moving. *I swear if he would just do what I tell him to do ...* I have another thought.

"Roy, what kinds of weapons are inside the tank?"

"Why?"

"Because I want them."

"No. They're my weapons."

"You've got the tank."

This seems fair to Roy. He climbs into the tank to see what he's got.

Meanwhile, back at the tank and Humvee compound, Sweetie tries to scurry over the tank. But, Darcy grabs Sweetie. "We're not risking two people to gather intelligence."

Sweetie yells to Mouth Wash, "Do you see Chevy?"

"Yes. He's on the ground. He's in his underwear too."

Crystal turns to Sweetie, "You attract all the freaks."

Mouth Wash yells, "Wait. Roy's climbing into the tank and Chevy is walking over to a crashed fighter."

Sweetie wants to see for herself, but Darcy blocks her. Sweetie yells to Mouth Wash, "What's happening?"

"Nothing. Wait. A uniform. Roy is throwing a uniform out of the tank to Chevy."

An OCP (Operational Camouflage Pattern) combat uniform flies out of the tank. It looks like a regular camouflage army uniform to you and me. First the shirt, then the pants. I take off the backpack and put them on. "Are you undressing someone in there?"

Roy's head pops out of the tank. "Shut up. You want to fight in your boxers?"

Roy comes out with M4's, extra magazines, and grenades. He now wears camouflage pants, but he hasn't put on a shirt. Show off. He hands me the M4's. "Be careful, they're loaded."

"No duh."

I look at Roy as I take the ammo and weapons. He still has the bulge in his pants. I laugh.

"What?"

"Nothing." I stuff extra mags and grenades into pockets on my shirt and pants.

"Why don't you load up your backpack."

"No. I don't want to crush it."

"Crush what?" asks Roy.

"Nothing. I'm going to leave it here."

"What's in the backpack?"

I shove the backpack under the broken wing of the jet fighter. I try to lift the wing. I can't move it. "Come on Roy, bring the tank over here and push on this wing. Hurry, while the balloon is still in range."

The tank doesn't move.

"Come on, Roy. I need your help." That might have been the hardest thing I've ever said in my life. Roy points at something. I follow his finger. Two Space Spiders come for us. They're pretty far away, but they're coming for us. Two, that's not so bad. We can take out two, but first I want to set up the fighter.

Roy doesn't move. Why doesn't he move? Probably because he realizes a tank is a big metal coffin. But I need him.

"Roy, Sweetie told me that she always loved you."

Roy looks at me. I got his attention. I put my hand on the jet wing. "Make the tank go forward. See this wing, push it so the jet wing tilts this way." I show him a 45-degree angle with the palm of my hand.

Roy disappears into the tank. "Sweetie, I'm coming inside you." The tank moves forward. It bumps into the broken wing of the jet. The wing bends and the whole jet tilts. Yes! I look at the dead pilot and then look up at the balloon. That's about a 45-degree angle.

"That's good. That's good."

I undo the pilot's harness and pull him out of the jet. Roy climbs out of the tank and stands behind the 50-caliber gun. He looks at the two approaching Space Spiders. He looks at me as I put on the varsity jacket that fell from the sky.

He shouts, "The missiles aren't pointed at the balloon."

"I'm not launching the missiles."

What? Then Roy sees the empty pilot's seat, the tilt of the jet, and the balloon above it. He gets it.

"Chevy, you're crazy."

"Roy, listen. If I … don't … you gotta leave Sweetie alone."

"I can't make promises I don't plan on keeping."

"Then I guess I won't die."

"Good."

We have a moment of appreciation. OK, maybe we're friends now. I look at the two Space Spiders and say, "I'll help you with these two first."

"You're all heart."

But what we don't see are the eight Space Spiders sneaking up behind us. The two Spacers we see stop advancing toward us.

Roy says, "They're just out of range. It seems like they're waiting for something." We wait. Roy says, "A strange time for school pride."

I look at the varsity jacket I put on. "It's going to get cold up there."

Sweetie takes off her sneakers and rolls off her yoga pants.

"What are you doing?" asks Darcy.

"That's how they got past hundreds of Spacers," says Sweetie, "in their underwear. They weren't seen as a threat."

"Are you serious?"

"If I'm going to help, I need to see what's going on. I think there are two ways to be safe and on the battlefield. Be in your underwear like Chevy and Roy or pee like Mouth Wash. I'm not peeing in front of everybody."

Crystal nods, *that's reasonable*. But Darcy blocks Sweetie.

"Listen," says Sweetie, "when SNAFU comes down you're going to run onto the field to help him. I'm not going to try and stop you from helping the man you love, and if I did, you'd just knock me out of the way." Darcy smiles. Crystal nods again. Sweetie continues, "If you want to, you can stop me from going out there. You are stronger and better trained then me. But I can't help by sitting back here. Maybe *there is* something I can do *right now*. Please, let me try and help the man I love."

Darcy moves out of the way. Sweetie climbs out of the tank and Humvee fort. Darcy unbuttons her shirt and looks at Crystal. Crystal shakes her head. "I'm not undressing. I'll cover you." Darcy waits for an explanation. Crystal sighs, "I sometimes don't wear underwear."

Darcy smiles and says, "And I shall call you Commando." Darcy gives her shirt to Crystal. Crystal can't stop from looking. "Nice."

"Thanks." #girlcrush

Darcy gives her weapon to Crystal. Darcy climbs out still wearing her camouflaged pants and army-issued boots.

"You're not going to take off your pants?"

"If they can't see I'm not a threat in a black lace bra, then they can eat me."

Sweetie walks up to Mouth Wash. His pants are still down around his ankles. "I guess I'm not going to finish peeing." He reaches for his pants.

"Wait. Leave them down," says Sweetie.

"Whatever you say, Princess." Sweetie shakes her head but steps closer to him so she can see Roy and me.

Crystal yells, "Not too close."

Mouth Wash looks at Sweetie in her panties. "Hello."

Sweetie says, "Focus."

"Yes. You're right."

"Look at my face when you talk to me."

Mouth Wash looks up. "I get it," he says, "we're not a threat when we're in our underwear."

"What's going on over there?" asks Sweetie.

Mouth Wash makes himself look in our direction. "Chevy pulled the pilot out of the fighter jet that the tank pushed. I don't know why. Now they're getting ready to shoot the two Space Spiders over there."

Mouth Wash points at the two Space Spiders who just stand there. Darcy arrives and stands on the other side of Mouth Wash. He stares at her.

Darcy says, "War makes you do crazy things."

"The crazier, the better."

Sweetie hits Mouth Wash. "Don't flirt with her."

Mouth Wash nods. "OK. You're right. I'm sorry. This is just very unusual and I'm having a hard time concentrating."

Darcy looks at the rising balloon. "I don't like it. It keeps getting higher and higher and he's not getting out."

Three Space Spiders scurry past Darcy, Mouth Wash, and Sweetie. The Spacers hesitate and look at them. Darcy, Mouth Wash, and Sweetie smile and wave. The Spacers shake their heads and move on.

Sweetie sees the eight Spacers sneaking up on Roy and me. She points at them. "Chevy and Roy don't see the ones sneaking up on them. The other two Spacers are waiting until the eight get the boys from behind."

Sweetie yells, "CHEVY! ROY! BEHIND YOU!"

But we don't hear her. The roar of the flames from the balloon, the distance between us, the random battle noises of gunfire, jets, and explosions, and our own breathing create a white noise background that drowns her out.

Crystal calls out, "Look what I found." Crystal stands on top of the Humvee. She holds up two shells the size of American footballs and shouts, "Mortars!"

Darcy says, "Shoot them at the Spacers."

"But I can't even see Chevy and Roy."

That's true. The crashed Chinook transport blocks Crystal's view of us. Sweetie points to the eight hop-scotching and leap-frogging Spacers. "Do you see the group of Spacers advancing on the left?"

"Yeah, but I can't hit them all. I only have two shells."

"You don't have to hit any of them, just get close so the boys turn around and see them."

"How many yards?"

Darcy shouts, "Eighty."

Crystal jumps to the ground inside the makeshift fort. She dials in 80 yards. She angles the mortar launcher a little and goes with her best guess. She drops the first one in.

Pffft.

It flies out. She moves the tube a few degrees to the right and drops the second shell in. It fires out.

Pfft.

Roy and I watch and wait. The two Space Spiders don't approach us. They shuffle side-to-side like crabs and twitch their fangs. I say, "Something isn't right."

"Yeah, and I can tell you what isn't right," Roy says. "Space Spiders are messing up my Prom with your girlfriend." He gives me a wicked smile.

What an idiot. He laughs.

I'm about to say, "It seems like they're stalling." When...

BOOM the first mortar explodes behind us. The explosion sends a Jeep into one of the sneaking Space Spiders. It splatters into goo. We see Spacers scurrying toward us. I realize the other two were distracting us so the ones sneaking up on us could fang us from behind ... BOOM. The second mortar explodes a little closer to Roy and me. Dirt rains down on us. The other Spacers take cover. I can't count them in the chaos.

Roy shouts, "I told you they were alright."

I see Darcy in her bra, Mouth Wash with his pants down, and Sweetie in her teal Prom panties. We wave to each other.

Roy yells, "Underwear friends!"

I knew they were back there by the Chinook. I could sense them. I look at the balloon. It's not lined up with the fighter jet, but it's still close. I've got to hurry, but this bunch of Spacers is too big for Roy to handle on his own.

"Go on," says Roy. "Get out of here. Go see your boyfriend."

"You sure?"

"I'll be fine. I'm the cock master."

I sling the two M4's Roy gave me over my shoulder. I climb into the cockpit of the fighter.

Darcy asks, " What's Chevy doing?"

Mash Wash says, "He's going to fire the missiles at the sneaking Space Spiders."

"No," says Darcy. "I don't think the fighter is pointed in that direction."

"He's going to shoot the missiles at the Spacers coming down the Cord."

"No, that's too dangerous."

"Then what he's doing?" says Mouth Wash.

"He's going up there," says Sweetie, "to help SNAFU."

Darcy nods. "They're going to ride the balloon up so they can protect it."

The cockpit of the A-10 Thunderbolt II fighter is super cool with lots of buttons and switches. I've been in my Dad's plane a lot. He's teaching me how to fly. But those experiences aren't helping me now. This is a complex bird of prey. I think back to all of the Fourth of July air shows I went to with my family. I remember climbing into fighters. "Dad, where is the eject button?" He'd always shake his head. He wanted to teach me how to fly and I just wanted to know where the eject button was. Thank God I asked him that over and over again. And, I'm glad he told me. *OK, where is it?*

Roy is inside the tank, he turns the big gun. *Oh man, that's going to be loud.* I plug my ears. BOOM! One of the Space Spiders explodes. Others zigzag their way toward us. *Serpentine serpentine.*

There it is. The time for talking is over. I throw the switch.

PFFT!

I shoot up and out with the pilot seat. Space Spiders watch me rocket into the sky. This gives Roy a stationary target. Stupid hairy beasts. BOOM. The Abrams tank shoots another shell. Three Space Spiders explode. They stood too close to each other. Oops. My Dad always said, "Making mistakes is part of life. That's one way we learn." After he said that, he always said, "It's OK to make mistakes. Nobody is going to die if you make a mistake." Well, he's not so right on that one.

I rotate and I watch Darcy, Sweetie, and Mouth Wash rush back to their tank and Humvee fort behind the Chinook troop transport. I can see their hideout now that I'm up in the air. Somebody hugs Mouth Wash after he gets into their stronghold. *Who's that?*

I reach for the balloon basket as I go up, but I'm not even close. I shoot past the basket and fly half way up the balloon. For a moment I hang in the air in the middle of the orange stripe. I realize that I did not think this out. I now have nothing under me except battlefield. I'm not even close to being above the web hammock. And, my angle was WAY off. I should have paid more attention to those cannon ball trajectory lectures at our annual summer Civil War reenactments. Who would have thunk mathematics and physics could have saved my life?

CHAPTER 42

DRESS UP IS FUN

EVERY SUMMER OUR SMALL town hosts The Battle of Fairland Reenactment. Visitors come from everywhere and they get to go "back in time" to the 1800s for three days. Throughout our town, cars are hidden and horses are tied to moveable posts that are setup outside shops in the main town square. Visitors get to eat wild game cooked over open campfires in cast-iron skillets and kettles. They also get to crunch on unsavory cracker-like biscuits that the Union soldiers called hardtacks. Tasteless, but big sellers. At the end of the long weekend is a big Civil War reenactment.

But the real fun for the visitors is everyone in Fairland dresses up in authentic Civil War costumes. We also act the part. Each one of us is an expert in something about the Civil War. Visitors can meet generals, captains, and soldiers who will tell them how they fought, slept, ate, and died. They can gather with women who talk passionately and freely about their 1800s dresses, corsets, and private undergarments. And, they can discuss trains and railroads with engineers that will tell them,

"It's the railroad that won the war."

Our whole little town participates all weekend long. It's fun and a big money maker for all the merchants. My Mom plays a Union Surgeon. It's the one time of year that my Mom gets dark. She puts clamps on tourists' limbs and waves around a jagged and rusty authentic Civil War saw. She goes on and on about amputating legs and arms. People scream and get grossed out, but they love it. It's crazy because when our family binge watches *The Walking Dead,* my Mom is the one who covers her face and says, "Tell me when it's over." When I was little, I'd have nightmares for a week after each reenactment weekend. I never told my mom the nightmares were about her. I knew she was having such a good time; I couldn't ruin it for her.

When Sweetie and I were little, we use to pretend to be farmers' kids. We'd run around barefoot with authentic, dirty, 1800's clothes our moms made for us. We'd ask visitors if we could, "Water their horses for five cents." We told them, "We accept postage currency since there ain't no more coins in-sir-cue-lay-shun because of the war." They'd take pictures of us and we'd point to their camera's and cell phones and pretend we didn't know what they were. Every time there was a flash, Sweetie would look up at the sky and say, "Is that lightning? It doesn't look like rain." That line always got a laugh. It's a good line and I always let her say it. I loved seeing her smile and laugh even when we were young.

I come back to the present moment. My upward movement slows. I reach out and try to touch the balloon but I'm not close enough. This is the end of my glorious blast into the sky. I'm at my zenith and I have a good view of everything. Three hundred and sixty degree Sky Roof, eat your heart out. I try to see Sweetie, but I'm facing the other direction. It would be nice to see her again. I wonder if she put her pants on yet. What a treat for Mouth Wash. I see so many dead humans and Spacers. The practice field isn't for practice any more. It's all real. No more do-overs. No more one-more-times. No more let's-get-this-one-right, boys. I see Spacers web-up Roy's tank. Hopefully, he's OK in there. The tank gets rolled a few times; maybe not. I fall and see the first jet that crashed with Little Bob. That's where it all started. I realize, even if I survive the fall the Spacers will surely take a break from rolling Roy's tank to fang me.

I look down at the ground. I might as well see death coming. It will be interesting to see what's on the other side. Then, I see something glorious. I'm not falling straight down. I went up on an angle and now I'm coming down on an angle. The Galactic Cord is going to be under me soon. The diameter of the Cord is 19 feet 3 inches. Mr. Giggin's grain silo is 16 feet around. SNAFU and I climbed up and ran on Mr. Giggin's silo when it was on its side before it was put upright next to his barn. We only slide off it a couple of times. *I can land on the Cord!*

But I'm coming down fast and I realize I'm going to overshoot it. I pull out the knife from the uniform Roy gave me. I reach for the Cord, but hand slides over the top of it. I jam the knife into the Cord as my legs bounce off it. The knife sticks and I hold onto it. The M4's strapped to my back slam against my spine. I dangle from the side of the Cord, high above Roy's tank and the Spacers. I can't see SNAFU, but I hear him yell, "Yeah, Chevy!" I gather my strength and pull myself up onto the Cord. I pull the knife out and sheath it. The Cord slopes down to SNAFU and the basket, but it's a gentle slope. SNAFU waves to me. I smile and catch my breath.

SNAFU blasts more flames and the balloon rises. If I had my skateboard, I could ride it down to SNAFU. (Or, I could ride my skateboard right off the Cord to my death.) The basket rises and lifts the Cord higher. The Cord is almost horizontal to the Earth now. Someone could walk along the Cord and jump into the basket. I hope that someone is gonna be me.

SNAFU points at me. I give a thumbs-up and I walk down the Cord to him. SNAFU raises his gun and points it at me. I think he's joking around, but I realize SNAFU would never joke around with a gun – loaded or not loaded. I turn around. Four more Spacers are coming down the Cord behind me. They burn off the last of their colors and unfurl. I shuffle toward SNAFU almost losing my balance. I need to get inside the basket so SNAFU can shoot them. I look over my shoulder; they're coming toward me too fast, I won't make it to the basket in time. The Space Spiders are going to slam into me and then we'll all crash into the basket and take down the balloon. I have to jump off so SNAFU has a chance to blast them, or I have to face the

417

Spacers coming down the Cord. Since I would prefer not to die, I turn and run up the Cord at the Spacers. They need to get past me so SNAFU can shoot them. The Spacers fire their webs and connect themselves around the Cord. The webbing is going to trip me up. I crouch low. No, I'm not low enough, and I was never good at limbo. I hear a high-pitched whistle and realize the sound is being made by the webbing that connects the Spacers as they zoom toward me. I jump as high as I can. The webbing between the two closest Spacers goes under me. But I jumped too soon, I'm going to come down and trip on the web line passing under me. One Space Spider looks at me with all eight eyes. Then I have an idea. As I come down I grab the webbing that connects two of the Spacers with both hands. I hold onto the webbing and it pulls me down the Cord as the four Spacers race toward SNAFU and the basket. It's like I'm water skiing. My feet slide across the top of the Cord.

SNAFU is ready but he can't shoot because I'm in the middle of two of the Spacers. It's up to me. *It's OK buddy, I've got these guys.* I continue to hold the webbing with my left hand while my right hand pulls my side arm, a Beretta 9M.

I point it at the Space Spider to my right. This Spacer holds the web line with its fangs. I blast the Spacer Spider in the head. BAM. BAM. BAM. I don't need to kill it, I just need it to release the webbing and disconnect it from the others. BAM. BAM. BAM. Let it goooooooo! Let it goooooooo! The cold never bothered me… The Space Spider's head caves in and it releases the webbing. The Space Spider slips away as gravity pulls it over the side of the Cord. The web line I hold pulls me toward the other Space Spider (it's butt) and the other side of Cord. I let go of the web line before I'm pulled off the other side of the Cord. I see the four Space Spiders fall to Earth. I continue to slide toward SNAFU, momentum continues to pull me toward him. He puts down his M4 and opens his arms. I hit the basket, flip over it, and slam into him. I push him to the far side of the basket. He looses his hold me and I flip over the other side of the basket.

CHAPTER 43

LATERS, BABY

SNAFU REACHES OVER THE basket and grabs me. He pulls me back in. I fall to the bottom of the basket. I lay there as the two M4s fall on top of me. Grenades roll and hit me in the face. Safety first. SNAFU pulls me up.

"I like what you've done to the place," I say.

"You're crazy."

"Me? You're still in the basket."

"They keep coming. If I'm not here they'll just slam into the balloon and take the whole thing down."

I stand up and look down. Space Spiders shoot Roy's webbed up tank with a couple of more web lines. They drag the upside down tank away. All I can think about are the unsatisfied mourning women around the world.

The balloon continues to lift.

The battlefield is relatively quiet. Or maybe we just can't hear the fighting so well now that we're up in the sky. Dead Spacers and soldiers are all over the place.

"Where did the rest of them go?" There were so many more Spacers behind the Web Wall.

SNAFU shakes his head. He doesn't know. I don't say it out loud but I think, *our town failed ... again. We let them retreat. We let them escape. We let them get away to fight another day.*

CHAPTER 44

THE CREED

A GROUP OF ABOUT 50 Space Spiders make it to the Medical Center. The Space Spiders stop for a breather now that they aren't being attacked. They rest in and around the parking lot. Maybe they can sense this is a place of healing. About half of the Spacers are injured. The healthy ones web up their comrades. They put web-cap-tourniquets on limbs where legs have been blown off so their mates won't goo out. Quick web-bandaging plugs are inserted into bullet holes on the Spacers that took the most damage. Some of the Spacer Medics rip off worthless, dangling legs before a web-cap-tourniquet is sprayed on. A mound of twitching legs pile up in one of the Visitor parking spaces.

When the Space Spiders are ready, they turn the corner around the medical building with the intention of crossing over into the state of Maryland. History repeats itself. Once again, the soldiers in our town cannot stop the opposition from retreating and escaping out of Pennsylvania. But something unusual happens. Something unusual even for a day like today. The 50 Space Spiders stop when they see a company of Civil War soldiers. There are about 90 men and women dressed in Union and Confederate uniforms. They form two straight lines. The front line is on bended knee. The second line stands behind the first. As the Spacers approach, the Civil War soldiers raise their muskets and take aim.

The Infantry Captain yells, "Steady."

The Space Spiders have not seen anything like this before. Two Union soldiers start playing Civil War battle drums. Ba dum, ba dum, ba dum dum dum. A musket is not my weapon of choice on a day like today, but the formation is impressive. The Space Spiders aren't sure what to do. The Captain raises her sword and yells, "Ready! Fire!" Muskets blast, gunpowder smoke rises from the rifles. Some of the Space Spiders wince as the small metal balls hit them. But as the smoke clears, they look at each other to see if anyone is hurt. Not really. One Space Spider reaches over with its mandibles and flicks a metal slug out of its Spacer buddy. *Only a scratch. It's just a flesh wound.* The Space Spiders laugh. High-pitched chirping and screeching fills the air.

The infantry captain's job is to lead her company into battle by giving the proper commands. The Captain yells, "Hold the line."

The brave men and women of our borough lower their muskets and attach bayonets. The company points the muskets at the Spacers. The Spacers legs are longer than the old rifles even with the blades attached. This isn't going to be pretty. This isn't going to be a fight. This isn't going to stop the Spacers. Sure, a few of them are going to get poked, but Team Human is at a big disadvantage. Sweat drips down the faces of the older infantrymen and collects in their straggly beards. This is a lot different than their staged reenactments. Breathing gets shallower. The Captain yells,

"I am the infantry!"

The company of soldiers responds,

"I am my country's strength in war, her deterrent in peace!"

424

At that moment, SNAFU and I blast our M4s at the next four Spacers running down the Cord at us. The contrast between the weapons of yesterday and today is significant. SNAFU and I yell,

"I am the heart of the fight, wherever, whenever!"

Less than a quarter of a mile away, Sweetie, Darcy, and Crystal unload their mag into two Spacers that try to climb into their tank and Humvee fort. Sweetie, Darcy, and Crystal yell,

"I am the queen of the battle!"

Back at the medical center, the Space Spiders are not impressed with the Captain, the drums, or the company of men and women reciting the infantryman's creed. The Spacers advance as the men and women continue,

"I am what my country expects me to be. The best-trained soldier in the world. In the race for victory I am swift, determined, and courageous. Armed with a fierce will to win!"

The Captain shouts, "Prepare for engagement!"

Nobody exchanges rings. The men put their Civil War rifles down and put on ear protection. *What?* Some put on fluorescent green noise canceling-earmuffs. Others press non-allergenic medical grade rubberized plugs into their ears. The company continues,

"Never will I fail my country's trust!"

Their 21st Century ear protection is not historically accurate but promises firepower more effective then their muskets.

"Always I fight on through the foe, to the objective, to triumph over all. If necessary I will fight to my death!"

The Space Spiders charge. The Captain orders, "Now." The frontline picks up their loaded shotguns.

"By my steadfast courage, I have won 200 years of freedom!"

The Space Spiders scurry with great speed, but not faster than modern technology. Pump action and semi-automatic shotguns fire. Remingtons, Purdeys, Winchesters, P. Barrettas, Brownings, and Ithacas to name just a few. The company releases their 12, 16, and 20-gauge fury on the invaders. It's crazy to see Civil War soldiers pumping shotguns. The Spacers don't know what hits them. But I do: slugs, birdshot, and double-aught buck shells, all fueled by the desire to be free.

"I yield not to weakness, to hunger, to cowardice, to fatigue, to superior odds, for I am mentally tough, physically fit, and morally strait!"

Most of the shotguns hold seven or eight shells. Some of them have an extra one in the chamber. For simplicity lets say 90 guns x 7 shells = 630 blasts. The Space Spiders are bigger then the humans. Each Spacer stands about 16 feet tall (5 meters) and each human approximately 6 feet tall (2 meters). But the 50-plus Space Spiders are no match for the blasts that literally push them back. Legs and other pieces of their exoskeleton fly off. Gooey and brutal.

"I will never forsake my country, my mission, my comrades, my sacred duty!"

By the time the Spacers realize what they're truly up against, they don't have time to run. Spacers trip and fall over each other. Screeching fills the air.

"I am relentless, I am always there, now and forever, I Am The Infantry!"

The last Spacers crumble. The company cheers.

The Captain yells, "**Follow me!**"

The Captain rushes forward. The drums beat on. The men and women of *my town* run around the Spacer mess in their quest to continue the fight.

CHAPTER 45

GRAVEYARDS ARE FOR DYING

FIFTEEN WORRIED MEN AND women dressed in hunting attire carry shotguns and walk past the old cemetery that's located next to the medical building. Even in the middle of the day, a graveyard is a little bit spooky. They stop and listen to the 630-plus shotgun blasts coming from the other side of the medical building. Humans fighting back with great force fuels their spirits.

Two teenagers with rifles are in the back of this little group of 15. The teens are bored. They were promised an opportunity to kill Spacers and so far nothing. The boy teenager picks up a random Space Spider leg and hits his younger sister with it. She grabs a downed tree branch and they duel. Their father, one of the older guys in camouflage, yells at them, "Hey! Self-control and target identification. You're carrying loaded weapons." The teens drop the hairy leg and branch.

The teen girl looks at the Civil War statue in the cemetery. The rest of the group moves on without her. The stone solider on horse back shines in the sun. She doesn't notice the movement off to the right by the bushes. She takes the rifle off her back and leans it against the short fence. There is more movement, but it's just beyond her peripheral vision. A Space Spider peeks out from behind a tall, family tomb marker.

Her brother yells, "Come on, Tracy. You'll be pissed if we get one and you don't." Tracy grabs her rifle and runs after the group. The Space Spider twitches its fangs. The Spacer decides to go after her. It scurries out of the cemetery and onto the road, but it hears the snort of a horse behind it. The Spacer turns and looks at the Civil War monument. The stone horse and stone solider remain motionless.

A young woman calls out, "Over here, Graveyard!"

The Spacer answers to its new name. Graveyard turns to see a short knight in a full suit of armor on a big brown horse. The knight flips up its visor. It's Rose, one of Sweetie's Prom Committee friends. You remember Rose. She is the teen who always reads the book about the first female knight. Rose sits on top of her dark brown award-winning thoroughbred. Champion snorts again. The horse is as brave as she is. Rose bought her suit of armor online and her uncle, a welder, helped custom fit it for her. Rose finally gets to be a knight. But, there are two unusual things about this knight, her footwear and her lance. She wears high-top sneakers and her lance is actually a pole vault pole. Rose's parents bought it for her because they thought it would be safer to practice with than a real lance. Rose raises her shield, which has a big "F" on it for Fairland High. Her broadsword is attached at her waist and rests alongside her horse.

The sun reflects off her armor and shines in all eight eyes of the Space Spider. This is the advantage she was hoping for. Rose raises her 12-foot fiberglass lance.

"En garde, Graveyard."

Graveyard twitches its fangs and scurries at her. Champion flares his nostrils and charges. The steed races past the old tombstones. The pole-vault-lance hits Graveyard. The impact stops the Space Spider and punches through its thick hide. Rose urges Champion forward. The pole drives into the Spacer's body right below its head.

Graveyard tries to hold its ground, but the gelding pushes the

Space Spider backwards. Rose yells and leans in. The front of the pole-vault-lance pops through the back of the Space Spider and gets stuck between gnarled branches of an old oak tree. Champion stops. Graveyard is skewered. I guess if you're going to die, it might as well be in a cemetery. But Graveyard isn't dead. The Space Spider grabs tombstones and monuments with its legs and pulls itself forward. The Space Spider slides itself down the pole+vault+lance toward the female knight and her noble steed. Rose raises her shield. Fangs hit the shield and knock her and the big brown horse over. Graveyard tries to fang Champion, but the noble steed gets up just in time.

"Champion, get out of here!"

The big horse holds its ground and snorts at the bigger Spacer. "Now! Home!" Champion listens to Rose and gallops away.

Rose stands tall, but Graveyard towers over her. The end of the pole-vault-lance sticks out of the front of the Space Spider's body. Mandibles reach for Rose. She raises her dented shield and swings her broad sword. She blocks the mandibles and fangs with her shield and counters with a slice that leaves a deep cut in one of Graveyard's front legs. Rose ducks so the pole-vault-lance that extends toward her swings over her head.

Graveyard gets an idea. The Space Spider backs up so the end of the pole-vault-lance sticks further out of its chest. Graveyard moves from side to side, using the pole-vault-lance as a weapon. Rose parries the attacks and blocks the thrusts with her shield. Graveyard turns *snapping* the end of the pole-vault-lance that is stuck in the tree. The lance end sticking out of the front of Graveyard *smacks* Rose's shield and sends her flying. Rose tumbles and comes up with both hands on her broadsword. Graveyard turns itself completely around so Rose now faces Graveyard's rear end. Graveyard blasts webbing. Rose dives behind a tombstone. Webbing hits the marker and sticks to it. Rose shouts, "That's a red card violation." Graveyard screeches.

Graveyard turns to face the feisty female. Once again they are face to fang. Two eyes to eight. Teen broadsword to Spacer pole-vault-lance. Attack, parry, thrust. Chips of fiberglass fly through the air. Graveyard lunges for Rose with its fangs. She blocks them with broadsword sending vibrations through the Spacer's head.

Rose ducks the next attack and the pole-vault-lance jabs the air above her. Rose rolls under Graveyard. The young knight thrusts her sword into the beast and turns the sword. The Spacer screeches. Rose rolls out as buckets of goo pour out of Graveyard.

Rose stands as the Space Spider collapses. She runs toward the Spacer as she raises her broadsword. She brings it straight down into Graveyard's head. Crunch. She smiles, victory in true *Game of Thrones* style.

In the background, the red, orange, and yellow striped hot air balloon continues to rise. The Cord now comes down from the sky, dips toward the Earth and then slopes up toward the basket.

Rose looks at the balloon lifting the Cord and yells, "Get that thing out of here!"

CHAPTER 46

BARUKH ATAH ADONAI

THE BALLOON CONTINUES TO rise. Except for being rather chilly, the balloon ride is pleasant. Floating is nice. And, when SNAFU doesn't blast the flames, it's quiet. Deep woods quiet like it's 5 a.m. on a Sunday morning. Everything is beautiful as long as I don't focus on the fact that I and every other human on the planet might die if this doesn't work.

The far end of the Cord is, of course, still attached to the moon. The moon is way off in the distance. At some point the Cord just disappears into the sky. The balloon is high enough now that the Cord dips to the Earth and then comes back up to the balloon basket. The Galactic Cord now looks like a smile. Yes, a smile with the balloon and the moon being its rosy cheeks. Thinking of the Cord as a smile is much better than thinking of it as a death slide or a zip-line for fangs.

SNAFU points at the Cord. "Get ready."

Four more Spacers burn off pretty colors. SNAFU points at the dip in the smile. "Maybe they'll get to the dip and drop to Earth from

433

there. Maybe they won't have enough oomph to come back up this side of the Cord toward us."

Maybe.

We watch the four unfurl, link up, rub their webbing against the Cord and slow each other down. The Spacers get to the dip, shoot past it, and kept coming up the other side toward us. Their momentum carries them up this side of the smile.

And maybe not.

I flip off the safety. The four Space Spiders continue up the Cord toward the balloon and us. No, wait. They're slowing. They slide back down the Cord and stop at the dip. I flip the safety back on.

"They're going to drop to Earth from the dip," I say.

We're doing it. The balloon has passed the point of no return. It's safe. We're safe. *Now SNAFU and I can think about getting out of here.* SNAFU pulls the lever. Flames blast more hot air into the balloon.

The four Space Spiders disconnect from each other, but they don't drop. They walk around the Galactic Cord at the dip taking it all in. I imagine they're weighing options and trying to figure out what to do. They stop walking around the Cord: one stands on top, one stands on the bottom, and one stands on each side of the Cord. It's like gravity and physics don't apply to them.

SNAFU says, "They're getting ready to jump."

Maybe.

The Spacers walk up all four sides of the Cord toward us.

And maybe not.

I flip the safety off. I say, "I've got the one on the right." They're still pretty far away. I aim and fire. BAM. BAM. BAM. I hit Righty. That's the upside of the Spacers being so big, they're easy to hit. I hear SNAFU counting. "One, two, three …" He must be getting ready to throw a grenade. I continue to blast Righty. BAM. BAM. BAM. Goo drips down to Earth.

"Seven," says SNAFU.

"Throw it!" I yell. I don't want him to blow us up.

He tosses the grenade. It hits the Cord in front of the top one and bounces off to the left. He misses them, but then I realize it's perfect. SNAFU was always good at skipping stones at Creeks End. The

434

grenade bounces up right between Topper and Lefty when it goes BOOM. Great throw. Lefty is blown up, only two legs remained attached to the Cord. The explosion also hits Topper HARD, ripping it up and knocking Topper off of the Cord. The Space Spider flies off into the sky and drops to Earth. I continue to blast Righty. It stops. It stands on the side of the Cord, than sags, than dies, than drops to Earth.

"Laters, Baby."

One more to go. The bottom one. SNAFU leans left. I lean right. We can't see it under the Cord. "Wait, I see a leg," I say. "Hold me." SNAFU grabs my varsity jacket and my legs. I lean out of the basket with my M4. I shoot. The Spacer pulls itself closer to the Cord. Maybe I hit it once or twice, but it's safe under the Cord.

SNAFU pulls me in. He blasts more flames. His focus is better than mine. I forgot what our mission is.

"We can't get it," SNAFU says.

"Yes, we can. Just not that way."

"I'm glad you're here," he says.

I pull on the thin, lightweight webbing that attaches the basket to the arrow SNAFU shot into the Cord. As I pull on the webbing the basket gets closer to the Cord. When the basket is close enough, I climb out of the basket and onto the Cord. I hold onto the basket, I don't want to slide down the Cord to the dip. The balloon and basket are high in the air. The slope of the Cord down to the dip gets steeper by the moment. I find my balance. "SNAFU, get two grenades. Pull their pins and throw them to me." SNAFU pulls two pins, and we count, "One, two ..."

He hands one to me. I put one leg back over the edge of the basket to make sure I don't slide down the Cord. SNAFU holds my knee with his free hand.

"...three, four..."

He hands me the other grenade. I roll over so I lay face down on the Cord. SNAFU holds both my legs.

"...six, seven..."

I hold out my arms, a grenade in each hand. SNAFU gets a glimpse of the Spacer under the Cord. "It's under Cord!" I drop the grenades.

435

They fall - one grenade on each side of the Cord - the grenades explode as they fall past the upside-down Space Spider - one grenade on each side of it. BOOM. BOOM. Goo splatters the underside of the Cord and rains down to Earth. The force of the blasts lifts the Cord and tosses me into the basket. SNAFU catches me but I'm too much for him. We fall down and I get wicker face from the basket.

He pulls me up. "Thanks."

The balloon rises and it gets colder. SNAFU shivers. I'm glad I grabbed the varsity jacket.

SNAFU says, "Damn, it's getting cold."

"Do you want to snuggle?"

SNAFU just looks at me.

I open my arms. "Come over here, you big lug."

But he doesn't come over. He gets closer to the flames as he blasts more hot air. We are really, really, high and we keep going up. We both stand closer to the flames to stay warm. For the third time I think, *this might work.*

SNAFU says, "I could really go for some of Mouth Wash's Challah bread right now."

My mouth waters. Stupid SNAFU. I wasn't starving until he mentioned the Challah bread. I wish I would have grabbed the trail mix out of the back pack. Mouth Wash brings the best homemade braided bread when we go on overnight hunting trips. Then on Saturday morning we always make awesome French Toast with the leftovers.

SNAFU and I look at each other and say, "Barukh atah Adonai."

I feel better. I always feel better whenever I say that. My shoulders relax, my breathing gets a little deeper, and my body calms. I guess that's why people pray.

Barukh atah Adonai. That's the first part of the prayer that Mouth Wash always says after he lights two candles on Friday when the sun goes down. He does a little wave over the candles welcoming in the Sabbath before he says the prayer. If you don't know, the Sabbath is supposed to be a day of rest and thanks and a time to remember God. I wonder if his family celebrated the Sabbath yesterday when the sun didn't set. The whole hunting group knows the first line of the prayer and we say it with him.

Barukh atah Adonai, Eloheinu, melekh ha'olam. This means: Blessed are you, Lord, our God, sovereign of the universe

Mouth Wash asks Crystal to light the candles whenever she's with us. She always accepts. I think she comes out on Friday nights just to do this even when she's not sleeping out and hunting the next morning. Mouth Wash asks her to light the candles because it's tradition that the woman of the household lights them. Everyone is quiet when she lights the candles. We're always calm and respectful.

Mouth Wash practices Judaism but he also goes old, old school. Not just the *Torah*, but the *Kabbalah*, which some say is the mystical roots of both Judaism and Christianity. We're talking Tree of Life old school.

For Jewish people, the Sabbath starts on Friday evening. Most Christians celebrate the Sabbath on Sunday. The early Christians used to start the Sabbath on Friday night because Jesus was Jewish. My Dad told me that the Last Supper was Jesus celebrating Passover with his disciples. Who would have guessed that?

The Romans, or someone, wanted Christianity to grow. They decided one way to do this was to make Christianity more appealing to the Pagans. I guess they were in the market for a new religion. So the early Christians moved the Sabbath to Sunday. Get it SUN-day, that was the big day when the Pagans chilled-out and celebrated the Sun.

The early Church also made the rabbit and eggs part of Easter. The Pagans celebrated spring with these fertility symbols. Christianity adopted the Easter rabbit and Easter eggs so Christianity would seem less different than the Pagan religion. I never would have guessed marketing and packaging could be so involved in a religion's growth, but I guess it is.

I think of chocolate rabbits and caramel eggs. I could really do some emotional eating right now. I shift my focus. I go for a better feeling thought, we are alive and we're going up. The better thought gives me a better feeling. There is only one thing that really bothers me right now. OK, let's make that *four* things. Four more Space Spiders stand on the Cord at the dip of the smile.

SNAFU says, "Maybe the second set will knock off the first four."

"What?"

SNAFU points. *Oh, I see what he's talking about.* Another set of four has burned off colors and come down the Cord fast. They're going to slam into the first set waiting at the dip.

The first four Spacers catch the second four. Nope, nobody falls off. Now there are eight Spacers standing on the Cord. I think, *it could be worse.* The balloon continues to rise. The Earth rotates or the moon pulls the Cord (or a little of both) and the Cord straightens out. This means the dip is no longer a dip and the Cord is now horizontal to the Earth. The Cord is now one flat path from them to us. The eight Space Spiders look at us. *Still, things could be worse.* Four more come down the Cord. The first eight Spacers catch the next four Spacers. Now there are twelve. We get higher and colder. The twelve Space Spiders march toward us.

We look at our ammo the same way a person looks in their fridge hoping more food has magically appeared since the last time they looked in the fridge - ten minutes ago - even though no one has gone shopping. We've got a few rounds left in each of our weapons and one more full magazine left. *Things can't get worse.*

I say, "Time to get out."

SNAFU checks his magazine and picks up the last one. "What?"

I jam my knife into the basket near the lever. I rig it so the flames will keep blasting. *The balloon might get out of the atmosphere before the Spacers get here.* I don't think they understand what's really going on, but who knows. Maybe they have figured it out. Either way, staying and fighting will not accomplish our goal.

SNAFU raises his M4. He's going to go out fighting, but he doesn't fire because they are too far away. "Chevy, we can't jump."

"Yes, we can."

I take off the varsity jacket and show SNAFU the jet pilot's parachute I'm wearing. "I brought a parachute."

"I love you."

"I know."

He shoots some rounds at the Spacers. He's not ending his turn with left over ammo.

"Hold tight. It might be a little rough. We're probably over the weight limit."

"What?" SNAFU says, "All these years you don't make fun of my weight and now you do?"

"I'm not making fun of your weight. I'm just saying hold on because … "

"Because I'm fat."

"Grab me and hold on." He won't get near me.

SNAFU blasts again.

"What are you scared of?" I say.

"Nothing."

"Are you afraid of heights."

"No."

"Are you concerned about your weight?"

He hesitates. "No."

"You've never been concerned about it before?"

"I've always been concerned about it."

That's new. I didn't know that. "But why are you sensitive about it now?"

He won't answer. He shoots out his mag, ejects it, and slams in our last one. He shoots a few more rounds. I aim and shoot until I'm out. I drop the gun and finally get what's going on. I say, "You don't want Darcy to see you naked."

"Shut up."

"She will still love you when you take off your clothes."

"I wish I would have known I was getting married. I would have started working out."

SNAFU blasts some more. The first Space Spider falls off the Cord. Nice shooting. SNAFU blasts again, but his magazine is empty. He tosses his gun over the side. The Spacers charge us. They scurry along the top, the sides, and bottom of the Cord. I grab SNAFU and shout, "I love you whatever your size."

"You're an ass."

SNAFU grabs me back, but we're still in the basket. We don't know how to hold each other *and* get out of the basket. The Spacers get closer.

"Lean," I say.

We lean, but we just press against the side of the basket. They get closer. SNAFU gets frustrated and yells, "Arrrrrrrrrrrr!" He picks me up and charges the side of the basket. We hit, tumble out, and fall over the edge and out of the basket as the Spacers attack. We drop like a rock. It's scary. I look up at the balloon, it's still going up.

The chute opens. SNAFU almost slips out of my arms, but he's smart enough to hold onto the parachute straps running over my shoulders.

I look up again. The Space Spiders jump on the basket and on the balloon. The balloon collapses on one side. A Space Spider bursts into flames and falls to Earth. The balloon crumples in slow motion. The balloon, basket, and the Cord fall back to Earth.

We failed.

We did the best we could and it just wasn't enough. It's quiet in the Command Center. The General doesn't say anything. People all over the planet watched the balloon lift the Cord. They figured out what we were doing. Now they watch their screens in silence.

It's quiet in the drone trailers across America. They see the balloon and Cord fall. The mission has failed. No one says anything in the New Mexico Command Drone Room until a 22-year-old stands behind his drone operating station and says, "Sir, permission to speak."

"Hansen, not now," orders the Commanding Sergeant.

"Sir, I request permission to drive my drone up into the balloon and to push it into outer space." All of the drones have used up their hardware. They are just serving as eyes for the General. Some of them are tracking Spacers going to town, literally.

Another drone pilot says, "One drone can't make a difference."

Mackenzie says, "No, but if we all work together."

The Sergeant says, "What are you all waiting for? You heard Mr. Hansen."

The pilots drive their drones up into the falling balloon. Hansen's drone leads 30 other drones up into the balloon. Hansen's battle yell fills the Drone room. "Aaaaaaaaaahhhhhh!" The drones catch the sagging balloon and push it up. Some of the Space Spiders fall off of the balloon and basket. One Space Spider climbs into the balloon and grabs a drone. The Spacer webs up the drone and the drone drops. Space Spiders reach for other drones.

A senior voice booms throughout the drone room, "This is Lt. General Spade. I request permission for my Global Hawk to join your drone party."

One of the youngsters says, "Global Hawks are the big ones."

The Sergeant says, "It would be our honor."

A Global Hawk drone, which is the same size of a regular jet, flies up and into the crumpling balloon. Space Spiders pop out in every direction. It works. The drones push the balloon into outer space.

When they get there, the balloon, the basket, the drones, the Cord, and one Space Spider floats weightlessly in space. Four more Spacers burn off colors as they come down the Cord. They stop burning off colors but the outer shells don't burn off. They don't unfurl. The space pebbles zoom off the end of the Cord, past the crumpled up balloon, and into outer space.

The drone pilots cheer. The citizens of Earth cheer. Mouth Wash and Crystal cheer.

Darcy and Sweetie don't cheer, they climb out of their stronghold as they watch SNAFU and I parachute to Earth. But a group of Spacers gather out on the practice fields.

Sweetie says, "Let go!"

"No," says Darcy. "There's too many of them."

Twenty or more Spacers look up. It seems like they're waiting for something. Maybe they don't know what to do if the Cord gets disconnected. Sweetie watches our parachute descend.

"We can't just stand here and watch," says Sweetie.

"What do we do?" asks Mouth Wash.

"We wait for an opportunity," says Darcy.

Even though a bunch of Spacers are gathering on our school ground there are many Spacers that flee the battlefield. There are many roads that go south from Pennsylvania to West Virginia and Maryland. The biggest one is the Pennsylvania Turnpike, which is a toll highway. Four Fairland citizens dressed in hunting camouflage with shotguns stand at the tollbooth. Today's toll is Space Spider goo. Buckets and buckets of it. These men and women are here to make sure Spacers attempting to cross over the PA state border pay the toll with their lives. This state borderline is also known as the Mason-Dixon line, which represents the cultural border between the Southern United States and the Northern United States. This is the line that had to be held a long time ago. This is the line that our little town couldn't hold during the Civil War.

Ten Space Spiders come through the woods that run along the state turnpike. The citizens blast their shotguns. The Spacers scurry left and right. Moving targets are harder to hit. The Spacers have learned that hunters and doomsday preppers are powerful, and it's dangerous to engage them head on.

The four Freedom Fighters flee the tollbooth, there are too many Spacers to fight. I guess there won't be a fee today for using the interstate highway. The Freedom Fighters run down the empty turnpike toward a jack-knifed 16-wheeler big rig. The Space Spiders scurry past the tollbooth as they gain on the fleeing Freedom Fighters. The 16-wheeler starts up and pulls forward onto the berm revealing ten civil war cannons and a bunch of men and women dressed in Civil War uniforms. Both Union and Confederate. Everybody works together today.

The Space Spiders try to stop, but they don't have time. An ex-Navy Seal in full dress uniform stands near the cannons. It's SNAFU's Dad. He yells, "Fire!" The cannons fire. The Space Spiders try to scatter, but they can't do it fast enough. Cannon balls rip through the first bunch of Spacers and keep going. They puncture the second set and slam into the ones in the back. Other cannons are angled a bit higher. Their cannon balls come down and wipe out the Spacers in the back. Space Spiders stumble and crumble as they pay the price for using the Freedom Turnpike. Today there is a fee, and the cost is a little more then usual.

The four hunters that led the Spacers to their demise grab rifles and blast the handful of wounded Spacers that try to crawl away. The Civil War soldiers leave their cannons and also join in the slaughter. They blast the survivors with their semi-automatic and pump action shot guns. They take no prisoners.

No escape. No retreat. This ends here, today.

CHAPTER 47

LRIGWOC

NOBODY TELLS YOU THAT falling with a parachute is still falling. I know, it sorta goes without saying, but professionals always make it look so easy. Sure, we drop slower than if we didn't have a chute, but SNAFU and I hit the ground hard. At the last moment I remember you're suppose to hit and roll. But, it's too late, we hit and bounce. SNAFU goes one way. I go another. When I hit the ground *the second time*, I don't come up. I believe I got knocked out. The next thing I remember is SNAFU shaking me, "Come on, you can sleep when you're dead." *Not funny.* Then I think, *am I dead?*

Then I remember the war as I see and smell dead Spacers, big holes in the ground, burning jets, and smoking Humvees. I remember the balloon. It's going to crash on top of us. I yell, "Down. Down, get down." I cover my head. Nothing happens. I look up; the balloon isn't in the sky.

"Where's the balloon?" I ask.

"I don't know."

443

"And the Cord? Where the hell is the Cord?"

"I don't know," says SNAFU. "Maybe it worked."

"How? We saw it falling back to Earth."

"Maybe it is a Prom Day miracle."

We had missed the whole drone up, up, and away show. I'm not sure how long we were out. I look toward the Chinook transport copter. I see a bunch of Spacers disperse in every direction. *What was that about?* I see Sweetie, Darcy, Crystal and some guy peek out from behind the Chinook. They have to wait for more Spacers to clear the field. I remember the backpack I hide under the fighter jet wing. I look for the fighter that was next to the tank that Roy was in. But Roy's tank is gone now. Roy's gone now.

"Chevy, what are you doing?"

"What?" I forgot what I was doing.

"They're coming for us," he says.

I look at Sweetie. Oh, ya, the backpack. *Where is that fighter?* I see a trail through the destruction where the Spacers dragged Roy's tank. I run to the trail and follow it backwards to the fighter that I launched out of.

"You're going the wrong way!" SNAFU yells.

I pull the backpack out from under the jet's wing. Yes! I run back to SNAFU. The field has a few Spacers scurrying around. Sweetie waves to us from behind the Chinook. I wave back. She points at me. I smile and stand tall, *that's right, I'm the man.* SNAFU taps my shoulder, "She's not pointing *at you.*" I turn. A lone Space Spider watches us. It's pretty far away, but then it heads for us.

I say, "It's only one."

"We don't have any weapons."

I look at Sweetie and Darcy. "Maybe they've got weapons."

"We're pretty far away from them."

"Let's change that."

We run toward Sweetie, Darcy, Crystal and a guy. *Oh, yes, that's Mouth Wash. I'm glad he pulled up his pants.* I yell to SNAFU, "Keep your eyes open for weapons."

"I am," SNAFU says. "You got anything in the backpack we can use?"

I laugh. Sweetie stops to pick up something. She gets down on one knee and puts the tube on her shoulder. She aims it right at us. *Oh, a missile launcher.* "Come on, faster."

Sweetie preps the rocket launcher. "Prepping Rocket." She takes a deep breath. *Slow is smooth. Smooth is fast.*

Darcy, Crystal, and Mouth Wash look around for other weapons. Nothing. Mouth Wash picks up a rock.

Sweetie says, "Rocket ready."

Darcy points to her right. It's another Spacer and this one is coming for their little group. It's far away, but it's heading straight for them.

Sweetie says, "You take that one, I'll take the one behind Chevy and SNAFU."

Crystal shakes her head no, she's out of ammo. Darcy says, "I've only got three rounds left."

Mouth Wash says, "I can hit it with a rock." Crystal looks at him.

"I only have one rocket," says Sweetie. She looks behind her to make sure all is clear. Crystal and Mouth Wash are behind her. Sweetie says, "Watch out. Get out of the way." They move. Sweetie says, "Back blast area all secure." Then she has an idea. Sweetie stands, looks at the Space Spider coming toward them. She turns her back so THAT Spacer will be approaching from behind them. She says to Darcy, "Tell me when its close." Sweetie whispers, "Come on, Chevy. Figure it out."

I see Sweetie stand and then point the missile launcher in a new direction, *away* from us. I shout to SNAFU, "Do you see another Spacer over there?" SNAFU and I look where Sweetie's pointing her launcher.

"No," says SNAFU, "nothing over there. But I see a Spacer heading for them. Now that Sweetie has turned, it looks like THAT Spacer is coming up behind her."

SNAFU pants. "Your girlfriend better have two rockets."

My girlfriend. I hope so. Then I get it. Sweetie only has one rocket, but there are two Spacers. I know what she's trying to do, and she calls me nuts. I yell to SNAFU, "Follow me. We've got to run to where Sweetie's pointing the rocket."

"That's stupid."

"No, it's not."

I change direction and run hard. He follows even though he disagrees. Our Space Spider scurries after us and closes the gap. I yell, "Don't turn toward Sweetie until the missile launcher points directly at us."

"That's really stupid."

"There are two Spacers and she's only got one rocket."

Darcy watches the Space Spider speeding up behind them. She shouts, "Fifteen meters!"

"I don't know what that means!" yells Sweetie.

"Fifty feet!"

Darcy is introducing the metric system to our class. She says the whole world uses it besides England and us. Going metric is another 21st Century thing she's trying to do with us. But today is not a good day for teaching metrics.

Sweetie says, "Huddle close. We need that thing all over me." Mouth Wash wants to say something, but wisely chooses not to. Crystal is in punching distance. Darcy steps toward Sweetie. Crystal and Mouth Wash move closer to Sweetie, but Crystal makes sure she's between Sweetie and Mouth Wash. There's no reason for 'accidental contact' even at a time like this.

SNAFU points. "Second Humvee to your left and then straight on till Sweetie."

SNAFU is a guy that never wants to grow up. I make the hard left around the second Humvee and turn toward Sweetie. There's *my dangerous princess*. She's on one knee and now she points her missile launcher right at me. Strong. Beautiful. Powerful. SNAFU and I run straight at her.

I yell, "Get ready to duck."

"Don't you worry about that!"

Our Space Spider scurries over the Humvee in hot pursuit of us. It doesn't round the corner. Cheater.

SNAFU says, "Come on Sweetie."

"She's got to be sure the other one is close enough."

Darcy yells, "Twenty feet!" Darcy shoots her last three rounds at the Spacer and tries to act concerned, which is not hard to do. Darcy

446

wants to make sure their Spacer keeps charging.

Sweetie says, "Back blast area NOT secure. Wave Chevy and SNAFU down!"

Mouth Wash and Crystal wave their arms.

"Rocket!" yells Sweetie as she pulls the trigger. The Space Spider charging from behind leaps for Sweetie. The back blast hits the Space Spider and knocks it backwards. SNAFU and I see the signal, but we can't stop running, our Spacer is right behind us.

SNAFU yells, "Aaaaaaaa."

The rocket streams at us as we dive forward. The Spacer behind us reaches for SNAFU. Its mandibles grabs one of SNAFU's leg as the missile zooms toward us. The Spacer's fangs reach for him as the missile hits the Space Spider in its face. The Spacer can't hold onto SNAFU, the missile pushes the Spacer back and then ... BOOM. The force of the explosion throws us forward. We roll and bounce.

I look up and see an angel looking down at me. "Thank you."

Sweetie smiles back at me.

The back-blast Spacer lies out-stretched on its back. Legs wiggle as Darcy pulls her knife and leaps over its head and fangs and lands on its stomach. She slices a three-foot incision down its belly. She raises her knife high and then jabs it into the Spacer's body. Both the knife and her hand disappear into it. All eight legs shoot straight out and the Spacer's body bucks. The last violent shudder throws Darcy off of the Spacer and onto the battlefield. All eight legs relax and fall into the dirt. It's spent. It's lifeless body gives up the fight.

Darcy sits, brushes off battlefield grime, and rubs her leg. She doesn't stand. She wipes her knife on her pant leg and then sheaths it. SNAFU picks her up and twirls her. She laughs.

I hug Sweetie. She feels and smells good, but she doesn't hug me back.

The bomber with the nuke is called off. The General and President don't want to wipe out civilians and a whole lot of valuable farmland and livestock with no guarantee of getting all of the fleeing Spacers. They also know the radiation from the bomb will drift to other states. That wouldn't be good for humans, and it might actually be good for the Spacers that scattered. There's a lot of radiation in space. Maybe

Spacers like radiation.

The General receives intel from the drones. He watches as the good people of our tiny borough contain many of the rogue Spacers. It seems only a small number of Space Spiders are crossing state lines. The real good news back-up has arrived. The President, the General, and the United Nations are working together. We didn't know it, but the international community dispatched fighters from around the world about 20 hours ago and they're just getting to Pennsylvania. Canada gave the OK to fly through their air space. Thank you, Canuks.

West German Tornado fighter jets and British Royal Air Force Eurofighters strafe Space Spiders as they run through cornfields in Ohio. French Dassault Rafale multirole fighters and Israeli F15 Strike Eagles bombard Spacers that climb through the mountains of West Virginia. Chinese J-10 Multi-role fighters and Russian Migs punish Spacers scurrying through Maryland.

The Space Spiders that escaped north are a little trickier to root out. But the Special-Weapons-and-Tactics units (S.W.A.T. teams) of the Pennsylvania law-enforcement agencies respond quickly and effectively. Thank goodness that the militarization of the police in the United States has gone relatively unchecked. The S.W.A.T. teams met the Spacers in the streets of the cities with submachine guns, assault rifles, breaching shotguns, and sniper rifles. On a side note, S.W.A.T. is also the mixed martial arts series promoted by the Lithuania Bushido Federation. Darcy took Bushido for a year when she was in college. SNAFU better watch out or she'll use the Two Leg Grab Defense on him. But knowing SNAFU, he'll probably like that.

The hunt for the stragglers continues, but not everyone wants to kill the Spacers. Large black vans and trucks with no insignia (or plates) roll through PA and the Midwest. Soldiers wearing black uniforms jump out, corner Space Spiders and electrocute them with strange weapons. The limp Spacers are then pulled into the black trucks. S.W.A.T. teams also help with the "bug collection" using their stun grenades to knock out the Spacers without killing them. I imagine the military wants to run tests on the Spacers to figure out their secrets. Stupid mistake. Didn't anyone see King Kong? Am I the only one that knows that keeping Space Spiders is not going to play out well somewhere down the line?

I keep hugging Sweetie even though she doesn't hug me back. She says, "OK, you can let go now." I hold on for one more second and then let go.

SNAFU puts Darcy down on the ground and says, "Hello wife."

"Hello sexy," Darcy touches his face.

Sweetie pushes me away. *What?!* Sweetie looks at Crystal.

Crystal says, "Yeah, we've got look out." Crystal scans the horizon. "Better than watching you two go all yuk yuk."

But Sweetie doesn't kiss me. I can't decide if she's being smart because she knows if we beso we might get eaten by a Spacer or if she's still not OK with me.

Mouth Wash walks over and we hug. He says, "Nice job, man."

"Thanks, you too." I look up. "The Cord's gone, right?"

"You didn't see it?"

"No."

"Bummer. It was a team effort and it was really cool. You see, the balloon was coming down and ... "

Crystal nudges Mouth Wash, "Come on, you can tell him later. Let's see if we can find something better than a rock to defend ourselves with." Mouth Wash smacks her butt. "Hey!" But she smiles. They search the battlefield.

I turn and Sweetie leaps on me. *That's more like it.* We wrap our arms around each other. *She was being cautious.* She feels so good. I wish our bodies could be stuck together for a 100 years.

She whispers, "We did it."

We did. Her fingers run through my hair. I pull her closer. We kiss and nothing else matters. I want to live, but it would be OK to die now.

Darcy says, "OK, let's get out of here." But SNAFU hugs and kisses her again. Crystal yells back to us, "Take your time guys."

I look at Sweetie. "You look great."

"So do you."

Neither of us comment on the fact that we're no longer dressed for Prom. She ditched the dress for something more comfortable and I traded my tux for a camouflage uniform. We couldn't save Prom, but we saved the world. That's something. I hope it's enough.

I say, "I'm sorry. I ... "

"Shhh." Sweetie kisses me again. "I'm sorry too."

I move a strand of hair away from her face. "Wait, let me say this, it's important for me to make sure you know what I realized." I hold her hands. "From now on, I'll do my best to know what is important to you and honor it even if I disagree. It's important that I respect all of you."

"Yeah. That's it. Thank you. That means a lot to me."

"I'll make it up to you," I say.

"You better."

We kiss again. Mouth Wash walks over. I ask, "Have you been hitting on Sweetie?"

"Not anymore." Mouth Wash looks at Crystal and smiles. *Damn. Mouth Wash and Crystal, that's amazing. I guess anything can happen on Prom Day.* Then I remember all those Friday nights and how she's an excellent candle lighter. I probably could have seen this coming. Crystal walks over to SNAFU and Darcy. Crystal holds out her quartz necklace; it swings back and forth.

She taps SNAFU on the shoulder and says, "You still love me."

Darcy tries to walk away to give them some space, but SNAFU holds onto her. In fact, SNAFU pulls Darcy closer to him. She's not going anywhere.

SNAFU says, "I will always love you."

"But Mouth Wash is the guy for me now," says Crystal.

"Good," says SNAFU, "because he does absolutely nothing for me."

Darcy smiles, but Crystal remains serious and says, "I wish you both the best." She sticks out her hand to Darcy. Darcy and Crystal shake. It's formal but nice. Crystal turns to SNAFU, "Can I hug you?"

"Sure."

He lets go of Darcy and hugs Crystal. It's a good hug. Crystal gets her last smell of SNAFU. The sun feels different. It's only been a short time since the Earth started rotating again, but everything feels better. It feels like everything is going to be all right.

Crystal wipes a few tears, "You're such an ass. Don't you know when you break up there is suppose to be a lot of yelling and screaming?"

SNAFU wonders how many times they're going to breakup. But he doesn't say that. He says, "That's 20th century breakups. It's the 21st century. Now when we breakup, we thank each other for being part of our adventure. We celebrate each other."

Darcy looks at her husband a little surprised. We all do. *Did SNAFU just say that?*

Crystal says, "Damn, what happened to you? Space Spiders must have messed you up pretty good in that hot air balloon."

"I guess I'm just *Reaching New Heights*," says SNAFU. Everyone groans. He just made a Prom theme joke.

Crystal moves the crystal back and forth. "Hey, it says you're still an idiot."

I think of Roy, and I can see so does Sweetie. She looks around, but doesn't say anything. She's not going to ruin the moment.

Crystal feels bad for being mean. She tucks the crystal into her shirt, "I'm sorry, you're not an idiot. You never were."

SNAFU laughs. "Now you're stretching it the other way."

Crystal turns to Darcy. "Can I hug you too?"

"Ah … sure."

Darcy and Crystal hug. Crystal whispers, "Thank you."

"What for?"

"I don't know. Everything. Your kindness. Your strength. For just being you."

Crystal turns and punches Mouth Wash in the arm for no reason. He says, "Hey, punch someone you don't love."

Crystal laughs, "Love? Already? Slow down Minty."

Sweetie says, "Maybe Crystal is immune to the Mouth Wash magic?"

"Impossible," says Mouth Wash.

"Come on," says Crystal as she pulls Mouth Wash away from everyone else, "let's go help clean up the town. All these mushy feelings make me want to kill something." Crystal and Mouth Wash jog and then break into a run toward town. Overachievers. Without turning around, Crystal points her middle finger in the air and shouts, "Have fun on your honeymoon!"

Sweetie turns to me. "Where's Roy?"

I shake my head. "He didn't make it."

Everyone pauses. We watch Mouth Wash and Crystal run.

SNAFU says, "Shall we join them?"

Darcy limps as she picks up her M4. "I need to sit down first." SNAFU looks at her leg and sees a six-inch piece of metal sticking out of her leg. "Whoa!"

"It's not a big deal," Darcy says. "I landed on something when that thing knocked me off it. I can still walk."

We look at the piece of metal sticking out of her leg. She's not going anywhere. SNAFU says, "I don't think we should remove it."

"Yes," says Sweetie, "let's wait till we find a clean bandage and first-aid supplies. There's a military base over here."

I look. It *was* a military base before the Spacers trampled it. I think it was called Free Earth HQ. We walk toward it. Hopefully we'll find some shelter from the sun, and some supplies.

SNAFU picks up Darcy. "You don't have to do that," she says.

"My pleasure."

We walk to the abandoned military base. It takes a few minutes. We walk slowly so SNAFU doesn't bounce Darcy around. Sweetie and I get to the base first and clear a way for SNAFU.

"You can put me down now," says Darcy.

"I'll carry you over the threshold."

SNAFU steps over busted-up equipment, and they enter the trashed military outpost. Sweetie and I pick up a table and pull it under what's left of a camouflaged tarp. We find chairs. SNAFU sets Darcy down on a chairs.

SNAFU looks at the soldiers as they clear debris away from a Humvee. SNAFU whispers, "How about the back seat of the Humvee?"

Darcy laughs. "I'm too wounded to walk, but not too wounded to celebrate?"

SNAFU kisses Darcy. They both say, "How'd I get so lucky?"

I kiss Sweetie and look into her beautiful eyes.

She says, "What?"

"I just want to look at you. You're so beautiful."

"I'm disgusting, filthy, and sore."

"That's how I like my women."

Sweetie smiles, "I know."

We look at Darcy's leg. We want to sit, but we don't, not yet. We search through the wreckage for first-aid supplies.

A few other wounded soldiers return to the base. They keep to themselves, loading and working on a Humvee. It seems like they have a plan and it doesn't involve us. Sweetie and I think about offering to help, but I need rest. We all do. Sweetie and I also realize we're not going to leave Darcy when she's wounded.

And, it's important to leave some of *the fun* for others.

CHAPTER 48

URBAN WARFARE SPACE SPIDERS

OPERATION CLEAN UP CONTINUES. Groups of Space Spiders scatter through town. Some enter from the north of the school on Front Street, some from the West on Paxton Church Road, and some from the east on Allentown Boulevard. The Space Spiders have learned from their engagements with the townies that it's stupid to line up and fight like the Civil War armies did, they've learned that shotguns and cannons hurt.

The Space Spiders enter Fairland proper, hiding behind cars, scurrying in and out of alleys, and crawling over the roofs of our tallest buildings. Note: our tallest buildings are only three stories high.

From the North

The Spacers come down Front Street. It's quiet. A little too quiet, but they don't know that. They're aliens from out of town. They aren't aware of our comings and goings, and it's going to cost them something fierce.

The United States Second Amendment grants Americans the right to own guns. The amendment is a little wordier. Here it is in its original colonial wording:

A well regulated militia, being necessary to the security of a free state, the right of the people to keep and bear arms, shall not be infringed.

It's not a well-regulated militia fighting today. It's just ordinary, freedom-loving citizens who grew up hunting. I'm sure our founding fathers never thought the Second Amendment would be so vital in stopping Space Spiders and saving the world.

Spacers wander down Front Street. Some hesitate and look around. Others start to back away, they sense something is wrong. A front door opens on a house halfway down the street. A young woman with short black hair and wearing a Fairland High sweat suit steps out of the house. Her sweats are black with gold trim on the collar and a gold stripe running down the side of her sweatpants. She stands on her front porch and looks at the Spacers at the end of the street. It's Falcon, one of the Prom Committee members. The one that is a track star. She yells at the Spacers, "Anyone of you freaks see my varsity jacket?" See, I told you, she always misplacing that thing. But she does look very official in her black and gold trimmed varsity sweat suit. She doesn't wait for a reply, she runs to the middle of the street and looks at them. Some of the Space Spiders are only five houses away.

Her mother comes to the front door and yells, "Yolanda, you get back here right now."

Falcon ignores her mother, smiles at the Spacers, and says, "Boo." Falcon runs away from Spacers - down the middle of the street. The Space Spiders forget their concerns and scurry after her. Falcon turns on the speed and pulls away from them. She's fast, but she's human; the Spacers gain on her quickly. Falcon collapses on the street next to a manhole cover. She's a goner, they are right behind … But the manhole cover gets pushed to the side and her father reaches out of the manhole and grabs his daughter, "Mija, estás loco." He pulls her into the sewer as Spacer fangs crack the concert just missing Falcon's legs. The Space Spiders screech at the open manhole, but it's too small for a Spacer to climb in.

Men, women and teens throw open front doors. They raise rifles and shotguns. More weapons poke out of open windows on the first and second floors. The citizens blast the Spacers standing in the middle of their street. The shooters hand empty weapons to older folks sitting in the shadows.

"Thanks, Grandpa."

"Give 'em hell, Jimmy."

Then grandpa and grandma exchange the empty rifles and shotguns with fully loaded ones. Families, who shoot together, stay together. Space Spiders try to get out of there, but there's nowhere to run or hide. They screech, goo, and drop.

From the West

Space Spiders enter our borough via Paxton Church Rd. There normally aren't dumpsters lining the shops on the northern side of the road, but the Spacers don't know that. The Spacers spread out because they have learned from the drones that if you bunch up, a rocket will kill you and your friends. They look jumpy, even for spiders. Deputy Rogers has the honor of stepping out of Mr. Taylors' Barber Shop. The red, white, and blue striped barber pole rotates inviting the furry Spacers to *come on in and get a little taken off the top*, like maybe their heads. Deputy Rogers blasts his shotgun into the air.

The Spacers face the Deputy. They see only one man with a gun, but oh that hypnotizing barber pole. For a moment, they just stare. The Spacers don't realize his shot is a signal. Before the Spacers can tear their eyes away from the barber pole, the lids of the dumpsters fly open. The dumpsters are full of men, women, and teens. They blast their rifles and shotguns ripping up the Spacers. The Spacers charge the dumpsters, but the closer they get, the more accurate the blasts become, causing even more damage.

A few Spacers hit the dumpsters hard. They tip over. The humans inside slam into each other. People get hit in the face with elbows and shotguns. Humans tumble out onto the road. Space Spiders climb over the dumpsters. The Spacers fang an old guy, a woman, and others as they try to escape. The fleeing Space Spiders scurry up walls of buildings. Some citizens scramble back into the dumpsters for cover. Others get up and shoot at the fleeing Spacers. Old Man Cassidy applies direct pressure to his friend who got fanged.

"Harold, don't you leave me," says Old Man Cassidy.

Harold looks at Old Man Cassidy's hands pressing against Harold's bloody fang wound on his leg. "What are you using as a bandage?"

Old man Cassidy looks at the baggie under his hands and says, "I think it's an old baloney sandwich."

"Aaaaaaah."

"Stop your moaning. It's in a plastic bag."

As Spacers scurry up buildings, guns poke out of windows and shoot them. One Spacer falls and hits the ground hard. It wiggles and then stops. Another leaves a trail of goo on the bricks as it goes up. The wounded Spacer lifts its front legs over the top of the building, and pulls itself up on to the roof. It stops when its eight eyes see something on the roof it's never seen before. A pink ballerina stands in fourth position. She wears pink leotards and a tutu, which match her pink ballet slippers. OMG it's Slippers. You remember her. She's the Prom Committee high school senior who always wears pink ballet slippers. She curtseys to the wounded Space Spider. Wounded looks around as if it's being pranked.

Slippers opens her arms and bends her knees outward with her back held straight. It's a beautiful plié (plēa-ā) that's wasted on the uncultured eight-legged freak. Her right knee bends as she slides her pointed-toe up her left leg. She can hear her instructor, "Passé" (pah-say). Slippers turns three times in position. Her body has good alignment, and for a moment she looks like a spinning coin on a table. This time the Space Spider is impressed by her triple pirouette. She smiles, she did it! Then she remembers Wounded. She dances across the roof before the Spacer snaps out of its daydream and hobbles after the prima ballerina.

She dances toward the edge of the roof. There is a ten-foot gap between her building and the roof of the next building over. There is an alley down below. Wounded closes in on her. Slippers picks up speed and leaps. She soars off of the roof over the alley. Her front leg straight out in front of her and her back leg straight behind her. It looks like she's doing the splits in the air. It's a *grand* grand jete (grāN ZHə'tā). But this show-stopping move doesn't stop Wounded. Inspired by the split jump, the Spacer leaps after her, spreading out all eight of its legs as it soars through the air after her.

Spider see, spider do.

Slippers lands on the roof of the next building, but she's got to much speed, she's going to crash. Mouth Wash steps in front of her and catches her. She knocks him down. Slippers ends up sitting on his chest.

"That was beautiful," says Mouth Wash.

Slipper blushes and catches her breath. She smiles, "Minty fresh."

The wounded Space Spider lands on the roof with a thud right behind her. Goo splatters out of its body with the impact. Wounded has a hard time standing.

Crystal steps next to Mouth Wash. She gives Slippers a *look*. Slippers gets off of Mouth Wash. He extends a hand to Crystal, but she doesn't help him up. Instead, she raises her M4 at Wounded. Mouth Wash gets up by himself. Slippers steps behind Crystal and whispers, "Thank you for helping me." Crystal softens, "You did good, tiny dancer." Slippers squeezes Crystal's shoulders and kisses Crystal on the cheek.

One wounded Spacer is no big deal to these proven warriors. But six more Spacers come up and over the wall right behind Wounded. Wounded finds the strength to screech. Mouth Wash, Crystal, and Slippers step back. Mouth Wash keeps his M4 trained on them as he blows a whistle. The whistle makes a Pintail-Wigeon Duck Call.

About twenty duck hunters, men and women in camouflage, step out from behind air conditioning units all over the roof. Crystal yells, "Get down!" Slippers hides as Mouth Wash and Crystal drop to one knee and shoot. The duck hunters also start blasting the Spacers. The Space Spiders try to hold their position, but there's too much metal flying at them. The hunters advance. The Spacers step backwards until they fall off the roof into the alley. Wounded is the last one to go over. *You see, the first shall be the last.* They hit the ground and splatter. The duck hunters cheer. Crystal, Mouth Wash, and Slippers hug.

From the East
Allentown Blvd. is lined with cute one and two-story houses with

well-manicured lawns and white picket fences. Deserted cars are parked in the street and in driveways. A police car with lights on and sirens blaring shatters the silence as it races down the street. It slams on its brakes and fishtails to a stop. Two police officers get out of the squad car with shotguns. Nothing moves. All is quiet. It looks like the Space Spiders aren't coming this way. The police officers lower their weapons. One leans into the patrol car and grabs the radio. Space Spiders scurry down the driveways on both sides of the street. They were hiding in the backyards of these quiet houses. This time the Spacers have set the trap.

The officers keep their backs to their squad car and raise their pump-action shot guns. They aren't going down without a fight. The Spacers charge them. But before the Space Spiders can get to them, two more officers sit up in the back seat and lean out the open car windows. Citizens pop out of the parked cars that line the boulevard. The Spacers don't know who to attack first. Fangs come down through roofs of cars. Citizens blast. One guy is dragged out of his car and fanged to death in the street. Four guys bust out of a van, but a Space Spider webs them.

The Spacers fight, but there are too many humans. Some Spacers go for the officers, but these Spacers crumble before they get to them. Others scurry behind parked cars for a moment to think, but more men and women hide inside the parked cars. They press shotguns against the windows. BOOM. BOOM.

Spacers have to get off the street if they're going to survive. Some scurry toward houses and crash through the big front windows.

One Spacer, Twitchy, who seems especially nervous, pounces through a double-paned front glass window and lands inside someone's living room. Shards of glass stick out of it's white furry head and arms. Twitchy looks one way, then the other, and then frantically does a complete 360. Pieces of wall, lamps, and furniture are knocked around the room. A young male teen pulls up his pants as he staggers out of the living room. *Did Twitchy hit him so hard his pants fell down?* A cabinet lays on the floor, a young woman pulls a shotgun out of the wreckage. She wears jeans and a T-shirt. It's Friendly. You may remember her. She was the high school senior on the Prom Committee sitting with Roy until he dumped her for Sweetie. You know, Friendly is the one with the high voice, mini-skirt, and tight clothing. But she looks different now. She's dressed casually, like she's not trying so hard.

Friendly cracks opens the Winchester shotgun and loads two shells, but Twitchy smacks her with one of its long Space Spider legs. Friendly slams into the couch and bounces off of it. The Winchester flies out of her hands as she falls onto the floor. Twitchy brings its other front leg down in an attempt to crush Friendly, but she slides out of the way. The Spacer's leg comes down so hard it breaks through the wood flooring.

Before Twitchy can pull its leg out of the floor, Friendly jumps on the long, white, furry leg. She wraps her legs around it and rotates as she slides down it. *What? Was that some sort of pole dancer move?* Twitchy stares at her, not sure what just happened.

Friendly scissor kicks her legs, rolls on the floor, and slowly stands. A Space Spider's leg is more slippery than a stainless steel pole. When people first start taking classes, they usually practice on a titanium-gold or brass pole because these are "stickier" and easier to do moves on.

But Friendly thinks of herself as a professional. She saunters toward Twitchy. Friendly has no fear, she's in her element, she's the one in control now. Twitchy looks at its leg to make sure she didn't damage or wound it. Twitchy doesn't know what's happening, Friendly doesn't seem like a threat. Does Twitchy need to attack her? Friendly leaps onto its leg again. She holds the white hair firmly with both hands and extends her body out, away from the Spacer. She demonstrates great core strength. She opens her legs in a splits-type-move and into a near perfect Iron-X. She must have abs of steel.

Friendly pulls on the Spacer's hair as she extends and holds her position. Twitchy grimaces. It's painful, but bearable. In fact, Twitchy finds the tug on its hair a tad bit exciting. I guess Spacers like it rough.

Moving like this is freeing, awesome, and a great workout, but once again Friendly is inappropriate with her actions. But this time, it looks like it's going to cost her a lot more than a broken heart. Make love, not war. Yes, but even Gandhi doesn't recommend pole dancing in the middle of armageddon.

But Friendly has just started her routine. She wraps her upper leg around the top of Twitchy's leg doing an outside leg hang. Friendly hangs upside down and smiles at Twitchy. Again, the Spacer hesitates. Friendly's hands extend down and touches the floor. She keeps smiling, as her hands sift through the debris and moves the wreckage around.

Gunshots echo in the street. Twitchy remembers it's a Spacer and screeches at Friendly. The screech blows back Friendly's hair. Boyfriend bounds back into the living room. Twitchy turns toward him. Boyfriend jumps and kicks his legs. He sings at the top of his lungs, "Hava Nagila! Hava Nagila!" He's dancing the Horah. *What?* That doesn't make sense. *Exactly.* That's what he's hoping for. Confuse the Spacer!

Twitchy sees something reflecting light in the boy's hand. Boyfriend's got a big kitchen knife. Twitchy screeches at him, but then remembers Friendly hanging on his leg. So much weirdness is happening at the same time. Twitchy looks down just in time to see Friendly load two shells into a Remington shotgun. She found what she was searching for in the rubble. Boyfriend was acting as a distraction to give her the time she needs. Friendly snaps the shotgun shut, but she doesn't have time to point it at Twitchy. Boyfriend yells, "Linda!" and throws the knife.

The Ginsu 8-inch stainless steel Chef Knife from his family's Quikut collection sticks the Spacer in the head. Boyfriend yells, "But wait, there's more!" This gives Friendly the time she needs. She raises her shotgun and with a tear in her eye says, "He said my real name."

She blasts the Spacer with both barrels. At that range, it's not pretty.

Twitchy shudders. With only one good fang left, it tries to pierce Friendly, but she rolls away as the fang hits the floor hard. Boyfriend grabs Friendly and pulls her away. They run into the kitchen. Twitchy attempts to stand, but hunters blast it from behind, through the busted window. It falls and stops twitching.

The street is quiet again. Nothing moves. Everyone cheers.

A 10-year old boy full of excitement runs into the street. He yells at a dead Space Spider. "Don't tread on me!" The dead Space Spider isn't dead. It stands on six legs. Goo leaks out. The Space Spider is 16-feet tall, the boy is just over 4-feet. The cheers stop. People take aim, but the boy is too close to the Spacer. Everyone with buckshot lowers their guns. A few of the older, more confidant hunters take aim, but it's unlikely single shots will kill it.

The Space Spider's fangs open and close. The boy trembles.

A 1969 Chevy zooms down Allentown Boulevard. It's my '69 Chevy. It heads straight for the Space Spider and the boy. The Spacer steps backwards to avoid being hit by the speeding car. This gives the expert hunters the opportunity they need to shoot. Men, women, and teens fire their rifles. Sure, they're only single shots from about fifteen guns, but they hit, hurt, and distract the Space Spider giving the '69 Chevy just enough time to slam on its brakes and slide between the Spacer and the boy. Seven-Thirty, my sister, drives. I'm glad I showed her where I keep the extra set of keys. My '69 Chevy comes to a stop separating the hairy beast from the boy. My Mom is in the passenger seat. She leans out her window and smiles at the boy.

She talks gently, as if she has all the time in the world, "Billy, I need you to turn around and run."

He nods.

My Mom smiles and says, "Now."

The boy turns and runs away from the Chevy and certain death. The Space Spider grabs the Chevy with its front legs. It's mandibles and fangs reach for my sister, but she rolls up the driver's window catching both of the mandibles. Fangs smack against the driver's window cracking it. The Spacer screeches in horrible pain as she tightens the window. She opens it a bit so the Space Spider can pull out its mandibles.

Seven-Thirty looks at the crack in window. "Chevy's going to kill me."

My Mom slides a shotgun in front of my sister. It hits the driver's side window. My Mom and Sister put camouflaged hunting earmuffs on for protection. Seven-Thirty rolls down the window. BAM. A direct hit that pushes the beast back. My sister grabs the pump-action shot gun and pumps. A shell ejects. My Mom pulls the trigger again. BAM. They work together. BAM. BAM. BAM. The blasts push the Spacer back. My sister slams on the gas. Squealing and smoke fill the air as my car leaves rubber on the road. My ride is fast. I knew that Holley 750 double-pumper carburetor was a smart buy. The hunters are ready for this opportunity. They've got a clean shot and they take it. BAM. BAM.

BAM. BAM. BAM. BAM. BAM. BAM. BAM. BAM. The Space Spider is hit from all sides. It crumbles to the ground.

My sister accelerates as she turns down Rosewood. My Mom says to her, "Drop me off at the medical center; then go find your brother."

My mom grew up hunting. She doesn't like it, but she knows how to shoot. My mom is also a nurse practitioner. When we were young, my mom stayed home with us. She realized she liked being a mom more than she thought she would. I heard that happens sometimes. A parent holds their baby and realizes their day job doesn't compare to the love they feel. It was also nice that we weren't living in a big city where both parents had to work to make the rent. So she stayed home and bandaged our cuts, bumps, and bruises with expert, professional care. She would always say to us that our co-pay was a kiss and a hug. I didn't know what that meant when I was little, but my Dad thought it was funny. He said we kids had the best insurance plan on the market. When we got to middle school, my mom went back to work a couple of days a week. She's headed for the medical center so she can help any wounded that might show up there.

CHAPTER 49

IT'S OUR CHANCE SOON

SNAFU AND I STAND behind Sweetie as she looks at the piece of metal protruding out of Darcy's leg. Darcy sits with her leg stretched out resting on another chair. I hold a first-aid kit. Sweetie slides a pair of scissors into the hole of Darcy's pants that the metal made. Sweetie cuts Darcy's uniform so they can see the wound better. Gross.

Sweetie says, "You ready?"

Darcy takes a deep breath and nods.

"OK, this is going to hurt so ... "

Darcy pushes Sweetie's hand out of the way. Darcy pulls the metal out of her own leg. "Rrrrrrrrr, let's not make this a big deal." Blood flows, but it isn't a gusher. SNAFU pours clear liquid on it. Darcy holds back a scream, but then she realizes there is no sting. The liquid bubbles and fizzes on the wound and her leg. Darcy grabs SNAFU's arm. "What is that?"

She looks at the bottle.

"All I could find is sparkling water. It must have been the

Commander's."

I hand Sweetie an alcohol wipe from the first-aid kit. "This is going to hurt." Sweetie wipes the wound to sterilize it. Darcy stiffens. Sweetie places a big sterile bandage over the wound. Sweetie and SNAFU work together to wrap an ace bandage around Darcy's leg. Up, over, under, repeat.

"You've got nice legs," says SNAFU.

"Thanks," Darcy turns to Sweetie, "Give me the scissors."

Darcy cuts off the blood-soaked pant leg. "Here, make it a pair of shorts." Darcy gives the scissors to SNAFU. He cuts off the other pant leg, but he cuts off too much, they're uneven.

Darcy takes the scissors from him. "How short do you want them to be?" See, 85% of our actions are directed by our subconscious. Now we know where SNAFU's mind is. Darcy trims more off the other side so they are even now.

SNAFU says, "I'm sorry."

"I bet you are." Darcy pulls him close and kisses him. Darcy hands the scissors to Sweetie and says, "Now we celebrate."

I hand everyone a plastic cup. SNAFU pours sparkling water in the cups, "Welcome to Free Earth."

Sweetie returns with a bag full of cookies. "We are living the life." She passes the bag around and everyone grabs a handful. We toast. Darcy says, "To everyone doing their part."

I say, "To creating what we want."

SNAFU says, "To beating alien scum."

We look at Sweetie. She wants to say something about Prom, but we didn't save it. A piece of equipment beeps. Sweetie looks at me. "To us." She looks at everyone, "To us."

We bump plastic cups and repeat after her, "To us!" We drink.

The equipment beeps again. We look around at the mess made by the Spacer exodus. *What's beeping?* Tables and chairs are flipped over. Monitors lay on the ground. Lamps are knocked over, a few are are still on. There must be a generator somewhere providing power.

Beep. Beep. Beep.

SNAFU rummages through stuff looking for the beeping. Sweetie decides she doesn't care enough to clean up. She sees my backpack.

"What's in the backpack?"

This is going to be the best. This is going to get me some action tonight. Guaranteed.

Sweetie sees my smile. "Did you get me something?"

My smile gets bigger. I grab the backpack.

SNAFU picks up a monitor. It has a big crack on the screen. He tries to move the computer so the monitor will reach the table, but the cables are tangled up. It beeps again. SNAFU says, "I found the beep." But no one cares.

Sweetie says, "Chevy, what you'd get me?" Sweetie moves toward the backpack. I turn and block her from grabbing it. Darcy leans trying to get a better view of the backpack. I unzip the pack slowly. Anticipation and wanting are very important for successful gift giving.

"That's not funny," says Sweetie. "What is it?"

Beep. On the limp over to the trashed military base, Darcy and Sweetie told us about the drones taking the balloon up, up and away. Amazing. Maybe the experts are right after all, it takes a village to save a planet. The radar beeps again. I'm thinking some of the drones are still out there.

Sweetie says, "Chevy!" She calls me back to the present moment. This is her "present moment" and she wants to see what it is.

SNAFU untangles the cords without unplugging the radar computer. He places the monitor on a table.. Darcy limps over to him so she can see, but she keeps an eye on the backpack. It's a small limp, but she should take it easy. I stick my hand into the pack. I pretend I can't find it. "I think it might have fallen out."

Sweetie punches me. "Stop it already."

The radar beeps again. A walkie squawks at us, "We've got incoming." I grab the item, but I stop. My hand is still inside the pack. "Is the balloon falling back down?"

The walkie squawks again. "Free Earth Ground Base, is there anyone left down there? Head's up. A chunk of the moon is coming down."

SNAFU turns the radar computer so we can see it. BEEP. It's a big blip, but they don't offer blip-ology as a high school elective, so we don't really know what we're looking at. If I was fishing with my Dad, and we saw a blip like that, I'd guess there was a big school of bluegills swimming under our boat. But I don't think there is a whole bunch of fish falling from the sky. Nothing crazy like *Sharknado* is going to happen now. We won. It's over. *Right?*

Darcy picks up the walkie. "This is … " Another walkie under the table SCREAMS with feedback. The two walkies are too close to each other. We cover our ears and wince with pain. SNAFU grabs the other walkie and turns it off. Darcy tries again, "This is Private First Class Meyers. We're at Ground Base. It looks big. What can you tell us?"

"We advise you to take cover."

"Is that really going to help?"

There is a long pause. And then, "No, it's too big. The impact will take out about a 30-mile radius."

Sweetie pulls my hand out of the backpack to reveal her surprise. I hold the Prom Queen's tiara. "Oh, my gosh. How'd you get that?"

I turn it so the faux diamonds sparkle. It's beautiful. "I got it from Ms. Meyer … Darcy's office. Come here." Sweetie steps forward with tears in her eyes. I place the tiara on her head and say, "You're my Dangerous Princess. You're my Prom Queen."

Sweetie looks at Darcy. Darcy smiles. "You look beautiful."

Sweetie and I kiss. I'm glad we get to kiss. We aren't going to have time for anything else.

"I love you."

"I love you."

I'd prefer a win-win scenario. You know, humanity survives AND we get to live. But I guess we'll have to settle for win-lose. Everyone gets to live, but us. I suppose it could be worse, we could all die. I take her face in my hands and look into her big, beautiful eyes. I kiss her again. She kisses me back.

The walkie crackles, "Private First Class Meyers, is my daughter there?"

Sweetie stops. "Dad?" Unbelievable. Even when we're about to die he interrupts us making out. Her father never liked me.

Darcy hands the walkie to Sweetie. "Dad, it's me."

"Honey, I'm so proud of you," says the Sheriff. "I love you. You did great today. You and all your friends."

See, he doesn't even mention my name. He knows my name.

"I love you too, Dad."

SNAFU points at the sky. "There." The moon chunk enters the atmosphere. It's big and it's burning up something fierce. He says, "Maybe it will burn up before it hits us." Look who's sounding like an optimist now.

Darcy stands. "That doesn't make sense. The moon is going the other way and the Earth is turning. There's no way a chunk of it would end up at ground zero."

Sweetie says, "Not unless it's aiming for here."

What???

The Sheriff says, "Honey, it's NOT going to burn up before it hits you."

Thank you for the uplifting clarity, lawman. Everything always 'by the book." The walkie crackles, the falling rocks causes interference. The static gets louder. Sweetie turns off the walkie. "Goodbye Dad."

You can kinda guess she isn't in a smoochie mood after that. We turn so we can watch the big thing hit. Sweetie stands in front of me. I wrap my arms around her. It's nice to hold her. It's good to smell her. I make a mental note to duck and turn my head when the chunk hits so the tiara won't poke me in the face. If we do survive the impact, I don't want to be running around with an eye patch having to explain how it happened.

Sweetie holds me tight as SNAFU and Darcy embrace, but overall we're pretty calm. I guess after you face death about ten times it's not such a big deal. It still sucks, but it's not the end of the world. Well ... not for everyone else, just us.

I pull Sweetie closer; her fantastic rear end bumps into me. She laughs and shakes her head. "Really? Now?" But she rubs against me on purpose. God, I love her so much.

Beep. Beep. Beep. SNAFU looks at the monitor. "The pieces are breaking up."

The big rocks burn as they zoom through the sky toward us. We wait. And then, we wait some more. Why does it take so long for them to hit? I get a bad feeling about this. I think back to what Sweetie said. *Could it be aiming toward us? But that would mean ...* Then I think, *what is worse than death?* I hear a voice inside my head and I don't like what it says. L*osing, losing is worse than death.* I say to myself, *"But we already won."* And the voice replies, *"Are you sure?"*

Darcy looks at the monitor, "There are six or seven big rocks coming down."

Each rock is about the size of a four-story apartment building and it looks like each rock has a parachute attached to it. *Why do they have parachutes attached to them?*

SNAFU says, "What are the parachutes made of?"

"Webbing," says Sweetie.

"That means they're not rocks," says Darcy.

I was just about to figure that out, but someone needed to say it out loud. These are not white, furry, regular-sized, Space Spiders. These things are shinny, black, and building-sized. They unfurl. Yup, they're Space Spiders that are hundreds of feet tall. Their bodies and legs are covered with what looks like black armor. Even with the web chutes they hit hard, but the good news is the chutes slowed them down, which means we may survive their impacts.

Darcy yells, "Take cover!"

I turn my head to protect myself from the tiara. We duck and cover. Even the two soldiers behind us dive behind the Humvee. The big, black Space Spiders release their chutes. Their long, powerful legs hit the ground first. They hit hard. The Earth shakes beneath us. Dust and dirt fly into the air. Sweetie and I crouch under a table. Dirt rains down on us. We wait. Everything settles. We're still alive and I have both my eyes.

We stand. *They are BIG.*

SNAFU says, "How many do you think there are?"

"Nine," says Sweetie. "There are nine Warriors."

We don't argue. They look like Warriors. Big, protected, and impressive. They stand in a circle with their backs to each other. Each one looks out toward the battlefield. They're focused and disciplined. Their huge fangs twitch in unison. They're ready for a fight, but there is none to be had.

The four of us remain very still. The soldier with the wounded leg limps up behind us. He lifts his M4. Sweetie looks at him. *Are you serious?* He puts it down. He notices her tiara. It takes him a moment, but he recognizes Sweetie. He says, "You're Prom Queen with a ... "

Sweetie smiles and put her finger to her lips, "Shhh." Wounded Soldier nods.

SNAFU whispers to me, "Any ideas?"

"Yeah, but I don't think Sweetie's in the mood."

Sweetie punches me.

Then we hear the fighter jets. The United Nations offered the General the command of the international fighters. The General accepted. He called the fighters back from their search-and-destroy missions. The *little* Spacers running around will have to be cleaned up later.

The Chief of Staff of the Air Force informed the General that every available Air Force fighter in the vicinity is in the air. More than two hundred American fighters join the international forces. A few of the pilots are seasoned Space Spider veterans. They fought earlier, but needed to refuel and get more ammo. Most of the pilots are new to the conflict.

The American fighters soar through the air, some of them at twice the speed of sound. The fighters include F-15 Eagles, F-16 Fighting Falcons, F-22 Raptors, and F-35 Lighting IIs. They each carry an impressive arsenal of weapons: sidewinder heat-seeking missiles, six-barrel rotary cannons with 480 rounds, 1,000-pound Joint Direct Attack Munitions, Paveway bombs, Brimstone anti-tank missiles, Cluster munitions (with Wind Correct Munitions Dispenser), Sparrow medium-range air-to-air missiles, 20 mm Vulcan cannons for close-range aerial combat and strafing.

They arrive from more than 20 different Air Force bases in the United States including: Vandenberg, California; Lewis-McChord, Washington; Laughlin, Texas; Grand Forks, North Dakota; and Cape Canaveral, Florida.

The American fighters approach from the south in an orderly manner and by the book. There is not going to be casualties from friendly fire.

The General orders the international fighters to a higher altitude to wait further instructions. He might have done this because they just had some action cleaning up the stragglers and their ammo might be running low, or maybe it's an American pride thing. The bugs landed here and our boys and girls want the first shot at them. *Not in our country. Not in our house.*

The American fighters come in waves. Maybe 20 or so at a time.

The lines of fighters shoot their missiles, bombs, and cannons. The General repeats his orders, "Not too close." Nobody really knows what that means with the Warriors, so they fire as soon as their weapons get in range. After they shoot, half of the fighters break off to the right and the other half off to the left. Then they circle around to the back of the line so they can make another run.

The Warriors just stand there and take it. Explosions happen all over their armor. We don't see any leaking goo. The General is concerned their armor-like skin is too strong for our weapons.

Then the Warriors rotate so the same ones don't keep taking the punishment from the American jets. Sorta like penguins. When it gets really cold in Antarctica the penguins on the outside of the group rotate to the center to warm up before they freeze to death. The General sees the Warriors rotating as a good sign. The ones taking the beating wouldn't move unless they're getting hurt. I wasn't too sure about that.

Sweetie says, "They keep doing the same thing." She's talking about the fighters.

"The same number approach," says Darcy, "flying at the same altitude, firing from the same distance, and then breaking off in the same pattern to return to the back."

I understand what the woman folk are saying. I nod. "They need to do something different. The Warriors are gathering intel."

SNAF says, "There, look. That one."

We see something beautiful. Goo runs down one of the Warriors. Missiles explode and another one springs a leak. It's working. It took some time, but it's working. Missiles and rounds blast through their armor. All of the fighters target their weapons on the crack in the armor of the Warrior. More bombs and missiles slide into the Warrior. Goo explodes out of the big crack and a piece of the Warrior is blasted off. The Warrior falls! The jets take one down! There is great rejoicing.

Emboldened with enthusiasm, the pilots fly closer and target the crack in another Warrior's armor. *No, don't get closer.*

The eight remaining Warriors crouch down low. One of the soldiers behind us says, "Look, the rest are getting ready to fall."

Sweetie shakes her head. "No, they're getting ready to jump."

Then it happens. The Warriors jump. They jump big and in different directions. The Warriors strike back. One of them leaps over the trashed military base we hide in. We duck when it goes over us. They leap at the incoming fighters. Two, four, six, eight fighters blow up as the fighters crash into the huge Warrior bodies. They use their bodies as battering rams. The Warriors swing their long legs and explode more jets.

The fighters take evasive actions and break formation. There is a lot of dodging and weaving now. The pilots won't underestimate the Warriors again. The fighters zigzag while their bombs and rounds take their toll on the big, black bugs. A giant leg falls off a Warrior and then another. Some of the Warriors leap again, some fighters outmaneuver swinging legs, others explode.

The General calls down the international fighters. They're happy to join in. They come in fast. They blast the attacking Warriors, but this seems too much for the giant, armored Space Spiders. The Warriors bury their heads in the Earth. We don't say anything. It's hard to believe that they're trying to hide in the middle of battle. We want to believe it, but it seems too good to be true. Then I see their abdomens flex.

"Get back!"

Webbing blasts out, but not in *lines* of webbing. Short controlled bursts. *See, even aliens know that.* The Warriors shoot out hardened webbing in the form of ninja throwing stars the size of cars. They slice through the air and through the fighters. Fighters explode. One web-ninja-star crashes into our trashed military base. The 10 foot multi-spiked, steel-hardened web star sticks in the ground next to SNAFU. It's taller than him.

"Damn."

A few of the Warriors turn around and smack down the scattering fighters. Legs swing, fighters do down. The remaining jets scatter, roll, and deploy counter measures. They continue to blast the giant Space

473

Spiders. Another Warrior falls. More cheers.

Sweetie says, "I think the fighters are going to win."

I hold her. "I think you're right."

More Warriors collapse. The last two Warriors screech as the remaining fighters turn and regroup in the sky. There are only 30 fighters left, American and International. Goo pours out of the Warriors as they hobble together. This goo forms rivers in our practice field. The fighters blast the last two Warriors. They huddle together and it looks like they hug each other. This is how they're going to die. I kinda feel bad for them. You know, like when King Kong finally falls at the end.

But then the stronger Warrior, the one with seven legs, throws the one with only six legs. Six Legger is a whirlwind of death and destruction. More than half of the remaining fighters explode, but each explosion takes its toll on the wounded Warrior. It lands and crumples into a dead pile of armor and goo.

The last 12 jets approach the last Warrior from all sides. They use up their ammo and then fly straight up into the sky. The last Warrior falls. The ground shakes beneath our feet as it hits Mother Earth. We wait, but the last Warrior doesn't get back up. The Jets have to leave, they have no more ammo and they're running low on fuel. The General invites them to land at Cleveland's International Airport. The pilots are greeted with a hero's welcome. Cleveland rocks! The world cheers, but it's not a loud cheer. The cost has been high and everyone is exhausted.

Sweetie and I hug. She still wears the tiara, so I'm careful. SNAFU squeezes Darcy's hand. She sits again with her leg propped up. Her bandage is bloody, just a little, but she's smart enough to know it's time to sit down and not push it. We did it. We don't have a lot of energy to celebrate, but we did it. Sure, there might be a handful of little Spacers scurrying around, but we'll hunt them down and get them later.

CHAPTER 50

EAT. PRAY. SHOOT.

THE MEDICAL CENTER PARKING lot is empty except for a few cars and a pile of Spacer legs. Flies swarm around the gooey limbs. An 18 year-old boy speeds through the parking lot on his dirt bike. There's a human skull on his black T-shirt. The shirt doesn't seem appropriate on a day like today. It's Jerry, Roy's best friend. This makes sense, he's seldom appropriate. He rides over a Spacer leg and laughs. He turns to spit on the leg. His spit lands on his shoulder. Gross. He wipes it off. By the time he looks forward again it's too late. He doesn't have time to swerve, there's a concrete parking block with RESERVED DR SPERLING on it. He brakes, but the puddle of goo he rides through doesn't give him the traction he needs. He hits the parking block and is thrown from his bike.

He lands in the pile of Spacer legs in the VISITOR parking space. He freaks out as he scrambles out of the mess. He curses and limps up the stairs. The automatic doors open for him as he enters the Medical Center. It's not too crowded. A few staff members assist patients. On a day like today, nobody is asking for insurance cards and co-payments. My Mom helps an elderly man sit down in the waiting area. His arm has a fresh bandage on it.

"Thank you," he says.

My Mom sees Jerry enter. "You can sit down right here," says my Mom. Jerry sits next to the old man. Jerry holds his leg. My Mom doesn't see any blood, but does notice the Spacer goo all over him from the pile of legs.

"Damn, Spacers," says Jerry.

"Are you all right?" says my Mom.

"Do I look alright to you?"

The old man rolls his eyes as he pages through the *Cosmo* magazine promising a better, faster, more satisfying O. My Mom pulls another chair over and gently lifts Jerry's leg.

"Easy lady. Easy."

"OK, let me see."

Jerry moves his hand so she can see. There is a tiny, little rip in his jeans with a little bit of blood on the palm of his hand. Jerry cries out in pain when he sees the blood. The old man gets up and moves two chairs away. My Mom looks at the cut. "You're going to be OK."

"How do you know? How do you know? It's deep I tell you."

My Mom decides to give the patient the benefit of the doubt. She moves his hand again to get a better look. "Is it deep? Did one of them fang you?"

"What? No way. I haven't even seen one yet. I mean, not one that's alive. I'm not stupid. I started running when I heard the reports. I pushed an old lady out of the way and she poked me with something she was carrying. These are my $150 jeans!"

My Mom holds her tongue. She's a better person than me. "I'll be right back," she says. She leaves.

"Get me something for the pain," he yells. Jerry looks at the old man. "It's so hard to get good medical care these days."

My Mom returns with a big pair of cloth cutting scissors, antiseptic cream, and a small bandage. Jerry sees the big scissors and recognizes my Mom. "Wait, I know you. You're Chevy's mom. You're that crazy Union Surgeon hack. Don't you cut off my leg."

My Mom is about to reassure Jerry that everything is going to be OK, but instead she smiles and slips into her Union Surgeon character. She flashes the scissors. Snip, snip and says, "I don't know, it looks pretty bad."

"No. No. It's just a scratch."

She laughs a wicked laugh. "I think the leg's got to come off."

The old man looks at my Mom and smiles.

"No no, it's fine." Jerry stands and does a couple of lunges. Then my Mom says her famous line that makes all the tourists squirm. "We've got to stop the black infection before it makes its way to your heart."

The old man rolls up his magazine and walks to Jerry. The old man says, "Son, don't you worry. You can bite on this while she ..."

Jerry runs out of the waiting room. The limp is gone. He's healed. Another Prom Day miracle! The old man laughs. My Mom realizes she crossed the line. She puts down the scissors and chases after the teen. "No wait. You're going to be fine."

Jerry runs out the Medical Center and down the steps. He picks up his dirt bike. He doesn't see the Space Spider standing only 20 feet away from him. The Spacer has only five legs. It looks through the pile of limbs in the VISITOR parking space. I'm not sure if it's looking for a replacement or what? Jerry has a hard time starting his dirt bike because his trembling. The Spacer hobbles toward him. Jerry is unaware of his impending doom. My Mom rushes out of the front doors.

"Wait," yells my Mom.

Jerry and the Space Spider stop. My Mom has a very powerful Mom-Jedi voice. Jerry notices the Spacer.

"You can make it back inside," says my Mom. "Just stay calm and walk backwards towards me."

Jerry could have made it, but he doesn't move. He just stands there. The Space Spider screeches at Jerry. Jerry trembles and drops his bike. The Spacer hobbles toward Jerry.

The doors slide open behind my Mom. B+ rushes out with his M4. He wears a minor bandage. My Mom steps back. B+ blasts the Space Spider. The five-legged Spacer charges past Jerry and up the stairs at B

+, but the rounds are too much. In battle, the side with the higher ground usually wins. The Spacer collapses. The shooting stops. The dead Spacer slides down the stairs and bumps into Jerry. Jerry screams.

"Thank you, Eddie," says my Mom.

"Sure thing, Mrs. W."

My Mom marches down the stairs, grabs Jerry's shirt, and pulls him up the stairs. "Enough already," she says. "Come in and sit down. I'm not going to cut off your leg."

B+ smirks and says, "Good luck, Union Surgeon."

Jerry whimpers. My Mom gives B+ a hard look, but she can't stop herself from smiling. My Mom pulls Jerry into the building. B+ realizes he hasn't been paying attention to the parking lot. He scans the area, but all is safe. He walks backwards into the Medical Center.

Chapter 51

Umph. There It Is.

SWEETIE SITS ON MY lap and we talk about barbecue chicken. We're hungry. Darcy sits on SNAFU's lap. She has her leg propped up on the table next to them. They whisper and giggle. It's nice and weird at the same time.

Both Marines change a tire on the Humvee. One of the ninja stars landed next to the Humvee and sliced a back tire. They ask for our help, but we tell them, "No." We're tired and we aren't in a rush to get anywhere.

The radar beeps again.

I say, "It's our helicopter ride out of here." We cheer.

SNAFU leans and reaches for the beeping monitor. He holds Darcy so she doesn't fall off of him. He turns the monitor and they both stop laughing as it beeps again.

Sweetie says, "What?"

Darcy remains silent. SNAFU turns the monitor so we can see it. Beep. Another big blip is coming for us.

SNAFU says, "Who do you think those Warriors were suppose to protect?"

I never thought of it that way.

"All the little ones," says Darcy. "They didn't come from the Warriors."

It would have been better if Darcy would have asked that as a question. You know, like, hey guys, do you think the little ones came from the Warriors? But she didn't. She knows the little Space Spiders didn't come from the Warriors. I don't know how she knows that, but if there is one thing we've learned, it's our intuition is stronger than knowledge.

The radar beeps again. The Marines stops tightening the lug nuts on the Humvee. One of them shouts at us, "Hey, stop that. It's not funny."

"Stop what?" says Sweetie.

The Wounded Solider says, "The beeping. Enough already."

We don't have the heart to tell them. The image on the screen is big. Maybe it's the whole freaking moon coming down on us. Darcy says, "It's not as big as the nine Warriors."

I take another look. She's right. It's not the whole moon; it's not that big. Let's not panic. Ford Perfect would be the first one to remind us not to panic.

Sweetie points at the sky. "There."

We can see it. A big ball of fire in the sky. It's going to land in the same spot where the Warriors hit. In fact, this is the same area that the small group of solider Spacers gathered when they looked up into the sky, before the Warriors dropped. Maybe the solider Spacers were 'dropping a pin' for everyone else. There's no time to do anything. Getting up and running would be a waste of effort and time. Sweetie and I hold each other. I say, "I don't see a web parachute."

Sweetie points. *Oh, ya, I see it now.* The flames were blocking it from my view. You'd think the flames would burn it up, but I guess we used up that wish already. I turn to try to protect Sweetie. My face pointed away from her tiara.

The big thing CRASHES. A wave of Earth hits our trashed base and knocks us over. Dirt covers us.

The battlefield is silent until we climb out of the dirt and gasp for air. SNAFU helps Darcy up. He finds something for her to sit on. We see a big round ball stuck in the Earth. It's bigger than three or four Warriors put together. Maybe it's as tall as a 10-story building. It doesn't look like a chunk of moon. It looks like another Warrior but bigger. A lot bigger. It doesn't move.

"Well, at least there's only one of them," I say.

"Always the optimist," SNAFU smacks my back. Dirt flies off my body.

"Maybe it's dead," I say.

We hope. But it shudders and legs unfurl. It's the Boss Space Spider. It's 10 stories tall. Its legs reach out almost half a block on either side. It turns in a full 360-circle looking in the sky. Fangs twitch. It relaxes when it realizes there are no threats from above. It walks over to the dead Warriors. The Boss pokes one and then another. The Warriors don't move. The Boss screeches. We cover our ears, but we can't stop the sound from almost shattering our eardrums. The Boss gently pushes a dead little Space Spider with one of its legs. Funny, we use to think the 16-foot Spacers were big.

The tiara is no longer on Sweetie's head. I think about saying something but I don't. I take a quick look around, but there's dirt and mess everywhere. I don't think we're going to find it.

Sweetie says, "I know it's gone. It's not important."

The Boss picks up a little soldier Space Spider with its mandibles and gives it a little shake. The little Spacer doesn't move. It's dead.

"Oh, it's sad," says Sweetie.

The Boss drops the little Spacer in its mouth. Crutch, crutch, crutch, swallow. That gives us a better idea of how big the Boss is.

"Or, it's hungry," says Darcy.

The Boss walks around the battlefield eating solider Spacers.

I touch Sweetie. "Sweetie, I've been thinking."

"What?"

"I'm going to take you to Prom."

Sweetie touches my forehead to see if I'm running a fever. "Oh, honey. I'm not sure if you're in shock, but I don't think there's going to be a Prom. Did you hit your head? Are you looking at the same thing we're looking at?"

"I'm sorry for not realizing what's important to you," I say. "In the future, my intention is to acknowledge what's important to you even if I'm not excited about it. You know why?"

"Why?"

"Because I'm excited about you and you're important to me."

Sweetie smiles and says, "And I acknowledge you were thinking about us when you bought the carburetor for your Chevy. I'll do my best to remember that you're usually thinking about what's best for us even if it doesn't initially look that way to me."

"There is going to be a Prom and I'm going to take you," I say.

Sweetie looks into my eyes. She sees I'm serious. "OK. I look forward to going with you."

Good. Our relationship is better than when all this craziness began. I take a big breath in and let it out. Now it's time for the hard part. I take hold of her hands. "But Sweetie, there's something I need to do first."

Sweetie's worst fear hits her. "You're going back out there."

"Yeah. I am. I get a feeling that *this* is mine to do."

She pulls her hands away from mine. It looks like she wants to fight, pout, yell at me, and walk away all at the same time. But she sees my conviction. She inhales and looks at the Boss Space Spider. She exhales and returns her eyes to mine. "OK, what's your plan?"

"I don't know yet."

She nods. This doesn't slow her conviction. She's a tough young woman; I'll give her that. "I'll come with you," she says.

I take her hands again. "I appreciate that, I do, but I need you to answer me one question first."

Sweetie nods.

"Do you think it's a good idea to go back out there?"

Sweetie doesn't say anything.

"Be honest."

Sweetie tries to pull her hands from mine. I won't let her go. She surrenders and tells me the truth.

"I think your idea is stupid."

I smile. I asked for honesty and I got it. That's Sweetie for you.

"Then you shouldn't go out there with me," I say. SNAFU and

482

Darcy get closer. Darcy puts a hand on Sweetie's shoulder to support her. I continue, "I do think it's a good idea … for me. That's why I'm going. You have to come up with your own *good idea*. And then do whatever that is."

She tries to pull away from me. She's pissed. I won't release her hands.

"I believe that's what will save the world," I say. "Everyone needs to come up with his or her own good idea. For some people it will be a better solar panel, for others it will be cars that run on blue-green algae," I look at Darcy, "Others will create a better way to educate kids. Maybe in a way that will engage more of their heart, their passions, and perhaps even their soul's purpose." Darcy nods.

Sweetie stops fighting. She looks up at the small, puffy clouds in the sky. She says, "OK, I get it. I'll see you later." *That was quick.* She kisses me on the cheek and I let go of her hands.

"What you're going to do?" I say.

"I've got an idea." I wait for more, but she doesn't say anything else. She picks up an M4 from the dirt and brushes it off. She ejects the magazine, looks at it, blows off some dirt, and slams it back into the rifle. She turns to the solider with the bandage on his leg, the one that picked up his M4 when the Warriors first landed. She says to him, "I need your help."

Wounded Solider says, "Anything, Prom Queen with a Shotgun."

Sweetie asks, "Did you get the Humvee working?"

"Yes, ma'am." He gets excited, "Are we going to ram the big bug?"

"No. No. No," says Sweetie. "We're gonna get out of here."

"Whatever you say, you're the A+ student." Rumors had spread about the infamous Prom Queen with a Shotgun. The Marine also thinks Sweetie knows seven different languages, tap dances, and talks to dolphins. Sweetie opens the driver's door of the Humvee and slides in with her M4. Wounded Solider hobbles around to the passenger side.

Darcy steps toward the Humvee but winces in pain. Blood seeps through the bandage. She stops. She wants to help but she knows she will be a liability. This is not hers to do. The other Marine watches with the rest of us as the Humvee drives off. I wish I would have told Sweetie that I loved her one more time, but that would have made it obvious that I'm not sure I'm going to survive this.

The other solider that helped fix the Humvee walks over to us and says, "She's getting out of here because she's scared. She's running." SNAFU punches the Marine. He goes down and stays down. Darcy shakes her head at her husband. It's not the first time and probably won't be the last.

I look at the Boss. It turns over a Jeep looking for more dead Spacers to eat. It sees a dead human solider. It inspects the lifeless body. Its mandibles toss the solider into its mouth. The Boss rolls the body around inside its mouth and then spits out the soldier's bones, side arm, and helmet. The Boss continues to eat dead Spacers and soldiers.

SNAFU says, "How are we going to try and stop that thing from going to town?"

The Boss pushes an upside-down tank. The tank flips over. The Boss reaches out its front legs and sweeps a Humvee and broken jet out of the away.

It continues to eat dead soldiers. I don't know how to stop it, but I'm not going to say that out loud. I'm not going to declare that. I am the creator of my world. If I say, "I don't know how to do something," then I don't. And, that isn't going to help me see a solution. Saying something like that will only shut me off from my genius. But to tell you the truth, I'm running out of optimism.

The Boss Space Spider moves one of the big dead Warriors out of the way. Darcy says, "Is it looking for something?"

The Boss claws at the Earth. Its front legs toss dirt behind it. "It's not looking for something. It's clearing a path," I say.

The Boss digs. Within minutes it dips down into the planet's crust.

SNAFU says, "Is it burying its dead?"

I don't know why SNAFU says that. We just saw it eat a bunch of the 16 foot ones. The Boss keeps digging.

Darcy gets it. "The Boss is doing what it did to the moon a long time ago. It's going to plant more eggs."

"But that's OK, right?" says SNAFU. "The shells of the Space Spiders won't burn off under ground. They'll just sit inside the Earth forever."

"Unless," Darcy says, "it gets close enough to the core. Then the heat of the Earth's magma will burn off the shells of the little fur babies and they'll crawl right up."

SNAFU says, "When will the Earth crack? When will they come out?"

"I don't know," I say. "Next month. Five years from now. When your grandkids turn one. I don't know." I watch the Boss dig. Dirt flies as the giant Space Spider lowers itself into the Earth. This is not good. Conviction and purpose well inside me. *This ends here. Today. Now. We have to stop its retreat.* "We gotta keep it above ground until reinforcements arrive." I remember our town's history. Being told over and over again about how the brave men of our town were outnumbered and outgunned during the Civil War and how they failed to contain the enemy. But today, the brave men and women of our little borough did it; they didn't let the Spacers retreat, well, not most of them. We fought and we held them until backup and our international friends arrived. #OneWorld

And now, it's my turn. No retreat for the Boss. Not today. Not on my watch. I get an idea. A crazy one, but sometimes crazy is what you need. I see handles of a dirt bike sticking out of a mound of dirt behind SNAFU.

"Give me all the grenades you can find," I say. I see the backpack that carried the tiara. I pull the backpack out of the dirt. We find grenades and put them in the pack. SNAFU helps me dig the bike out of the dirt. Darcy locates a weapons storage unit. She gets it open and loads six more grenades into my backpack.

Darcy says, "You're going to ride a dirt bike with that on your back?"

"We haven't been safe for the last three days, why start now?"

SNAFU says, "I'm coming with you."

"What? On the handle bars?"

SNAFU looks around and sees an abandoned school bus not so far away. "I can take the bus."

"That's stupid. I am not taking a school bus onto the battlefield." I look at the Boss, but I can't see it. I only see dirt fly out of the hole. It's digging pretty fast.

"You stay here with wifey. I may need backup."

I put the backpack on and tighten the straps. I get on the bike, slide the fuel switch over, and open up the choke. It's gonna need the extra gas. I bring my weight down on the kick-start peg. The bike roars to life. Good. It sucks trying to start a dirt bike with an audience and not being able to do it. I look at SNAFU and Darcy. The bike is loud. Talking is no longer an option. We nod. That will have to do.

I gun the engine and ride toward the hole. I weave in and out of bomb craters and busted-up vehicles. I jump small rivers of goo left over from the Warriors. The grenades inside my backpack rumble around and slam against my back. The path up ahead is blocked with tanks and stuff. I don't see dirt flying out of the hole anymore. Geez, the Boss is moving fast. I have to hurry, but how am I going to get around this mess? I see a fighter jet buried in the dirt; one wing stuck in the ground, the other wing rises up into the air toward the busted-up tanks. I adjust the choke since the bike is warmed up now. I open up the throttle and race for the jet-wing ramp. I get good speed and the bike zooms up the wing that's stuck in the dirt. I drive the bike over the cockpit and straight up the other wing. I see a bomb still attached to the jet. At first I think it's Little Bob, but then I remember the jet with Little Bob crashed a lot closer to the road. This jet has a "normal" bomb. No problem. I'm sure it's safe to ride over. I turn on the speed and zoom into the air. The bike and I fly over a few broken tanks and Humvees.

I land and swerve through more wreckage on the way to the hole. I think of Roy. Maybe the Spacers that dragged him away made him Emperor of Ohio. I hope so.

I stop the bike near the edge and peek in. The Boss is pretty far down, but it's easy to see. It's big and continues to dig. I realize I could gun the bike and jump into the hole. I could land on its back. I decide to slow down my attack plans. No need to do something stupid right away. Let's save stupid for later and only if I really need it.

I take off the backpack and dump out the grenades. They roll around. One rolls into the hole. I yell at myself. Aaahhh! *Slow down, Chevy. Don't waste your ammo.* I put the rest of them in a line. Ten left. OK, let's increase my energy and alertness with some yogic Bellow

Breathes. I inhale and exhale rapidly through my nose keeping my mouth closed. I do it for 15 seconds. I can feel a wave of energy course through me. Good. I'm more alert. Thanks, Bender. All the best on your next adventure.

I pull the pin from the first five grenades and count, "One …two . …" I pull the pins out of the next five grenades. "Three… four…" I toss all ten into the backpack. "Five… six…" I zip it up and toss the backpack into the hole. "Seven… …eight." I duck behind a busted up Humvee. Nine… ten!

BOOM. BOOM. BOOM. BOOM. BOOM. BOOM. BOOM. BOOM. BOOM. BOOM.

I figure the first grenade will penetrate the Boss' hard armor. The next one will blow away the next layer. The next grenade will break through the muscles and tissues. And so on until the ninth and ten grenades will get down to its heart and then BOOM BOOM. Then there will be one big Space Spider in a grave it dug for itself.

The booms stop. I don't hear anything. No digging noises. No movement. Just silence. It worked! I walk to the edge as two giant, black armored legs plop down on either side of me. The Boss's head rises in front of me. We are face to fang. I can see my entire reflection – from my sneakers to the top of my head – in one of its big red eyes. I look small. It screeches and I stumble backward. Its mandibles and fangs reach for me. I scramble into a broken Humvee and close the door. It grabs the Humvee with its mandibles and pulls it close. I jump out of the other side and fall to Earth as the Boss fangs the vehicle. It crushes the Humvee as easily as SNAFU crushes an empty beer can.

I hide behind a tank that's balanced on its side. The Boss drops the Humvee near the edge of the hole. It sees me. A mandible reaches over and pushes the tank over with the intent to crush me. The tank topples over and I scurry backwards just in time. The Boss pulls itself all of the way out of the hole. It's BIG. It stops and scans the sky. I think it's checking for jets. It knows jets are dangerous. It doesn't see any, but the Boss is cautious. It's on its own. The Boss lowers itself back into the hole, but stops to look at me. It sizes me up. It doesn't look concerned. The Boss looks at the sky one more time and then looks back at the hole. *Oh, no.* The only thing worse then it coming for me is it going back into the hole.

I yell, "Hey. Hey. Where you going? The fight is right here."

It looks at me one more time and then lowers itself into the hole. I throw a rock and it bounces off the Boss's face as it descends. It screech-laughs at me. It disappears back into the hole. Dirt flies up and rains down on me.

I run to the edge of the hole. It's getting pretty deep. The Boss digs fast. I see a hot tub sized wound on its back. The wound is filled with bubbling goo. Well, at least the grenades wounded it. I get on the bike and ride away from the hole. I stop and turn the bike around so I'm facing the hole. I gun the engine.

SNAFU tightens his grip on Darcy. "Oh man, he's going in."

I drive my dirt bike toward the edge of the hole. Luckily, my brain kicks in. *What am I going to do?* Jump into the Jacuzzi of goo and swim down into its innards and strangle its heart with my bare hands? That's insane. If the grenades can't blast through it, I'm not going to be able to claw my way into the beast with my fingernails. I race by bike toward the hole as I figure this out. But, maybe I can get it to come back up. I jump off the bike as the bike leaps into the hole. The bike flies in. I land on the edge and almost roll in. I watch the dirt bike explode on the Boss's back. I pull myself up and get ready to run. The Boss screeches at me, but it doesn't come up. The explosion didn't even scratch it. The Boss continues digging.

I need something bigger. I look around. *Yes!* The tank the Boss tried to crush me with, now sits right-side up. I watched Roy drive. I'm good with cars. *Piece of cake.* I climb onto the tank. Sweetie, I'm ... I stop myself. We don't need to continue that tradition. Let's hope this baby has some gas. I start it up. *Yes! Slow is smooth. Smooth is fast.* Just like driving the Chevy, but different. Hands on the wheel at ten and two, even thought the tank doesn't have a steering wheel. Check and adjust the mirrors, even though the Abrams tank doesn't have mirrors. I say a little prayer for a safe and successful journey, always a good idea: tank or car. I push the controls forward. The tank moves forward. I scream like a little girl with excitement. My dad always said it's important to celebrate each accomplishment no matter how small.

Darcy and SNAFU watch it jerk forward. "If he shoots the tank gun, the shell is going to fly right over the hole," says Darcy.

"He's not going to shoot the tank," says SNAFU. "He's going to try and squash the damn bug." SNAFU rushes to a turned-over table and rummages through dirt and equipment.

It's not easy to drive a tank. I finally turn it around. I hear SNAFU's voice, "Chevy, can you hear me. Don't do it. Don't do it." I look around for a walkie. I pick it up. "Hey SNAFU, I'm driving a tank."

"Good for you. But don't do it."

"What are talking about?"

"Don't try and squish it. You won't kill it. It's too big."

I hadn't thought about trying to squish it. I had dropped the idea of sacrificing myself because I didn't see it getting me the result I want: a dead Boss Space Spider. But his comment makes me realize I haven't figured out how to point the tank down into the hole. If I shoot the tank now, the shell will just go right over the hole. Time to look for an opportunity. I stop the tank and pop my head out of the hatch. "Don't worry, I'm not going to do that." I see the crushed Humvee that the Boss dropped near the edge of the hole. I could push it into the hole, but it's not going to hurt the Boss. Then I have another idea. The Humvee's close to the hole, but not right on the edge. This might work.

I call SNAFU again. "I'm not driving the tank into the hole. You're right, the tank won't smush it. It's too big and hard."

"Said the actress to the bishop," replies SNAFU.

Darcy grabs the walkie from SNAFU. *Enough of that.* I laugh. Darcy has no idea what she has signed up for when she married SNAFU. I drive the tank toward the crushed Humvee.

SNAFU tells Darcy, "He's going to push the Humvee into the hole."

"No, he's going to use the Humvee so that the tank will point down at the Boss." Darcy is smart.

I slow down when I get to the smashed Humvee. I go only four miles per hour when the treads grab the crushed Humvee. The tank tilts up as it climbs and crushes the Humvee even more. The tank balances on top for a moment. I push the controls and give the tank a little more juice. The tank leans forward and tilts down as the front of the tank climbs over the Humvee. The front of the tank hits the ground hard. I stop the tank right at the edge of the hole. I pull back hard and hope the tank doesn't slide into the hole. I wait. The tank doesn't fall in. The tank now slants down at a forty-five degree angle over the edge. The large-caliber tank gun points at the Boss. I can see the Boss in the cross hairs of the scope. It worked! I scream again like a little girl.

Goo splashes out of the grenade wound on the back of the Boss as it continues to dig its way down. I turn my attention to the firing controls. Now it's time to shoot a kinetic-energy-penetrator round into the Boss. I push some buttons just like Roy. I pull the do-thingy just like Roy and fire. But nothing happens.

SNAFU helps Darcy to a standing position so she has a better view. SNAFU says, "What's he waiting for?"

"He doesn't know how to shoot it."

"That's crazy. He knows how to drive it. He wouldn't have gotten into it if he didn't know how to shoot it."

SNAFU's walkie crackles. It's me. "SNAFU, put Darcy on."

SNAFU hands the walkie to Darcy. "Hello Chevy. How can I help?"

"Darcy, do you know how to shoot a tank?"

"No, I don't," says Darcy. "I never trained to do that. I've only been inside a tank once."

"With Roy?" says SNAFU. Darcy doesn't answer him. This is not the time for jealously or stupidity.

"I watched Roy shoot it," I say. "I thought I knew how to do it."

"Chevy, hold on. You saw Roy shoot the other Abrams tank?"

"Yes."

"Then I think I can help you," says Darcy. "If you watched Roy shoot it then your subconscious knows how to do it. You have all the information you need. You just need to access it."

"How do I access my subconscious?"

"Don't think," says Darcy.

"That's not helpful."

"Sing and act like Roy," says Darcy. "Pretend you know what you're doing and you've done it before. The body should just do the right things in the right sequence."

490

SNAFU looks at Darcy with awe. Smart, strong, and beautiful.

I look at the Boss through the viewfinder. The tank gun still points at it. I'll try it. I make up words and start singing. "Oh, I drive a tank all the time. I know what to do. I'm acting like Roy. This is my tank Sweetie. I love to climb all over her." I feel stupid, but I'm not going to let that stop me. At least I'm alone. I don't realize I'm sitting on the walkie and pressing the talk button. Darcy and SNAFU hear every verse. Darcy cringes, SNAFU laughs.

Someone else also listens in; a Sergeant scans through the walkie channels at the Mountain Base. He hears me singing. "Let's blow up the big Space Spider ..."

The Sergeant runs to the command center. The General confers with other military men and women. The Sheriff sits by himself in a chair on the other side of the command center. An uneaten sandwich wrapped in plastic sits in front of him on a small table. He looks at it.

"General, I've got something," shouts the Sergeant with the walkie. "I believe it's coming from someone on the ground. The Sergeant holds up the walkie for all to hear. "I like being inside Sweetie. I'm hitting buttons. I hope I'm going to hit the right one so she'll shudder and go BANG! I like it when things go BOOM BOOM BOOM."

The General says, "Give me that thing."

The Sheriff, a.k.a Sweetie's father, pushes his chair away from his tuna on white bread sandwich. The chair scrapes the floor. I continue singing, "I'm just turning, pressing, and pulling on things. I'm new at this, but I've got a good heart and I'm eager to learn."

The General and Sheriff don't laugh. The rest of the command center wants to laugh, but they follow the General's lead.

"Who the hell is that fool?" shouts the General.

"That is my daughter's boyfriend, sir," says the Sheriff.

The General says, "He was one of the guys that was skipping around in his underwear. Right?"

"Yes, sir."

The General shakes his head. "I'm so glad I'm not a parent. I thought fighting a war was hard."

Inside the tank, my subconscious kicks in. I press the correct sequence and flames shoot out of the tank and into the hole. Not what

I wanted, but I'm getting it. Then I remember how to shoot the big gun. I yell, "I got it!"

I look through the viewfinder. *Good, bossy pants is still there.* I shift in my seat and release the walkie. I hear SNAFU and Darcy singing, "I like being inside a tank. It feels so good." *Damn, I must have been pressing the talk button.* Then the tank is hit by something. I look through the viewfinder, but can't see anything. I pick up the walkie, "What the hell was that?"

Darcy answers, "The Boss just hit the tank with webbing. Your blast of flames gave you away. The webbing might be blocking the tank gun."

I look through the viewfinder. The Boss is still in the cross hairs. That's the one good thing about the Boss being so big. I decide to shoot because I've got the shot.

The General booms out of my walkie. "Everyone stop talking so I can say something. Son, do not fire. Do you hear me? That is an order. Stand down. If your gun is blocked, your shell will explode before it leaves the tank. You will die and the giant Space Spider will not."

I stop and pull my hand away from the controls. That order makes sense. I'm afraid to ask, but I do. "Who is this?"

"It's the General."

I pause. "General, what do you want me to do?" Then I remember, "Sir."

"One moment, son." The General turns to discuss options with his advisors. The Sheriff walks up to the General. The Sheriff is not part of the war discussions. The Sheriff points to the walkie. The General gives it to him. The Sheriff walks away from the military pow-wow and says, "Chevy, this is Sheriff Meeks."

"Sheriff, sir. Did you hear me singing?"

"Yes, Chevy we did. We can talk about that later."

"I'd prefer we don't."

"Son, you're not in trouble. You did good getting the Cord off our planet."

"Thank you, sir."

There's a long pause and then he asks, "How's Sweetie?" For the first time ever, the Sheriff sounds vulnerable.

"She's good, sir. Very good … but not in that way." I stammer. "Nothing happened in the RV, sir. I mean, she's fine. She's safe. She left the battlefield, sir."

"Thank you, Chevy."

I don't have the heart to tell him that she's up to something. The General gets back on the walkie "Son, we're not done with you yet. It seems like you're the last man that we've got in play down there. We need you." Notice it's the General who says that. Not the Sheriff. The Sheriff never says he needs anything or anyone. That's part of the reason why Sweetie's mom left.

The General says, "Son, you need to get out of the tank and see if the webbing is blocking the gun. If it is, then you abort the mission. Just keep the walkie with you and we'll help you come up with another plan. This fight isn't over yet."

I like the General's resilience and optimism.

I take the M4 as I open the hatch and climb out. The M4 isn't going to win the war, but I feel less naked with it. The tank slants down toward the hole so I have to balance. A glob of webbing covers the front of the tank. Yup, the big gun is covered. I take the walkie from my belt. "It's a no-go, General. The gun is blocked." A web line shoots up. The tank shudders when the web line hits it. I almost fall off the tank and into the hole. The Boss sees me on the tank. Its legs pull the web line. The tank lurches forward. I run and jump off the back of the tank as the tank slides into the hole. I leap through the air as the tank lands on the Boss. I grab hold of the edge of the hole. Umph. My M4 and walkie get knocked out of my hands and fall into the hole. A SCREECH blasts up and out of the hole.

I pull myself up. The tank looks like a tiny plastic toy on its back. The Boss doesn't care. It continues digging.

SNAFU and Darcy hold each other. SNAFU says, "Well, Chevy's still alive; that's something." Optimism can be catchy because it feels good.

The General barks over the walkie. "Son, are you still there?"

I don't answer because I don't have the walkie.

Darcy replies, "General, this is Private First Class Meyers. It looks like Chevy is OK, but we believe he lost his walkie."

493

"Meyers, are you in communication with the operative?"

"No sir, we are stationed at the abandoned command center. We can see him, but we cannot communicate with him. I screwed up, sir, and got myself a million-dollar wound." A million-dollar wound is not fatal, but it's a wound that is big enough to get a solider sent home.

The General says, "Private, you said 'we.' Who are you with?"

"My husband, sir."

"You mean the kid you just married."

"Sir, with all do respect, he's not a kid anymore."

There is silence in the control center.

"Private Meyers," says the General, "I stand corrected. And, Private
…"

"Yes, sir?"

"You and your team preformed honorably today."

"Thank you, sir."

"But it's not over yet. I need you to be my eyes and ears and I need you to help Chevy in whatever way you can."

"Yes, sir."

"Now tell me, what's our boy doing now?"

CHAPTER 52

HE'S DOING WHAT?

I LOOK DOWN AT the Boss. It digs itself deeper and deeper. *Come on,* I think, *I don't need 50 options, just one good one.*

SNAFU pulls up a chair and urges Darcy to sit. Darcy sits on the edge of the table. SNAFU tries to lift her wounded leg, but she stops him. Darcy says, "One moment, General." Darcy turns to SNAFU, "I need to get out there."

SNAFU shakes his head no. "You dying is not going to help him. I don't care what Five Star says." Darcy looks at the white bandage with red blood. SNAFU says, "We'll have to figure out a way to help Chevy from here. We're still in this." Darcy nods, and lets SNAFU lift her leg so it rests on top of the table.

SNAFU looks through his binoculars, "He's standing at the edge of the hole looking at the Boss."

"General, he's thinking," says Darcy.

"Tell him to think faster."

Darcy taps SNAFU on the shoulder and he hands her the

495

binoculars, she wants to see for herself. She gives SNAFU the walkie. SNAFU holds the talk button for her. Darcy says, "Hold on. Chevy is doing something."

"Be more specific," says the General.

"I think he just undid his belt." Darcy stands, favoring her bandaged leg. She's trying to get a better look.

SNAFU also tries to see. "What's he doing?"

They can't see what I'm doing because my back is to them. I'm glad for that. SNAFU says, "I think he's peeing."

"That's stupid," says Darcy.

"Yeah, that's what he's doing. He's insulting it."

The General yells over the walkie. "You can't insult a spider!"

SNAFU and Darcy watch me run away from the hole. I zip my fly as I haul ass. The Boss Space Spider LEAPS out of the hole, all eight legs land around the perimeter. Its massive body hovers above the hole. The tank tumbles off its back and falls into the hole. The Boss shakes its head and water drips from its face.

SNAFU says, "That's not water."

The Boss screeches. I scramble backwards, away from it. I look in the sky. It's blue with puffy white clouds. It's quiet and peaceful. I look at the battlefield. Everything is still. The General is right. I'm the only one left in play. Backup isn't coming ... not yet anyway. That's what I tell myself. Backup *is* coming; it's just not here *yet*. I just need to buy some more time.

"Come on, Bossy. Come on, we've got all the time in the world." I pick up a M4 on the ground. I eject the magazine. Good, it's not empty. I SLAM it back in. "Let's play!"

The Boss looks at me, and then the sky. I'm not a threat. Not really. I'm just annoying. I see a dead, soldier Space Spider a few feet from me. It's only sixteen feet big. ONLY. I used to think they were big. Oh, how I long for the good old days. The Boss decides to lower itself back into the hole. I kick the soldier Spacer. It doesn't move, but I get the Boss's attention.

"We did this," I yell. "We only have *half* of the amount of limbs you guys have, but we've got *twice* the amount of brains. Your party is over. I'm the one who killed the first one. Yeah, that's right, me. And my friends cut the Cord. And now they," I kick the 'small' dead Space Spider again, "are all dead. What you going to do about it?"

The Boss stops its descent. It comes toward me. I run. The Boss picks up the Spacer I kicked and tosses it into its mouth. The Boss eats it. Perhaps one of the ways they recycle on their planet. *Damn, I missed that opportunity.* I could have shoved a bomb into that Spacer. The explosion would have killed the Boss. That's it. I'll kill it from the inside out.

The Boss slams a leg down next to me. The earth shakes. It screeches at me. It wants my attention. I look at the Boss as it raises its legs and leans to the side. It wants to show me something. *What?* It moves a flap of hairy skin from under its legs. *Too gross* and *too intimate* for me, we just met. Under the Boss's hairy skin is a layer of translucent skin.

"Hey, we don't need to get personal."

The Boss leans a little further and its internal organs push against the translucent skin.

Darcy asks, "What the hell is it doing?"

SNAFU says, "It wants to show Chevy its pancreas."

"No thanks," I say. "I don't need to see more." Then the bumps under the Boss's clear skin become more recognizable. I see round, 16-foot orbs under its skin. Then, the *things* inside the round bumps move. *Those aren't internal organs.* Rows and rows of soldier Space Spiders are inside the Boss.

"Oh, there are a lot left," says Darcy.

"We shouldn't be able to see through the shell. We shouldn't be able to see each Space Spider," says SNAFU.

"Maybe the Boss doesn't put on the outer shell until the Spacers comes out of the Boss's butt," says Darcy.

I pick up a second M4 with a grenade launcher, but it's out of grenades. I shoot the Boss in the face a couple of times to be annoying. I yell, "Eat me."

Darcy says, "He's just standing there. He's not fighting."

"He's saving his ammo," says SNAFU.

"For what?"

"He's saving it until he gets eaten. He's going to kill it from the

497

inside out."

The Boss looks at the sky and then at the hole in the ground. *Come on, focus. Focus on me.* I yell, "I helped do this. They're all dead. You are not taking over our world. Eat me!"

The Boss doesn't move. Maybe I said too much. Maybe it can tell I'm ready to shoot it up from the inside out. Maybe it just wants to get deep underground where it knows it will be safe. The Boss takes a step toward me. *Good, bring it.* But it doesn't bend down to grab me with its mandibles or fangs. Instead it swings a front leg and hits me. I fly into the air. I lose the grip on my M4. I drop it as I tumble and bounce. It takes me a moment to get my bearings, but I stand. It smacks me with the other front leg. I fly and tumble the other way.

The General says, "What's going on?"

"The Boss is torturing Chevy for killing all of the Space Spiders," says Darcy into the walkie. "It's not going to eat him."

I look at the Boss. *It's not going to eat me. It's not stupid.* The giant Space Spider smiles and twitches its fangs.

The General says, "We've got to get that boy some help."

The Marine that SNAFU had knocked out steps forward. SNAFU holds his ground.

Tough Marine says, "That was a lucky shot."

SNAFU nods. "I agree."

The Marine salutes Darcy's walkie and responds to the General, "Sir, yes, sir." But before Tough Marine can rush into battle my 1969 Chevy Camaro races toward them. SNAFU grabs Darcy and pulls her out of the way. The Marine steps back. My '69 Camaro fishtails, throwing dirt. It stops very close to where everyone was standing. Seven-Thirty gets out of the car.

"Sorry," she says. "It's got a lot of power."

"Seven-Thirty!" says SNAFU.

"Hey SNAFU, I figured you would be close to the action."

SNAFU introduces her. "Darcy this is Seven-Thirty, Chevy's older sister. Seven-Thirty this is Darcy, my wife."

Seven-Thirty can't talk, because her brain freezes up. *Did he say wife?* Darcy doesn't say anything, but she nods and gently touches Seven-Thirty on the arm which helps her to focus. Seven-Thirty says, "OK.

Sure. I mean congratulations."

Tough Marine is smitten with Seven-Thirty. She's wearing some really colorful hip-hop clothing. He wants to introduce himself, but he takes too long.

Seven-Thirty says, "Where's Chevy?"

SNAFU points to the Boss. Seven-Thirty watches as the Boss smacks me again. Seven-Thirty says, "He has a way of getting in over his head."

Tough Marine stands tall and proud, "I'm going to help him."

"Wait," says Seven-Thirty. "We need something yellow."

"What?"

"The Space Spiders are afraid of yellow things," says Seven-Thirty. There must be something dangerous and yellow on their home planet."

"There's nothing yellow on the moon," says SNAFU.

"The moon isn't their home planet. They come from somewhere else."

"Oh."

Darcy says, "How do you know they don't like yellow?"

"A group of Spacers wouldn't attack kids that took shelter in a school bus. I saw it on the news. And, when I was with Mark we tested the theory and chased a few Spacers down Rosencrantz in the town's short school bus."

Tough Marine says, "Who's Mark?"

But Seven-Thirty is lost in the memory: She drives a short yellow school bus. It has only eight seats. The front windshield has been shot out. Mark, a handsome Marine sits in the first seat. The little yellow bus chases three soldier Space Spiders down the street right into twenty townies with shotguns. The townies blast the Spacers. Seven-Thirty and handsome Mark high-five. But their high-five turns into hand holding and they share a moment.

Seven-Thirty catches her breath as she recalls the memory. Darcy and SNAFU look at the full-sized school bus not too far away. Seven-Thirty sees it. "Perfect," she says.

SNAFU gives Darcy a quick kiss and says, "I want dinner ready for me when I get home, and I want you to be wearing something sexy."

"Do they make sexy bandages?"

"I think you'd look good with a couple of well placed Band-Aids." SNAFU gathers together weapons and ammo.

Darcy shakes her head, but can't stop herself from smiling. Seven-Thirty pulls her M4 with grenade launcher out of my Chevy. Tough Marine grabs a few weapons. "Come on," says Seven-Thirty. She and Tough Marine run for the school bus.

"You know I'd go with you if I could," says Darcy as she gives him another loaded magazine.

"Without a doubt," says SNAFU.

He's glad his hand bandage is still white. SNAFU runs for the bus. Darcy sits and watches. She hates doing that. Tough Marine is in the driver's seat, but he doesn't know how to drive a bus. Seven-Thirty says, "Get out." The Tough Marine moves to the first seat and says, "I never learned how to drive a stick." *City folk, worthless at crunch time.* SNAFU bounds up the stairs.

"Never thought I'd be in one of these again," he pants.

The bus pulls out before SNAFU can grab a seat. Seven-Thirty negotiates the bus around obstacles. She crashes though things that will move. The quickest way between two points is a straight line. Tough Marine and SNAFU bounce around.

"You want me to drive?" says SNAFU.

"No."

Seven-Thirty turns the bus around a tank. The Boss seems to fill the front windshield and they still have some distance to drive. It's BIG. The Boss smacks me again. The Marine points, "Your friend is doing it. The big Spacer is moving farther and farther away from the hole."

It's true. With each hit, I fly backwards, closer to the road with the blown up RV. This means with each hit the Boss has to walk farther and farther away from the hole. But my success is taking its toll on me. This time I stay down, not as a tactic, but because I can't get up.

"Is he dead?" says Seven-Thirty.

"No, he's just resting," says SNAFU.

Seven-Thirty guns the engine and drives the bus right at the Boss.

The Marine shouts, "You're gonna hit it!"

"I know."

The Boss steps forward to give me one last flick. *Oh, how many bugs have I flicked.* I hear a bus horn. The Boss turns and sees the yellow school bus rushing toward it. It jumps back. I never thought I'd be saved by a school bus. The bus roars up between the Boss and me. Wheels lock as the driver slams on the brakes. The bus screeches to a stop. That's the type of screech I like to hear.

The driver's window slides open. Seven-Thirty leans out, "Hey bro, what are you doing?" I smile, but I don't move. She continues, "Come on, you're either on the bus or off the bus." My Mom use to shout that to Seven-Thirty and me when we were young and rushing to catch the bus in the morning.

I pull myself up. The Boss screeches at the bus, but the Boss doesn't approach it. Tough Marine remains tough. He checks his weapons. The back door of the bus swings open and SNAFU and Seven-Thirty jump out. They help me climb into the bus. Seven-Thirty gives me a bottle of water. Tough Marine watches the Boss, ready to provide cover.

I say, "How am I doing?"

SNAFU shakes his head. "Terrible, but you *look good* doing it."

"You're doing great, it's not underground laying eggs," says Seven-Thirty. She was raised an optimist too.

"What are you doing here?" I say to Seven-Thirty.

"Taking care of my little brother."

"How did you know the school bus would scare it?"

"Mark and I tested my theory on some small Spacers."

"Who's Mark?"

Seven-Thirty blushes, but doesn't answer.

SNAFU says, "How much longer do you think you can keep this up?"

"Not much," I say.

SNAFU turns to Seven-Thirty. "How much longer before it realizes we're not a threat?"

"I don't know."

The Boss approaches the bus. Darcy's voice booms out of SNAFU's walkie. "Hurry up. What are you waiting for?"

Seven-Thirty jumps into the drivers seat, but I say, "If we drive away, it just goes back to the hole."

The Boss pokes the bus with its front leg. The Marine says, "It's figuring out yellow *is not a big deal* on this planet."

Seven-Thirty turns to the Marine. "We're not running."

Tough Marine smiles. He considers himself *a big deal* on this planet. He sticks his M4 out of a bus window and shoots. The Boss steps back, but it's only tiny metal bullets that hit its armor. The Boss pokes the bus again and the bus rocks. Seven-Thirty lays on the horn, but the Boss laughs this time. The Maine nods, and Seven-Thirty swings open the side door. He jumps out of the bus and launches a few grenades. They explode on the Boss, but don't scratch it. The Boss grabs Tough Marine with its fangs. Blood shoots in all directions. The body slumps. The Boss shakes the dead solider. Helmet and weapons fly off the body. The Boss waits.

I count. "Three ...four ....five."

"What are you doing?" asks SNAFU. But I don't reply. I hold up my hand telling him to wait. I continue counting, "Eight ...nine ... ten."

The Boss waits one more second and then drops the Marine's lifeless body into its mouth. The Boss moves the body around in its mouth and then spits out sparkling white human bones that fly out and bounce off the bus. The Marine's skull cracks a window.

I say, "It was counting in case the Marine was holding a grenade."

"They're that smart?" asks Seven-Thirty.

I nod. "It seems if one of them learn something, they all do." The Boss pokes the bus again. Seven-Thirty grabs her M4 with grenade launcher.

SNAFU asks, "What's the plan?"

I say, "We've got to keep it out of the Earth until back up arrives."

"I don't think help is coming."

Seven-Thirty remembers something and hands me her M4. She says, "Mark gave me something."

SNAFU and I say, "Who's Mark?"

Seven-Thirty grabs her bag that she left at the front of the bus. She pulls out an olive drab grenade with an aluminum skirt. She says, "Here." I take the oversized grenade with mini-wings. She's happy to give it to me. She was never that good at shooting. Not her thing, she's more of a dancer, not a fighter.

"Only one?"

"You should only need one. This is a HEDP, a High-Explosive Dual Purpose Round grenade. It penetrates at least 5 cm, which is about 2 inches, when fired straight at *steel armor* at 150 meters or less. We're a lot closer to it right now. The HEDP causes casualties within a 130-meter radius, and has a kill radius of 5 meters.

"What does that mean?" says SNAFU.

"It means," I say, "If I shoot this thing into the Boss, I'll blow up about a third of it. It may not kill it right away, but it will die and it will die quickly."

"That's what Mark said." SNAFU almost asks, but I stop him. She continues, "All you have to do is find an access point. Who knows, you may not even need to hit soft tissue. The HEPD might be able to penetrate the Boss's hard exterior, but that should be your last resort because we don't really know how strong its shell is."

I look at her.

"Any questions," she says.

SNAFU can't stop himself. "Who's Mark?"

She blushes. *Why do people get romantic when the world is ending?*

The Boss hits the bus again. This time the bus tilts over and slams onto its side. Windows shatter and glass flies. Metal crunches. Seven-Thirty, SNAFU, and I bounce around. The bus is on its side. We moan. The Boss screech-laughs.

I try to pull myself up but I can't. I yell in pain, "Aaaaaaah." I think I broke my arm. SNAFU and Seven-Thirty help me up.

"My arm, I can't move it," I say.

My left arm hangs from my side. SNAFU studies me for a moment. He puts a hand on my shoulder. I yell.

SNAFU says, "I think you dislocated your shoulder."

Seven-Thirty brushes the glass off her cool shirt and jeans. She picks up a varsity jacket that someone left on the bus. Glass falls off of the black and gold jacket. I see "Falcon" written on the front. *Anyone see my jacket?* The Boss screeches at the bus again. We prepare for impact, but nothing happens. I think the Boss is declaring victory over the bus.

I say, "Where is the H.E. whatever round?"

SNAFU points. "The Boss is leaving."

The Boss turns around and starts for the hole again. It stops here and there to eat the dead. Both human soldiers and little Spacers.

I find the M4 and confirm the penetrating round is still loaded inside it. I hand the M4 to Seven-Thirty.

"No," she says. "You of all people know that I'm not that good of a shot."

"It's big. You won't miss," I say.

Seven-Thirty ignores me and puts on the varsity jacket and says, "I'll slow it down."

"I'm going to do something that is either brilliant or stupid. I'm going to buy you some more time so you can take that shot."

Seven-Thirty climbs out of the bus and runs toward the Boss.

I yell, "Seven-Thirty!" But I can't chase after her.

I look at SNAFU. "She's too fast for me, bro," he says. "I can't catch her."

I hand him the M4 with the HEPD grenade round. He shakes his head no and holds out his right hand for me to look at it. A big piece of glass sticks right through his trigger hand. Oh, geez. I reach for the shard of glass.

"No, don't," he says. "I'll bleed less if it's in."

Seven-Thirty moves fast. She ran the 100-yard dash in high school and qualified for State. Combine that with her hip-hop, and she maneuvers the battlefield in very interesting ways. I say to SNAFU, "Do it."

"I've never done it before."

I lean against a bus seat. My left arm dangles over it. "Do it."

SNAFU had a few "accidents" when he was younger. He dislocated his shoulder a few times while "playing in the backyard." After his mother left, he never had an accident or broke another bone. *Strange coincidence, eh?* I remember one time that I went over to his house when I was eight. I had a mouthful of gooey chocolate chip cookie. My Mom gave me two for SNAFU, but I ate one of his because they were so good. That's why I didn't call out when I ran up his drive. I didn't mean to sneak up to the house, but my mouth was busy chewing. I saw his father "pop" his shoulder back in place through their screen door.

They were in the living room and SNAFU's arm hung over their dark green couch. His mother was in the kitchen crying. His father gently pulled and moved SNAFU's arm until he said, "Ow." Then SNAFU turned toward his mother and said, "It's OK, mom, I'm OK. Everything alright." I couldn't believe it. After everything that happened, *he was taking care of her.*

Years later, when we were drunk, SNAFU told me his father learned how to put his shoulder in after watching real doctors do it. "Why drop $250 in emergency room fees when you can do it yourself?" That's when I said something really stupid. I said, "Thank God she left." SNAFU swung at me, but his fist only caught a part of my shoulder. His momentum carried him into a tree and knocked him down. That was the only time I've seen SNAFU cry, and I don't think it was the tree that was causing the tears. I never said anything bad about his mother after that.

"Chevy, are you ready?"

"Yeah, go ahead."

SNAFU takes a firm hold of my shoulder with his good hand.

"Don't baby me. I like it rough."

SNAFU holds out his hand with the glass shard. He needs me to pull the shard out before he can put my shoulder back in. He sees the concern on my face.

"It's OK," he says. "I'll put direct pressure on it. Just make sure you blow up the Boss."

I take hold of the glass shard, pull it out, and toss it aside. Blood flows into his hand and drips. He grabs my arm leaving a bloody handprint on my uniform. He lifts my arm and gently moves it.

"I think you have a shoulder subluxation," says SNAFU.

"What?" I don't like it when SNAFU uses big words. It's not right.

"No, that's good. That means the top part of your arm bone," he holds up his bloody fist to demonstrate, "the ball part, is only *part way out* of the socket."

We look at his bloody fist. Gross. He takes hold of my shoulder again and gently pushes and pulls. I wait for more. SNAFU says, "That's it. It wasn't that bad."

SNAFU pulls his uniform shirt tails out of his pants and wraps his wounded hand. He says, "It will be sore, you should put ice on it."

"Thanks, doctor. I'll get right on it." I grab Seven-Thirty's M4.

"Remember, you've got to get that explosive-grenade-thing *inside it*, past its armor," says SNAFU. "You going to shoot it in its mouth?"

"No. This is a time for K.I.S.S.?"

He steps away from me, but then realizes I'm not going to kiss him. SNAFU asks, "K.I.S.S., as in the old rock group?"

"No. K.I.S.S. as in Keep It Simple, Stupid. The Boss is walking away from us. I'm going for the rear."

SNAFU winces. I look out the window. The Boss has stopped, I see it's big butt. I look for Seven-Thirty, but can't see her. We step on broken glass, crunch, crunch, crunch as we make our way to the back door. I climb out the back with SNAFU right behind me.

"There she is!" We watch the colorful and talented Seven-Thirty sneak past the Boss as it eats more dead Spacers and humans. My big sister dashes ahead of the Boss hip-hoping over, under, and around obstacles. I don't know what she's doing, but the best way for me to help her is to get close enough to blow the Boss up. Blood soaks through SNAFU's shirttail and drips onto his pants.

"Go back to Darcy," I say. "Get a real bandage."

"No. I'll come with you. I'll cover you."

"You'll bleed to death."

"You can't stop me," says SNAFU.

I don't have time for this. No, wait, that's a terrible affirmation. If I think I don't have time, then I don't. What did Gandalf say? "A wizard is never late or early. A wizard is always right on time." *I have the time I need.*

"SNAFU, the vision I'm holding includes you celebrating with us."

"Cool. Let's go."

I try something different. "Does coming with me sound like a *good idea* to you?" I say.

"Yes."

I look at his bloody hand. I can't ask him to be honest. He's not like Sweetie. He lies all of the time. I try again. "Right now, I need you to go back to Darcy. If *another idea* comes to you then do it." I raise his bloody hand. "You should keep this higher than your heart, so you won't bleed to death. If that happens you're not useful to anyone."

"But ..."

"No buts. Today is not a day for buts!" We both smile. "You know I'm right." I run before he can answer. I carry the M4 with the high explosive round. The Boss hasn't gotten to far ahead of me, it continues to eat. Seven-Thirty gets in front of Boss. We can't see her, but she stands on top of a webbed-up tank that is in-between the Boss and hole. She stands tall with both her arms behind her back.

The Boss looks for more dead, but can't find anything else to eat. He turns toward Seven-Thirty. My sister waits. Sweat drips down her face and she tastes the salt. The Boss reaches for Seven-Thirty with its mandibles and fangs. Right before the Boss grabs her, Seven-Thirty stretches out her arms showing the varsity jacket's *yellow-gold* sleeves. She flaps them up and down and screams, "Ka ka. Ka ka." The Boss jumps back.

Holy geez, it's going to land on me! I run back toward the bus so the Boss doesn't crush me. *What did my sister do?* I didn't expect it to jump backwards. The Boss lands and the earth shakes. I look at the Boss' big butt right in front of me. Perhaps today is a day for butts. My sister has set me up for success. I call her actions genius, but I need to act fast or her crazy stunt will probably become stupid.

I lean against a busted-up Jeep for stability. My left arm doesn't like holding up the M4, but it can do it. I target the Boss' aperture.

The Boss walks cautiously toward Seven-Thirty. My sister pops and locks and does other hip-hop dance moves on top of the tank. She waves her arms. I hear another, "Ka ka, ka ka."

I blast the high explosive round. Pfft! Yes! Right into its web spinner. Game over! "Get off my planet!" I yell.

The Boss turns and glares at me. Sensitive. Seven-Thirty takes advantage of the distraction. She jumps off the tank. She hits the ground, but she doesn't get up. She grabs her ankle and rolls back and forth. She must have landed wrong. *It doesn't matter; it's all going to be over in a few seconds. Take cover older sibling, a big wave of goo is coming.* Gratitude washes over me. Thank you Seven-Thirty for setting this up. Thank you for teaching me how to read when I was little. Thank you for making me brownies when ... I stop, I'm getting emotional.

I take cover. The Boss blasts webbing at me. Fortunately, I was already ducking. If I hadn't been in motion, I'm sure it would have hit me.

The webbing blasts over my head and sticks to the underside of the school bus behind me. *Ha, missed.* I look at the webbing on the bus. I see a dull, metal thing in it. The HEPD grenade is in the webbing. *Oh, no.* The round explodes. BOOM. The explosion hits me from behind and lifts me off of the ground. The bus blows up next. BOOM. The force of the second blast throws me toward of the Boss.

I turn in the air and see something yellow through the trees that line the highway. *Oh, look Martha's, I mean, Slippers' car.* I'm close to where it all started. I hit the ground and tumble. It hurts, but I'm already hatching a plan. I remember Slippers' little yellow car is close to the RV. I know the RV blew up but there might be a few weapons still lying around.

I pull myself up with the help of a busted-up jet. It takes me a moment to read the upside-down words written on it. Little Bob. Wow, *this is* where it all started.

The Boss doesn't care about me. I'm not a threat any more. It returns to Seven-Thirty. She limps now. I don't want to see my sister die. The Boss reaches for her, but a Humvee races up and stops between the Boss and Seven-Thirty. A handsome Marine leans out of the driver's window and points two guns at the Boss. Handsome blasts the Boss in the face. BAM. BAM. BAM. ETC. Yes! The Boss screeches. It wasn't expecting that. Seven-Thirty opens the passenger door of the Humvee and climbs in. She smiles, "Hi Mark."

So that's Mark. Good timing – I think of Mouth Wash – good timing always does. I'm glad he's with Crystal now. Because if he touches Sweetie, *both* Crystal and I will pound him.

Before Seven-Thirty can close the passenger door, Mark hits the gas and yells, "Seat belt." The wheels on the Humvee spin, but it's too late. The Boss picks up the Humvee with its mandibles. The Boss crushes the Humvee with its fangs. Large pointed fangs pierce the metal frame of the Humvee, just missing the human passengers. Seven-Thirty clicks her seat belt as the Boss passes the Humvee to its big legs. Its legs turn the Humvee over and over while the Boss webs it up.

Mark and Seven-Thirty hold on. It is like an out-of-control carnival ride. The Boss drops the big ball of Humvee-webbing. It bounces a few times before it rolls to a stop. *They might be alive in there. Right?*

I hide behind the jet with Little Bob. I need to get another weapon. I see a pile of bones, weapons, and helmets that the Boss spit out after eating soldiers. The bones are clean and white. Four helmets, two M4's, and a walkie-talkie. No grenades or missile launchers. I need something powerful. I need a bomb. Where can I get a bomb? *Come on Chevy. Opportunities are all around you.* Then I see the words again. Little Bob. Little Bob is a bomb. It's a big one. I bet I wouldn't even have to jam the Boss in the ass with Little Bob. I edge myself closer to the pile of pretty white human bones. I stick my hand into them and pull the walkie from under a hipbone. I try to pretend they aren't human. A shiver runs through me. I call on the walkie, "Darcy, you there?"

"Go ahead, Chevy."

"Darcy, you can disarm bombs, right?"

"Yes. I can."

"Disarming bombs has to be similar to arming them, right? You just do the steps backwards."

"Ahh ... maybe. I don't know. I mean ... Chevy, what are you talking about?"

I peer into the cockpit to look at the instrument panel. I try to ignore the dead pilot still strapped in it.

"I want you to help me to arm Little Bob," I say.

"Chevy, that's above my pay grade. And you don't have the tools to do that. I don't even know what kind of tools you need to do that."

"Come on, Darcy, think. There has to be a way."

"Don't give up, Chevy."

"I'm not giving up. I'm going to take the Boss out."

"But Chevy, don't give up."

"I'm not giving up!"

"Chevy, YOU ARE giving up on you and Sweetie! You promised her that you'd take her to Prom. How are you going to get away from a blast that big? And, if you set the timer for 20 minutes the Boss will be back down the hole and half way to China, literally, and it will be safe from the blast. Chevy, what I'm saying is *don't give up on Sweetie and yourself.* Look for a way to defeat the Boss and survive."

"There is no other way," I say. *It's time to do something stupid.*

Darcy says, "There is no other way ONLY if you think there's no other way."

"Maybe, but blowing Little Bob just feels right." I wipe the sweat from my face, "Don't tell anyone I said that."

I don't hear Darcy's response or SNAFU's laugh. The Boss flips the jet over. I scurry for cover, but there is none. *That's what I get for not paying attention.* The other wing breaks off as the jet flips. The dead pilot almost tumbles out of the cockpit. Fuel spurts out of the jet and drips onto the torn off wing.

I don't know why the Boss came back for me. Maybe one of Seven-Thirty's last thoughts was, "I hope Chevy's safe." Maybe it's personal now or maybe it knows I'm planning something big. All I know is that it's big mandibles reach for me. I undo the pilot's seat belt and turn the body just in time. The Boss grabs the dead pilot and shoves him into its mouth. The Boss spits out bones and a helmet. They rain down on me. *I am too close to it.* I hear a buzzing. That's funny because my head doesn't hurt that much. The Boss swats at something in the sky. Something falls next to me. I jump. But it's only a coil of rope. *Where did that come from?* I look up. My Dad's biplane zooms overhead. The Boss reaches for it, but my Dad is smarter than that. He's up pretty high.

I look at the coil of rope. *Why would he drop me a coil of rope?*

The Boss turns to watch the biplane. The Boss searches the rest of the sky for other dangers. *My Dad always gives me what I most need at the moment.* When I was young, if I needed help with math, we'd search the Internet for the right answers. If I needed to know how to wrap a burrito, he'd show me how to fold it so the insides wouldn't fall out the bottom. And now, rope. *So the question is, what do I most need right now?* The Boss reaches for my Dad with its front legs. The biplane rolls in the sky to avoid the swatting legs. I didn't know my old man could fly like that.

I yell, "Get out of there. You're too close. You can't do anything when you're that close." I laugh. *That's it.* My Dad says that whenever I yell at someone, I'm usually telling myself that same thing. I never

510

understood that before. But I just yelled that he's *too close* to the Boss. *And that's the same with me. I can't do anything this close.* I need to get out of here. I see the banner cord that trails behind the biplane. Thank God my Dad doesn't have a banner attached, this is not the time to make a few bucks advertising. *But why would he attach the cord with the hook without a banner?* The line trails about 12-feet behind the plane. A red cloth is tied to the banner hook at the end of the line. The red cloth flaps in the wind. I get it.

I need something about 10-feet high if this is going to work. To my right is a Humvee that leans against a tank. The rear end of the Humvee stands 12-feet high. I see a couple of steel poles with a piece of blue fabric between them. *Oh, man that's a piece of the Sky Roof.* The poles and Sky Roof are about 14-feet high.

I throw one end of the rope over the bumper of the Humvee. I toss the other end of the rope over the Sky Roof metal poles. Good. The rope stretches between the backend of the Humvee and the poles. I pull the ends of the rope until the rope becomes a taunt horizontal line about 10-feet off the ground. It looks like the make-shift volleyball "net" Seven-Thirty and I made in our backyard when she played on her middle school team.

The Boss watches my Dad's plane. He will never be able to swoop down and get me without being crushed by its fangs. He needs a distraction.

Two missiles stream out of the abandoned military base and hit the Boss. SNAFU and Darcy are back in the game. The missiles don't wound the Boss, but they sure get its attention. The Boss turns and screeches at the newlyweds. *Oh look, matching bandages.* Darcy has her white and red leg bandage. SNAFU has his white and red hand bandage. I hope they're not going to be one of those couples that dress alike. SNAFU and Darcy load more rockets. My Dad dive-bombs me. *Here he comes.*

I hold the rope ends, but then I realize the tug will pull my arms out of my sockets. I tie the ends of the rope to my belt and hold the ropes. Darcy and SNAFU fire two more rockets at the Boss. They hit and explode.

The biplane zooms toward Earth. Let's hope the rope is high

enough for my Dad to snag it. I duck as he swoops over my head. I hear the banner hook whistle past my head. It catches the rope. Yes! The plane zooms away and the coiled rope goes with it. I wait to be picked up. The Boss turns and reaches for me with its fangs. I run away from the Boss and jump. The fangs just miss me. While I'm in the air, the rope tightens and the plane pulls me up. The Boss lunges for me again, but it's too late. I'm up and away. The giant fangs pierce the air behind me. *Too late, sucker.* The plane lifts me high into the air.

My Dad's plane climbs. I'm flying! I can feel the banner crank working. My Dad pulls me closer to the plane. I watch the Boss give up on me. It turns. I see the busted-up RV below me. Black, burnt parts all over the road. I look for leftover weapons, but I'm moving too fast. I see Slippers' yellow car again. *Dance and Know God.* Darcy was right. I had given up on Sweetie and me. I hear a voice inside me, sorta like when Obiwan told Luke to run for the Millennium Falcon. The voice says, "Come on Chevy, you've got to picture dancing and celebrating WITH Sweetie." It's true. I need to *see it* if I am going to *create* it. But I don't have time to make a vision board or an ideal scene. I need to get my Dad to land so I can find a weapon by the RV. I look for a piece of road or a flat field that can be used for landing.

A web line shoots out of the Boss' rear end at me. I don't see it coming, but I feel it hit me. It feels like SNAFU running into me. The force from the web line sends me into the tail of the plane. Umph! I try to hold onto the plane, but my hands slip off it. I fall, but not to far. The crank has pulled me pretty close, but the Boss' webbing now pulls me the other way. The webbing stretches me. I'm going to rip in half. The Boss laughs and makes a single popping noise, "Pop." I try to unbutton my shirt, but I can't, the webbing pulls on my uniform. I can't wiggle out of it.

My Dad sees me being pulled back. He stands in the cockpit of the plane and raises his Winchester shotgun. He may not like hunting, but he's smart enough to bring a gun to a spider fight. He aims the shotgun at me. *That's not a good idea.* I duck. He aims higher, but I know there's no way he's going to hit the Boss, and if he does, a shotgun blast ain't going to slow it down. My Dad doesn't shoot. Instead he aims for the back of the plane. *No, Dad. A plane can't fly without its tail.* BAM. He shoots the tail of the plane. He pumps the shotgun and shoots it again. BAM. The tail of the plane breaks off. My Dad smiles at me as the webbing pulls me back towards the Boss. The tail of the plane comes with me. My Dad tosses the shotgun and scrambles into his seat. The plane nose-dives.

"Noooooo." I fly backwards over the highway and watch his plane crash. See, sometimes you try really, really hard and you still can't get what you want.

I pull myself around so I can see where I'm going. I grab the webbing that's attached to my back. I'm zooming toward the Boss. The good news is I'm falling fast. I'm going to hit the pavement before I get to the Boss. The bad news is I'm going to hit the pavement. I need something to break my fall. I see a blackened rectangle on the ground. That has to be the double sized mattress from the RV. But I'm going to hit the ground way in front of the life-saving box springs. I pull on the webbing, hand-over-hand and reel myself in faster. The mattress gets closer. I come down. Yes. I hit the mattress. The tail of the plane hits the pavement behind me and busts into pieces. That could have been me. I bounce up, off of the mattress. I feel the walkie on my belt slam into my side. That's going to leave a bruise. I rip off my shirt as I turn in the air. The webbing pulls my shirt away. I hit the ground and roll. I'm back to wearing a tank top. I'm glad I'm still wearing pants. I look for cover. Slippers' yellow car. *That's it.* I run for the love bug. The Boss crashes through the line of trees that border the highway; it's coming for me. Giant legs snap the tallest elms. The Boss glares down at me. I slide under the little car.

SNAFU yells to me, but only Darcy hears him, "No Chevy, it's not afraid of yellow any more. It learned yellow is no big thing here."

But I'm not trying to hide. I'm looking for what rolled under it. *There it is, but can I reach it?* The Boss picks up the yellow car with its mandibles and tosses it away. I lay on my back. I hold the grenade I dropped. I'm ready to pull the pin.

"Your move!"

Once again, I'm face-to-face with the Boss. "You going to pop me into your mouth? We can end this right now."

But what Darcy said bothers me. Killing the Boss *and myself* no longer feels right. I would be giving up on Sweetie and me. *But how can I bypass this opportunity especially if this is the only one I get?*

There's got to be other opportunities available. I think about *tossing* the grenade in its mouth. That could work. If it goes down its throat the shrapnel from the explosion might kill it and I'd be safe. The shrapnel wouldn't be able to blast through the exterior body armor and get me. But the risk is too big, if the Boss turns or if I miss, the grenade will just bounce off a fang and never get inside it. I only have one grenade. And right now, it's the only thing stopping the Boss from turning me into a pile of spiffy, clean bones.

The Boss screeches at me. It has a BIG mouth. I can make the throw, I know I can. I have a good arm. Then I realize the Boss might be able to spit it out. A lot of animals can spit as part of their defenses. *Do spiders spit or swallow?*

The Boss's mandibles pick me up. I see my reflection in its red eyes. I'm ready to pull the pin. I get closer to its fangs. "Come on, get closer. Let's see how that works for you." What does the Vulcan say? "The needs of the many out weight the needs of the few ... or the one." But the Boss looks at the grenade and decides eating me is not a good idea. It drops me. Luckily the roof of a Nissan Quest minivan breaks my fall. Crunch. Ohhhhhhh. Not as soft as a burnt mattress. The Boss turns and heads back to the hole. My heart races, my body shakes, my trembling hand almost pulls the pin out of the grenade.

I lay in the metal hammock. The walkie on my belt screams with SNAFU's voice. "Chevy, can you hear me?" I don't move. "Chevy, are you alive?"

I move my hand away from the grenade. I sit up. The Boss is on its way back to the hole. I raise the walkie, "SNAFU, I need your help." I roll off the roof, down the cracked windshield, and onto the hood. I pause for a moment and then I roll off the hood and hit the road. Umph!

"How can I help?" says SNAFU.

I pull myself up and stumble after the Boss. I reply, "I'm not sure what to do." I start to jog, I can't let it get too far ahead of me.

SNAFU hesitates but says, "What do you have available?"

My Dad taught me this game, I taught it to SNAFU. But this is the first time SNAFU and I are playing it with him asking me the questions. Usually, SNAFU's upset and depressed and I ask him, "What do you have available?"

I look at the grenade and the Boss' rear end. *OK, I'll play.* "I've got a grenade but I've got to make the blast bigger if it's going to do any damage to the Boss." I climb through the trees that line the side of the road. I look at some of the big ones that the Boss snapped like twigs.

SNAFU says, "What do you have available?" I don't respond. He says, "Come on, Chevy. What do you have available?"

Darcy gives SNAFU a funny look.

All of a sudden, I'm tired and defeated. "Nothing is available." I think of my Dad and yell at the walkie, "Everything and everyone is gone. I'm all alone and I've only got one lousy grenade."

"What do you have available?" says SNAFU.

Darcy looks at SNAFU. She whispers, "You're not being helpful." SNAFU ignores her. He repeats into the walkie, "What do you have available?"

I hate myself for teaching SNAFU how to do this. I want to punch him. "Nothing. I've got nothing. Nothing is available."

Darcy hits SNAFU. He shakes her off. She reaches for the walkie. He turns and holds it away from her.

The Boss stops to eat more Space Spiders. Maybe the more it fills up, the longer it can hibernate. I see the jet with Little Bob. *Stupid useless bomb.* I see jet fuel leak out of the jet. Jets usually have a center fuel tank located under the cockpit. Fuel leaks out of the jet and runs over the wing. Fuel gathers around the wing. If you don't know, jets wings are also fuel tanks. I watch the jet fuel overflow from this wing's fuel tank. There's a hole in the wing, I can see the fuel. The whole wing is full of fuel. *Stupid leaky jet.* I look at the jet fuel leak out of the busted jet wing. *Stupid busted ...*

"Come on, Chevy," says SNAFU. "What do you have available?"

Wait ... jet fuel is explosive. I say, "Stop talking, something's coming to me."

SNAFU prompts me. "Say it, Chevy. You always make me say it. This is payback time."

SNAFU is such an ass. I'm suppose to say, "I've got everything I

515

need right now to take the next action in the direction I want to go." But I'm not going to say it out loud for SNAFU. It's stupid and I hate him for being a jerk.

Darcy says to SNAFU, "Say something."

SNAFU turns to Darcy. "No. Chevy does this all the time for me. He asks and then waits."

"Really?"

"Yeah, I'm creating the space to let him think. Everyone has access to what they need if they can just be quiet and listen. Chevy's Dad says sometimes you can help the most by NOT talking."

Darcy says, "I know what it means to *hold* for someone."

SNAFU gets frustrated, "Then why did you just make me say all those words?"

"Don't get upset with me," says Darcy. "I didn't know what you were doing."

SNAFU breaks the tension with a smile. "Wife, I'm full of surprises." Darcy returns the smile. SNAFU confesses, "This is the first time I'm doing it, and I feel stupid saying the same thing over and over again."

"It seems like you're doing great," says Darcy. "I'll help you." She reaches for him. SNAFU pulls the walkie away from her, but she isn't going for the walkie. She takes his hand and holds it. The time for talking is over. They hold in the silence.

I look at the jet and the jet fuel. Another thought comes to me. The jet is pretty close to the Boss. If I can get the Boss to stand next to the jet, then maybe I could get the grenade in the jet and the explosion will blow up a part of the Boss.

I raise the walkie. "Thanks, SNAFU. I got it."

SNAFU squeezes Darcy's hand. "Thanks." Darcy gives SNAFU a kiss. They watch me run toward the Boss. Darcy says, "What's he going to do?"

"I don't know, but that doesn't matter. He knows."

I slide the walkie onto my belt. I'll toss my grenade in the jet fuel. I'll blow up the Boss or at least enough of it. I jog toward the Boss, but it walks away from the downed jet. No, I'm too far from the jet to throw the grenade. I run and yell, "Hey, hey! Wait up!" The Boss looks at me, but it resumes its travels to the hole. It doesn't care about me anymore. I'm within range, but the Boss is too far away from the jet. Damn, I missed the opportunity. *Chevy stay positive. All I need is a miracle.*

Suddenly a cherry red glider – you know a small airplane without an engine – comes out of the sky and hits the Boss. The Boss gets knocked sideways into the air. It lands on its feet and now stands directly over the jet. The glider bounces off of the Boss and continues flying.

Sweetie has always been my miracle.

CHAPTER 53

30 MINUTES EARLIER

SWEETIE AND THE WOUNDED Solider stand in the middle of one of the open grass fields of the East Atlantic Soaring Center. They stand next to a big round machine that stands about 10-feet high. Their Humvee is parked a few feet away. The machine looks like a giant fan. Sweetie attaches a hook with a cable to the machine.

"This is a winch," she says. Sweetie points to the cherry red glider that is far away in the field. She holds up the cable. "I'm going to attach the other end of this cable to that glider. When I wave and yell, you press this green button." She taps the green button on the winch.

"Are you sure?" says the Wounded Solider. "That thing doesn't have an engine."

Sweetie wraps her end of the cable around the side view mirror of the Humvee until it's secure.

"It's a glider," she says. "I've been flying since I was sixteen. I'll be fine." She climbs into the Humvee and starts it.

"Yes, ma'am."

Sweetie drives to the glider. The Wounded Solider watches the Humvee pull the cable to the glider. Sweetie gets out, unwraps the cable from the mirror, and clips the cable to the front of the glider. She takes her M4 and with the butt of the gun smacks the shinny red glider under the cockpit window. She hits it over and over again until she makes a hole in the glider. The Wounded Soldier hobbles toward her so he can help, but then remembers his orders. He looks at the green button and moves back toward the winch. Sweetie sticks her hand through the hole she made in the glider and touches the pilot's seat. *That will do.* She tosses the M4 into the cockpit and climbs in.

Sweetie orientates herself to all of the controls and then waves and yells, "Now!"

Sweetie slams the cockpit cover shut. The solider waits a second and then presses the green button. The winch screams. The high-tensile steel wire pops up from the ground as it gets sucked into the winch at a very fast speed. The winch quickly pulls the glider toward it. Sweetie pulls back on the glider's stick. The wing edges flip and in a matter of seconds, the cherry red glider quickly climbs to 1,200 feet. It's a short, steep ride into the sky. Sweetie presses the release button and the cable disconnects. A little parachute attached to the end of the cable opens. This way the cable won't fall to Earth too fast. Don't want to hit anyone on the ground in the head with a steel cable. Sweetie and the sailplane fly off.

The solider salutes her.

CHAPTER 54

FREE TO SOAR

THE BOSS STANDS OVER the jet. The full wing of fuel is right under it. *Thank you, God.* I get ready to throw.

The radio crackles. "Chevy, this is the General. Don't throw that grenade. The explosion won't be big enough to terminate the Boss."

As soon as he says it, I know he's right. Not even with the jet fuel. I could probably catch it on fire, but I doubt that will kill it. It would just roll or web the flames out. SNAFU and Darcy have already hit it with rockets. And, ten grenades only gave it a flesh wound. I also saw what kind of punishment the Warriors took. Fighters crashed into them and they were OK. But even though I know he's right, I fight back, "No, this has to work. It's all I've got."

The General says, "Chevy, I have someone here from the Air Force that I think you'll want to talk to. I believe we may have another option for you. Chief Master Sergeant James, this is Chevy."

The Boss watches as the cherry red glider turns in the powder blue sky. This is the first time a Space Spider has ever seen a silent Earth

521

bird that doesn't flap.

Chief Master James says, "Chevy, I hear you want to arm Little Bob. I believe we can override the safety mechanisms and blow it up even though the jet is grounded."

"No Chevy," says Darcy. "There is no way you'll survive that kind of blast." I forgot she and SNAFU are listening.

The General orders, "Stand down, Private Meyers."

SNAFU says, "You can't order me to stand down."

"No, I can't," says the General, "you're a civilian, but Chevy can tell you to stand down. Do you think he's going to pass up this opportunity to save the world?" The General is good. That's why he's the General.

There's silence and then I say, "Stand down, SNAFU."

The Chief Master says, "OK, Chevy, you'll need access to the cockpit." I shove the grenade into my pants pocket. I run toward the jet and the Boss. I'm getting used to rushing toward the most dangerous situation available. Sweetie catches a thermal under a big, white, cumulous cloud. The glider goes up. The Boss watches her. The Boss hasn't moved. It's gathering intel on Sweetie. The Boss continues to stand over the jet.

I run past the Boss' legs to get under it. It's legs are as thick as 50-year-old oak trees. I step into the Boss' shadow. "OK, I'm at the jet."

"We're going to switch the bomb settings from exploding on impact to a timed explosion," says Sergeant James. "We can then fool the bomb into thinking that it has been dropped."

Sweetie swoops down and gets closer to the Boss. *Not too close.* The Boss crouches down; it's going to jump. I duck as the underside of the Boss comes down over me, but its belly is still way over my head.

Sergeant James tells me what to do. I do it. He checks my work, step by step, just like my Mom use to do with my third grade math.

The glider pulls up into the sky. Sweetie must have found a ridge lift or a lee wave. She told me once about the air currents that gliders use, but I wasn't listening so I can't tell you about them. The glider climbs four meters per second. That's fast. The Boss stands. Jumping is no longer an option. The red silent bird is out of range.

"We're almost done," says the Sergeant. I look up. Sweetie banks the sailplane. She's coming back around. *Keep your distance. You're defenseless.* The Boss gets bored and remembers its mission. The Boss walks away. I'm no longer in its shadow. Bright sunlight hits the instrument panel in the cockpit. The sun's reflection off the glass makes me squint. Sweetie glides right in front of the Boss cutting off its escape. Front legs, mandibles and fangs reach for the shinny cherry-red glider. Sweetie sticks something out of the hole in the glider near the cockpit. It's the muzzle of her M4. Sweetie unloads her weapon into the Boss' face as she banks the glider. RATT-A-TAT-TAT-TAT. The rounds don't score real damage points, but the Boss doesn't like being hit in the face. The Boss steps backwards. Perfect. Once again, I'm working in its shadow.

The Chief Master Sergeant says, "That's it. You're all set. Just push it."

"How many seconds do I have before Little Bob explodes?"

I hear whispering. The General says, "Tell him."

Sergeant James says, "I don't know. Probably around a minute but it could be less. With the crash and the jerry-rigging, you get what you get. It might just detonate when you push the button."

"OK."

I was wondering what I would say if it came to this. And, I just found out. *OK.* I've read that acceptance is the first step on any spiritual journey. Supposedly you've got to accept *what is* before you can do anything about it.

One minute is not enough time to run and find cover. It's going to be a big explosion. I hope Sweetie will forgive me.

"SNAFU, Darcy, are you guys clear?" I say into the walkie.

SNAFU and Darcy drive a jeep away from the bomb and me. The army jeep drives off of the battlefield and onto a dirt road. SNAFU accelerates as he raises his walkie and talks to me. "We're good. Thanks, Buddy."

"Tell Sweetie I love her."

"Of course."

SNAFU puts the walkie down between Darcy and himself. She puts her hand on his knee.

I look up at the glider. *I love you.* The glider flies away from the Boss. *Good.* Get some distance, Sweetie. I hold my breath and press the launch button. No boom. And then, on the console I see 57, 56, …

Sergeant James says, "What do you got?"

"54 seconds now."

The General says, "Keep the Boss near the plane."

He's all business. I guess we aren't going to exchange any warm, mushy words.

Again I hear myself say, "OK."

The glider turns and comes back toward the Boss and me. That's not good. I need Sweetie to get out of here. There's no reason we both need to die. I get out from under the Boss and step into the sunlight. It feels good. Maybe I'm making a memory so that I can remember how warm it feels after I'm dead. I look back at the cockpit. 49 seconds. Most people don't get to know when they're going to die.

Something falls out of the sky and lands next to me. I look up, the glider flies off. *Good.* She's getting away. I'm sure she doesn't want to but the clouds are moving. Without thermals, a glider will not stay up. I look at the thing that fell, Sweetie must have dropped it. It's an empty M4 magazine with what looks like a piece of paper rubber-banded to it. Sweetie wrote me a note. She's so cool. I look at the timer, 42, 41 … I pull the note off of the mag and unfold it. It's a drawing of two stick figures. They have smiley faces and hold hands. Under the figures are the words "Me and YOU." The word YOU is in all caps and is underlined three times. Sweetie is yelling at me. I need to hold THIS picture inside my head. I need to picture BOTH of us together at the end of all this.

Damn, I'm giving up on Sweetie and me again. I look at her drawing. I look at the console, 36 seconds. I don't have much optimism left, but I say out loud, "Sure, plenty of time to figure out how to blow up Little Bob and the Boss without killing myself." I don't believe it yet, but it's a possibility now. That is a whole lot better than me preparing to die. I look around for what I have available.

The Boss moves a giant leg. It bumps me. I trip and step onto the wing overflowing with jet fuel. *That's not safe.* The Boss walks away. No! No! No! I look at the counsel, 32 becomes 31. I yell, "Hey, hey."

The Boss looks surprised to see me. I need to keep the Boss close to Little Bob AND I need to save myself. *Come on, the present moment supposedly has everything I need.* I step back and bump into the jet. I feel the grenade in my pocket. I look at the jet fuel. I *could* blow up the jet fuel, but that isn't enough to kill the Boss and an explosion wouldn't make the Boss want to stay for more. In addition to all that, I'd probably die a fiery death.

The Boss turns toward me. Maybe it wants to eat me. I pull the grenade out of my pocket. I smell the leaking fuel.

Why do I keep thinking about the grenade and jet fuel? It's stupid, I need something bigger and better. A jet fuel explosion will just blow me away. Wait a second. Blow me away. *That's it.* Blow me away. That's what I need. I need to *get away* from here. *But how can I do that safely?*

I look over at the Humvee with Mark and Seven-Thirty. It's still webbed up. Then I think about Hope. Not the hope that most people might embrace at a time like this, I mean Hope the goat. The timer counts down to 19 seconds.

This is possible! I just need the Boss to help me.

I hold the grenade behind my back. I yell at the Boss, "I know you don't want to eat me. Too quick of a death. I get that. I respect that." The Boss hesitates, it doesn't trust me. It knows I have something behind my back. I glance at the timer. 16 seconds before Little Bob explodes. I pull the pin and start the grenade count down in my head. The grenade will blow up about five seconds before Little Bob.

TEN. I yell, "I hope you don't take me down in the hole with you."

NINE. I step forward and drop the grenade into the hole in the wing behind me. I hear the grenade kerplop into jet fuel.

EIGHT. I hold up my hands to show they're empty.

SEVEN. "I wouldn't want your kids to eat me as a snack when they're born."

SIX. "That would suck." The Boss screech-laughs.

FIVE. "I am not Spacer snack!"

FOUR. The Boss grabs me with both mandibles and fangs me. Ahhhhhh!

THREE. I get paralyzed. The mandibles pass me to its legs.

TWO. The legs twirl me as it webs me up.

ONE. I continue to flip around. Webbing covers me.

The grenade explodes. BOOM.

I hear the explosion in some sort of weird dream state, but I continue to get flipped around and webbed up. The jet fuel explodes KA-BOOM. The force of the giant explosion knocks the webbed-up me out of the Boss's legs. I feel the force of the explosion, but I'm safe inside the webbing. The blast throws me into the air. I can't see anything and I'm all drugged up on Spacer venom, but I know I'm flying.

Flames shoot up and cover half of the Boss. It dances in the fire trying to stomp it out. The Boss has no idea Little Bob is coming to the party.

I'm in the air when I hear the big explosion. Little Bob goes BOOM. Half of the Boss is ripped away. I'm glad I don't get to see that.

The force of the explosion hits cocoon-me and keeps me flying. Some of the poles of the Sky Roof still have a piece of blue cloth draped on them. I fly into it and the section of Sky Roof acts like a baseball glove. It catches the webbed-up me. I rip through the fabric, but it slows me down. You gotta love the Sky Roof. I hit the ground, tumble, and pass out.

The blast also hits the webbed-up Humvee that holds Seven-Thirty and Mark. The ball of webbing rolls and bounces away.

Space Spider eggs fly out of the Boss as it rips in half. The General and the rest of the world hold their breath. The eggs don't open. Everyone cheers. The other half of the Boss crumbles. Target neutralized. More cheering.

During clean up, it's reported that the Military gathered all of the "good" eggs in unmarked trucks. *Idiots.* I'll say it again, that is not a good idea.

The explosion pushes Sweetie's glider up and away.

As soon as Little Bob explodes, SNAFU and Darcy make a U-turn and head back to the battlefield.

Sweetie finally turns the glider and lands it in a wheat field as close as she can. She runs until she's exhausted. She walks/jogs the rest of the way holding her side. She hopes to find me. It takes her almost an hour to get to ground zero and the dead, smoking Boss. She tests walkie-talkies as she looks through the rubble for me. The seventh walkie works. SNAFU and Darcy hear her calling. They tap on the Jeep's horn. Sweetie turns and sees them. They drive to her.

"Where's Chevy?" asks Sweetie.

SNAFU and Darcy don't say anything.

"He's not dead," says Sweetie. She turns and looks at the mess. "Help me find him." SNAFU and Darcy aren't sure what to say. They've been driving around since the explosion looking for me. No one knows that I got the Boss to wrap me up to-go.

Sweetie walks away from the jeep. She's not giving up.

SNAFU says, "Sweetie." She ignores him. SNAFU runs to her and grabs her arm. She rips it away from him. She yells, "Don't! Don't you try to stop me!"

SNAFU holds up a water bottle and says, "I wouldn't think of it." She wipes her eyes and drinks. "Thanks." She gives the bottle back to him. They continue the search.

I lay in the sun for another two hours. I sweat, because it's hot in the sun and I'm all wrapped up. I must sweat out some of the venom. It wasn't the deadly stuff, just the paralyzing stuff, so the Boss could feed me to its young. I feel like a high school wrestler wearing 4 sweat suits in a steam room trying to make weight for a competition. I think I lost three or four pounds of fluid. I'm not sure, but it seems like I'm waking up more often now. I finally wiggle my fingers and toes. I'm not as freaked out I was.

The sun starts to set. Everyone around the world is so happy. All Sweetie can think about is how much harder it will be to find me in the dark. She slowly turns and points. "What's that?!"

She points to a big, white, webbed-up me laying between burned-up RV parts. She runs toward cocoon-me. SNAFU pulls the Jeep next to her and Sweetie jumps up onto its side running board. He drives as fast as he can. Sweetie leaps off the Jeep before it stops. She runs to me. SNAFU and Darcy follow. Darcy tries to keep up, but has to move slow. She tells SNAFU to go ahead without her. SNAFU and Sweetie rip away the webbing. SNAFU uses both hands ignoring his wound. He bleeds through the bandage and gets blood on the webbing. Sweetie sees it and freaks.

"It's OK. It's my blood."

Sweetie and SNAFU remove enough webbing to find the back of my head. They roll me over and remove the webbing from my face. I don't move.

"Chevy! Chevy!" yells Sweetie.

I wake again and open my eyes. They cheer. But Sweetie says, "He's not moving." She's wrong. I moved, she just missed it.

"I think he's been paralyzed," says SNAFU.

"Blink if you got fanged," says Sweetie

I blink. Sweetie falls on me and hugs me. The venom is wearing off, I can feel her crush me.

They rip off the webbing and grab a leg or arm. SNAFU says, "Be gentle with his left arm." Sweetie shifts from my left arm to my right arm. SNAFU and Darcy bend and move my legs. Sweetie bends and rotates my right arm. They move my limbs with the intention of pushing the toxins out faster. I open and close my hands. Sweetie shouts, "It's working." She grabs my face with both hands. She smushes, squeezes, and pulls my face. I'm finally can say, "OK, OK." They stop. I can feel my body now except for my left arm, which is probably good. I imagine it's going to hurt a lot.

Sweetie kisses me and then wipes drool from my face. My lips aren't 100% under my control yet. I wiggle and stretch. SNAFU grabs my right hand and gently pulls me up. He looks at the hole in the front of my shirt made by a big fang. He turns me and sees the same sized hole in the back of my shirt.

I touch my belly. *It's still numb. I'm going to hurt when the venom wears off.*

Sweetie hugs me. I give her a one-arm hug.

"Thank you," I say.

"What for?"

"For everything. Showing up with your glider when I needed you, giving me the time I needed, and reminding me of what I already knew."

"That's what friends are for."

"We're a lot more than just friends."

"I know," she says.

We kiss. My lips are back to maximum effectiveness. But I think a little more practice is still a good idea. I want to say, "Let's keep kissing," but I know Sweetie doesn't want to make out in front of SNAFU and Darcy. And to be honest, it would be good for me to sit. As the venom wears off, the numbness in my body is replaced with an overall feeling of pain.

SNAFU lifts my left arm as Darcy slips a piece of blue Sky Roof over my head and shoulder. She's adjusts the all-weather fabric sling until my left arm cradles comfortably against my chest.

"Thanks."

I see something in the distance. A man walks toward us while the sun sets behind him. A bandage is wrapped around his head. I realize he's coming from the direction where my Dad's plane went down.

"Dad?" I say.

Everyone turns. Sweetie finally confirms it, "It *is* your Dad."

My Dad sorta runs to me. I want to run too, but a saunter is all I can muster. We hug. He's careful to not hug too hard, but I'm not. I give him a big hug.

"Ow," he says.

"Dad, are you all right?"

"I'm great. My body needs time to recover, but I'm great. How about you?"

"I'm good," I say. "I can barely feel anything. Damn thing fanged me." I lift my shirt so he and the others can see the matching puncture wounds: front and back.

"That's gross." Darcy pulls my shirt down.

"Thanks for your help, Dad."

"Anytime. That's my job as a parent, to do the best I can. Nothing more, nothing less." He smiles, "You did good son." He turns to everyone. "You all did real good."

My Dad hugs Sweetie while favoring his right arm. "Nice work, Prom Queen." My Dad extends his hand to SNAFU, but SNAFU opens his arms. My Dad hugs him. Another first on Prom Day. My Dad turns to Darcy, "Ms. Meyers." He knows her from teacher meetings.

"You can call me Darcy, sir." She extends a hand and says, "I'll go with a hand shake right now. Maybe a hug later when we're both feeling better."

My Dad and Darcy shake. He says, "You can call me Wayne."

Someone behind us yells, "Hey! Save me some loving!"

Seven-Thirty rides piggyback on Mark. They look like they're having a good time. Mark lowers Seven-Thirty. She limps toward me favoring her ankle. We hug. I ask, "What about Mom?"

"I dropped her at the hospital. She should be fine."

My Dad and Seven-Thirty hug. "Oww," my Dad says. Seven-Thirty shakes her head, "Stop being so old." Seven-Thirty and Sweetie hug.

I shake Mark's hand, "Thanks for saving my sister."

"My pleasure. Anytime."

Seven-Thirty laughs and punches him in the arm. He feigns being hurt. They're good together. I can see that already.

CHAPTER 55

THREE DAYS AFTER PROM

TOO MANY FUNERALS, SITTING shivahs, wakes, memorial services, and "life celebrations."

The rest of the world has been partying for three days and we got stuck with cleaning up the physical and emotional mess. I don't remember much during these days. I slept a lot, held Sweetie's hand a lot, and nodded my head a lot. The only thing I remember someone saying is:

Love never dies. Friends do.

I found this both disturbing and comforting. I'm doing my best to focus on the first part.

Love never dies.

CHAPTER 56

PROM PROPOSAL

AT SOME POINT AFTER a traumatic experience, everyone has to ask themselves, "OK, when do I start living again?" My experience is the answer to that question is always, "Now." I think the key to this, and I'm no expert, is each person has to wait until they ask *themselves* this question. Then, and only then, is the answer now.

Twenty-one days after Prom Day and our house is the cleanest it's been in a while. We always tidy up before guests come over, but we've never hosted a Prom before. The coffee table, love seat, and my Dad's reclining chair have been moved to the back porch. It's not a huge dance floor, but it should be big enough. I stand by the living room window and look out at the night. I have always liked night, but now I'm very happy when the sun sets.

I look down the drive to Miller Creek Road. No headlights. Chicks are always late. I guess some things don't change. I look up at the starry sky and the moon. They say you can't see the crack anymore. A lot of rubble shifted when the Warriors and Boss left the moon. It's true the rubble filled it in, but I can still see a faint outline of the crack even though everyone says it's gone. The moon isn't full now. Not with Spacers and not in the traditional sense either. It's waxing. It's on its way to being a "full" moon again. Time moves on.

SNAFU walks up to me. We both wear tuxedos and we both look good. "Do you see any of them out there?"

"What?"

"Did you hear about the Spacer they found in the abandoned gas station in Georgia? Some experts say there are as many as two hundred still roaming the states."

"Shut up. That has to be a gross exaggeration," I say. People just want another Big Foot out there so they can freak themselves out every time they take out the garbage." It's gonna be the first full moon after the invasion. The world is a little jumpy.

"What're you looking for then?" says SNAFU.

"I'm not looking for anything. I'm looking at the night."

SNAFU nods. "It's nice to see dark."

Technically you can't see dark. Dark is the absence of light. Dark only exists when there isn't light. Our job is just to bring the Light. We did. And, that is why we're still here.

"Yeah," I say. "It's nice to see dark."

We look at each other and laugh. Who would have thunk we'd *help save the world?* He flicks my bow tie and says, "This is stupid."

"So stupid."

My Mom, Dad, SNAFU's Dad, and the Sheriff enter the living room from the kitchen. They laugh at some lame parent joke that probably isn't funny, but it's great to hear them laugh. The Sheriff doesn't laugh, but I see him smile. That's progress. My Dad's right arm is in a cast. SNAFU's Dad is dressed in his Navy Seal uniform. He looks sharp. SNAFU and I have a bet on how many days he will wear his uniform. I say another ten. SNAFU says till the end of the month. We'll see who's closer.

The Sheriff also wears his uniform. He always wears his uniform when he's out. He told Sweetie that you don't ever stop being the sheriff. I saw him in an old concert T-shirt once when I visited Sweetie during junior year. I stopped over her house with flowers and chicken soup that my Mom made. Sweetie missed a couple of days of school because she was sick. I surprised them because I didn't want Sweetie to go through the hassle of making herself up. The Sheriff disappeared into his room and came back out with his uniform on. He still wore the black T-shirt under it. I wish I saw the name of the rock group on the front of his shirt. Sweetie won't tell me and she's right not to. I'd sing some lyrics or bring it up in some inappropriate joke and her old man would take it as an insult. But I think about him and that concert shirt when my Mom and Dad listen to *their old time* music. I wonder, does he feel more like himself when he wears that black concert shirt or his uniform?

The Sheriff doesn't wear his gun tonight. He left it at home, which is good considering my intentions involving his daughter. My Mom puts chips on the dining room table near the burgers, corn-on-the-cob, and other fixings. My Mom walks over to us.

"You both look so handsome." She kisses my cheek and gives me a hug. I hug her back. I smile. This is the thousandth time my Mom has hugged me since we won.

"I'm OK Mom."

"I know you are. I love you and I just want to give you a hug and kiss."

"I love you too." I don't want to make her feel bad so I add, "And, you can hug and kiss me anytime you want."

My Mom looks at SNAFU. "You both look so grown-up and handsome. Come here, Robert." My Mom hugs SNAFU. He gets a big silly grin on his face, "Thanks, Mrs. Wright."

My Mom hugs me again. I roll my eyes, but I hug her back.

There's a knock on the door and then it opens. A young woman walks in with straightened hair wearing a beautiful Prom dress. She looks great, but I don't recognize her. Did someone invite other seniors I don't know? Mouth Wash walks in behind her wearing a tux. Oh, geez, I look back at the young woman, it's Crystal.

SNAFU says, "Crystal, you look great."

Crystal's eyes sparkle. I think she wants to say, "See what you're missing." But instead she says, "Thank you. So do you." Crystal looks at Mouth Wash, "You should see all the crazy things this guy has me doing."

Crystal blushes. "I don't mean things like that." Mouth Wash smiles and nods. *Yes, things like that!* Crystal blushes even more. She takes his hand and pulls him toward the adults. "Let's say hi, and behave yourself."

"Never," says Mouth Wash. She laughs.

There's another knock on the door and B+ and Benji enter. They look great in matching tuxedos. B+ *could* be a tuxedo model. SNAFU and I hug them.

B+ says, "Where's the after party?"

"The barn," I say.

"Super."

"What you got to eat?" says Benji. "I can't seem to eat enough."

"I know what you mean," says SNAFU. "Food is on the table by Mouth Wash and Crystal."

B+ and Benji walk over to dining room table. We hear them say, "Damn girl, you look good." Crystal hugs them.

My Mom hugs and kisses everyone.

The screen door opens and Sweetie and Darcy enter. They look great. Sweetie wears the tiara I gave her. *Did she go back and find it?* SNAFU says, "I take it all back. This is so cool."

I smile. "Very cool."

I look at Darcy. "Hi Darcy, you look good."

"Thanks, Chevy. So do you."

It's still a little weird calling Ms. Meyers, Darcy, to her face. But I'm getting use to it.

SNAFU smiles at Sweetie. "If I wasn't married ..."

Sweetie laughs. "You look good too, SNAFU."

I take Sweetie's hand and pull her away from SNAFU and Darcy. I want some private time with my girl.

"You look great," I say.

Sweetie spins for me. She's absolutely beautiful. I want to hug and kiss her, but I don't want to mess up everything she's got going on. Out of the corner of my eye, I see SNAFU bow to his lady. Darcy curtseys and then they kiss.

I lean in to kiss Sweetie but stop.

"It's OK if you kiss me," says Sweetie. "Just don't maul me. At least, not yet. We haven't taken any pictures yet."

"I love you," I say.

"I know."

We kiss. It's not a long kiss, but it's not too short either. Just enough so I can remember how great her lips are. I feel electricity run through my body. She's fantastic.

I look at the tiara. "Did the military find it for you?"

"No. Darcy ordered me another one online."

"She's a good friend."

"She is," agrees Sweetie. "We've spent a lot of time together the last few days while I couldn't see you." Sweetie looks concerned. She touches my left arm. "Are you OK? Did they hurt you?"

"No, I'm OK. It was annoying and long, and I think they took more blood than the Spacers did, but they didn't hurt me."

The military prodded and tested me for the last two days. Sweetie and I texted and talked, but we couldn't see each other. I think they would have kept testing me, but I said I needed to go to Prom. The General told them to let me go.

"Look," I raise my left arm and rotate it, "I'm better than new." She wraps her hands around my bicep and squeezes. She says, "You're so strong." I smile and continue, "Theoretically, they say I shouldn't be able to do this for two more weeks." I lean in and whisper, "And, I can even curl 55-pounds with *each* arm, even my left arm, which is crazy because the most I've ever been able to curl was 35."

It seems like the Boss' venom repaired and rebuilt my body when it paralyzed me. Maybe it does that so its prey is healthy and strong before it gets eaten by its young.

Sweetie says, "Let's go say hi to everyone."

"Thank you."

"Chevy, you don't have to keep thanking me."

"Yes, I do. You saved me."

"I would like to take responsibility for that so you'll owe me for the rest of our lives," she smiles. "But you did it. Sure, my little drawing reminded you, but you're the one that ..."

"Sweetie, that's not what I'm talking about." I step closer to her.

"You save me every time I look at you."

We kiss.

My Dad brings a small, mirrored ball into the living room. It's on a little stand with its own built-in LED light. SNAFU's Dad turns off the lights in the kitchen. My Mom dims the lights. My Dad sets the mirrored ball on the table and turns it on. Tiny reflections of light dance around the room. It's amazingly effective considering its size. We clap.

My Dad joins my Mom by the food table. She says, "It's perfect."

My Dad kisses her. "You're perfect."

Get a room.

The screen door flies open and Seven-Thirty and Mark enter. Seven-Thirty yells, "Party crashers in the house!" Mark wears a tux and Seven-Thirty wears a funky gown. Beautiful, but different. Very Seven-Thirty.

Seven-Thirty pulls Mark to Sweetie and me.

"You look great," says Sweetie.

"Aren't you a little old to be going to Prom," I say. Sweetie punches my arm. She's getting weaker or I'm getting stronger. I barely feel it.

Darcy and SNAFU join us. Everyone says hey to each other.

Seven-Thirty says, "I never went to my Prom."

"Me neither," says Darcy.

"I went to Prom," says Mark, "but someone left with my date." Sweetie, Darcy, and Seven-Thirty sympathize with him. "Awwww."

"Or maybe I left with someone else's date," says Mark. "I don't remember."

Seven-Thirty punches him. Mark grabs her and kisses her.

SNAFU whispers to Darcy. "You know," he says, "Seven-Thirty and Mark were in that webbed-up Humvee for awhile."

"Yes, they were," whispers Darcy. "And, they were all pumped up on adrenaline and desire."

SNAFU pulls Darcy closer. "They knew they could die at any moment."

Darcy acts innocent. "What do you think they did in that webbed up Hummer?"

"People do crazy things when they think the world is ending."

Darcy closes her eyes and prepares for a kiss, but SNAFU doesn't kiss her. She opens her eyes.

"What?"

"I got you a present."

Darcy smiles.

SNAFU pulls something out of his pocket. "I've never given one of these to anyone before."

Darcy stops smiling. *That's what Crystal said he would say.*

SNAFU shows her the nail pendant. *It's the same one!* Darcy crosses her arms. She says, "And did you make it yourself?"

SNAFU hesitates. "No, a designer guy named Matthew Moir makes them."

He didn't lie. He didn't say he made it himself.

SNAFU looks hurt and confused. Darcy looks at the nail pendant. *Wait, it's not the same as Crystal's.* This pendant has two nails wrapped together. She says, "It's not the same one."

"Oh, you heard about the other ... I'm sorry, I shouldn't have ..." SNAFU puts the pendant back into his pocket.

"No, wait," says Darcy, "you didn't lie to me."

"No, I'm not going to lie to you. I realized if I lie to you, and you like me, then you won't be liking the *real* me, you'll be liking the lie. I need to tell you the truth. I'm *always* going to tell you the truth. This way, if you like me, I know you like the real me. And if you don't like something about me, we'll work it out. OK?"

"OK," says Darcy. "Let me see it."

SNAFU hands her the pendant. It's two nails, one wrapped around the other. He says, "This one is called a soul pendant. This is you and me. We are both tough as nails and we're together."

Darcy smiles. "Who's *wrapped around* whom?"

"Either way it's a win-win."

Darcy laughs. "How do I put it on?"

"It's got a magnet clasp." SNAFU pulls it apart. Darcy turns around and he puts the pendant on her. Click.

She touches the nails. "I love it."

"I love you." They kiss.

My Mom turns on a big, round wireless speaker and a dance beat rocks the house. Everyone starts moving.

I turn to Sweetie. "Can I have this dance?"

"You can have them all."

Everyone dances. We have fun. A slow song comes on. We press our bodies against each other and move.

"I'm sorry I couldn't save Prom for you," I say.

"Shut up. This is great."

"I got you something."

Sweetie smiles, "You know how to get into a girl's heart."

"That's not where I want ..."

Sweetie gives me a look and I stop. I get back to what I was saying, "We have always talked about going to Spring Break. I think we should go next year."

"Really?"

"Yeah, I know you like to plan ahead. And, I think Spring Break would be a great place to have an all-week, simultaneous bachelor and bachelorette parties."

Sweetie stops dancing. "SNAFU and Darcy are already married? Whose bachelor and bachelorette parties would we ..."

Sweetie looks at the box I pull out of my pocket.

"That's *not* an early birthday gift is it?"

I get down on one knee. We're in the middle of the dance floor. The others stop dancing when they see what's happening. Little white reflections dance around us. Someone turns down the music. Everyone stands still. The Sheriff touches his empty holster.

"Sweetie, I've realized that there is nothing like impending doom and death to make me realize what makes me feel most alive. You are, and have always been, my miracle. I want to continue creating my life with you." I open the ring box. "Will you marry me?"

There is a bang on the screen door. Everyone jumps. The moment is lost. Then something SLAMS into the screen door. I stand and slide the ring box into my tux pocket. *What the* ... The screen door creaks open. A Spacer leg reaches into our living room. Now I wish the Sheriff had his gun.

I look for a weapon, but all I see is cheese dip.

A second Spacer leg enters through the front door. The two long, hairy, white legs bump into each other. The Spacer must be wounded ... We hear growling, "Grrrr grrrrrr." That's strange. And then we hear laughter – female laughter. One of the legs falls to the floor and a young woman says, "I dropped mine. Do you think they noticed?" Then more giddy laughter.

The other Spacer leg comes into the house, but we're not freaking out any more. Roy walks in waving the big, hairy white leg. It hits the lamp near the couch. The lamp crashes to the floor. *Idiot.* He wears a tux with tails. He also wears a gold Spacer fang on top of his head. He must have hollowed it out and painted it, or maybe they come hollow. The only thing I know about Spacer fangs is how they feel.

Roy hands his Space Spider leg to SNAFU.

"Cool," says SNAFU.

Roy's date steps over the Spacer leg she dropped. I don't recognize her. Late twenties, Asian. She wears a formal dress with a slit all of the way up her leg. She wears it well. She also wears Roy's top hat. Sorta goofy, but she looks good with it. Her heel catches on the fallen leg and she trips. Roy turns and catches her just before she hits the ground. They kiss as her top hat flies off her head and rolls to my feet.

"My BIG hero," she says to Roy. She's been drinking. Maybe you have to if you're dating Roy. I realize his international dating plan worked. I hope she won't be too disappointed later. Roy may be an idiot, but he's our idiot and I don't want him to be sued for false advertising.

I pick up Roy's top hat and hand it to him. Roy says, "You and Sweetie may be the king and queen, but I am the Prom Emperor!"

His date claps with joy, but no one else does. Roy doesn't notice and she doesn't care. They seem perfect for each other.

The music starts again. She takes the top hat from Roy and puts it on her head. Everyone dances.

Sweetie touches my arm. "It's not going to be easy."

"I think we've established that."

"And, you've got to promise me a few things."

"Go ahead," I say.

Sweetie takes a deep breath and says, "When I push you to be the best you can be, you don't get angry and call me a bitch."

It was pretty rough growing up in Sweetie's house. She doesn't like that word. "OK," I say. "What else?"

"And when you want something, *anything*, you tell me and we'll work together to figure it out. Your hopes, dreams, and desires should benefit us both."

"Sounds good. I'm on board with that," I say. "Anything else?"

"That's all I've got for you right now. How about you?"

"When I tell you to slow down and take care of yourself, don't tell me to stop telling you what to do."

Sweetie laughs. "I'll try, but I can't make any promises on that one."

"And when you want something, *anything*, you tell me too."

"I promise," says Sweetie. "Give me the ring."

"Give me your face." I lean in to kiss her, but Sweetie doesn't kiss me.

"Give me the ring first."

"You've got to say it."

She smiles the best smile I've ever seen and says, "Yes Chevy, I will marry you." Everyone applauds and hollers. I didn't realize they were listening.

Sweetie leans in and whispers, "Chevy, I will be your lady and your freak."

I kiss her and say, "I love you so much."

"I know. I love you too."

I put the ring on her finger and we kiss.

"You know," I say, "it's our chance soon."

"No," Sweetie says. "It's our chance *now*."

The music gets louder and we dance.

We dance until the ex-Navy Seal leaves.

We dance until the Sheriff goes home.

We dance until my parents go to bed.

And then, it's the best Prom ever.

Want More?

Finishing a book is great, but sometimes I'm bummed because it's over. Well, I'm here to tell you it's not over, it's just starting. Do you want more? If you do, here are few ways to keep the fun going. First, let's talk about the next Chevy & Sweetie Adventure…

Sand Sharks on Spring Break

Chevy proposes to Sweetie and she says YES! The next big question is where are they going to have the bachelor and bachelorette parties? What if they're held at the same time? And, what if the bachelor and bachelorette parties last for a whole week? Perhaps at the beach?

Chevy, Sweetie, SNAFU, Darcy, Mouth Wash, and Crystal go to Spring Break to celebrate! It's HOT on the beach. *If you know what I mean.* But there's something else going on. Something strange. Something that's threatening Spring Break. Sharks have mutated and now swim through the sand!

Just when you thought it was safe to lay out on the beach. Chevy & Sweetie survived Prom. Can they survive Spring Break?

Go here for more info
www.SandSharksOnSpringBreak.com

Posters, T-shirts, and More

Another way to keep the good times going is to get some *Space Spiders on Prom Day* stuff.

If you'd like to see some really cool *Space Spiders on Prom Day* posters, T-shirts, shower curtains, and other neat stuff, check out the Society 6 online store: **society6.com/ SpaceSpidersOnPromDay** Space Spider *shower curtains*? Really*? Yes.* A mug that has *Minty Fresh* written on it? *Yes, of course,* and sooooooooo much more.

Sweetie's Empowering Song

You can listen to Sweetie's song, *See Me* which was inspired by Sweetie's heated conversation with the General in Chapter 35 in the *Space Spiders on Prom Day* novel. What's really neat is the name of Chapter 35 is also *See Me*. If you want, you can re-read the chapter and see if you can find some of the song lyrics.

Lyrics from the song *See Me* include:

See me for who I am,
Not what I've done,
what you think I can
See me, my hopes, my dreams;
There is only
one of me

You've been in charge
You had your turn
It's our chance now.
We don't have to ask
We're free to soar

Sweetie wrote and recorded this empowering song with her musical friend, Paul. You can checkout and purchase the song *See Me*, on Bandcamp here:

www.PaulBabin.BandCamp.com/track/See-Me

Special Thanks & About the Illustrators

Special thanks to all these good people who listened, read, discussed, corrected grammar, re-read, and gave feedback. Your support, fun, and caring inspired and fueled me. I literally could not have done it without you. Thank you Jeff Youngs, Trisha Kuhlmey, Ben Miller, Erin Behan, Mike Polek, Elana Christiansen, Patty Hruby, Chris Gebo, Nancy O'Leary, Chris Freyer, Connor Hruby, & Cayden Hruby. Special thanks to Ellen Karpenkova for the awesome cover designs. Special thanks to Eliza Swords, Angus Ross, Barry Alden Clark, Kurt Christiansen, & James Philip Cox. You're the best Tuesday Lunch Writing Group ever. What good and productive times we had. And, a BIG thank you to Amy Hruby, my soul-mate-wife, for all the fun and support. What an adventure, eh? Amy, you're beautiful and I love you. I look forward to more…

Greg Hain created the *Prom Queen with a Shotgun* comic book illustration. He can be reached at: **greg@greghain.com** To see and purchase posters (and T-shirts, shower curtains, ties, mugs, etc.) with his print and other *Space Spider on Prom Day* images and phrases from the book, check out **www.Society6.com/spacespidersonpromday**

Liwiljo created the front cover image of Chevy & Sweetie, the back cover image of the Space Spider, and all of the other sketches in the book (except for the *Prom Queen with a Shotgun* comic book illustration). Liwiljo can be reached at: **liwiljo@gmail.com**

The Story Behind the Story

About the Author: John J. Hruby

John J. Hruby is a screenwriter who decided to write a short story because his family (and most of his friends) don't read screenplays. His short story turned into *Space Siders on Prom Day*. As he wrote his epic novel, he realized he was using *screenplay* story structure to write a *book*. He wasn't sure it was going to work, but it did. John had so much fun sharing his story in book form, that he wanted to help other screenwriters share more of their creativity by writing novels. John wrote an ebook showing how he used screenplay story structure to write *Space Spiders on Prom Day*. His ebook, *If You Can Write a Screenplay... You Can Write a Novel*," can be found on Amazon.

About halfway through *Space Spiders on Prom Day*, John realized his "short story" was turning into a two-book story (which is now ONE big epic novel). John knew he needed to spend more time writing or he'd never finish. With this realization, he decided to embrace some ideas and daily-practices he calls "Trading Your Addictions for Creativity." This new way of living helped him *trade* some of his *time consuming habit-patterns* for *creative activities*, specifically writing (and rewriting). It worked. He successfully completed his book while working a full-time job, being married, raising two young kids, and walking a dog. John believes part of his mission is to help others be more creative. He gives talks, facilitates workshops, and coaches writers and artists one-on-one, so they can be more productive.

Here is a short excerpt from one of John's presentations.

"As I become more creative in my life, I experience more joy. I encourage others to be more creative, not because they *should*, but because it feels *really good* to be creative. I have also discovered that life becomes more fun. And, I believe that when ordinary, regular people (this includes you and me) are creative and have fun, we make the world a better place."

If you're interested, you can listen to a free audio recording "Creativity & Addiction" on his website: www.JohnJHruby.com

John was born in Cleveland, Ohio and now lives in Los Angeles with his wife and two boys. John thanks you for reading his novel. He had a lot of fun writing it and hopes you had a good time reading it.

You're invited to contact/follow him, if you'd like. And, he'd love to hear from you. Especially what you liked about *Space Spiders on Prom Day*.

Website: www.JohnJHruby.com

Email: John@JohnJHruby.com

Facebook: JohnJHrubyAuthor

Instagram: HrubyNow

Snapchat: johnjhruby

Be Creative!

#Chevy&Sweetie

I request your help with being part of the creativity and empowerment movement that's happening all over our planet at this time.

Here are some ways you can make a difference:

Post a review of this book on Amazon, add *Space Spiders on Prom Day* to your goodreads account (or start a goodreads account if you don't have one yet @ goodreads.com and add *Space Spiders on Prom Day* to the list of books you've read), tell your friends why you like this book, take a picture with the book and share it with #Chevy&Sweetie

Remember, word of mouth is one of the most powerful ways to influence the world & make a positive difference. You have a lot of power. Remember that.

The time for talking is over. Or, perhaps in this case, the time for talking has just begun. :)

One of the most important things you can do right now is to be creative and have fun. When you do this, you make the world a better place.

Chevy & Sweetie thank you for being part of the adventure.

John J. Hruby, author of *Space Spiders on Prom Day*

43963773R00334

Made in the USA
Middletown, DE
24 May 2017